THE
IMMIGRANT
Brides
COLLECTION

9 Stories Celebrate Settling
in America

THE
IMMIGRANT
Brides
COLLECTION

Judith Miller,
Irene Brand, Kristy Dykes, Nancy J. Farrier,
Pamela Griffin, JoAnn A. Grote,
Sally Laity, and Janet Spaeth

BARBOUR
PUBLISHING

Capucine: Home to My Heart © 2006 by Janet Spaeth
The Angel of Nuremberg © 2002 by Irene B. Brand
Freedom's Cry © 2002 by Pamela Griffin
Blessed Land © 2000 by Nancy J. Farrier
Prairie Schoolmarm © 2005 by JoAnn A. Grote
The Golden Cord © 2002 by Judith McCoy Miller
I Take Thee, a Stranger © 2000 by Kristy Dykes
Promises Kept © 2000 by Sally Laity
The Blessing Basket © 1999 by Judith McCoy Miller

Print ISBN 978-1-62416-243-5

eBook Editions:
Adobe Digital Edition (.epub) 978-1-62416-421-7
Kindle and MobiPocket Edition (.prc) 978-1-62416-420-0

All scripture quotations are taken from the King James Version of the Bible.

This book is a work of fiction. Names, characters, places, and incidents are either products of the author's imagination or used fictitiously. Any similarity to actual people, organizations, and/or events is purely coincidental.

Cover Photo: Ramon Purcell, photos.com

Published by Barbour Publishing, Inc., P.O. Box 719, Uhrichsville, Ohio 44683, www.barbourbooks.com

Our mission is to publish and distribute inspirational products offering exceptional value and biblical encouragement to the masses.

ecpa Member of the
Evangelical Christian
Publishers Association

Printed in Canada.

Contents

CAPUCINE: HOME TO MY HEART

by Janet Spaeth

Dedication

For my family: You are my treasure and my heart.

"For where your treasure is, there will your heart be also."
MATTHEW 6:21

Prologue

I am afraid, and yet I know I must go forward,
not just for my sake but also for Aliette and my mother.
I am a child and a woman. I am lost and I am found.

One nun stood behind the others, her tall, thin body swathed in the black habit. Her dark eyes studied the two girls expressionlessly, and instinctively Aliette shrank against Capucine.

"That woman, she scares me," Aliette whispered into her sister's side.

Capucine didn't answer. She shoved her hands deeper into the pockets of her apron until her fingers closed protectively around the small rectangle—the leather-bound journal her mother had given her before they'd been separated. She stared at the gaunt nun and then whispered back. *"Non,"* she said. "She is strong, that one, but she is fair."

"She has the light of God in her eyes, eh?" Aliette looked up, her guileless blue gaze as innocent as a kitten's.

"Perhaps." Capucine's mouth straightened into a thin line. *The light of God?* Somewhere her mother cried for her lost children. Was the light of God shining on her? Or had it dimmed?

God seemed to have forgotten the Louet family. When the British had stormed in, they killed her father, took the two girls from their home in Acadia, and dropped them in this convent in New York.

Their mother—what had happened to Mama? Capucine had been literally torn from her mother's arms, and now she rubbed her wrists as if she could still feel Mama's fingers in their last futile grasp as they were wrenched apart. *"Moi, je prierai pour vous!"* she had called to her daughters in Acadian French. *I will pray for you.*

Capucine blinked back the tears. She would not cry. Tears would get them nowhere.

Once again she touched the beloved diary, as if the soft leather would somehow connect her with Mama. In it, her mother had written in her lovely flowing penmanship:

"Car là où est ton trésor, là aussi sera ton couer." Matthieu 6:21.

Then, she hadn't realized how close her treasure was, let alone her heart.

Capucine made a promise. *I will find you.* And then, as ice began to wrap her heart, she added, *I will make sure the British pay for what they have done. I cannot forgive them. I will not forgive them.*

"Capucine?" Aliette tugged on her sleeve. "I am scared."

"I will take care of you," she answered softly.

The nun's face softened a bit and she swept toward them, not unlike a large raven, Capucine thought. From her great height, she bent her head slightly. *"Bonjour. Je m'appelle Soeur Marie-Agathe."* Then she added the words that sounded so wrong: "Hello. My name is Sister Marie-Agathe."

English, the hated language. There was no music in its words, only spread out vowels and sharp-edged consonants.

Aliette tugged fiercely at Capucine's sleeve. "She speaks to us!"

Capucine lifted her chin proudly and answered her in Acadian French. "My name is Capucine Louet, and I will never forget."

Chapter 1

Mama said that God does not forget His children,
but that His children forget Him.
Does He remember me now?

Capucine's fingers ached. Aliette's grip was relentlessly tight, and every time Capucine tried to wiggle her hand free, her sister shook her head in a fury of blond curls.

"Aliette," she whispered furiously, "if you don't let go of my fingers, they'll fall off."

The young girl giggled nervously. "Why does she want to see us? Have you forgotten morning prayers again?"

"How could I? You've been with me every time, and she watches me to make sure I don't miss a single amen."

"Did you bow your head?" Aliette persisted. "Put your hands together? You know that—"

"*Sssh!* Here she comes."

Sister Marie-Agathe motioned them into a sparsely furnished room and sat in a heavy mahogany chair. She looked at them first, one at a time, quite seriously, but saying nothing. Then she held out her arms. "Come to me, children."

Hand in hand, the two girls approached the nun. Capucine's stomach twisted in dread as Sister Marie-Agathe wrapped them in her black-robed embrace. Capucine buried her face in the dark folds and breathed in the smell that she'd come to love, a mixture of lavender and soap. It was distinctly Sister Marie-Agathe's.

"I have something to tell you," she said to them, and from the way her voice broke, Capucine knew it was going to be bad news. "My uncle Claude has passed into our heavenly Father's hands."

Aliette breathed softly. "God rest him and save him."

"Bless you, child, for your prayers. Our kind Lord hears them all." The nun sighed. "My uncle and I were the only members of our family on this side of the ocean. The rest of my family still resides in France. The abbess, with her infinite good heart, has agreed with me that I can best serve by seeing to his estate on their behalf."

There was more coming. Capucine could sense the nun's tension.

"I will be leaving the convent to do this."

"You'll be back." Aliette patted the nun's arm.

Sister Marie-Agathe didn't answer. Capucine's heart froze in her chest, and her hands clenched into tight knots. Aliette would *not* be abandoned again. As the older sister, she'd manage somehow, but Aliette was different. She didn't have the independent heart that Capucine did. She needed an adult to guide her.

You're an adult. She heard the words as clearly as if they had been spoken, and she knew their truth. She would do whatever was necessary to make sure that Aliette was cared for.

But how?

She squeezed her eyes shut and tried to formulate a prayer. *Mon Dieu cher,* she began. *My dear God—*

"Take us," Aliette begged in her piping voice, and Capucine's eyes sprang open. God certainly was quick to answer! "Take us with you!"

The nun stroked their heads. "I am going to New Orleans."

New Orleans! The very name was mystery and intrigue and vivid color. Plus it was French, and in an instant, a longing for her own history washed over Capucine.

"It's very far away," the nun continued. She paused for a moment. "And I must speak honestly. There is unrest there. The Spanish—"

"Spanish?" Capucine laughed. "Don't you mean the French?"

"It is difficult to explain to young ears. You will find French and Spanish and British there, and sometimes they get along, but sometimes. . ." She shrugged and let the sentence finish itself.

"You must not go, then." Capucine clutched the nun's gnarled hands. "If it is not safe for us, then it is not safe for you."

"Oh, it's safe enough. I would not be in peril."

"Then take us." Aliette was more insistent. "You must."

"Aliette!" Sister Marie-Agathe reproved gently. "Such a way of speaking is impolite."

Capucine pulled out of the embrace and dropped to her knees, still grasping the nun's gnarled hands. "Please, please, Sister, take us with you."

"I can't—"

"Please," she implored. "We can help. We will be your servants. We will cook and clean and say our prayers three times a day."

"Three!" A smile twitched around Sister Marie-Agathe's lips. "Well, that is an enticement."

Capucine held her breath as the nun smiled at them both. "Aliette is a blossoming cook, and Capucine, your needle skills are above compare. I suspect that I might find a use for you."

"So may we go?" Capucine asked.

Sister Marie-Agathe nodded. "Yes. We shall all go to New Orleans, to Claude Boncoeur's house."

Aliette stole a look at Capucine. "Boncoeur!" she whispered. "It means *good heart*. Surely it is a sign from God Himself!"

The nun rose to her feet. "Indeed. Claude Boncoeur was one of God's finest men, and I am proud to claim him as my uncle. Well," she finished briskly, "we leave tomorrow."

"Tomorrow?"

"There's no sense in waiting, is there?"

Capucine and Aliette shook their heads. "No, Sister Marie-Agathe," they chorused.

"Then start to ready yourselves." She touched their shoulders tenderly. "I am glad you're going with me, girls. Very glad."

Chapter 2

New Orleans, 1767

*I have determined to live my life as fully as I am able,
and to use my talents as I can to bring me forward.
Who knows what may happen to me now?
But I am ready to meet my future!*

T he breeze off the bay ruffled the stray curls around Capucine's face. No matter how hard she tried, her hair simply would not stay bound in a sedate bun. Sister Marie-Agathe had sighed and poked more and more pins in, until even her patience had been tested to its limit, but to no avail.

Her hair had a mind of its own.

Like the head under it.

The wharf teemed with activity, and three languages melded into one that was uniquely New Orleans. Spanish and French and English. After four months here, Capucine was beginning to gather the Spanish words together into something she understood, but her French and English were flawless, thanks to the daily lessons at the convent, and she turned her head slightly as words floated her way.

". . .will change the order of things." The speaker's English was faintly tinged with a familiar inflection.

She tried to isolate his voice from the other sounds of the wharf. A very interesting conversation might be underway, one that she could find of value.

But the rest of his words were lost as a shout went up. A ship had come in, and from the way it sat low in the water, Capucine knew it was heavily loaded.

What could its cargo be? Perhaps bolts of fine satin and rich velvet from France, or silken embroidery threads from Italy, or perfumed oils from Spain, or tea scented with jasmine from China?

Her imagination soared, although she knew that with the limits of shipping, the contents were probably nothing more exciting than wine and flour.

The ship was quickly docked, and almost immediately the crew leaped onto the wharf. A stout man with an air of authority shouted a few words at the men—words that the wind mercifully carried away, for she suspected they were quite rough—and the men turned back to the ship. Soon bale after bale began to pile up on the wharf.

They *could* be bolts of fabric.

One of the bales had broken open, and something was poking out of it, something silvery that caught the sun's gleam. She moved in for a closer look.

Wham!

A white-wrapped packet crashed into her shoulder, throwing her off balance. She was knocked to the wooden planks, and very ungracefully somersaulted backward, landing on the back of her head, with her heels on the top of the packet.

"Mademoiselle?" a solicitous voice inquired.

She opened her eyes cautiously. Stars and lights spun in front of her, and a pain that alternated dull thuds and sharp pangs began to gain momentum behind her ears. A man's face, his bright-blue eyes soft with concern, blurred in and out of focus. She was vaguely aware that his light-brown hair was being ruffled by the breeze off the water, and she wanted to smooth it back into place.

For some reason, she felt she had to explain to this incredibly handsome man why she was sprawled in such an unladylike position. "I fell." The words sounded garbled to her, and she winced as the mere act of talking sparked an entirely new set of fireworks.

Other faces joined his, those of the crew members who had been unloading the ship. One of them asked, "Is she injured, LeBlanc?" With a few words he dismissed them and turned his attention back to her.

"Mademoiselle? Miss? *Señorita?*"

She tried to laugh at his accent as he tried all three languages, but the sound came out as a dry croak.

"J'ai." Her voice came out as a dry croak, each word pronounced separately. *"Tombé."*

"So I see. You fell." He spoke in French as he rocked back on his heels and studied her, a tiny frown wrinkling his brow. "Would you like to see a doctor?"

She shook her head and winced. "Ow. No."

"Would you like me to help you to your feet?"

"That would be nice."

Soon she was standing, albeit a bit unsteadily.

"Can you walk? Do you want to walk? Would you rather stand here for a moment? Is anything broken?"

His words swam past her scrambled brain like tiny fish. She didn't attempt an answer.

"Let's take a few steps and see how we do."

His words struck her as very funny, but laughing was out of the question. Not when her head felt as big as an apple basket.

With his arm around her waist, they took a few tentative steps. The ground seemed spongy, and Capucine felt buoyant, like a delicately bouncing bubble bobbing along the uneven wharf.

He frowned at her when they stopped. "I don't like your head."

This was too much, and despite the throbbing that threatened to explode her skull, she laughed. "Well," she answered, touching his elegant forehead, "I like yours."

And with those words, the world went dark.

❧

Michel walked along the tree-shadowed street. Evening was coming with its relief from the heat of the day, and the air was heavily scented with the rich aroma of the white flowers that grew in the bushes beside him. He had no idea what they were called, which was silly, he realized, considering how long he had lived in New Orleans.

Perhaps the young woman at the wharf—Capucine Louet—knew their names. She had seemed like the kind that might. Her clothing was thick with her well-known embroidery, and her hair, which had shaken loose of its bun in her fall, flowed around her head like an ebony river. He could see a white flower tucked behind her ear.

He ran his hand across his eyes. His thoughts were as fanciful as if he had gotten hit in the head himself! The poor woman had gotten quite a wallop, and he was glad that he had been there to help her, and to take her to her home.

Nothing happens without a reason. God knows. God is in control.

The irony of what had happened struck him, and he had to smile. He, a mere boat builder, had come to the aid of Capucine Louet. He shook his head in amazement. He knew who she was, of course. Her beauty, so dazzling in the streets of New Orleans, had attracted as much attention as her embroidery had.

He'd known where to take her, to Boncoeur House. A nun, Claude Boncoeur's niece, he'd learned, had met him at the door, thanked him, and taken Capucine from his arms as easily as if she had been a bird.

Since then, he'd been walking, unable to go back to the close confines of his small cottage, preferring instead to roam the streets of New Orleans as the cooling night draped the village in darkness.

His stomach growled, reminding him that he hadn't eaten since noon, and he turned toward home.

He found himself unable to stop thinking about Capucine. He knew, even as he entered his own cottage, that he would be back to see her.

❧

"Capucine?"

A disembodied hand touched her cheek, and automatically Capucine turned toward the welcome scent of lavender and soap.

"How is your head, dear?"

She lifted her head slightly from the cool pillow and stopped as the blood began to thump wildly against her skull. "It hurts, Sister."

"I'm sure it does. You took quite a tumble on the wharf."

"Is there some tea?" Her mouth was as dry as paper.

"Aliette has just brought you some. It should be cool enough to drink a few sips."

Capucine struggled to push herself up and winced as her shoulder flared into pain where the bale had struck her.

Sister Marie-Agathe shook her head as she helped Capucine sip some tea. "Move carefully at first."

Capucine sank back into the pillow. "I don't know if I will have a choice in it. I'm certainly not about to skip or twirl right now."

"True. You have enough bruises and scrapes to keep you in place for a while, but none of it seems too bad. Praise our dearest Lord that Michel LeBlanc was at the wharf today."

The name LeBlanc rang a faint bell. "Who is Michel LeBlanc?"

"He is the man who came to your aid. Do you not remember him?"

"Does he have kind blue eyes?" She smiled at the memory.

Sister Marie-Agathe moved uneasily in her seat. "I don't know that I looked at his eyes, but yes, I suppose they are blue."

"As blue as the delphiniums that grew at the convent?"

"Oh, those delphiniums!" The nun laughed. "How I struggled with them to make them grow."

"But they did," Capucine answered. She took Sister Marie-Agathe's hand in hers, and pressed it to her lips. "They were like me, struggling to die, yet you were there, struggling to keep me alive."

A flush stained the nun's cheeks bright red. "I was doing the Lord's bidding."

Disappointment sank into Capucine's heart. She and Aliette had come to love Sister Marie-Agathe as if she were family—in fact, she had become their family, since the chances that they'd ever be reunited with their mother were remote.

The nun had never said that she loved them. Perhaps it had been too much to ask, but growing up without parents had been painful for the girls, and Sister Marie-Agathe was the surrogate they'd found.

Sister Marie-Agathe must have seen her distress because she leaned closer. "And do you know what the Lord's bidding was?"

Capucine shook her head slightly, just enough for the pounding pain to start again.

"The Lord bid me to love you. I hadn't thought that would happen, my dear. I thought I would tend to your needs, both spiritual and physical. I would make sure you had food, clothes, a dry and warm place to sleep, and the knowledge of our gracious Lord and that you would come to be able to live with forgiveness. But He saw a need that I hadn't recognized."

Too many words. Her mind was still groggy, and the conversation was wrapped in a gauzy aura of unreality.

Speaking had tired her, and she couldn't quite follow what Sister Marie-Agathe was saying. Love. Something about love. And forgiveness?

Her head hurt too much to think about it now. Later, later she would, when the world wasn't filled with thundering drums and crashing cymbals and painful light.

Chapter 3

I have met someone intriguing. He makes me laugh,
which may be the most wonderful thing on earth—or the most dangerous.
Only time may tell.

"Capucine, would you mind going to the market for me?" Aliette's golden head peeked around the doorway. "I'd like to have the chicken done before the day gets too hot. It's already too warm for my comfort."

Every morning Aliette asked the same question, and every morning Capucine gave the same answer. *"Mais oui!"*

"And see if you can find some cabbage while you're there. If there's not cabbage, then look for a turnip. No, two turnips. Wait, a cabbage and two turnips."

Capucine nodded. "Yes. Cabbage and turnips."

"Now hurry!"

As wonderful as Boncoeur House was, she felt stifled inside its whitewashed walls. A walk in the fresh air was welcome.

Summer mornings in New Orleans were blessed with only a touch of the blanketing heat that would follow in the afternoons. The city woke up with beauty. Flowers spread their petals, merchants opened their shops, and the streets were busy with people going about their daily business.

She paused outside the market and tried to remember what Aliette had asked her to purchase. She should have asked her sister to write it down, but Aliette had been in an unusual hurry to return to the kitchen and start the chicken stewing.

Capucine shrugged. Whatever she bought, Aliette would make it into a delicious dish. She had quite a talent for cooking.

What *had* Aliette wanted?

She reached for a cluster of onions, and at the same time, so did another hand.

"Oh, excuse me," she said, pulling back. "I didn't—"

"Mademoiselle Louet!" Michel LeBlanc tilted his head in greeting. Sunlight touched his honey-colored hair. "I see we have the same taste in onions."

"One onion, I suspect, tastes the same as another," she answered.

He grinned. "You are right."

His words had a familiar accent, and her heart raced.

"You are Acadian." She steadied her voice so that it would not quiver and give the secret of her heritage away.

"Yes, I am. I'm proud of it, although there are those here who are not as accepting." He tilted his head slightly toward the group of men who lounged against the wall.

The men stared back at them, their gaze challenging.

Probably British, she thought. It was hard to know how alliances were drawn, and that was the reason she was guarding herself so cautiously. So far, no one except a select few knew that she spoke English and Spanish as well as French, and even fewer knew that she had been born Acadian.

With each passing day, the chance that she would ever be reunited with her mother grew smaller. Mama could have been relocated anywhere, perhaps put in prison, or even—she swallowed hard—dead.

Capucine hated the British with a fiery anger that gnawed at her. The only appeasement was her dream that one day she would find other Acadians who had made their own community again, and she could rejoin with them.

"I understand that there are many Acadians in this area," she said, carefully nonchalant.

"Many of them have settled in this area."

"They've established new lives, I understand."

"Not at all." His words were clipped. "They are the same lives they had before, but they are living them here."

From the way he spoke, and the fervor behind his words, she knew she had found a compatriot who would be able to help her go there. But his hesitation was natural. She'd have to overcome his suspicions of her motives.

She changed the subject.

"I do feel that I am eternally indebted to you for saving my life." She laced her fingers over the edge of her basket to hide their trembling.

"Saving your life? You overstate my actions."

"If you hadn't been at the wharf and acted so quickly. . ." She let the sentence trail off.

He brushed away her gratitude. "Please, speak of it no more. A man who didn't come to your aid would have been no greater than a beast."

Her fingers twisted together. "Nevertheless, I thank you."

"I must admit, Mademoiselle Louet, that I find it a fortunate calamity."

"A fortunate calamity?"

"I was able to make your acquaintance."

She took a deep breath. Her plan had to work. If only he would stop watching her so intently with those brilliant-colored eyes, she could focus on the task at hand.

"And I, yours."

An awkward pause followed, until he picked up the bunch of onions and placed them in her basket. "I wish they were roses."

She couldn't help herself. She took the onions from the basket, held them to her nose, and inhaled deeply. "So do I."

He chuckled at her grimace. "Shall I select some daisies for you?" He gave her a cluster of carrots. "Some violets?" He dropped a handful of beans into her basket. "Or perhaps an orchid?" An oversized cabbage joined the other vegetables.

"Aliette will be delighted with such a bouquet," she said, totally charmed.

"Aliette?"

"She is my sister. As you know, we are staying at Boncoeur House. She cooks. I sew and do needlework." She held out the edge of her shawl, a delicate lace as fine as a spider's web.

"Your reputation as a needlewoman precedes you. I don't believe that anyone here doesn't recognize your work."

"Why, thank you!" she answered, a pleased smile lighting her eyes. "And you? What do you do in New Orleans?"

"I've been here only a few months. I am helping my cousin build boats at his shop."

"Ah. That's why you were at the wharf that dreadful day?"

He grinned. "That's right. But why were you there? What would an elegant woman like yourself be doing at such a place?"

She looked at him sharply. "I like watching the arrival of the ships and wondering what they carry as cargo."

"Inquisitive, eh?"

"Sadly, my downfall." She laughed at her own words. "Literally, my downfall that day!"

"You're as inquisitive as a cat," he said with amusement, "and as quick."

Capucine couldn't believe she was being so bold. She should simply thank him for his help and walk away, but before she could stop herself, she said, "Oh. And do you like cats?"

"Yes," he said. "Of all the animals, I admire them the most. It must be handy to have nine lives." He glanced past her shoulder. "And there is my cousin, looking stern. If I don't hurry, I'll wish I had nine lives."

He quickly paid for his onions, and as he left, he called over his shoulder, *"Au revoir,* Capucine Louet. *À demain!"*

Until tomorrow? What on earth did he mean?

🐾

"Michel, are those stars I see in your eyes? Has the uncatchable been caught?" Pierre escaped his cousin's jab.

"She is a friend." He knew that his words wouldn't convince Pierre. They certainly didn't convince him.

"A friend? *Une amie?"* Pierre guffawed. "A certain kind of friend, I believe."

"She is an acquaintance. I barely know her," Michel protested.

"Ah. I see. First the young woman is a friend, and now she's been demoted to an acquaintance? Hardly the compliment, LeBlanc!"

20

"She is the one I helped at the wharf, the one who was hit by the packet and then struck her head on the planks. Whatever you care to call it, I know her to some extent. And that is all."

Pierre slapped Michel's back. "I'm teasing you. I must say that I'm glad to see you looking like a calf in love."

"A calf in love? What a terrible—"

"Don't be so serious about everything! Let me say one more thing, and then we will be through speaking of this. You've been alone too long. *Le bon Dieu* did not mean for us to spend our time on the earth alone. He gave Adam a helpmate, and He gives you one, too. Perhaps you are this woman's helpmate—as she is yours."

Michel opened his mouth to speak, but Pierre waved away his comments before he could speak. "We have work to do. No more talk about women, or *l'amour*. Go now, and see if you can sand the side of that boat more smoothly. Your mind hasn't been with your hands lately, and although I am your relative and forgiving, I do have a business to run."

"*Oui, oui.*"

Michel bent over the curved wooden slats, and with each stroke he repeated in his mind the prayer that had been his for months. *Thy will. Thy will. Thy will.*

For too long he had been living with a different prayer: *My will.* But age was seasoning his heart with wisdom. *Thy will.*

❧

Night fell upon the city like a blessing. The heat lingered, but it was bearable. Up in her room at the top of Boncoeur House, Capucine stared out the window, her embroidery forgotten on her lap. Lights glimmered, bobbing across the landscape like bright fireflies.

Somewhere out there were those from her homeland. They lived together, bonded by the past and by the terrible scourge that had thrown them into this terrain so unlike their own.

And, perhaps, somewhere was her mother. If, in fact, she was still alive. Not knowing was perhaps the worst state of being.

The tears rarely came any more. She'd learned quickly that tears changed nothing. They were simply a way of washing emotion out of the body.

She didn't want her emotion washed out. She wanted to hold it, to keep it near to her heart where it could boil and keep her resolve clear. Hatred was a strong, driving force. She intended to use its power.

With a sigh, she folded the fabric on her lap and laid it aside. It was a blouse for Madame Dubois, adorned with vibrant leaves and flowers, and it needed to be done soon, but now the light was gone, and her head was beginning to ache.

She wouldn't write in her journal tonight. Not the way she felt.

Once her mother had told her that hate festered and ate into the soul. Love, she had said, was redeeming and healing. Love seemed so far away, though, distant and small like a tiny star that faded in and out of her vision.

A small knock on her door was followed quickly by Aliette peeking inside. "Capucine? Are you asleep?"

"Non. Come in. I was just looking out the window."

Aliette crossed the room and knelt beside her. "This is an amazing place. I feel so free here, don't you? New Orleans is such a mixture of people."

Capucine stiffened. "No one is free," she said. "As long as there is war, there will be conquerors—and the conquered."

Her sister touched her hand. "We aren't conquered. Even when we were, we weren't. No one can take your heart from you." She laughed slightly. "Except, of course, when you fall in love."

"Even then," Capucine chided her, "no one should *take* your heart. It's your treasure."

" 'For where your treasure is, there will your heart be also,' " Aliette quoted. "Remember when Mama taught us that?"

"I couldn't understand why it wasn't the other way around, why it didn't read: Where your heart is, there will your treasure be also. That seemed to be more logical, but Mama assured me that some day it would make complete sense."

"Does it?" Aliette whispered.

Capucine paused. "It's beginning to," she said softly. "It's beginning to."

Chapter 4

Some people express themselves in music, or painting, or poetry.
I record each moment in my embroidery, the green minutes, the blue hours,
the black days. I see the rhythm in the flow of the thread and
the dip of the needle as it weaves its way in and out.

I f only he could come up with some excuse to go to Boncoeur House, Michel thought, he would be able to stop this insane habit he'd developed of lingering by the market on his way to his cousin's shop.

But the residents of Boncoeur House—a nun and two young women—hadn't much use for a boat, and he spent way too much of his time mooning over anything that reminded him of Capucine. When he caught himself smiling at an onion, he knew that the time had come for him to act or forever abandon this fancy.

He tugged on his jacket and straightened his shoulders. Pierre would tease him endlessly about his side trip on his way to his job, but he'd understand that the course of true love sometimes took a detour.

The solid outline of Boncoeur House stood before him, and he paused at the foot of the stone pathway as he ran through possible scenarios to explain his presence.

"May I help you?"

He spun around as the voice spoke behind him and found himself face-to-face with a tall, black-garbed nun. He recognized Sister Marie-Agathe, whom he'd met when he'd brought Capucine home after her injury.

"Michel LeBlanc!" She beamed at him. "Please, come inside! I'm sure that Capucine would like to see you again."

He was swept into the house before he could object. "She's in the garden. Follow me, please."

Michel had only a hurried glance at the interior of the house as he trailed after the nun. Soon they were in the back garden.

Capucine sat in the morning sunshine, her head bent over a length of linen. A few ebony curls had escaped the loose bun that was knotted at the base of her neck, like black lace around an ivory cameo, he thought, surprising himself with the poetic image. A silver needle flashed in the light, dipping in and out of the fabric.

"Capucine, you have a visitor," Sister Marie-Agathe announced.

She looked up, squinting against the sun, and then sprang up, tucking the errant tresses into place. They promptly dropped down again.

"Michel! I mean, Monsieur LeBlanc!"

Sister Marie-Agathe looked at Capucine, at him, and then back at her. She smiled a little but only said, "Ah," before ducking back inside the house.

"She's watching from inside," Capucine said with a meaningful glance at one window where a drapery fluttered.

"She's making sure that you're safe."

Capucine tilted her head at him. "Are you saying that I might not be safe with you? Why, I thought you were quite a gentleman."

He knew he was blushing. It was one of the curses of being fair skinned. "I live my life as a God-fearing man should," he answered. "I would never do anything to hurt you."

"You're a Christian, then."

"I am."

She didn't respond right away. Instead, she took the fabric she was working on and shook it out and studied it critically. The snowy white linen was festooned with bright threads and ribbons in what seemed to be an abstract design.

"What are you sewing?" he asked. "It's quite pretty."

"I'm embroidering a tablecloth." She resettled the swath of cloth onto her lap and took the needle in her fingers again. "I prefer to work on it during the morning when it's a bit more comfortable, and when the light is good."

The needle dipped in and out of the material, leaving a trail of vivid green across the white fabric.

"Is it your own design?" The question was less from curiosity than the need to break the overwhelming silence.

She looked up at him, a half smile on her face. "I always do my own designs."

"Interesting." He picked up a corner of the cloth, which was almost touching the ground, and examined the needlework. "I don't know much about embroidery— actually, I don't know anything about embroidery—but this is quite lovely."

"Thank you."

Neither of them spoke, and only a bird's song decorated the silence.

He swallowed. What was he doing here?

"You seem to be doing well. Are you recovered?"

"Completely."

"Well, then." He was completely out of things to say. He stood up abruptly. "It's been quite pleasant visiting with you."

She also rose to her feet, gathering the embroidered fabric to her. "I've enjoyed this, too."

Together they walked through the house, past a smiling Sister Marie-Agathe and to the entrance. Capucine opened the front door and called to a young woman coming up the stone path.

"Aliette, this is the fellow who saved my life that day at the wharf, Michel LeBlanc! Michel, this is my sister."

Aliette was as blond as Capucine was dark, and she cheerfully met him with an immediate and effusive greeting. "We all owe you quite a debt, *monsieur*. Would you do us the honor of joining us for dinner this evening?"

Capucine tapped his shoulder. "Aliette is a marvelous cook. You must come."

Was it her touch? Was it the invitation? Was it the chance to see her again?

Whatever the reason, Michel's spirits soared. "It would be my pleasure."

"We shall see you, then, at the close of the afternoon." Capucine's eyes twinkled as she leaned in and said in a stage whisper, "Be prepared to eat until you cannot stir. Aliette cooks enough for an army every evening."

Strands of her hair, softly scented with some floral aroma, curled around her face and brushed against his cheek as she moved away from him.

He bowed, unable to hide the smile that captured his face. "Au revoir—until this evening, mademoiselles."

His feet barely touched the paving stones as he returned to the street. Then, under the cover of the thick shrubbery that surrounded the house, he glanced back. The two women were turning to return to the house, and something flashed in the sunlight in front of Capucine.

It was the needle, hanging from the embroidery thread, and she quickly caught it up and returned it to the cloth, weaving it safely into the fabric.

From the far reaches of his mind came the uneasy feeling that he had missed something rather important, but the thought of spending more time with the fascinating Capucine drove back the thought.

Tonight would be more important than any bit of silver. Much more important.

☙☞

The sun was at its peak, driving Capucine from the garden. Moist and intense, the damp heat was too much for her to work comfortably outside.

In the house was not much better. The rooms held the humid closeness, and eventually she was forced to put her head back on the settee in her bedroom, a wet cloth on her forehead to cool her, and close her eyes.

Sleeping was out of the question. Too much had happened today—all of it beginning and ending with Michel LeBlanc.

He was Acadian. The lilt in his words took her back to the precious years of her childhood, before she was separated from her mother and her friends. He would understand. He might even be able to help her.

She rubbed the bridge of her nose, trying to ease her headache that had begun to gather. There were times when her goal seemed so clear, and others when it was a garbled mess.

First, she had to find out what happened to her mother. Logic told her that she had probably died, either in those terrible days when the British had come sweeping in, or in the dark days afterward.

But thinking what might have happened and knowing what really happened could be poles apart.

She owed it to her mother to try to find her. In her heart, she knew that Mama must have tried everything within her power to find her daughters, but her resources would have been limited. The realization that her mother missed her and Aliette as much as they missed their mother struck like a poisoned arrow. Was Mama, at this very moment, thinking of her daughters?

Capucine had heard murmurs that some Acadians had been sent to this area. She heard the sounds of their voices on the streets, in the markets, at church. None had been even faintly familiar, though, and her careful questioning of the few whom she trusted hadn't indicated that her mother or friends were near.

One settlement in particular had her attention. *Bayou Teche.* The name was coming up in overheard conversations more and more.

The name took on a golden glow.

Bayou Teche.

She heard it in the stir of her skirts as she walked. *Bayou Teche.* It was whispered from tree to tree. *Bayou Teche.* The birds in the garden chirped it. *Bayou Teche.*

Somehow she had to get there. She had to see once again what had been taken from her. She was Acadian in her blood.

Of course, it might be, as rumors often were, untrue or only partially true. These days, with Spanish control of the city in the offing, the streets were abundant with rumor and speculation.

But as long as the slightest chance existed, she would continue in her pursuit, for her mother and for her people.

Michel LeBlanc might be just the person she had been looking for.

"Capucine!" Aliette spoke from the doorway. "I need to run a quick errand. Sister Marie-Agathe is out, so she can't help me. Can you come to the kitchen and watch the soup for me?"

"Me?" she asked, sitting up and letting the damp cloth slide from her face. "You trust me with your soup?"

"Silly goose!" Her sister laughed. "Everything's taken care of. All you have to do is stir it once in a while, and if you could peek in at the bread, that'd be wonderful, although I should be back before it's done."

Reluctantly, Capucine stood up and grumbled as she made her way into the stifling kitchen. She knew nothing about cooking, nothing except that the kitchen was her least favorite place in the house. How on earth Aliette could stand this heat was beyond her.

"There probably isn't any errand," she muttered as she moved the spoon slowly through the bubbling mixture. It smelled wonderful, but the cloud of steam rising from it just intensified the warmth of the room. *Aliette couldn't stand being in here one second longer—not that I blame her, not one bit—and she's gone in search of a breeze.*

The wisps of hair that refused to stay in place soon turned from spry curls to lank strings. Her dress stuck to her, and her face streamed with perspiration.

She muttered as she checked on the bread. "I can't believe Aliette left me here. How am I supposed to know if this bread is ready? The soup smells done, and—"

She wiped her hands on her skirt. She probably should have worn one of Aliette's aprons, but this dress would have to be washed anyway.

This dinner was so important. How could her sister abandon her like this? If anyone could ruin a dinner, she could. She'd have a stern older-sister talk with Aliette before bed tonight about responsibility.

She turned gratefully at the sound of someone at the door. "Aliette, you may have your kitchen back. I am as thoroughly baked as one of your roasts."

Michel laughed.

Capucine gasped. She knew that she looked terrible, red and sweating and covered with splotches of soup. She wanted to grab one of the kitchen cloths and throw it over her face.

"Monsieur LeBlanc," she said, trying desperately to repair the damage as well as she could. She smoothed her hair back and wiped her cheeks with her fingers. "You've caught me by surprise. I'm afraid I'm not—I'm not at my best right now."

He shook his head. "On the contrary, mademoiselle. You are lovely, if I might say so."

"Lovely? I hardly think so, especially now."

"I disagree. Your cheeks are pink, your eyes are sparkling, and your skin is glowing."

Her dismay at being found in such condition evaporated into laughter. "In other words, I'm overheated, near tears, and perspiring."

He chuckled. "Aliette should be back soon. I passed her on the way here."

"Yes, she said she had some errand to run."

"Ah. Yes, she was just coming out of—"

"Michel LeBlanc!" Sister Marie-Agathe swept into the room. "It's so good to see you again." She frowned at Capucine, clearly noting her unkempt condition. "My dear, are you sure you should be receiving guests?"

"Sister, the blame is all mine. I'm afraid I was lured in here by the delicious aromas. My path had crossed with Aliette's, and she told me that you were out, so I was to let myself in."

Capucine growled softly. She was certainly going to have that talk with Aliette, but it was now going to include the folly of what she had done. Not only was it highly improper, but she had also created this awkward situation.

Sister Marie-Agathe murmured a few conciliatory words and led Michel from the kitchen. Moments later, Aliette arrived and within minutes had an apron on, the bread out, the soup off the fire, and her sister calmed down.

"*Sssh, sssh,*" she said, shooing Capucine out the door and waving away her complaints. "Later. Right now you need to put yourself to rights. Dinner will be served in a few moments."

Capucine scurried up the stairs and washed her face, re-brushed and pinned her hair, and changed her dress. Within minutes, she entered the main room of

Boncoeur, where Michel and Sister Marie-Agathe sat.

He rose to his feet. "Mademoiselle!"

She dipped in a small curtsy. "We are delighted to have your company tonight, monsieur."

"My pleasure." He coughed. "I must apologize for intruding into your kitchen—"

"My kitchen? Hardly! I have no cooking skills. For food I rely upon my sister, Aliette. What I would do without her—"

Sister Marie-Agathe cleared her throat. "Capucine. . ."

Perhaps the heat had gone to her head, she thought, as she heard the words coming from her own mouth. "Well, it's true. When Aliette was born, the angels must have realized that they slighted me with culinary talent, so they gave mine to her."

The nun's lips twisted as she clearly fought an amused smile. "Capucine, that is not—"

Aliette appeared at the doorway. "I may cook, but my fingers turn to thumbs with a needle. The good Lord, le bon Dieu, has gifted us all differently."

"That is so," Michel agreed. "I'm afraid I would also be a catastrophe with an embroidery needle and thread, and in the kitchen I can prepare only the most basic foods, but give me a length of wood, and I will happily build you a boat."

"A boat!" Aliette laughed. "I will remember it should the need for a boat arise, although I must honestly say that I cannot foresee such an occasion, right, Capucine?"

Capucine nodded, although the truth was that indeed there might be a call for a boat at some point. One never knew when the least bit of information might play a crucial role.

"Now, let us go eat, before the day's heat cooks the food even longer," she announced.

After they had seated themselves, Sister Marie-Agathe asked Michel if he would like to lead them in asking a blessing.

"Mais oui! Of course I will!"

Capucine peeked out of the corner of her eye as she bowed her head. He didn't seem to struggle to find the words, as she did when Sister Marie-Agathe occasionally asked her to pronounce the blessing.

His grace was short and direct. "Lord of all, we ask Thy blessing and Thy touch on all who are gathered here today."

Sister Marie-Agathe looked a bit taken aback, as if the brevity surprised her, but Capucine breathed a sigh of relief as the nun seemed to accept it.

The dinner was, as usual, splendid. Aliette had outdone herself, and how she managed to look cool and relaxed was incomprehensible to Capucine. She seemed to blossom with the extra attention, and Capucine looked quickly between her sister and their guest. Could it be Michel's presence that was causing Aliette's extra vitality?

But nothing passed between them. No shared glances, no coy smiles, no lingering touches as dishes were handed around the table.

"This is a lovely tablecloth," Michel said, touching the hem of the linen. "Is this your needlework, Capucine?"

"It is. I'm afraid it's an old one, but it's held up well."

"Wasn't this one of the first ones you made?" Sister Marie-Agathe asked as she took a piece of bread. "This is one of the convent designs, I believe."

"Yes, it is." Capucine picked up the corner of it and showed it to them. "This is the dove of peace."

"So I see," Michel said. "There are never enough doves, are there?"

She bit her lip to keep herself from responding as sharply as she wished.

Sister Marie-Agathe filled the uneasy silence. "Peace is something we all must work for." She laid her napkin across her plate and caught Capucine's gaze with hers. "Doves or no doves," she added sternly.

❧

The sun was sinking into the horizon as Michel prepared to leave, and Capucine walked with him down the cobbled path to the street. Overhead, the weeping willows whispered to each other as a faint breeze ruffled the long strands. He couldn't think of a time when he had been happier, or more at ease.

"When Aliette first came here, she called these 'sweeping willows,'" Capucine said.

"That fits them better, I think," he answered. "They sweep, not weep."

They walked a few more steps, and he stopped. "May I ask you a question?"

"Yes."

"Will you answer it?"

"Perhaps."

He paused. This woman was at times so oblique that there seemed no chance of knowing her, and at other times so friendly that he felt he had known her since birth. "You speak French with your family and with me, but do you also speak English?"

Was he imagining it, or did her laugh have a tinny ring of nervousness? "Why on earth would you ask such a question?"

"The part about sweeping and weeping willows. That's English."

"Yes, I suppose it is."

"So you do speak English."

"Enough to know what the difference is between a sweeping willow and a weeping willow."

"And enough to tell me my answer, although you think you do not."

"I did not answer."

"Ah, but you did."

The repartee was frustrating.

He continued. "You must have learned languages other than French in the convent."

She shrugged. "These are no more than games, *mon ami*. Perhaps if you keep your eye on me, you may even catch me speaking Egyptian, or perhaps Chinese." She

29

laughed. "Although my talents, I'm afraid, do not go quite that far."

"You are a fascinating woman, Capucine Louet." The last rays of the sun illuminated her rich ebony hair. "May I see you again?"

She tilted her head and studied him. "You do so at your own risk."

His breath caught in his throat. "It is a risk I am willing to take."

"Then yes, you may see me again." She leaned in closer to him. "But be aware, I am not one to fall in love with, for I am not one to fall in love."

And with those mysterious words, she turned and left him.

Chapter 5

Only in the silence do we hear.

Capucine sat on the stone bench at the edge of the courtyard, her embroidery spread out across her lap. Conversations flowed around her like water from a fountain, some in French, some in Spanish, and some in English. Months of experience had helped her sort through the barrage of words, to pick out exactly what was useful and what was not.

The government changeover was going well, but she knew that nothing was perfect. There would always be someone looking for a way to make his or her own nest a bit better feathered.

One cluster of three men in particular had her attention. They spoke in the flat, broad tones of English, and when they talked of the Spanish and the French, the disdain in their voices was clear. They had something in mind, something that would disrupt the smooth flow of New Orleans.

With a quick tilt of his head, a short, stocky man in the group indicated her. "We need to be careful. She could—"

"*Pffft.*" The man with the oversized moustache waved away the other's concern. "She is French."

The third man hooted in derision. "Plus she is a woman. What danger can she be?"

What danger indeed?

Her fingers flew as her needle outlined an egret with fantastic plumage. Crimson, gold, and coral—the threads dipped in and out of the fabric, filling the bird's feathers with a rainbow of warm colors.

"I'll not leave here without what's due me," the barrel-shaped man declared. "I've come too far from my homeland to slink back like a beaten dog."

"I'm with you." The tall fellow rubbed his moustache thoughtfully. "And I have a plan, a smart plan, to make sure that this city pays me what I'm owed."

"You've got a plan?" The third man, nondescript in his work clothes, leaned in closer. "Let's hear it then, my good man. Time's wasting, and I'm not getting any younger."

31

The first man snorted. "That's the truth. Come on, Will, now let's hear it."

The three put their heads together and began to talk. Capucine couldn't make out the words clearly, just bits and pieces of sentences that didn't make much sense, but as the men grew cocky with their cleverness, they drew apart and their voices grew louder.

Her needle flashed in the sunlight, gaining in speed as she glared at them under the cover of her eyelashes.

What danger indeed?

At last, with a great shout of laughter, the men slapped each other's backs and swaggered away. It took every ounce of willpower for her not to stand up and follow them, repeating their conversation in English—and translating into Spanish and then French.

Someday, she thought as she folded her sewing, they would get their comeuppance. Heaven wouldn't hold them, that was for sure.

She shot a dire glance at the retreating figures.

Sister Marie-Agathe would tell her to pray for them.

She couldn't. She just couldn't.

🐝

Michel stood at the side of the courtyard. Surely he wasn't mistaken. That was Capucine, sitting on the bench, her constant embroidery in her hands. Nearby her a trio of rough-dressed men, known in the town for their wild ways, carried on an animated conversation as they walked slowly out of the sunlit area.

Yet she seemed to be totally unaware of them. Or was she? Had she just raised her head a bit, to look at them with what was clearly contempt?

The men were British. Most of the British in New Orleans were gentlemen, but these three had come in on a vessel filled with rats and spoiled goods. He remembered it well.

The townspeople had taken the situation into their own hands. They'd towed the boat, a rickety thing called the *Gull*, well out into the water, far enough away that the rodents couldn't swim ashore, and sunk it. The owners had been furious and had vowed revenge. Fortunately—or not—they spent most of their time filling their mouths with ale, and their plans never progressed past idle threats.

He moved toward her, edging around the border of the courtyard. He didn't want to seem as if he were watching her, although of course he was. Somehow he knew that she would not accept his watchful attentions. She was too independent.

Yet these men were well known to him, and although they'd never caused any more real trouble, he knew that even an old powder keg could explode. He always acted with caution around them.

"Michel!" She called to him as she stood up. He apparently hadn't been as stealthy as he'd hoped. *"Comment t'allez vous?"*

"Bon."

His nightmare seemed to spring into reality. The three men turned around.

"Bone, bone, bone, who's got the bone?"

"Take no notice of them," he said to Capucine in a low voice. "Their stupidity is exceeded only by their stench."

She tucked her embroidery into her apron pocket and looped her arm though his. "I'd noticed that."

"Bone, bone, bone!" The men continued their taunt.

"Why do they keep doing that?" she asked, frowning.

"They are ignorant. No more reason needed. Shall we go?" He held her arm tightly at his side.

"Mammy-zelle, show us your pretty stitches!" one of the men called.

"You fool," one of the others said, poking his companion in the side, "she can't speak English. You might as well be barking like a dog or snorting like a pig."

The third man took a bold step forward. "I'll go get that fancy needlework from her. I'd look pretty with a stitched-up cloth on my collar!"

Michel gripped her arm closer. "They are all bluster. Act as if they're not there."

"Michel, are you sure?"

Help me, dear Father in heaven. Help us. Show us the way out of this.

The mustachioed man shook his head. "Aw, that old cloth is probably just a rag she's making into a hanky. Let's go have us some refreshment, what do you say, men? This heat is causing me a mighty thirst."

With a show of laughing and shoving, the three confronters left the courtyard, apparently in search of more ale.

"Oh, Michel," Capucine said, sagging with clear relief against him, "I thought for sure they were going to come after us."

"Well, we were in the middle of this courtyard. I don't think you had much reason to be really afraid that they'd hurt you," he said.

"I wasn't afraid of that," she said. "But I—now, you're going to think I'm foolish for saying this—I was afraid they'd take my embroidery."

"You treasure it that much?" He couldn't keep the amazement out of his voice.

"It's my livelihood," she explained. "And I suppose, yes, it's my treasure. You know what the Bible says: 'For where your treasure is, there will your heart be also.'"

"I wonder if the gospel was referring to embroidery," he said lightly.

Capucine stared up at him, her eyes so dark brown they were nearly as black as the waters at night. "Why wouldn't it?"

He didn't have a good answer. Instead, he did what any good man would do—he changed the subject. "Were you returning home?"

"Yes, I was. Today is the day Sister Marie-Agathe is refreshing all the linens and draperies, and Aliette is furiously cleaning her precious kitchen and roasting what must be half a pig."

"Half a pig?" He tried to visualize that in the small kitchen, and failed.

"Maybe not half a pig, but it's a huge chunk of something pork, and between Sister Marie-Agathe's pounding of the drapes and Aliette's blazingly hot kitchen, I decided the best thing for me to do was leave them in peace."

"They don't expect you to help?" The question popped out before he could stop it.

"I did my part earlier. I'm taller than Aliette, so I emptied the cupboards for her, and I'll put them back to rights later. Sister Marie-Agathe and I took the linens down to the garden to air, and I'll have the distinct privilege of putting them in place again when she's finished. So no, I haven't been a sluggard, if that's what you're asking."

"I didn't mean to imply that at all!"

She shrugged. "I know what I do, and that's what matters."

He had the terrible feeling he was losing ground, and it mattered to him very much.

"Are you going home now? I would be glad to walk with you."

"Don't you have boats to build?" she asked, the humor returning to her voice.

"Possibly."

"Oh," she said, laughing, "you're being as circumspect as I! Actually, I'm not ready to go home at all. Would you mind showing me where you build your boats? I'd like to meet your cousin, too."

Michel's world shuddered to a stop. Taking her to the shop and introducing her to Pierre would set him up for a daily barrage of teasing. It was a terrible thing to do, just terrible, but worse would be to tell her no, that he wouldn't bring her there.

He pasted on a smile that he didn't really feel. "*Allons!* Let's go!"

The boat shop was only a few blocks away.

"Pierre, I've—" he began as he entered the doorway, but his words were cut short as his cousin exploded from the back room.

"Michel LeBlanc, you are a fool! I send you for a simple—oh, hello!" Pierre stopped in the middle of his angry spate of words. "What is this? Or should I say, *who* is this? Michel, please introduce me to your lovely companion."

"Capucine Louet, this is my horrible cousin Pierre LeBlanc. He is a slave driver, and a terrible flirt. You should always be careful around him."

"Mademoiselle Louet, it is a pleasure to meet you." Pierre delicately balanced Capucine's hand in his and bowed deeply, dropping a kiss on her fingertips as he rose. "You are always welcome in my humble shop, even when Michel, my bullish apprentice with two left hooves, has wandered off."

Capucine laughed. "The pleasure is mine."

Pierre winked openly at Michel. "She is charming, this one is. Take good care of her."

"He's already rescued me this morning," she said.

"Really?" Pierre glanced quizzically at his cousin. "What is this story?"

"Nothing. The crew from the *Gull* was a bit too interested in her embroidery."

"So you ran them off?"

"Not exactly. Their taste for ale got the better of them, and they left on their own. You know how they are."

Pierre rolled his eyes. "Mademoiselle, I regret that you had such an unlucky experience."

"Michel assures me that I was never in any danger, but this is the second time he has come to my assistance."

"Capucine—" Michel tried to protest, but she spoke over his objections.

"It's true. First by the water, and now this. I am indebted to you. I can never repay you."

Pierre's eyes twinkled. "Give him your heart, *cherè*."

She looked at Michel, a speculative gleam in her gaze. "My heart? Would you want it?"

Why not? he thought. *You already have mine.*

Instead, he shook his head. "I warned you. He is a romantic dreamer."

"Dreams are good," she said, "and romance is good, but I must agree they're not enough. They're not food, or a shelter over your head."

"She is practical," Michel said. "Practical enough to know that someone must buy the threads for her embroidery."

"Oh, yes," his cousin responded. "Her embroidery, which the men from the *Gull* found intriguing. I would be very interested in seeing it myself."

Capucine withdrew the folded cloth from her pocket.

"I won't spread the thing out. I don't want to get any sawdust in it, but you can see from this bit here what it's like. I'm just starting the pattern, making it as I go. Right now it just looks like a crazy rooster, but it's actually supposed to be an egret."

"An egret?" Pierre looked confused.

"It's a big bird that was in one of the books at the house. I must confess I've never seen one, so I've made up the colors myself."

"These spots of blue and green to the side?" he asked.

She put the cloth back in her pocket. "Those are the marks where the flowers will be."

Michel had the feeling that he'd just walked into the middle of a discussion that he didn't understand.

Capucine said to him, "I think I've stayed away long enough. I should get back and help Sister Marie-Agathe and Aliette."

"I'll walk with you—"

"No, no reason to. I'm perfectly safe. Thank you again for saving me once more. Monsieur Pierre LeBlanc, I'm glad to have met you. Au revoir."

With that, she turned quickly and walked out of the shop.

Michel frowned at his cousin. "Did I miss something?"

Pierre rubbed his beard thoughtfully. "Perhaps yes, perhaps no. I'm not sure, but I think our Capucine Louet might need a protector more than she realizes."

"What? Why?"

"I won't say, not yet, but we should pray for the young woman. Is she a Christian?"

"She grew up in a convent and lives with a nun."

"I grew up on a poultry farm and live behind a boat shop. That doesn't make me either a chicken or a sailing vessel."

The analogy wasn't quite sound, but Michel knew what his cousin meant. "I'm not sure," he acknowledged at last. "I do wish you'd tell me what this is all about."

A little line of worry etched its way into Pierre's forehead. "Not yet." He busied himself with some scraps of wood from the floor. "You do know she's Acadian. I can hear it in her voice."

"Are you sure?" Michel frowned. "I've thought it myself, but I couldn't be sure."

"I believe she is. She would have been very young when she left Acadia. There are, however, enough subtle nuances in her speech." Pierre met his eyes squarely. "I might be wrong. But promise me that you'll be careful. Very careful. All is not what it seems. Pray for wisdom, my cousin."

Chapter 6

A small cottage in the country, away from others, just my loved ones around me,
and a dog and a cat to keep my feet warm—my desires are simple.

The Place d'Armes buzzed with rumor. Men huddled together in animated conversation. Certain phrases broke free of their conversations and floated in the air.

"—never allowed!"

"He would be wise to watch his—"

"—a stranger to us! What does he know?"

"He must be mad! Insane! *Dérangé!*"

Capucine bent over her embroidery, her fingers swiftly guiding the needle as she eavesdropped.

She knew whom they were talking about. All of New Orleans was talking about him.

Antonio de Ulloa. Spain had sent him to be the first Spanish governor of New Orleans. Capucine was vague about what had happened—it had all occurred before she had arrived—but somehow New Orleans now belonged to the Spanish, not the French. Nothing had changed after the signatures had dried on the page, and the French, she'd been told, had lived as they always had. Now Spain was starting to flex its muscle, and de Ulloa was the fist.

She put her head closer to her embroidery as she put the last touches on a brilliant lily. The Place d'Armes was usually not this busy on a weekday. On Sundays, of course, people would stroll through it after services at the St. Louis Church, and Capuchins, the spiritual leaders after whom she had been named, were often there, too, trying to find some relief from the stifling heat.

Capucine kept the jail carefully out of her vision. She did not want to know what went on in there, nor what the men who were housed in it had done. There were some things best left unknown.

A shadow broke the sunlight across her fabric, and she looked up. It was Madame Dubois's maidservant, a charming young woman with skin the color of *café au lait*. Her voice contained the lilt of islands far away when she said in patois French, "My madame, she would care to know if the blouse, it is finished."

Capucine reached down for the carefully folded blouse that lay in a parcel at her feet. "Please tell her I hope that she wears it with health."

The servant's nod was barely visible. "Oui, ma'm'selle. *Merci.* A'voir."

With a quick bob of a curtsy, the maid took the parcel and was gone.

The sun was nearing its zenith, and the shade Capucine had enjoyed was vanishing. Droplets of sweat were becoming rivulets, and she gathered her embroidery to leave.

"Capucine!"

With a quick intake of breath, she sprang to her feet, spilling her threads across the stones of the plaza. Then she slumped in relief.

"Michel LeBlanc, you nearly scared the life right out of me!"

She knelt to pick up the skeins of floss at the same time he did, and their heads bumped.

"I'm sorry. I saw you here and—"

A scuffle broke out near them.

"You cannot speak of what is right, not when you say that he—" one of the combatants growled.

"This is what must be—" another responded, but the rest of his sentence was interrupted when a blow struck his jaw.

Michel stuffed the last bits of thread back into her satchel. "Allons! We had better hurry to avoid getting knocked down ourselves. I don't look forward to an exchange with those fellows."

She allowed herself to be hustled out of the plaza, his arm protectively on her back.

"Do you often come to the plaza?" he asked.

"I like the vigor of it," she answered and then laughed. "Sometimes, like today, there was a bit too much vigor, though!"

"I agree." As they strolled back toward Boncoeur House, he commented, "I assume that you are firmly sided with the French on the issue."

She shrugged noncommittally.

With fury, he swatted at an insect that flew by his face, and the beetle barely escaped his hand. "It does seem right to side with the French, does it not, since this village has been French for so many years and is even named after a Frenchman, the Duke of Orleans, not a Spaniard."

She glanced at him covertly. He was quite serious about this.

"Plus," he continued, "I am dismayed, of course, that this exchange, if indeed it is an exchange, was done in secret, but more than that, once again we are being treated as if we are mere property to be handed back and forth."

She could see his teeth clench, and then he added, in a softer tone that was no less impassioned, "This happened to us once before, in Acadia, and now. . .now we are expected to bow and scrape and say, *Sí?* This is not going to go easily for de Ulloa, and I fear for the repercussions that he will suffer for his country."

"Your anger surprises me," she said when he had paused.

He smiled a bit. "I am sorry, Capucine. I suspect that we all have one part of our lives that are our—how to say it? The one thing that we cannot compromise on. For me, it is justice and fairness and truth. I do not tolerate lies. Not at all."

Her blood ran icy cold as he continued. "Those who live in the shadow of secrecy and untruths and even half-truths will have to explain their actions to their Maker one day. A lie is a detestable twisting of what is real, and I, for one, have had enough of that."

He rubbed his hand over his face. "I'm afraid the heat is getting to me. I usually don't pontificate like this to lovely young ladies."

Their footsteps had taken them to the walkway of Boncoeur House, and she paused. "You speak of what is important to you. I would not expect less of you, Michel LeBlanc, not at all."

Somehow she walked into the house, out of the oppressive midday warmth, and collapsed into a chair. What would he think of her when he found out what she was doing?

And why did it matter to her so much?

❧

Capucine put the fabric in the box beside her bed. Within a week, it would be done and she could deliver it to the woman who owned the shop where she bought her embroidery materials. In exchange for the tablecloth, she would receive several hanks of brilliant thread and a handful of coins.

She couldn't make her stitchery fast enough for the demand. More and more, she had visitors asking for garments and household linens. She needed more than two hands.

She couldn't do this forever. Her eyes burned, her fingers cracked, and her neck ached. Plus the stress of the deadlines was nearly unbearable.

And it wasn't safe. The other day she'd seen a flicker of knowledge in Pierre's face. What did he know? And how did he know it?

She shuddered as she thought that perhaps she wasn't as skilled as she thought she was. Her designs might be growing too obvious.

An egret? What had she been thinking?

Things were changing too quickly for her comfort. In her grand plan for revenge, she'd never considered Michel LeBlanc. She'd told him that she couldn't fall in love.

But she'd forgotten to tell her heart.

Already he was moving into her mind. She'd never met anyone like him, a fellow who lived honestly, who respected his fellow human beings completely. And who seemed to find her appealing.

Could it be that at last she had found someone to love?

But her mission wasn't completed. She couldn't fall in love, not yet.

A gust of wind blew the curtains from her open window. A thunderstorm, bringing blessed relief from the heat, was moving in.

Capucine dropped into her bed. From her pillow, she could watch the rain fall on the trees. The long graceful branches of the weeping willow, caught by the storm's winds, stood at an unnatural angle to the earth.

Thunderstorms were wonderful. She'd always loved to watch the power they unleashed, to hear the rumble of the thunder, to see the mighty flash of lightning. When they'd been little girls, huddled in the convent, Aliette had told her that the thunder was God's voice. Capucine, always the practical older sister, had asked her to explain lightning.

The little girl had looked at her with wide eyes and explained that the lightning was God's way of pointing at a wrongdoer, much the way Sister Marie-Agathe did when she was angry.

I have some suggestions for You, she thought, *starting with three men. You can point at them.*

Michel had explained about their boat, the *Gull*, being sunk, and she could almost feel a bit sorry for them. It wasn't fair, not really, that they lost what little they had, but on the other hand, the townspeople were right to stop the boat from docking there and releasing its pestilence on the area.

Maybe their anger was somewhat justified. Still, after a while, one needed to lay it aside and move on.

Something prickled at her heart.

Not everything needed to be laid aside, she qualified. Some things could not be forgiven. Nothing would be changed if someone forgave and forgave and forgave.

Nothing?

She picked up the small picture of Jesus that Sister Marie-Agathe had placed at her bedside.

You forgave and forgave and forgave, didn't You? And we're so slow that we still don't understand. I don't understand.

How could Jesus have done this? And how could He forgive even after His death?

He'd been hurt worse than she'd been. Yet still His arms were outstretched, welcoming, even loving those who had killed Him.

"I'm sorry," she said softly to the picture. "I'm sorry."

Deep inside her heart, a bit of ice melted.

Chapter 7

Forgiveness has a medicinal quality to it—and an equally medicinal taste.
I struggle with this daily, keeping the hate close
and not letting mercy temper my heart.

Days grew into weeks, and the weeks passed in a fast parade. The market burst with late-summer bounty, and Michel found himself stopping on the way to the boat shop in the morning to pick up some fresh produce for his lunch.

Capucine was usually there, and the two of them chatted as they shopped together, occasionally stopping to share some bread and tea. The days that she wasn't there seemed to be covered with a gray pall, while the mornings that they were able to linger sparkled with joy.

It wasn't enough. He wanted to steal away from the shop in the afternoon and spend some time with her, but he and Pierre were busier than ever with a spate of orders for boats. Michel left the shop exhausted, but his footsteps often took him to the Boncoeur House. It was a circuitous route home but one he took at the close of business every day.

It was a busy road. He'd often see Aliette hurrying toward the house from one direction just as Capucine was returning from the other. Now that the weather was cooling somewhat, Capucine had explained, she was spending more time in the area by the marketplace. The bustle and colors of the wares being traded there were inspiration for her embroidery designs.

Her patterns were increasingly vivid. The last apron she wore over her dress had an abstract design of swirls and speckles in black and red and green on a snowy white background. He shook his head. God hadn't given him a creative eye like hers, one that could invent and concoct so freely. Instead, He'd gifted him with the ability to saw wood and nail it into the shape of a boat. It wasn't the same at all. He'd tried his hand once at painting a landscape, and when he had finished, it looked less like a tree-lined stream and more like a line of giraffes beside an oversized earthworm.

"You look as if you are thinking very hard." Capucine's voice had an amused lilt to it.

"I am. I was thinking about painting."

"Really?"

"Or not. Not painting. I am a terrible painter."

She grinned. "As am I. My skill is with my stitching, not with a brush. What scene were you thinking of painting?"

He looked at her, her dark eyes shining like black marbles, her hair, as always, struggling to escape the knot at her neck. Her cheeks were highlighted with a sun-warmed bloom.

More than anything, at that moment he wanted to take her in his arms and hold her, to clasp to him her beauty.

"I'd paint you, just as you are now."

"Truly? You wouldn't put me in a grand chair, my hands primly folded in my lap, with perhaps a bird in a cage at my shoulder?"

"No. I like you the way you are." He felt like a schoolboy.

"You are too kind."

There were so many things he wanted to say, but the words wouldn't form. He wanted to see her more, spend hours with her instead of these "accidental" meetings, but he couldn't bring himself to say it. Instead he stood like a puppet, waiting for the heavens to open and supply the syllables he couldn't find.

"Aliette will be furious if I am late for dinner," she said at last. She started to walk toward Boncoeur House and stopped. "You could visit later tonight—if you wish. Aliette has made cake."

If he wished?

He knew he was grinning like a fool. "I like cake."

❧

"Michel might stop by after dinner," Capucine announced as she took a slice of pork from the serving platter.

Sister Marie-Agathe looked up sharply. "You've been seeing that young man quite a bit."

"Our paths cross regularly, but it's not as if we've been spending much time together," she protested.

"You might want to think about this," the nun cautioned. "He is a pleasant fellow, and I suspect that he would be very interested in pursuing something beyond a friendship."

Capucine knew that she was blushing, and she studied the beans on her plate, pushing them around intently.

"Are you equally as interested, my dear?"

"He hasn't said anything," she muttered, still rearranging the beans.

"And I suspect it might take him some time to do so. I do believe Michel is a bit shy." The nun leaned across the table and grasped Capucine's hand. "Don't toy with his heart."

"I—"

"And don't toy with your own." Sister Marie-Agathe pushed her chair back and stood up. "The heart is a sacred thing. Guard it carefully."

Oh, mine is guarded, Capucine thought. *It's encased in ice and metal. No one, absolutely no one, will ever intrude.*

🐝

Michel stood outside the Boncoeur home. Perhaps this was a bad idea. He should turn around and leave, go back to his own small cottage, and think this through again. His hands clenched and unclenched in fists of indecisiveness.

Instead his feet marched forward, and his hand rose and knocked on the door.

Capucine herself opened the door.

"Might we go for a walk?" he asked immediately.

"I'd like that."

They walked slowly, commenting on anything and everything. The wall that needed repair. The flowers that bloomed in the moonlight. The dog that barked at everything that moved, including the leaves on the trees.

At last they were back at the house.

"I'm not ready to end this evening," he said, feeling extraordinarily bold.

"Shall we sit in the garden, then?" Capucine asked. "Let me get a shawl from inside."

They sat on the bench under the stars, neither saying a word until the silence was too heavy for Michel to bear. "Will you stay here forever, in New Orleans?"

She shook her head vehemently. "No. At some point—" Her words broke off, and then she started again. "At some point, I will find my mother, or at least my people."

"Your mother?"

Capucine stiffened, and she turned her face away from him. "I haven't told you, although I suspect you've already determined it, but I was born in Acadia. The British killed my father, and then they took Aliette and me and sent us to the convent in New York. I don't know what happened to my mother."

"Is she alive?"

"I—I don't know. I don't have any idea where anyone went, except for Aliette and myself."

He glanced at her. "Don't you know where they are? Your people, I mean?"

"No. I know that there are Acadians in this area. Have you heard of Bayou Teche?"

"Yes, of course."

"I often wonder if she is there." She bit her lip.

This was the chance for him to ask the question that had been eating at him. "You're an enigma, Capucine. You don't acknowledge in public that you are Acadian, yet your entire being is dedicated to your heritage. Why is that?"

"I can be who I want to be." Her voice was firm.

"That's true. But why deny being Acadian?"

She stood up suddenly. "I have never denied being Acadian. Never."

But you've never acknowledged it in public. In fact, she had never told him.

Still, there was pain here, pain and a deep, unquenchable ache of questions left unanswered.

He touched her arm. "We are much alike, you and I. Acadians far away from our homes, but see how we've created our lives anew?"

For a moment she didn't speak. Then, in a voice so faint he couldn't be sure he'd heard it at first, she began to talk. "How do you do it? How do you go on with your life? Do you forget the lost ones? Do you forgive those who came in and ripped our families apart?"

"I pray. I pray and pray and pray. God has helped me heal. I can't imagine doing this without Him. Capucine, have you prayed?"

She made a small sound. "Pray. Oh, I've prayed, and do you see my mother? No. He listens to the prayers of the British, not the Acadians."

The desolation in her words gnawed into his soul. "He listens to all of us, no matter what our heritage."

"He hasn't listened to me."

"Perhaps you haven't listened to Him."

"Perhaps He needs to speak louder."

Michel laughed. "One day He might. One day He might."

"He will speak French, will he not?"

"Mais oui!"

She gripped his hand. "I do want to go Bayou Teche."

"What about Sister Marie-Agathe?"

"She is finding her calling here, tending to those who live in poverty and need. I am welcome to stay with her, yet she does not expect me to stay here forever."

"And Aliette? What about her?"

"She will come with me, of course."

"She wants to?"

Capucine shrugged. "She will come with me. I am her older sister. What else does she know? She cooks here; she goes to church. She barely knows the world."

Aliette's daily furtive rush to the Boncoeur House suddenly made sense. Capucine clearly didn't know that her sister was leaving the house every afternoon, and Aliette didn't seem as if she wanted her to know.

"Have you given any thought to the fact that she might want to live on her own, perhaps here in New Orleans?"

Capucine looked at him sharply. "No. She won't. Aliette doesn't leave the house if she can avoid it. Why would she want to be independent? She even has me run her errands for her."

"What would you do if she, oh, fell in love?"

Capucine hooted. "With whom? She doesn't even see the poultry man!"

Be careful, he warned himself. He had no proof, only the vaguest suggestion that something was happening with Aliette.

He quickly changed the subject. "Aliette is a cook, and you are a needlewoman. How did you start on that?"

Her eager smile told him that she was grateful for the switch in topics. "My mother started me, of course, but I owe my growth to Sister Marie-Agathe, who encouraged me to master the basics and then explore the possibilities."

"You've been very fortunate to have her."

"I know. When I needed her, she was there for me. You know, I have a vague memory after I was struck with the bale at the wharf. I was in my bed, and she was at my side, and she said the oddest thing. Or at least I think she did." Capucine frowned.

"What was it?"

"She said that she was doing what God wanted her to do, not just to feed and clothe and shelter me, but to love me. I find that unusual, don't you?"

He thought about it. "We are instructed to love one another."

"But it was what I needed. I wonder if we can force ourselves to love someone."

"What do you mean by that?" He leaned forward.

"The Bible tells us to love each other, but it doesn't tell us how to do that. We are human, after all. How do we make ourselves feel that way? I can't order you to love me."

The cover of darkness hid his flush. "If I were a lovable person, it would certainly be easier. You know, that may be why the Bible doesn't tell us to love *everybody*. It tells us to love *each other* so that there's a flow of emotion among all involved."

"The village of New Orleans could use less emotion right now," she said.

"It is all coming to a head, *ça, c'est vrai*," he answered, reverting to Acadian French.

She stood up. "No politics tonight, please. I want to have only the most pleasant of dreams."

"Yes. Politics does not make for a restful sleep, nor does sitting in the moonlight, no matter how lovely the companion."

He didn't want the evening to end, but if he was not going to fall asleep over his work at the boat shop in the morning, he'd have to get home.

They returned to the house, where Sister Marie-Agathe and Aliette sat reading by a lamp.

"May I see you again?" he asked as he opened the door.

"Yes," she said softly. "Yes."

Chapter 8

My treasure, my treasure. Have I lost my treasure?
And in doing so, have I lost my heart?

The plaza was filled with even more people. Madame Frenier, who held the tablecloth that Capucine had embroidered for her, looked around in growing apprehension.

"Capucine, are you not concerned?"

Capucine settled herself in her usual spot and took out her embroidery. "I am quite fine, I believe."

The older woman sat beside her. "Capucine, listen to me!" She scooted closer. "It's getting increasingly dangerous. I know that you think you are perfectly safe, but you are not. I hear murmurs of suspicion. 'What is she doing in the plaza every day?' 'Michel LeBlanc is a well-known oppositionist to the Spanish—why is she spending so much time with him?' 'What is her sister doing near the Corps de Garde?'"

"My sister? What is this about Aliette?"

"Aliette is seen every afternoon in that area. I do not know if that's her destination, just that she is—"

"Aliette? How can it be? She spends every afternoon in the kitchen. Why, she doesn't even leave to go to the market. . . ."

Her voice faded out as the blood froze in her veins. She had been so focused on her own mission that she had not been paying much attention to her younger sister. What had she been up to?

"Capucine, these are dangerous days," Madame Frenier said, tucking the tablecloth into her bag. "Be careful."

As she walked away, voices came from behind the shrubbery.

"The sixth. It is the sixth."

This was the fourth of September. She knew what this meant.

Capucine didn't even fold the fabric. She wadded it up, shoved it into her apron pocket, and quickly fled the Place d'Armes.

God, if You are still with me, I need You now. She hadn't prayed for so long that the words were wooden at first but then began to flow with intensity as she rushed to Boncoeur House. *This is beyond my control. Please, let it not be beyond Your control.*

She remembered how indignant Michel had been about the political situation, and she knew that he would be involved. He could be hurt, even killed!

I know what will happen. It is all told in my embroideries, and I have sewn my fate into each stitch. But I never, ever meant to hurt Michel. And I don't know what Aliette is doing, but please, please, spread Your protection over her.

She took a deep breath. *I cannot do this alone.*

She ran all the way to Boncoeur House, only to find Aliette happily singing in the kitchen. There was no way that she could have been all the way to the Corps de Garde and back and still have dinner well underway.

"Capucine, why are you so flushed? Come and sit in the garden, where it's cooler." Sister Marie-Agathe led her to the back of the house. "Sit now, and tell me what is going on."

The entire story poured out of Capucine, like water from a jug, and soon she was wrapped in a lavender-and-soap-scented embrace. "There, there," the nun soothed her. "We will put this in the Lord's hands. His reach far exceeds our own."

And then, as Sister Marie-Agathe rocked Capucine, she whispered in her ear, "But I will see to Aliette myself."

🕊

Michel hummed to himself as he made sure his shirt was presentable. Tonight he intended to declare himself to Capucine.

Perhaps, if she was receptive, he might even ask her to marry him.

The thought elated him—and terrified him. A lifetime with Capucine would be one filled with laughter and excitement and energy. She would be a wonderful mother, involved with her children and encouraging them to strive to greater heights.

If only he knew how close her relationship was with the Lord. Her doubt was understandable—he certainly had known those reservations himself. He had a vague feeling that she really was a Christian, but an unwilling one.

That made him smile. Only Capucine would be in that position!

There was one unanswered question—did she love him?

On that matter, he could not be as sure.

He straightened his shirt one last time, ran his hand over his hair in case some strands had decided to go astray, and left the house to proclaim his heart.

🕊

Aliette's *fricot* was magnificent, Capucine knew, but she could barely taste the Acadian stew, lush with chicken and vegetables and dumplings. Too much was on her mind tonight.

"Are you all right?" Sister Marie-Agathe asked Michel who, like Capucine, was only picking at his food.

Aliette's delicate forehead creased with worry. "Does it not taste good? Is something wrong with it?"

47

"No, no," Michel and Capucine chorused together.

Sister Marie-Agathe poked Aliette and nodded at them meaningfully. "This is not a time to worry about food, I think."

Aliette nodded knowingly and smiled.

Capucine could feel her neck reddening and pushed her chair back suddenly to hide her embarrassment. "Michel, let's go into the garden."

He wiped his mouth. "Yes, let's."

As soon as they were seated, he faced her. "I have something to discuss with you."

"And I with you." She was about to explode with nervousness.

"I must say this, Capucine." He took a deep breath and exhaled. "I love you."

She couldn't speak. This was what she had wanted to hear—and what she had dreaded to hear.

"Did you hear me?" he asked. "I said I love you."

"I heard." If her heart didn't stop beating so loudly, it would fly right out of her chest. "But I'm not what you think I am."

He shook his head. "Are you sure of that? Perhaps I know exactly who you are."

Tears stung at her eyes. "If you knew, you could not love me."

"There cannot be something so terrible that it would stop me from loving you."

"There is."

"Let me ask you one thing. Do you love me?"

If she lied, it would be easy to move on. Once again, the truth was the hardest. "Yes," she whispered.

"Then perhaps you should marry me."

"Marry you! Michel, I—" She leaned over and grasped his hand. "Michel, take me to Bayou Teche. Tonight. Or tomorrow."

"Bayou Teche? Whatever are you talking about? Is this about marrying?"

"I want to go there, as soon as possible," she said.

The intensity of her voice worried him. "What is wrong?"

"Take me, take all of us, out of New Orleans. Let's go to Bayou Teche, where we can be among people who are like us."

"Sister Marie-Agathe and Aliette?" he asked stupidly. "They want to go, too?"

"They will go. I can ensure that. Please, please, *je, je plaide*, I am pleading!"

He shook his hand free. "You are talking like a madwoman. If you truly want to leave New Orleans and go to Bayou Teche, then let's plan it by the daylight sun, not in the shadows of the night."

She didn't answer. A small sound in the darkness startled him.

"Capucine, are you crying?"

She still did not respond, and a heavy sadness came over his heart, as if it were suddenly weighted down with stones. "Capucine," he whispered, "if you truly want to go to Bayou Teche, let's go in two weeks. Then it will be nearly the end of September, and Pierre will not need my help as much."

"I will find someone else, then, to take me."

"You don't have to. I will take you, but I can't leave—"

Her whispered response as she rose to leave was swallowed by the rustle of the weeping willow, but he thought she said, "Too late."

He sat in the garden of Boncoeur House alone and watched as she entered through the doorway and stood there, silhouetted against the golden glow of a lamp.

He loved her. With all his heart and soul, he loved her, and he'd heard in her voice the raw need to leave New Orleans.

If he did not take her, he would lose her. And that he could not bear.

☙

A young man, barely whiskered, ran into the boat shop. "Pierre LeBlanc!" he called. "The day of infamy is at hand!"

Michel poked his head out from the back of the shop. "My cousin is not here. May I help you?"

The fellow leaned against a half-built boat as he struggled to catch his breath. "The sixth. The seventh. *Je ne sais quoi.* But the plan is for the Spanish to make a great show of power. They will march through the streets of New Orleans and make a proclamation."

"About what?"

"Trade. Antonio de Ulloa says it is for the good of the people, so that we are not charged so much for that which comes from France, but in the market, the anger grows. All I know is that the message is for all of us to be at the Place d'Armes, to show who we are!"

His stomach twisted, but even as it did, he knew that he would be there. He also understood why Capucine wanted to leave New Orleans so desperately.

He returned to the back of the shop. There was much work to be done.

Chapter 9

Often what we've been waiting for has simply been waiting for us.

The September day was clear and warm early on. Pierre hung a sign on the boat shop door, announcing that it was closed. Then he and Michel walked to the Place d'Armes.

A crowd had already gathered. The sound of a drum, its steady beat like the thud of men's pulses in their ears, broke through the morning. The crowd grew silent as a line of soldiers, bayonets in their hands, followed the drummer. On they walked, through the streets of the village, many of the townspeople following them.

Voices rose again. Protests and arguments filled every inch of the plaza.

Michel saw a familiar face beside the church.

"Go," Pierre said, motioning to her. "Your heart is over there."

He crossed the plaza to where she stood. "Capucine, this is what you feared, am I right?" he asked her straight out.

"Yes. I knew—"

He put a finger across her lips. "There are ears everywhere. But I don't think we are in such danger after all. There will not be an open revolt, not today."

She sagged in relief.

"Do you still want to go to Bayou Teche?"

"Yes, of course. I love New Orleans, but I want to be with Acadians again. I've lived this duplicitous life too long. And perhaps I can find my mother."

"I will be bold here. You said you loved me. Is that true?"

"It is."

"I have arranged for us to go to Bayou Teche in four days. Capucine, we—we are in front of a church. Inside is a priest. We could be married, now, today, here."

She stepped into his arms. Her voice, muffled against his neck, said only, "Yes."

Capucine stood outside the church. She had gone inside as Capucine Louet and had come out as Capucine LeBlanc. This man at her side was her husband, and soon she would be on her way to live, once again, in an Acadian settlement.

50

How quickly life could change!

Soon they were in his cottage. "Look," he said, "I've set this up for us. A chair for you by the fireplace, and one for me. We won't be here long, but we will be comfortable."

The sweet gesture took her heart by surprise.

Then he gripped both of her hands in his.

"I will tell you again," he said, his voice cracking with emotion, "as I did before God in the chapel, that I love you with all of my being, and if I cannot have your love, I will accept your happiness."

"We are so different," she whispered, blinking back the tears that stung her eyes. "You are so noble, so kind, so honest, and I am. . .not."

"Dearest Capucine, you slight yourself."

"No, I am a deceiver. You don't know." Shame washed over her in a hot flood. She did not deserve this wonderful man.

"You deceive yourself."

She shook her head furiously. "I have been lying to so many people. The embroideries are—"

"Maps. Yes, I know this."

"You do? How?"

"Pierre noticed it first. The curve of the egret was the same as the river, and the green and blue stitches were encampments of British discontents. Am I right?"

She sank to the small chair by the fireplace. "You're right."

"It's time to stop." His words were gentle.

"I see that." She could barely speak. "My work is over. It's no longer as concealed as it was, and that's dangerous. I don't want to hurt. . .anyone."

"It's also time to stop hating." He pulled his chair up beside hers. "Let the wounds heal."

"The only thing that can heal me is Bayou Teche."

"No. The only thing that can heal you is in yourself. Capucine, let God help. Allow His healing touch—"

"I can't. When the British killed my father, when they tore Aliette and me away from our mother, God wasn't there."

"He was."

Tears streamed down her face. "How would you know?" she lashed at him. "It's not like—"

He put one finger over her lips. "I was there. Remember, I'm Acadian, too. That's how I ended up with Pierre."

"You were—" In all this time she'd known him, she'd never asked how he'd come to live in New Orleans, questioned why he hadn't mentioned parents or brothers or sisters, had no stories about where he'd lived before.

"Yes, my family was ripped apart, too."

"And you don't hate them?"

He shook his head. "I can't. I did for a while, but I can't any longer. I hate what

51

they did, but I can't hold onto that hate for them. It's like a vicious animal that snaps and eats at your soul until nothing is left but shreds."

She thought again of the picture of Jesus, His arms open and inviting. "It's not that easy."

He wrapped her in his arms and murmured into her hair, which had once again escaped its moorings, "It is that easy. It is just that easy."

🐝

"Thank you for everything," Michel told his cousin. "Are you sure you don't want to join us?"

Pierre shook his head. "No. My place is here, in New Orleans, building boats. But I will come visit you, once I find someone who will be as strong a partner as you were."

They clapped each other on the back and then embraced. "Au revoir." The words stuck in Michel's throat.

He walked slowly back to the cottage. He would miss his cousin. Pierre had been his entire family for a long time.

His little cottage had been emptied. The packets were in the yard, ready to be loaded, and words, strident and furious, echoed from the open windows.

"Traitor! You are no better than the men who killed our father!" Capucine's voice was strained and angry.

"Don't say that!" Aliette's teary response was faint. "Please don't say that."

"It's true. How can you call yourself Acadian? How can you expect me to take this monster into my home? Will he be welcome in Bayou Teche? Think about it, Aliette! Think!"

A man spoke, but his voice was too low for Michel to make out his words.

Capucine burst from the house, her hair sprung free from the bun. It stood out in a wide black spray, and she looked like a madwoman. "Get away from me!"

Aliette, followed, begging, "Please listen to me! You know what it's like to be in love."

"Love? Don't talk to me about love! You don't know what it means."

"I do, too. Capucine, listen!"

Michel felt like he was watching the scene from a distance. What on earth could have caused such a rift between the sisters?

The answer walked out the door of his house. A man strode to stand beside Aliette, his arm around her shoulders.

"Get him out of here!" Capucine's voice had dropped from a scream to an even deadlier stage whisper.

"Capucine!" The venom in her voice terrified him, and he ran to her side. "Capucine, what is the meaning of this?"

"This man, this beast, has married my sister! This is what she was doing each afternoon, sneaking out to see this man! Not only that, she is his wife!"

"Aliette?" He turned to her in confusion.

"This is John Powers, Michel. We were married three days ago." She smiled at her new husband and then back at Michel. "It's all right. He speaks French, too."

The realization of what had happened dawned on him. "He's British. That's what it is. Am I right? He's British."

Capucine stood beside him, hands on her hips, glaring at the newcomer. "Not only that, he's the son of an officer!"

If Aliette had married the king of England himself, it couldn't have been worse.

He put his hand on Capucine's elbow. "Aliette, Mr. Powers, I think Capucine and I need some time alone."

"Good," Capucine said. "Get him out of here."

There was one table left inside the cottage, and he drew their chairs up to it.

"Capucine, if you refuse to see your sister because of him, then you have lost."

"Lost?"

"You will have lost her to the British, too."

"Then she must have the marriage annulled." She sat back in the chair, her lips in a tight line.

"No. When you were a child, the troops came in and tore your family apart. You had no choice in the matter. You were a scared little girl who did the best she could, am I right?"

She nodded as a single tear traced its way down her cheek.

"Now, if you make Aliette decide between Mr. Powers and yourself, you will lose again. Either way, you lose her. If she chooses him, she is gone. If she chooses you, that will be a stake in your closeness that might never heal."

"He's *British*, Michel."

"He's British, but he could just as easily have been Spanish. Or German. Or Chinese. I think they love each other." He touched her hand. "And she loves you. Walk in the way of the angels, Capucine. Choose love."

"They want to come with us," she said.

"Then they shall. And we will welcome them, will we not?"

She managed a faint, watery smile. "We will try."

❧

The sun set with a glorious radiance. "Our last night here," Capucine said, cradling a cup of tea in her hands. "Are you sad?"

"I must admit that I am, a bit," Michel answered reflectively. "I'll miss Pierre, of course."

They sat in front of the small cottage, watching the colors shift across the sky from luminous pink to glowing orange to vibrant scarlet.

She reached across and covered his hand with her own. "I know. Sister Marie-Agathe has been with me for many years, and I can't imagine life without her. But she's going back to the life she knows, in the convent. I know it's for the best, but still, I will miss her dreadfully."

"She leaves, though, knowing that her girls are happily married and returning to their heritage." He looked at her. "You are happy, aren't you? Or you will be when you get to Bayou Teche."

Capucine sat the tea down on the ground beside her and faced her husband. "Michel, I love you. With all my heart, and with all my soul, I belong with you. I love you."

The final slants of light caught the tears in his eyes. "Capucine, dearest Capucine, my own Capucine. . ."

❧

The wagon creaked over trails and through soggy areas that Capucine was sure teemed with wildlife that she didn't want to see. Some she did see: snakes that slithered past with silent intent, frogs that jumped out of nowhere and disappeared as quickly, birds that cawed overhead.

John Powers was, amazingly, a nice fellow. He gladly spoke French with them and had quite a store of tales to share with them of life in Florida, where he'd grown up. As they traveled together, she came to realize that once a nameless hate has an identity, it will either explode or it will die out. In this case, it changed into an appreciation of the man who was sharing her sister's life.

Love, she discovered, was indeed stronger than hate. Her love for her sister far outweighed any hatred she might retain for the British. And, even more oddly, once she let that go, the remainder dissolved.

"You're writing in your journal again," Michel said to her as he looked over her shoulder. "More patterns?"

She laughed. "Any new patterns that go in there will truly be just that—patterns. There'll be nothing secretive or furtive about them at all."

"Will you miss it?"

"I'll have other things to keep myself busy," she answered. "Starting our new life together, for one thing."

He planted a kiss on the back of her neck. "Are you ready to meet your new home? Bayou Teche is just ahead."

Bayou Teche. After all this time, she was going to Bayou Teche!

She moved to the front of the wagon and leaned as far forward as possible to watch for her new home.

Suddenly, she was there. The wagon was surrounded by people. The distinctive Acadian accents filled her ears, and welcoming hands offered to help her down.

Capucine stood on the lush green expanse, her fingers laced with Michel's. Behind her, Aliette stood with her husband. "We're home," she whispered.

A woman broke through the crowd and dropped to the ground at their feet. Her face was familiar—Capucine had seen it a million times in her dreams.

"Mama!"

"Capucine! Aliette!"

The tears of the reunited women joined together. "It's been so long," Capucine murmured through the tears.

"I was almost afraid to hope," her mother said as she hugged her daughters to her, "but I never quit. God was watching over us, all of us."

Capucine touched the small cross around her mother's neck as a wave of memories swept over her.

"Do you remember it?" Mama asked gently. "I was wearing it that terrible day we were separated, and I've never taken it off since."

She kissed the forehead of each daughter and sighed. "I thought I'd lost everything—my husband, my daughters, my home—but I knew I could not lose God. He would be with me, no matter where I went, and He would be with you, no matter where you went."

The ice surrounding Capucine's heart fell away. All these years, God had been with her. She'd known that, and no matter how she'd pushed Him away, He'd never left.

The arms of His Son were open, as they'd always been, and she walked into them, into the peace of trust and certain faith.

"I never gave up on God," Mama whispered.

"And He never gave up on us," Capucine added. "Never."

She held out her hand to Michel and breathed a wordless prayer of thanks. Love was triumphant, and she was home.

Epilogue

I have found my treasure, my heart.
And all along, God has not only been watching over me,
He has been leading me by the hand. I am so happy!

The cabin seemed to burst with life. Laughter and song filled every corner. But the baby slept on.

"She's beautiful," Michel said. "As beautiful as her mother."

A tall figure swooped toward them. "May I hold her?"

"Sister Marie-Agathe," Capucine said, laughing as she handed her daughter to the nun, "you're going to spoil her."

"This is a special day for a baby," Sister Marie-Agathe said as she nuzzled the baby. "Her christening day! Comforte Acadie LeBlanc, we are delighted to have you with us."

"I'm so glad Sister Marie-Agathe was able to come and be with us for Comforte's christening," Capucine said as the nun carried Comforte into the sunlight where Aliette and her husband, John, and Mama were sitting. "It makes the day complete. I'm going to write this all in my diary, so that even when I am old and Comforte is grown, I can relive these moments." She leaned against Michel's shoulder. "I would never have thought that it would be possible to be this happy."

"God has blessed us, indeed," he said, kissing the top of her head.

" 'For where your treasure is, there will your heart be also,' " she said softly. "I have found my treasure, and my heart."

THE ANGEL OF NUREMBERG

by Irene Brand

Dedication

Be not forgetful to entertain strangers:
for thereby some have entertained angels unawares.
HEBREWS 13:2

Chapter 1

Trenton, New Jersey, 1776–77

Hoping to avoid the German soldiers who had occupied Trenton during the night, Comfort Foster slipped quietly from the hospital and hurried across the backyard to the family home. Oliver Foster had never allowed his daughter to enter the hospital before, but he'd needed help this morning with feeding the convalescing soldiers under his care. With the approach of the enemy, the three Patriot soldiers who'd been assisting her father had returned to the Continental army.

To discourage any impropriety from the soldiers, Comfort had disguised herself as a middle-aged woman. Powdered hair, pock marks on her face made with dye, a pair of clouded spectacles, a matron's cap, an untidy dress, and a feigned rheumatic limp had fooled the patients as she'd served their gruel. Proud of her ingenuity, Dr. Foster assured her no one would suspect that beneath her outlandish costume was a petite eighteen-year-old brunette with extraordinary brown eyes full of life and a rosy mouth set in a delicate, yet strong face.

Entering the back door of their stone house, Comfort started upstairs to check on her younger sister, Erin, when a knock sounded at the front door. With the town full of enemy soldiers, Comfort was tempted to ignore the caller. When a more demanding summons followed, Comfort walked across the kitchen floor and cautiously cracked open the door.

The biggest man she'd ever seen in her life towered over her. With a gasp, she slammed the door in his face and dropped the latch. *A Hessian soldier!* With pulse racing, Comfort backed up to the door, knowing the flimsy hasp would be a feeble defense if he tried to force his way in. She needed to warn her father, but she shouldn't leave Erin alone in the house. Her chest heaved in anxiety as she remembered the things her brother, Marion, had said about the ferocity of these foreign soldiers George III had imported to crush the colonial rebellion.

He tapped again, and the sound seemed as loud as a thunderclap. The possibility of molestation flooded her mind, and Comfort started shaking.

"Go away!" she cried in an agitated voice.

"Frau Foster." His words came clearly through the wooden door. "I mean you no harm." In spite of her fear, Comfort detected sincerity in his composed voice. How strange that a German soldier spoke English with only a slight burr in his smooth voice!

"Frau Foster," he persisted, "are you still there?"

She didn't answer.

"I have a paper that explains why I'm here. Please take it."

"God, protect me," she whispered, then lifted the latch and opened the door an inch, fully expecting him to force his way into the house. Instead, a thin piece of paper was extended through the opening. She grabbed it and latched the door again. It was a document ordering the Foster family to house and feed one Hessian soldier.

"Will you wait until I bring my father?"

"Ja," he answered.

Comfort ran lightly across the backyard to the log hospital, opened the door, and called her father, who was inspecting the poultice on a soldier's leg. Perhaps the tone of Comfort's voice alarmed him, for her father jumped to his feet and came to her immediately.

"There's a Hessian soldier at the house with this paper ordering us to shelter and feed him."

Father's haggard face paled, and his sensitive lips straightened as he scanned the paper. Her father was a kindhearted man, dedicated to saving lives, and it startled Comfort when a savage look overspread his face.

"I won't have this man in our house with you and Erin at his mercy. I should have sent you out of town when I heard the enemy army was approaching."

"He said he won't hurt us, and I believe he's telling the truth."

As they neared the back stoop, Father scanned Comfort's untidy appearance. "If we have to take this man in, you stay in your disguise. Erin's probably safe enough, but you might be bothered."

When Father jerked open the door to confront the Hessian, Comfort was reminded of Goliath and David. Short and slender, her father was wearing gray woolen breeches, woven stockings tucked into his heavy shoes, and a loose-fitting coat over his blouse.

The soldier must have been seven feet tall. A high, miter-shaped brass cap adorned with scrolls and heraldic emblems on the front fit snugly on his head. He wore a long, medium-blue wool coat with turned-back skirts. White buttons splashed down the front of the pink-lined coat, and its collar, cuffs, and lapels were made of the same rich color. The soldier's white waistcoat was long and belted. His breeches were tight, fitted into black gaiters with brass buttons, and tucked into thick leather boots. A short-sword was strapped at his side.

The magnificence of the man overwhelmed Comfort, and she drew a quick breath. She felt like a dowdy sparrow in the presence of a bird of paradise.

The two men locked gazes for several moments, each measuring the intent of the other, until her father stepped back and motioned the visitor inside the large kitchen. The Hessian bent almost double to get through the door. He removed his pointed headgear, revealing fair skin and light hair and lowering his height by several inches.

Hearing five-year-old Erin coming down the steps, Comfort moved into the back room and held a hand to her lips. She hid Erin behind her skirts and moved into an unobtrusive corner that provided a view into the kitchen where the two men stood.

"My name is Nicolaus Trittenbach."

"We aren't equipped to take in visitors, Mr. Trittenbach," Father said in a steely voice. Comfort admired his courage.

"Nicolaus. Call me Nicolaus, please."

"I'm Doctor Foster. I'm not willing for you to stay here."

"I apologize for intruding, Doctor Foster." The soldier's voice was even, but Comfort sensed he was uneasy, for he fingered the powder pouch attached to his belt. "Colonel Johann Rall commands three Hessian infantry regiments, fourteen hundred men in all, occupying a ten-mile stretch along the Delaware. The town's barracks won't accommodate half that many soldiers, so Colonel Rall is billeting the rest of the troops in private homes. If you turn me away, your family may be evicted and your home confiscated for the army's use. I won't cause you any trouble."

Father glanced at the paper in his hand. "It seems I have no choice; but I have two daughters living in this house, and I demand that you respect them."

Was it anger or a flush of embarrassment darkening Nicolaus's face?

"I won't cause any trouble," he repeated.

Their father motioned Comfort and Erin into the room. He placed his hand on Erin's tousled hair. "This is the baby of the family, Erin." He gestured toward Comfort. "My other daughter, Comfort, is the hostess of my house and will see to your needs."

Nicolaus bowed from the waist. "I'll return this afternoon."

"We'll do our best to make you comfortable, Mr. Trittenbach," Comfort said.

Nicolaus darted a quick glance at Comfort. Had he detected that her voice was out of character with the rest of her appearance?

Comfort had estimated that the soldier was about their father's age, but he flashed a smile that revealed youthful lines in his somber face.

"Call me Nicolaus, please."

His beaming smile flustered Comfort, and she didn't know what to say, but she nodded assent.

When the door closed behind Nicolaus, Comfort and her father stared at one another in dismay.

"What are we going to do with him?" Comfort whispered. "Put him in one of the attic rooms?"

Father shook his head. "Not with you and Erin sleeping up there. Prepare my room for him, and I'll sleep upstairs."

He peered out the room's only window. "I see soldiers everywhere. I'm not easy in my mind about this man, but what else can I do? I can't oppose the whole German army." Awkwardly, he cleared his throat. "You do understand why you must be on guard all the time, don't you?"

Comfort felt her cheeks grow hot. "I'll be cautious; but, Father, I don't believe he'll harm us. We must be kind to him." She dropped to her knees beside her sister.

"Erin, remember that we've been invaded by the enemy. You stay with me all the time."

Wide-eyed, Erin promised, "I will."

"Good advice," their father said. "For the time being, stay away from the hospital. I'll find other help. But for your own protection, keep wearing that outfit to disguise your youth." He opened the door, peered up and down Queen Street, then whispered in Comfort's ear. "Washington is gathering his army on the other side of the river, so the Hessians may not be here long."

After their father went back to work, Comfort stirred the fire, for a chill had crept into the kitchen.

"How about a piece of gingerbread, Sister?" she asked, motioning Erin to the warmth of the fire. "I haven't had time to prepare corn cakes this morning."

"I like gingerbread," Erin said, climbing up onto a stool near the fire.

"Marion bought this gingerbread from Mr. Ludwick. Just imagine, our German neighbor from Philadelphia showing up in Trenton as a baker for the Continental army."

Chewing slowly on the gingerbread, Erin asked, "Who's Mr. Ludwick?"

"Oh, I keep forgetting you were born after we moved to Trenton. Mr. Ludwick came from Germany several years ago and set up a bakery in Philadelphia. He soon became known as the Gingerbread Baker, and Mother used to buy his products."

Comfort set a bowl of porridge on the table. "You finish eating while I prepare Father's room for our visitor."

The bedroom was cold, so Comfort placed fresh logs in the fireplace and started the fire. She carried her father's clothes and other belongings upstairs. She swept the wooden floor until no trace of dust was evident. She fluffed the straw mattress, arranged fresh sheets and blankets, then covered the bed with a colorful quilt her mother had made. She pulled her father's favorite chair close to the fireplace, took a bayberry candle from the cabinet, and placed it on a table beside the chair. She arranged a pitcher of water and a bowl of soft soap on a cabinet with other personal necessities and surveyed her preparations. The room should provide a pleasant haven for Nicolaus.

As she worked, Comfort contemplated her reaction to having the soldier in their home. One of the complaints voiced against the king of England in the Declaration of Independence, passed a few months ago, was the king's importation of foreign mercenaries to complete the death and destruction already started in the Colonies by the British. According to her brother, Marion, a soldier in the Continental army, the Hessians had no mercy on their enemies, and his hints of how they mistreated women had alarmed Comfort. She should be frightened to have a Hessian living in their house, but she wasn't.

When Nicolaus had been talking to her father, Comfort had watched him closely. She'd detected a hint of loneliness, perhaps homesickness, in the steady gaze of his dark-blue eyes. Considering his generous, kindly mouth and the tenderness of his voice, she didn't believe Nicolaus would be cruel to anyone.

Comfort contemplated the Colonists' efforts to gain independence from Great Britain as she mixed bread dough. Was freedom an impossible dream? The American soldiers had been defeated in almost every battle, and even now, Washington's army had retreated across the Delaware River, leaving New York and New Jersey in the hands of the British.

After she placed five loaves of bread in the oven to the left of the kitchen fireplace, Comfort hung a pot of cabbage pudding on the crane. To complete the meal, she cut the top off a small pumpkin, removed the seeds and pulp, spooned a mixture of sugar, butter, and nutmeg into the opening, placed the top back on the pumpkin, and covered it with hot ashes.

While Erin took a nap, Comfort prayed, asking God to protect her family. Jesus had said, "Love your enemies." And when He'd been teaching how His followers could be recognized, He said, "I was a stranger, and ye took me in." And she recalled another Bible verse that cautioned, "Be not forgetful to entertain strangers: for thereby some have entertained angels unawares."

If Comfort understood these Scriptures correctly, it was her Christian duty to entertain Nicolaus as she would treat Jesus if He came to her door. But by midafternoon, when his hesitant knock sounded and Comfort opened the door to admit Nicolaus, she wondered fleetingly if that was the only reason she smiled brightly and said, "Welcome to our home, Nicolaus."

He stepped inside, a hint of uncertainty in his gentle blue eyes. When his lips parted in an apologetic smile, Comfort knew that Nicolaus would never seem like an enemy to her.

Chapter 2

A large leather bag hung from Nicolaus's shoulder, and he carried a flintlock musket with a bayonet. Her father was opposed to firearms in the house, but Comfort knew she mustn't protest.

She pointed to the bedroom. "You may put your belongings in there," she said. With Erin hanging on her skirts, impeding her progress, Comfort moved to the doorway.

"I hope you'll be comfortable here," she said as he walked past her into the room.

Nicolaus's incredulous glance swept over the neat, pleasant room. *"Nein! Nein!* I didn't expect this luxury," he protested. "I'm not used to it. I won't misplace any of your family. I'll sleep on the floor somewhere."

"Father told me to prepare this room for you."

"You humble me," Nicolaus protested. "I'm an intruder, and you're treating me like a guest."

A slight smile touched Comfort's lips. "But you're under orders from Colonel Rall, just as we are. I do not blame you personally."

"Then I'll accept your hospitality, but I'm not worthy of it. *Danke schön.*"

From her association with Christopher Ludwick, Comfort recognized these words as "thanks very much."

He stood uncertainly in the center of the room. "You may join us in the kitchen whenever you wish to," Comfort said, pulling the door shut behind her.

❧

Dumbfounded, Nicolaus lowered his long frame to the wooden chair and stretched his sturdy legs toward the warmth of the fire. He'd expected nothing more than a cubbyhole, but the Fosters had given him this comfortable room. He'd been invited to enjoy the fellowship of the family circle by sharing their meals.

"Danke, Gott," he prayed, "for providing a refuge in this foreign land." He thought of his favorite psalm and quoted softly, " 'Thou preparest a table before me in the presence of mine enemies.' "

The last two months of fighting and marching had been rough, and Nicolaus welcomed the opportunity to relax for a few minutes. Taking advantage of the first privacy he'd experienced since he'd left his homeland six months ago, Nicolaus reflected on the circumstances that had brought him to this place.

When his parents died, his oldest brother had inherited the land, so there seemed nothing he could do except become a career soldier. He'd accepted that as his destiny until he'd received a letter from a kinsman, Christopher Ludwick, who had served for years in the German army and navy. On a voyage to America, Christopher had visited Philadelphia and liked it enough to settle there. His glowing report of the advantages of living in America had started Nicolaus wondering if his own fortune lay in the American colonies.

When the British asked Hesse's ruler, Frederick II, to provide troops to fight in America, Nicolaus had volunteered. If his reception in the Foster home was indicative of the treatment he could expect in this country, he didn't want to return to Hesse.

Since he'd considered cutting ties with his homeland, before he left Germany, Nicolaus made a nostalgic pilgrimage to two ancestral sites. He'd heard all of his life about the village of Dinkelsbühl, where Nicolaus Trittenbach, for whom he'd been named, had lived as a child. It had been rewarding to walk the streets where his ancestor had played many years earlier. He'd then traveled to Engelturm, a castle in the Black Forest, where the first Nicolaus had received his training for knighthood. The castle had been partially destroyed in the Seven Years' War, twenty years earlier, but he welcomed the opportunity to ride along forest paths his ancestor might have enjoyed before he became a landowner in Hesse.

The warmth of the room eased Nicolaus's tired body, and he dozed. The face of Comfort Foster floated in his subconscious mind. How old was she? This morning, she'd walked like a tired, aged woman; but this afternoon, while her face still showed the marks of maturity, she'd moved freely without limping at all.

A slight tapping disturbed Nicolaus's slumber.

"Nicolaus," a childish voice said.

He roused and hurried to open the door. Erin spoke around the finger she held in the corner of her mouth. "Sister says come to eat."

"*Danke schön.* I'll be there shortly."

Nicolaus removed his sword and heavy coat and hung them on the rack in the corner. The Hessians had been warned to stay armed at all times, but he wouldn't abuse the Foster hospitality by wearing weapons to their table. He pushed his hair back from his forehead and unwrapped the black cloth from the foot-long thin strip of hair hanging over his back. He laid a heavy log on the dwindling fire before he entered the kitchen.

❧

Wishing she could have entertained Nicolaus in more pleasing garments, Comfort had put on a clean overskirt and straightened the muslin cap on her camouflaged hair. She wondered how long such a mediocre disguise could fool Nicolaus.

"Father can't leave the hospital right now. Please be seated," she added, motioning to the table, where only one place was laid.

Hesitating, Nicolaus said, "Have you already had your meal?"

"No. I'll serve you. Erin and I will eat later."

"I'd be pleased if you'd share the meal with me. Or would your father object?"

"I don't know." *Be not forgetful to entertain strangers.* A biblical admonition? Should she ignore it?

Hearing Erin's approach, Comfort made a quick decision. "Come, Erin, we'll join Nicolaus at his meal." She tied a large towel over Erin's dress and helped her up on a high stool.

"Would you like a cup of cider, Nicolaus? Cider is a specialty of the region. We have lots of apple orchards in Trenton."

"Ja. Danke."

Comfort filled a mug with cider. She heaped large servings of cabbage pudding and baked pumpkin on Nicolaus's plate and passed him a wooden tray holding freshly baked bread. Erin, normally talkative, was subdued in Nicolaus's presence; but she kept eyeing him, finding him of more interest than her food.

Finally, Erin said, "That funny hat made a red streak on your face." She leaned forward and traced the indentation on his forehead. "Why'd you wear it?"

A smile lit Nicolaus's face, and he touched Erin's little round nose with his long, delicately tapered finger. "To make me look taller and meaner than I actually am to scare saucy little girls."

Erin nodded seriously. "You scared me when you came this morning, but I'm not afraid of you now."

He tenderly touched Erin's brown hair. "You don't have to be afraid of me, but. . ." He hesitated as if he were choosing his words carefully. "There are many *soldaten* in Trenton now, and you might need to be afraid of some of them. You and your sister shouldn't go out in town unless I'm with you." He looked piercingly at Comfort. "Do you understand?"

"Yes. Maybe I shouldn't ask this, but how long will your troops stay in Trenton?"

He smiled. "That depends on your general Washington, but right now, it looks as if we'll be here all winter."

"It's obvious I can't stay in the house that long, so Erin and I will welcome your escort when we go to the market or to worship services."

"I've been assigned midnight-to-dawn sentry duty, so I can accompany you during the daytime." He turned back to Erin and said teasingly, "Now I'll tell you the real reason for our brass hats. I'm a grenadier, a member of a company that was formed a hundred years ago when soldiers tossed grenades in battle and wore soft, floppy headgear. They couldn't throw the grenades without knocking off their hats, so the heavy helmet I wear was designed to take care of that problem. We don't use grenades anymore, but brass hats are still part of our uniform."

"Marion told me that all German soldiers are seven feet tall and have two sets of teeth."

"Erin!" Comfort reproved. "Don't repeat things Marion said."

"And who's Marion?"

"Our brother," Comfort explained.

"Erin," Nicolaus said, "a lot of reports about the Hessians are untrue, just as I imagine that some of the things our troops have been told about Americans are false."

"What, for instance?" Comfort asked, surprised.

"That Americans are savages and cannibals," Nicolaus said, a humorous glint in his blue eyes. "And that we should kill them as fast as we can if we don't want to be captured and eaten alive."

"Oooo," Erin said.

"That isn't true," Comfort protested. "Some Indians are reported to be cannibals, but I even doubt that."

"Our commanders often give the troops false or, at least, exaggerated information to get us to fight fiercely. I suspect American leaders do the same thing."

"Nicolaus, I'm surprised at your excellent command of the English language."

"My mother was English, and she taught me. Knowing English has proven beneficial on this assignment. I've been helpful to our commanders, as well as the common soldiers, who can't speak English."

"Comfort is teaching me my letters," Erin said, "but I don't know any German words."

"Then I'll teach you some."

Comfort stood, saying, "While you're having a German lesson, I'll clear away the supper dishes."

Nicolaus jumped to his feet. "I'll help. I don't want to cause you any extra work."

"You'll be helping if you keep Erin occupied," Comfort assured him.

Nicolaus sat again and pointed to the general family room behind the kitchen. "Such a room in our home is called a *scheff.*"

Erin rolled her tongue around the word several times, but she couldn't get it right.

"Let's try an easier word. The German word for friend is *freund.* I would like to be your *freund,* Erin."

"*Freund!*" Erin tried the word, and she appeared disappointed when the pronunciation didn't sound the way Nicolaus said it.

"German isn't an easy language to learn," he encouraged, "but you can learn it. Since Christmas is only two weeks away, why don't we learn some Christmas words? In my homeland of Hesse, we have big celebrations at Christmastime."

"Our family has never observed Christmas," Comfort said. "We had Puritan ancestors a generation or so back, and their beliefs came down through the family. Celebrating Christmas is anti-Christian, isn't it?"

"Not to Germans. Why, it was our countryman, Martin Luther, who encouraged the children to learn the song 'Away in a Manger' for Christmas festivities. Do you know that song?"

"I've never heard it," Comfort answered, "but we do sing Luther's 'A Mighty Fortress Is Our God.'"

Drawing his chair closer to Erin, Nicolaus said, "Someday, I'll teach you to sing the song, but now I'd like to tell you about Martin Luther." He glanced toward Comfort. "That is, if your sister has no objection."

He noticed that Comfort wasn't limping now. She moved between the hearth and the table, taking care of the chores, as sprightly as a youth. The woman mystified him.

"Erin loves stories."

"Martin Luther was a great preacher, but he was also a family man, happiest when he gathered his children around him and taught them to sing. 'Away in a Manger' was a favorite of his son, Hans."

Erin listened intently to Nicolaus and clapped her hands when he finished. "Sing the song, Nicolaus, sing the song."

"Erin, you've bothered our guest enough for today. If he goes on duty at midnight, he needs to rest."

Nicolaus wondered if that was Comfort's way of telling him he'd overstayed his welcome, so he said, "Just one verse, Erin, and then I must go to my room. My mother taught me the English words, but I can't recall them at the moment. I'll sing a few lines in my native language."

He stood, somewhat awkwardly, as if embarrassed to be performing, but Comfort's hands paused at her work as she listened to his mellow baritone.

"Weg in einem manger, legte keine Krippe fü ein Bett der kleine Herr Jesus seinen süssen Kopf nieder; der Sterne im Himmel schauten unten, wo er den der kleine Herr Jesus legt, schlafend auf dem Heu."

"That was beautiful," Comfort said. "We'll look forward to learning the song. Perhaps you can sing it at our church."

"Would I be welcome at your services?"

"I really don't know," Comfort admitted. "But since you're one of the conquerors, I don't suppose anyone could stop you from entering if you wanted to."

"I'd rather not be called a conqueror. Our ruler hires his army to any country that needs us. On the battlefield, I have enemies, but I don't have hatred toward the citizens." He started toward his room. "Since there's an outside door from my room, I won't be bothering you as I come and go at night. *Danke* for the tasty meal—I haven't had any food like that since my mother died. It's good of you to make me welcome."

He paused in the doorway. *"Gute Nacht,* Erin," he said; and when the child looked mystified, he translated the words into English. "Good night."

"Good night, *freund,"* Erin answered, her face alight with happiness.

Chapter 3

C omfort put the leftover food in a cupboard and hung a pot of porridge on the crane to cook through the night. She added extra logs to the fire to keep the embers alive until morning, and then she and Erin went upstairs to their bed and snuggled together under several comforters. Heat from the fireplace, filtering through the cracks in the ceiling, took the chill off the room.

Their bed was directly above the room Nicolaus occupied. After Erin slept, Comfort's thoughts dwelt on the enemy in their house. He seemed like a gentle man, so why had he taken up soldiering? She'd heard that many German rulers drafted their men and sold their services to other countries, so perhaps Nicolaus didn't have a choice.

In his words, she'd detected a warning that not all of the Hessians were as harmless as he, so there was more than one reason for her to wear a disguise. Still, she wished Nicolaus could see her as she really was.

Comfort was still awake when her father came into the house.

"Are you awake, Comfort?" Father whispered at the opening between the two attic rooms.

She eased out of bed and followed him to the cot he'd laid across the landing of the stairway.

"How'd it go?"

"All right. He has picket duty at midnight, but I don't believe he's left the house yet."

"How's his behavior?"

"He's courteous, and Erin likes him. He's going to teach her to speak German. His mother was English, so that's why he speaks our language so well."

"I've heard reports that some of the soldiers have looted Patriots' houses. And a few women have been insulted."

"That's probably true, for Nicolaus suggested that Erin and I shouldn't leave the house unless he's with us."

"Well, thank God for sending a gentleman among us." He paused, a speculative gleam in his eyes. "If Nicolaus is that friendly, perhaps you can learn British plans, and we can send them to General Washington."

"I won't spy on a guest in our household," Comfort said coldly.

"I hardly consider Nicolaus a guest. We didn't invite him to come here."

"But he's offered to protect us from his fellow soldiers, and I won't repay that courtesy by betraying his trust. I favor American independence as much as you do, but the Continental army will have to wage war without my help."

She went back to her room and got into bed beside Erin. Why had her father's suggestion made her so indignant? She didn't remember she'd ever before talked to her father in that tone of voice. Nicolaus was only a brief diversion in her life, so she shouldn't antagonize her father by treating Nicolaus as more than an unwanted visitor.

🐝

Comfort was preparing Father's breakfast the next morning when she heard Nicolaus enter his room. When her father sat at the table, she whispered, "Do you want to invite Nicolaus to eat with you?"

Father turned an angry face toward her. "No. They can make me house an enemy, but they can't force me to eat with him."

Remembering her decision of the night before, Comfort said no more. Without answering, she placed bread and preserves and a bowl of porridge on the table for her father. She brought him a cup of warm cider from the hearth. Then she prepared a similar tray for Nicolaus and carried it to his door. He had no doubt heard her father's comments, and she was embarrassed. She knocked on the door, and she heard his steps approaching.

"Here's your breakfast," she said. His eyes were weary from lack of sleep. "Would you like some coffee? We keep coffee beans on hand."

"*Nein, danke.* I'll drink water from the pitcher in my room."

He took the plate from her, nodded kindly, and closed the door. He probably didn't expect any better treatment, but she did wish her father hadn't voiced his opinion so loudly. Comfort sat across from her father and nibbled on a slice of bread spread with plum preserves. She poured hot water over tea leaves. Although the beverage wasn't popular in the Colonies since that ruckus over the tea tax in Boston a few years ago, Comfort still liked to start her day with a cup of tea.

Her father wouldn't meet her gaze, and she knew he was sorry for the remark he'd made, but she expected no apology either to her or to Nicolaus.

Comfort tried to work quietly so she wouldn't interrupt Nicolaus's sleep, but Erin pestered her all morning, wanting to talk to him. After their father's comment, she didn't believe Nicolaus would voluntarily come into their living quarters, and she didn't know if she should invite him. What would Father do if he came into the house and caught her and Erin eating with Nicolaus?

She took Erin into the room behind the kitchen and wrote a few sums on the slate for the child to tally. Then she read a chapter of the Bible aloud and helped Erin learn a few of the words. Their mother had taught both Marion and Comfort to read, and she was passing that meager knowledge along to Erin.

Comfort had a pot of vegetable stew simmering over the fire, and when it was almost time to eat the midafternoon meal, she hadn't heard anything from Nicolaus.

She gave Erin permission to knock on his door, but he didn't answer.

Later, when she heard his steps in the other room, she called, "Nicolaus, we'll be eating in a short while."

He opened the door and stood on the threshold. "I went to the barracks. I ate something there."

Comfort didn't meet his gaze. "I'm sorry you heard what my father said."

Nicolaus shrugged his shoulders. "I understand his attitude."

Erin ran in from the back room. "Come, Nicolaus," she said, grabbing his hand. "I want to hear more stories."

Nicolaus looked pointedly at Comfort. "Perhaps she can come to my room."

"I don't want to defy my father," Comfort said, "but I think he's sorry for what he said. If you prefer to eat in your room, I'll serve you there, but Father didn't say you couldn't eat in the kitchen. Until he does, I don't see why you can't come to the table for your meals."

"C'mon," Erin said, tugging on his hand, but she couldn't budge him. "Time to eat."

"I promised not to cause you any trouble," Nicolaus said, scanning Comfort's face for signs of anxiety. He wished she would remove the clouded spectacles so he could see her eyes. But her even white teeth were evident as she smiled, a gesture that eased his loneliness.

"We'll face that trouble if and when it comes," she said. "Erin has been pestering me all morning to have you tell her a story."

Capitulating, he swooped Erin up in his arms, and she squealed as he strode into the kitchen.

"But there'll be no stories until we've eaten," Comfort said in mock severity. "I've made a pot of stew, and I expect it to be eaten."

While they ate, Comfort said, "I've never lived in a city occupied by the enemy, so what should I expect to happen?"

"Contrary to what you've heard, Hessians don't wage war on women and children. However, there are always a few self-willed soldiers; and if they get drunk, they may disregard orders."

"And you might be here all winter?"

Nicolaus squirmed uncomfortably. "I suppose there's no harm in telling you what is common knowledge."

"I'm not asking for secret information," Comfort protested.

"I don't know any secrets, but how long we stay here depends on the Continental army. War is like playing cat and mouse. If General Washington moves, we move. It's as simple as that. But it's not customary to fight in bad weather like this."

"Then I *may* have to impose on you to escort me to the market. I go on Fridays when the farmers bring in supplies."

"I can go with you as soon as I return from sentry duty." He extended his bowl for another helping. "The stew is very good, and as you see, it takes a lot of food to satisfy my appetite."

71

"If preparing meals for you is the worst imposition the British put upon us, I'll have gotten by very well. I like to cook for people who enjoy their food. Father and Erin are both picky eaters, but Marion makes up for that when he's home. He's a big eater."

He started to say that she seemed young to have so much responsibility, for when he listened to her youthful and vibrant voice, he often forgot her apparent age. Instead, he said, "How long have you been responsible for running the household?"

Comfort reached for Erin's hand. "Our mother died when Erin was born. I was only. . ." She flushed and stopped just short of saying that she was thirteen years old when her mother died.

"It hasn't been easy, I'm sure, but you make a wonderful hostess. I appreciate the comfort you've provided for me."

"Thank you," she said shyly.

She'd never had any thanks from anyone else before. Their father and Marion took for granted that it was her responsibility to provide for them, and she supposed it was. Still, it was pleasing to have someone notice her work. She'd had a few men court her; but if she married one of them, she'd just go from one fireplace to another. She'd never thought before about marriage being exciting; but with a man like Nicolaus, life wouldn't be humdrum. *Yes,* she mentally mocked herself, *it wouldn't be humdrum following a soldier from one battlefield to another.*

❧

Erin had been taught to be quiet when her elders were talking, so she hadn't interrupted Comfort and Nicolaus, but she'd been fidgeting on her stool and had almost fallen off once.

Laughing, Comfort said, "All right, Erin, I'll stop talking. You can have Nicolaus to yourself while I go to the cellar to get vegetables for tomorrow."

Nicolaus turned toward Erin. "So, Fräulein, what do you want to hear today?"

"Tell me about your country. How far away do you live from Trenton?"

Nicolaus chuckled in amusement. "Far enough that it took six months for me to arrive in America."

"Six months!" Erin counted on her fingers. "That was way back at the beginning of summer."

"We were on ship only two months, but it's been a long time since I left my home in Hesse."

"Hesse?"

"Germany is made up of lots of little principalities, and Hesse is one of them."

❧

Erin was singing "Away in a Manger" with Nicolaus when Comfort reentered the house. It was a pretty tune, and Comfort hummed along with them as she swept ashes from the hearth and filled a bowl with water from the huge pot hanging on the crane. She applauded when they finished the song.

"Do Germans do anything except sing at Christmas?" Erin demanded.

"Oh, lots more things. Have you heard of the *Belsnickel?*"

"The bell what?" Erin asked, puzzled.

Comfort picked up her sewing box and pulled a chair close to the fireplace for extra light while she knitted woolen socks for Marion.

"It's warmer near the fire," she said, pointing to a chair that their father usually occupied.

Nicolaus hesitated before he took the chair. Erin sat on a low stool near him.

"The *Belsnickel* is associated with Saint Nicolaus, so I'll tell you about him first."

"Were you named for Saint Nicolaus?" Comfort asked.

"*Nein.* My name came from an ancestor. But I consider it an honor to bear the saint's name. He was a bishop who lived in the fourth century and became the patron saint of children. When we celebrate Saint Nicolaus Day, December 6, the children fill their shoes with straw and carrots for the saint's horse. The next morning the shoes are full of toys and cookies."

Erin grinned widely, and Nicolaus tapped her lightly on the head. "That is, if they've been good children. If they haven't been, that's where the *Belsnickel* comes in."

"I've been good," Erin assured him with a serious expression in her brown eyes.

"When Saint Nicolaus makes his rounds, he's sometimes accompanied by *Belsnickel,* a boy with blackened face and a beard, who carries rattling chains and walks on his hands and knees to represent the donkey the *Christkind* rode. The Christ child is often represented by a little girl dressed in white."

"*Christkind* is the German word for the Christ child?" Erin asked, pronouncing the foreign word correctly.

"That's right," Nicolaus said, "you're learning fast."

A satisfied expression overspread Erin's face as she crowded closer to Nicolaus's knees.

"*Belsnickel* goes from house to house with the *Christkind* and gives each mother a switch to discipline her children during the coming year. When *Belsnickel* arrives, if the children kneel and say their prayers, he treats them with nuts or apples. This visiting goes on until Christmas Eve, when Saint Nicolaus arrives with the real Christmas gifts."

"Wouldn't it be nice if Saint Nicolaus comes to Trenton this year?" Erin said, her eyes gleaming with excitement. "With so many Germans here, he might."

Nicolaus stood to his full height, and Comfort gasped as she experienced a delightful tingle in the pit of her stomach. She was intensely aware of his superb masculinity. Was she attracted to him because she'd never seen such a well-built man before? It must not be more than that. Attraction to Nicolaus would lead to nothing but heartbreak.

Nicolaus must have heard her gasp, for he turned toward her, and his penetrating blue-eyed gaze traveled over her face, taking in each detail. She was keenly aware of his scrutiny, and she wondered if he suspected that she wasn't what she pretended to be. Comfort held her breath, dreading what he might say, but Nicolaus turned his attention back to Erin and patted her on the head.

"The *Belsnickel* might come," he said. "But if he does pay a surprise visit, it might be a good idea for a certain Fräulein to be sure she gets candy and nuts instead of a switch."

"I'll be good," Erin promised.

Flustered by the smoldering flame she'd seen in his eyes, Comfort lowered her head and busily plied her knitting needles. She didn't look up when she answered his *Gute Nacht*.

🍂

When Father came for his meal, the harried look on his face disturbed Comfort.

"Do you need any help?" she asked.

"Yes, but you've got enough to do. Where's Erin?"

"Already in bed. She's been asking Nicolaus questions about Germany."

"You're trusting him too far, Comfort."

"That could be true, but we may need an ally in the Hessian camp before this winter is over. So far, he's given me no reason to distrust him, and until he does, I'll take him at his word. He's offered to escort me to the market on Friday, and I accepted his offer."

"I'll just have to trust your judgment in the matter, for I'm worried about what will happen to my patients if the Hessians find them. These men fought at the Battle of White Plains in October, and the Hessians lost a lot of men there."

"So did the Americans."

"That may not make any difference." He drew a long breath and closed his eyes. "I must spend the night in the hospital, but if Nicolaus is on night duty, you should be all right."

Comfort would have felt safer if Nicolaus was in the house at night, but she didn't voice the thought. She didn't want their father to be suspicious of her interest in Nicolaus.

Chapter 4

The frigid weather intensified during the night, and as the wind pelted sleet against the roof, Comfort fretted about Marion and the other Continental soldiers sleeping in crude shelters. She also wondered if Nicolaus had to stand outdoors all night long.

The sleet had stopped by morning, but the house was cold. After she stoked the fire in the kitchen, Comfort knocked softly on Nicolaus's door. When she received no answer, she cracked the door and saw that he wasn't in bed. She laid several logs on his fire, stirred up the coals, and took a pitcher of hot water to his room.

Their father had finished his porridge and was swigging on a hot mug of cider when Nicolaus passed the window and entered his room.

"You and Erin bundle up good if you're going to market. It's raw outside." Their father wagged his head in concern. "I don't know how Washington and the boys will manage. Too bad they let the British take Trenton, or they could have lived in the stone barracks built by the British during the last war. Instead, our enemies are quartered there."

"I'm worried about Marion."

With a sigh, her father drained his cider mug. "And I'm worried about you, too. I don't like leaving you and Erin so much, but I feel I have to stay at the hospital most of the time. I'm uneasy leaving my patients if the Hessians should attack, and I don't want our enemies to get the medications Congress allotted me." He lowered his voice. "I've got a lot of bed sacks, sheets, blankets, and shirts, too."

"Are they hidden?"

"I don't know where I can hide them. But," he said, dropping his voice lower, "it's reported that the Hessians haven't made any entrenchments. Colonel Rall scoffs at the Continental army and doesn't think he has anything to fear. The officers drink and play cards all night and sleep through the day, so that makes the regular soldiers lax. There's been a lot of looting, but I'm hoping they'll leave the hospital alone."

He wrapped his heavy coat around his shoulders and gestured toward the bedroom. "If our visitor starts drinking, you and Erin leave the house immediately and come to me."

Comfort agreed with a nod. She called up the stairs and told Erin to get up, and then she prepared a plate for Nicolaus and knocked at his door. He and Erin arrived in the kitchen at the same time. Nicolaus ate heartily of the bread and porridge, and Comfort served him extra portions.

"Did you spend a miserable night?" she asked.

"It wasn't too bad. We've taken over a cooper's shop on the edge of town, and we alternate the patrol. It's very cold, though. Must you go to market?"

"I usually go on Friday when Mr. Stone comes to town. He brings butter, milk, and eggs for us. We have plenty of vegetables, fruits, and cured meat in the cellar, but I like to have fresh farm products. Do you want to rest before we leave for the market?"

"Not if you want to get there early."

Comfort bundled Erin into a long woolen shawl, and she put on a heavy coat and pulled a shawl low over her head. She didn't want any of her acquaintances to see her and reveal her youthful identity to Nicolaus. But she wondered if he was really fooled by her dowdy garments because she occasionally caught him watching her with a speculative gleam in his eye.

Nicolaus walked a few paces behind Comfort and Erin as they hurried northward along Queen Street and turned eastward on Fourth Street. Only a few farmers had braved the cold to bring in supplies. Thankful that Mr. Stone was one of them, Comfort approached his wagon. Shivering from the cold, he paid no attention to her until she spoke.

"I hardly recognized you, Miss Comfort. Are you ailing?"

She warned him with a shake of her head, and Stone looked quickly from Comfort to Nicolaus, his keen glance taking in the situation. "I've got your things. The colder the weather, the less milk and eggs I get, but I'm still providing for my best customers."

He placed the items in her basket, and Comfort handed him some paper notes issued by the Continental Congress that Father had received for operating the hospital.

Mr. Stone kept eyeing Nicolaus, who stood several feet away from them.

"What's he doing with you?" he growled.

"He's billeted in our home, and he offered his escort this morning. Watch what you say," Comfort cautioned. "He speaks and understands English."

"What do you hear of Washington?" the farmer whispered.

"Not much. Marion hasn't been home for a couple of weeks, and I hope he doesn't come while the Hessians control the town."

"The Germans think Washington has sneaked away like a dog with its tail between its legs." He winked conspiratorially. "They might be in for a surprise."

If Washington was planning an attack, Nicolaus would be in danger. It had been disturbing enough to worry about Marion and the soldiers in her father's care. Now she'd added Nicolaus to her concerns.

Mr. Stone handed Erin a cookie. "Here's a sorghum cookie, Missy. Fresh baked yesterday."

Comfort thanked Mr. Stone, and Nicolaus fell into step behind them as they left the market area.

Glancing over her shoulder, Comfort asked, "Do you know where I can find the roving army baker who was in Trenton when your troops arrived? I've heard your colonel detained him before he could leave town."

A smile spread across Nicolaus's generous mouth. The rare smile always transformed his somber countenance to pleasant features and made him appear friendly and trustworthy.

"*Ja*. His ovens are in a shack near our headquarters along King Street. Colonel Rall likes his food, and when he tasted the baker's bread, he said he hadn't eaten anything to compare with it since he left Germany. He's posted guards to keep the baker from leaving Trenton."

"If the colonel hasn't seized all of the bakery products, I'll see if Mr. Ludwick has some gingerbread. He was a neighbor of ours in Philadelphia, and we've been eating his good pastries for years."

"Ludwick, did you say? I have a cousin by that name living in Philadelphia. And he's a baker. The few messages he wrote to our family about the English colonies encouraged me to volunteer for service in America."

"Then let's find Mr. Ludwick, and I'll introduce you."

The tantalizing aroma of fresh pastries greeted them when they entered the bakeshop where two Hessians stood guard. Christopher Ludwick was a short, portly man, and when the Foster sisters entered with the Hessian, an angry look crossed the baker's round face.

German, though he was, Ludwick was an outspoken critic of George III and the foreign soldiers he'd sent to the Colonies. Christopher had prospered in Pennsylvania, but he'd donated much of his fortune to the colonial cause. And he'd volunteered to provide bread for the army, refusing to draw either pay or rations for his work.

The baker was in a bad humor, and he paid no attention to Comfort's disguise when she asked for some gingerbread. "It's an outrage," Christopher stated in broken English that was difficult to follow in spite of his many years in the Colonies, "that these foreigners have moved in on us. The Continental army is starving for my bread, and I'm forced to cook for these scoundrels."

"Hush, Mr. Ludwick," Comfort said, fearful of what else he would say that Nicolaus would understand. "I've brought you a surprise. This *gentleman*," she emphasized the word, "is lodging in our house. He's a kinsman of yours."

Christopher cast a sharp glance at Nicolaus.

"Meet Nicolaus Trittenbach," Comfort added.

The baker scuttled closer to Nicolaus and peered upward at him. " 'Deed you could be my kinsman, but you have grown up, way up, since last I saw you." He threw his arms around Nicolaus's waist. "It is good to see one of my kindred once more."

"Your success in America made me want to come here."

"But I would have preferred that you didn't come to fight us," Christopher said severely.

"I'm under orders from the King of England. If I should meet you in battle, I will fight fiercely against you, but I won't attack a peaceful citizen."

Mr. Ludwick motioned to the two guards. "Not all are like that." Turning his attention to Comfort, he said, "How much gingerbread do you need?"

"Two loaves, please. Erin is very fond of it."

The baker smiled at Erin. "Then you shall have my best. I have just taken some loaves from the oven. Colonel Rall has ordered that all my products be kept for his men, but I do what I want."

Comfort wrapped the two loaves in a cloth and put them in the basket with the farm produce. She paid him with Spanish coins. Mr. Ludwick handed Erin and Comfort each a gingerbread man and one to Nicolaus also.

"Come and talk to me whenever you can," Christopher said to Nicolaus. "We have much to say to one another."

As they left the building, the guard by the door guffawed and spoke to Nicolaus. Comfort didn't understand his words, but somehow she thought they were directed toward her. Nicolaus's face darkened in anger, and his retort was harsh and surly. The incident revealed another side of Nicolaus, and Comfort realized that he could be ferocious if provoked to anger. Of course, Nicolaus wouldn't have made a good soldier if he didn't have this characteristic. How thankful she was that he hadn't vented his anger on her family.

❧

Nicolaus stayed in his room the rest of the day, and his presence was welcome, for rowdy soldiers prowled the streets. One stopped by the house and peered into the kitchen. Comfort shrank against the wall, and he didn't see her. He pushed on the door, but the latch held, and he moved on. One group of soldiers passed, their arms loaded with plunder.

By nightfall, the soldiers had banded together in a mob, and Nicolaus was called out early. Before he left, he cautioned Comfort, "Stay in the house with the doors locked. I'll try to keep an eye on your home, but I don't know where I might be stationed. A farmer brought in a load of whiskey this afternoon, and our soldiers are drinking."

Comfort sent Erin to bed early, but she stayed up to guard the house, since Father had to remain in the hospital all night. With Nicolaus and her father away from the house, Comfort took the opportunity to wash her hair. The powder that she'd used to disguise her appearance made her head itch, and if only for a short time, she wanted to freshen up.

After she washed her hair, she bathed her face with some scented soap her father had bought from a French merchant. In the darkness of the back room, she took a quick wash and put on clean clothing. She was tired of wearing the dirty dress she'd worn for the past week. She sat by the fire to dry her hair, intending to relax an hour or two before she replaced her disguise.

Comfort dozed before the fire, and she didn't know how long she'd slept before she heard the mob approaching. They bypassed the house and headed toward the hospital and built a fire in the yard. Father locked the doors at night, but this mob could easily wreck the building or burn it.

A hospital window shattered, and the drunken soldiers roared with laughter as they advanced on the building, their voices demanding and piercing. Frightened, Comfort stood in the middle of the dark room and wrung her hands, wheeling at a sound behind her. Nicolaus rushed into the house and strode purposefully toward the back door, his face hard as granite. He was in full uniform, and the brass headgear made him look like a giant. He carried his musket, fixed with the bayonet. With a mighty thrust, he swung open the door, slamming it against the side of the room.

Nicolaus fired his musket.

"Anschlag!" Shouting in German, he advanced on the mob, his bayonet threatening. He was a terrifying apparition in the glow of the fire as smoke swirled around him. He thundered at the soldiers in a coarse voice, and they turned tail and ran out of the yard with Nicolaus in full pursuit.

Throwing a shawl around her shoulders, Comfort ran toward the hospital.

"Father," she called. "Are you all right?" The door opened cautiously. "They're gone. Nicolaus chased them away." She pushed by her father and into the room.

"No damage, except the broken window," Father said in a shaking voice. "Two of the men got slight wounds from the flying glass, but nothing else. I'll put out that fire before it spreads to the buildings."

Now that the danger was past, reaction set in, and Comfort's legs trembled until she could hardly stand. She stumbled into her father's office and sat behind the desk, leaning her head on her hands. Comfort had heard of avenging angels, and when Nicolaus advanced on the mob brandishing his musket and bayonet, he could have been the archangel Michael. What if Nicolaus hadn't come when he had? Would the recuperating soldiers have been killed and the hospital destroyed?

"Be not forgetful to entertain strangers: for thereby some have entertained angels unawares," she murmured. Had that Bible verse come true tonight? Maybe angels didn't have to wear wings and a halo like the ones she'd seen in paintings. Tonight, she believed an angel, in the guise of a Hessian soldier, had helped her family.

"Comfort," her father called, rousing her from her reverie.

"In your office," she answered and stood to greet him, thankful that her limbs were steadier now. Father rushed into the small room with the tall figure of Nicolaus towering behind him. Both men stared at her as if they'd never seen her before, and Comfort couldn't imagine what was wrong until she lifted a hand to her smooth cheek. Fingering her clean hair, her face flamed.

"Oh, Father, I forgot. My hair was so uncomfortable, I just had to get rid of that powder. With the house empty, I thought it was safe to wash my hair."

He waved his hand impatiently. "We'll talk of that later. Did you have trouble in the house?"

Comfort's gaze wandered to Nicolaus, who stared at her in astonishment. A look of wonder, admiration, and a glimmer of hope shone from his blue eyes, but he said nothing.

"No problem at all, but I must hurry back in case Erin is awake. Thank you,

Nicolaus," she said. "If you hadn't come, we might have lost everything."

"Colonel Rall gave orders for the renegade soldiers to be locked up until they're sober. That should stop the rioting."

Clearing his throat awkwardly and without looking at Nicolaus, Father extended his hand. "I owe you a lot for this night's work. Thank you."

Nicolaus gripped her father's hand. "When I'm in battle, I'll fight my enemy as fiercely as any Hessian, but I won't stand by and see the wounded and innocent molested. Now that I know you're all right, I'll return to my patrol."

After Nicolaus left, Comfort helped her father nail a blanket over the broken window before she returned to the house. Father hadn't mentioned the lack of her disguise, and unless he ordered her to further conceal her true identity, Comfort didn't intend to do so. Nicolaus knew the truth now, and she would have given a great deal to know how the revelation had affected him.

Chapter 5

The grenadiers were ignobly reported to be seven feet tall, but as Nicolaus spent the next hour patrolling Queen Street, he felt as if he lived up to that reputation. He had the sensation of floating on air, his heavy boots hardly touching the ground.

For the past week he'd puzzled over Comfort's appearance, wishing he could see behind her dark spectacles, but he hadn't been prepared for the vision he'd encountered tonight when he entered the hospital. He'd thought she might be younger than she looked, but he was unprepared for her loveliness. Comfort was young, beautiful, and desirable.

Oliver Foster had shaken his hand tonight, but Nicolaus doubted that the man would look favorably upon him as Comfort's suitor. He'd been drawn to her the first day, but now that he knew she was a maiden instead of a middle-aged woman, Nicolaus realized the depth of his interest. How did one court a girl in America?

Nicolaus's father had met his mother when the British had hired Hessian soldiers during the Scots Rebellion in 1745. They were married, and she returned to Hesse with him when the rebellion ceased, apparently without any looking back. Would history repeat itself in Nicolaus's case? But he didn't want to take Comfort to Hesse—he'd be content to stay with her in America.

❦

Comfort was amazed but relieved to find that Erin had slept through all the commotion. She couldn't believe any soldier, drunk or sober, would deliberately harm a child, but she felt the need to protect Erin anyway.

Wondering what Nicolaus had thought when he'd discovered her real identity, Comfort both anticipated and dreaded seeing him again. She checked to be sure he wasn't in the house before she entered his room and stirred the fire. She didn't intend to go to bed until she knew the Hessian soldiers had been subdued, so she left the door open between Nicolaus's room and the kitchen, hoping he'd come to talk to her when he returned.

Her mind was in turmoil, so to occupy her hands, she mended a pair of her father's breeches. Her hands stilled over the workbasket when she heard Nicolaus's steps. He paused, then turned toward the kitchen.

"Comfort," he whispered.

"Yes, come in," she said. "I couldn't go to bed until I knew we were safe."

"The riot involved only twenty men, but they did a lot of damage. Everything is quiet now."

"I'm grateful you came before they ransacked the hospital. Father doesn't own a firearm, but he wouldn't have shot at them anyway."

He came closer, and Comfort motioned to a chair. "You're probably cold, so sit near the fireplace."

Nicolaus sat down, sighed, and stretched his feet toward the fire.

"*Sehr Gut!* Very good," he repeated. "It's been a difficult night."

"Is this apt to happen again?"

"Not if Colonel Rall keeps these men confined until after Christmas. Some Germans celebrate Christmas by carousing."

The silence lengthened between them as Comfort nervously plied the needle in and out of the breeches.

"Why did you change your appearance?" Nicolaus asked.

She spoke eagerly, hoping for understanding. "With enemy soldiers in town, Father thought I'd be safer if I appeared to be middle-aged."

"A good idea," Nicolaus agreed.

"It's obvious now that the disguise wasn't necessary in your case, but we didn't know what to expect."

"You had no reason to trust me. Your father was wise to guard you."

"But he didn't tell me to resume the disguise. I'm glad to get rid of that powder in my hair, as well as those blotches on my face."

"How old are you?"

"Eighteen."

"I'm twenty-six," he said.

The room lightened as daylight approached, and Nicolaus stood. "I should go to bed."

Comfort laid aside the sewing basket. She moved close to him and laid her hand on his forearm, the first time she'd touched him. A delicious tingle moved up her arm.

"Thank you for what you did for us tonight."

His fingers were warm and strong as they wrapped around hers, and she wondered how such a large hand could convey so much gentleness.

"It's my pleasure to serve you." Smiling tenderly down at her, he continued, "You are very beautiful. I'm happy that beauty won't be concealed from me any longer."

He whispered *"Liebchen"* when he left the room. A spark of undefinable emotion gleamed in his eyes, and she feared to ask what the word meant.

❧❧

A few days later, Nicolaus returned from a sortie into the country, carrying a large evergreen tree. He left the tree on the stoop.

"With your permission, Comfort, I want to set up this *immergruner Baum*—evergreen tree—for Erin. I'd like to decorate it the way we do in my homeland."

"I'll have to ask Father."

Nicolaus nodded in approval.

While he waited for Comfort to finish the midafternoon meal, for they ate only twice a day, Nicolaus told Erin the story of the Christmas tree.

"Decorating a tree was a pagan custom before Germans started it. The ancient Romans decorated with evergreens to honor one of their gods, and that's the reason early Christians refused to decorate a Christmas tree, called *Weihnachtsbaum* in our language."

Erin tried the word and, after a few tries, pronounced it correctly.

"An English missionary, Saint Boniface, brought Christianity to Germany in the eighth century, probably the first person to use an evergreen tree as a symbol of Christ. But Martin Luther is thought to be the first man to decorate a tree in his home during the Christmas season."

"What can we use for decorations?" Erin said.

"You can hang fruit on it," Nicolaus suggested.

"We have apples in the cellar," Comfort said, getting excited about the idea, hoping their father would approve it.

"We can put some of Ludwick's gingerbread men on the tree. Or take pieces of colorful fabric, put them on strings, and wind them around the branches."

"Let's put up the *Weihnachtsbaum* now, Comfort," Erin begged.

Comfort shook her head. "Not until Father gives permission. If he does, we can put it in the room behind the kitchen. It's cooler there, and the needles won't wither."

"I have something in my room we can also use," Nicolaus said. He left the kitchen and returned with a wooden angel that fit in the palm of his hand—a slender angel that stood tall and straight in a pleated-foil gown with outstretched arms, holding an evergreen wreath in each hand.

"Our word for angel is *engel*—not much different from the way you say it. This Nuremberg *Engel*," he explained, "has been in our family for generations. Before my father died, he gave it to me."

"It's beautiful," Comfort said, running her finger down the face of the fragile angel. "Is it very old?"

"More than a hundred years old. It belonged to my ancestors, who lived in Dinkelsbühl. Legend has it that the first Nuremberg angel was made by a German doll maker in memory of his daughter killed during the Thirty Years' War. Now, most every German home has a Nuremberg angel on its *Weihnachtsbaum*. It would be an honor to place my *engel* on the first tree you've had in your home."

"That's kind of you, Nicolaus. I'll talk to Father about the tree, and if he approves, we can start decorating it tomorrow." Comfort reached for the tablet on the mantel where she tabulated the days of the month. "Today is December 18. One week from today will be Christmas."

"When you talk to your father about the tree, perhaps you can mention a

Christmas feast, which is also traditional in our country."

Erin smiled broadly. "I like feasts. I'll beg Poppy to let us have one."

🐝

Comfort hadn't been in her bed long when she heard her father's footsteps on the stairs. He usually stayed until after midnight, then left an elderly Patriot to guard the hospital. She wondered why he'd left the hospital so early. She'd started to get out of bed to ask if there was any trouble when she heard him stumble at the head of the steps and fall heavily onto the cot. The cot was where it had been for a week. Why had he forgotten it?

"What's that cot doing there?" an angry voice mumbled.

Marion! Comfort's heart almost stopped beating when she realized her brother had come home—into a town controlled by the enemy. She slid out of bed and scurried into the next room.

"Be quiet!" she whispered sternly. She heard her brother disengaging himself from the comforter. "What's my cot doing over here?" he demanded.

"Hush, I tell you!" she repeated in a harsh whisper. She reached his side and took him by the arm. "What are you doing here? Don't you know this town is full of Hessian soldiers?"

"Yes, I know it. That's why I'm here. General Washington wants me to find out what they're up to."

"Do you also know there's a Hessian soldier sleeping downstairs in Father's room?"

"What!" Marion shouted. "He won't be sleeping long." With all the bravado of a seventeen-year-old, Marion started downstairs with Comfort at his heels.

At the foot of the stairs, she forcibly pushed him out the back door. "You're not going to bother him," she hissed. "The man protected our property last night when other Hessians were attacking the hospital, and I won't have you fighting with him. Besides, he's a huge man, a foot taller than you are. You're no match for him."

"There's not a Hessian I can't whip with one hand tied behind me!" Marion said loudly.

"Yes, just like the Americans did at Fort Washington," Comfort jeered. She grabbed his arm. Marion struggled, trying to throw off her grasp. Exerting strength she didn't know she possessed, Comfort prevented him from returning to the house. "Come to the hospital. Maybe Father can talk some sense into you. You need to get out of Trenton."

She tapped their secret signal. Her father opened the door, and Comfort quietly pushed Marion inside. Her brother was trembling, and Comfort thought it was from anger until he said, "I haven't had anything to eat for two days or you wouldn't be able to shove me around like this."

"Son, you shouldn't be here!"

"Just what I told him," Comfort said.

"I'm not here to visit my devoted family, who certainly don't seem glad to see me," Marion said angrily. "I'm on assignment from General Washington. He sent me to scout out Trenton, and I'm not leaving until I find out what he wants to know."

"That puts a new light on the situation," Father agreed.

"He can't stay at the house with Nicolaus there," Comfort said.

"Why'd you let a Hessian move into our home?" Marion demanded of his father. "I wanted to put him out, but Comfort threw a fit about it."

"Don't be foolish, Son. If you start a fight with Nicolaus, German troops will be on us in no time. You can't serve the Continental cause if you're killed or taken prisoner, so use what sense the good Lord gave you. Besides, the Foster family is indebted to Nicolaus Trittenbach."

"Make Marion stay here, and I'll go back to the house and bring some food for him."

"I'm about starved to death, Sis. In fact, the whole Continental army is hungry."

"I'll be right back," Comfort promised.

🐝

She lit a candle and moved quietly about the kitchen, filling a bowl with beans that had been left over from supper. She put a half-loaf of bread and some butter in a basket and a jar of plums she'd brought from the cellar intending to use them for a plum cake tomorrow. She filled another jar with cider and carried the provisions to the hospital.

The three Fosters moved to the office. While Marion wolfed the food, his father said, "We're in a tight situation. As a soldier, Marion has to carry out the orders of his commander. He can hide here in the hospital until I find out what Washington needs to know."

Between swallows, Marion said, "That Hessian at the house ought to know something. What's he told you, Comfort?"

"Nothing!"

"I don't want Comfort mixed up in this," their father said. "I'll send word to a few Patriots, and they'll pick up information. Go back to the house, Comfort, and try to act normally."

"Not until Marion promises that he won't attack Nicolaus."

"Your brother isn't going to leave this building until tomorrow night. By that time, Nicolaus will be on duty, and Marion won't even know where he is."

"Nicolaus wants to help Erin decorate a tree for Christmas like they do in Germany. Will you agree to that? If so, we can keep busy with that tomorrow and divert his attention from activities at the hospital."

"That smacks of paganism to me," their father said, "but under the circumstances, it might be the best way to keep him occupied."

While she had her father in an agreeable mood, Comfort pushed for another concession. "He's mentioned a feast on Christmas Day."

"All right! All right!" Father shouted. "If you keep him in the house and away from this hospital until Marion rejoins General Washington, I don't care what you do."

Smiling, Comfort hurriedly returned to the house. The town crier, a custom

Trenton had borrowed from Philadelphia, walked down Queen Street calling out the midnight hour. Comfort paused in the kitchen until she heard Nicolaus stirring, and then she went up to her bed.

Why had she forcibly prevented Marion from harming Nicolaus? She'd known this foreigner less than a month, but their association had been so intense, she felt as if she'd known him all of her life. Comfort's friends had sometimes talked of love; but among her people, love had never played a part in the decision to marry. The life cycle was set, and one lived by it. You were born, lived as a child, and when you were of marriageable age, you took the most likely prospect.

Love, as she understood it, was the passionate affection of one person for another. She'd never felt about anyone like she did about Nicolaus. Was that love? Was it possible to love a person after knowing him only a few weeks? She didn't understand her feelings, but she wanted to prevent trouble between Marion and Nicolaus. Thankfully, Nicolaus had slept through all the commotion.

❦

As Nicolaus took up picket duty beside the cooper's cabin, he reviewed the night's activities. He remembered the light touch of Comfort's fingers on his arm and her fragrance—a light rose scent that must have come from the soap she'd used to wash her hair. Thoughts of Comfort brought peace to his mind, but he was troubled about the Fosters' late-night visitor.

He hadn't been asleep when Marion had stumbled over the cot. Short-sword in hand, he'd opened the door into the kitchen. He'd heard Marion's threat against his life and Comfort's efforts to get her brother out of the house.

Marion Foster was in Trenton to spy on the Hessian army. As a loyal soldier, was he guilty of betrayal by not reporting to Colonel Rall that there was a spy in their midst? He'd watched as Marion and Comfort had gone to the hospital, and he knew Marion was sequestered there. Was it his duty to arrest the boy? He knew it was, but he couldn't bring himself to make any more trouble for Comfort. Never before had he vacillated in his duty toward the country that had hired his services. At no time had he let personal bias interfere with commitment to his commander. But in a choice between distressing Comfort Foster and fulfilling his oath to serve the British, he had chosen Comfort. Why? He puzzled over the weighty question all night long.

Chapter 6

Try to keep Marion hidden? If the Hessians found out that her father was harboring a spy, the whole Foster family, as well as the convalescing soldiers, would suffer for it.

She tried to act as excited as Erin when Nicolaus nailed the evergreen tree to a board and brought it into the house. She brought a basket of red and yellow apples from the cellar. She cut stars from scraps of colorful fabric left over from dresses she'd made for Erin and herself.

She gave needles and thread to Nicolaus and Erin to string the fabric into a chain. Erin laughed at Nicolaus's clumsy efforts to thread the needle. Comfort tied strings to the apples, and Nicolaus lifted Erin to attach some of the decorations at the top of the tree. Sometimes amid their laughter, when Comfort suddenly remembered the danger hanging over the Fosters, her hands paused in their tasks and a frightened feeling overtook her.

After Nicolaus had repeatedly observed her agitation, he stepped close to her and took her hand. "Comfort, I told you when I came here that I am not a threat to you or your family. Don't you believe me?" he asked softly.

She lifted her eyes to meet his steady, tender gaze. The blue of his eyes had intensified until they were as dark and luminous as midnight. *He knows about Marion!*

"Yes, I believe you," she murmured and dropped her gaze in confusion, realizing suddenly why she'd defended Nicolaus from her own brother and why she trusted Nicolaus completely. The realization was two-edged. She was happy to at last experience this special affection for another person, but she was wretched to be so fond of a man who might be gone from her life in a short time—a man who in reality was her enemy.

❧

Marion made it in and out of Trenton without incident, but their father and Comfort despaired of having him return to the army. The weather had turned fiercely cold, and the signs were right for a big snow. Erin and Comfort stayed in the house most of the time, and she accepted Nicolaus's offer to bring the farm products from Mr. Stone on Friday, including a plump goose—a traditional Christmas food in Germany.

Besides the goose, she intended to cook a mixture of beans and dried corn, baked squash, oyster soup, and a sweetened rice pudding that Nicolaus told her how to prepare. He had persuaded Christopher Ludwick to make a *Schnitz* pie—a layer of sour dried apples covered with cinnamon, sugar, and orange rind baked in a thick pastry crust. Christopher had also sent two loaves of rye bread and some gingerbread cookies.

The ornaments on the *Weihnachtsbaum* increased as Nicolaus and Erin thought of new items to add. By Christmas Eve, it was a heavily laden tree, and Comfort was pleased that it had provided so much enjoyment for Erin.

⁂

On Christmas Eve, Nicolaus arranged for one of his friends to appear in the role of *Belsnickel*. Nicolaus had coached Erin on what she should do if *Belsnickel* did show up. Even then, she rushed to hide behind Comfort's skirts when the back door unceremoniously opened and a huge figure, wrapped in a shaggy bearskin coat and wearing a mask, entered the room. He carried a handful of switches.

The *Belsnickel* laughed fiendishly, swung one switch, and exploded into a spate of German words. Nicolaus answered in English, "We have only one child here, and she says she's been a good girl this year."

He motioned to Erin, who somewhat reluctantly left the safety of Comfort's skirts, knelt, and clasped her hands in prayer.

Standing up, Erin stayed close to Nicolaus when the *Belsnickel* patted her on the head and gave her some gingerbread cookies that looked suspiciously like those made by Ludwick, a bag of maple sugar candy, and a wooden figurine of a woman wrapped in red cloth.

Shouting, *"Frohliche Weihnachten,"* the man exited.

Nicolaus answered, "Merry Christmas to you."

After Nicolaus went on duty, Comfort placed more coals in the oven to keep the goose roasting through the night. But listening to the wind and experiencing the chill from the window and the cold draft under the door, Comfort went to bed with a heavy heart. How could she enjoy a feast tomorrow when Marion and his fellows were camped outdoors?

⁂

Colonel Rall declared Christmas a holiday, and the streets were empty of Hessians. Erin begged her father to eat Christmas dinner with them, and because the town was quiet, he agreed to leave his patients untended for a few hours. Comfort set the larger table in the back room for the occasion, where they could also enjoy the scent of the *immergruner Baum* that permeated the room.

For the first time, their father sat at table with Nicolaus, seemingly without animosity. Comfort blushingly accepted the praise of both men for the delicious meal. She read the Christmas story from Luke, and Nicolaus took a prayer book from his pocket and read a blessing in German. Smilingly, he translated it into English.

"God's blessing upon those who give shelter from the storm to weary travelers

88

passing their home. May God's favor always shine upon them and bring peace to their hearts. Amen."

His gaze passed from Father to Erin and to Comfort as he softly repeated the words. "I sincerely pray that God will grant that blessing because of your kindness to me."

After the meal, they gathered around the big fireplace in the kitchen. Father stayed at the house until almost dusk, and Comfort was delighted to see the congeniality between the two men. Her father plied Nicolaus with questions about Germany and answered Nicolaus's queries concerning opportunities in America.

After he left, Nicolaus taught Erin the English words to "Away in a Manger." It took more than an hour, but soon Erin could sing the English translation. Nicolaus sang one line in German, and Erin would take the following phrase in English.

Comfort even joined them on the last line. When Nicolaus sang, *"die Sterne im Himmel schauten unten, wo er den,"* she and Erin concluded, "the little Lord Jesus, asleep on the hay."

Erin soon went to sleep on a blanket in front of the fire.

"Thank you, Nicolaus, for making this such a wonderful day for Erin. She'll never forget it." Then she added slowly, "And neither will I."

Comfort roused Erin and sent her to bed, then peered out the window. "It's snowing again." The window was frosty, and wind gusts whistled around the house. "Your assignment is going to be miserable tonight," she said to Nicolaus.

He shook his head in dismay. "I'm not concerned about the weather, but it's frightening that Colonel Rall and the other officers are taking our position here for granted. The majority of our soldiers are already drunk. We'll not be a fit army to defend ourselves in case of any attack. Some of us requested additional pickets, but the commanders laughed at us. 'Armies don't fight in this kind of weather,' was the answer we received."

Giving Nicolaus a hot mug of cider, Comfort said, "I took the liberty of making you a gift. You've served our family well this week." She handed him a pair of mittens. "I hope they aren't too small for you."

Obviously pleased, he put on the mittens, which fit snugly. "Just my size. Thank you. I'll wear them tonight."

He walked into the back room and returned with the Nuremberg angel. "This is for you. I've enjoyed seeing it atop the *Weihnachtsbaum,* and I pray that it may decorate many more trees in the Foster household."

"But, Nicolaus," she protested, "this belongs in your family. I can't take it."

He closed her hand around the angel. "My father gave it to me, and I want you to have it. If I should fall in battle, the angel would become part of the plunder. I'll be happier knowing you have it."

"Why would you give me such a treasure?"

He laid a hand on her cheek. "Because you've become very important to me." His blue eyes shone, and his brow wrinkled in wonderment that echoed in his voice. "It's hard to believe that in such a short time I've learned to care so deeply for you, but there's no mistaking the message of my heart."

"Oh," Comfort said, breathlessly.

"If my term of enlistment ends while I'm still in America, I'll request parole in the Colonies. If I'm no longer a part of the British army, will you forget that I'm your enemy?"

Bravely meeting his gaze, in a tremulous voice, Comfort answered, "You've never seemed like an enemy to me."

Cupping her chin, Nicolaus bent down and brushed her lips with a soft kiss. *"Guten nacht. Frohliche Weihnachten."*

"Good night and Merry Christmas to you, too," she replied softly.

❧

As he strode briskly toward the outpost in the cooper's house, Nicolaus wondered if he should have kissed Comfort, but she hadn't resisted his caress. He didn't regret his boldness, for his body still tingled from the sensation of the touch of her lips.

His excitement cooled immediately when he reached the outpost. His fellow soldiers were grouped around the fireplace in earnest discussion.

"Nicolaus," one of them said. "A loyal farmer brought word that the rebel army has crossed the Delaware to attack Trenton."

Nicolaus slapped his thigh in disgust. "I've had the feeling all day that something was wrong. Why didn't the colonel anticipate this?"

Leutnant Wiederhold, commander of the post, said sharply, "He should have. Small rebel parties have been crossing the Delaware and pestering our patrols for days. A cousin of mine was killed in one of the skirmishes."

"Surely the colonel knew that," Nicolaus said.

"Ja," Wiederhold said, "but knowing that Washington's troops are half-starved and exhausted, he didn't figure they'd march during this harsh weather. Herr Trittenbach, go warn the colonel and return here as soon as you can."

The cold wind chilled Nicolaus in spite of the heavy coat he wore over his uniform. Freezing rain coated his musket with ice, and he tried to shield the weapon beneath his coat as he quickly retraced his steps into Trenton.

He heard the celebrating soldiers before he reached Rall's headquarters in the stone barracks on King Street. When he hurried into the anteroom, he was greeted with cheers. One soldier, mug of ale held high, saluted him.

"Where've you been, Nicolaus? You're missing all the fun."

The roistering soldiers sickened Nicolaus, but he didn't have the authority to tell them to prepare for battle. "I have a message for Colonel Rall."

Laughing and cheering greeted his remark as another soldier delivered a toast. Nicolaus strode outside, uncertain what to do until he saw Ludwick's bakeshop across the street. The baker was working at his ovens with only one Hessian on guard when Nicolaus entered. The soldier seemed sober, and Nicolaus asked him quietly, "Where's Colonel Rall?"

"At the home of Abraham Hunt. That's the big brick house down the street."

"Thanks," Nicolaus answered and waved to Ludwick, who watched him curiously. Outside, he was greeted by another onslaught of snow and sleet.

Nicolaus had admired the Hunt mansion more than once as he'd patrolled the streets of Trenton. He approached the rear of the mansion, and when a servant answered his knock, he asked for Colonel Rall.

"Mr. Hunt and his guests are playing cards, and they are not to be disturbed."

Playing cards when his whole contingent of men might be captured! Nicolaus considered shoving the servant aside and breaking in on the party, but he knew he'd be punished if he barged in on his superior officer.

"Will you take an urgent message to him?"

"I can take him a note when I go in with food and drinks."

"May I step inside to write the message?"

Nicolaus was shown into a small room, where he found paper and a quill pen. He hurriedly scribbled in German, "Washington is bringing his men across the Delaware. They're approaching Trenton." He started to add, "The troops need to be rallied," but he didn't go that far. All he could do was sound the warning—the rest was up to the commander. Nicolaus thanked the servant and rushed back to his post.

🙂

The two dozen Hessians at the outpost didn't relax their vigilance all night. By daylight the snowfall had intensified, and their vision was limited to a few yards. The howling wind kept them from hearing the approaching column led by Washington until it was almost upon them.

Nicolaus heard shots, rapid footsteps, and a sentry's cry, *"Der Feind! Heraus! Heraus!"*

"The enemy! The enemy! On your feet!" The Hessians rushed toward the Americans, but when *Leutnant* Wiederhold saw the weaving line of Colonial soldiers, he shouted, "Men, we're outnumbered. Fall back and join the other troops."

Nicolaus retreated with his comrades, trying to fire his musket, but his gunpowder was wet. He thought of Comfort and Erin, wishing he could warn them of the impending battle, but a Hessian soldier couldn't help them today.

Chapter 7

Comfort learned of the Continental advance when her father rolled out of his blankets to answer an imperative pounding on the door.

"Comfort," Father called, and she hurried to the top of the stairs. He motioned for her to join him.

"That was Marion. The Continental army is attacking. Take Erin and go to the root cellar."

"But, Father. . ."

"Do what I say," her father demanded, interrupting her protest. "Immediately."

Hurrying to obey him, she asked, "Will you keep me posted about what's going on? The enemy could burn the house over our heads."

"Washington's men will keep the Hessians too busy for that. Fortunately, the enemy soldiers are disorganized. I'll bring you word when I can, but you must hide. I don't know what I'll face today, and I can't be worried about you and Erin."

Comfort dressed Erin in a heavy layer of clothes, put on several of her own garments and wrapped woolen cloth around their legs and shoes. She handed Erin a jug of milk to carry. Toting a basket filled with bread, cheese, and some candles, she hurried her sister along the stoop to the cellar door.

The cellar was damp, but not much colder than their attic bedrooms. The frigid weather had entered every nook and cranny of Trenton; and thinking of the soldiers fighting in the streets, Comfort knew she should be thankful for shelter of any kind.

Erin was crying, and Comfort put her arms around the child.

"Don't fret. We won't be here long. General Washington will soon drive the Hessians out of town."

"Nicolaus?" Erin said. "Will they drive him away?"

"Probably so," Comfort answered, a cold sweat breaking out on her body as she suddenly realized what a personal calamity it would be to never see Nicolaus again. How could he have become so important to her so quickly?

Throughout the morning, they heard intermittent firing and the sound of many footsteps sloshing along snow-covered Queen Street. More than once Comfort was tempted to peer out and see what was going on, but she knew her father was right. A battleground was no place for her, and she was responsible for Erin's safety.

About noon, their father opened the door and called down, "We're still safe here.

Most of the fighting is on King Street. Are you all right?"

"We're awful cold, Poppy," Erin whimpered.

"It's cold everywhere. I'm sorry, but you'll have to stay hidden a little longer."

By midafternoon, their father called again. "It's safe enough now, I think, but you must still be cautious."

Comfort's feet felt like blocks of ice. She could hardly climb out of the cellar, and Father had to carry Erin up the ladder and into the kitchen. Comfort unwrapped Erin's feet and took off her shoes so the child could extend her cold toes toward the fire blazing on the kitchen hearth.

"The Colonials have apparently won the battle," their father said. "I don't have many details, but it seems that Colonel Rall has been killed and the Hessians have surrendered. I'm going to find out what happened. Don't open the door to anyone until I get back."

"What about Nicolaus?" Erin said through chattering teeth, asking the question that trembled on Comfort's lips.

With a quick look at Comfort, Father said, "I don't know."

The afternoon dragged by, but Comfort kept busy. She went into Nicolaus's room and stirred the fire, cleaning the room as she always did. Even to herself, she couldn't admit that she'd never again hear Nicolaus's firm step on the threshold. She walked into the back room and looked at the Nuremberg angel atop the tree. Was that all she had left of Nicolaus?

She pared carrots, onions, and potatoes, mixed them with the leftover goose, and placed the stew in an iron skillet over a bed of hot coals. She heated the oven and prepared loaves of bread for baking.

Darkness had fallen when their father returned with a jubilant Marion. "We got rid of the dirty foreigners," he shouted. "The cowards! The whole battle didn't take much more than an hour."

"Son," Father said, "it is a great day for the Colonies, but the outcome would have been a lot different if the Hessians had been prepared. When Colonel Rall learned of the attack, it was too late to rally his troops. If he'd heeded the warning he received last night, we might be mourning instead of rejoicing."

"You mean he was warned?" Comfort asked.

"Some soldier took a message to Colonel Rall," Marion said, "but he stuck the note in his pocket without reading it. It was unopened when he died."

"I'm not discounting the bravery of our troops," his father said, "but you'd have been no match for the highly skilled Hessians if Rall had heeded the warning and been waiting for you. Don't gloat over your victory."

But Marion was heedless to his father's opinion. "Forty Hessians killed, including Colonel Rall, about that many wounded, and we've captured nine hundred more. We're going to win this war."

Their father darted a quick glance at Comfort, and she knew he was aware of her interest in Nicolaus. She was pleased that the Continentals had won, but her heart was divided.

What had happened to Nicolaus? Was he dead, wounded, or a prisoner?

"Well, you don't look overjoyed," Marion said to Comfort. "Don't we get any thanks for releasing the citizens of Trenton from the cruel Hessians?"

"It's been a long day for me, Marion, worrying about what was happening. I have a meal ready for you—that should be thanks enough."

Erin looked at her brother, a slight pout on her mouth. "Nicolaus wasn't cruel to us. He taught me lots of things about his country. Hessians are Christians just like we are."

"You wouldn't think so if you'd see the way they fight," Marion said testily. "And who's Nicolaus—that scoundrel who forced his way in here?"

"Nicolaus Trittenbach wasn't a scoundrel," Father said. "He was courteous and served our family well. I agree with Erin. Some of the Hessians might be cruel, but it's un-Christian to judge all the soldiers by those who haven't been merciful. Let's change the subject."

Comfort stood by the fireplace and nibbled at a bowl of stew. Although she'd had very little to eat that day, she had no appetite. As soon as she washed the dishes and put away the food, she left her father and Marion before the fire talking about the battle. As she took the sleepy-eyed Erin upstairs, she heard her father say, "Marion, listen to me. This is only a symbolic victory for the Colonials, and I'm sure General Washington realizes that. Winning one battle won't end the war—we still have a long way to go."

❧

Marion left before daylight to join Washington's troops. By then, Comfort had come to a decision. Through the long, sleepless night, she'd decided that, with or without Father's permission, she was going to search for Nicolaus.

When her father came from the hospital for his breakfast, Comfort had once again assumed the disguise that transformed her into a middle-aged woman. Father surveyed her appearance, but he asked no questions.

"Washington's army is retreating across the river," he reported. "His troops aren't fit to fight—they've gone for days without adequate sleep, food, or clothing. But they captured enough Hessian stores to provide food and clothing for a while."

"So Trenton is without any protection?"

"Some Hessians escaped to join General Cornwallis's army north of here, so I suppose we're still at the mercy of the British if they advance on our town. As soon as the Colonials have rested, they'll attack the British again."

"When Erin has eaten her breakfast, I'm going to find out what happened to Nicolaus."

"That's no job for a woman," Father protested. "I'll do what I can."

"No," Comfort stated flatly. "I'll do it. Erin can sit in your office."

"I'm going to be busy, for I have several new patients—the ones wounded yesterday."

"Erin won't need much supervision, but I don't want to leave her alone in the house until I return."

"Daughter, what is this man to you?"

Comfort evaded her father's stern gaze. "I don't want him to go out of my life, never knowing whether he's dead or alive."

"If you choose him over your countrymen, you'll be considered a traitor."

Comfort didn't answer, and her father sighed deeply. "It's times like this when I miss your mother. When I don't understand women's emotions, how can I advise you?"

"I'm not asking for advice, Father. Just a little understanding."

Her father pushed back his chair and rose from the table. "I'll keep an eye on Erin," he said as he left the kitchen.

❧

When Comfort stepped out on Queen Street an hour later, she hardly knew which way to go. Nicolaus could be dead, wounded, a prisoner, or he might have escaped from Trenton. In her disguise and carrying a basket over her arm, Comfort hoped she'd appear as a housewife buying supplies.

She went to Ludwick's bakeshop first. He was loading his ovens into a wagon, preparing to follow Washington's army.

"Great news, Fräulein," he shouted when she entered the building. "So why are you sad? Is there trouble?"

"I'm concerned about your cousin, Nicolaus. He and Erin became friends, and she's worried about him." She hoped that wasn't being deceitful, for Erin was fretting over Nicolaus's absence.

"I don't know what happened to Nicolaus. He's a good man. I hope he's safe."

"Do you know where the prisoners are? Or the wounded?" She couldn't bring herself to ask where the dead Hessians had been taken.

Mr. Ludwick motioned his pudgy hand to the barracks across the street. "The wounded Hessians are in that building. Washington took the other prisoners with him into Pennsylvania. I'd help you, but I'm ordered to join the Continental army."

"Do you have time to see if he's among the dead?" She took his hand. "Please do that for me. I must know. I'll check among the wounded."

An hour later, Comfort came out of the barracks, enraged and disappointed. She'd had to fight her way past the Continental soldiers guarding the barracks to look at the faces of forty or more wounded Hessians. Nicolaus wasn't among them.

Mr. Ludwick was fidgeting from one foot to the other, apparently eager to be on his way, when Comfort emerged from the building.

"Did you find him?" he asked.

She shook her head. Nicolaus must not be among the dead either, or Mr. Ludwick would have known she had not.

"I will send you word if Nicolaus is with the prisoners," he promised. He started to climb aboard the wagon, but with one foot on the wheel, he paused and stepped back to the ground. Looking around, he said slowly, "I should not tell you this, but I've heard that some escaped soldiers are hiding in the old Webster barn outside of town. Webster is sympathetic to the British. But you should not go there alone."

His words brought a ray of hope to Comfort. Her depression lifted, and she experienced the unerring conviction that she would find Nicolaus at the Webster farm. She waved good-bye to Mr. Ludwick and started the long trek along Princeton Road. The sun was shining now, glinting off the icy snowdrifts. She pulled her scarf more tightly around her face and stuck her hands in her pockets for warmth. For encouragement, she repeated over and over a favorite verse from the Bible, "For He shall give his angels charge over thee, to keep thee in all thy ways."

Two hours later, she topped a small rise and saw the Webster farm before her. Should she try to sneak into the barn or walk boldly up to the Webster home and state her business? She'd seen Mr. Webster a few times, and she hardly thought he'd harm a woman; but if he saw her sneaking into his barn, he might shoot first and ask questions later. The long walk through the slippery snow had sapped her strength, but Comfort took a deep breath and headed directly toward the residence.

A woman with unkempt gray hair opened the door cautiously. Her brown eyes shifted uneasily as Comfort introduced herself. "A Hessian soldier is a friend of my family, and I've heard that some Hessians are hiding on this farm. Will you tell me if the man I'm looking for is among them?"

"I know nothing," the woman said and started to close the door. Comfort stuck her foot in the opening.

"Ma'am, I appeal to you as one woman to another. Have you ever lain awake all night wondering if your loved one was dead or alive? If you have, you'll know why I'm concerned. I'm a Patriot, but when you love a person, it makes no difference which army he serves."

Comfort gasped in surprise. She'd told this stranger a fact she had barely admitted to herself. But it was true; she *did* love him.

"I'm not going to betray you, and I'm not interested in anyone else in your barn. If you tell me that Nicolaus Trittenbach is not here, I'll be on my way."

"Let her in," a deep voice said. The door widened enough for Comfort to slip inside to be confronted by Mr. Webster, holding a musket. He looked Comfort up and down, perhaps trying to determine her sincerity.

"Don't let her leave the house," he said to his wife and exited through a rear door.

Comfort's legs wouldn't hold her any longer. She leaned against the wall and slid slowly to the floor. Resting on her haunches, she dropped her head to her knees.

"You can sit on a chair," Mrs. Webster said in a kindly voice.

"I'm all right. I've walked all the way from Trenton without stopping, and I can't stand any longer."

"Do you want something to eat?"

"Yes, please."

Mrs. Webster soon handed Comfort a thick slice of brown bread, generously spread with preserves. She accepted the food with thanks and ate it swiftly.

"War is harder on womenfolk than it is on our men," Mrs. Webster commented.

"They decide to fight; women sit at home and worry. It melted my heart to know that you laid awake all night. I haven't slept for two days, wondering if the rebel army will come and get my husband."

"I understand the Continental army is west of the Delaware now, so he's probably safe for the time being." Comfort hoped she wasn't giving away important information to the enemy, but the woman had been kind to her. The wait seemed interminable. Comfort decided she must have dozed, for she was startled when Mr. Webster appeared before her.

"Trittenbach is out there, and he wants to see you, so I guess you're all right. God forgive you if you betray those men."

Offering a silent prayer of thanks that Nicolaus was alive, Comfort said, "You have nothing to fear from me."

Chapter 8

Nerves tingling, Comfort followed Mr. Webster down an ice-covered path. He motioned her inside the barn and stood guard at the door, his eyes surveying the surrounding countryside.

The scent of animals and hay stung Comfort's nostrils. When her eyes adjusted to the dark interior, she saw Nicolaus lying on the dirt floor. Rushing to his side, she dropped to her knees beside him. He lay on an improvised stretcher—a blanket tied around two long poles. He managed a weak smile.

"Nicolaus, are you wounded?"

"My leg," he said. "I can't walk. My friends plan to carry me with them, but I'm trying to persuade them to leave me behind. I'll just delay them."

Comfort pulled back the thin blanket that covered him. His uniform had been cut away below his left knee, and the leg was swollen to double its size. He felt feverish to her touch.

She looked up at the tall soldier beside Nicolaus. "You can't take him like this. He'll die of exposure."

He said something in German, and Nicolaus translated. "He says if I stay behind, the Americans will take me prisoner."

"Not if I can help it. Father will tend your wound."

"Nein," Nicolaus protested. "You'll make trouble for your whole family."

"Nicolaus," she pleaded, "let me take care of you." She called to Mr. Webster. "Will you help me take him into Trenton? My father is indebted to him. We'll shelter Nicolaus until he's able to walk."

"I want these men out of my barn right away," Webster said testily. "I'm in enough trouble with the rebels. If they find out I'm harboring enemy soldiers, they'll burn me out."

"You may already be in trouble for sheltering them, so one more act of kindness won't make that much difference. If you'll bring Nicolaus into Trenton after dark tonight and help me smuggle him into our house, these other soldiers can go on their way now. Will you agree to that, Nicolaus?"

"Why are you taking such a risk?" he asked her.

"You'll die if you try to escape with these men. And if you're captured, you'll be living out in the open without any medical attention. You're safer at our home until you get well."

"Why are you taking such a risk?" he repeated.

She turned her eyes away and wouldn't meet his gaze, but her face flushed with embarrassment. What must Nicolaus and these other men think of her pleading for him to go home with her?

Nicolaus reached for her hand and squeezed it tenderly.

"Danke. I'll stay behind." He turned to his friends and spoke to them in German. Comfort assumed he'd told them to leave, for they saluted, picked up their weapons, and hurried from the building.

Mr. Webster still hadn't said whether he would help or not, so Nicolaus turned to him. "I have some gold in my pack at the Foster home. If you'll provide transportation into Trenton, I can reward you for your services."

"What's a good time to bring him?" Mr. Webster asked.

"Two hours after nightfall. My father will be at the hospital, and the Continental soldiers are exhausted. No one is apt to see you."

Webster wasn't wholehearted in his agreement, but Comfort thought he would keep his word. She told him how to access the Foster home without being detected.

"You know where my pack is," Nicolaus said. "There's a bag of coins inside it. This is a risky move, and I won't blame you if I'm taken prisoner."

She bent forward to kiss his feverish cheek, but he moved his head suddenly, and her caress landed on his lips. His eyes twinkled a bit when she drew back quickly.

"You tricked me," she said, but her lips parted in a smile, taking any sting from the words. "Try to rest this afternoon."

She made final plans with Mr. Webster and started the long trek home, but the journey wasn't nearly as difficult this time. Nicolaus was alive!

❧

Comfort reached Trenton in late afternoon. She went to the hospital and called for Erin. Her father followed them to the house.

"Did you find him?"

"Yes."

"Alive?"

"Yes, but I won't tell you anything else right now. What about Marion?"

"He's on the western side of the Delaware River, but I expect the army to return as soon as the men have rested. If Washington doesn't push forward, he'll lose the advantage he gained at Trenton."

"Will the Continental army return to Trenton?"

"Probably—I don't know."

That information concerned Comfort, and she fretted the rest of the day about the best place to put Nicolaus. With his wound, she couldn't get him upstairs. And how would her father react to having Nicolaus occupying his room? Would he refuse to treat Nicolaus if Comfort was successful in smuggling him into the house?

With these problems flooding her mind, nightfall came before Comfort was ready for it. After they'd eaten, Father gave Comfort a long speculative look before he returned to the hospital. She read Erin a Bible story before hustling her off to bed. She started a fire in the bedroom and took two gold coins from Nicolaus's pack to pay Mr. Webster for his trouble.

Bundling into heavy garments, Comfort monitored the progress of the town crier. When two hours had passed, she slipped out of the house and headed into the darkness. Would Mr. Webster keep his word? She breathed a sigh of relief when she rounded the side of their barn, heard a horse snort, and sensed the outline of a wagon.

"Mr. Webster," she called softly.

"Here," he answered.

"Nicolaus, are you awake?" she whispered, moving close to the wagon.

"Ja," he answered, and a moan escaped his lips. "It's been a rough ride."

"Can you walk to the house if Mr. Webster and I support you?"

"I didn't agree to nothing except bringing him to town," Mr. Webster complained.

"You'll get paid when he's in the house. If you're quick about it, you can leave soon."

Nicolaus slid to the edge of the wagon.

"Mr. Webster will hold your right side, and you can put your hand on my shoulder."

"Nein. I'm too heavy to lean on you," he protested.

"I'll just support you. Drag your wounded foot and walk on the other one."

Nicolaus slipped once in the snow, almost pulling Comfort and Mr. Webster to the ground. The farmer swore, but after that near mishap he held Nicolaus more securely. Progressing slowly, they kept at it until the wounded soldier lay exhausted on the bed, his breath expelling in guttural wheezes.

Comfort handed Mr. Webster the two coins. Since hard money was scarce in the Colonies, he seemed pleased with his reward. He hurried from the room, and Comfort turned to Nicolaus and touched his face. His hot, dry skin was feverish.

"I have some herbal tea brewing. It's good for fever and contains a light sedative for pain. I'll bring it in, and then I'll call Father to treat your leg."

"It's broken, I think."

Comfort brought the mug of tea, and Nicolaus leaned on his elbow to drink it.

"Tastes good," he said. "Can you tell me what happened? A few of us were separated from the rest of our troops during the fighting, and when the main body of Hessians surrendered, we escaped."

"If reports are to be credited, the Continental army took nine hundred prisoners, and when the Patriots moved across the river to rest, they took the prisoners with them. The river was partly frozen and very treacherous. I'm glad you weren't with them."

"What will happen if I'm discovered here and taken prisoner?"

"I don't know, but I hope we can keep you hidden until you're able to walk."

When he finished the tea, over his protest, Comfort knelt by the bed and removed his heavy shoes. "Now take off your coat, and cover yourself with this quilt. I'll go tell

Father you're here. If you hear an explosion coming from the hospital, you'll know he's displeased. If not, he'll come and check on your injury."

Still wearing her disguise, Comfort hurried across the backyard. Seemed as if she'd spent most of the past month running back and forth between the hospital and the house.

The patients were resting, and when she didn't see her father in the ward, she entered his office. He sat dozing, his chin on his chest. He looked so tired that Comfort hesitated to awaken him, but Nicolaus needed immediate attention.

She touched him lightly on the shoulder. He straightened, his eyes glazed with sleep.

"I have Nicolaus at the house."

"Are you out of your mind? Washington's army will be back in Trenton within a few days."

"Come and look at his leg," Comfort insisted. "I think it's broken."

With a resigned look, Father notified his helper that he was leaving for a few minutes and followed her into the house.

"I'm better off not knowing how you happened upon Nicolaus, but I took an oath to heal the sick in spite of circumstances, so I'll check on him. But he can't stay in this house. Some American soldiers are unscrupulous, and they might burn the house if they hear an enemy soldier is lodged here."

"Jesus said we were to love our enemies."

"Yes, but I doubt He was speaking of the same kind of love you are," her father said dryly.

"Nicolaus," Comfort said. "Father is here."

"*Danke schön*, Herr Foster."

Father pushed the quilt aside and gently massaged Nicolaus's leg. Nicolaus's muscles tightened with pain, but he didn't make a sound.

"It's broken a few inches below the knee. With so much swelling, I can't tell if the fracture is a clean break, but I think it may be. It's going to be very painful to fix it, for it should have been set right away, but you could lose your leg if I don't act immediately."

"Two legs are a necessity for a soldier," Nicolaus said with some humor. "I trust you. The decision is up to you."

"First, we'll have to find a safe place to hide you."

"Isn't this room safe enough?" Comfort asked.

"Daughter, use your head. If Marion comes home and finds Nicolaus, you know what a commotion that will cause. And he can't stay in the house without Erin knowing it. He has to hide."

"I don't want to make trouble for your family," Nicolaus stated through clenched teeth. His face was the color of ashes.

"There's no one in the isolation room at the hospital," Father continued. "If Nicolaus gets rid of his uniform and puts on other garments, he can pass as an American. His command of the English language will be in his favor."

"That's a good place to hide him," Comfort agreed. "But where can we find garments big enough for him?"

"I'll find some clothes for him, but, Nicolaus, we'll have to move you to the hospital where I have my equipment. I'll help you take off your uniform. Find a blanket to wrap around him, Comfort."

Nicolaus clenched his teeth as they moved him. When his leg hung down, it was apparent that he was in great pain; but leaning on Comfort and her father, he made the trip into the surgery room. He was barely conscious when they laid him on the table.

"Now, Comfort," Father said, "you're going home, and you will stay there."

"I want to help."

"No. You've done your part—the rest is up to me."

Nicolaus lay with his eyes closed, and a pulse beat rapidly in his forehead. While Father prepared the bandages and splints for the fracture, Comfort touched Nicolaus's hand, and his long fingers curled around hers so tightly that she winced.

"I'll be praying for you, Nicolaus. You're in good hands. My father received his training in Philadelphia, and he's been practicing for years."

Looking to be sure her father was occupied, Comfort leaned over quickly and kissed Nicolaus's cheek. Without opening his eyes, his lips parted in a tender smile, and he whispered, *"Guten nacht."*

"Good night," she answered softly.

🐝

"He's sleeping now," Father reported when he came for breakfast. "He bit on a bullet while I set the fracture, bandaged the area, and placed the wooden splints on it. He didn't make a sound, but when I finished, he was sweating like I'd thrown a bucket of water on him. I dressed him in a large pair of trousers and a blouse that another patient had left behind and gave him a small dose of opium that should keep him sedated most of the day."

"Thank you, Father. I hated to involve you, but I don't want him to die."

Her father encircled Comfort's waist with his left arm and drew her to his side. "You've only known the man a few weeks, but I guess time doesn't matter that much. *I* knew the first time I saw your mother walking along a Philadelphia street." He pushed back his thin hair. "But go slow. Times are too uncertain to make lifelong decisions."

🐝

That evening, her father allowed Comfort to visit Nicolaus. "He's alert and not in much pain, so you can see him. But after this, I want you to stay away from the hospital. If you visit a lot, the other patients might become suspicious. I'll sit with Erin until you get back."

Comfort had shed her disguise again, but she pulled a shawl over her face as she hurried through the general ward of the hospital into the private room that was reserved for very sick patients. She carried a pumpkin tart and a bowl of stew in her basket.

Nicolaus lay on his side with the injured knee half bent on a pillow.

"Good evening," she said. "You look better."

"I am better, but according to your father, I won't be walking much for several weeks."

"You can stay here until you're well. To avoid suspicion, Father says I can't visit again, but I'll send food each day. Can you sit up to eat?"

"Yes," he said, scooting to a sitting position with the injured leg stretched out on the bed. "I'm to keep the knee on a pillow as much as possible to take pressure off the fracture, but I can change positions."

Comfort tucked the pillow under his knee and watched as he ate heartily.

"Let's have a prayer together and thank God for saving you," she said, and God seemed very near as they clasped hands and offered their thanks.

A few days later, when once again Washington led his bedraggled army across the Delaware, Trenton braced for another battle. The British were marching southward under the command of General Cornwallis, who was under strict orders to defeat the Continental army.

On the second day of the new year, Cornwallis's troops reached Trenton. Her father warned Comfort to stay hidden, for he expected another fight in town. But Washington tricked Cornwallis by circling the British army during the night. The next morning the Colonials attacked other British troops at Princeton, eleven miles to the north. By the time Cornwallis organized his troops and returned to Princeton, the Americans had won another battle.

After two defeats in less than two weeks, the British command decided to relinquish the territory along the Delaware and withdrew eastward. Before they did, they stopped in Trenton to release Hessian prisoners.

Father feared the British might take vengeance on the citizens for their defeat at Princeton, so he ordered his daughters to stay inside. Comfort was terrified when a tall Hessian appeared at the door, reminding her of the day, almost a month earlier, when Nicolaus had stood there. But this man also seemed courteous, no more of a threat than Nicolaus had been.

"I'm Conrad Holstein," he said in broken English, and Comfort thought he said, "I was here as *Belsnickel*. I'm Nicolaus Trittenbach's superior. I want to see him."

"He isn't in our home now," Comfort said truthfully.

Again Comfort found it difficult to interpret his words, but she decided he'd said, "Do you know where he is? I have checked the names of prisoners, and Nicolaus is not listed."

Why did this man want to see Nicolaus? If she told him where Nicolaus was, would he take Nicolaus with the retreating army? Comfort didn't want Nicolaus to risk injuring his leg by traveling, but did she have the right to keep him hidden from his comrades?

She shifted from one leg to the other, getting colder as snow whirled into the room.

"Will you come in? I must talk to my father," she said. She handed the Hessian a cup of cider and left him sitting before the fire.

🔉

The swelling on Nicolaus's leg had reduced considerably, and Comfort's father was tightening the bandage. Comfort closed the door behind her and blurted out the news about their visitor. She looked from Nicolaus to her father. "I didn't know what to tell him."

Oliver motioned to Nicolaus, indicating the decision was up to him.

Nicolaus rubbed his forehead. "I'm not any good to the army this way, and I don't want to fight against the Colonies anyway. I believe if I talk with Conrad, he might arrange for me to be paroled here in the Colonies. He's a reasonable man."

"You can't bring him to the hospital," her father said. "I won't risk having my other patients imprisoned."

"I've been walking very well with the crutch you gave me," Nicolaus said. "I can make it over to the house."

Oliver replaced the splint, and Nicolaus stood gingerly, holding on to the wall until he got the crutch under his arm.

Looking her father straight in the eye, Nicolaus said, "If I am paroled here, I'd like your permission to marry Comfort."

Oliver's eyes gleamed humorously. "But does Comfort want to marry you?" He turned piercing brown eyes on his daughter.

Her face flushed, and she refused to meet his eyes. "I think so," she whispered faintly.

"Well, I won't give any such permission! You haven't known each other long enough to make a decision about marriage, but I will permit you to court Comfort. Will you both agree to trust my discretion in the matter?"

"*Ja*," Nicolaus said. "We couldn't marry soon anyway. The only profession I know is soldiering. I'll need a means of livelihood before I can support a wife."

"Go talk to your superior officer, then," Oliver said. "I won't insult you by asking you not to betray my patients, but I'm trusting you to be discreet."

Nicolaus rested his hand on Comfort's shoulder to balance himself as they went to the house, but it was still painful for him to jostle the leg. *Leutnant* Holstein stood quickly as they entered the kitchen and reached for Nicolaus's hand.

"*Danke Gott,* you still live, Nicolaus. I feared you were dead."

"Only wounded, Sir. I've been well cared for by Comfort and her family." Nicolaus spoke slowly in English so Conrad might understand and as a courtesy to Comfort, so she would know what they were saying.

Conrad said that the British were leaving Trenton the next day and asked if Nicolaus could travel with them.

"I'd be a liability to the British now, for I won't be fit to fight for several months.

And I don't really want to fight against the Americans any longer. Can you arrange for me to be paroled?"

Conrad looked from Nicolaus to Comfort, smiled slightly, and spoke in German. Nicolaus smiled and translated for her. "He said, 'I'm not sure I want to return to Germany either, and I may stay here after the war is over—especially if I have the same incentive you do.'"

Comfort blushed and lowered her eyes.

Leutnant Holstein spoke in German again, and Nicolaus raised his hand. "If I am paroled in America, I swear that I will not take up arms against the British in their current conflict with the rebel Americans."

After promising that the parole paper would be delivered the next day, *Leutnant* Holstein clicked his heels together and exited the room with a salute. With a nostalgic twinge in his heart, Nicolaus returned the gesture. It was sad to part with the past, but he turned to Comfort—his future—put his arm around her, and drew her into a tight embrace.

"I'm committed to America and to you. *Ich liebe Sie*—I love you, Comfort. *Heiraten Sie mich?*"

"I love you too, and if your question means 'will I marry you?' the answer is yes. But I agree with Father that we should wait, at least until you find employment."

Nicolaus laid his crutch aside and sat at the kitchen table. "Christopher Ludwick asked me to join him in providing bread for the army. If I work with him, I'd not be fighting against the British, but I would be helping the Colonists win independence—a cause I believe is just."

Comfort put her arms around Nicolaus's shoulders and leaned her head against his face. "That sounds like a good opportunity, but it means you'll be on the move a lot. I won't like that, Nicolaus, but it will be several weeks before you're able to walk. That will give us time to become better acquainted."

"*Danke Gott*, that He brought me to America, or I wouldn't have found you."

"Yes, I thank Him, too. Who knows, perhaps Father will relent and let us marry before you join Christopher."

Nicolaus's eyes brightened at the possibility, and he pulled Comfort down on his uninjured knee. His mouth covered hers hungrily, and Comfort responded to the touch of his lips.

Nicolaus had come to this house as an enemy, but the perilous experiences of the past few weeks had plunged them into an intense friendship that was blossoming into a satisfying love. He knew that for the time being, Comfort would shove aside her concern about the days when they would be separated. War still loomed on the horizon; but tonight, they were together, with no storm clouds to threaten their love.

FREEDOM'S CRY

by Pamela Griffin

Dedication

First, I want to say a special thank you to all the courageous men and women in the military who've fought for our country. You are very much appreciated, and my prayers are with you. May God bless America!

And to my wonderful critique partners on this project, Tracey Bateman, Paige Winship Dooly, Tamela Hancock Murray, Jill Stengl, and my mother, Arlene Trampel—I never could have done any of this without your help and encouragement. Also to my historical researcher and brother, John Louis, and my dad, John Trampel, who designs my bookmarks and website—thank you, all of you.

As always, I dedicate this story to my Lord and deliverer, Jesus Christ, who freed me from the bondage of sin that once ensnared me and gave me victory over all the powers of the enemy.

Chapter 1

1777 Philadelphia

S arah Thurston hurried from the humid kitchen, her grip tight on the platter of steaming dishes. Swiftly she moved down the dim corridor toward the dining room, where the master entertained his guests.

"Best look lively," Belle, a housemaid, warned as she bustled by Sarah. "He looks to be in a foul mood despite the occasion. Likely because his wife lies abed."

Grimacing, Sarah turned the corner. The master's five-year-old son stood near the entrance to the dining room and peeked around the doorframe.

"Rupert," Sarah scolded quietly, "away with you. If your father catches sight of you spying on him and his guests, there will be trouble—and well you know it." Soon Rupert would be six and ready for breeching, the step initiating him into manhood. Sarah would miss seeing his blond curls, which would be shaved off so the boy could be fitted with a wig, as the gentlemen of the township wore.

The child spared her the briefest of glances, then looked back into the well-lit room. "They are toasting the thirteen colonies now," he whispered. "Mr. Rafferty belched horribly after Father toasted Maryland. Father doesn't look happy."

"Nor will he be if he catches sight of you. Run along."

Rupert reluctantly moved away. "Will you play quoits with me later, Sarah? It is so dull here, and Father will not allow me to go into town to watch the celebration."

"If my duties allow it. Now go, Child," Sarah whispered before entering the room.

Wealthy gentlemen in powdered wigs, colored coats, knee breeches, and white stockings sat around the long table. Frills of lace or scarves in white donned their throats above their buttoned waistcoats. Sarah's master, Bartholomew Wilkerson, stood at the head, his wine glass raised high. Catching sight of Sarah, his heavy-lidded eyes remained on her seconds longer than usual, and Sarah shuddered. How thankful she would be when her indenture was completed and she could be away from this place.

"And finally, I propose a toast to the Commonwealth of Pennsylvania," Mr. Wilkerson said. "And to our most esteemed town of Philadelphia, the City of

Brotherly Love, which William Penn founded almost a century ago, establishing this great township for religious and civil liberty—that all therein should not suffer persecution of the same."

Sarah clenched her teeth as she served the twelfth cake for dessert, unable to bear the man's hypocrisy. It was common knowledge that shipping magnate Bartholomew Wilkerson had friends who were loyal to King George. Though he spoke of liberty, Sarah suspected Mr. Wilkerson of secretly being a Tory sympathizer. With recent local arrests of pro-British citizens, two of whom were Mr. Wilkerson's friends and prominent men such as he, it stood to reason he would now hide any sympathy he might feel toward the British.

"On this fourth day of July, in the seventeen hundredth and seventy-seventh year of our Lord," Mr. Wilkerson said, "we declare to Great Britain our right of independence. No, we demand it! And as the most esteemed John Adams decreed a year previously, upon the signing of our Declaration of Independence, we shall celebrate the day with great rejoicing, with parade and cannon fire—this, our Independence Day. May God hasten this war to a glorious end, so that we may not only declare our freedom but live it in the fullest sense."

"Hear, hear," a portly gentleman cried.

"And may the Tories return with all Godspeed to their native England—and keep their accursed tea with them," another man exclaimed. His remark brought a round of laughter from all except the master.

Sarah saw Mr. Wilkerson frown, then quickly give a feeble smile to his comrade who turned to speak with him. The tea incident in Boston led to the start of the war two years ago and was still talked about in drawing rooms. She had heard how the Sons of Liberty disguised themselves as Indians and dumped a ship's cargo of highly taxed tea into the harbor.

Though she herself was a native of England and had sojourned in Pennsylvania only five years, Sarah felt the people's cry for freedom deep within her heart. Soon she would be free from her indenture, free to pursue personal interests and no longer bound to serve a wealthy family's every whim. That the master's interests had not been of a more personal nature these five years past was a blessing to Sarah; he exerted those particular interests in another direction. Sarah felt sorry for the young and beautiful indenture named Grace, who at twenty-one was four years younger than Sarah. However, lately Mr. Wilkerson had been eyeing Sarah the same way he eyed Grace.

Determined not to dwell on ill thoughts, Sarah hurried to the kitchen to resume her duties to Mrs. Leppermier. The elderly cook was bossy at times but had a fondness for Sarah, and Sarah knew it was because she reminded the woman of her daughter, now deceased.

Once dinner ended, they worked in the kitchen, scrubbing dishes while quietly conversing. Suddenly Belle swept into the room. "Where is that young scamp Morton? I have searched and searched for him!"

"Whatever is the matter?" Mrs. Leppermier asked.

"The matter?" Belle screeched. "The mistress has run out of her tonic, and whenever she lies in such ill humor with her complaints, without fail she asks for it the following morning. If I tell her she has no more, she'll cause a ruckus we'll all regret. I have need of Morton to hasten to the apothecary's shop at once."

"I'll go," Sarah said, removing her water- and gravy-spotted apron. "I know where the apothecary resides."

"You?" Belle said in shock.

"Aye, 'tis a good thing for Sarah to go," Mrs. Leppermier quickly intervened. "If Mrs. Wilkerson doesn't have her tonic, the entire household will suffer her ill temper come morning."

"Very well," Belle said to Sarah, her thin lips compressed in disdain. "I suppose there is no other recourse, but do not dawdle." Because Belle had willfully signed a contract of indenture, unlike Sarah, she considered herself superior and let Sarah know it at every opportunity.

"Take your time," Mrs. Leppermier corrected after Belle exited the kitchen. "Mrs. Wilkerson will have no need of the tonic until the morrow, and Katie and I can finish here. Linger and watch the celebration if you so desire."

"You are too kind," Sarah murmured with a grateful smile, looking forward to the reprieve. Before setting off, she adjusted her ruffled mobcap, which had gone askew during her work. Hurriedly she tucked a few errant tendrils beneath the white puffy circle of cloth that was fitted to her head by use of a drawstring. Smoothing her ankle-length gray skirt, she hurried outside into the sunny afternoon.

The Wilkersons' home, a stately two-and-a-half-story Georgian manor of buff stucco and red brick with gabled roof and dormers, was in Fairmount Park, as were other mansions. Tall poplar trees lined the walk, shielding the sun's brilliance. Beneath the fresh smell of grass and flowers, the acrid odor of gunpowder filtered through the air. In the distance, Sarah could see white fogs of smoke drift toward the delft blue sky, marking where guns had been discharged. Throughout the day she'd heard muffled explosions of cannon and musket fire, and the revelry had not yet ceased. Nor would it until the day was spent.

The glaring sun had dropped a couple of notches by the time Sarah drew near the heart of the city. Loud huzzahs and more reports of musket fire rang through the air. Buildings of red brick trimmed with white-painted wood, soapstone, and marble lined the straight, paved streets. Charming gardens and shade trees were in abundance. White towers could be seen on the roofs of a few important public buildings, and inside the belfry of the State House on Chestnut Street, the great Liberty Bell hung.

To Sarah's left, three boys laughed and raced along the cobbles, propelling their hoops with their sticks. A dirty terrier scampered at their heels. To her right, a group of men stood in a circle, cheering the day with loud acclaim. One decreed certain victory for the Patriots and discharged his pistol in the air to the excited cheers of others. A few men threw their tricorn hats upward in jubilation.

Sarah strode the crowded footpath, paying little attention to any horses and carriages that traveled the road alongside her. Only men of means and men of trade used coaches or wagons. Most, like Sarah, walked everywhere they needed to go. In honor of the holiday all businesses were closed, and she wondered too late if she would have trouble finding the apothecary.

Through the thin soles of her shoes, Sarah could feel the heat radiating off the cobbles in the stifling summer day. Five years she had worn these shoes and was in dire need of another pair. When she left the Wilkersons, she would have to acquire a job. Widow Brown ran a coffeehouse near the wharf. Perhaps Sarah could find work there. Once she gained enough money to provide for her immediate needs, she could save up her guineas to do the one thing she desired, the one thing she longed for each night as she stared at the moon suspended above tree-dotted hills. . . .

"Well, gentlemen, what have we here?"

Sarah came to a halt, startled by the mocking voice. Three guests from the Wilkersons' dinner party moved to block her path.

"I'm on an errand," she stated with an air of false bravado, her heart skipping a beat. "Please, stand aside and let me pass."

"Bartholomew's estate must be in a sorry state of affairs that he would send his kitchen maid on an errand," Samuel Fenston, the biggest of the three, said. His dark eyes narrowed beneath his tricorn hat. "Why does Morton not attend to such a task?"

"Me thinks I detect treachery afoot," William Reilly inserted, the odor of liquor heavy on his breath. A smirk distorted his pockmarked face. "Mayhap the girl lies and has slipped away to meet a lover. Perhaps we should interrogate the wench. We owe it to our friend to right a wrong if we discern trouble in his household."

"Aye," Clay Riggs, the youngest, agreed. "A private interrogation might be just the thing to loosen her tongue."

Alarmed by the sudden gleam in the eyes of all three men, Sarah backed up a step. "I tell the truth. The mistress needs a potion for her ails, and I've been sent to the apothecary to fetch it."

"A likely story," William sneered.

Clay reached out to fondle the curl hanging by her face. Sarah tried not to flinch, but the brand of fear was leaving a deep impression on her soul. People flocked everywhere. Yet if she cried out, the merrymakers would likely think her cries ones of revelry in the day and not pleas spurred from alarm. Indeed, jubilant screams, along with repeated gunfire, filled the city streets.

"My friends, let us not judge the lass too quickly or too harshly," Clay said, his gaze never leaving her face. "The matter is easily settled. We shall retrieve Samuel's coach and return with the wench to the estate to inquire there." A slow smile spread across his face, and he grabbed her arm above the elbow. "A most expedient solution for all involved, I daresay."

William laughed. "An excellent suggestion, Clay. I do admire your rapier intellect."

Sarah panicked when William took his place on the other side of her and also grasped her arm. "Please," she said, the word lost in the surrounding din as she was forced to move with them to a narrow alley between brick buildings. She struggled to be heard. "Unhand me! I have done no wrong."

"We shall soon see," Clay said. "Do not be anxious, Sarah. We will deliver you safely to your master. In due course."

At this the other men laughed.

"You heard the girl," a calm, masculine voice spoke from behind. "Unhand her."

Along with the others, Sarah turned. . .to observe the most handsome man she'd ever seen. One hand behind his back, he stood with a casual, masculine grace she had not perceived in many of his gender. Though his shirt, breeches, and leather jerkin were those of a commoner, he filled the clothes out well. His pleasing face was strong, unafraid. His head was bare, and Sarah would wager that the thick, dark hair gathered back to hang in a queue and tied with a black ribbon was his own and not a wig. His deep blue gaze briefly lit on her, then made a scan of each of the two men holding her against her will.

William tensed. "You dare to address us in such a manner? Do you know with whom you speak? Be gone with you, Cur!"

The man did not move a muscle, only stared at them in a way that showed he wasn't easily intimidated. Sarah felt her heart flutter with both interest in him and fear concerning her predicament.

"Though it's true I'm not aware of the identity of those I address," the man said, his rich voice sending flutters through Sarah again, "I am well acquainted with the manner of men to whom I speak. I repeat, unhand the girl."

Samuel stepped forward, his face a mottled red. "You, Sir, are overstepping your bounds! By your manner of dress it's plain to see you're nothing more than a common laborer. What entices you to presume that you can address us in such a manner?"

Clearly unruffled, the handsome stranger calmly brought his arm from behind him. He held a pistol, which he raised to aim at Samuel.

"This."

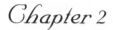

Chapter 2

His grip on the weapon strong, Thomas eyed the last man to speak. The woman fidgeted, but Thomas did not risk glancing her way again. Her loveliness was engraved upon his mind, and he feared that if he looked into her pale-green eyes once more—eyes so clear and riveting they could disarm a man—he would forget why he was there.

"You dare draw a weapon on us?" the tallest of the three asked. "I'll have you dancing on the end of a rope for this!"

"When a woman's honor is at stake, Sir, there are a great many things I dare," Thomas replied smoothly, though he felt anything but calm. The woman gasped in what sounded like surprised awe.

"She is an indenture. Hardly worth this bother," the light-haired one who held one of her elbows explained almost cordially. "We were in the process of returning her to her master when you came upon us."

Thomas spared her a glance then. The girl trembled, her breathing labored, as revealed by the rise and fall of her chest underneath the laced bodice. Golden-brown hair, the color and shine of honey, escaped in damp ringlets from her mobcap. Although she was not classically beautiful, there was an appeal to her oval-shaped face, which rivaled the color and purity of cream just skimmed off milk. A few light freckles dotted her nose and the apples of her cheeks. Her eyes, thickly rimmed with long, sable brown lashes, beseeched him.

"The lady doesn't appear to desire your company, gentlemen," Thomas said quietly, watching her.

"Lady? Perhaps you misunderstood. She is an indenture—a common servant."

"Ah, but it is you who misunderstood. As my mother once said, a true lady isn't characterized by class but rather by her actions and modesty," Thomas countered softly. The girl's eyes widened.

"What drivel is this you speak?" the man holding her other elbow intoned.

"And yet what more can one expect from a man of such questionable character?" the light-haired man put in with an air of condescension. "Far be it from me to verbally spar with one lacking intellect in the merits of social standing."

"Well said, Clay," one of the men spoke.

Thomas gave a slight mocking bow. "Be that as it may, it's not my character that

114

is in question. I must insist that you release this woman and take your leave, Sirs. Otherwise, you leave me no recourse but to locate the constable. When last I saw him, only moments ago, he was strolling down this very block."

"Call the constable?" one of the men sputtered. "You would dare—what impudence! He would not believe your word over a gentleman's!"

"You may be correct in that assumption. However, I'm willing to find out." Thomas motioned with the gun for them to precede him. "Oh, did I mention that the constable and I are long-standing acquaintances?"

Suddenly the men did not look so cocksure. Thomas was disgusted with their arrogance.

"The wench isn't worth the trouble," the tallest man grumbled. "Let us depart."

The other two seemed about to protest but were silenced by the look in their leader's eyes, and they released the woman. She crossed her arms, rubbing the long sleeves where they had grabbed her.

The leader turned his cold gaze once more to the pistol aimed at them, then upward to Thomas. "Have a care. This is not the end of the matter."

Thomas watched as the three grimly moved away, back to the crowded street, before lowering his weapon.

"Thank you, Sir," the woman said, her voice shaky. "I am in your debt."

Thomas gave her a faint smile. "It is my pleasure. Yet I find it a good thing that your attackers were ignorant of the fact that the pistol is not loaded."

Her eyes widened. "Not loaded?"

He shook his head, rueful. "I doubt this relic would have discharged a lead ball had I tried. The frizzen spring has been defunct for some time."

"Defunct?"

He nodded. "This flintlock was my father's long ago. I also own a matchlock, but alas, I have no match."

"Oh, my."

She looked as if she might swoon, and Thomas put his hand out to steady her. "Are you well?" He scanned the area, looking for a stoop or crate—something for her to sit on—but nothing of that nature was in evidence.

Pink flushed her face, and she moved her arm from his fingers. "I must be about my business, Sir. Again, I thank you." Though her words were steady, her eyes held a trace of lingering disquiet.

"Might I presume to ask permission to accompany you?" Thomas inquired softly. "Merely to offer protection, of course."

"Oh, but. . .really I don't wish to be a bother—"

His smile grew wide. "It's no bother. All the shops are closed in honor of the celebration—mine as well. I have a wagon I keep at the livery to help me with my deliveries and would gladly take you wherever it is you need to go."

Shyly, she averted her gaze. "I do not know you, Sir."

"How remiss of me! My apologies. I am Thomas Gray, a cabinetmaker. My shop is on the next street." He motioned in that direction with the hand that held the pistol, looked at the weapon wryly, then glanced at her. "Perhaps you would feel more assured if we seek out the constable to give you a character reference on my behalf? I normally don't carry a weapon—much less one that is disabled—but I brought it with me at my young nephew's request."

She regarded him with surprise. "Did you say your name is Thomas Gray? I overheard my mistress tell her company that she acquired a Thomas Gray's services to fashion a bookcase with the faces of the statesmen carved along the top."

"Am I to understand your mistress is the wife of Bartholomew Wilkerson?"

She nodded. "The same."

"Then you are correct. It's the latest fashion among the wealthy to have busts of popular statesmen predominant in their furniture."

The girl's brow lifted. "You must be quite skilled in your trade. Only the finest joiners are capable of such a task, from what I have heard."

"I was an apprentice to Hermann Unger, one of the most talented cabinetmakers there was. Everything I learned was under his tutelage." He shifted. "But let us not stand in the street and converse. Will you not accept the offer of my aid?"

"I do not wish to detain you."

"Detain me?"

"You mentioned a nephew."

He smiled. "I've been invited to my sister's home to partake of a meal with them this evening. First, I thought to enjoy the festivities and should welcome the company."

She hesitated before giving a shy smile. "Then I shall be pleasured to accept your offer, Sir."

❧

Once they secured his wagon and horse, a placid-looking beast with a rough coat of dappled gray, Sarah took a better look at her self-appointed escort.

The sun shimmered off his ink-dark hair and highlighted the clean lines of his profile. His features were most pleasant, though a minor bump at the bridge of his nose prevented his countenance from being too perfect. His mouth was thin, well formed, with a slight tendency to lift at the corners, even when he wasn't smiling. Sarah guessed he must smile often, judging from the laugh lines creased alongside his lips. Realizing she was shamelessly staring, she turned her attention to the road, thankful he'd not caught her frank appraisal.

The traffic on the street was congested. Hearing the *rat-a-tat* of drums, the piping of wind instruments, and the tromp of many boots, Sarah sat up straighter and craned her neck, trying to see the road intersecting the one on which they traveled.

"I believe there is a parade," Thomas said. "Would you care to take a closer look? With this crowd, we would need to walk and dispense with the wagon."

Sarah hesitated. Mrs. Leppermier had made it clear that she should take the opportunity to enjoy the festivities. The mistress's potion would not be needed until the morrow, and Sarah had never seen a parade.

She turned to him and smiled. "I should like that."

This time he hesitated. "Might I ask your name? I know not how to address you."

She flushed. "Oh, of course. 'Tis Sarah. Sarah Thurston."

"A pleasure, Miss Thurston," he said, smiling. With agile grace, he alighted from the wagon and came around to her side, offering his hand.

Sarah felt her cheeks go hot as her fingers touched his warm, rough palm when she stepped down. He treated her like a lady, instead of the commoner she was, and it made her wonder. Very few gentlemen would treat a servant with civility. Though Thomas claimed to be a tradesman and not a gentleman, his deportment stated otherwise.

Curious, Sarah sent sidelong glances his way as they strolled toward the spectacle. Once they reached the flagstone street crowded with commoners and the wealthy alike, Sarah looked over the man's shoulder in front of her. She had to stand on tiptoe to see, but it was worth it.

At the front of the procession, a boy on horseback carried a flag that Betsy Ross was reputed to have created for the budding nation. A circle of stars on a square of blue sat in the uppermost corner, and red and white stripes horizontally filled the cloth. The sight of it made Sarah's throat clench with emotion.

A group of young men followed, playing their instruments, and Sarah saw four drummers and other men with clarinets, fifes, and oboes. Rigid lines of soldiers, each holding muskets and bayonets over their shoulders, marched in rows of four behind them, looking stately in their brown uniforms with blue facings.

The gentleman in front of Sarah, obviously wealthy, as denoted by his fine coat and the metal buckles on his shoes, turned to his companion, who wore an expensive gown of blue cotton. "The Hessian band that played at the dinner for Congress was much more accomplished than these musicians, do you not think so, my dear?" he asked.

"Yes, my husband. Quite." She gave a disparaging glance at the pressing crowd around her. "Let us be away from this dreadful heat. I've seen enough."

"As you will."

The two left, and Sarah stepped up with Thomas to take their place at the front. It was nice not to have to crane her neck to see. First came the infantrymen, followed by soldiers who rode horses. The animals' coats gleamed in the sun from the currying they'd received. A corps of artillery, hauling cannon and other weapons, trailed behind.

"God bless 'em," Sarah heard the man at her side say to his comrade. "I hear tell they're on their way to join the grand army."

"God go wi' ye," an elderly woman from the crowd cried out. "An' give ye victory over them Redcoats!"

Sarah looked in the woman's direction and suddenly caught sight of her three attackers in the crowd on the other side of the parade. She froze, unable to look away. Clay caught her eye and gave a slow smile fraught with the promise of retribution.

Thomas turned his head toward Sarah, and she flicked a glance in his direction. His brows drawing down in concern, he gently grasped her elbow. "You've gone as white as parchment. Is this heat overly much for you?"

117

Sarah shook her head, somewhat amused by the prospect. As a kitchen maid, she was accustomed to worse heat than this. "Nay, Sir. I am well. Truly," she added when he looked unconvinced.

His gaze went to the crowd on the other side of the marching soldiers. Sarah knew when he caught sight of Clay and his acquaintances, for his hand marginally tightened around her elbow. Thomas turned to her, understanding in his eyes.

"Perhaps you would care to seek out the apothecary at this time?"

"Aye," she said, relieved. "That I would."

He nodded, keeping his hand on her arm while he accompanied her back to the street where he had tethered the wagon's horse to a lantern post. Sarah appreciated the warmth of his hand for more than the protection offered. Once he dropped his hold from her sleeve, upon helping her into the conveyance, she missed his touch.

Her cheeks grew hot. What folly! This man was a stranger, a kind stranger, to be sure, but still a stranger. Had her aunt known what wayward imaginings traveled through Sarah's mind, she would think her little worse than a doxy.

Thoughts of family made her sober, and tears clouded her eyes. Impatiently, she brushed them away with the heel of her hand, but Thomas had already seen.

"Here, what ails you?" he asked, his words laced with worry.

Knowing it would be inconsiderate to give no reply, as benevolent as he'd been, she spoke. "I was thinking of home. I miss my brother and sister."

"Do they reside in Philadelphia?"

"No. In England." She shook her head. " 'Tis a long, sad tale. I do not wish to burden you with it."

"It would be no burden, I assure you. However, if you do not care to speak of it, then let this be the end of the matter. I have no wish to upset you further."

His words were kind, and Sarah studied his profile. Would he understand? Or would he judge her based on titles alone?

"We shall have to backtrack and take another street." Thomas flicked the reins and turned the horse around. He looked her way again. "Have you family in town?"

"Not a soul." Her gaze dropped to her lap. "My father was a scholar and was killed in a carriage accident when I was but three and ten. My mother died a year later. Afterward, my two siblings and I were taken in by poor relations—an elderly aunt and uncle in Dorchester. Besides them, I'm alone and have been alone for five years, since first I came to America."

"You do not sound pleased with the arrangement," he said, perplexed. "Why, then, did you leave England?"

Sarah balled her hands in her lap and for a moment chose not to reply. She looked at him then, noticing his brow creased in puzzlement. His midnight-blue eyes regarded her sympathetically, and she wondered if they would remain so once he knew the truth.

"I had no choice in the matter," she said slowly. "I did not come of my own free will. I was transported on a convict ship."

"A convict ship?" he repeated, taken aback.

"Aye. I was sent to the colonies to serve out my sentence."

Chapter 3

Thomas's mind brimmed with questions. He struggled to contain them and waited for Sarah to continue.

"My sister has been sickly all her life," she said and looked away, as if the memory were painful to recall. "One day we were at the market. I was procuring vegetables for my aunt, who's an invalid. Dorrie, my sister, who was then ten and six, had left my side. I heard a ruckus and looked up to see an elegantly dressed, old gentleman holding Dorrie by one ear and yelling. Dorrie was crying."

Moisture filmed Sarah's eyes when she looked at Thomas again. "He accused her of stealing his wallet. Dorrie insisted it fell from his waistcoat and that she was returning it to him at the same time he discovered it missing. Yet he didn't believe her and called a constable. Though I didn't know it at the time, Dorrie's accuser was visiting our city and was a prominent man from the House of Lords. He demanded a high sentence."

Sarah let out a mirthless chuckle, her eyes despondent. "You see, the fault was mine for Dorrie being there in the first place. I thought the outing might do her good. They were going to take her away and put her on a convict ship, and I begged them to let me go in her stead."

"And they allowed it?" Thomas asked in surprise.

Sarah nodded. "I was in full health, and anyone with eyes could see my sister was not. She was still weak from a recent illness and continuously coughed. Her skin had a gray pallor. It was apparent Dorrie would not last the voyage on such a ship and they would receive no payment for her labor."

He stared, silent. Again she looked away, obviously uneasy. "After a harrowing voyage, with sickness and death abounding everywhere, the convict ship arrived in Philadelphia. Mr. Wilkerson paid the asking price for me and acquired me to be one of his kitchen maids."

"A remarkable story," Thomas said pensively.

Her chin sailed up. "You don't believe me, but I shouldn't be surprised. Few people who know my story do."

"I didn't say I doubted you," he quickly inserted. "Only that your story is remarkable. There are few people—blood related or not—who would willingly take another's sentence."

Sarah gave a slight shrug. "Dorrie is my sister, and I've always taken care of her. I could not let her be sent away to die."

He eyed her with respect. "A commendable action on your part, Miss Thurston. And how much longer is your indenture?"

"Three weeks." Her eyes sparkled with anticipation. "And then I shall be rid of the Wilkersons, though I must admit I'll miss young Rupert's company. He has taken to me since his father and stepmother show him no interest. I spend time with him when my chores are done."

"What will you do once you leave?"

"I shall find work here in town and save my money so that I may send for my sister and brother one day."

"You will not return to England?"

"No." Her expression sobered. "I am a Patriot at heart. I admire this nation's fight for liberty, as I have long wished to be free, and want to call such a land my home. England never held anything for me except my siblings, of course."

Thomas nodded, thinking of his older sister, Anne, whose husband was off fighting in the war. She was looking for a cook, and Thomas wondered if she would consider Sarah for the position. He planned to bring up the topic that night.

When they reached the apothecary's shop, Thomas pulled on the reins. The building's two narrow windows were shuttered, and he frowned. "It appears empty. I'll look into it." He stepped down to investigate, finding the shop was indeed vacant. Noticing a group of children nearby, Thomas approached them.

"Have you seen the apothecary?" he asked a freckle-faced little girl nibbling on a chunk of rock candy. Blue ribbons adorned her light hair.

She nodded but did not speak. The boy next to her, sharing the same facial characteristics and coloring as she, pointed down the road. "Last I saw, Sir, he was heading in that direction, he was. He closed up shop, due to the holiday."

"Did he mention where he was going?"

"Why should he speak to the likes of us?" an older boy responded. "We ain't his keepers."

Thomas nodded stiffly. "Thank you," he said to the first boy, then headed back to the wagon and told Sarah the news.

She sighed. "Well then, that is that. I thank you for assisting me in my quest." She made as if to get down.

"You are giving up so soon?"

"No, I shall look for him—I must. Yet I cannot take up more of your time and ask you to search with me. You've done so much already."

"I have nothing else to occupy my time at present. I don't mind." Thomas slapped the reins against the horse's neck before she could exit the wagon. He did not approve of her wandering about town alone.

"Oh!" A surprised gasp escaped her lips as the conveyance lurched forward, and she moved her hands to the seat to hold on. She looked at him curiously. "Well, Sir, if you are sure you don't mind. . ."

"Quite sure," he said, sending a grin her way.

🦋

Rather than be alarmed that Thomas would not allow her to continue her quest alone, Sarah was relieved. She felt secure in his company, something she had never experienced with other men. Despite their short acquaintance, Sarah instinctively knew Thomas could be trusted. Why else would she have told him her history, when she had told so few? Had this man not saved her from possible disgrace? Memory of her encounter with Mr. Wilkerson's acquaintances brought an involuntary shudder, and she silently thanked God for Thomas's intervention.

They slowly drove along the road, searching the people walking along the sidewalks. Thomas came to a stop before a tavern. "I'll look inside. You stay here."

Relieved, Sarah nodded. She preferred to avoid such places. Alehouses in the colonies were the same as in England, with men well into their cups, foul language afoot, and frequent brawls. Her uncle frequented just such a place, and it was due in part to his ill reputation that the convict sentence Sarah had taken for Dorrie was so stiff, she was sure.

Within minutes, Thomas was back. "The apothecary was here but left a short time ago. We shall find him."

The glowing ball of the sun had dropped lower toward the horizon by the time they found the portly, ruddy-cheeked man walking with a taller gentleman along Cherry Street. The apothecary's wig hung askew, and his clothes appeared rumpled, but Sarah was relieved to see he was not inebriated. She explained her reason for seeking him out.

He clucked his tongue in disgust but said a farewell to his companion and moved to take a place beside Sarah. Quickly she slid over to make room for his wide girth on the short bench. Pressed up against Thomas's solid build as she now was, Sarah found it hard to draw breath; the pulsing of her heart reverberated in her ears. His clothes had a fresh, musky smell coupled with the aromatic odor of wood shavings, and she inhaled his pleasing scent, feeling a trifle lightheaded.

When they pulled up in front of the apothecary's shop, Sarah found it difficult to stand. Her limbs were shaky from being in such close proximity to Thomas. He said nothing, yet his eyes questioned as he helped her down. Embarrassed, she looked away.

Inside the dim shop, the apothecary went to a back room behind the counter. Avoiding Thomas's gaze, Sarah studied the shelves filled with labeled jars and bottles containing colored liquids and powders. Several stone mortars and pestles were strewn atop the wooden counter, one mortar still bearing grains of white powder. A huge jar of live leeches sat at the other end, and Sarah hurriedly turned her gaze away from the sight of the blood-sucking creatures crawling inside the glass.

"Here it is," the apothecary said when he rejoined them, a bottle of dark liquid in his hand. "I realized Mrs. Wilkerson's supply would be running low and had the foresight to prepare this a few days past. I'll put it on her account."

"Thank you, Sir," Sarah said, slipping the bottle through a slit in her skirt to one of two bags suspended from a rope tied around her shift. The pockets, as they were called, helped her carry all manner of things and leave her hands free.

She strode to the door, Thomas behind her. At the wagon, she turned his way. "You've been of great help to me, Mr. Gray. Again, I thank you."

His expression was incredulous. "You don't think I'll allow you to walk to the Wilkersons' estate when I have a wagon to drive you?"

"But you've spent so much time helping me already," Sarah protested. "Look, it's approaching nightfall. You'll miss dinner with your family."

"Anne will understand. I cannot let you traverse these streets alone, especially with night falling as you have pointed out."

The sound of many bells pealed throughout the streets, interrupting their conversation, and Sarah started in surprise. The great gongs of the Liberty Bell, hanging in the State House a few streets over, mingled with the more delicate sound of hand bells the excited townspeople rang. The mellow tones of nearby church bells added to the delightful clamor.

"The sweet sound of liberty," Thomas said, his gaze meeting hers.

Before Sarah could reply, a small urchin with the biggest and brightest dark eyes scampered between them, laughing. Her short black curls bounced under her ruffled cap and over the collar of her gown as she shook her brass hand bell. Her older sister trotted after, catching up with the plump child and scooping her up and onto one hip. The toddler giggled and rang her bell some more.

"Shall we join in the fun?" Thomas asked, smiling.

Though to spend more time in this man's company was exactly what Sarah did want, she knew she shouldn't. "I've been gone a long time. I best return before they think I've run away."

"As you will." He stepped toward the wagon and held out his hand to assist her. She hesitated but accepted his aid, reasoning he could get her to Fairmount Park much faster than she could walk.

Thomas drove slowly along the roads to avoid hitting the people—children mostly—who sometimes darted across the street. Everywhere citizens rang their bells and gave loud huzzahs. Sarah smiled, wishing she, too, had a bell to ring. On such a day as this, it was easy to get caught up in the merriment.

The dusky purple twilight had deepened to inky darkness by the time the bells stopped ringing, though throughout the town a few could still be heard, the merrymakers not wanting to cease in their revelry. All of a sudden, myriad explosions of color shattered the air to Sarah's left, painting spectacular starbursts of light against the dark sky.

"Oh, look," Sarah gasped in awe, taking hold of Thomas's shirtsleeve, barely cognizant of the fact she'd done so. "Let us stop and watch."

Thomas pulled the wagon to the side of the road, and they lifted their faces toward the heavens. For the next several minutes, they watched the vibrant rockets explode above the commons, one by one.

"How exquisite," Sarah whispered. A spark lit inside her, quickly fanning into flame. "America must win this war and gain her freedom. She must!"

Thomas turned her way, his eyes understanding. "She will. God is for us. He forever stands on the side of justice."

"Aye," she whispered. "That He does."

During her absorption with the display, Sarah hadn't realized that she had moved closer to Thomas. Against the backdrop of the illuminated sky, she could easily see the dark lashes that framed his eyes, feel his warmth, smell the sweet scent of herbs on his breath. A colorful finale of numerous fireworks filled the heavens beyond, highlighting his features all the more. His eyes were gentle, soft, like liquid velvet might appear if there were such a thing. . . .

Feeling faint, Sarah moved back, putting distance between them, and averted her gaze. "We should go."

He lifted the reins from his lap where he clutched them. "Aye. The day is long spent." His words seemed terse and rocked Sarah a great deal more than the deafening bangs from the fireworks had done.

As the wagon bounced along, Sarah shot several discreet glances his way. The flame-lit globes of lantern posts that lined the wide streets shed a pale glow over Thomas's sober profile, until the wagon moved into the shadows between posts once more. Would she see him again? Or was the scope of their acquaintance destined to be limited to this one extraordinary day?

At the manor, the wheels crunched over pebbles while Thomas drove to the side of the house, as Sarah directed. Once the vehicle came to a stop, she looked at him. "It has been wondrous, and I appreciated the company."

He inclined his head. "My pleasure."

Before she could say more, he leaped down and came around to her side to assist her. This time, his hands briefly spanned her waist as he lifted her from the wagon and set her on the ground in front of him. The action took no more than a few seconds, yet his touch flustered Sarah, sending her heart racing.

She opened her mouth to frame a cordial farewell, but the faint sound of crying coming from the vegetable garden stopped her.

S arah stared at Thomas, wondering if her mind was playing tricks on her. "Do you hear?"

"Yes," he said, already ahead of her. Sarah followed him to the garden, the moon lighting their way. Upon leaving the cloak of trees, they came to the grassy clearing. With bowed head, Grace sat on the ground near the rows of vegetables.

"Grace! What ails ye?" Sarah asked in alarm, rushing over to the young woman. She knelt before the housemaid, feeling the reassuring presence of Thomas behind her.

The girl lifted a face wet with tears, her dark eyes forlorn. "Sarah," she murmured. "Whatever shall I do?" Suddenly she threw her arms around Sarah and buried her face in her shoulder, starting to cry again.

"I should be going," Thomas inserted quietly, obviously recognizing Grace's need for privacy.

Sarah nodded, already missing his company.

"We will meet again, Sarah Thurston." His eyes glowed with promise in the moonlight. "Farewell."

"Farewell," she breathed, watching his tall form move away. Even concern for her friend could not dispel the flutter of her heart at his words.

When Grace's tears were spent, Sarah pulled back. "Tell me," she chided gently, "what causes you to weep as though the world were coming to an end? Have you ill word of your family?"

"I am with child," Grace blurted out numbly. "Which means another year will be added to my indenture, as the law states." Like Sarah, Grace's servitude was almost at an end.

Indignation rose up in Sarah. "You must take this to the constable, Grace. You mustn't let Mr. Wilkerson get away with such a deed."

"I'm only a servant, and he's an important man. Who would give heed to what I say?"

Such deeds were common among masters, Sarah knew, to prolong an indenture's servitude. Yet there had been cases of a penalty being slapped on the offender and the servant being removed from his custody. "You must try, Grace. You don't want to work for him another year, do you?"

Grace helplessly shook her head. "I've not your courage, Sarah. I'm afraid to let my plight be known. Likely, I will be publicly whipped and ostracized." She clutched Sarah's arms, and her tone grew cautious. "Your indenture ends soon. Now that the deed is done, the master will look to others for his entertainment. You must be on your guard, Sarah, lest he do the same to you."

Sarah clenched her teeth. "He dare not try!" Remembering her earlier encounter with Mr. Wilkerson's three friends and her timidity in the face of danger, she sobered. "I will be cautious. And I'll consider a solution for your dilemma, as well, though I know not what. You shouldn't be forced to serve that ogre another year! But come, let us talk of this no more. The night air grows cold."

Helping Grace, who leaned heavily on her shoulder, Sarah rose with her friend, keeping an arm around her waist. Together, they moved toward the house.

❧

Tuesday was baking day. Up at four, Sarah and the other servants served the family scrapple, eggs, and other foods to break the fast, then made quick work of building a fire inside the oven, using finely split wood. After the fire burned awhile, Katie scraped the oven out, swept the ash away, and stuck her arm into the heated box to test the temperature. Both her arms were smooth, the hair singed off them long ago from this practice. First in went foods that needed more baking time—the meat pasties, the duckling, and the mutton. Sarah turned the hourglass upside down to let the sand trickle to the bottom. When that was accomplished, the breads would go in.

Swiping her forearm over her moist brow, Sarah released a weary breath. Next came making the fruit pastries and sweet breads of which Mrs. Wilkerson was so fond.

As Sarah stirred the ingredients for another piecrust and lifted the bowl to dump its contents to be rolled out, Mrs. Leppermier spoke. "Tell me, Sarah. Did you have a good time at the festivities? Did you meet anyone special?"

Sarah almost dropped the bowl. The celebration was a week ago, though she had not ceased thinking of Thomas since. Feeling her face flame even more than the heat in the room had already caused it to, she stared. "Pardon?"

"Grace mentioned a man brought you home that night," Mrs. Leppermier said as she sliced the apples thin. "Would ye care to talk of it?"

Sarah immediately focused on her job, rolling out the dough. "Aye, there was such a man. He saved me from a dangerous situation and helped me to find the apothecary."

"What's this?" Mrs. Leppermier stopped chopping, her knife still. "A dangerous situation?"

Sarah nodded and told the woman all that had transpired. The cook looked thoughtful. "Perhaps it was a mistake to let you go into town alone on such a day of revelry. . .then again, perhaps not." Her smile was mysterious. "Whatever the case, the good Lord protected you, Sarah, and He will go on doing so."

"Aye." Sarah smiled. In her prayers, she'd pleaded with God for protection in

125

light of what had happened to Grace and had felt His reassurance. Had He not sent her Thomas when she needed him? Sarah wished she could share the gospel with Grace, but when she'd tried in the past, the woman had shaken her head.

"We are the masters of our own lives, Sarah. As such, we are responsible for our destinies," Grace had said, a sad smile on her face, as though she felt sorry for Sarah's gullibility. "Besides, how can a God who is real allow horrible things to happen to people?"

Sarah hadn't been able to respond, since that same question sometimes filtered through her mind. It made her ashamed that she also harbored doubts. Growing sober, she focused on her work.

The hours passed with dogged slowness, like a stubborn mule with a burden upon its back, plodding along a trail. Once the food was baked for the week, Sarah used a wooden peel to scoop the items from the oven. Afterward, she and Mrs. Leppermier cleaned the mess they had made, washed pots and pans, and swept flour and other food droppings from the flagstones. Katie, her skirt pulled up and tucked in to give her some relief from the oppressive heat, put bread pudding into a fabric bag to steam over a kettle. Pepper pot, the spicy beef and vegetable stew everyone in the family loved, boiled in the container.

"Fetch the butter, Sarah," Mrs. Leppermier ordered. " 'Tis soon time to put the meal on."

Sarah exited the house, carrying a basket laden with perishable food they would not eat that day. Rupert came skipping out of the trees to join her.

"Play with me, Sarah?"

She shook her head, never diverting from her trek. "This is baking day, and there's still much to do." At his downcast face, she relented. "Tonight, I will tell you a story."

His face beamed. "Will you tell me more about the celebration? I heard a friend of father's say thirteen galleys and armed ships were gathered in the harbor, all with red, white, and blue streamers, and each of them fired thirteen cannon! Did you see it? That must have been what made all the noise and scared the hens from laying eggs."

"I don't doubt it," she said with a laugh. "No, Child, I didn't see the ships. That must have taken place afore I arrived. Now off with ye! There is much to be done."

Once she entered the springhouse, Sarah set the basket down. The soothing sound of the stream rushing over small rocks filled the building. She turned to retrieve the container of freshly churned butter from the cool water. A shadow filled the door, and she looked up in surprise.

Mr. Wilkerson stood in the entrance. "Sarah. We have need to talk."

Sarah's body went as cold as the brook. "Something I've done displeases you, Sir?"

"Nay, your conduct has been exemplary. Rather, I have looked through my papers of late, and I see that your term of indenture is almost at an end."

"Aye," she said through numb lips.

He regarded her where she knelt by the gurgling spring. Slowly, he walked closer and came to a stop beside her. Reaching out, he laid his hand upon her shoulder.

Petrified, she looked up at him.

"Would you consider signing another contract, this one of your own will?" he asked, his voice silky. "The boy has taken a liking to you. Therefore, I would give you a different position, as a companion to Rupert. You would find such an arrangement comes with numerous benefits, especially the closer our acquaintanceship grows. Know ye what I am saying, Sarah?"

"Aye," she said stiffly, clenching her teeth. She averted her gaze to the clear water, wishing he would go. Fear struggled with resentment for first position in her mind.

A long, unnerving pause followed. Sarah swallowed over the lump that had formed in her throat.

"Think on it," he said finally, his voice harsh as he wrenched his hand away.

After he exited the small building, Sarah took time to gather her composure before returning to the house. She uttered a brief prayer for safety during her remaining days in Mr. Wilkerson's employ but couldn't help feeling apprehensive about her future.

�

"I did it!" Rupert cried with glee, clapping his hands and jumping up and down.

"That you did," Sarah said with a congratulatory smile. "And now we shall see if I can fare as well."

She lifted her wooden ring, brought it back, and slowly lifted it again, her eye on the stake. Quickly she drew back her arm and flung the ring at the target. The edge of the wooden disc bounced on top of the stake and went awry.

"Oh too bad, Sarah!" Rupert sympathized.

"Your stance is incorrect," a masculine voice said from behind, startling Sarah into dropping the rings in her other hand. Spinning around, she spied Thomas standing near the flowering dogwood trees.

"Forgive me," he said. "I delivered the bookcase and heard the sound of laughter so decided to investigate." The noonday sun painted silvery-blue highlights in his dark tresses. Again he wore no tricorn, and his trim form was clad in a billowy white shirt with leather vest and breeches. He looked magnificent.

Sarah dropped her gaze to the rings on the ground. Hurriedly she bent to retrieve them, not overly surprised when Thomas joined her in the task. He picked up two and placed them in her hand. Their eyes met, and Sarah felt a jolt go through her.

"Would you care for me to give you some pointers? I was quite accomplished at quoits in my day." He grinned, his laugh lines becoming more pronounced.

Sarah's heart flipped. If his referral to "in my day" suggested he was advanced in years, he was obviously jesting. He could be no older than his late twenties, she was sure.

"Sarah?" Rupert asked. "Are you going to swoon? You look ill."

She sent a rapier-sharp glance to the young scamp. "I am fine." Turning to Thomas, she said, "If you care to coach me, I'll not refuse you." Sarah looked away from the amusement dancing in his eyes as he moved beside her.

127

"Put one foot in front of you and bend slightly at the knees," Thomas instructed. "Now, raise your arm to shoulder level—slightly bend it—keeping your back straight. No, you're too stiff. Permit me."

Before Sarah knew what he was about, she felt his warm touch on her wrist. He came alongside her while lifting her arm and pushing against the inside of her sleeve to bend her elbow, as though she were pliable clay and he were the potter. Indeed, she felt as stable as mushy earth. He stood so close she was aware of his form lightly pressed against her side. She tried to draw a firm breath, but it, too, felt shaky.

"Steady," Thomas said close to her ear. "Steady. . ." He pulled her arm back until the disk brushed her skirt. "Now bring the ring up swiftly and release it!" He let go of her wrist but otherwise did not move.

Sarah brought her arm up with a snap and let go of the ring. Her hand was trembling so that she was surprised the ring made it as far as it did, though it came nowhere near the stake.

"You are too tense," Thomas said. "You need to relax."

Ha! As if she could do such a thing with him standing so near, reminding her she was a woman and he was a man. "I think I have the gist of it," she said, not daring to look his way. In the position they were in, his lips would be at a level with hers if she faced him. She continued to stare at the stake until it swam before her eyes. When at last he moved from her side, she was relieved. Almost.

"Will you play with us, Sir?" Rupert asked hopefully.

Sarah stole a peek at Thomas and felt another bout of lightheadedness when she noted him staring at her.

"No, Lad. I'm in the process of making deliveries. I thought only to bid you good day." He nodded at Sarah. "Again, it was a pleasure."

Sarah's heart raced as she watched his erect form stride toward the front of the house. *Aye. A true pleasure.*

"Sarah?" Rupert asked, his voice holding a superior air. "Should you not offer him cider? He looks thirsty, and the day is hot."

Already he was beginning to sound like a master giving orders. Sarah had noted the perspiration beading Thomas's fine brow when he stood close. And the boy was right. The day was hot.

"Mr. Gray!" she called, taking a few running steps after him. He turned in surprise.

"Would ye care for refreshment before you go? We have cider." She motioned to a nearby decanter sitting on the step.

Something lit the deep blue of his eyes, as though a candle's glow shone beyond them. "Yes, thank you."

Feeling suddenly flustered, Sarah quickly turned to the task at hand.

Thomas watched her flurry about. Her upswept hair was in disarray underneath the mobcap, several damp curls sticking to the slender column of her neck. Her cheeks glowed from exercise. Or was it from embarrassment?

Thomas realized he had inadvertently made her ill at ease, standing close to her as he had while showing her how to throw the wooden rings. At first his action had been one of courtesy. Yet when he stood near her, inhaling the sweet apple scent that undoubtedly came from the cider she'd prepared, and felt the brush of her silken curls against his cheek, he had not wanted to leave. Propriety demanded he step away, and he had, albeit reluctantly.

Sarah handed him a brimming glass. Thomas was surprised to see shaved ice floating in the liquid. Yet it shouldn't astonish him that the wealthy Bartholomew Wilkerson owned an icehouse, where huge blocks of ice from winter's frozen river were stored in hay and buried deep within the ground to provide refreshment in summer.

Thomas gratefully swallowed the tangy, cold mixture, draining the glass without removing it from his lips. Afterward, he handed it to Sarah. She smiled, a twinkle in her eyes.

"More?"

"No, thank you. I need to complete my deliveries." Normally, he might have let such a task fall to Jeremy, his apprentice. Yet the hope of seeing Sarah again had Thomas going in Jeremy's stead.

"Thank you for coaching me in quoits." Sarah's face reddened, and Thomas grinned and gave a small bow.

"My pleasure. Good day, Miss Thurston."

"Good day."

Thomas resumed the trek to his wagon. Before entering it, he again looked toward the mansion. Mr. Wilkerson stood at the front, his gaze raking over Thomas. Thomas wasn't sure why, but he felt the man boded no good. Hesitating, Thomas returned the stare, then climbed into his wagon.

Chapter 5

Several days later, Sarah had just finished preparing a currant pudding when Mrs. Leppermier came sailing into the kitchen. "Sarah, put away your apron. You have need to accompany Morton into town."

Sarah looked up in surprise. "Morton?"

"Aye. Mrs. Wilkerson was so pleased with Mr. Gray's work that she wants him to design another piece of furniture." She handed Sarah a slip of paper. "This tells what the mistress wants. You're to give it to Mr. Gray along with a small advance." She placed a guinea in Sarah's hand.

"I don't understand," Sarah said, looking first at the guinea and paper, then at the cook's wrinkled face. "You want me to go with Morton to talk to Mr. Gray? Mrs. Wilkerson asked this of you?"

"No, Belle spoke of it," Mrs. Leppermier corrected. "And since you answer to me, I'm ordering you to go." She winked, smiling. "That young scamp Morton is not to be trusted; yet, since he's the master's illegitimate son, he gets away with more than most. With you along, I know Mr. Gray will receive his guinea—and that it won't go toward a round of drink for Morton and his disreputable friends."

Moved, Sarah nodded, putting her hand through the slit in her skirt and sticking the note and money in the pocket. Mrs. Leppermier's faith in Sarah spoke volumes to her.

Hurriedly she untied her apron and fixed her mobcap. The thought of seeing Thomas again brought excitement, something she tried to hide. Yet the knowing smile on Cook's face when Sarah bid her farewell proved her efforts were useless.

Morton, who was all of eight and ten years, regarded Sarah with effrontery when she joined him on the lawn. "So, Cook won't let me go on my own, won't she?" He snorted, fixing his flop hat over his head. "Well, you best keep up then. I won't be trailin' behind for the likes o' you!"

Sarah rolled her gaze heavenward, then quickly followed Morton as he turned on his heel and kept a few paces ahead of her the entire way. Morton was an enigma. Though he held the station of a servant, he was treated better than all of them combined and given finer clothes. It would seem that to be so blessed, his attitude might be kinder. Yet he was often surly—aided, no doubt, by his desire for rum. Or perhaps his dour behavior stemmed from the fact that the master barely acknowledged him, though Morton was his offspring.

As they approached Thomas's street, a sense of alarm made Sarah halt in her tracks. Columns of thick gray smoke rose in the humid air over the rooftops of the buildings, and she could smell the fumes from where she stood. Picking up her skirts, she ran ahead of Morton.

In the distance, flames licked a roof not far from Thomas's shop. A volunteer fire brigade worked to put out the flames. Axmen opened and stripped the roof, hookmen pulled down burning timbers, and others manned the two-handled pump on the engine and held the hose. The townspeople helped. One long row of men passed full water buckets in the direction of the blaze, while an opposite row of women passed the empties to children, who filled them at nearby pumps.

Sarah searched, shading her eyes from the sun with one hand. Relief seized her when she spied Thomas's strong form in the long line of men, though she was alarmed at how close to the burning structure he stood. Wanting to help, she filled buckets, then ran with them and transferred them to the last man in line.

Finally, the crackling flames dwindled. A loud hiss filled the air, as though the dying fire were protesting, while gallons of water continued to be tossed upon it.

When all that remained was smoke, several men closest to the fire moved away, their faces blackened. The crowd began to disperse, the people finding and taking their leather-covered buckets, which each household was required by law to possess.

Thomas moved from the crowd, and Sarah hurried to join him. Now that the danger of the fire had passed, she suddenly realized she'd lost Morton. Exasperated, she made a quick scan of the crowd before continuing her trek toward Thomas.

Soot covered his face and streaked his white shirt, the sleeves of which were rolled up, exposing sinewy forearms. His queue hung askew, long strands of dark hair hanging near his lean face, but he looked no less striking.

"Miss Thurston," he said, surprised. "What brings you here?"

"Business—with you," she said, averting her eyes from his steady gaze. She felt somewhat embarrassed by the admiration she felt toward him upon surveying his form and wondered if he could sense her thoughts. "Mrs. Wilkerson wants you to fashion another piece of furniture. I have the description with me."

"Really? Well, come along. I need to find my bucket, and we will talk. Thank the good Lord the fire is out. Old Mr. Fogherty is a kindhearted man, and I would have been dismayed had he lost his livelihood, though surely there will be damage to his merchandise."

Sarah walked behind Thomas to the fire-blackened, smoking building. Several bystanders eyed the ruined structure. One man gazed at the fire plaque on the outside wall, the symbol of an eagle showing from which company the fire brigade would receive their reward for putting out the fire. Along with other townspeople, Thomas searched through the pile of discarded buckets on the ground until he found the container with his initials. Straightening, he headed Sarah's way, his expression sober. "Did you come alone?"

Sarah thought she detected a note of disapproval in his voice. "I came with another servant. Yet he seems to have disappeared."

"He knows my shop was your destination?"

"Aye." She hesitated. "Perhaps I should wait on him."

"He will show. Come, and I'll have a look at what Mrs. Wilkerson desires."

Sarah accompanied him to his shop. Several people greeted them along the way. Most mentioned the recent fire and the relief that it had not spread. Many looked at Sarah with raised brows and curiosity plainly written on their faces.

Their frank appraisal made her wonder. Did Thomas have an understanding with a woman? Was that why they looked at Sarah so? Or was the opposite the case? That he was rarely seen in the company of the fairer sex, and so the prospect provided interest to his neighbors?

Sarah hoped the latter were true, though as attractive and kind as Thomas was, she doubted it.

☙

Thomas led Sarah into his shop, his gaze darting around the room to make sure everything was in its proper place. He winced when he noted his dark coat draped over the bench instead of hanging from the wooden peg in his living quarters above his shop. When the fire had started, he had been in the process of donning his coat. An empty tankard and pewter plate sat nearby, an old, dog-eared copy of Franklin's *Poor Richard's Almanac* beside it, and both table and floor were littered with wood shavings.

Thankfully, she made no comment, and Thomas began to roll down his shirtsleeves, at least hoping to make himself presentable. He stopped upon catching sight of his blackened hands and forearms. Realizing for the first time that his appearance must be shocking, he hurriedly excused himself and rushed upstairs. After using the washbasin to cleanse his face and hands to the best of his ability, changing into his one spare shirt, and redoing his queue, he clomped down the wooden stairs, worried he had taken too long and Sarah would not be there. Her form was bent over a maple candle sconce he had recently carved, and relieved, he shrugged into his coat.

"Now, then," he said, out of breath. "What is it your mistress fancies?"

Sarah withdrew a note and coin from within her skirt, handing them to him. His brows lifted at the advance of the guinea, and his eyes skimmed the missive: *A chest press carved to portray "The Fox and the Grapes" from Aesop's Fables.* And she wanted it in two weeks.

Thomas frowned. "I can deliver the item she requested, but I'll need more time than she's allotted me." He looked up from the paper. "I have orders from other customers to fill."

"I'll deliver the message," Sarah said, her gaze on an unfinished secretary in one corner of the room. She strode toward it and moved her hand over its many pigeonholes. "What beautiful work! And such fine detail!" She turned her shining face his way. "How long have you been a cabinetmaker?"

"I became an apprentice at the age of thirteen. When I was twenty-four, I opened my own shop, using all that Mr. Unger taught me. He died three years ago." Realizing she was still standing, he motioned to the bench beside the table. "Please, have a seat."

She stared, her expression curious, but did as he asked.

He inclined his head. "You wish to say something?"

"Aye. But I don't want you to think me impertinent."

Thomas chuckled. "I could never think that of you, Sarah." Realizing his slip of the tongue, he sobered. "Pardon me, Miss Thurston."

"I don't mind you using the name given me at birth," she assured. "All at the estate call me Sarah. You're the only one who addresses me otherwise." A curious expression lit her face. "It does make me wonder—and that is the question I wish to ask—how can a tradesman have the manners of a gentleman?"

"Ah," he said with a smile. "I'm a mystery in need of solving?"

At this, she blushed. "Aye."

" 'Tis a simple matter. My father was the youngest son of an English earl. As such, he did not stand to inherit the property or the title. He was given an allowance and came to the colonies to pursue his living as a practitioner at law. Soon patriotism fired his blood, and he joined the cause, though he was a nobleman's son—unheard of, you understand. For his 'impudence and betrayal,' as my grandfather posed it, my father was ostracized from the family. Being raised a gentleman, he taught his sons that same trait."

"Sons?"

"I have two brothers. I am the youngest of all my father's children."

"And your mother?"

"She died in childbirth, as did the babe. My father never remarried."

Sarah nodded, her eyes sad as she studied the room filled with the tools of his trade. "And so this is the life you lead, though you were born to one of wealth?"

"Do not pity me, Sarah. I am satisfied with my 'plight,' as some have called it. Since I was a small lad, I was fascinated with the exquisite carvings on the mahogany furniture in my father's house and even took a kitchen knife to a block of wood one day to fashion one of my own. I was but seven at the time, and this is what I received for my troubles." His words were light as he held out one hand to show her the long white scar racing along his palm.

"Oh," she murmured in sympathy.

What Thomas did not expect was for her to lift her fingers and brush the old wound with lingering feather softness, sending his nerve endings tingling into awareness. Stunned, he yanked his hand back before he could think twice. She looked up, her eyes full of embarrassed dismay.

"Forgive me," she blurted, hurriedly rising to her feet and moving across the room.

Feeling like a fool, Thomas shook his head. "There's no need. You've done nothing wrong." Though she was by proxy a customer, they were alone, nevertheless. Because of this, he considered it wise to keep his distance, as attracted to her as he felt.

She moved toward the sash window and gazed through the square-shaped panes of glass. "Morton is taking a long time. I should look for him."

"Sarah, please stay," Thomas encouraged, his voice steady. "I don't think it wise for you to wander the town alone."

"I've done so before. What happened with those men during the celebration was the first time such an incident had occurred," she said, addressing the window.

"It is my hope you'll not invite a second incident. I may not be there to protect you."

Her gaze swung his way, her face flushed. "Tell me, why is it that one in such fine form as yourself and forever spouting of protection is not off fighting in the war?" As soon as the rash words left her mouth, she looked distressed, as though she wished she could take them back.

Her soft question struck him hard, ramming at the door of his defenses. "I make a better craftsman than I do a killer."

"A killer?" A trace of censure filled her tone. "Then you secretly despise the men who are fighting for freedom, yours included?"

"Not at all. I have great admiration for them. Would I could do as they have done."

"I fail to understand your reasoning, Sir." Her eyes brimmed with confusion and, Thomas was saddened to see, disappointment. Before he could reply, the door swung open and a young man half stumbled inside.

"There you are," he said, his words full of reproach. "I been lookin' for you."

Sarah eyed him without flinching. "Then you have searched the wrong place, Morton. You would not have found me in the alehouse." She wrinkled her nose at the strong stench of liquor that cloaked his breath, her expression one of disdain. "Imbibing in rum again, I see. Never mind. I have taken care of all the necessary arrangements. We are free to take our leave."

She looked at Thomas, her manner detached. "I wish you good day, Sir. I will deliver your message to my mistress." She swept out the door, Morton in her wake.

Thomas stared into space, his mind replaying her cutting words. He thought of another day, another time. . .two mischievous lads, nowhere near old enough to shave, behind the springhouse—one the master's son, one a servant's. The master's pistol in the son's hand. . .the curiosity and excitement involving the danger of being caught with the forbidden weapon. . .the haughty order from the master's son for the servant's son to shoot first. . .the blood when the gun misfired.

Thomas had been to blame for the death of his young friend, a heavy load he still bore. Turning his gaze to the mantel, he looked at his father's old pistol. He kept the relic as a reminder that human life was precious. And because of those feelings mingled with those of his faith, he had never killed a man. As a child standing beside his friend's grave with tears running down his cheeks, Thomas had vowed never again to be responsible for another's death. Yet neither had he reckoned that, one day, the land he dearly loved would be at war in a fight for its freedom.

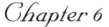

Chapter 6

B efore retiring, Sarah lit a candle and went upstairs to bid Rupert good night, as she always did. The boy was so often lonely, and Sarah felt sorry for the young scamp. His eyes stared up at her with love as she walked toward his cot.

"Have ye said your prayers?" She smoothed his golden locks from his forehead.

He nodded. "Will you tell me a story?"

"Aye." Sarah smiled. "That I will."

She related the Bible account of the Israelites gaining freedom from the wicked pharaoh and thought of her master. Though Mr. Wilkerson had toasted religious freedom, he forbade his servants from attending church on the Sabbath, claiming it a lot of nonsense designed to prevent them from doing their chores. Yet once a week, a handful of indentures and slaves took a few minutes to gather by the springhouse and hold their own service, while Mrs. Leppermier recited Scripture from her Bible.

"The Is-il-rites wanted freedom, like the colonies do from England," Rupert murmured sleepily when Sarah paused after relating how Moses had taken God's people across the Red Sea.

She smiled and kissed his cheek. "Aye. Something like that." When she straightened, he regarded her sadly.

"I miss my mother. She used to kiss my cheek every night."

Tears stung Sarah's eyes at the admission. "I'm certain she looks down from her home in heaven every evening to blow you a kiss on that same cheek."

Her words erased his frown, and he closed his eyes. "Good night, Sarah. I'm glad you'll never leave us."

Alarm shot through her, but before she could question him, Rupert turned on his side and burrowed into a ball. She picked up the candle and left. Did he know her indenture was almost at an end? She had not told him. Yet what did he mean by those last words?

Telling herself she was looking for problems that did not exist, Sarah sank to her mat above the kitchen where the kitchen servants slept. She had been given permission by Cook to go into town the next morning and search for employment. Less than a week remained until her term was complete.

Smiling, she floated into sleep but was troubled by disturbing dreams that woke her well before four, when she usually began her day. Sarah decided to get an early start. She donned her clothes over her shift and laced up her bodice in the dark, not bothering to light a candle.

Quietly, she slipped downstairs and tore off a hunk of bread from the shelf. A rustle and series of footsteps from beyond the wall caused her heart to lurch. Gathering courage, she peered into the main room. No one spoke to her from the still darkness. Uneasy, she let herself outside.

❧

The air was cool against Sarah's skin. Up ahead in the distance she could see ships' masts, their mammoth bows almost touching the row of buildings facing the harbor. The vessels were outlined in the lanterns' glow against the sky, now lightening from inky black to murky gray.

"Sarah! Is that you?"

Without realizing it, she had walked down the street with Thomas's shop and was not overly surprised to hear his voice quietly call out.

In the stillness, his footsteps echoed on the cobbles as he approached. Early morning mist from the Delaware River clouded the air but not so much as to make it impossible to see. Thomas's expression was one of surprise as he came upon her. "Whatever brings you to town so soon? It is not yet daybreak."

"I've been granted permission to seek future employment and have only the morning to do so. I thought I would get an early start and ask at the coffeehouse the Widow Brown runs."

"It is early," Thomas agreed. "Many have not yet tumbled from their beds, though I notice several are up and about now." With a wry grin, he motioned to the tobacconist, who swept his stoop across the street and cast interested glances their way.

"Your neighbors watch you often?" she asked. "Are they so inquisitive?"

"Only when their curiosity is aroused. I am not often in the company of an attractive woman."

The soft compliment made her eyes widen. He took her elbow. "Come. Let us walk and not provide Mr. Coppel with further information to tell his wife. I have something I need to discuss with you."

"Oh?" Sarah asked, her heart tripping a beat at his light touch. He turned her away from the direction of the river, and they began walking.

"I spoke with my sister. She is married to an army officer and has a fine house in town. At present, she has much to do with six children to look after. Her cook has departed, and Anne is helpless at the craft." He grinned. "In short, she's open to the idea of hiring you."

Tears pricked Sarah's eyes. Was there no end to this man's benevolence? Memory of how shoddily she'd treated him when they last parted made her face go hot, despite the cool mist bathing her skin. Thomas did not lack courage. Whatever his reason for separating himself from the fighting, it must be a worthy one.

"I owe you an apology," she said softly.

"An apology?"

"Aye. I never should have spoken to you as I did when last we were together. I was mistaken."

"Never mind, Sarah," he said, his voice gruff. "Let us put the matter behind us."

She nodded, relieved.

"Would you care to meet my sister? She, too, is an early riser. Her house is on the other side of town, though, so you might prefer for me to fetch my wagon."

"No." Sarah sent him a shy smile. "I think I'd rather walk with you."

"As you will." His voice was as soft and warm as the look that suddenly lit his eyes.

When they finally reached the large, two-story plain brick building, the sun, visible through the leafy boughs of sycamore trees, was just peeking over the horizon. Thomas sensed Sarah was nervous and gave her a reassuring smile. "Never fear. Anne is quite companionable," he said before knocking at the door.

A sour-faced woman answered and glared at them. Sarah started, obviously taken aback. Thomas quickly spoke. "Good morning, Matilda. Is my sister available?"

The maid opened the door to let them in, but her stiff countenance did not change. "She's in the garden."

When Matilda continued to stare, Thomas blew out a quiet, exasperated breath. "Then if you will not announce us, we shall go and make our presence known."

"As ye will." The maid turned her back to them.

Thomas caught Sarah's shocked gaze at Matilda's disrespect. "She, too, is an indenture," he explained. "And as lazy as an old hound."

At the back of the house, they found Anne kneeling on the soil in a losing battle against a carrot that refused to be tugged out of the earth. Her belly was great with child, and Thomas caught Sarah's surprised gaze toward him before she hurried to his sister.

"Milady, allow me." Sarah knelt beside her and gave one hard tug to the carrot Anne had let go of in surprise, freeing it from the earth. His sister smiled.

"Thomas, please tell me this is of whom you spoke."

He grinned. "Anne, may I present to you Miss Sarah Thurston. Sarah, my sister, Mrs. Anne Rollins."

Sarah nodded and averted her gaze, obviously still uneasy. Anne touched her arm. "Let us go inside for coffee, though perhaps I've had too much of that already." She shook her head. " 'Tis a craving I've had since first I was with child. The weakness that has come upon me in months past is also due to the babe within my belly, I suppose—"

Thomas cleared his throat and looked away, uncomfortable with the womanly conversation. Anne laughed. "But, lo! I've offended my brother's sensibilities. Without a man around the house of late, my talk has become quite frank." She gave Thomas a grin sparked with mischief, then faced Sarah. "Come, let us get acquainted."

Thomas hurried to help Anne to her feet, a trifle amused at how awkward his normally graceful sister had become. The three went into the hall, and Sarah admired the small glazed pictures, framed in black molding with gold-leafed corners, on the whitewashed walls. "How lovely," she murmured.

"Aren't they? I procured them from the Kennedy's Print Shop on Second and Chestnut. I do so love the one showing Jesus with the little children."

Almost as if on cue, Nancy and Frank, the two youngest of Anne's brood, ran into the hall still in their bed gowns. Seeing Sarah, they stopped in surprise. Anne smiled and held out her arms to the pair, who shared the same dark hair and hazel eyes as their mother. "Come along, children. 'Tis all right."

Frank ran across the hall and hurtled himself into his mother's arms to receive his usual morning kiss, but Nancy moved more slowly, her wide gaze fastened to Sarah.

"Hello," Sarah said with a smile.

Nancy giggled shyly and, after receiving her mother's affection, scurried from the room, Frank close to her heels. Immediately Martha came to the door, the eldest of Anne's children. Where Anne was dark, Martha was fair like her father.

"Oh, hello," Martha said, first looking at Sarah, then to Thomas and her mother. Her pale-blue eyes were curious. "I've started the porridge, and Fran has set the table. Willis is chopping more firewood, and Clive is gathering the eggs."

"You are a blessing, Child." Anne glanced at Sarah. "I had no need to learn to prepare food until our cook left, shortly after Phillip went to war," she explained. Her eyes clouded, but only momentarily. "Tell me about yourself, Sarah, and why you wish employment here."

"Will she be the new cook?" Martha asked hopefully. Thomas hid a smile. Neither his sister nor his nieces knew how to prepare food. Thomas had endured charred meat and stew with vegetables boiled to mush more times than he cared to remember.

"She might," Anne said with a conspiratorial grin at Thomas. Yet his sister's look said more. Realizing she wanted to interview Sarah alone, Thomas rose. "When last I visited, you mentioned the window shutter in the girls' room sticks," he said. "I will see to it."

Before leaving, he glanced Sarah's way. She smiled, her shoulders relaxed, all anxiety vanished. Anne had that way about her, putting people at ease. He was certain this arrangement was an answer from heaven. Returning Sarah's smile, Thomas strode from the room.

※

Humming a little ditty, Sarah let herself in through the servants' entrance. The interview had gone well, and both women admitted they eagerly awaited the day when Sarah would join Anne's family. Though Sarah's title would be cook, Anne had also asked for help with the children after hearing of Sarah's experience with her siblings and with Rupert. As such, her wages would reflect both positions. God was good!

The cook turned from stirring the stew in the kettle over the fireplace trivet, her actions edgy.

"I received a position!" Sarah exclaimed, her words brimming with happiness.

The woman did not reply. The uneasiness in her countenance and the warning look in her eyes alerted Sarah that something was amiss. "Mrs. Leppermier?"

The door banged open, admitting the master of the house. His features were grave. "Sarah," he clipped. "I would have a word with you."

Before she could speak, he exited the room. Aghast, Sarah looked at the cook, hoping for an explanation.

"I'll be praying, Child." The woman's look was sympathetic. "No matter what is said, I hold ye in high regard."

Sarah gave a faint nod, moving to the door on stiff legs. The fangs of dread bit deeply into her soul.

Chapter 7

M r. Wilkerson looked at Sarah grimly from where he stood behind his desk. "You are a thief, and I have the proof," he said quietly.

Certain she'd not heard correctly, Sarah stood frozen in disbelief. His accusation sank to the bottom of her being like a heavy rock disturbing peaceful waters.

"Sir?" she said, her voice raspy.

Mr. Wilkerson arrogantly surveyed her, his hands clasped behind his back. "You were seen skulking about the house this morning and entering the room where the ivory frame was kept. I have no alternative but to believe you are the thief."

Sarah shook her head. "I took no ivory picture frame. You have my word on that."

"You were seen, Sarah. Why else would you move about in the dark without lighting a candle if you were innocent of the crime?"

Sarah desperately tried to think of a reply. Only Mrs. Leppermier knew of Sarah's quest for another job. Sarah had purposely kept the fact from her master for obvious reasons. Yet for all her caution, she stood here, accused.

He narrowed his eyes in speculation. "You do know the punishment for such crimes, Sarah. The least you can expect is a day in the stockades."

Dread dug its talons deeply into Sarah's heart. "Please, Sir, you must believe me! Search my sleeping area, if you so desire."

"For what purpose?" He slowly shook his head, as though addressing a child. "You could have transferred the frame to your partner—perhaps the man I saw here recently? The cabinetmaker. Are you conspiring with him, Sarah? Do you sell stolen merchandise for money?"

"No! I would do no such thing—nor would Thomas."

His brows bunched at her familiar use of Thomas's name, and then his forehead smoothed and he offered a tight smile. "Very well. I am a reasonable man. I'll turn you over to the constable to be publicly punished. Instead, I will lengthen your term of indenture by one year and issue a contract for you to sign."

Sarah's eyes widened. Was such an action lawful? Yet it made no sense. If he considered her a thief, why would he want her to continue working for him?

The answer was obvious, so obvious it kindled her anger. He knew she had not taken the frame. This was only a scheme devised to keep her here.

140

"No," she said bravely, lifting her chin. "I will sign nothing."

His fleshy lips narrowed. "You'll do as I tell you!" He walked over to her and grabbed her elbow. "Or I'll see to it that you are publicly whipped—forty-nine lashes to be carried out at one time. My three friends, whom you met during the celebration, would be most eager to testify to the constable on my behalf and swear how you've also stolen from them. Especially after the unforgivable treatment you and *your friend* meted out to them."

Sarah's blood turned cold. Few people survived so many lashes given at one time. No one would believe the word of an indentured convict against that of four prominent gentlemen.

Mr. Wilkerson began to walk with her to the door. She dragged her feet, now very afraid.

"A night in the springhouse might help you think differently," he said, forcing her to move as he tugged her arm. "When you're given time to dwell on the choices, another year of indenture might not seem so horrible in comparison."

Tightness clenched Sarah's throat, but she couldn't speak. He pulled her, struggling, to the springhouse. Roughly he pushed her inside, and Sarah went tumbling to the ground. Her palms stung as they scraped hard earth. The door slammed shut, and the suffocating cloak of darkness fell. A heavy thump and scrape of a wooden bar being dropped across the outside of the door sounded ominous in the chilled room.

Disbelieving, her mind too numb to grapple with the enormity of the plight that had befallen her, she struggled to sit up and stared into the darkness.

🙚🙘

Sarah was unaware of the passage of time, though she knew it must be hours. Crossing her arms, shivering, she determined to escape. The cry of freedom demanded to be heard, its peal reverberating throughout her soul. If she would not be granted liberty, then she would seize it! She had waited too long for the day.

Despite her doubts and questions of how God could allow such a thing to happen, she breathed a prayer. "Heavenly Father, help me! If I am forced to stay, You know what he will do. Please protect me from the evil intentions of that man. . . ."

Sarah staggered in the direction of the door, careful to avoid the narrow brook that bubbled to her right. Her hands made contact with stone, and using it as a guide, she slowly walked along the wall until she found the door. She pushed against it, though such efforts proved futile since it had been barred from the outside. From earlier visits to this structure, she knew the walls were strong. The place was as secure as a fort.

In frustration, Sarah repeatedly banged her fists against the door, until her hands throbbed with heated pain. Angry tears filled her eyes. "Why, God? Why did You let this happen to me? Why?" At last, spent, she allowed her fists to slide down the wooden door while her forehead dropped to its rough surface.

"Sarah?"

The voice was weak, muffled, coming from the other side. Instantly alert, she lifted her head, her eyes going wide with hope. "I'm here! Rupert, is that you?"

"Yes," the boy replied. "I waited for you to come bid me good night, then said my prayers without you. I heard a voice in my head telling me to go to the springhouse."

The hairs on the back of Sarah's neck prickled, but she didn't dwell on his words. "Rupert, you must let me out. Can you lift the bar?" Sarah's brows drew together. The boy was so small, and the beam was heavy.

She heard a grunt and the slight scraping of wood, followed by a thump. "I can't," he said, his words remorseful.

Sarah closed her eyes and tried to think. "Find Mrs. Leppermier or Grace and bring one or both of them here. But tell no one else."

There was a pause. "Sarah? How did you get in there?"

She clenched her hands on the wood. Despite the truth—that Bartholomew Wilkerson was a horrid man with wicked motives—she could not hurt his son by telling him so. "Never mind. 'Tis not important you should know. Go find help, there's a good lad."

Silence met her plea. Sarah prayed that the boy would not be offended but would do as she asked. Intolerable minutes passed before she heard the wooden bar slide up. In sudden caution, she backed away from the entrance as the door creaked open. What if the master had returned with an even more despicable act in mind?

A cloaked form stood silhouetted against the starlit sky, the smaller form of Rupert behind it. Sarah stood still, her heart hammering in her ears, her fist pressed to her mouth to still the scream that wanted to escape.

"Sarah?" Grace whispered.

Relief melted through Sarah, dissolving the ice that had frozen her blood. She stepped forward and hugged her friend.

"What will you do?" Grace whispered solemnly.

"I don't know." She clutched Grace's forearms. "Yet I cannot stay."

"But you have only a few more days left of your contract!"

In the hours she had sat in the dark, pondering her dilemma, Sarah had reached a decision. "I would rather risk being publicly whipped or put in the stockades than to stay here and wait to see what he will do to me."

"Sarah, the penalty for an escaped convict may be death—"

"So be it," Sarah stated firmly. "This country's brave men are fighting to the death to procure our land's freedom. I'll do no less when it comes to mine. Though my oppressor is of a different nature than the foe that the colonies wage war against, it is through meditating on this country's courage that I have found a measure of my own. Do ye understand, Grace?"

Grace shook her head, her brow wrinkled in confusion.

Sarah attempted a smile. "Never mind. I must go."

"Sarah?" Rupert asked, his voice fearful. "Will they kill you?"

She knelt to better see his face in the moon's glow. A pang struck her heart at his woeful expression. "I pray not. You mustn't tell a soul about tonight, especially the part you played."

He nodded, and Sarah kissed him on the forehead. She clutched Grace's arm once more, then hurried away.

🙏

Thomas bade a late good night to Jeremy, his thirteen-year-old apprentice, who slept on a mat in the shop. Wearily, Thomas climbed the stairs to the loft, a copy of *The Pennsylvania Evening Post* in one hand, a candle in the other. He made himself comfortable, pulling the ribbon from his hair, then sat upon his cot to read any latest news of the war.

One column held an update concerning a recent battle. As Thomas read the numbers killed and wounded, a strong sense of self-reproach came over him. He lifted his gaze from the print and stared at the opposite wall, watching the shadow from the flickering flame dance on the whitewashed surface.

How long he sat, staring, he did not know, but when the frenzied pounding came at the shop door, it was shocking enough to make his hands jerk and tear the half sheet of crown paper.

Irritated, he laid aside the ruined newspaper and hurried downstairs in his stocking feet, the pounding at the door never ceasing. Jeremy stood near his mat and stared at Thomas, his eyes wide.

"Think you, Sir, that the Redcoats have come?"

Before opening the door, Thomas offered a reassuring smile. "Nay, Lad. Nothing so tragic." He lifted the beam and stared at the dark figure on the doorstep—a woman. She stepped forward into the light. "Sarah!" he exclaimed in shock.

A mass of tangled ringlets covered her shoulders, and the mobcap was missing. Her dress was dirty as though she had lain on the ground. Smudges of dirt covered her pale cheeks. Her eyes were wide with fear, but something else as well. Determination.

"What happened?" he asked. "Are you hurt?"

She shook her head, as if she didn't want to discuss it. "I need sanctuary. Will ye help me?"

"Is there trouble at Wilkerson's estate?" Thomas asked, confused.

"Nothing of that nature," Sarah stated impatiently. "Please, Thomas. I've nowhere else to turn!"

Knowing he must calm her before he could get her to make sense, Thomas put an arm around Sarah's shoulders and shepherded her to the low fire. Jeremy had not moved, but curiosity had replaced the fear in his eyes as he stared at Sarah.

"Stop your gawking, and make yourself useful, Lad," Thomas said quietly as he helped Sarah sit at the table's bench by the fire. "Bring her a cup of that coffee you made earlier."

Jeremy nodded and scurried toward a high shelf. He pulled down one of two pewter mugs and set about his task.

"Now," Thomas said, turning his attention to Sarah, who stared blankly at the waning fire. Her eyes focused on him, traveling to his unbound hair that touched his shoulders and reminding Thomas he was unfit for company. Rather than bring attention to that fact by rising to tuck his shirt into his breeches and fasten the shirt's top four buttons, he tried to focus on the problem at hand.

"Tell me, Sarah. What tragedy brings you here in the middle of the night—and in such disheveled condition?"

Jeremy walked over to her, offering the pewter cup. Accepting it, she took a steadying drink before staring into Thomas's eyes. "I will tell you everything, but, in turn, will ye promise to help me, no matter what I say?"

Thomas felt a twinge of unease, but the anxiety in her eyes stilled his qualms. "Aye, Sarah. You have my word."

Chapter 8

The boy apprentice, seeming to realize his presence was not desired, went upstairs. Once Sarah told Thomas everything, including her fear of Mr. Wilkerson doing to her what he'd done to Grace, she waited for his response. His eyes had deepened to a stormy blue, and his mouth was drawn tight in anger. Sarah thought his ire might be directed at her, so she opened her mouth to defend her actions, but he shook his head.

"It's not you I'm angered with, Sarah. I understand your reasons for escape." His features softened with concern. "Yet you have put yourself in a precarious position. A runaway is still a runaway and subject to punishment by law."

"Think you they will truly give me forty-nine lashes?" she all but whispered.

Again Thomas's expression grew grim. "Is that what he told you?"

She nodded.

"Sarah, I seriously doubt they would give a woman accused of theft forty-nine lashes on her first offense."

"But they would not see this as a first offense. Few people know I took my sister's place. I'm looked upon as a true convict."

To her shock, he dropped down on the bench beside her and took hold of her hand. "Then, if necessary, I'll testify on your behalf. My word holds some merit because of who my father was." His voice was low, determined. "However, you must return to the Wilkerson estate. Otherwise the sentence could be extreme."

The wave of gratitude that first swept over her was replaced by one of fear, and she snatched her hand away. "How can you say such a thing? You know I cannot go back."

"It's the only way. To escape makes you appear guilty. Such an action will not aid your case."

"And what if he attacks me?" she asked, her voice strained. "What if he does to me what he did to Grace?"

A flicker of anger shot through his eyes, then disappeared. "We will pray to the heavenly Father and ask Him to bestow on you His divine protection."

Giving a faint nod, she looked down at her lap.

He put his hands to her shoulders, startling her into meeting his gaze. "You must put your hope in God, Sarah, as all of this land is doing in its fight for liberty. Trust

145

that He will take care of you and that His righteousness will prevail so that you may win your own freedom."

" 'Tis a hard thing," she whispered, the tightness in her throat cutting off her voice. "And yet, I do so want to trust. . . ."

Sympathy gleamed in his eyes, and he drew her close. Suddenly the swift beating of her heart stemmed not from fear but rather from the powerful feel of his arms encircling her. Her ear lay against his solid chest, beneath which his heart pounded just as erratically. The soft brush of his hair tickled her cheek while the pleasant musk, combined with the sweet aroma of wood shavings—a scent uniquely his—made Sarah woozy, yet strangely alive.

In wonderment, she lifted her head. Her stomach tumbled when he touched his warm lips to her brow. Their gazes briefly met before he slowly dipped his head to brush his lips across hers. Sarah's heart ceased beating. The kiss lasted mere seconds, but she knew she would remember this moment for a lifetime.

When he pulled away, self-consciousness wouldn't allow her to meet his gaze. "I'll see you home," he said after a long moment, his voice strange.

At this, she swiftly looked up. "Please, Thomas. I promise to return, as you have advised. But I need time—just this night—to reconcile my feelings in the matter."

"Sarah," he said, his voice hoarse. "You cannot stay here."

Her cheeks flamed at what he must think of her after she so readily accepted his kiss. Embarrassed, she pushed him away and rose from the bench. "Never fear, Sir. I am no doxy to seek a man's bed! I thought only to sleep by the fire. If you won't help me, I'll find another place to rest my head. I've slept beneath the stars before and in worse places than that, I assure you."

He also stood to his feet. Still feeling the sting of humiliation, she stepped back—and came against the wall.

"Sarah, I never gave nor suggested any ill construction to your words," he said patiently. "I know you're a woman of pure heart." He stepped forward and gently pulled one of her stiff hands from her crossed arms. "Regardless of how innocent it may seem to let you take my cot for the night while I sleep down here with Jeremy, the townspeople are likely to misconstrue the situation and regard you as a woman of ill repute."

The truth of his words made her bow her head in shame. "Forgive me, Thomas. I didn't think."

He placed a finger beneath her chin, lifted it, and offered a tolerant smile. "It's understandable. You are overwrought. I'll take you to my sister's house for the night. There you'll be safe."

Grateful, she nodded.

⁂

When Thomas collected Sarah from Anne's the following morning, she was quiet. Later, as he guided the wagon onto the road of Wilkerson's estate and she still had not spoken, Thomas looked at her. "You are silent this morn."

Brow furrowed, she turned to him. "I've been mulling over the conversation I

146

had with Anne." She paused, ashamed. "I hesitate to speak so, but I was having a difficult time understanding how God could let this happen to me."

When she didn't expound further, Thomas nodded. "Permit me. Anne told you that God wasn't responsible for bringing misfortune but rather it was the result of evil men who make evil choices. Since man has been given the gift of free will, God will not interfere with those choices. Yet to His children who obey His commands and confidently rely and trust in Him, He will deliver them from the hands of the enemy and to a place of safety."

She lifted her brows, surprised. "She spoke of our discussion?"

"No. Anne would never divulge a confidence. In years past, she has also told me as much. My sister is an intelligent woman of strong spirit. Tell me, has she eased your fears?"

"She answered the question that has long plagued me, 'tis true. Yet I am still apprehensive of the future."

"Shall we pray?"

To Sarah's amazement, Thomas pulled the wagon over and held out his hand. Shyly, she gave hers to him, and he bowed his head. His words were confident as he asked God to give them peace, wisdom, and protection, also asking for His divine intervention.

"Thank you," she said, touched.

His eyes reassured, and he squeezed her fingers before returning his hand to the reins. "Remember, Sarah. God is bigger than the difficulty you face."

Once they arrived at the estate, Sarah clung to Thomas's words as she watched Mr. Wilkerson storm outside. She had barely stepped off the wagon before the man grasped her arm and pulled her toward the house.

"You'll be greatly sorry for attempting to escape," he snarled.

"I returned of my own free will," Sarah argued, trying to wrest her arm from his iron hold.

"Tell that to the constable when he arrives. I have sent Morton to fetch him." He shoved her inside, but before he could shut the door behind them, Thomas moved to the entrance.

"Be gone," Mr. Wilkerson said. "This is none of your concern."

"I beg to differ, Sir. Anything relating to Sarah is of the utmost concern to me."

Despite the grave situation, Sarah's heart leaped. Had Thomas stated his intentions, or was she reading more into his words than was there?

"Sarah is my indenture. She is under a convict's contract, and as such, she has sorely abused the law."

"As have you, Sir, in your treatment of her, as well as other indentures in your household—namely a woman named Grace," Thomas rejoined quietly.

Mr. Wilkerson regarded him in incredulous anger. "You dare speak to me in this manner and in my own home? I have broken no law!"

"I speak not of the written law man has devised, but rather of God's Law, as revealed in His holy Word."

"What insolence! Leave my house at once!"

Thomas did not budge. "I shall not go until I am assured of Sarah's safety."

"Now you accuse me?" the older man sputtered. "What lies has the wench told you?"

"I merely state the facts as I perceive them."

"Though he may not accuse you," a sober voice abruptly announced from the doorway, "I, and others, most certainly do."

Sarah turned in shock to see the constable standing near the open door, a solemn expression on his lined face.

Her master pointed an accusatory finger Sarah's way. "This indenture has stolen an item of worth from my household. I demand you arrest her. And this man," he continued, pointing his finger at Thomas, "I suspect to be her accomplice."

"I have stolen nothing," Sarah countered firmly. "Nor has Thomas. You have no proof."

"My proof is my word. I am a gentleman of means, and that should be testimony enough against the word of a convict and her, her. . ." He sought for a fitting word to describe Thomas.

"Father?" a small voice broke into the discord.

Everyone looked toward the entrance near the stairwell. Rupert stood in his bed gown, sleepily rubbing his eye with one fist. With the other hand he held an ivory picture frame clutched to his chest.

"What have you there, Lad?" Thomas asked, moving his way. "May I see?"

Rupert eyed Thomas, uncertain, then nodded and held his treasure out. " 'Tis my mother, Sir." He looked toward his father. "I know I wasn't supposed to take it, but. . ."

His words trailed off in fear, and Sarah stepped forward and knelt before him. Remembering their conversation the previous evening, she finished the boy's sentence. "But you were lonely for your mother and slept with her likeness since you couldn't have her with you. Is that not true, Rupert?"

Hanging his head, a great tear rolling from his eye, he nodded. Thomas faced Mr. Wilkerson. "Is this the item which you accused Sarah of taking?" The older man frowned, gave a stiff nod, and Thomas turned to the constable. "Then it would appear there is no longer a need for an arrest. Correct, Edward?"

"Unfortunately, Thomas, that is not the case."

Shocked, Sarah watched the newcomer step in front of her master. "Bartholomew Wilkerson," the constable said, "through the authority invested in me by the township of Philadelphia, I place you under arrest for a suspected liaison with the enemy, as well as for harboring pro-British sympathies."

"Outrageous!" the accused man sputtered. "I'm as much a Patriot as you are."

"On the contrary, several highly venerated men have come forward stating otherwise," the constable rejoined. "Will you leave peaceably, or need I exert force? I have men at my disposal to aid me, should such a task prove necessary."

The estate owner opened his mouth to speak, cast a look at his son staring up at him in confusion, then shook his head and marched out the door. The constable followed.

Sarah blinked, startled by the speed with which events had progressed. Only seconds ago she'd stood accused, and now her master was going in her place?

Sensing the child tremble, she gave him a hug. "Go ask Mrs. Leppermier to give you a dish of plum pudding. Tell her I said it was all right."

The boy's eyes widened. "Before breakfast?"

She grinned. "This time only."

The thought of a sweet in the morning brought a smile to his face. After he left, Thomas spoke. "You truly love him."

"Aye," she said, as Rupert skipped to the kitchen with thoughts of his father temporarily forgotten. "Think you that Anne would agree to Rupert coming to visit? His stepmother cares naught for him, so she would likely condone the arrangement."

"I believe Anne would agree."

She hesitated, then looked at him. "I have a second favor to ask. Would your sister consider hiring another indenture? I believe Grace would be an asset. Her term here as a housemaid is almost at an end as well."

"Anyone would be an improvement over Matilda," he said with feeling. "I'll discuss the matter with Anne."

"Thank you." Suddenly the enormity of what had transpired struck Sarah fully. "God answered our prayer," she whispered. "He delivered me from the hands of my enemy, as Anne said He would."

Thomas nodded. "Yes, He did. . .as He will do for all who serve Him."

Something about his manner made her peer at him more closely. "Is anything the matter?"

He was quiet a moment. "I had not thought to tell you at this time, but in light of the circumstances. . ." He released a breath. "Let us go to the garden and talk."

Perplexed, she rose to go with him.

They walked side by side in the shade of the chestnut trees. Thomas gravely stared ahead, clasping one of his wrists behind him. "For long weeks I have agonized over a decision. A childhood tragedy shaped my beliefs, and I made a vow never to take a life. Yet I can no longer idly stand by and watch while my friends and neighbors fight for this country's freedom." He halted on the path and faced her. "I'm going to join the war."

"Oh, Thomas," she breathed, feeling faint. She clutched her skirt. "When?"

"After my last work order is filled. A month, perchance." He took her hand. "Do not fear for my life, sweet Sarah. God will protect me."

Before she could formulate a response, he volleyed another cannonball through the unsteady foundation of her whirling emotions.

"Forgive me if I speak too rashly, but I must say more. I care deeply for you, Sarah—nay, I love you and want to protect you always. Bartholomew Wilkerson is detained, but for how long? Then, too, there is the matter of those who harassed you during the celebration. . . ."

She only stared, the chambers of her mind still echoing with his words, "I love you and want to protect you always."

Thomas paused, seeming to realize he'd lost her. "Sarah, I'm asking you to consider becoming my wife and marrying me before I go to war. In bearing my name, you'll be protected from those who mean you harm. Until my return, you shall live with Anne as a member of the family, not as a servant."

His *wife*? Sarah struggled to retain his words, but she could not think. Everything was happening so fast.

"I respect your desire to bring your siblings to America," he continued, "but until this conflict is over, it is impossible to do so. Yet I give you my word that I will acquire passage for them as soon as is feasible." His hands tightened on her fingers when she did not respond. "What say you, Sarah? Will you have me?"

She looked away from his penetrating blue eyes and down at the grass while she endeavored to express herself. "I know not what to say, Thomas. My heart is full, and my thoughts are in a muddle." She shook her head, overwhelmed. "So much has happened this morn—"

Dismay clouded his face, and briefly he closed his eyes. "Forgive me. I spoke too soon. Attribute my blunder to my eagerness at the prospect of sharing my life with you as well as to my concern for your protection. I'll not speak of the matter again." Swiftly he brought the backs of her hands to his lips, released them, and turned away.

Bewildered, Sarah watched him go, the sun's rays highlighting his striking form. Nowhere had she met such a benevolent man, a man who lived his faith without apology, who was not afraid to face danger for righteousness' sake. . .and soon he would be entering the very heart of danger. He was going to war.

The thought frightened her. Would she see him again?

With each step Thomas took away from Sarah, her heart beat harder within her breast, as though punishing her for her foolishness. *Dear Father in heaven, what should I do? I need Your guidance. I do care deeply for him. . . .*

With astonishing clarity, her rampant thoughts melded into one, and she was assured of the course to take.

"Wait!" she cried.

Picking up her skirts, she ran down the path and came to a stop in front of Thomas, where he, too, had halted. "Aye, Thomas," she murmured, suddenly bashful. "I will have you."

His eyes were tender, his smile sad. "No, Sarah."

No? She blinked, certain she had misunderstood. Did he not just ask her to marry him?

"I was wrong to seek your response so soon," he explained. "I see that now. I don't wish you to speak in haste, only to regret doing so later. 'Tis my earnest hope that should you ever seek me out it will be love that compels you. I know many enter a match for convenience's sake, but I want mutual love to be the bond that holds us together."

Awed, Sarah stared at his handsome countenance, convinced of one thing. It didn't matter how much time passed, whether it be a day or a year. Thomas's unselfish words only further persuaded her that this was the man God had chosen for her. She wanted no other.

Placing her hands on either side of his face, Sarah looked deeply into his eyes. "I never have been more certain of anything. And I do love you, Thomas Gray."

Hope lit his features. "You are certain?"

She grinned, her heart buoyant. "Aye."

To her delight, he pulled her into his strong embrace and kissed her, sealing the pledge of their future together.

Sarah didn't know what lay ahead in their land's fight for freedom, but she vowed to be grateful for the moments God gave her with Thomas. Every day was a gift, and she would treasure each one.

Epilogue

In the darkening twilight, Sarah stood on the grassy hill and scanned the crowd of merry-goers. Grace's daughter, Hannah, played with Phillip and Anne's seven children, while Anne strolled nearby, carrying her newest daughter, Beulah.

Laughing, the children stood in a circle and threw a ball to one another. Hannah's hands were too small to catch it well, and she could only throw it a few feet; but everyone loved the cheerful six-year-old and couldn't refuse her in the game. Grace stood nearby, looking at her child with a mother's loving pride. In the years she'd worked for Anne, she'd responded to the love and kindness showered upon her and grown to know the Lord.

Sarah sighed. So much had happened in the past few years. Two weeks after Thomas left for war, her old master, Mr. Wilkerson, had been banished, though his wife and son were allowed to stay behind. The next day, Sarah had heard the guns of battle at nearby Chadd's Ford. On September 26, the British marched into Philadelphia and occupied the town for nine months. During the following five years, as all other soldiers' wives did, Sarah waited, wept, and prayed for word from her husband. Then last year, two months after the war's end, her beloved had come home. A short time later, Thomas kept his promise to Sarah and answered another strong desire of her heart. That of bringing her family to America.

"Sarah?" Her sister, Dorrie, hurried her way. "Have you seen Charles?"

"I imagine our young brother is with Thomas," Sarah said with a smile. "The two are inseparable since Charles has shown an interest in woodworking."

"Would they have gone to the shop this night?" Dorrie asked in surprise.

Though still frail, she was beautiful, with her cobalt eyes and ginger-brown hair. Happiness made her face glow. That and the attentions of a certain young blacksmith who lived nearby.

"All the shops are closed," Sarah said. "Though I know Thomas is eager to finish the cradle before the time arrives."

Several loud, popping explosions interrupted their conversation, and both women looked toward the heavens, where brilliant starbursts of color painted the evening sky.

"Oh," Dorrie murmured in awe. " 'Tis beautiful."

"That it is," Thomas said, coming up behind them. Charles and a smartly dressed, thirteen-year-old Rupert flanked his sides.

"A wondrous spectacle," Rupert agreed, his voice cracking with manhood.

In the shielding cloak of night, Thomas looped his arm around Sarah's waist, gently drawing her back so that her shoulder blades rested against his chest. " 'Tis the triumphant cry of freedom," he said softly. "One this nation has longed to hear."

Suddenly the babe within Sarah's belly kicked hard against Thomas's arm, and he chuckled. "It would seem our son agrees."

"Aye," Sarah said with a smile, leaning back against him. "How thankful I am that our child will be born in a land that is truly free." Her hand covered Thomas's where it rested against her swollen stomach. "And how thankful I am for you, and men like you, whose bravery made it possible."

She felt his lips brush the top of her head.

"I pray all generations, henceforth, will remember this day and hold it in high regard," Sarah said, watching the rockets light the sky. "That the meaning is not lost and the sacrifices made are not forgotten. . . . Thomas, do you think our country will ever again have to fight a war?"

"Sarah. . ." He turned her to face him. "Why question what we cannot possibly know? I cannot predict the future, yet I can tell you this: God stands for righteousness and looks after His own. Let us thank Him for our liberty this Independence Day and put all worries behind us."

"Aye," she murmured, grateful for this man. Thomas was a strong tower when she needed reassurance, and he was right. God would take care of them, come what may, as He had always done. Through past years, Sarah had finally learned that lesson, and her faith had grown.

"I love you, my husband."

"And with all that I am, I love you."

The glow from the fireworks lit his tender expression as he lowered his head. His lips met hers, and myriad explosions—both in the sky above and in her heart—filled Sarah with joy.

At last, freedom was theirs.

"Proclaim Liberty throughout all the land
unto all the inhabitants thereof."
INSCRIPTION ON THE LIBERTY BELL
FROM LEVITICUS 25:10

BLESSED LAND

by Nancy J. Farrier

Dedication

To Anne, who had so much fun
plotting the story with me.
To Dell and Audrey, who read it in a hurry.
For John, with whom I am blessed.

*In that I command thee this day to
love the L*ORD *thy God,
to walk in his ways,
and to keep his commandments
and his statutes and his judgments,
that thou mayest live and mutliply:
and the L*ORD *thy God shall bless thee
in the land whither thou goest to possess it.*
DEUTERONOMY 30:16

Chapter 1

Spring 1854

The big dun horse whickered softly and stomped his foot. Antonio Escobar grinned and rubbed Grande's neck. "Sorry, amigo. You must be the most jealous horse in all of Tucson. I'm only looking at the señorita, not asking her to marry me."

Antonio continued to brush Grande as he looked back down the stable aisle where his cousin, Chico, talked to a young woman at the entrance of the building. Chico lifted his horse's leg off his knee and stood slowly, like someone whose back has been bent in an awkward position for too long.

Smiling, Antonio watched his handsome cousin at work. Chico, with his silver tongue. Chico, the man at whom all the women flashed their eyes as he swaggered down the street. A chuckle welled up, threatening to burst forth. For once, Chico had met his match. This young woman refused to buy his sweet talk.

The quirt in her hand snapped rhythmically against her skirt. The tip of her long braid swung slightly, showing beneath the scarf she wore over her head. From the cut of her clothing and her proud stance, Antonio gathered she came from a wealthy family. Although he couldn't see her face clearly, he knew she was a stranger to their small pueblo. He watched all the señoritas who came to visit Chico, and this one was new. Perhaps she would be the answer to Antonio's prayers. Despite his assurance to Grande, he hoped that someday the Lord would answer his prayer for a wife and family.

Chico moved around the horse closer to the girl. She lifted the quirt like a weapon and stepped back. Chico flashed his infamous grin, the one designed to set hearts thumping and fans whirring. But to no avail. The girl continued to gesture toward the small adobe house in front of the stables, where Antonio lived and had his workshop.

Grande nickered again and nudged his shoulder. Antonio patted him absently on the neck. "I think I will have to finish you later, amigo. It looks to me like this lady in distress needs rescuing." Antonio nodded his head toward the pair near the door. "Or, perhaps, this time it's Chico who needs help." He laughed softly and sauntered down the aisle, past horses boarded in stalls and others waiting to be shod. Yes, this just might be the one time Chico would lose and he, Antonio, would win.

He could see the young woman more clearly now, even if the view was from the side. He noted the tilt of her head, her slender neck, the smooth, dusky cheek that made him long to run a finger across it. She lifted a slim hand, gesturing once more as if trying to make Chico understand the importance of her mission. Antonio couldn't take his eyes off her. A longing to help and protect her nearly overwhelmed him.

❧☙

Her hand ached from the desperate grip she had on her quirt. Paloma Rivera forced herself to loosen her fingers, trying at the same time to rid herself of the longing to use the small whip to wipe the idiotic grin from this hombre's face. She could feel the anger starting at the pit of her stomach and working its way throughout her body like a living thing. Why wouldn't he help her? Instead, the imbecile seemed to think he could wink at her, and she would swoon at his feet like some empty-headed buffoon.

"Rosita Lopez. I'm looking for my sister, Rosita Lopez," Paloma repeated for what seemed like the hundredth time. "Her husband's name is Pablo. Have you seen them?"

"Is there a problem, Chico?"

Paloma swiveled around to face the newcomer now sauntering down the stable walkway. Her breath caught in her throat. For a moment, she forgot her mission. Gunmetal-black eyes, glinting with humor, captured hers. She noted the stranger's strong arms. Muscular arms. Probably strengthened from his hours of physical labor running the blacksmith shop. His hair, combed straight back, fell in raven waves that dipped and shone in the afternoon light. Paloma gave herself a mental shake, trying to remember why she was here.

Standing straight and as tall as she could at five-one, Paloma blurted, "I explained to this mor. . .um, this man that I'm looking for my sister, Rosita Lopez. Do you know where I can find her?"

She didn't miss the fleeting glance directed toward Chico or Chico's answering shrug. What was going on here?

He bowed slightly to her and said, "Allow me to introduce myself. I'm Antonio Escobar, owner of this establishment."

She nodded in greeting. "Paloma Rivera. As I said, I'm looking for my sister. I must find her."

"And why do you think you will find your sister in a stable?" Antonio grinned, and she noted the slight gap between his front teeth. Why did he have to be so handsome?

She sighed, allowing her gaze to wander over the walls lined with tools and tack for use with the horses. "This was the last address that my sister gave when she wrote home."

"And may I ask how long ago she wrote?"

Paloma shifted uncomfortably. "We haven't heard from her in three years."

"Three years?" Antonio's eyes widened. "And you think that after three years she might still live here—at this address?"

Clenching her jaw, Paloma fought back the tears of frustration. Nothing was working out right. She had ridden to the small pueblo of Tucson, hoping to convince her sister to come back home to Mexico. When Rosita and Pablo moved up here, Tucson was still a part of Mexico. Now, with the Gadsden Purchase signed and the ratification nearly finished, Tucson would soon become a part of the United States of America instead of the United States of Mexico. Hatred welled up inside. She couldn't bear for Rosita to be a citizen of America. She had to bring her back home to Mexico where she belonged.

"Please, Señor Escobar, it's the only place I had to begin my search. I didn't think I would have any trouble finding her. I know she hasn't written, but sometimes the mail is very slow making its way to us."

Antonio's gaze softened as if in sympathy for her plight. "Your sister and her husband aren't here. Perhaps they chose to move on. Many people have trouble making a living in Tucson."

"But Pablo was always good with horses. I thought maybe he worked for you."

Antonio shook his head. "The only one who helps me here is my cousin, Chico." He indicated the young man leaning on the partially shod horse. Chico flashed his idiotic grin at her.

"What did your sister say in her letter to you?" asked Antonio.

"She said they were doing fine, described the town, and mentioned Pablo either getting work at a stable or at a ranch as a blacksmith."

Antonio gestured outdoors with his hand. "There's your answer. Perhaps he's working for one of the big ranchos down south of here."

Paloma felt as if the wind had been knocked from her. How would she ever find Rosita? How many ranches were there to search?

"How long have you lived here?" she asked. "Do you remember Pablo and Rosita at all?"

Antonio smiled softly. "I've only lived here four years, but Chico has lived in Tucson all his life. Do you remember her sister, Chico?"

Paloma turned hopefully to Antonio's cousin. Chico frowned, as if deep in thought.

"Some of the women might have known your sister. Have you asked them?"

With a sigh of resignation, Paloma shook her head. "No, I came here first, hoping she would be here. I'm staying with Señora Fernandez. Perhaps she will know something. Thank you for your help."

Paloma stepped out into the late-afternoon sunlight. Its warmth wrapped around her, giving some slight comfort. Where should she go now? She trudged slowly down the dusty street, lost in thought. A dog slinked out from the side of a building to nose at her skirt, tentatively waving its tail. She smiled and patted the dog, its tail now wagging enthusiastically.

Wait a minute! She straightened so fast the dog scurried off, tucking his tail between his legs. Antonio and Chico had to know something about Rosita and

Pablo. She remembered seeing a saddle and blanket at one side of the stable. Yes, she was certain. They belonged to Rosita. They had been a gift from her father when Rosita and Pablo married. The saddle had been hand-tooled by one of the men who worked for her father. There couldn't be another one like it.

Paloma swiveled around, retracing her steps to the stable. Chico still leaned against the horse's haunch. Antonio's back was toward her, and the two men were apparently having a heated discussion. Chico noticed her and nodded in her direction. Antonio turned.

Paloma strode into the stable, angry at their deception. "I believe you do know my sister," she blurted. "I want to know where she is."

Chico moved to the far side of the horse, as if hoping to escape her anger. Antonio studied her, then spoke quietly, "What makes you think we know of your sister?"

"This saddle," Paloma hissed, gesturing to the saddle not quite covered by the red and gray blanket. "This was a gift to Rosita from my father on her wedding day. I recognize the pattern. The blanket is hers, too. Now, where is she?" Paloma moved to the saddle and jerked the blanket off. She ran her hand lovingly over the roses and leaves carved into the leather.

"I, too, am a maker of saddles," Antonio said softly. "What makes you think I didn't see the pattern somewhere and copy it?"

Unwanted tears burned Paloma's eyes. "This is Rosita's. See these initials carved in the rose petal? I did that the day she left for Tucson. I told her that way she would always remember me."

She wanted to bury her face in the saddle blanket and weep. Where was Rosita? What had happened to her? Why was her saddle here, when these men denied ever knowing her?

"Please," she begged. "You have to tell me where she is."

Antonio studied her for a long moment without speaking. He rubbed the back of his neck. Chico picked up the horse's hoof again and began to scrape away at embedded dirt.

"You will have to ask some of the women around town about your sister." Antonio's eyes reflected an inner sadness. "I can't tell you where this saddle came from. I can only tell you that your sister and her husband aren't here."

Resignation overwhelmed her. She knew she wouldn't get any answers here. Suddenly, exhaustion from the long trip north drained her of strength. Her whole body relaxed, and the daylight faded to darkness. Paloma tried to stop herself from falling, but her muscles refused to respond. She barely felt the strong arms that caught her and lowered her gently to the ground.

As if from a great distance, Paloma heard Antonio and Chico talking.

"Is the señorita all right?" Chico asked.

"I think she's just fainted. Bring some water, and we'll see if we can revive her."

"What will you tell her about Rosita and Pablo?"

"I'll tell her nothing. You won't say anything either, Chico. Understand?"

"But she seems very determined."

Paloma felt a hand gently brush the hair from her face. A finger traced a path down her cheek. She felt a tingle run throughout her body and struggled not to move. She didn't want them to know she could hear what they were saying. She nearly cried out at Antonio's next words.

"We'll just have to be *more* determined, then." Antonio sounded angry. "Rosita's life depends on it."

Chapter 2

Antonio tightened his arms around Paloma. What a beautiful name, Paloma. This young woman appeared as graceful as the dove—her namesake. Although small in stature, she carried herself with a dignity that spoke of determination.

He studied her, noting the gentle curve of her round cheeks. Her full lips were slightly parted, giving a glimpse of small, even teeth. Delicate eyebrows framed what he knew to be large, expressive eyes the color of well-worn leather. Her scarf slipped slowly back on her head. A wisp of nut-brown hair drifted down across her cheek. Tenderly, he smoothed the wayward tendril back into place.

Paloma stirred and groaned.

"Where's the water, Chico? I think she's starting to come around." Taking the dipper full of cool water, Antonio lifted Paloma up and slowly dribbled water into her mouth. He handed the dipper back to Chico and gently wiped the water from her chin. When he looked up, her eyes were open. An unreadable expression clouded their depths.

"Are you feeling better?" In a way, he wished that she would faint again. He could go on holding her all day and never tire.

As if suddenly realizing her whereabouts, Paloma sat up. She gasped and grabbed her head, covering her eyes. For a moment, she leaned once more against his chest, then slowly straightened.

"I'm fine." She sounded disoriented. "My weariness from my long journey has just caught up with me. I need to get back to Señora Fernandez."

"Let me help you up." Antonio slowly lifted her to her feet. She swayed slightly; he hoped, in vain, to catch her again. "I'll walk you to the Señora's house."

The fact that she agreed told him she still wasn't herself. He tucked her arm into his and set off at a leisurely pace.

"I'm sure you know where my sister is." Paloma's soft words barely reached him. "I have to find her. You don't understand how important this is."

He studied her, seeing for the first time the dark circles under her eyes. Her face seemed paler than when she had first walked into the stable. Perhaps she did have a good reason for finding Rosita. Maybe he should listen to her. Try to understand.

"Why don't you tell me the reason it's so important for you to find your sister? You must have traveled a long way to get here. I hope you didn't travel alone."

She shook her head, wincing as if it hurt. "I came with my brother, Berto. He dropped me off at my mother's cousin's, Señora Fernandez. He and some of my father's vaqueros continued on to a friend's rancho to purchase some horses."

For a moment she walked in silence. In the distance, Antonio could see the walls of the *presidio* where the Mexican soldiers kept watch for raiding parties of Apaches. Although Tucson was relatively safe, many of the surrounding ranches had been abandoned due to the fierce attacks.

"Did you live in Tucson during the war?" Paloma asked.

Antonio frowned. "No, I moved here after the end of the war in 1848. Chico and my uncle and aunt were glad to have me come."

"Then perhaps you can understand my reason for needing to find Rosita." Paloma looked up at him, her eyes sparkling as some of her passionate fire returned. "You see, my family lived near the Nueces River, in the territory disputed by the two governments. The Americans," she nearly spat out the words, "wanted the land between the Nueces and the Rio Grande for themselves even though the Mexican government refused to sell to them. The Americans decided to fight for that land. They stole it from us and killed many fine Mexican men."

She stopped, obviously struggling to get her emotions under control. Antonio wanted to wrap his arms around her and take away the pain that must be tearing her apart. He put his hand over hers and tightened his arm.

Her eyes brimmed with tears. "My brother died in the war. Our beautiful home was taken from us. Of course, the American government promised that we could keep our homes, but they lied. They used trickery to swindle us out of our lands and our homes."

"Where do you live now?" Antonio asked.

"We live in Mexico." She raised her head and stared at him. "I wouldn't live anywhere else. My mother's health was ruined by the hardships of the war and the aftermath. My father struggled to rebuild what we had in a different location. Only by the grace of God do we have food to eat and a place to live."

"Then perhaps the grace of God should be enough." Antonio stopped as she turned to him, jerking her hand free from his arm. Anger sparked in her eyes.

"How can you say that? Is the death of my brother, the ruin of countless families, and stolen lands nothing to you? Don't you care about what the Americans have done? I will never live in America, and I won't stand for my sister living here either. This is now American territory. I will find Rosita, and I will bring her home."

Antonio watched Paloma stride across the street to Señora Fernandez's small adobe house. The riding crop that had dangled from her wrist moments before, she now used to hammer an angry tattoo against her skirt. He smiled. This was the woman for him. He had always longed for a woman with passion, one with intelligence who would challenge him at every turn. Paloma Rivera was that woman.

❧

Paloma stepped through the thick doorway of the small adobe house. She leaned back against the wall, closing her eyes, fighting back tears of frustration. She had hoped that, by appearing to be a little disoriented, she could trick Antonio into telling her what he knew about Rosita and Pablo. Instead, she had lost her temper and ruined everything. Now, he would never talk to her. How would she ever find her sister before her brother returned to take her back to their home in Mexico? She didn't have much time, two to three weeks at the most.

A wave of anger swept through her again. How dare Antonio suggest that God's grace be enough? Didn't he understand the hurt and destruction Mexico had suffered? He probably lived in some remote area unaffected by the war. But she had seen the devastation firsthand. She'd heard the cannons. She'd seen the bloodied fields. She remembered the graves visited by weeping mothers, widows, and orphans. These haughty Americans had much to answer for. She couldn't wait to get Rosita and escape from here.

"Señora Fernandez?" Paloma walked through the main room to the kitchen, where she could hear the rattle of dishes.

"Si, *mija,* please call me *'tia.'* I know you aren't really my niece, but your mother and I were as close as sisters when we were young." Elena Fernandez smiled, her eyes crinkling into mere slits. "Come sit down. How do you like our little pueblo Tucson? You haven't even told me what you went to find. Did you just want to walk around?"

Paloma smiled as she sat down. Her mother had told her that Elena could talk the legs off a donkey. That was why she hadn't questioned her before setting out on her search for Rosita. She'd been so sure of where to find her sister, she didn't want to be detained by a lot of useless conversation.

"Tucson seems very nice, tia." Paloma paused, not wanting to offend. "I only wish it would stay a part of Mexico."

Elena patted a ball of corn *masa* between her fingers, flattening the dough into a rounded tortilla. "I think it will not be so bad to be in America. If it's God's will, then He will make it right." She tossed the small tortilla on the hot stove, flipping it quickly to brown both sides. "Will you stay here, mija? There are many fine young men here who would make good husbands for you. I can ask my friends, and we will introduce you. Maybe we can have a small fiesta just so you can meet someone."

Paloma sighed. "I don't want to live here. I want to live in Mexico. It's where I belong. It's where all Mexicans belong. I wouldn't marry someone who is willing to live as an American."

Elena's eyebrows arched, and her eyes widened. She picked up another ball and began to shape it. "But, what of God's will? Didn't He even lead the Israelites to other lands? Those who were faithful to Him were blessed no matter where they lived."

"They were slaves for the most part." Paloma was having trouble keeping her temper. "I don't want to be a slave to the Americans."

Elena stared out the window, a dreamy expression on her face. "I would think to have God's blessings one would be willing to endure anything. Even America might be a blessed land."

Her quiet words pierced Paloma's heart. Was her anger against the Americans keeping her from God's blessings? She shook her head, forcing the thought from her mind.

"Tia Elena, I came here to find my sister, Rosita. I thought I knew right where she lived, but she isn't there anymore. The man who lives there says I have to ask the women in town about her. Do you know where I can find Rosita?"

Elena grabbed at the bubbling tortilla, preparing to turn it. Her fingers missed, and she jerked them back from the hot stove, a look of pain on her face. Quickly, she recovered, plucked the tortilla, and flipped it.

"Are you all right?" Paloma jumped up from her chair and grabbed her aunt's hand. The tips of her fingers showed the red marks of a burn that would probably blister.

"It's nothing, mija." Elena pulled her hand away and lifted the finished tortilla from the stove. "It happens all the time when I'm cooking."

Paloma once more caught her aunt's plump hand firmly in hers, stopping her from picking up another ball from the pile. Elena fidgeted nervously for a moment, then looked up.

"Tia, do you know where Rosita is?" Paloma tried to speak softly. But she really wanted to shake someone and get the answers she needed.

"If Antonio said you should talk to some of the women, then that is what you should do." Elena spoke as if the matter were settled. "Some of my friends get together to do embroidery. Maybe we could take a few minutes to drop by and talk with them before I finish our supper." She pulled her hand from Paloma's and covered the balls of masa with a damp cloth, then led the way out the door.

An hour later, Paloma followed Tia Elena back into the dim interior of the house. Silently, she watched as her aunt lit a lantern in the kitchen and added wood to the fire in the stove. The last hour had been a lesson in frustration. All of the women had been very polite and eager to talk with her until they found out her real reason for being there. They longed for news of Mexico, but when it came to Rosita and Pablo they refused to talk.

She didn't know so many women at once could have an unspoken agreement to stop talking or change the subject. Every time she mentioned her sister, one of the women would totally ignore her and begin talking about a certain young man courting a young lady. . .or how soon the newest señora would become a mother. . . or some other subject that had nothing to do with Rosita. They only talked to her when she willingly told them about the people she knew in Mexico.

She hadn't missed the furtively exchanged glances when they must have thought she wasn't looking. The quick shake of the head here and a glare of warning there told her more than their words could have. These women knew something about Rosita, and Paloma had to find out what.

In the midst of stirring beans for supper, Paloma stopped her spoon in midair. Poised above the pot, the utensil dripped bean juice in a steady rhythm. She swiveled around to where Tia Elena was just cooking the last of the corn tortillas.

"Tia?" Paloma let out the breath she'd been holding unconsciously. "You knew where Rosita lived. If you didn't know about Rosita, how did you know Antonio was the one I talked to?"

Paloma grasped both of her tia's hands in hers. "Tia, please, you must tell me what you know about Rosita."

She watched as her aunt began to tremble. A look of pure fright crossed Elena's face. Tiny beads of sweat dotted her forehead.

"Oh, mija, don't make me say this. If you love your sister, don't make me say things I shouldn't."

The acrid scent of burning corn filled the air. Elena tugged her hands free and whirled around to the stove to toss the scorched tortilla away from the heat. Her hands shook so bad Paloma feared she might burn herself again.

"I just want to find my sister. Is that too much to ask?" Paloma fought to keep the frustration from her voice.

Tia Elena turned back to her, tears filling her eyes. "Yes, mija. I know you don't understand right now, but you must trust me. Your mother and I were best of friends. I would never mislead you. But right now, you have to listen when I tell you to give up your search for Rosita."

Paloma began to stir the beans again. Before her trip to Tucson, her mother had insisted that she stay with her old friend Elena. Had her mother known something she hadn't known? At the time, she only thought her mother wanted to learn how her childhood friend was doing. No matter what, Paloma knew her tia Elena could be trusted. Still, she had to find Rosita. How could she vanish like this? Why would it hurt to look for her?

Tomorrow she would return to the stable. Antonio wouldn't give her the information, but perhaps, if he wasn't there, she could convince Chico to help her. With his empty-headed ways, all she had to do was smile at him, and he would tell her anything she wanted to hear. She frowned and shrugged away the thought that such a move would be deceptive. Hopefully, he would tell her the truth.

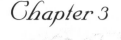

The next morning Paloma helped her tia clean the dishes. "The morning is a fine one for a walk, Tia Elena. Do you mind if I go for a stroll after we finish here?"

Elena smiled broadly. "Not at all, mija. Just remember not to go outside the edge of Tucson by yourself. The Apaches and banditos can be dangerous."

"I'll just look around close to home," Paloma assured her.

A few minutes later she slipped out the door and strolled slowly until she couldn't see the small adobe anymore. Then she quickened her pace. With purpose in her stride, she headed directly for Antonio's stable. Her full skirt swished softly, dancing with the swirls of dust raised by her feet. The ever-present quirt brushed softly against her side.

She stopped just outside the open doors of the stable. The steady bang of a hammer told her that Chico must be working on a horseshoe. The quiet murmur of voices from the side of the building stirred her hope that Antonio was discussing business with someone and wouldn't notice her. If so, this might be the right time to corner Chico and get some information from him.

She stepped from the bright sunlight into the dim interior. Standing still, she allowed a few moments for her eyes to adjust. Chico, his back to the stable door, pounded a red-hot horseshoe on an anvil. A sweet-faced sorrel mare tied nearby turned to stare at her. She couldn't see Antonio anywhere.

The sharp clangs of the hammer beating the horseshoe stopped suddenly, and quiet enveloped Paloma. She wiped her sweaty palms against her skirt. As Chico turned her way, she forced a smile on her face.

"Good morning, Chico." She hoped he couldn't read her intense dislike of him in her eyes.

"Paloma, you look so beautiful this morning." He picked up the horseshoe with a set of tongs, then dropped the hot metal into a bucket of water. His idiotic grin showed through the steam that boiled up in a cloud. He stepped closer to her, and she fought the urge to back away.

"Your eyes could make a man's heart melt." Chico reached out to touch her. She flinched, and he dropped his hand. His grin wavered only slightly. "I love the challenge of taming a wild mare," he spoke softly, swaggering over to stroke the sorrel mare. "Perhaps you would accompany me to dinner this evening. I can show you a wonderful time."

Repressing a shudder, Paloma knew she couldn't carry out this ruse. How could she even pretend to like this man when he was so full of himself? Comparing her to a horse. Indeed! Anger boiled up, and she resisted to no avail.

"I want you to tell me where Rosita and Pablo are," she snapped, her quirt slapping rapidly against her leg. "I won't give up, and I'm sure you know something. Now, tell me before I lose my temper completely." She glared at him. "Remember, sometimes a mare can pack a mighty kick."

Chico tried to laugh, but it came out more like a strangled squawk. "I think Antonio told you to talk to the women, my pretty."

"I'm not your pretty," she hissed, "and I have talked to the women. They refused to say anything." Paloma closed her eyes, fighting for a modicum of self-control. "Why won't anyone tell me about my sister? Is there some dark secret about her? I'm beginning to wonder if the whole town has done something shameful. Maybe you've all decided to lie to protect one another."

Chico lost his grin as she spoke. He looked wary and perhaps a little afraid. "I have to get back to work." He headed toward the water bucket and the now-cooled horseshoe.

"No." Even she was surprised by the forceful tone with which she spoke. "You have to help me."

"Perhaps I can help you instead, Señorita Rivera." Antonio's voice sounded close behind her, stopping her from saying more.

Paloma spun around. Antonio stood with the sunlight at his back, his face mostly in the shadows. Still, she couldn't help but notice her response to him. It wasn't just his good looks or the way his broad shoulders complemented his narrow hips. There was something else that attracted her to him. She just couldn't quite figure out what. She found herself wanting to stand here, simply looking at him. She loved the way his homespun shirt hung loosely over his muscular frame. The accent of the bright red sash he wore heightened the effect. She couldn't look away.

"How can I help you, Paloma?" Antonio sounded amused, as if he had read her thoughts.

"I–uh. I—" Paloma stuttered. Then, forcing herself to look away, she managed to regain control of her thoughts. "Tell me where to find Rosita. I'm sure you know where she is. No one I've met seems to want me to find her, but I have to. I won't quit until I do. I explained to you yesterday why." She stopped, knowing she was rambling on without making much sense.

Antonio stepped closer. She could see his dark eyes flashing.

"Have you prayed about all this?" He spoke so softly, she might have thought she imagined his words if she hadn't seen his lips move.

"Of course, I prayed," she retorted. "I prayed with my mother before I even began my journey to Tucson. We prayed that I would find my sister and get her safely back to Mexico, where she belongs."

He studied her silently. "I guess what I'm asking is, did you pray about God's will in finding your sister?"

She stood straight, clenching her fists at her sides. "And why wouldn't it be God's will? Doesn't He want her to be where she belongs? How dare you question whether I'm seeking to do what God wants?"

"I'm sorry, Paloma. There are circumstances you don't understand. But I will help you look for your sister."

Paloma swallowed the fresh tirade of angry words forming on her lips. "You what?"

"I said, I will help you look."

As he spoke, she studied his face before nodding her acceptance of his offer. "All right, where shall we start?"

"Why don't you accompany me to a couple of the ranches near Tucson? We could ask if Pablo is working there."

She nodded. "That's fine. Maybe on the way you can tell me these circumstances I don't understand."

He smiled, and her heart fluttered. "I'm sure there are many things we can find to discuss."

❧

Antonio secretly watched Paloma as she rode. She sat astride the horse in an easy manner—one that only came with hours of time in the saddle. For an instant, he wished her horse would become lame so that he could insist on her riding with him. He longed to hold her again. All afternoon, she had pummeled him with questions about her sister and the circumstances he had so foolishly mentioned. It had taken his every effort to dodge her inquires.

He hated leading her on. Hated making her think that he was helping her when he really wasn't. He knew Pablo and Rosita weren't at the ranches they visited. But he couldn't let Paloma know that. He had to keep up the pretense of a search until her brother returned to take her home to Mexico. After all, he'd given his promise to a dying man. He couldn't reveal what he knew.

Moving his horse, Grande, closer to her mare, Antonio noted that Paloma's long-legged horse was nearly as tall as his. As slight as Paloma was, it would take no effort at all to scoop her out of the saddle and deposit her in front of him. He smiled, wondering what her reaction would be.

Earlier he had asked her if she had prayed about finding her sister. Now, his conscience pricked and reminded him that he hadn't really prayed about Paloma. He just assumed God had answered his prayer for a wife, but he hadn't checked to be sure. What if she wasn't the right one? After all, she insisted she wouldn't marry a man who lived in the United States of America. And he didn't intend to move back to Mexico. Too many bad memories were there for him. He wanted to stay right where he felt the Lord had placed him.

Oh, Lord, I don't talk with You enough. I'm just like I believe Paloma is. I assume I know what You want and rush ahead with it. I'm afraid I follow my will sometimes instead of Yours. Please, show me Your will clearly. Help me to walk in faith and to trust You with my every step.

"I think this was a wasted effort." Paloma's velvety voice cut through his thoughts.

Antonio looked into her doelike eyes and could find nothing to say. She had thrown him off-guard again, and he couldn't afford that. Finally, he managed to ask, "Why is that?"

"Since we left the Hidalgo ranch, I've been thinking. You don't want me to find Rosita and Pablo. None of the women in the pueblo want me to find them either. Even Chico is being secretive. So, why would you suddenly agree to help me look for them?"

"You tell me." Antonio hoped she didn't notice the strain in his voice.

"I think it's because you knew they wouldn't be there. You knew no one at the ranchos would have heard of them. You only did it to pass the time until my brother comes back. You hope that, by then, I will concede defeat and return to Mexico."

Antonio held his breath and stared into her beautiful eyes. Could this woman read his thoughts?

Paloma leaned across the narrow space that separated them and put her hand on top of his. "Listen to me," she spoke slowly and forcefully. "I will never give up. Never."

Chapter 4

The interior of the small chapel wrapped Paloma with a welcome coolness. The weather had turned very warm today. Walking around the small pueblo of Tucson and inquiring after her sister had caused her to perspire in a most unladylike fashion. Now, sinking into the narrow pew felt like a piece of heaven. The quiet helped her to relax for the first time in the week since she'd arrived here.

"God, I don't know what's happening here. I have tried to find Rosita, but no one will talk. I think I've asked every one of the people who live here. Yet, they either deny knowing her or they tell me to ask someone else. Why, Lord?" Tears traced a path down her cheeks.

What more could she do? Every day she had tried to get Chico to talk. He acted as though she only wanted to see him because he was so wonderful. Ridiculous! Antonio had been of no help, either. He hadn't even offered to search with her since taking their visits to the two ranchos near town. Of course, he was always polite, always acted like he hoped she found her sister. But deep down, she knew he was doing everything he could to ensure that she didn't find her. After all, she had heard him tell Chico that first day that he wouldn't tell her anything. Perhaps if she had confronted him right away, he would have said something, but she doubted it. The man was mule-stubborn.

Despite that, she couldn't help but like him. He worked so hard. He loved the Lord. He seemed honest and was obviously well-loved in town. Plus, every time she saw him, her heart skipped a beat. She found herself longing to touch him, to feel his arms around her as she had on the day she fainted. She cherished that memory.

"God." Her whisper echoed in the quiet building. "This afternoon, I'm going with Tia Elena to visit with some of the women. I know they're keeping something from me. Please, help me to convince them to tell me what it is. You brought me here for a reason, and I'm sure it's to find Rosita and bring her back home. Time is running out. I have to know today."

Paloma stalked from the small church, trying to ignore the fact that she was angry with God over His obvious reluctance to do what she wanted. Determination gave a spring to her step. This afternoon, God would show her everything.

After a light lunch, Paloma hurried to wash up the dirty dishes. Tia Elena was gathering her things, and then they were leaving for Mrs. Garcia's house. There they would meet the same women she had questioned earlier. Only this time, she wouldn't do the asking. God would make them talk. She was sure they knew something.

"Ready, mija?" Tia Elena clutched her embroidery under one arm as she fastened her scarf.

"I'm just finished." Paloma smiled. She had come to love this friend of her mother's. Tia Elena would do almost anything for anyone. She visited the sick and took them food. She helped the young mothers with their children, and the children loved the sweets she gave them.

After a short walk in the heat, Elena and Paloma were welcomed into Mrs. Garcia's adobe house. Paloma loved the way the thick earthen walls kept out the heat. It felt like walking into a cave.

Settling into a chair, she watched as the women pulled out their embroidery and began stitching. She tried to fade into the background, hoping Rosita's name would come up. As she relaxed, the tension and stress of the last few days began to catch up to her. She struggled to keep her eyes open. She *must* remain alert. Gradually, the light chatter of the women faded to a drone. Then silence, as sleep overtook her.

Paloma didn't know how much time had elapsed, but she woke slowly to soft, murmured whisperings. Keeping her eyes closed, she pretended to still sleep. Breathing deeply and slowly, so as not to alert the women that she was awake, she slowly opened one eye just enough to see. The women had abandoned their chairs and were huddled together on the opposite side of the room. She longed to lean forward to catch more of their conversation, but knew that would give her away. Instead, she sat quietly, straining to hear something.

"...sister... Does she know...Franco...Pablo?"

"...sees the gravestone...keep her away."

Paloma leaned slightly forward, frustrated at only catching a few words here and there. What were saying about Pablo? Who was Franco? She'd never heard of anyone by that name.

The material she'd been stitching earlier now shifted, and her scissors clattered to the floor. The talk ceased abruptly. Paloma opened her eyes, knowing the women realized she was awake. She yawned and stretched, trying to make it appear as if she'd just woken up.

"Ah, Paloma," Tia Elena's light laugh sounded strained. "You had a little siesta. Come here and see Mrs. Garcia's scarf. We were all admiring it."

Paloma walked over and pretended interest in the intricately embroidered cloth, but she really wanted to leave. She needed to think about the words she'd overheard. Somewhere there was a clue to finding Rosita. She was certain.

❧

"Antonio, we have to talk." Chico's serious tone cut through the haze that surrounded Antonio. He hadn't been able to concentrate on the saddle he was tooling. The rancher who had placed the order wanted the work finished before his son's birthday in two weeks. Antonio knew time was growing short, but he couldn't get his mind off of a certain pretty señorita.

"What is it, amigo?" Antonio beckoned to a seat across from him, and Chico sat down.

"I can't do this anymore." Chico kneaded his work-blackened hands as if thoroughly agitated.

"You are tired of shoeing horses?" Antonio looked at him in surprise.

"No. You know I love working with the horses."

"What is it, then, that you can't do?"

"I can't continue to deceive Paloma. Is it so wrong to let her see her sister? What would their meeting hurt?"

Antonio studied the saddle beside him, polishing it gently with a cloth. "I, too, am having trouble with all this deception, amigo. But you know what happened to Pablo. He was my best friend. I can't go back on the promise I gave him when he was dying."

"But would he want Paloma and Rosita kept apart?"

"I don't know." Antonio felt miserable. He didn't know what was right anymore. "On one hand, I feel that I should take Paloma to Rosita. But you saw what that monster did to Pablo. What if he does the same to Rosita—or Paloma? I can't let that happen."

He paused, studying the forlorn expression on Chico's face. He leaned forward, placing his elbows on his knees, wishing God would show him a clear way to do the right thing.

"Chico, you know I can't take back what I said to Pablo. He died in my arms." Antonio fought to swallow around the lump in his throat. "I still have his bloodstains on my shirt."

"But Paloma is Rosita's sister. They're family." Chico protested. "Maybe Rosita needs family right now."

Antonio began to pace, his hands knotted behind his back. He wanted to kick something. Why all these questions? He felt as if he were being torn in two. On one hand was a promise to his best friend, and on the other was the need of a sister looking for her sister. What was the right thing to do?

"Chico, I'm not doing this out of cruelty." He hoped his passionate plea wouldn't go unheeded. "That killer promised to find Rosita. You know we can't let that happen. I have to protect her. I know he's watching me, and he's watching everyone who knows me. We have to wait a little longer."

Chico's shoulder slumped as he leaned back against the wall. "All right, I'll wait, but I want you to know, I don't like it."

"I know, amigo. I don't like it either. I just don't want to see Rosita dead like Pablo." Antonio whirled around to look out the window. "Did you hear something?"

"No." Chico stood and crossed to look out. He groaned. "It's Paloma. This time you have to talk to her. I can't stand her prying for answers again."

"Wait here." Antonio clapped him on the shoulder as he headed for the door. He squinted as he stepped out into the brilliant afternoon sunshine. Paloma stood near the stable door, her back to him. Something was wrong. Could she have heard them talking? *Lord, please don't let her have heard,* he prayed.

"Paloma?"

She turned slowly. She wiped her eyes with the edge of her scarf.

"Is something wrong?"

She shrugged, not meeting his eyes. "You know how the dust can be." Her voice sounded choked.

"Can I help you with something?" He had to fight back the urge to sweep her into his arms. The desire to protect her nearly overwhelmed him.

"No, I. . .I wanted to ask you something, but I'm not feeling so good right now. I think I'll head home." Paloma turned and nearly ran toward the street.

"Would you like me to walk with you?"

"No." Her sharp retort held a note of desperation. "I need to be alone."

🐝

Paloma halted her headlong flight and leaned against the shady side of a building. Her knees shook so badly, she didn't think she could stand much longer. She had wanted to scream at Antonio. How could he deceive her about something so important? Now she understood the snatches of conversation she had overheard from the women. They had mentioned a gravestone. Surely, it was Pablo's.

She covered her mouth, fighting for control. *Oh, God, how can Pablo be dead? He was always so kind. He loved to laugh and have fun. I've never known him to get in a fight. Who killed him? Why?*

She made her way slowly back to the church where she had prayed that morning. She remembered a small courtyard beside the church with several headstones. Maybe she would find her answer there.

The streets were deserted as she passed through the gate into the small graveyard. Her heart pounded. *Please don't let this be true, Lord. But, if it is true—keep Rosita safe.* She walked slowly through the yard, reading those small crosses that bore inscriptions. As she neared the far side, she noticed a grave with freshly mounded dirt. Her tight fists causing her knuckles to turn white, she dragged herself closer.

"Pablo Lopez, 1854." She sank to the ground next to the cross. A sob shook her as her fingers traced the name. "Oh, Pablo, what happened? I remember the day you left to come here. You were so happy and full of dreams. You loved Rosita so much. How could you be dead? What's happened to Rosita?"

She could no longer hold the tears at bay. Covering her face with the loose end of her scarf, Paloma cried for what had been and would never be again. She barely

175

heard the footsteps approaching. Strong arms lifted her from the ground, and she found herself held in a powerful embrace. The familiar smell of leather and horses surrounded her.

"Palomita, my little dove." Antonio's soft words warmed her. "I'm so sorry. I thought, perhaps, you heard us talking. I loved him, too." He softly rubbed her back. Slowly, her tears subsided. She wanted to stay close to him, to feel the solid strength he gave her. Reluctantly she pushed away, wondering at these feelings she was experiencing for someone she barely knew.

Brushing the tears from her cheeks, she stepped back. "Now I am even more convinced—I must find Rosita. I told you America is bad. See, already I have lost someone I loved here."

Chapter 5

The first fingers of rose-colored dawn stained the cotton clouds in the eastern sky as Paloma slipped from the house the next morning. Tia Elena still slept. Paloma didn't want to waken her and face all the questions about where she was going, alone, so early in the morning. After a sleepless night, she couldn't face the thought of answering questions from anyone.

Hurrying down the deserted streets, she pulled her shawl snugly around her shoulders. Although the days were warm, the nights cooled drastically. Only a couple hours of sunshine could chase the chill from the air. Paloma shivered. She didn't think even direct sunlight could warm the cold that had settled deep in her heart and soul.

"God, I hate this place," she whispered as she walked. "I know Tia Elena is wrong. You couldn't possibly bless such a cruel land as this. Please help me find the answers that I need. Quickly."

The dry, crisp air brushed like a cool cloth against her face as she passed through the shadows of the church. The gate to the churchyard stood slightly ajar. She slipped through and slowed her pace, trudging past the row of crosses that led to Pablo's grave. She stared at the ground, hating the thought of seeing the rectangle of disturbed ground that now covered her brother-in-law's body.

"Good morning, Paloma."

She jumped and clamped a hand over her mouth to stifle a shriek. Antonio rose from where he had been squatting next to Pablo's grave. Her heart pounded—she didn't know if from fright or from the strange attraction she had for Antonio.

He smiled. "I didn't mean to startle you."

She fought the urge to run as he moved closer. "What are you doing here?" Paloma bit her lip and looked away, wishing her words had sounded less demanding.

"I come here for a few minutes every morning."

"Why would you do such a thing?" she asked, meeting his eyes again. She immediately regretted that. The memory of being held in his strong embrace was too fresh. It took an iron will to keep from flinging herself at him, begging him to hold her and help ease her hurt.

The smile left Antonio's face. He turned back to the grave, running his fingertips along the top of the small cross. "Pablo was like a brother to me. I loved him."

"Then you lied to me." She wanted to scream at him.

"I didn't lie to you. I said Pablo isn't here, and he isn't. Neither is Rosita."

"But you led me to believe that you didn't know Pablo or Rosita."

He studied her before he nodded. "I suppose I did. Perhaps I was wrong, but I made a promise to Pablo."

"A promise that includes refusing to tell Rosita's sister of her whereabouts?"

A sad smile flickered across his lips, then faded. "I suppose, in a way, yes."

Clenching her fist, Paloma wished she had brought her quirt so she could take out her frustrations with it. "I have no idea why you're doing this, but I do know you don't understand the pain my family has been through already. The war was cruel. So many we knew died. My brother suffered a horrible death. It took him hours to die from his wounds. If the Americans hadn't been so greedy in their lust for land, those fine young men would be alive today. All the Americans could say was that they had a 'Manifest Destiny' to own the land. As if they're the only ones who count."

She turned away, blinking back tears of anger and frustration. "I'm sorry for being so passionate about this. I don't believe anyone understands unless they've been through such trauma."

His hands, warm on her shoulders, startled her. He gently, but firmly, turned her to face him. His palm, smooth from hours of working with leather, cupped her cheek. He wiped a tear from the corner of her eye.

"Look at me, Palomita." His voice was soft, undemanding. She looked into his serious eyes. "I understand. Believe me; I do understand."

"How can you understand?" she barely managed to choke out the question around the lump in her throat. With his touch, her anger fled and was replaced by a longing to stay close to him.

"Sit with me for a few minutes." Antonio beckoned to a bench near the fence that surrounded the graveyard.

Paloma sat nervously on the edge of the stone bench, trying to put some distance between them. For some reason, this man had an effect on her unlike any other man. He frightened her, in a way. She didn't know whether she should run toward him or away from him as fast as possible.

"I, too, lived in Mexico when the war broke out." Antonio's statement surprised her and grabbed her attention.

"Did you fight in the war?" she asked.

Antonio shook his head and leaned forward to put his elbows on his knees. "I begged my father to let me fight with the army. He said no. Said he needed me at the ranch. Said I was too young. I scoffed at his words. I was fifteen and thought I was already a man. Others younger than I were fighting."

He paused and rubbed his face with his hands. When he glanced at Paloma, she could see the pain etched in his expression. She wanted to reach out and comfort him. Instead, she forced herself to sit still.

"I knew my father needed me. I was the only boy in a family full of girls. My sisters were all younger than I. My father had been injured in a fall from a horse. He couldn't do many of the necessary chores around the ranch. As the only son, I helped him with the work."

He stopped as if battling with strong emotions. When he continued, his voice had a raspy quality that wasn't there before. "At sixteen, I ran away to join the army. Selfishly, I thought my family could do without me, but my country couldn't. I had to fight against the Americans who were trying to take away our beloved Mexico. For days, I wandered through the hills looking for the army so I could join. I had no idea how to do it, just a determination to do so. Finally, God showed me I shouldn't have left my father when he needed me. As I was heading home, I got my wish. But the war found me, not the other way around."

"Did you join the army?" Paloma wanted to reach out to him but couldn't.

"No, I entered the city of Monterrey as the Americans were battling to take it over. The sight of the bloodshed in the streets sickened and frightened me. You see, in order for the American army to reach Monterrey, they had to pass very close to our ranch."

"What did you do?"

"When the fighting ended, I slipped out of town and hurried home as fast as I could. Although the main army had passed by without going to my hacienda, a group of renegade soldiers couldn't resist. I watched helplessly as they burned our house. My family lay in the yard, murdered. I knew the old musket I carried would never stand up to those killers, and my family was beyond my help."

Antonio bowed his head, burying his face in his hands. Paloma touched his shoulder lightly, wanting to ease his pain with a desperation borne of sorrow. "I'm so sorry, Antonio. I had no idea."

When he looked up, the sheen of unshed tears brightened his eyes. He nodded. "I left for Tucson that day. I buried my sisters and my parents, and then I rode away and never looked back. The bitterness and anger in my heart took years for God to erase. I had to learn to forgive, which wasn't easy."

"Forgive?" Paloma jerked her hand from his shoulder. "How can you possibly forgive something so horrible?"

"My mother always told me that if I kept anger and hatred in me it would turn to bitterness. 'Bitterness is a root that will dig down into your very soul and ruin you,' she would say. I didn't want those murderers to kill me, too, because of a root of bitterness that I allowed to grow. Paloma, you need to ask God to help you get rid of your bitterness against the Americans."

A wave of anger washed over her. "I am not bitter; I'm angry at what they've had the gall to do. They deserve my anger. I don't know how you can forget your family so easily. They died for their country. Maybe it would have been better if you had tried to defend your home when you had the chance." Paloma practically ran from the churchyard, tears streaming down her face. *How dare he suggest I should act like they did nothing wrong?* she fumed, trying to ignore the voice in her heart that said Antonio was right.

For the rest of the day, Antonio fought a battle with himself. Had he been too hard on Paloma? Had he been out of place to tell her she needed to forgive the Americans for what they had done to her family and all the others she had known? Should he go to her and apologize, or should he give her some time to think about it?

All day as he worked, he watched the door, hoping she would come to the shop so they could talk. *Oh, God, give me wisdom in this,* he prayed over and over. But, no matter how much he prayed, he didn't feel any wiser. He still didn't have the answers.

Lord, You know I'm falling in love with her. I feel she's the one You've sent to me, but how can that be when we can't even agree on where we would live? I'm sure she has feelings for me, but she won't admit them for fear she would have to stay in America with me. What am I to do? And, Lord, I want so much to take her to Rosita. Please show me what's right to do. As always, I pray for Rosita's safety.

The last golden glow of the sun was fading from the sky when Antonio closed up the shop and headed toward the Fernandez home. He had to talk to Paloma. His footsteps were nearly silent on the dirt road. Rounding a corner, he saw Paloma step out into the twilight. She didn't look his direction but turned the other way and set off at a brisk pace.

Antonio opened his mouth to call out to her, but something stopped him. What if she had seen him and deliberately turned the other way to avoid him? Maybe she was still mad and refused to talk to him. He stood watching as the distance between them grew. Well, he would follow her, and if he got the chance, he could apologize for offending her this morning.

Hurrying to catch up, Antonio nearly missed the turn Paloma made. When he reached the corner, he could only see the white of her shawl as the darkness swallowed her. Loud laughter rang out through the evening as a door across from Paloma burst open, bathing her in golden lamplight. A man stumbled out, almost knocking her over. He grabbed her, and they both staggered to one side to keep from falling.

Antonio began to run, wishing he had stayed closer to her. He could see Paloma pushing the man away, but he seemed to be pulling her closer. Paloma's scarf drifted from her head into the dirt of the road. Both appeared unaware of him rushing toward them.

"Rosita, my sweet. I've missed you. I knew you would come back to me."

The man's slurred words reached Antonio's ears, filling him with fear. *Oh, God, it's Franco. Please help Paloma. Help me protect her, Lord.* He felt utterly powerless as he watched the outlaw drag Paloma into the alleyway beside the house.

Chapter 6

Paloma could barely breathe. The only good thing about the hand clamped over her face was that it blocked some of the odor of alcohol that surrounded this man. Who was he? What did he want with her? Why did he think she was Rosita?

God, why, when I finally find someone who will talk about Rosita, is it like this? What is happening here? she prayed.

She pulled at the sinewy arm, trying to loosen his hold, but he laughed. Grabbing her dangling quirt, she tried to swing the whip around. He wrenched it out of her hand and threw it in the dirt.

"I always loved your spirit, my little Rosita. Only you would pretend to fight against Franco." He pulled her close against him, dragging her around the corner of the house. "You know, my sweet, the other women are so jealous of you."

Panic gave way to desperation. Paloma kicked back hard. She heard the man's grunt of pain as her heel connected with his shin. His grip tightened, squeezing the breath from her lungs. His hiss of anger sounded loud in her ear. She knew she could never defeat him on her own.

Twisting to one side, Paloma tried to remove his hand from her mouth. She had to find out what he wanted. How did this vile excuse for a man know her sister?

"Easy, Rosita." His hoarse whisper in her ear sent a shudder rippling through her. "I love the way you act like you don't want me, when you really do."

Paloma managed to open her mouth slightly. The fleshy part of his palm pressed close, and she clamped her teeth into his skin as hard as she could. He let out a grunt of pain and jerked his hand away, then slapped her across the mouth. Stunned, she stood mute for the precious few seconds when she could have talked. Once more, his hand covered her mouth.

"If you bite me again, my sweet, I'll give you more than a little love tap."

She closed her eyes, fighting the fear that threatened to overwhelm her. *Oh, God, I need help. I don't know what's happening. Please send someone.* As she flung her silent prayer toward God, a picture of Antonio came to mind. How she longed for him right now.

"Franco, let her go."

Paloma's heart skipped a beat. Could God have answered her prayer so quickly?

Was Antonio really here to rescue her?

Franco whirled around to face Antonio. He turned Paloma sideways, shoving her face against his chest. "She's mine," he snarled. "I won her fair and square. All you've done is try to interfere in my business. This time I won't allow it."

Pushing away from Franco, Paloma tried to turn far enough to look at Antonio. For some reason she had to see him. She knew the sight of his solid presence would comfort her.

In answer to her twisting, Franco whipped her around, pulling her back against him. He removed his hand from her mouth but wrapped an iron-muscled arm tight around her neck. Breathing became a chore. She still couldn't speak.

"What's this, Franco? Hiding behind a woman? I thought you were more of a man than that."

Paloma drank in the welcome sight of Antonio as he stood splay-legged, his back to the street. Shadows made his face a black mask, but she knew every feature by heart. An overwhelming urge to touch him made her lift her hand, reaching out to him.

Franco jerked his arm tighter around her neck, forcing her to instinctively claw at the obstruction to her breathing.

"Forget it, little Rosita. Your coward of a husband couldn't stand up to me, and neither can this lily livered hombre."

"You're so sure that's Rosita in your grasp." Antonio's mocking voice cut through Franco's tirade. "I'm telling you that isn't who you're hiding behind."

Like a feral animal, a growl of protest ripped through Franco. "I think I should know the woman who loves me."

"Well, I know the woman I love, and that's her. You don't think I would bring Rosita out of hiding this soon, do you?"

Paloma's heart pounded so hard she didn't think she would hear anything else. What had Antonio said? Had he really referred to her as the woman he loved? And, what did he mean about bringing Rosita out of hiding? If only this baboon would loosen his hold on her so she could talk.

"Don't think you can trick me, Antonio. You thought I left town for California like I said I would. Well, I lied, and now Rosita is mine."

Antonio's hands were clenching and unclenching. Paloma wondered if he longed to get them around this Franco's neck. At this point, that would be fine with her.

"Look at her, Franco. This is Rosita's sister, Paloma, not Rosita."

Franco's arm tightened more. Paloma's vision dimmed. *Please, God, don't let me faint. Help Antonio, Lord.*

Muttering an oath, Franco twisted Paloma around, his grip loosening enough for her to gasp some air. Before she could cry out, she found herself staring into a shadowed, ruggedly handsome face. A heavy mustache drooped past his chin, giving Franco a sinister appearance. A shaft of fear pierced through Paloma. This man would show mercy to no one. She felt as if she were staring evil in the face.

"Who are you?" Franco shook her until her teeth rattled. "Where is Rosita?"

"I don't know." Paloma couldn't keep her voice from shaking. "I've been looking for her, too."

"Are you her sister?" he demanded.

She could only nod.

"Then you're lying," he roared. Grabbing her neck, he nearly lifted her from the ground. She felt her eyes strain, and blackness begin to descend again. "Tell me where she is before I kill you."

Something seized her from behind, pulling her from Franco's hold. She fell back, stumbling slightly. The next thing she knew, familiar arms were around her. She clung to Antonio, praying this Franco would leave her alone.

"She isn't lying, Franco. Rosita is beyond your reach. Now, get out of here. Why don't you just leave for California like you said before."

Franco snarled a reply, but Paloma heard little of it as she buried her face against Antonio's chest. Footsteps retreated, and she fought to still the trembling in her limbs.

"Ah, Palomita, my little dove." Antonio gently stroked his hand over her hair. His arms tightened around her comfortingly. "I'm sorry you had to meet Franco. Everything is all right now."

"Who is he?" Paloma wanted to scream, but instead her question could barely be heard. She looked up at Antonio. The moon, now peeking through the branches of a nearby Palo Verde tree, lit his face. His loving expression took her breath away. "I have to know," she whispered.

"I gave my promise to Pablo, my sweet. I can't tell you, but I will pray about taking you to someone who will tell you what has happened."

"What about Tia Elena? Why hasn't she told me? Did the whole town make the same promise?"

"Your tia Elena and many of the other people of the town don't know all of what happened." Antonio frowned as if considering his answer. "They only know they must carefully protect Rosita."

Paloma gripped the front of his shirt in her fists. "Don't you see, Antonio? If Rosita needs protecting, what better way than to get her out of here and back to her home in Mexico? My father has many vaqueros. Each one would lay down his life for my sister or me. She must return with me. Now."

Antonio's smile glinted in the moonlight. "Palomita, I love your spirit. You never give up on an idea." He lifted a finger and traced a path down the side of her face.

Paloma knew she should move away from him and the feelings he stirred inside of her. After all, she had to stick with her plan, the plan to find Rosita and be ready to ride for Mexico as soon as her brother returned. She couldn't let her feelings for Antonio interfere.

Antonio watched the moonlight play across Paloma's perfect features. He'd been so afraid that Franco would hurt her. *Thank You, God. I know You protected Paloma from that rogue. I've never known him to give up so easily. Please help me to protect her from him should he try to hurt her again.*

Paloma's doe-eyes reflected a shaft of light. Her full lips, darkened in the evening light, proved irresistible. Antonio bent his head, pulled her close, and gave her a slow, soft kiss. Fire raced through his veins. He longed to draw her close and kiss her again. Instead, he cautioned himself to retreat. He didn't want to frighten her.

"I love you, Palomita." He couldn't believe he blurted those words out when he had just determined to restrain himself. "I've prayed so long for a wife, and I believe you are the answer to my prayers." He desperately wanted her to understand his serious feelings for her.

"No, Antonio." She pushed away from him. "I have to get back to Tia Elena's. I have to go now."

"Wait." He grasped her arm, turning her back toward him. "I'm sorry. I didn't mean to upset you. I can't help how I feel. Let me walk you home. I don't trust Franco."

She glanced fearfully around the shadowed streets then nodded her ascent.

He grinned and extended his arm to her. "I promise I'll be the perfect gentleman."

The walk to her aunt's house proved peaceful. No one bothered them. Paloma appeared lost in thought. She didn't speak again until they reached the Fernandez house. Antonio simply enjoyed watching the play of shadows and moonlight wash across Paloma's face.

"Thank you for rescuing me." Paloma tilted her head to one side as she looked up at him. She lifted a hand and softly cupped his cheek. He fought to keep from grabbing her and covering her face with kisses. He didn't want to frighten her again.

"It was my pleasure, Palomita." He turned to leave.

"Wait, Antonio."

He stopped.

"You promised to take me to someone who would tell me about Rosita."

He glanced around the seemingly deserted streets. "Tomorrow," he spoke softly, hoping the words wouldn't carry far. "I will take you to my tia Isabel tomorrow. She will tell you what you want to know. Then you will understand why you need to leave without Rosita."

"I'll never leave without my sister." Paloma disappeared inside the house, her words echoing through his head and his heart. No matter how he felt about her, she still planned to leave. In fact, she acted as though she couldn't get away from there fast enough.

Antonio trudged through the streets to the little adobe that served as his house and workshop, his heart heavy. He felt sure she cared for him, but then she pulled away and wanted to leave. Would life in the United States of America be so awful?

Inside the house, he sank onto his bed and buried his head in his hands. *Dear God, help me to accept this if it is Your will. Lord, You know how I feel about Paloma. I feel sure she's the one You have for me—the one for whom I've prayed. Please, help me to have faith if she isn't, Lord. And, if she is the one, I trust You to work things out.*

As he prayed in the dark, Antonio remembered his tia Isabel talking about his uncle's favorite Scripture passage. He loved to hear about the Israelites going to the Promised Land. Tia Isabel always said the Promised Land could be anywhere, as long as you were there with God.

His voice far from steady, Antonio began to quote aloud the verse his *tia* had helped him memorize. "In that I command thee this day to love the Lord thy God, to walk in his ways, and to keep his commandments and his statutes and his judgments, that thou mayest live and multiply: and the Lord thy God shall bless thee in the land whither thou goest to possess it."

Lord, help Paloma to see that, as long as she walks with You, the land where she lives will be a blessed land. It's knowing You and following Your ways that makes our homes a blessing. And, Lord, please work out what's right concerning Rosita. Thank You, Lord.

Contentment surrounded him, and for the first time since meeting Paloma, he slept peacefully through the night.

Chapter 7

Paloma rose early the next morning. She had slept fitfully. Memories of Franco's near-abduction haunted her dreams. She would wake in a cold sweat, but the thought of Antonio's loving protection comforted her each time.

She gazed out her window at the mountains standing tall in the distance. The sun barely peeked over the tops of them, but it held the promise of a warm, beautiful day. The dark, scary night faded.

A low, buzzing sound startled her. She jumped back, then laughed lightly as she watched a hummingbird thrust its long beak into the bright orange flower of a trumpet vine near her window. She hoped she didn't jump at every little sound today. Humming to herself, she headed for the kitchen.

"Good morning, tia." She leaned over to give her tia Elena a quick kiss on the cheek as she entered the kitchen.

"My, you are cheery this morning." Tia Elena smiled and stirred the meat sizzling in the skillet. "Is there a reason for all these smiles?"

"Antonio promised to take me to meet his tia Isabel. She will tell me all about Rosita." Paloma paused, seeing a frown cross her aunt's face. "What? What is it?"

Tia Elena sighed and shook her head. "Nothing, mija. I just pray you don't have your hopes up for nothing. There may be nothing you can do for Rosita."

"I know she is having trouble here, tia. I can take her back to Mexico. There, she will not have trouble." Paloma sensed her aunt's scrutiny as she stirred eggs into the spicy Mexican sausage.

"Are there no bad people in Mexico, mija?" Paloma turned to look into the frowning face of her tia Elena as she spoke. "Does everything always run smoothly? I seem to remember a government that has trouble running the country. I've seen the poor get poorer and the rich get richer. Is this the best way?"

Paloma stalked across the kitchen and stared out the window. She breathed deeply, wishing people would understand. "At least in Mexico we don't try to take what is someone else's. We only want to hold onto what we have. The Americans see something they want, and they take—without thought of whose it really is. They're greedy and evil."

"In some ways that's true," Tia Elena agreed. "Or, at least, for some of the people.

I don't believe all Americans are like that, just like I don't believe that all Mexicans are power hungry. You, mija, have been blessed with a family who has much. Think of all the poor of Mexico who struggle. Do the wealthy give up their riches to help them?"

"Do the Americans do that?" Paloma shot back.

Tia Elena tipped the skillet, scooping some of the chorizo and egg mixture onto two plates. "No, mija, I'm not saying they do." She handed Paloma a plate and beamed a smile at her. "All I want you to think about is this: Maybe Americans and Mexicans aren't so different. We all have faults. God doesn't say that only Americans are sinners, mija. We have all sinned and need to ask His forgiveness."

Paloma scooted her breakfast around on her plate. Was Tia Elena right? Could it be that Mexicans were just as bad, in their own way, as Americans were in theirs? Had she been judging when she shouldn't?

A picture of the bloody street of Monterrey, Mexico, came to mind. She shuddered at the forever-etched mental image. That day, September 23, 1846, the Americans and Mexicans had fought the final full day of the Battle of Monterrey. She and her family had taken refuge with some of their extended family members in that small town, hoping to escape. Instead, the war had hit them full force. For two days, the battle had raged outside of town. Then, the hated Americans had come into the city and began to force their way into homes, looking for Mexican resisters.

Paloma remembered her brother fighting bravely to defend their family. As the only male left in a house full of women and children, he had considered it his duty to protect the family. The Americans brutally shot him, ran him through with their bayonets, then threw him into the street to die. She would never forget her mother's sobbing as she held her dying son, his blood covering her hands. For years now, her brother had been the hero of the family. She wouldn't allow anything to change that or to detract from his sacrifice.

No, Paloma thought to herself as she resolutely began to eat her breakfast, *the Americans are much worse than the Mexicans. I will never live among the people who stole my home and killed my brother. And Rosita won't either.*

A knock at the door startled Paloma from her reverie. She could hear the husky rumble of Antonio's voice as Tia Elena greeted him. Her hands trembled slightly, causing the eggs to tumble from her fork. She pushed the plate aside, excitement taking away her appetite. Was it Antonio or the thought of hearing what his tia Isabel would say that affected her this way?

"Good morning, Palomita." Antonio's smile lit the room. His gunmetal-black eyes glinted with laughter. Everything else faded into the distance, and Paloma found she couldn't look away from his warm gaze.

"Sit down, Antonio." Tia Elena's order broke the spell. "Let me give you some breakfast."

"I never turn down your good food. I could smell your cooking long before I arrived at your door." His words were for her tia, but his eyes told Paloma how much he had missed her.

Paloma turned away and busied herself with cleanup. She couldn't help but remember the sweet kiss he had given her last night. She found that, once again, she wanted him to hold her in his strong arms. She wanted to lean against his broad chest and feel protected from whatever might come. She wanted him to kiss her again.

Stop this, she scolded herself. *You can't fall in love with Antonio. He'll break your heart. He'll never leave Tucson, and you must never agree to live here. Wait and find someone who is willing to live with you in Mexico. Perhaps when you get back home Father and Mother can suggest the perfect husband.* She determined to speak with her parents as soon as she got back to Mexico. It shouldn't be too hard to forget Antonio and his declaration of love for her.

❧

Pretending interest in the food Elena Fernandez set before him, Antonio couldn't take his eyes off Paloma. She hadn't braided her hair yet this morning, and it hung free in a glorious mass falling below her waist. He longed to run his fingers through her hair and feel its softness on his arms as he held her in his embrace. He loved the way the light glinted and sparkled in her silky locks.

From time to time he caught her glancing at him. His heart soared with hope. *God, are You working on her heart? Lord, I pray that You are. I will try to wait patiently, even though I want the answer now.* He sighed, longing to know quickly if Paloma would be his. He knew waiting patiently would not be easy for him.

"Are you ready to meet my tia Isabel?" He watched Paloma's eyes light with excitement as he asked the question.

"Yes." She grinned at him. "I'll be ready in a moment."

She rushed from the room, and Elena frowned at him. "Are you sure this is wise, mijo? You will be careful to protect Rosita, won't you?"

"I gave my word," Antonio reminded her. "Did Paloma tell you what happened last night?" Elena looked fearful as he continued, telling her all about Franco. "He may be getting close to finding Rosita. Please pray that I will know how to protect her. I wish that sending her back to Mexico were the answer." He stood and gave Elena a quick kiss on the cheek. "I'll be careful with them both," he assured her.

On the walk to Tia Isabel's house, Paloma constantly tugged at his arm. He wanted to stroll slowly, extending his time with her. Yet, she seemed to want to race like the wind.

"Easy, Palomita." He laughed, tugging on her hand to slow her down. "We'll both be so out of breath when we get there that we won't be able to talk."

She slowed and slipped her hand into the crook of his arm. "I'm sorry." Her smile dazzled him. "I have looked for Rosita for the last week and a half. Now, I feel she is very close. I want the answers, and I guess I want them now."

"I understand," Antonio agreed.

"I want you to know, I appreciate your willingness to keep your word to Pablo." She spoke so softly, he had to lean close to hear. "At first I was angry with you for

188

keeping things from me. Now, I think I understand a little. A man should always keep his word. I believe that is a good quality about you."

Antonio tugged on her arm and pulled her slightly closer. "So, you have been thinking about my good qualities," he joked. "Have you found any more?"

She grinned. "Not that I would tell you about. Obviously, you are already full of yourself. Perhaps I should make a list of your bad qualities and read them to you."

"Ah, but that list would be very short, indeed." Antonio laughed as Paloma rolled her eyes. "Here we are, Palomita. This is my tia's house."

In a short time, they were inside the cool adobe house and seated around the kitchen table. Tia Isabel, a short, rotund, motherly figure, sang softly to herself as she fixed a plate of sweet breads for Paloma and Antonio. Antonio smiled, seeing the frustration on Paloma's face. He knew she would rather talk than eat.

"Tia Isabel, I told Paloma that you would talk to her about Rosita and Pablo. She met Franco last night, and I believe she needs to know everything."

Isabel slipped into a chair across from Paloma, clutching her hand. "My Chico and Antonio have talked to me about your search for Rosita. For reasons you will soon understand, we had hoped you would tire of your search and leave. We have done this for Rosita's sake. I hope you will forgive us."

Paloma nodded, and Isabel continued. "When Rosita and Pablo came to Tucson, we all fell in love with them. Rosita has such a love for God and is always looking for ways to help others. Pablo had a quiet strength and a love for people. He worked hard to support not only themselves but also the others Rosita wanted to help. They were such a blessing to our small pueblo."

Isabel bowed her head for a moment then began talking again. "Rosita, in the goodness of her heart, didn't see the bad in others. She has always been very trusting. That is what got her in trouble."

Antonio watched Paloma. He ached to hold her, knowing what she would hear next would be painful for her.

"That bandito, Franco, came to town a year ago." Isabel spoke softly. "He and his men caused much trouble. They always fought, either ganging up on someone else or bickering amongst themselves. Anyway, one day, they were fighting, and Franco was shot several times. He nearly died. But Rosita decided she should save him. She talked Pablo into bringing Franco to their home, where she could nurse him back to health. She assured Pablo that if she did this, it would give her a chance to tell the outlaw about Jesus. Perhaps lives would be saved."

Isabel shook her head. "There was never any good in Franco. He did recover, thanks to your sister. And, in doing so, he fell in love with her. For months he pursued her, trying to get her to leave Pablo and run away with him. Rosita couldn't leave her house without Franco finding her."

A tear traced a path down Isabel's cheek. "Finally, Pablo could take no more. He tried talking to Franco, telling him he must stop bothering Rosita. Franco laughed and said Pablo was the only thing standing between him and his love. That despicable killer pulled out his gun and shot Pablo. Then, he laughed as he kicked him around and told him to die fast so he could have Rosita for himself."

Paloma began to sob. Antonio scooted his chair close to hers and put his arm around her, cradling her close.

"Antonio and Chico ran to help, but they were too late. Pablo died in Antonio's arms. My nephew promised to protect Rosita no matter what. That is why he hasn't told you anything. In fact, that is why the whole town is silent about Rosita. If we let Franco know where she is, he will kidnap her, and she will be lost—his to do with as he pleases."

Isabel paused until Paloma looked up at her. "Now, you see why you must go back to Mexico and leave Rosita alone. Only by forgetting about her can you help her."

"No!" Paloma exploded. "Don't you see? Only in Mexico will she be safe. America is wrong for her."

Chapter 8

"Antonio, you've got to listen to me." Paloma turned away from Isabel to face him, placing her hands on his chest, fighting a desire to grab his shirt and shake him. "I've got to get Rosita away from here. My father has many vaqueros who work for him. All of them would lay down their lives to protect Rosita. There is nothing Franco could do to her in Mexico."

Gazing into her moist brown eyes, Antonio longed to give Paloma whatever she wanted. If only he could. "You don't understand, Palomita. I'm sure your father and his men could protect Rosita once she got to them, but what about before then? He would follow you. How many men does your brother have with him? Think. They will be spread thin watching the horses they are buying. Rosita wouldn't have the protection she needs."

"I can use a gun. I'll protect her."

Antonio wanted to hug Paloma close for her determination to care for her sister. Instead he explained slowly, "Franco has many men, my sweet. He will promise them anything—your horses, your father's wealth—" he hesitated before adding "—you. It doesn't matter that they fight among themselves; they are very loyal to Franco. They will lay down their lives to get what he wants."

"But there must be a way." Paloma's tearful whisper tore at his heart.

"The best way is to keep her in hiding until Franco gives up," Isabel interrupted. "Perhaps, if we pray, that villain will lose interest. Maybe something will make him forget."

"It's up to you, Palomita. Will you do *anything* to help Rosita? Even if it means leaving her here?"

Paloma's fingers wrapped tightly around the soft folds of Antonio's shirtfront. She leaned her head against his solid chest, and he leaned his cheek against her hair. He could feel her shaking as if a battle were raging inside her. *Please, God, help her make the right decision,* he pleaded.

Lifting her head, Paloma looked up at him. "I have to see her." The quiet force of her statement startled him.

"But it isn't safe."

"There has to be a way. Please?" she pleaded.

Antonio glanced over at Tia Isabel, who nodded. "I think she has the right to see her sister before going back home, Antonio. We'll work out a way. I'll talk to the other women, and we'll work out a distraction. Then, you can spirit her away for a short visit."

"We'll have to do it soon, tia. Her brother is due back to pick her up anytime. He may not be willing to wait."

※&

Paloma nervously smoothed her skirt for what seemed like the hundredth time. She glanced over at Tia Elena and Tia Isabel and then around at the other ladies from the sewing group. They were all in on the plot to get her safely to where she could visit with Rosita. Two of the ladies, who were almost as small as she, were dressed exactly like her. Hopefully, the dim evening light and matching clothes would fool Franco.

In a group, the ladies began walking toward the church. To anyone watching, it would appear as if they were off for a time of prayer and worship. As the chattering women turned into the church, Paloma slipped into the churchyard. Antonio pulled her into the shadow of the wall. They waited breathlessly until the rest of the women passed. At Antonio's gesture, Paloma followed him through a back gate. In the shade of a mesquite grove, Chico waited with horses for them.

"Here you are cousin," Chico handed them the reins and helped Paloma into the saddle. For once, she wanted to kiss him, despite the silly grin on his face. "My mother and the other ladies will pray long and hard. I think they will also visit long and hard."

"Thanks, amigo." Antonio leaned over to shake Chico's hand. "We'll take the back way and try to stay out of sight. For Rosita's sake, I hope this works."

Paloma allowed her horse to follow Antonio's. The clop of the horses' hooves was muffled in the soft dirt of the side streets. Glancing from side to side, Paloma tried to watch everywhere at once. Every little noise caused her to jump. What if Franco hadn't been fooled? Although some people were in the streets, she couldn't see anyone who looked suspicious. Perhaps all would be safe.

Full dark had turned everything to shadows by the time Antonio stopped his horse in front of a long, low adobe ranch house. Paloma anxiously fidgeted, not at all tired after the long ride. Lantern light flickered in the windows. A slight breeze rustled the branches of the trees. When Paloma's horse turned to look behind them and nickered softly, she knew there must be other horses nearby.

Antonio swung down from his horse. He reached up to help her down. Her heart pounded, and she couldn't decide if it was the excitement of finally getting to see Rosita or Antonio's nearness. He pulled her close and whispered in her ear.

"Follow this walkway to the end of the house. There's a separate small house there. That's where Rosita is staying. I'll take the horses to the stable and let the rancher and his wife know we're here."

Clenching her quirt tightly, Paloma eased along the semivisible path. A break in the wall told her that she'd reached the end of the main house. A small house stood close by, joined to the main house by only a section of roof. She knocked at the door, holding her breath in anticipation of seeing her sister.

"Come in, Carmelita; the door is open."

Paloma pushed the door open. "Rosita? Rosita, is that you?"

A slight, dark-haired woman jumped up from a chair, her sewing scattering over the floor. "Paloma?"

She rushed forward, and suddenly, Paloma had her arms around the sister she had missed so much. "Oh, Rosita, I missed you so much. I've tried so hard to find you. Are you all right?"

Rosita backed away a step, holding on to Paloma's arms. Her dark eyes searched Paloma's face.

"What are you doing here? How did you find me?"

"Berto brought me to find you and take you home to Mexico. When I found out you'd disappeared, I didn't know what to do. Antonio finally agreed to lead me here." Paloma grinned. "I have to admit, I almost met my match. You have more friends than you know in Tucson. They all want to protect you."

"Paloma, you must go back home and forget about me. There is an evil man who is trying to capture me. If you stay, he might get you, too."

"I've met Franco." Paloma watched the look of horror cross Rosita's face. "Sit down, Rosita, and I'll tell you all about it."

Rosita picked up the piece of material she had been stitching and sank back into her chair. She clutched the bit of cloth in her shaking hands.

"I have come to bring you back to Mexico, my sister. You know how I hate America and all it stands for. When I heard that Tucson was to become a part of America with the Gadsden Purchase, I knew I must bring you home. Now that I know of your troubles with Franco and about Pablo being killed, I know this is the best thing. You must come back to Mexico. We will return with Berto in a few days. When we are home, Papa won't let anything happen to you."

Slipping to the floor beside Rosita, Paloma took her sister's trembling hands in her own. "Please say you'll come back," she begged.

"I can't come back with you." Rosita freed one hand and reached to smooth the hair from Paloma's forehead. "This is my home now. This is where God wants me to be. Pablo is buried here. I can't leave."

"But you can't possibly want to be a part of America," Paloma protested. "Think of our brother who died in the war. The Americans killed him. They're evil people."

"Paloma." Rosita lifted Paloma's chin. "There are evil people everywhere. American's aren't the only bad ones."

"But look at Franco. Tucson has barely become a part of America, and already the wickedness is spreading. If you stay here, he will find you and take you for his, no matter what you want, just like the Americans took part of Mexico because they wanted it."

"Hush, sister." Rosita's calm pierced through Paloma's panic. "Franco isn't an American. He is Mexican. And he has always been evil, even before Tucson belonged to America. He comes up from Mexico on raids with his band of men. You know, Paloma, that there are wicked people everywhere. Although not all of us are like Franco, still we all sin against God. Only by believing in Jesus are we made clean."

Paloma buried her face in Rosita's lap. *Oh, God, help me convince her,* she prayed. *I have to take her back with me. I know You want that.*

"I have another reason for not going back with you," Rosita said.

Paloma lifted her head and wiped a tear from her cheek. "What else is keeping you here?"

"This." Rosita spread her sewing on her lap. There lay a tiny nightgown, embroidered with bright flowers. Each stitch showed a mother's love waiting for a child.

"Rosita, you're going to make me an aunt? When?"

Eyes glowing, Rosita held the tiny bit of fabric against her breast. Tears glittered in her eyes. "Six months," she replied. "Pablo didn't even know before he died."

"But you must come home to have the baby. Mama and Papa will be so happy. This will be their first grandchild."

"No." Rosita shook her head. "You didn't know that I've already lost two babies. I can't take any chances with this one." She leaned close, holding Paloma's face in her hands. "Don't you realize? This is all I have left of Pablo. I want to have this baby."

Paloma rose up on her knees and folded Rosita in her arms. "I do understand. I can't make you return to Mexico and run the risk that you would lose the baby on the way. But I will stay with you," Paloma insisted. "Then, as soon as the baby is born and you are able, we will go home to Mexico. I'll have Berto come back for us."

"Sister of mine." Rosita laughed. "I'm glad to know you haven't changed at all. You always were determined to have your way. Do you even tell God what to do?"

Although she smiled at her sister's joke, Paloma felt a check in her soul. Did she tell God what to do? When she had asked Jesus to come into her heart and guide her life, she'd wanted so much to live as He directed. But somehow she had simply continued to run her own life and tell Him what she planned.

No, she thought, *I'm sure God wants me to get Rosita away from here as soon as possible.* The only problem would be spending another six to eight months around Antonio. How would she ever tear herself away from him then?

Muffled sounds scraped against the door. Paloma's heart skipped a beat as she turned to greet Antonio. Instead, in one swift motion, Franco slipped into the room and closed the door.

"So, my sweet, I've found you at last." His devilishly handsome face broke into a villainous grin.

Chapter 9

Paloma jumped to her feet, standing in front of Rosita. She raised her quirt in a vain attempt to stop Franco. "Stay away from my sister," she snarled. "If you don't, I'll scream and Antonio will come running to help us."

"No, Paloma." Rosita gently pushed her aside and stood up. "This is between Franco and me."

A shiver ran down Paloma's spine at Franco's sinister laugh. He sauntered toward Rosita. "So, my sweet, you're ready to go with me? I knew you would admit how much you love me as soon as I got that no-good coyote, Pablo, out of the way."

Rosita paled. Paloma feared she would tear her skirt; her fingers gripped it so tightly.

"My husband was an honorable man, not a villain like you. He loved me enough to die defending me. That's more than you would ever do for anyone."

Twining his fingers in Rosita's hair, Franco jerked her to him. "Don't make me mad, my sweet. I worked long and hard to find you. Why don't you show some appreciation? I know you've been waiting for me."

"Leave her alone," Paloma demanded. "She wants no part of you."

Franco's maddened eyes raked over Paloma. "So the sister has more fire than you, my Rosita. Maybe I'll take you both. After all, she is the one who so obligingly led me to you."

"We were very secretive," Paloma gasped. "I don't know how you could have followed us."

Franco leaned closer and grinned wickedly. "I didn't watch you, sassy one. I had men watching all the exits from the pueblo. You see, I knew Antonio left Tucson with Rosita. When you rode out tonight, one of my men followed you while another came back to get me—just like a fox catching chickens." His maniacal laugh chilled Paloma.

She thrust herself between Franco and Rosita. "Get out of here," she warned. "I won't let you hurt my sister. I'm taking her back to Mexico."

Still holding a fistful of Rosita's hair, Franco seized Paloma under the chin. His large hand encompassing half of her face, he squeezed hard. "So, my sweet, your sister is in competition for my affections. Apparently, she wants to come with us, too. Now, I'll have two women instead of one."

Without thinking, Paloma raised her quirt and slashed the outlaw across the face. Franco let out a roar. He freed her chin only to backhand her, knocking her across the room. Rosita began to sob.

"Please, Franco, don't hurt her. I'll go with you. Just leave Paloma alone."

"I knew you were looking for an excuse to go with me, sweet Rosita. You long for the exciting life of the outlaw. We'll ride together. What a team we'll make."

Paloma lay on the floor trying to get her breath back. Her head hurt where she had slammed against the wall. Her cheek stung from the blow. When she touched it, she could feel the welt that Franco had raised. She looked up to see Franco, once more clutching Rosita close to him. The tiny embroidered nightgown still dangled from Rosita's fingers as a pathetic reminder of the small life that depended on the outcome of this confrontation.

Pushing up from the floor, Paloma stifled a groan. She knew every muscle in her body would be sore tomorrow. Steadying herself against the wall, she called on all her determination to do what she knew she must do.

"Franco, take me instead of Rosita. I'm a good shot with a gun. I can ride a horse as good as anyone. I can help you with many things."

The outlaw paused in his attempts to kiss Rosita. "You see, my sweet. Your sister can't resist me. All women find me attractive."

"Don't fool yourself," Rosita retorted. "She just wants to protect me. There isn't a decent woman alive who would have anything to do with the likes of you."

With one hand, Franco picked Rosita off the floor. Like a wounded animal he snarled, "Enough of your talk. You say, 'I won't die for you.' How would you feel about dying for me? If you don't start pleasing me, this just might be the end of you."

Rosita's face turned dark as the villain's hand closed tightly about her neck, cutting off her air.

"No!" Paloma screamed. "Let her go! You're killing her!" She leaped across the room toward the pair as the door crashed open.

"Franco," Antonio roared.

Franco dropped Rosita and whirled to face his opponent. Paloma slipped to the floor next to her sister, throwing her arms around Rosita to protect her from the violence she knew would erupt.

Crouched in a fighting stance, Franco began to circle toward Antonio. Antonio glanced at Paloma, then Rosita, as though trying to determine if they were all right. Before Paloma could call out a warning, Franco picked up a chair and brought it crashing down on Antonio's head. Paloma gasped as Antonio slumped to the floor. She tried to run to him, but Franco grabbed her, flinging her back to where Rosita huddled. He bent over Antonio, now lying motionless on the floor.

"Leave him alone," Franco thundered. "He can't help you. Now, we're getting out of here."

Paloma fought back tears as Franco herded the two sisters out the door. Antonio lay so still. Was he hurt bad? Maybe even dead? *God, where are You now?* she cried from deep within her soul. *Every time I try to make things right, they only get worse. Don't You care?*

The drone of a hundred bees echoed through the room as Antonio tried to open his eyes. Even the dim flickering lamplight burned his eyes, and he let his lids drop closed. The droning sound grew louder, and he realized that a steady moan was coming from him. His head ached. He lifted a hand and traced his fingers across his temple. A tender spot indicated where Franco had hit him with the chair.

He opened his eyes again. This time, the light didn't hurt as much. From what he could see, the room was empty. How long had he been unconscious? Had Franco taken both Paloma and Rosita? Where had they gone? He forced himself to sit up, but the room spun in nauseating circles.

Dragging himself to his feet, he tried to reach the door. The room whirled, and a veil of darkness descended. He woke to find himself stretched out on the floor, his hand touching the partially open door. How long had he been unconscious this time? Gritting his teeth, he pulled himself to the wall next to the door and sat up, leaning against the wall for support.

Oh, God, how will I ever help Rosita and Paloma if I can't even stand up. Father, all I ever wanted to do was to protect them. I don't want them to end up dead like my family. I couldn't help my mother and sisters. But, please! Let me help Paloma and Rosita.

Tears burned his eyes as he remembered the helpless feeling of watching his home being burned, seeing his family dead in the yard. Now, he felt just as helpless. He had no idea where to look for Franco and his captives. He didn't know how much of a head start they had on him.

God, I can't be everything to Paloma, even though I want to be. I have to trust You with her life, Lord. I think I haven't fully trusted You since my family died. I guess I blamed You, when I know You had a purpose. Lord, forgive me. Whatever happens with Paloma and Rosita, I want to trust You.

Resting his head back against the wall, Antonio pressed his fingers against his eyes. One of Tia Isabel's favorite verses from the prophet Isaiah echoed through his mind. "Thou wilt keep him in perfect peace, whose mind is stayed on thee: because he trusteth in thee."

"I do trust You, Lord. I trust You with Paloma and Rosita. And I trust You with my love for Paloma. I know You will work everything out according to Your will. Thank You, Father." A feeling of complete peace washed through Antonio. Despite everything being in a mess, he knew God was in charge. He need not worry.

The night air had turned cool. Antonio eased his way along the path leading to the stables. He planned to get Grande and follow Franco to the ends of the earth, if necessary, to rescue Paloma and Rosita. He could still see their frightened faces— Rosita huddling on the floor, Paloma standing over her, ready to protect her to the end. He smiled. He loved the way Paloma stood up for herself and what she believed. He loved her spirit. He loved her beauty. In fact, he couldn't think of anything he didn't love about her.

Approaching the stable, Antonio slowly shook his head, glad to find the dizziness gone. The spot on his temple would be sore for a few days, but he could live with that. Now, he had to be ready to go where the Lord would lead him. That would be the only way he could rescue his love.

A shout rang out from the stable. Lantern light cast a dim eerie glow. Two figures were struggling and the horses next to them danced nervously. Antonio slipped quietly up to the door, sensing that he had come across Franco and the sisters.

"You will get on that horse, or I will kill you," Franco's voice grated harshly.

"You can't make us go." Paloma crouched like a fighter, ready to defend Rosita, who was already seated on a horse.

Rosita leaned forward, trying to soothe the horse and get Paloma's attention at the same time. Paloma pointedly ignored her and continued to face Franco.

As if by magic, a long-bladed knife appeared in Franco's hand. He waved the dagger in front of him, its point coming ever closer to Paloma. "We'll see how much fight you have when I carve up your pretty face." His handsome features twisted into a mask of hate.

Paloma backed against her sister's horse. Her dark eyes glittered in the lamplight. She watched Franco as if trying to judge what he would do next.

"First you hide behind women and now you're fighting them. And I thought you were a rough sort." Antonio stepped into the light as he spoke. Franco swiveled around to face him.

"I thought you were dead," he snarled. "I guess I'll have to make sure this time."

Paloma reached to help Rosita from the horse. They slipped into an empty stall. Antonio sighed with relief, knowing he could concentrate more on Franco with them out of the way.

"You won't catch me off guard this time, Franco. I know you don't fight fair, but I'm not letting you take Paloma and Rosita with you, either."

Franco leaped forward, his knife blade flashing in the light. Antonio dropped and rolled to the side, coming up behind Franco as he rushed past. In one swift motion, Antonio grabbed Franco around the neck, jerking him nearly off his feet. With his other hand, he caught hold of the wrist of the hand holding the knife and squeezed. Hours of working with his hands had given Antonio a strong grip. Franco's knife clattered to the stable floor.

Throwing himself to one side, Franco knocked them both to the floor. Antonio refused to let go, and the two fighters rolled under Franco's horse. The stallion whinnied loudly and reared high above them. Antonio looked up at the flashing hooves, released his hold, and dove out from under the terrified animal. Franco began to turn over as the horse's hooves descended. Antonio knew he would never forget the sickening crunch as the horse's hoof connected with Franco's skull.

"Antonio!" Paloma screamed.

He tried to block her view of Franco, but she rushed to him before he could position himself. She glanced past him at the blood pooling on the floor and covered her mouth with her hand. When she buried her head against his chest, Antonio wrapped his arms around her trembling shoulders.

"It's all over with, Palomita. Rosita will be safe now."

Rosita slipped out of the stall, staring out at the night as if avoiding the gruesome sight on the stable floor. Antonio rested his cheek against the top of Paloma's head. "You'll be fine now, Rosita. If you want, I'll take you to your tia Elena's. You won't have to hide anymore." His hand slowly stroked Paloma's back.

Paloma pushed away from Antonio. Her small hand caressed his cheek. "Thank you for saving us." She gave him a watery smile then turned to Rosita. "I've decided I'll leave you at Tia Elena's until the baby comes. Then I'll come back for you and bring you both home to Mexico. You'll be much happier at home where you belong."

Chapter 10

The overcast sky, with its heavy gray clouds and chilly wind, matched Paloma's spirits. Yesterday, Berto and the vaqueros arrived with the herd of horses purchased from a ranch up north. Today, Paloma would join them on the long ride back to Mexico and her home. This was what she had longed for, so why did her heart feel like a lump of lead sitting in her chest?

For the past week, since Franco's death and their rescue, both sisters had spent hours talking about their lives, their expectations, and their faith. Antonio dropped by nearly every day with some excuse or another. Every time Paloma stepped out of the house, he would "accidentally" show up to escort her around. Each encounter only made her fall more deeply in love with him.

She had tried her best to convince him to move back to Mexico with her. Her father would welcome him, and a leather worker and blacksmith would always be needed on a ranch. But Antonio insisted that Tucson was the place God put him, and here he had to stay until God said otherwise. She respected his willingness to do God's will but thought he might pray a little harder about going with her. Had he even asked God?

Rosita firmly stated that, while Paloma was welcome to come and visit after the baby came, she wouldn't return to Mexico. Rosita wanted to be here in Tucson because Pablo rested here, and this had been the home he had chosen for them. Here, a town full of people loved her and would watch over her.

Packing her few belongings, Paloma struggled to swallow the lump in her throat. Her eyes burned with unshed tears. *God, why didn't You work this out better? I thanked You for saving our lives and for Antonio's help. But, Lord, I don't know how I can live without him. I love him. Please, help him to realize that he needs to come to Mexico to live. That's where we belong.*

"Paloma, Berto is ready to go. He's asking if your bag is packed."

Forcing a shaky smile, Paloma turned toward the doorway. "I just finished packing." Her voice quivered from pent-up emotion. She hoped Rosita hadn't heard.

Rosita crossed the room and took Paloma's hands in hers. "Are you sure you're doing the right thing by going back to Mexico?"

"I have to." Paloma fought back the tears. "I can't live here in America. Not after what they did to our people."

"Paloma, remember what I said? The Bible tells us that God is in charge of the governments."

Paloma nodded and Rosita continued. "That means God allowed the war between America and Mexico. He knew what would happen. But He didn't do it to punish us. God loves us."

"So He allowed us to be beaten by a country that only thinks of itself. The Americans demand what they want and don't consider anyone else. Is that for our good?"

Rosita smiled and cupped Paloma's cheek in her hand. "Isn't that a human trait?" she asked softly. "Follow God, my sister, and He will lead you in the right way. Wherever you go, you will be blessed by Him."

"I know He wants me to be in Mexico, not America," Paloma said stubbornly. "I'm certain."

❧

An hour later, Paloma gripped her horse's reins tightly, determined not to cry as she followed her brother toward the edge of Tucson. Antonio hadn't even come to say good-bye. She would return in six months to convince Rosita to come to Mexico. By then, her heart would be healed. For now, her very soul was breaking in two.

God, I asked You to help with this and You haven't. Why am I hurting so much?

"When did you ask?"

Paloma glanced quickly about, wondering where the voice had come from. Then she knew. God had spoken to her soul, and He was right. Her shoulders bowed with the weight of the realization.

"You're right, Lord," she whispered. "I never asked You; I told You. I promised to give You my life, but I've only given You what I want to give. I allowed a root of bitterness to sway my thinking. Please forgive me."

The desert at the outskirts of Tucson opened its wide arms to welcome her. The vaqueros herding the horses were slightly ahead and to one side, waiting for Paloma and Berto to come.

Jesus, I see how wrong I've been. Just like the Americans, I hate. I've demanded my own way. I didn't think of what Antonio or Rosita wanted. I thought I was right, and I didn't consider anyone else, not even You, Lord.

Paloma bowed her head and closed her eyes, allowing her horse its head. *Show me what You want me to do. Lead me, Lord.* The steady clop of the horses' hooves and the yells and whistles of the vaqueros faded in the distance as the Lord spoke to her heart, showing her His will for her life.

❧

Despite the heaviness in his heart, Antonio relished the peace deep inside him. He had watched Paloma ride from town with her brother, but he couldn't bring himself to talk to her. Staying in the shadows, he knew a part of him went with her this morning.

I guess this wasn't Your will, Lord, he prayed. *I tried for the last week to convince her how much I love her and would care for her as my wife. She couldn't see that for her vision of returning to Mexico. I'm trusting You to heal this hurt, Father. Thank You for allowing me to know Paloma. Perhaps, when she returns in six months to see Rosita, I can convince her of my love.*

Absentmindedly rubbing at the same piece of leather he'd been polishing for the last hour, he sighed and pressed his fingers against his eyes. He hadn't slept at all last night, choosing to spend the night praying for Paloma instead. He'd prayed for wisdom, but he still didn't feel very wise—only saddened by his loss.

A beam of sunlight broke through the cloud covering and streamed through the open door. Antonio looked up at the brightness and blinked. Paloma's silhouette stood quietly outlined in the golden sunrays. He started to rise then realized it could only be a vision. Paloma was riding toward Mexico at this very moment. He'd seen her leave. Antonio sank back in his chair, but he couldn't take his eyes from the realistic image.

"Antonio."

The vision spoke. He staggered to his feet, and suddenly she was flying across the room, flinging herself into his arms. This was the most lifelike illusion he'd ever experienced. He pulled her tightly to him, breathing in the scent of fresh rain-laden air. *Thank You, God; she's come back.*

"Why are you here, Palomita?" He feared to ask.

She smiled up at him, her cheeks tearstained and dusty. "I'm following God's desire for my life. He showed me that you are His will for me, and He'll bless us both if we follow Him."

Antonio cupped her cheek and kissed her. He looked into her sparkling eyes filled with love and peace, and couldn't resist another long kiss. "I'm truly blessed," he whispered.

PRAIRIE SCHOOLMARM

by JoAnn A. Grote

Dedication

For Vicci and Joey Danens,
two special children who are wonderful
teachers in my own life.
For my relatives who show their commitment to,
and love for, children through teaching:
Jody Kvanli Capehart, Fran Olsen Strommer,
and Heather Adamson Olsen.
And for Sophia (Sophie) Olsen Fletcher.
Welcome to the family, little one!

*I can do all things through Christ
which strengtheneth me.*
PHILIPPIANS 4:13

Chapter 1

May 1871

M arin Nilsson leaned against the ship rail, turned her face into the May winds, and spoke in Swedish to her older sister, Elsbet. "There it is—the United States. I'd begun to think we'd never see it."

Elsbet's gaze rested on the nearing shore, but Marin could see no joy in her sister's blue eyes.

The lack of expression cut into Marin's heart. Would Elsbet's pain last the rest of her life? Two years had passed since her fiancé, Anton, left for America with the promise to send for her when he'd saved enough money for her passage. Two years since Elsbet had word from him. One year had passed since the news came through friends that he'd married a young woman he'd met in the new land. In the year between, Marin had watched Elsbet's joy and her faith in Anton's love slip slowly into fear—fear he'd been hurt or killed. She rejected speculation from friends and relatives that Anton had abandoned her, as so many men who emigrated had abandoned fiancées, wives, and families in Sweden.

At first, Marin was relieved when news came of Anton's marriage. Perhaps now, she thought, Elsbet would forget him and find someone new. Instead, Elsbet wrapped herself in her pain, in her longing for the love in which she'd believed so strongly. It seemed to Marin that rather than recover from the loss, her sister died a little more each day.

I'll never give a man my heart, Marin promised herself. *Not if I live to be one hundred. When Moder and Fader get old and die, Elsbet and I will take care of each other. Better two old maids than two women with broken hearts.*

Marin had made the same promise almost every day for the last year. Each day her resolve grew greater as the light in Elsbet's eyes failed to return.

"Maybe her heart will heal in America," their mother had said. "Plenty of young Swedish men are there looking for brides."

Marin wasn't so certain America held the remedy.

A young man's wide, smiling face slipped into Marin's view, pushing away her memories. The wind caught at his blond hair as he leaned against the rail on the other side of Elsbet. His gaze met Marin's. "Hello." He addressed the sisters in the lilting language of their homeland. "Exciting, isn't it? Soon we'll walk on American soil."

Elsbet ignored him.

Marin pulled back slightly, dropped an invisible veil over her eyes, and made her voice cool. "Yes, it is exciting." This wasn't the first time Talif Siverson had attempted to start a conversation with her during the crossing. She'd politely rebuffed each effort. It wasn't as though he was a family friend. He wasn't even from the same part of Sweden as the Nilsson family.

She'd noticed him before he approached her the first time, noticed him before they boarded. His handsome face beneath the wide-brimmed, brown felt hat and his gaze filled with excitement at the prospect before him had drawn her attention more than once. *It's natural that a good-looking man should catch a woman's attention,* she assured herself. *It doesn't mean I want to know him better.*

Talif made another attempt. "Maybe we'll see each other in the new land. Where is your family planning to settle?"

"Minnesota," Marin replied, though she was certain Talif already knew the answer. She'd seen him talking with her father and brothers.

"That's where I'll be homesteading. Where in Minnesota is your family headed?"

"Mankato. Our family will stay with another family while Fader looks for land."

Talif's eyes brightened. "That's my plan. My friend, Afton Thomton, says he knows of good land about one hundred miles to the north and west of Mankato, near the Minnesota and Chippewa rivers. We're going to look at it as soon I arrive."

"I hope you find what you want." Marin turned her back to the man and her gaze back to the water. Against all wisdom, her heart insisted on quickening in this man's presence. It was all she could do to keep the welcome from her eyes.

A long pause met her action. She was sorely tempted to shoot a glance back at where he'd stood, but she refrained herself with discipline. Was he still there?

A clearing of his throat finally broke the silence. She heard the pain of her rebuff in his voice. "I'd best be getting my things together. I want everything ready so my time is free to stand up here and watch as we near shore. Good day to you, ladies. I hope to see you in America."

Marin heard his boots smack softly against the deck as he walked away. Her throat burned from holding back her response. She didn't want to see him in America. She didn't want to see any men in America who might threaten her heart.

Chapter 2

Chippewa County, Minnesota—January 1873

M arin heaved a sigh of frustration. "Einer, pay attention," she demanded in Swedish. She glared at her fifteen-year-old brother, who sat across from her at the homemade wooden table in the one-room sod house. Light from the kerosene lantern played across his hair, which was pale brown like their father, Hjalmar's. "I've asked you three times to read the verse from Philippians in English. How do you expect to improve your English if you don't try?"

"What does it matter? We've been in America for a year and a half, and never leave the farm or see anyone but other Swedes."

August, twelve and the youngest of the Nilsson family, leaned forward on the barrel he used as a chair. "That's not true. Sometimes you go to town with Fader. You see people who aren't Swedes there."

Einer grunted. "I've gone to town with Fader exactly twice since we moved here last spring."

"More than me," August insisted. "And all our neighbors aren't Swedes. The Andersons are Norwegian. And there's the bachelor on the homestead to the south who came from New York."

"We won't stay so isolated forever," Moder broke in. "New people keep moving into the area."

Marin nodded. "Yes. Besides, we all agreed it's important to learn the language of our new land."

Anger smoldered in Einer's eyes. "None of my friends study English every night." He pushed the family's only copy of the precious Swedish-English translation of the New Testament from in front of him, narrowly missing the kerosene lantern.

"Watch out!" Moder grabbed for the lamp's clear glass base.

"I didn't hit it." Impatience filled Einer's defensive words.

"Einer." Fader's deep voice, low but stern, tumbled through the one-room soddy.

Silence filled the air in the wake of Fader's gentle reproof. Fader never allowed the children to speak with disrespect to Moder.

Einer crossed his arms over his chest and glared at the table.

Marin shifted her weight, uncomfortably aware that everyone was staring at Einer: Moder, who sat beside Marin on the crude log bench; Elsbet, on Marin's other side; August, who sat beside Einer; and Fader, who stood talking in quiet tones with their neighbor, Talif Siverson, beside the large, Dala-painted trunk at the end of Moder and Fader's bed. Normally Fader would be at the table with the rest of the family during the English-learning hour, but he'd excused himself when Talif arrived a quarter-hour ago.

Only with difficulty had Marin kept her gaze from Talif and her attention on the lesson. As their nearest neighbor, it wasn't uncommon for Talif to visit with Fader after the day's work was done.

Moder touched Marin's hand. "Marin, let's begin again."

Marin hesitated. No doubt Einer thought he should be visiting with the men instead of sitting with the women and youngest child. Was he embarrassed that Fader reprimanded him in front of Talif?

As the family member who knew English best, Marin led the family's daily English-learning hour. She knew Einer wouldn't dare chance Fader's disapproval by leaving the table, but perhaps she shouldn't insist he read the verse. She cleared her throat and repeated the verse in Swedish from memory before asking, "August, would you read the verse in English?"

The tow-headed boy pulled the New Testament near. "Which verse was it again?"

"Philippians, chapter 4, verse 13."

August frowned at the pages before him and read haltingly, " 'I can do all things through Christ which strengtheneth me.'"

The class continued only a few minutes longer. As the four gathered about the table stood up, Moder asked Talif, "Would you care for some bread and coffee before leaving, Mr. Siverson? There's quite a chill in the air tonight."

Marin smiled. A guest never left the Nilsson home without such an offer, regardless of the time of day or the amount of food available or even whether the Nilssons liked the visitor. Hospitality was as much a part of Fader and Moder as their faith.

"*Tack*, Mrs. Nilsson. A little warmth in my belly would be welcome against the cold. Besides, your coffee is always better than mine." He grinned at her and sat down on the barrel Einer had vacated.

As Moder put water in a huge graniteware kettle to heat on the stove, Fader headed to the sod barn to check on the cow and oxen. Einer and August, always glad to leave the dark little house that they considered the womenfolk's place, followed.

Talif reached for the New Testament. "I received one of these from a representative of a Lutheran church in New York when I arrived in America."

"That's where we got this one," Marin told him.

"Your fader tells me your family studies English for an hour each day."

"Yes, it's true, except for *Söndag*. We take turns reading in both Swedish and English. Then we choose a verse to memorize in English."

"That's a good plan. Does your family also speak in English around the house and while they work together each day?"

"We say we will, but it's easy to fall back into Swedish, as you heard tonight."

"Still, it is important to learn English. Those Swedes who know the language best will be able to get along best with Americans in business. Einer knows that. He's just tired."

Marin nodded. "I think he's right about other parents not requiring their children to learn English or even to read and write Swedish, as is required in the homeland."

"It's understandable. Everyone is so busy establishing their fields and homes. It takes all the time and energy available for parents and children alike."

Marin rested her forearms on the table and leaned forward. "But everyone will pay in the end if the children don't learn. How will the parents feel when the children are grown and still unable to communicate easily with the merchants, for instance?"

"I agree with you, but there isn't a school near enough for the children to attend. Chippewa City is the nearest village, and it's too far for the children to walk. The county doesn't have money to build a school here or pay another teacher."

"I know." Deflated, Marin sat back, her shoulders slumping. "For months I've been asking our heavenly Father to provide a school for the children in the area."

"Perhaps you should start one."

"I. . ." Marin stared at him, stunned. "But I'm not a teacher."

Talif shrugged. A smile lit his wide face. "You certainly sounded like one tonight."

"That was only with my family. I've no training to *truly* teach others."

"You've the knowledge that others need, and from your father's comments, I've no doubt you've the ability to share that knowledge with others. What else is required to teach?"

Marin spread her hands. "I don't know, but surely some test must be passed or permission received from the county school superintendent." Still, prickles ran along her skin at the possibility.

"You have a dream, a dream for a school for the Swedish children, and you've asked the Lord to grant this dream. It seems to me the best way for Him to do that is for you to do what you can toward building that dream. If it's to be, He will show you the next step and the next."

"What steps?" As soon as she asked the question, ideas popped into her mind. "Maybe I can talk with Miss Allen, the school teacher at Chippewa City. I can ask her what I need to do to become a teacher in this county—whether I need more training or to take a test."

"Yes, that would be a perfect place to start."

"But it won't be possible for me to get more training if I need it."

"Now you're trying to cross a bridge you don't even know needs to be crossed."

"You're right." Another problem loomed. "There's nowhere to hold lessons."

"You teach just fine right here."

"But this is our home. There isn't room for students."

"We hold church services here sometimes, and in other homes, too, some smaller than this."

She couldn't argue the truth of that. Excitement started to build, even as other problems came to mind. "We've no supplies."

"If the Lord can provide the teacher, students, and building, He can certainly provide whatever else is required."

Marin sat quietly for a minute, her mind racing. "Do you truly think it's possible?"

Moder set a cup of coffee on the table in front of Talif. "Didn't we just read tonight that 'All things are possible through Christ'?"

All things. Even a school, with herself as teacher? A thrill of hope ran along Marin's spine.

A minute later, Fader and the boys returned. Moder poured a cup of coffee for Fader and explained Talif's idea. Marin watched her father's face closely, knowing he was good at hiding his true feelings, good at using tact to give a gentle refusal.

"Sounds like a fine idea, Marin. Would you be agreeable to it?"

At Marin's surprised, cautious nod, he continued. "You couldn't give all of your time to it. Moder and Elsbet need your help, too."

Marin nodded again.

Fader glanced up at Moder and smiled. "What do you think, Tekla? Could we share our humble home with the neighbor children a few hours each day?"

"I think we could." Moder's smile lit up Marin's heart.

Marin's gaze darted to Talif, and caught him grinning back at her like a coconspirator.

"We'll need to rise early tomorrow, Marin," Fader advised, glancing at her over the rim of his pottery cup, "if we're to make it to Chippewa City so you can talk with Miss Allen."

"Yes, Fader." Joy bubbled within Marin's chest. A trip to town, a visit with the teacher, Moder and Fader agreeing to let her use their home as a school, and above all, her parents and Talif's belief in her ability to teach. It seemed too good to be true.

❧

Excitement, ideas, possibilities, and fears churned in Marin's mind, keeping sleep at bay for two hours after the rest of the family fell asleep. Pushing aside the bed curtain, Marin slipped out from under the heavy quilts, careful not to disturb Elsbet, who shared the bed. One of their brothers grunted and rolled over in the bed above Marin and Elsbet's, and Marin held her breath until all was again still.

She trod in stocking feet across the cold dirt floor to the window between the end of her parents' bed and the door, the window by which Fader and Talif had conversed earlier. A cotton curtain hid the bed from view, just like the curtain around the children's bed.

Marin picked up a quilt from the top of the trunk and climbed onto the wide window seat formed by the three-foot-wide blocks of sod. A woven rug of red and blue brightened the sill, and warmed the dirt a bit. She pulled her knees up, glad to have her feet off the cold floor, and wrapped the quilt around herself.

The sky was bright with starshine, clear of clouds. *The way the path of my dream appears tonight,* she thought, *bright, guided by starlight, clear.*

Her gaze drifted over the snow-covered prairie. There wasn't much to see, not even one tree. The sod barn, which sheltered the oxen, horse, and cow, stood silhouetted against the night sky. If the hour were earlier, a small point of light would be shining from Talif's window. No light there now. He'd be sleeping, of course. Without the light, his sod house was too far away to see even in the starlit, snow-bright night.

Even so, Marin's gaze searched the prairie where she knew his home stood. Gratitude filled her chest, warming her heart. In all the months they'd lived as neighbors, she'd treated him with a cool politeness. In return, he'd shown her how to reach for her heart's dream: to establish a school for the Swedish children. "Forgive me, Lord," she whispered. "Forgive me, Talif, and *tack*."

Chapter 3

Marin studied her image in the silver hand mirror Moder had brought from Sweden and patted the blond braids wrapped in a coronet from ear to ear on top of her head. "Do I look proper, Elsbet?"

Elsbet's usually sober face sparkled with laughter. "Like a proper school teacher, yes, and beautiful besides. It's time to quit admiring yourself and get ready to greet your students."

"*My* students." Marin handed Elsbet the mirror. Wonder and dismay battled for supremacy. "Do you truly believe I can do this?"

"Of course. You'll be a blessing to your students."

Marin pressed the palms of her hands down the skirt of her best plaid dress, straightened the prim black ribbon bow at the neck, and took a deep, shaky breath. "I hope so."

She pushed back the curtain that divided the beds from the main room, walked to the table, and looked down at her few supplies: the Swedish-English New Testament; the small slate she'd bought at the general store last week when she visited Miss Allen; an old, well-read Mankato newspaper; the few letters they'd received from relatives and friends in Sweden and other parts of America; and the faithful kerosene lamp. The lamp would be needed, for even during the day there wasn't enough light in the sod house by which to read. Marin sighed. "Not much to begin a school with, I'm afraid."

Moder patted Marin's shoulder. "Beginnings are often small."

"Another Swedish proverb, Moder?"

She gave a sweet chuckle. "No, my own."

Marin glanced about the room. Who had ever heard of a schoolroom with the only desk a table on which the family had eaten breakfast an hour before school was scheduled to begin? The odor of corn cakes, ham, and coffee lingered in the air. The stove lent welcome warmth to the room.

August sat on the trunk, his eyes wide with anticipation. Einer leaned against the wall beside the window, trying to look uninterested, but Marin could see his excitement.

Fader entered the room, letting in a blast of chill January wind before he shut the heavy door. His cheeks shone red beneath his fur cap. "Here, Marin. It's time to announce that school will begin in a few minutes." He held out a cowbell. "Every schoolmarm needs a bell to ring."

Marin accepted the cold bell with a laugh and hugged him. "*Tack*, Fader."

"English, daughter." He shook a finger at her playfully.

Moder placed a thick, gray wool shawl about Marin's shoulders. Marin took a deep breath and opened the front door, bell in hand. A sign Elsbet had tatted hung on the outside of the door: SCHOOL. Marin smiled, feeling wrapped in her family's love. Each member of the Nilsson family had contributed something to the new school.

The clear sky above the horizon was still bathed in dawn's pale lavender and rose above the snow-swept prairie. At the sight before her, Marin's heart missed a beat. Children waded through the foot-high snow toward the Nilsson house, their jackets, scarves, and hats dark or colorful splashes against the white background. Some of the students were almost to the Nilsson yard. Others were still distant enough that Marin couldn't make out their faces.

With a grin, she closed the door behind her and began to ring the bell. At first, in her excitement, she barely felt the chill. The family's black-and-white dog jumped up on her, barking the news that he saw people coming. "Shush, Sven," she scolded, pushing him down. "It's the school children. You must be nice to them when they arrive. No jumping on them."

Soon the cold from the air and the metal bell handle seeped into her bones, but she continued ringing the bell until the first group of children arrived at the door. Sven ran circles about them, barking in joyful greeting. Marin recognized the students as the Skarstedt children who lived over two miles to the east.

"*God morgan*, Eva, Anders, Sture. *Stig in*, come in."

"*God morgan*, Marin," ten-year-old Anders and eight-year-old Sture mumbled as they stepped over the threshold. "*God morgan*, Miss Nilsson," Eva greeted in her quiet, shy manner.

Marin was torn between the desire to stay outside until all the children arrived or to go in where it was warm. Warmth won. It wouldn't do for the teacher to come down ill on the first day of school. Besides, the other students were on the way and not likely to loiter in the winter morning. She could greet them beside the door inside as well as out.

Ten minutes later, she stood at one end of the table and stared in amazement. Children filled the sod house to bursting. *Students*, she reminded herself, a thrill warming her chest, *not just children, but students. Nineteen of them.*

Marin was glad her plaid skirt hid her knocking knees. She'd longed for this day, and now that it was here, she was terrified. *Don't think about the fear*, she ordered herself. *Just do what you planned. The Lord will take care of the rest.*

"*Velkommen.* Let us begin our first day of school with a prayer of thanksgiving." She clasped her hands and bowed her head. "Our heavenly Father, we thank Thee for granting us a place to gather and learn. Help us to use this opportunity to grow in knowledge and wisdom. Amen."

A murmur of *amen*s echoed in the little room.

Marin looked up and smiled brightly. "Now, then, we're ready to begin." She immediately faltered once more at the sight of nineteen pairs of eyes concentrated upon her.

The youngest children sat on the beds, their legs dangling over the sides, boots and shoes on the floor. Students' coats and scarves were piled on the quilts behind the children. Elsbet sat on the sod window seat between the bedsteads, keeping watch for the moment over the little ones for Marin. The older boys, including Einer, stood along the wall. Orpha Stenvall and Viola Linder, the oldest girls at thirteen and ten, claimed the top of the Dala-painted immigrant trunk. The in-between-aged children sat at the table. Every child watched her intently.

She swallowed hard, keeping the smile in place. *Just follow your plan,* she reminded herself again. *They're only the children from the church. You know them all. Your family and Talif and the children's parents all believe you can do this.* "We'll begin with the school rules. Each day will begin with a prayer or hymn. In the beginning, we'll speak mostly Swedish, but you'll be required to speak English more as you learn that language. Often I'll say something in Swedish, then repeat it in English. That way you'll become accustomed to hearing both languages and perhaps learn English more quickly. There will be no whispering. You will raise your hand and wait for me to call upon you to speak. When I do call upon you, or when you are to recite a lesson, you'll stand. You will address me as Miss Nilsson. Do you understand?"

Most of the students nodded. Jems Stenvall and Knute Linder, two of the older boys, shifted their feet and stared at her without nodding, but they didn't challenge her, either. Marin noticed that the youngest children frowned or looked confused. Was it too much for such little ones to remember at one time? She smiled at Sophia Linder, the tiniest of the students. "Don't worry. If you forget the rules, I'll remind you."

A relieved smile spread across the round face between thick blond braids. "What if I need to go the necessary?"

Snickers filled the air.

Marin bit back a grin. "You raise your hand and ask permission."

Sophia shook her head, her eyes wide. "I don't like to go alone." She grasped the hand of the seven-year-old girl beside her. "Can my sister, Stina, come with me?"

"Yes."

"Does she have to raise her hand, too, or just me?"

"Just you, Sophia."

Sophia frowned. "I'm thirsty."

"The water pail and dipper are by the wall beside the barrels." Marin pointed to the place. "Students must also raise their hands when they need a drink."

Sophia raised her right hand high.

"Yes, Sophia?"

"I need a drink."

"May I have a drink, Miss Nilsson?"

Sophia shook her head. "I'm not Miss Nilsson. You are."

The other students burst into laughter. Marin swallowed a chuckle. "I meant, the proper way to ask for a drink is, 'May I have a drink, Miss Nilsson?'"

"Oh." Sophia didn't repeat the question. She only looked more confused.

"You may get a drink if you wish, Sophia."

All smiles, Sophia slipped off the bed and headed across the room.

Marin began to relax and turned to the other students. "Your parents were asked to send along with you any books or supplies they had available. Let's see what everyone's brought. Everyone please stand." She looked over at the older boys. "We'll start with you, Jems. Then Knute. Everyone follow in an orderly manner and set your items on the table."

When all the students had passed the table and returned to their seats, Marin's heart sank. The supplies were meager: Marin's small slate, five Swedish-English New Testaments, one well-read and torn Swedish newspaper, and one book of Swedish poetry. She'd known supplies would be limited, but how could she teach so many students with so little?

It wouldn't do to let the students know how discouraged she found their offerings. She forced another smile. "Wonderful. I'm glad to see that each family has a Swedish-English New Testament. That means every student can study reading both languages at home, not only here at school. Now I'm going to talk to the oldest student from each family to find out what education each of you had in Sweden and America. While I do that, my sister, Elsbet, will lead the rest of you in an exercise, memorizing a Bible verse in Swedish and then in English."

The school day went by faster than Marin anticipated. It seemed the day had barely started before the students were filing out the door toward home. Marin stood just inside the door, smiling at the departing children in spite of her exhaustion. *"Vi ses i morgon,"* she repeated again and again. "I'll see you tomorrow."

She leaned down to tighten the ties on little Sophia's red crocheted headband beneath the girl's pointed chin. Sophia smiled her thanks with a charming grin made of little teeth with big spaces in between. *"Tack,* Teacher."

Marin's heart took a little leap. *Teacher.* "Ingen orsak, Sophia. You're welcome."

When the last student had left, Marin leaned back against the door, closed her eyes, and heaved a sigh of relief. The first day was over, and she'd lived through it. She'd been called "Teacher" for the first time. She was living the role she'd asked the Lord to give her. She'd expected it to bring joy, and it did. It also terrified her.

❧

Marin was helping Moder and Elsbet clear the dinner dishes from the table when Talif arrived that evening. As usual, he visited with Fader, Einer, and August at the table, where light from the kerosene lamp chased away the darkness of the winter evening. All four enjoyed cups of Moder's coffee.

Marin felt her gaze drawn to Talif continually while she worked. Each time she looked in his direction, she saw him watching her, a smiling curiosity in his eyes though he continued chatting about farm topics with Fader. She longed to share with Talif the experiences of her day. After all, he'd helped make the school possible.

"Elsbet and I will do the dishes, Marin," Moder said as she took a large wooden bowl from Marin, "while you prepare tomorrow's lessons."

"*Tack,* Moder." Marin smiled her gratitude and walked to the immigrant trunk to pick up the New Testament and her slate.

Talif stood, looking contrite. "I should be going. I'm intruding on your English hour again."

Fader pushed himself up from the barrel on which he'd been seated. "No. We've agreed to pass on the family English hour while Marin is teaching. Moder, Elsbet, and I will take time when possible to join Marin's class for our English lessons. Marin doesn't need an extra hour of teaching us each evening in addition to her responsibilities to her students." He reached for his coat hanging on a nail on the wide wooden door frame. "I'd best check on the beasts. Einer, August, come along."

While the brothers put on their coats, Fader lit a lantern. Moder handed him a plate of scraps for the dog. A swirl of cold air entered the warm house when the men left, chasing away a bit of the chicken stew and dumpling odors, and the warm smell of heat from the stove. Marin shivered as she sat down across the table from Talif.

Talif smiled at her. "One good thing about sod houses, they keep the cold out."

"*Ja,* that is true when the door isn't open."

"How did your first day of school go?"

"Wonderful!" Marin leaned her forearms against the table's edge, her hands clasped. "And awful." She laughed at the dichotomy.

Talif's grin answered her mirth. "Like most things in life, part good, part not-so-good, huh? Tell me about it."

"I'm afraid I didn't think my plan through well. Including Einer and August, I've nineteen students. Nineteen!"

"That's a roomful, I'd say."

"They're all ages. Sophia Linder is the youngest. She's five. Knute Linder and Einer are the oldest at fifteen. Most of the older students know some math and geography, and how to read and write in Swedish. The youngest students need to learn everything. Some of the students can speak a bit of English, but none of them can read it except my brothers." Marin spread her hands, palms up. "How can I teach so many children who start with such different abilities?"

"With patience," he replied promptly, "and wisdom and ingenuity. The Lord wouldn't have put you in this position if you weren't able to do it."

"I hope you're right." She leaned forward. "We've barely any supplies beyond the Swedish-English New Testaments."

"What supplies do you most need?"

"A blackboard would be wonderful. Slates for each of the children." Marin began ticking items off on her fingertips. "A globe for geography. Math books and readers." She sighed. "Not that it does any good to wish. There's no money for these things."

"Doesn't hurt to make a prayer list for them, does it?"

Marin opened her mouth to protest. It seemed impossible that God could furnish the supplies. The families needed all their money for their homes and fields, yet Scripture assured that nothing was impossible with God. "You're right; it won't hurt to ask. After all, the Lord answered my prayer for a school even though it's not what I expected."

Talif laughed. "Things seldom are what we expect. Tell me more about your first day."

She told him of the mixture of excitement and fear with which she'd started the day, of her fear she wouldn't know how to handle the older boys if they chose not to respect her authority, and of Sophia's funny comments. "The best part of the day was when the students left."

"You don't mean it!" Talif raised his blond eyebrows in astonishment.

"Not the way you think," she hastened to assure him. Marin touched the fingertips of her right hand to her throat and swallowed. "When Sophia Linder left, she called me 'Teacher.'" Marin almost whispered the word. "It's the first time anyone's called me that."

Talif met her gaze and smiled into her eyes, a sweet smile that wrapped around her heart.

Marin dropped her gaze to the table, feeling suddenly vulnerable and a bit foolish. "It probably doesn't seem like much, but it is to me. I've always thought teachers such special people, and now..."

"Now you are one."

She bit back the words on the tip of her tongue: *If I'm capable of meeting the challenge.* Talif would only repeat that God wouldn't have put her in the position if she weren't able to meet the duties. Talif was right, of course, but it was going to be more work than she'd ever imagined. Well, she wasn't afraid of hard work. She squared her shoulders and met his gaze. "Yes, now I am one."

Warmth, contentment, and faith spread through her chest as she and Talif shared smiles across the flickering flame from the kerosene lamp.

❧

The joy that shone from Marin's eyes when she proclaimed herself a teacher shone again in Talif's memory an hour and a half later. He stared out the wavy glass in his window, looking across the prairie to where the lights from the Nilsson home gleamed. Marin's happiness stirred his soul.

What an extraordinary woman she was, to take on such a challenge! He'd been attracted to her from the first moment he saw her, but he hadn't known then what a strong, giving person lay hidden by her outer beauty. She'd made it plain from the beginning by her cool attitude that she didn't want him to court her. He'd bided his time, offering only friendship. During that year and a half, his attraction had grown into love. At least lately she acted more friendly toward him. Was he a fool to hope she'd one day return his affection?

He'd encouraged her to believe that with God all things are possible, to believe the Lord would make her dream a reality. Yet Talif didn't quite trust that his own dream of making a home and building a family with Marin would come true. What if the Lord had other plans for her? Even if it was best for them to be together, the Lord allowed people free will. Talif remembered many times seeing people make choices he felt weren't in their best interests.

With a sigh, Talif turned from the window and crawled beneath the heavy quilts on his cornhusk mattress. He slipped his hands beneath his head and stared at the once-white cloth covering the ceiling. Moonlight rested gently on his face, but he didn't notice. His thoughts remained with Marin: *Miss Marin Nilsson, teacher.* A twinge caught at his heart. He envied Miss Nilsson's students, the time spent in her presence.

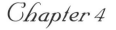

Chapter 4

Talif laughed at the sight before him as he approached the Nilsson's soddy. Driving his runner-mounted wagon from his place to theirs across the snowbound prairie, he'd wondered what all the people were doing in the yard. Now he knew. Letters and words were carved into the snow. Marin had found an ingenious solution to the lack of a blackboard and slates.

Sunlight bounced off the snow-covered yard and off the young students' red cheeks as they looked up from their work to greet him. Marin glanced up, too, from where she knelt beside Sophia and shot him a quick, small smile before turning her attention back to Sophia's attempts at spelling. *En. Två. Tre.* The little girl was obviously learning to write her Swedish numbers.

His chest constricted in a warm, pleasant way at the sight of Marin so involved with the child. He welcomed the feeling but didn't dwell on it as he directed the horse toward the sod barn.

Talif barely reached the barn when Mrs. Nilsson came out of the house, carrying the cowbell. Within minutes, laughter drifted through the cold air as children of all ages headed toward home. Boys teased and chased girls and tossed snowballs at each other. Swinging metal lunch pails glinted in the sunshine. Marin stood in the doorway, still in her coat and scarf, watching the students depart.

"Get along there." Talif urged the horse toward the house, stopping only feet from the door. He nodded at Marin. "I apologize for interrupting your class."

"Classes were almost over anyway, as you can see. Are you looking for Fader? He's in the barn."

"*Nej.* I've come bearing gifts." He climbed over the wagon seat and into the wagon bed.

"Gifts? For us?" Curiosity filled Marin's eyes as she walked toward the wagon.

"For your school. For you and your students." Talif's heart picked up speed. Would she like his gifts? All the while he'd worked on them, he'd imagined the pleasure he'd see reflected in her face. Now he doubted the worthiness of his gifts.

He lifted the largest of them and held it up above the side of the wagon for her to see. "Do you know what this is?"

She frowned slightly, studying the gift, and disappointment began to seep into his hope. Then the frown cleared, and her eyes gleamed with excitement. "It's a blackboard. You made us a blackboard."

"*Ja*. Not a fancy one. It's just boards painted black."

"But it will work, don't you think?"

"*Ja*. It will work just fine. It won't be as smooth as a real one to write on, of course, though I sanded it down as best I could." He refrained from mentioning the hours and hours he'd spent smoothing the wood with a piece of broken glass.

"Oh, it's a wonderful gift, Talif. The students will be so excited tomorrow when they see it. No more need to write in the snow."

He chuckled as he lowered the blackboard over the side of the wagon bed. "They may not appreciate that part so well. Seemed to me they were enjoying themselves out here."

"It's nice for them to get out of the house. I've tried having them write in the dirt floor, but it's too dark to see well, and Moder doesn't appreciate the way it loosens the dirt. Wherever did you find extra boards for this? Surely you didn't go to the expense of buying them for us?"

"There's an abandoned homesteader's shack, barely larger than a necessary, a couple miles to the west. I took the wood from there. The homesteader headed to the Black Hills after the grasshoppers left. Said he's never coming back. Rather take his chances on finding gold dust than farming. He won't be needing the wood."

Marin's smile blazed. "I never thought I'd be thanking God for the grasshoppers. Imagine the Lord using them to help the school I didn't know last summer would exist now."

"That's our Lord, not one but many steps ahead of us. If we remembered that, we'd trust Him a lot more." Talif leaned down and picked up a small pile of wood from the wagon bed. "Here's some more supplies for your school." He handed them over the side, and Marin took them from him.

Surprise and wonder swept over her face, and a laugh erupted. "You made slates for the students."

"More like tiny blackboards."

"The students will love them. So do I. I'm so grateful for your kindness and the way you've supported this school from the beginning."

Talif shrugged, unexpectedly self-conscious about his offering. "It's little enough compared to the hours you give to the students." He climbed down from the wagon and lifted the large blackboard. "I'll help you get these inside."

Once inside the sod house, he glanced around at the crowded floors and wall space. He hadn't considered the limited space when making the blackboard.

Marin didn't seem to have any misgivings about the cramped conditions. "Set it in front of that curtain at the end of the double bedstead." She flashed a smile at Moder and Elsbet. "Look what Talif brought; a blackboard and slates for the children. He made them himself."

Talif tried to discount the joy and pride that flooded him at her words, but he wasn't successful. He set the board down where she'd said and removed his hat.

Mrs. Nilsson and Elsbet came over to "ooh" and "aah" over his work, making him feel foolish but happy. Soon they moved back to the kitchen area to continue preparing the dinner of pork roast and potatoes that was filling the house with mouthwatering odors.

Marin turned her shining blue-eyed gaze on him. "How can I ever thank you for all you've done?"

Talif pushed the hand not holding his hat into his jean's pocket. He'd been waiting for an opportunity to tell her what he wanted. He knew this was the right moment, but it was still hard to say. "There's one thing you can do for me. I'm not a child like your students, but I need to learn how to speak and write English better. If you want to thank me, you can tutor me."

"No!" Shock widened Marin's eyes, and she stepped back, clutching her tan shawl.

Disappointment twisted through Talif. He struggled to keep it from showing.

Marin's gaze darted in one direction and then another. Her refusal to meet his gaze told him she was embarrassed about her sharp and instant refusal. "I—I can't tutor you," she started to explain. "Teaching the students takes all my time." Her words rushed over each other. "I spend every evening planning the lessons for the next day. And I need to help Moder with duties around the house, too."

"Of course." Now it was Talif who looked away. "It was thoughtless of me to think you'd have time. Your obligation is to your students and your family. I understand." He put on his hat and stepped around her toward the door. "I'd best be going. Evening, Mrs. Nilsson, Elsbet."

"I–I'm sorry."

"Don't give it a thought," he reassured Marin, not looking back.

Disappointment cut through him, keen and sharp, as he climbed into the wagon and headed the horse toward home. Marin's excuse was true; he knew that. How she found time to prepare lessons for nineteen students with such a vast difference in needs was beyond his comprehension. He should take her words at face value.

But it wasn't the words that hurt. It was the expression on her face, her first reaction to his request. The horror that spoke of more than a mere lack of time. The repulsion in her eyes and the explosive "No!" said she couldn't bear the thought of spending time that close to him.

"And I can't bear the thought she feels that way," he whispered into the early evening dusk, his gaze on his lonely little sod house on the rise ahead of him, pain tugging at his heart.

❧

Moder stared across the room from her place beside the hot stove, a wooden spoon in one hand. "Marin, how could you be so unkind?"

Marin glanced at her mother, then away. The fingers of one hand twisted her gray woolen skirt while guilt skittered through her. "I wasn't unkind. I haven't time to tutor him. You know better than anyone how much time the teaching takes me."

"You could have been gentler in your refusal. Talif has given so much support to your school, to say nothing of the many ways he's helped your father out of friendship."

The truth in Moder's words deepened Marin's guilt and caused a strange discomfort. She usually got along so well with her mother. They shared ideals and interests, and seldom had sharp words for each other. Marin wasn't accustomed to Moder's disapproval. "I didn't mean to speak unkindly. His request seemed so impossible to grant, and—"

"I'm going for a walk." Elsbet stepped toward the door, slipping her coat on. "I won't be long. Don't worry, Moder, I won't go far." She was out the door before Moder or Marin could say good-bye.

Elsbet's actions didn't surprise Marin. Her sister often went for walks in the dusk, before night settled too darkly on the prairie and covered potential dangers such as wolves and coyotes. Marin knew Elsbet liked to spend time away from everyone else in the quiet with her own thoughts. She hated disagreements, also, and that was probably the true reason she'd left now. The knowledge didn't add to Marin's comfort.

Moder's gaze rested on the door. "You don't want to become like Elsbet." Her voice was quiet, filled with sadness.

Marin studied Moder's face. The sadness in her voice shone in her eyes. "Elsbet is a good person. She has such a kind heart. I'd be glad to be more like her." *Elsbet wouldn't have spoken so roughly to Talif. She'd probably have made time to tutor him if she wasn't attracted to him.*

"Elsbet is a lovely person, yes." Moder reached for Marin's hands. "But her heart is closed to love. You don't want to end up like that."

Marin tugged her hands away. "Talif didn't ask me to love him; he asked me to tutor him."

"You said no to him as a man as well as to his request," Moder admonished. "I'm not only a mother but a woman. It is unfortunate that the man Elsbet loved treated her so harshly. My mother's heart aches for her every day. I hate that she was hurt by him, but I hate just as much that she continues to hurt herself."

"How does she do that?"

"By keeping a wall around her heart and refusing to believe that any other man might truly love her. A heart blocked off from love grows cold, Marin. Remember the proverb, 'A life without love is like a year without summer'? I don't want both my daughters to live their lives without love's warmth."

"But I'm not—"

"Talif Siverson cares for you, that's easy to see. He's a good man. Perhaps you truly don't care for him in the way I hope you will one day care for a man, in the way I care for your father, with a love that makes your life larger and better and more beautiful. Yet you could choose to treat Talif more kindly and to entertain the possibility of falling in love with some young man. You've turned down every man who's expressed an interest in courting you."

Marin slipped off her shawl and gave her attention to carefully folding it.

"I haven't time for courting. I'm teaching. My first responsibility is to the students."

Moder sighed. "Perhaps it would be best for them to have a teacher who is not only good at English, Swedish, arithmetic, geography, and history, but courageous enough to keep her heart open to love."

"Moder, I—"

Her mother pulled her close in a hug. "I love you just as you are. I only want you to be happy."

"I am happy."

"Then I'll keep my thoughts to myself." Moder loosened her hug and patted Marin on the shoulder. "Why don't you ring that school bell and call the family in to dinner? By the time they get inside and we finish setting the table, the meal will be ready."

The clang of the bell didn't overcome the words whispering in Marin's heart. She'd had no idea Moder knew so clearly how she felt about men and marriage. Her mother's perceptions made Marin feel vulnerable.

Moder was right about Talif, of course. Marin knew the true reason she'd refused to tutor him wasn't lack of time, though her time was filled to overflowing. The true reason she'd refused was that she liked him too much. If she allowed herself to spend as much time with him as tutoring required, she might do exactly as Moder wished and allow her heart to open to him.

"That I will never do," she promised herself, glancing at Talif's house in the distance. Determination hardened like rock inside her chest. "Never."

Chapter 5

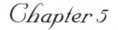

Marin looked up from the opening prayer and glanced around at the students stuffed into every corner of the house. Wind and snow whistled around the corners of the sod house and down the stovepipe, though even a winter storm had no power to penetrate the three-foot-thick sod walls.

It always encouraged her to see the students show up in inclement weather. Their dedication to learning gave her strength to work long into the night to plan lessons.

She smiled at the children. "Since you all walked through the stormy weather this morning to get here, I think for our first lesson we'll work together to learn the English expressions regarding weather. I'll say the expression first in Swedish, then repeat it in English. After I say it in English, you will all repeat it in English together. Understood?"

The children responded with nods

"Good. We'll start with a description of today's weather. *Det är kallt*. It is cold."

"It is cold," the class repeated.

"*Det blåser*. It is windy."

"It is windy."

"*Det snöar*. It is snowing."

"It is snowing."

"Good, class. We'll repeat—"

The door opened, and surprise stopped Marin's speech as Talif entered, a windy gust of cold and snow following him inside.

Talif removed his snow-covered, wide-brimmed hat and nodded at her, a polite, challenging smile on his wind-burned face. "*God morgon*, Miss Nilsson. I'm sorry to be late." He walked to where Einer leaned against one wall. "I'll just take a place here and join the class, if you please."

Marin bit back the response that leaped to her tongue. *If I please? I don't please at all, and he knows it.* Anger roiled through her at his presumptuous action, yet she refused to make a scene over it in front of the students. Likely Talif was counting on that. Well, she'd act like she'd expected him today, and tell him after school that under no circumstances was he to return.

The other students stared at Talif and at her, clearly as surprised as she at the presence of a grown man in the classroom. She ignored the fury in her chest and forced a smile. "Of course you may join us, Mr. Siverson. We're learning English terms for weather today." She turned her gaze deliberately away from him. "We'll repeat the phrases all together once more. Then I will write them on the blackboard, and we will break into small groups to memorize the spelling. Tomorrow we will have a quiz on the terms."

A groan erupted from the older boys.

Marin ignored it. "Repeat after me, *Det är stormar*. It is storming." *Storming inside and out,* she raged silently while the students chanted the phrase.

Talif's deep voice made its way through all the others to her ears no matter how many students spoke at the same time. Even when the students broke into groups and she helped the youngest girls with the weather phrases, the sound of Talif studying aloud with the older boys distracted her.

Once Marin caught Elsbet watching her with sympathy in her eyes. The knowledge that Elsbet saw through Marin's defenses only added fuel to her anger. Her mother's comment flashed through her mind: "A heart blocked off from love grows cold." *Better cold than fiery with pain like Elsbet's.*

Little Sophie tugged at Marin's sleeve.

Marin pushed away her uncomfortable thoughts and smiled down at the girl with the blond braids. *"Ja?"*

"Did I say it right, Teacher?"

Warmth spread over Marin's cheeks. How could she let Talif fill her thoughts to the point she didn't hear her student? "I'm sorry, Sophie. Would you repeat it for me?"

It took a few times for Sophie to learn to drop the *t* that ended the Swedish *kallt* when she said *cold*, but in the end, she said it properly and beamed when Marin praised her.

The day seemed long to Marin and more difficult than usual with her constant awareness of Talif's presence. By the end of the school day, the anger she nursed created an unfamiliar fatigue within her. Still, she stopped Talif as he prepared to leave with the other students. "Mr. Siverson, I'd like to speak with you."

For a moment he hesitated, and she thought he'd refuse, but then he nodded. "Certainly, Miss Nilsson."

As they'd grown to know each other better, they'd fallen into the practice of calling each other by their first names. It sounded strange to hear him address her formally, though she grudgingly appreciated it in front of the students.

She waited uncomfortably while the other students left before turning to him beside the closed door, with a glance at Moder and Elsbet standing by the stove talking while they started dinner. "What do you think you are doing?" Marin kept her voice low and stood closer to him than she'd like, hoping to avoid her mother and sister overhearing the conversation, an almost impossible task. She hated the way her voice shook with the anger she'd held inside for hours.

"Two weeks ago I asked you to tutor me." His spoke quietly, evidently as eager as

Marin to keep the conversation between the two of them. "You said—"

"I said I hadn't the time, and I don't."

"I realize that. It was inconsiderate of me to ask you when you're so busy with the school."

"If you believe that, why did you barge into my classroom today?"

His gaze met hers evenly. "I came because I want to improve my English, and I don't know how to do that on my own. I figured if I'm just another student in your school, my learning won't make any extra demands on your time."

The guilt she'd originally felt at refusing to tutor him began to creep back. He'd helped her start the school, he wanted to learn, and she'd turned her back on his request for her assistance. Still, that didn't change the fact that she didn't want him around constantly, and she wasn't ready to let go of her anger at him for shoving his way into her class.

She glared at him, tapping one high-top booted toe against the hard-packed dirt floor. "The school is for children, not men."

Something akin to anger flashed in his blue eyes, and his lips pressed together firmly before he spoke. "I thought the purpose of the school was to help people learn. I may be a man, but I'm a student when it comes to learning the language of my new country, and I need help. I plan to attend class and study hard, like any of the other students." He placed his black hat on his head and nodded grimly. "See you tomorrow morning, Miss Nilsson."

She stepped back quickly to get out of his way as he opened the door.

Then he was gone, leaving Marin frustrated. Her head throbbed. She'd meant to insist he not return to her classroom. Wasn't that what she'd done? It had been the intent behind her words, and certainly Talif Siverson knew that. Through the weeks of teaching, she'd grown accustomed to students acquiescing to her demands. It hadn't occurred to her he'd attend class if she made it clear he wasn't welcome.

She looked toward Moder and Elsbet. Elsbet turned quickly back to the stove and dumped the onions she'd just chopped into a hot, cast-iron frying pan, but Moder returned Marin's gaze. Obviously the women knew what Talif and Marin had discussed in spite of their attempts at privacy.

Marin lifted her arms, feeling helpless. "What can I do, Moder?"

"Teach him."

"But he's a man. He doesn't belong in the school."

"Then tutor him."

"You know I haven't time!"

Moder wiped her hands on her apron. "Would you refuse to allow him in class if he were any other man?"

"Of course." In spite of her instant response, the question caught Marin off guard. Would she truly mind if, for instance, Sophie's father wanted to join the class? Honesty made her admit to herself that, rather than be angry, she'd likely be flattered. But then, there was no man whose presence affected her like Talif's.

Moder still watched her intently. Did she again know what Marin was thinking?

Marin blushed. "It doesn't matter whether I 'allow' him in class or not. I can hardly force him out if he shows up, and he says he intends to continue attending."

Moder shrugged. "Then there's nothing to do but accept the fact and teach him, is there?" She put a coat over her shoulders. "I'm going to see whether Einer has the cow milked yet. We need some milk for the cooking."

When Moder had left, Marin walked about the room, picking up the small board slates students had used during the day. Another sign of Talif's help with the school. Another reason to feel guilty for not wanting to teach him.

With a sigh, she set the boards on the floor beside the large blackboard, then walked over to Elsbet and reached for a paring knife. "Let me help you slice those potatoes."

"*Tack.*"

For a couple minutes, they worked together in silence, the only sounds the sizzle of the sharp-smelling onions in the frying pan and the crack of burning wood in the cookstove. Marin's thoughts swirled about Talif, his declaration of intent, and her powerlessness to stop him.

"What do you think, Elsbet? I mean about Talif. Do you agree with Moder?"

Elsbet's gaze stayed on the potatoes as she pared. "Do I agree with what? That you should accept the fact that he is going to attend school, and teach him as you do the other students? Or that you would not be upset if it were any man other than Talif?"

If anyone but Elsbet had asked the question, which so directly struck at the heart of the matter, Marin's anger and embarrassment would have increased. But Elsbet's gentle voice and manner made it easier for Marin to accept the probing questions. "You believe, like Moder, that I care for Talif?"

Elsbet shrugged one shoulder, her attention still on her work. "As more than a friend, perhaps. Are you in love with him? Perhaps not. At least, not yet." She lifted her gaze to Marin. A little frown cut between her brows. "Why don't you allow anyone to court you, Marin? Don't you want to be loved, to be married, to have your own family one day?"

Marin looked away. "Because a man wants to court a woman doesn't mean he loves her. All husbands don't love their wives." She refrained from saying that Elsbet, of all people, should know those things. "Some men only want a woman to take care of things like cooking, cleaning, and sewing."

"I think Talif likes you very much. I think he'd court you if you let him and not just to get a housekeeper."

"I don't want to be courted by him, or marry him, or be his housekeeper. I don't need a husband. I'm a teacher. I don't make enough to live on now, but maybe when I have experience and more settlers come here, I can get a teaching job for the county. Then you and I can live together. We'll be just fine, the two of us, without any men."

Elsbet added the sliced potatoes to the onions in the skillet. "You've never been in love. You don't know what it feels like to love someone."

"I don't want to know what love can be like if it can hurt someone as much as it did you."

"Is that why you don't let anyone court you?"

"Maybe." Marin hadn't meant to let Elsbet know how she felt. She took plates out of the cupboard and began setting the table.

"I still think about Anton," Elsbet said quietly from behind Marin.

"I know." *If she didn't think about him,* Marin thought, *Elsbet wouldn't be so sad.*

"Sometimes I think awful things."

"What do you mean?"

"Sometimes I wonder what would happen if Anton's wife died, whether then he'd want me back."

Marin didn't know what to say. The thought of sweet Elsbet having such thoughts stunned her. Is that what loving someone could do to a person? All the more reason not to fall in love.

"I know," Elsbet continued, "it sounds horrible. I don't truly want her to die. I just want Anton back. I know it's not her fault he left me. If he hadn't married her, he would have married someone else. He simply didn't love me as much as I love him."

The emptiness in Elsbet's voice told Marin how much the truth hurt. An old Swedish proverb slipped into Marin's mind. *A wound never heals enough to hide a scar.* "You aren't the only woman whose intended left them behind in Sweden. It happens too often. Men can't be trusted."

"Not all men are like Anton. Some men truly love their wives—men like Fader."

"Yes." Anyone could see how much Fader and Moder loved each other. Marin weighed her words carefully before speaking. "If a woman could be guaranteed a man would love her the way Fader loves Moder, every woman would gladly fall in love. If you believed another man would love you that way, you'd let someone else court you, too, Elsbet."

Elsbet winced. "We're talking about you. You're nineteen, and you haven't started a hope chest."

"I'm too busy teaching." Not for the world would Marin remind Elsbet that her own hope chest, filled with so many hours of loving work, was still under one of the beds, its contents untouched. She linked her arm through Elsbet's. "One day I'll start that hope chest. You and I will need some things when we start our own home."

Elsbet smiled but didn't look convinced.

Time would prove the truth of Marin's intent. For now, she'd just do as Moder said and accept Talif's presence in her classroom. She'd treat him like any other student. Spring was just around the corner. Field work would soon demand Talif's time and require he abandon his plans to attend school. That would be the end of it.

Chapter 6

Teaching had been a heady combination of joy, fear, study, and lack of sleep for Marin before Talif joined the classroom. Now every day challenged her emotions. She was challenged to keep her attention on the other students and their lessons. She was challenged to keep her gaze from darting to Talif whenever she heard his voice or laugh. The greatest challenge came during the part of each day she spent with the older boys on their specific lessons.

Three weeks after Talif began attending class, Marin approached the older boys with dread. Talif, along with Einer, Jems, and Knute, made up the class. Marin kept her gaze carefully away from Talif as she approached them.

"We'll be working on English words with especially difficult spellings and sounds today," she informed them. "We'll start with words that begin with the letter *k*, but the *k* is silent."

Jems, leaning against the wall with his arms crossed, sneered. "Why would a word have a letter that's silent? That's stupid."

"Be that as it may, there are such words." Jems had been challenging her more lately. He'd started school as excited as the other students to learn, but the last week or so his attitude had changed, and she didn't know why. "We'll start with *kniv*, which is spelled *k-n-i-f-e* in English." Marin picked up one of the small board slates, wrote the word, and held the board for the four to see. "It sounds like *nif* with a long *i*."

"So the *e* is silent like the *k*?" Talif asked.

"Yes." She nodded toward Knute. "If you pronounce the word like we do Knute's name, with a *k* sound, you'll be proclaiming your ignorance of the language."

Knute grinned. "That makes it easy for me to remember."

"For all of us," Talif agreed.

Funny how the simple recognition that she'd made learning such a small thing easier for them filled her with pride. "Another word is the English word *know*, which in Swedish is either *veta*, to know something, or *känna*, to know someone."

"The same word is used for both in English?" Talif questioned again.

"Yes." She wrote the word on the board below *knife*.

"It sounds the same as *no*," Jems protested, "the opposite of *ja*. How do we know which form of the word to use?"

"By the way it's used in a sentence," Marin explained, trying to keep her patience.

Jems should know that rule by now. "Why don't you try using each version in a sentence for me right now? Say the entire sentence in English, of course."

"*No*, I won't." Jems grinned. "I don't *know* how to say it."

Knute and Einer laughed, and Marin could see Talif brush his hand over his face to hide a grin. Marin found Jems's play on words rather amusing, also, but the teacher in her wondered whether the action was inappropriate and disrespectful. Best to let it pass, she decided.

"Very good. Now you, Einer."

Einer and Knute each copied Jems by coming up with twists on the two words. The boys' laughs soon drew the other students' attention. "Back to work, everyone," Marin admonished in her most teacherly voice.

Some of the students turned reluctantly away. Others continued to watch, albeit in a less obvious manner. *Oh, well,* Marin thought, *at least they may learn something listening.*

Then it was Talif's turn. When he didn't speak at once, Marin glanced at him. He looked like he was struggling to come up with the sentences. She was about to ask if he needed her to clarify something when he said, "He know she will say no if he asks to court her."

The class erupted into laughter. Marin felt her cheeks grow warm. Was he teasing her? The other students obviously believed he was speaking of himself and her. His eyes glinted with poorly suppressed laughter.

At least his grammar error allowed her to correct him rather than address the meaning of the sentence. "In that use, you would need to add an *s* to the word *know*, Mr. Siverson. 'He knows she will say no.' Please repeat the sentence using the word correctly." Anger cooled her voice.

"He knows she will say no," he repeated, his eyes still laughing though not his voice.

"Correct." *Let him wonder whether I mean he said it correctly, or whether he's correct in thinking I'd say no,* she thought, triumph overcoming the anger.

She proceeded to explain the way the word *know* changed depending upon singular or plural references, and how *knew*, the past tense of *know*, also had a sound-alike word in *new*. She instructed Talif and the boys to work together using the words in more sentences and practicing pronouncing and spelling the words.

When she finally turned to go back to the younger children and begin an arithmetic class, she gave a sigh of relief.

❧

Talif watched Marin walk away from himself and the older boys, and over to a group of younger children. Her shoulders, which inched closer to her ears while talking with his group, lowered back to their normal position.

Did she always feel uncomfortable teaching the older boys? Certainly it couldn't be easy trying to teach her brother Einer. Brothers didn't often like to learn from sisters, especially in front of other boys.

Marin probably worried that Jems and Knute were too close to her in age to respect her knowledge. That would make teaching them tough for her. Lately it seemed Jems was testing her. Not a lot, just pushing a little more than was proper. The situation would bear watching. Talif wasn't about to let Jems or any of the other students cause problems for Marin.

She'd been a good sport about the humorous sentences they'd come up with today. He'd considered using a less volatile sentence, but to subtly tease her had been too tempting in the end. He smiled, remembering how she'd responded with an even more subtle jibe. It was the first time he'd experienced her wit.

After his first day at school, he'd more than half expected Marin to recruit her father and insist he demand Talif quit attending the school. Instead, she taught him every day just as if she didn't wish him gone. Of course, her cool reserve and her reference to him as Mr. Siverson instead of Talif told him clearly that she hadn't changed her mind about his attendance.

The clang of the oven door drew his gaze from where Marin bent over young Eva. Mrs. Nilsson was preparing the stove for baking. Her face looked tired in the dim light of the soddy. The realization of how difficult it must be for Marin's family to go about their daily business with the house filled with students jolted through him. There was barely a minute during the day for the Nilssons to relax and spend alone. Not many families would so graciously disrupt their lives for that of other people's children to have the opportunity to learn.

A memory slipped into his mind: Marin telling him how she hoped to have "a true schoolhouse one day." His gaze slipped back to her. Her earnest expression as she explained an arithmetic problem to Eva caused a little catch in his heartbeat. Marin's dedication to the students never ceased to amaze him.

She deserved that schoolhouse. But how, since neither the county nor church could afford one?

His heart sent up a prayer. *Dear Lord, please provide the schoolhouse for which Marin longs. If there's any way I can help, please show me. Amen.*

A picture of the homesteader's old shack flashed into his mind. Was that meant as an answer to his prayer? He dismissed the thought. That tumble-down place wasn't fit for skunks, let alone a school, and nowhere near as large as this little soddy.

An elbow nudging his side caught his attention. "You plan to study these words with us like the teacher said?" A glint in Jems's eyes added sly innuendo to his question.

"Of course. Just remembering something that needs doing." Talif turned back to the group, disgusted at letting himself get caught by a student, especially Jems, watching Marin.

At noon, the students relaxed and talked while they ate the lunches they'd brought from home. Some children had only buttered bread; others had baked potatoes they'd carried hot to school and left on top of the stove to stay warm. The Nilssons waited to eat until the students were done. Then the family sat down at the table while the students went outside for fresh air.

Talif let Eva and Sophie sweet-talk him into playing fox and geese with the younger children. He'd forgotten the joy of simple play in snow under a blue sky, with cold temperatures crisping the air and wood smoke adding a pleasant, warm fragrance.

Marin's ringing the cowbell brought an end to the games. Talif entered the home-turned-school with the children. Students took advantage during the last minute or two of chatting and laughing together while they removed their coats, mittens, and scarves.

As always, Talif's glance caught sight of Marin. She was picking up the small board slates the ten-year-olds had been using before lunch, nodding and smiling as Sophie regaled her with exaggerated tales of Talif's attempts at fox and geese.

Marin's face changed suddenly from a smile and a pleasantly distracted air to frozen shock. She stared down at the small slate in her hands, the color draining from her cheeks.

Shocked at the sudden change, Talif slipped up behind her and looked over her shoulder at the slate. He was dimly aware of children snickering. "What is it?" he asked, his voice discreetly low.

"Nothing." Marin flipped the board over and stepped briskly away.

But not before he saw it. Someone had drawn a heart, and inside, the words "Teacher + Talif."

He swallowed a groan. This wasn't going to do his cause any good at all.

Chapter 7

One evening two weeks later, Marin rested her elbows on the table, her chin on the palms of her hands, and stared at the open New Testament. She was so weary that the words seemed to swim in the wavering light from the kerosene lamp. The warmth from the stove behind her only made her more tired.

Her gaze slid to the small board slate beside the book. She'd meant to make notes on the slate for tomorrow's lessons, but it remained blank. Her mind refused to follow her intention to plan.

Elsbet sat down opposite her. "You look exhausted. Perhaps you should go to bed."

"No." Marin shook her head. "I haven't planned tomorrow's lessons."

"You'll be too tired to teach if you don't get some sleep. Something will come to you for the lessons tomorrow. It always does."

Did it seem so easy to everyone else, Marin wondered, *to find ways to teach?* "It would be easier if we had proper supplies. I'd like to teach geography, but how, without maps or a globe? I draw maps on the blackboard, but there isn't a way to save them so the students can study them again later. I considered asking the students to write letters to people back in Sweden telling them in English about their new life here. How can they do that on these small board slates? Paper is too precious to expect their parents to allow them to use any for just a lesson."

"Maybe you can have them work on a letter together and write it on the large blackboard."

"But I wanted them to write the words themselves, to practice writing English."

Elsbet's eyebrows lifted in question. "Can't you have a different student write each sentence? Or have them write a sentence on their slates and then you write the sentence on the large board so they can see whether they've written it correctly?"

Marin smiled wearily. "You came up with a solution so easily. I should have asked you for help earlier. Perhaps you should be the teacher."

"Oh, no." Elsbet shook her head, smiling. "That's not for me. I can help you with the simple, everyday things children need to learn, but I haven't the head for schooling you've had since you were a wee one. I wish I could be more help to you. I've noticed Talif helping lately."

"Yes. He's quite smart and completed his schooling in Sweden. He only needs help with his English. Since he can spend more time during these winter months away from his farm, he offered to help teach the older boys arithmetic. It's such a help. Knute is usually a conscientious student, but Einer and Jems prefer to tease and cause trouble sometimes. I suppose they're bored or don't like to learn from someone so close to their own age, and a woman at that."

Elsbet casually brushed at a bread crumb that had escaped the after-dinner wipe-down of the table. "So perhaps Talif's insistence on attending school is a blessing in disguise."

Marin's back tensed. "Not such a blessing that it overcomes the difficulties he brings along. At least no more hearts have shown up on students' slates since that awful experience a couple weeks ago, but I hate the students' sly looks and snickers every time I need to talk with Talif."

"Children are like that. Anything which looks like possible romance amuses them. You know that. It will pass."

"I hope you're right. Teaching isn't nearly as much fun as before the innuendoes began."

"What advice would you give a student in a similar situation, Marin?"

"To ignore it. That to give the teaser a reaction only increases the teasing." Marin laughed, realizing Elsbet's point. "See, you're a natural teacher."

"Only in practical, everyday matters, as I said before." Elsbet stood up as a loud knock interrupted them. "Not in reading, writing, and arithmetic," she said over her shoulder as she hurried to open the door.

Talif entered with the winter cold. Marin was only dimly aware of their greetings as her gaze met Talif's across the room. Annoyance slipped through her veins. Since Talif began attending school, his evening visits with Fader had almost stopped, and from the look in Talif's eyes, he wasn't here to see Fader now.

Marin felt herself tense as Talif removed his hat and gloves and crossed the room to the table. A cylindrical object under one of his arms caught her attention. "*God afton*, Miss Nilsson. I mean, good evening."

"Good evening, Mr. Siverson." Marin straightened her spine and allowed an invisible wall of reserve to slide over her face. "What can I do for you?"

He shifted his weight from one booted foot to the other. "I'd like to do something for you and for the other students." He took the roll of cloth from beneath his arm and handed it to her across the table.

"What is this?" Suspicion made her frown. She accepted the material reluctantly when he didn't respond. Pushing aside the New Testament and slate to make room, she began to unroll the object. It was rectangular in shape and only two-thirds as long as the table's width. The off-white material contrasted sharply with the rough pine boards of the table. Bright-colored embroidered letters began to appear. "A sampler?" When the whole was revealed, she gasped. "Oh!" She covered her cheeks with her fingers.

A picture of a small, white cottage with a thatched roof and a barn decorated the top of the sampler. Beneath the picture the Swedish alphabet marched primly, and beside that the English alphabet. Marin ran her fingers lightly across the finely wrought, colorful letters. "It's beautiful. Where did you get it?"

"My sister, Karin, made it for me before I left for America." Talif pointed to the picture at the top. "That's our parents' place in Sweden."

Marin's conscience struggled for supremacy. The sampler would make a wonderful teaching aid, and the school desperately needed such things. Yet. . .

"I can't possibly accept this." Setting her jaw as firmly as her determination, she began rolling the sampler back up. Such mementoes from loved ones in the homeland, people who might never again be seen, were precious, even priceless. "A gift from your sister. . ." She shook her head.

Talif reached out and stopped her from continuing to roll the sampler. "Now it's her gift and mine to you and to the students." He glanced at the curtain that hid the beds and behind which Elsbet and Mrs. Nilsson had discreetly disappeared. He leaned closer and lowered his voice. "You give of yourself every day to others who have come to this new land, to help them have a better life. Please, allow me the pleasure of giving to the students, also. *Var god.*"

"But it must be so special to you."

"It is." A grin lit his blue eyes. "Isn't that the best kind of gift to give?"

Marin ignored the question. "This sampler is part of your family's heritage now. You should keep it to pass it down to your children and their children."

A strange, almost hurt look filled his eyes for a moment, then disappeared behind a thin reserve. "Perhaps by the time I have children of my own, the students will no longer need the sampler." He cleared his throat. "I promise you, my sister will love knowing her sampler is helping students in America."

Marin gently held the sampler against her chest. "Just before you came, I told Elsbet how badly we need supplies for teaching." She tried unsuccessfully to keep tears from welling up in her eyes.

"You keep adding to that prayer list of things you need for the school, and pretty soon there won't be anything left God hasn't provided."

It seemed to Marin that God supplied most of the things through Talif. The thought ran through her mind that perhaps God found it amusing to do so, to keep bringing the one man who attracted her into her life. Had God also brought this man into her life because she was meant to be attracted to Talif? Her heart skittered away from the possibility.

"Thank you, Talif, for your thoughtful gift." She couldn't simply dismiss him after this, couldn't say "thank you, and good-bye now." She gestured toward the table. "Let me get you a cup of coffee and a cookie before you go."

"*Tack.*" Talif sat down on one of the upended packing boxes beside the table.

Marin set the sampler down and turned to the stove. She reached for the large graniteware kettle, which still held warm coffee from dinner. Marin poured some for herself and Talif, then took from a tin in the homemade pine cupboard some of the eggless cookies Elsbet had made earlier in the day.

When she finally seated herself across from Talif, he said, "I overheard some of the students' parents speaking to you at church last Sunday, telling you that you're doing a good job."

"Yes, it's nice they think so."

"They're right."

His praise pleased her, and she realized it meant more to her than the parents' praise. After all, he saw her teaching every day. None of the parents had visited the school.

The thought of Sunday meetings brought less pleasing recollections of comments by the adults in the congregation. More than one student's mother had asked her whether she and Talif were courting. Of course, Marin denied it in emphatic terms, but the questions made it obvious students and parents alike found Talif's presence in the classroom curious.

"The Linders told me their children are helping them learn English at home," Talif told her. "I suspect the same is happening in the other families. Your teaching is touching lives beyond your classroom."

Marin had never thought of that possibility. She lifted her cup to take a sip of coffee and, looking over the rim, found Talif's blue-eyed gaze intent on her. Suddenly, unexpectedly, she felt shy.

"Moder, Elsbet," she called out, "come see what Talif brought for the school."

The women admired the sampler, then sat down to have coffee with Talif and Marin. The embroidered picture of Talif's home in Sweden stirred the Nilssons' memories, and soon they and Talif were sharing stories of life in the homeland.

While the others talked, Marin discreetly studied Talif. Why hadn't she ever noticed the smattering of freckles on the bridge of his nose, or the way little lines— were they from laughter or squinting against the sunshine while working in the fields, or both—fanned out from the corners of his eyes? She'd never considered him a handsome man, but he had a fine, broad, honest face. He'd grown obviously stronger since they met, likely from plowing never-before-plowed land with its tangle of prairie grass roots.

Maybe she'd reacted too strongly to his choice to study with her class. After all, he only wanted to learn to better speak and write English. What was so awful in that? He'd helped her get the school started, made the blackboard and slates, assisted with teaching the other students, arithmetic, and now given the school that wonderful alphabet sampler. Surely, if anyone deserved to take part in her class, Talif Siverson did.

After all, just because she wasn't in love with the man was no cause to be un-friendly toward him, was it?

Chapter 8

Talif ran the palm of his hand over the board he'd been smoothing with a piece of broken glass. His lips stretched into a tired smile of satisfaction. No students would end up with slivers in their backsides from this bench seat.

He laid the board on the packed-earth floor and rubbed his right shoulder. Working on that board for hours left its mark on his muscles.

Talif let his gaze wander about his small sod house, lingering on one homemade bench after another. He'd spent hours and hours the last month tearing apart the departed homesteader's shack, hauling the wood home, cutting and pounding it into small benches for the school. He'd made good progress on his plan for Marin's schoolhouse...or rather, on the plan he believed the Lord had given him for the schoolhouse.

Rain spattered against his only window, in front of which he sat on one of his homemade benches while working, taking advantage of the little sunlight the clouds and rain let in. If this spring storm kept up, the roof would be dripping water and mud soon.

Mud. April's warmth had melted the last of the snow, chased the frost from the ground, and turned solid ground into squishy, boot-sucking mud. Too wet for planting or for building sod houses. When the rains stopped and the ground dried out somewhat, he and the other farmers could get into the fields.

It would be late summer or early fall before the schoolhouse became a reality. Impatience tugged at him as though he were a puppet with annoying strings tied to his limbs. Through each step of preparing for the school, he daydreamed of the expression he'd see on Marin's face when she first viewed the building.

There were still things to do—ordering the window glass and the wood for the window frames and door, for instance. He'd need to do that in Benson, thirty-odd miles across the prairie, the nearest town with a sawmill. There wasn't enough wood left from the homesteader's shack to use for the frames and door, and what was there wasn't good enough quality for such use anyway. No telling when the land would firm up enough for the Benson trip. He'd need to work the trip in after planting. Some things in life couldn't be put off, and planting fields was one of them.

He wished he could put all his energy into building Marin's school, but that wasn't possible. It would all come about in God's timing, of course, but waiting was difficult.

Marin's heart pounded as she looked about the crowded building at the congregation. She could barely believe this day had finally arrived: the first Sunday in May, the day of the school program signifying the end of the school year.

It seemed a good time for the school year to end. Spring heralded an end of the old and beginning of the new. Hadn't the community just celebrated the coming of spring on April 30, with the Swedish Walpurgis Night celebration? Everyone had gathered about bonfires and enjoyed good food while singing and talking about plans for the warm months ahead.

Students would be busy preparing fields and gardens soon. Too busy for school work. The longer, warmer days had already melted the snow cover and left the land so muddy many of the students found it difficult to traverse the prairie to school. Yes, it was time to end the first school year.

The Skarstedt family owned the largest sod house in the area, and they'd graciously offered it for this special Sunday. In spite of its size, parishioners filled it to overflowing. Unlike most of the sod houses, this house had a separate bedroom. There the students gathered after morning church service, waiting for the program to begin.

Marin's gaze wandered over the students, meeting their bright, eager gazes, noting the cheeks red with anticipation, admiring the Sunday-best clothing, and listening to the excited whispers. She knew the importance of the choice of clothing, how it made one feel better about oneself and more capable. She herself wore her best dress, with a new lace collar made by Elsbet especially for this occasion and Moder's precious silver pin, which had been passed down for three generations.

Even Talif wore a suit today. It wasn't new. *My*, Marin thought, *he looks handsome.*

Talif hadn't much part in today's program. She'd thought it might appear improper to the parents or at the very least cause more speculation by adults in the congregation. He'd agreed to help her keep the program running according to plan and take a small part in one skit. To her relief, he seemed satisfied with that.

She lifted an index finger to her lips. "*Shhh*. It's time for the program to begin. We'll do everything just like we practiced. When others are performing, those of you waiting here are to show them respect and keep quiet. No more whispering. If you've any questions while you wait, ask them of Talif. When it's your turn to perform, don't forget your curtsies and bows." Marin took a deep breath and gave the students a big smile. "I'm so proud of each of you. You will all do wonderfully."

Talif, moving to stand beside her, reaffirmed quietly, "*Ja*, they will."

Marin glanced at him. The calm certainty in the gaze that met hers spread sweet serenity through her. In spite of her assurance to the students that they would all do wonderfully, her desire for them to make her look good had caused her to worry. Now the knowledge hit her that whatever the students did would be fabulous in their parents' eyes, truly wonderful simply because the students had worked so hard to learn and to put on this program.

Yes, of course everything will go well, she thought. "Now, Eva, Sophia, and Stina, since you're the first to perform, come stand here by the door and wait while I introduce you."

Faces beaming, the girls hurried forward.

Sophia, blue eyes sparkling, put her plump hands over the coiled braids above her ears. "See my ribbons, Teacher? They match the black stripes in my dress."

"The ribbons are very pretty, Sophia, and so is your dress. You look beautiful." Marin smiled at Eva and Stina, then turned the smile on the rest of the class. "All the girls look beautiful, and all the boys look handsome." She winked at Sophia and dropped her voice to a whisper. "Be very quiet now while I go tell the parents what you and Eva and Stina are going to do, all right?"

Sophia nodded, her hair ribbons bouncing against her shoulders.

Marin entered the other room, walking over to the square oak table covered with the fine lace cloth. The table served as the altar during the church service. She could smell the comforting scent of the candle that had burned on the altar during the service.

She stood beside the table and faced the congregation, her hands folded primly in front of her green dress with tiny white lace edging the collar. Off to one side sat a special guest, Miss Allen, the teacher from town who had so kindly given Marin advice and encouragement months earlier. She'd made the long trip today to see the students' program. Marin hoped she could return the favor in a couple weeks when the town students gave their own program.

The parents' faces look as excited and proud as the students', Marin thought. She greeted them in Swedish. "Welcome to the first program of our congregation's school. The students have worked hard over the last months, and each one should be proud of what he or she has learned. They've also worked hard on this program. We hope you'll enjoy it. For our first presentation, Stina and Sophia Linder and Eva Skarstedt will sing a song in English about the days of the week."

The song set the program off to a good start. Marin had written the song with its simple tune. The lyrics told of common housekeeping duties for each day of the week. The students performed actions indicating laundering, baking, and such, which made it apparent to those in the audience who only spoke Swedish which day of the week was represented.

When the ditty was over, the audience burst into applause. At the appreciation, the little girls smiled widely and curtsied again and again, bringing enchanted laughter from their admirers.

Knute Linder, one of the most intelligent of Marin's students, read in Swedish an essay on the beginnings of their new country. The congregation listened wide-eyed and intent while he told of the Stamp Act, the Boston Tea Party, and the Revolutionary War.

The lesson on the United States continued with Orpha Stenvall and Viola Linder, thirteen and ten, reading the Declaration of Independence in Swedish. Marin had spent many long hours, working long into the night by the wavering light of the kerosene lamp, translating the work from English into Swedish. She and Talif had debated whether it should be presented in the new language or the language of the homeland, and Swedish won. Learning to speak English was important, but the adult immigrants—and even Marin's students—hadn't enough knowledge of the language to understand such a long and involved presentation. More important, Marin and Talif decided, that the audience understands one of its new country's most important documents.

When Orpha and Viola were done, the listeners affirmed Marin and Talif's decision by not only clapping but also cheering. Obviously they agreed with the sentiments of their new country's founders. Marin lifted her gaze above the crowd and searched out Talif where he stood at the bedroom door. His grin and wink made her laugh from the joy of sharing in the wonder of this special moment.

Other students followed with songs and recitations. Finally it was time for the largest event. Marin introduced it. "Next is a skit. The class wrote it as a joint project, and they did a fine job indeed. It involves situations in which we all find ourselves, simple things like greeting people, asking for directions, and buying things in stores. You'll hear common English phrases, phrases we will all use many times in the years to come. Every student in the class will take part. Talif Siverson will play the part of a store clerk. And now, the Prairie School Players perform for your pleasure."

As Marin walked away, she passed eight-year-old Sture and ten-year-old Anders Skarstedt as they headed to the stage area. She knew her own brothers, Einer and August, were coming from the other direction. The four would begin the first scene, greeting and introducing each other.

"Good morning. How are you, Anders?" Marin heard Einer ask as she reached her place in the back of the room behind the audience.

As she watched, contentment at her students' presentation filled her heart. *Did all teachers feel this incredible sense of satisfaction at their students' accomplishments?* she wondered. Her gaze rested on Miss Allen. She didn't speak Swedish, so she couldn't have understood everything. Yet judging from her expression, she was enjoying the program. Marin hoped this experienced teacher felt the students were doing as well as Marin did.

At the end of the skit, Marin joined the students. They all faced the congregation and recited together Psalm 23 in English. Then Marin invited the audience to join them in reciting the psalm in Swedish.

Before they were done, tears glittered in some of the parents' eyes, and tears blurred Marin's sight as well. Marin thanked the audience for coming and the students for their hard work. She spoke of the things the students had learned during the months of schooling, of how far they'd come, and of the goals she hoped the school could help students achieve in the future. Her own parents' faces gleamed with pride, making Marin feel humble in response.

She was about to dismiss everyone when Talif stepped forward. "Excuse me, Miss Nilsson. There's something I and the other students would like to say."

Surprise kept her from speaking, but she nodded at him and began to step back.

Talif touched her elbow, stopping her, then moved his hand away.

"You came today," he said to the audience, "to honor the students for the efforts they've put forth over the last few months and to listen to examples of what they've learned. They deserve your respect, and it's easy to see they've received it. There's someone else here today who deserves your respect and that of the students, as well as all our thanks. Miss Marin Nilsson, one of the finest teachers on the prairie."

The congregation rose as one, clapping and smiling. Calls of "*Ja*," and "*Många tack*, Miss Nilsson" reached Marin's ears and heart.

Before the ovation died down, Talif faced Marin and continued. "The families wanted you to know how much your devotion to their children means to them, so they've bought you a gift." He looked over at Jems Stenvall. "Jems?"

Her heart lodged in her throat, Marin watched Jems walk over to the stove and pick up from beside it what appeared to be a packing box covered with a woven rug. He brought the box over and held it in front of her. His expression was sober, his eyes serious as he spoke. "Miss Nilsson, all of us students thank you for all you've done for us. We can't truly repay you, but we hope this will show you how grateful we are for your teaching."

Marin covered her lips with her fingers and swallowed twice before she could respond. "Thank you, Jems." She recognized it as an extraordinary speech from the often rebellious student. Who had selected him as the gift giver? The choice was a lovely gesture.

She reached out shaking fingers and lifted the brown-and-tan-striped rug. At the sight of the gift beneath it, she dropped the rug to the floor with a cry.

Jems, Talif, and the other students laughed, and Marin, recognizing their laughter as joy at her response, joined them. She lifted out the gift: a globe of the world. She held it high to show the crowd.

Turning to Talif, she asked, "How did you ever. . . ?"

She didn't need to finish the question. Talif grinned. "All the families contributed to it. Miss Allen sent for it. More than that, she told the county school superintendent about our plan. He decided that since the students' families went to such trouble to start a school, the county could spare a little of their funds to make up for what we hadn't raised in the cost of the globe."

Marin's gaze darted to Miss Allen. The town teacher rose and joined Marin and Talif. "You and the students deserve this gift. You are to be commended, Miss Nilsson. Your dedication to the students is inspiring. I feel privileged to know you."

Marin murmured her thanks as the congregation once again broke into applause.

Marin could barely keep her emotions in control while the parents, one by one, thanked her before leaving, and the girl students stopped to give her hugs.

Standing in the background, Talif watched it all, sharing in Marin's happiness from afar. Miss Allen's words rang true: Marin well deserved the praise.

The rest of spring and summer loomed long ahead of him, months without seeing Marin in class every day. But the thought of the surprise gift awaiting her before classes resumed next fall made his heart quickstep. The next school program wouldn't be held in anyone's home but in a school, as was proper. In Marin's school.

He'd spoken with Einer, Knute, and Jems after the program, and they'd agreed to help. Their eyes had shined with excitement at the idea. He knew they'd find time to slip away from their chores and field work to help him when the time came.

Talif leaned back against the wall, arms crossed over his suit front, a smile on his face, joy in his chest, and Marin in his sight and heart.

Chapter 9

Marin knelt in the late August twilight, weeding the garden in the cool of the evening. She was grateful for the light breeze that rustled through the corn and kept the mosquitoes away. Crickets and cicadas sang their songs for her as she worked. Scents of moist earth, green plants, and humid air surrounded her.

Standing up, she stretched, pressing her hands against the small of her back as she lifted her gaze and stared over the land toward Talif's home. His roof was barely visible over the tall prairie grass and her father's field of corn. Grasshoppers had invaded the county again, destroying many crops but for some reason sparing the Nilssons', Siverson's, and other nearby fields.

Talif's plowed land lay on the side of his home opposite the Nilsson farm. A small rise hid his fields from her view even in the early spring before the wild grasses and crops grew high. Sometimes on windy days during the spring, she'd seen thin clouds of dirt in the air and known he was working his fields. Now no such signs disclosed his actions.

She hardly dared acknowledge to herself that she missed seeing him every day as she had during the school term, hardly dared acknowledge the ache that tugged at her heart when she remembered all his kind assistance with the school. Last winter, even before school began, Talif had stopped at the house often to visit with Fader. Field work kept all the homesteaders busy during the summer. She knew Talif was no exception. They all worked late into the evenings. Only when rain kept Talif from the fields did he stop by the house to see Fader now. Talif always greeted Marin pleasantly when he stopped, asking after her, but it wasn't the same as when they worked on his lessons or he helped with the class in some way.

Would he join the class again this fall? He hadn't said, and she wouldn't ask.

Soon she'd need to begin planning lessons again. Likely fieldwork would prevent any but the youngest boys from attending the first fall classes. She expected the parents would allow most of the girls to come to school except during harvest when all female hands were needed to bake and serve the men when they came from the fields.

The black-and-white dog came running out of the cornfield and across the garden rows, eager to greet her. "Sven!" Marin grabbed at the dog. "Come. The garden is no place for you. If Moder sees you among the beans. . ." She let the warning stay unfinished as she urged the dog across the furrows.

"Where've you been, Sven? Did you go with Einer? You're as mysterious as he's been, heading off every night as soon as the evening meal is over, refusing to tell me where he's going. I can't believe Fader lets him go like that."

It wasn't like Fader to let Einer leave that way. The cows needed milking each evening, and Fader and the boys often worked in the fields late. Besides, where could Einer possibly go? They lived too far from town for that to be his destination. She'd asked Fader where Einer went, but he hadn't told her.

Petting Sven's head, she looked out over the prairie, then up at the sky where the love star announced the coming of night. Something strange was going on, that was certain.

🐝

Talif lifted his hat with one hand and wiped the sweat from his forehead with his opposite forearm. Einer, Knute, and Jems imitated him.

Talif grimaced to hide a grin. Almost nine in the evening and still warm enough that he and the boys broke a sweat working on the building. Of course, cutting prairie sod into three-by-two bricks and laying them up two layers thick to build a house would probably make a man sweat in the midst of a Minnesota winter.

He took a tin dipper of water from the bucket beside him and drank down a refreshing swig. Einer followed suit.

Talif rested his hands on his hips, surveying the building. "You've done a good night's work, boys." Talif studied the cloudless sky. "If the weather holds, we can start the roof tomorrow. Once that's on, we should be able to finish the school by this time next week."

Einer wiped his hands on the back of his jeans and grinned. "Marin's going to be mighty surprised."

"She'd better be." Talif looked from boy to boy. "You've all kept your word? Haven't told anyone but your fathers?"

They all nodded.

"Good. It'd be a crying shame if Miss Nilsson caught wind of what we're doing."

"I haven't told anyone else, but. . ." Knute cleared his throat. "Fader told Moder."

Talif wasn't too surprised. "Well, that's to be expected. Seems men can't keep secrets from their wives no matter how hard they try. Besides, I imagine your mothers insisted on knowing where you boys have been going each evening."

Knute nodded, looking relieved by Talif's response. "Moder wants to help. She's a Dala painter. She thought, if it's all right with you, Talif, she could paint pictures on the door and window lintels."

"Sounds like a great idea. It would sure make the school more attractive. I'll talk with her about it at Sunday service."

Knute leaned over to grab the water dipper, but Talif figured the boy did so more to hide his pride in Talif's response to his mother's offer than because Knute wanted the water.

Soon the boys left for home, leaving Talif alone with the soon-to-be schoolhouse. He walked inside the roofless building, imagining it filled with benches, students, and the most beautiful Swedish teacher on the prairie.

He sighed deeply. "Oh, Lord, please let her love it as much as I think she will."

❧

Marin sat with her brothers and sisters in the bed of Fader's spring wagon as they bounced across the prairie under the Sunday-morning sun. The straw beneath her softened the jolting somewhat but poked through the blanket she sat on and through her stockings, making her calves itch. The back of her head hit the side of the wagon with a *thump* as the wagon went over a particularly rough bump. "Ouch." She winced and pressed the palm of her hand against the back of her favorite blue sunbonnet. "How much longer before we're there, Fader?"

"Soon. Have patience."

She could hear the laughter in his voice. She wasn't amused. She glanced at Elsbet, who sat beside her, and didn't bother to disguise her disgust. "I don't know why it's such a secret where services will be held today. It's never been a secret before."

Elsbet smiled and patted Marin's calico-covered knee. "May as well enjoy the ride and let Fader enjoy his secret."

They'd passed Talif's home minutes earlier, so obviously the meeting wouldn't be held there. The Linder and Stenvall families lived in the direction they were headed. She hoped the meeting wouldn't be the Stenvall home, which was more cramped than most of the congregation members' houses. Immediately she felt ashamed for her attitude. What could be more crowded than her own home when she taught school?

Marin stretched her neck, trying in vain to see over the wagon's side. The sounds and smells didn't help. The prairie was filled with the scent of earth and sound of wind rustling through crisping leaves of corn. With a half sigh, half inelegant snort, she gave up and let her mind drift to lesson plans. She mentally listed English words for the everyday lives of her students: fields, plows, crops, farm, farmer.

She felt a smile tug at the corners of her mouth. Talif would say this showed she was a God-made teacher. A trickle of sadness slid through her. She missed his presence in her life, missed his encouragement for her teaching. Well, no sense dwelling on that. She forced her mind back to the list. *Trädgård*, garden; *växa*, grow; *grönsaker*, vegetables; *ko*, cow.

Entertained with the list, she didn't notice the wagon slowing and stopping. "Everyone out," Fader called.

Marin stood, looking about. In front of them sat a sod house, one she'd never seen. Rectangular, it had a door in the middle and a window on either side. Someone had cut down the prairie grass in front of the house, and half-a-dozen horse-drawn wagons stood in the yard. She recognized a number of the teams as belonging to church members.

"Who lives here?" she asked as Fader helped her from the wagon.

245

"No one."

She opened her mouth to question further, but the twinkle in Fader's eyes told her it would be useless.

The planks making up the door stood unweathered against the prairie winds and still held the smell of newly cut wood. Fader held the door for the family, Marin entering last. She paused a step past the threshold, her gaze wandering over the congregation-filled room as curiosity grew stronger instead of lessening.

The freshly whitewashed walls added light and cheer. The unusual luxury of a window on each end of the building let in additional sunlight and warmth. On the wall facing her hung a painted blackboard like the one Talif had made for the school. Below it, a crate stood on end, three books on the only shelf as though the crate were intended as a bookcase. A metal stove stood square in the middle of the room. Primarily women and children sat on the crude benches facing the far wall. Men and older boys with hats in hands stood along the walls. A small table between the benches and far wall served as an altar. A white cloth with a cross made of hardanger embroidery covered the table. Two silver candlesticks held candles for the service, and a Bible lay between them. The pleasant scent from the warm candle wax mingled with the odor of fresh earth.

"Good morning, Marin." Talif's whispered greeting came from beside her.

She turned her head to smile at him but didn't think to answer, her mind still attempting to understand where this place came from and why Fader had kept it a secret.

"Come, Marin." Fader's hand against the small of her back urged her forward. She followed her mother and siblings to the front row of benches, which for some reason remained empty in spite of the standing members.

Marin found it difficult to keep her attention on the service and the pastor's words about the Lord bringing all things to a time of harvest. Her gaze and mind kept wandering about the room, noticing every little thing, trying to figure it all out. When the service was over except for the final blessing, the pastor finally mentioned the building.

"The Lord has brought much to harvest in our little congregation this year," he began, "including this wonderful new *kyrka*, church, in which to worship. One day we will have a building of wood or brick, but for the moment, we have a temple filled with love and devotion, and I am sure that makes it a magnificent temple in the eyes and heart of the Lord."

Murmured *amen*s and nodding heads showed agreement.

"Our gratitude goes out to the one who conceived the idea for this building, who gave the land for it, and who gave of his own labor and funds to build it. Talif Siverson, please accept our thanks."

Marin whipped her head around in stunned surprise to look at Talif, who still stood beside the door, his face now a ruddy red from the attention and applause of the congregation. Talif had done this, created this place, given it from his own land and labor?

"Every family has contributed something," the pastor continued. "I especially want to honor Einer Nilsson, Knute Linder, and Jems Stenvall, who helped Talif build the church."

Marin's gaze found Einer's face with its pleased but embarrassed expression. This was where he'd disappeared all those evenings!

The pastor lifted his right arm in a sweeping motion. "Mrs. Linder decorated the lintels with Dala painting."

Marin liked the cheer added to the otherwise plain walls by the typical Dala-picture elements: a simple, almost childlike style, oversized flowers, bright colors, and people wearing traditional Swedish outfits.

"The Stenvalls contributed a water bucket and dipper," the pastor continued. "Mrs. Nilsson and Elsbet made curtains for the windows and Mrs. Skarstedt sewed a curtain for the bookshelf. The women brought their gifts today."

Marin stared in amazement as the women carried the items to the front and laid them reverently on the makeshift altar. When had Elsbet and Moder found time to make the curtains without Marin's knowledge?

After thanking the women, the pastor said, "There are some here who still don't know of this building's complete purpose."

Marin brought her gaze to his and was surprised to find him smiling at her.

"Specifically," he continued, "Miss Marin Nilsson and most of her students. Einer?"

Einer stood and, carrying a rectangular plank, walked to stand beside the pastor. Then he held the plank for everyone to see.

Marin gasped. PRAIRIE CHURCH AND SCHOOL, she read. The words were in script, in two lines, the top in English, the bottom in Swedish. She covered her lips with her fingers. Tears blurred her vision. Through her wonder, she heard the pastor's words. "This building began as a school, a place for our children to learn, a place for our own dedicated Miss Nilsson to teach them."

She missed the rest, the few additional words or phrases, the final blessing. She wanted to turn, to look at Talif, to thank him. How could he possibly have done this marvelous thing? She'd scorned his attentions. In return he'd only given good back to her, encouraged her dream, assisted with teaching ideas, and now built a school.

The wonder of the new school paled beside the other thoughts and feelings flooding her, crumbling the walls she'd built around her heart. Such a man as Talif would never betray a woman as Elsbet's fiancé had betrayed her. A man like Talif would remain devoted to the woman he chose to love.

Marin caught her bottom lip between her teeth. Had she given away any chance of Talif's love? Her chest felt as though squeezed in a vise. She'd hardly seen him the last few months. Had he lost interest in her? But he'd built this school. Had he done so because he loved her or because he, also, cared deeply for the students? Hope fluttered in her heart. If she received another chance at Talif's love, she wouldn't be so foolish as to refuse it again.

❧

Early the next morning Marin hurried down the ruts that formed a road between the Nilsson farm and Talif's place. She breathed a sigh of relief as she passed his home apparently undetected and continued along toward the new schoolhouse.

She saw the sign hung above the schoolhouse door long before she reached the building: Prairie Church and School. It sent joy humming through her.

A long piece of carved wood rested on the large flat stone Talif had placed for a doorstep. The sight of the wooden piece brought Marin to a breathless stop six feet from the house. She recognized the piece. Not that specific piece, but the design, like a long, beautiful chisel. Any Swedish woman would recognize the traditional courting request. Bring it inside, and she agreed to be courted by the giver. Leave it on the doorstep, and the giver knew his heart's request was rejected.

Her breath came short and quick as she walked toward it, step by slow step. She stared at it long and hard before kneeling to examine the intricate carving of hearts and flowers with a trembling index finger. It was Talif's work, of course. She lifted the piece and hugged it to her heart, whispering silent thanksgiving to the Lord for the second chance.

Marin carried the courting board inside with her, began to set it down on the desk, then changed her mind. With one hand, she untied her bonnet and laid it on the desk, then began slowly walking around the room, glad to at last be alone to absorb the wonder of this school built for her and her dream.

※

Talif leaned against the doorframe of the open door, watching Marin walking about the room, lost in her own thoughts. He'd known as soon as he saw the courting board gone from the doorstep that she'd accepted his request, but his heart stumbled in joy at the way she clutched it to her. Warmth spread through his chest at the reverence with which she ran her fingers across the simple desk and the back of the barrel chair he'd made her.

Even knowing she welcomed his courting, he felt tentative stepping inside, as if entering new territory. And weren't they? A territory filled with new joys, and new challenges, as well. He walked slowly across the packed-dirt floor toward where she stood with her back toward him. "Marin?"

He'd spoken quietly so as not to startle her, but she swung about like a frightened bird, her blue eyes first wide with fright, then shining with welcome and something similar to embarrassment. Instinctively he reached to comfort her, his hands on her arms. "I didn't want to frighten you."

"You didn't. I mean, you did, but only for a moment."

His touch made her nervous, he could see. Disappointed, he removed his hands from her arms, reminding himself they were only beginning the move from friendship to courtship.

Marin's lashes hid her eyes from his view as she glanced down at the board she still carried. "I–I'm honored you wish to court me. Thank you for this. It's beautiful."

"You're welcome. I'm honored you agreed."

Her gaze darted about the room. "And this. . .the school. . .everything. I don't know how to begin to thank you."

"By using it for the teaching God created you to do." He took the board from her and set it on the desk. Then gently, he brushed the fingers of his right hand over the curve of her cheek, rejoicing when she didn't flinch from his touch. "I wish it could be a wooden building, but I couldn't afford that now and neither could the congregation."

"That will come in time."

He saw belief in her eyes, and it reinforced his own. Would they help build that school one day together? Would their own children attend it? He swept the thought away. Moving too fast again. She'd only just agreed to court.

Yet unless he was mistaken, there was more than belief in the school to come in her eyes. There was joy at the thought of *them*, of the two of them as a couple. Anticipation? Faith?

His hand slid to the back of her neck, and he leaned close until, an inch away from her lips, he locked her gaze in his and whispered, "May I kiss you, Miss Nilsson?"

"Y–yes."

He touched his lips to hers tenderly, lost in wonder at the gift, the treasure that was Marin, at the hope that she offered him in agreeing to court. One kiss grew to two, gentle, questioning. Then to more, exploring, thanking. Until with a sweet sigh, she leaned against his chest, and his chin rested against her hair. And forgetting all over again not to move too quickly, he said, "I love you, Marin Nilsson. Is that all right?"

Marin shifted her head until he could see the joy shining in her eyes. "It's perfect."

As he drew her into another embrace, he could only agree.

Epilogue

June 1874

The summer breeze tugged playfully at the wildflowers tucked into Marin's coronet braid and tossed the heads of the flowers she carried as she stood outside the church and school, waiting impatiently for the ceremony to begin. Delicate blue, pink, and yellow flowers dotted the prairie grass surrounding the building and growing from the roof.

Marin smiled at Elsbet. "Was any chapel or home ever decorated so beautifully for a wedding?"

Elsbet's gaze held laughter, but she agreed as she smoothed the arms of Marin's dress of dark-green silk.

Lovely strains from a violin inside the building reached them, and Marin took a shaky breath. She smiled at Sophia. "Time to begin. Are you scared?"

Wide-eyed, the little girl shook her head no. "Mother says I've the most important job of the whole wedding."

Marin bit back a laugh and avoided looking at Elsbet. "Your mother is right."

Sophia grinned and started toward the church to spread wildflowers from her basket onto Marin's path. At the door stood Fader, waiting to accompany Marin to the altar.

Elsbet slipped her arm about Marin's waist in a quick hug. "I'm so happy for you. Talif is a good man. Seeing his devotion to you. . ." Her voice broke. Marin waited patiently while Elsbet took a deep breath and continued. "Seeing the way he treats you. . .it makes me believe that maybe. . .maybe there's a man somewhere who might love me that way."

Elsbet's hope caught at Marin's heart. She hugged her sister close. "Of course there is," she whispered fiercely. "Can't the Lord do anything? Isn't love His favorite gift?"

Marin saw tears glitter as Elsbet broke away and followed Sophia toward the church.

Moments later, Marin's vision was free from tears as she stood beside the altar and the man who would become, in only minutes, her husband. Seeing the love in

Talif's eyes, standing with him before the Lord and her family, and the congregation in the church and school built by Talif's love, she knew her words to Elsbet were true.

That truth sang inside Marin's heart as she and Talif vowed that the love they had for each other would continue forever.

THE GOLDEN CORD

by Judith Miller

Dedication

To Mary Greb-Hall,
for her valuable and timely assistance,
her quick smile, and her friendship—
thank you!

Chapter 1

Pearl River Delta, China, 1885

Panting and drenched in perspiration, Suey Hin sank back onto the cot, the birthing finally over. Another girl! For the fifth time, she watched her husband place a pair of shoes outside the window. This was a custom with which she had become all too familiar. Only once had her husband placed shoes facing inward under the bed, signifying the birth of a son. Her heart ached with the knowledge that the birth of this child meant the departure of her eldest daughter, Qui Jin. There were always mouths to feed, but there was never enough food. The sale of Qui Jin would provide additional funds to feed those mouths. It was a way of life, this peddling of females. Sons were the revered children. Suey Hin despised the practice, but she accepted it. She had no choice. Wives of peasants quickly mastered the ability to safeguard their hearts where daughters were concerned. It was less painful when the day of parting arrived.

❧

Qui Jin glanced back one last time, capturing a final look at her family who stood peering from the doorway. *I'll see them again,* she thought, scurrying along behind her father. But deep in the recesses of her heart, she knew she wouldn't. Quickly brushing away a tear that escaped one of her dark, almond-shaped eyes, she momentarily considered inquiring about their destination but censored the idea as quickly as she had brushed away her tear. Such behavior would not be tolerated from a daughter. Silently, she hurried onward toward her father's unknown goal, with fear and sadness her constant companions.

Several hours later, the bedraggled pair arrived at the water's edge near the outskirts of Canton. Qui Jin stood silently behind her father, watching as merchants and sailors swarmed about them while a mixture of noises, smells, and sights assaulted her senses. Spellbound, she listened to the instrumental music of bamboo flutes, zithers, and chimes that floated through the air from the flower boats. Soon the clanging gongs and chattering voices of the boatmen broke the spell. She had never been so far from home, and the flurry of excitement was astonishing. Her attention darted from place to place until her gaze finally rested upon a cluster of factories that appeared to balance in midair.

"I wonder why those buildings don't topple into the water," she murmured.

No answer came, but she expected none. Her father and a strange-looking man with round eyes and pale skin were too busy with their own conversation.

"That's as much as I'll give you," the stranger replied in a determined voice. "Take it or leave it. I don't have time to haggle."

Qui Jin watched her father nod his head in reluctant agreement and take the money being offered. Instinctively, she cowered behind him, but the man reached around her father and pulled her forward.

"Go with this man, and do as he tells you. You now belong to him," her father ordered, shoving her toward the stranger. As soon as he spoke the words, she watched her father turn and scurry away without so much as a backward glance.

Qui Jin cautiously studied the captain's features. Sometimes, late at night after her parents were in bed, she had listened to them talk about the Gold Mountain in America and the round-eyed people who lived there. This sailor's appearance confirmed that he was from *Gam Saan*, the Gold Mountain. A large man with rough-looking hands and dirty clothes, his unshaven face and matted, brown hair attested to his need for soap and water. Beads of perspiration trickled down his forehead until they reached the cotton bandanna tied around his head. Qui Jin looked into his eyes. She thought she saw a glimmer of kindness, but she couldn't be sure. She had never before seen an American, and she was afraid to trust her instincts.

Breaking the silence, the man pointed toward the water. "They're built on piles. When you get around to the other side, you'll see them—long, slender columns of wood hold up the suspended parts of the building."

"What?" Qui Jin asked, staring at him wide-eyed.

"The factories. They don't fall into the water because the part of the building that overhangs the water sits on top of tall, wooden pillars. Isn't that what you asked about earlier?"

"Yes. But I didn't think anyone was listening," she softly replied.

"I hear everything going on around me. It's the only way to survive as a captain in the shipping business. Now, come on! We've got to get moving," he ordered as he pulled her along toward a junk at the water's edge. Lifting her with one arm and jumping onto a small junk with a practiced ease that amazed Qui Jin, he shouted orders to the boatman. The brightly colored craft slid quietly through the water, making its way toward one of the large clipper ships anchored several miles offshore.

"What's your name?"

"Qui Jin. Suey Qui Jin," she meekly replied.

"Well, Suey Qui Jin, here's the way things are between us: Your father sold you to me. I guess you already figured that out for yourself. I'm not in the business of buying and selling humans. In fact, I'd much rather haul cargo than people—fewer problems. Sometimes I break my own rules, and I'm usually sorry for it later. Don't make this be one of those times. I don't want any problems on this voyage."

Qui Jin listened intently. He spoke her native language with relative ease, and most of the time, she could make out what he was saying. . .or at least she believed she understood. "I think I am the one with a problem," she murmured, careful to keep her head bowed.

He emitted a deep belly laugh. "You may be right about that, little lady. You'll likely have more problems than you know what to do with when we arrive in California. But don't blame me. Your father was determined to sell you—if not to me, then to someone else."

She met his gaze briefly and nodded. Her young heart ached at his words; she could not deny the truth—but why this decision to sell her to a foreigner? Why couldn't her father have sold her to another Chinese family? She would have preferred to become a servant in a Chinese household rather than this banishment to another country. Becoming a *mui tsai* for a wealthy Chinese family wouldn't have been nearly as dreadful as being forced to leave her family and her homeland. In every way, her father's choice seemed painfully unfair.

Custom forbade her to question a man, yet fear would not allow her to remain silent. "What will become of me?"

The captain leaned back and stared at her for several moments. "I don't know. It's certain that I'll not be keeping you. If I can manage to get you past the immigration officials when we dock in San Francisco, I'm sure you'll fetch a pretty penny."

"You will sell me to someone else? To someone in *Gam Saan?*"

One side of his mouth curled upward into an ugly sneer, and any sign of kindness had disappeared from his eyes. "Most likely. There's lots of Chinamen in San Francisco who would enjoy having a pretty young thing like you working for them."

The thought sent her heart soaring. Perhaps this wouldn't be as difficult as she had anticipated. If she could work as a servant for a Chinese family in Gam Saan, it wouldn't be so bad. "I will be living with Chinese people?"

"You might put it that way," he replied. The junk maneuvered alongside the anchored clipper ship. "Come on—I'll help you up."

"You'll be staying down below," the captain stated when they had finally boarded the vessel. He pointed toward a small, dark stairway. Carefully, Qui Jin walked down the steps and made her way through the narrow passageway, which was flanked by several doors on each side.

"That one," he said, motioning toward a small doorway of rough-hewn timber at the end of the hallway. The captain shoved the door open, permitting a slender shaft of light to fall across the room. Qui Jin moved forward. Squinting as her eyes adjusted to the semidarkness, she focused on a narrow bunk that was bolted to the cabin wall. "Once we've set sail, I'll come back with some food. Do you understand?"

Qui Jin nodded.

"You can wash up if you like," he remarked, pointing toward a washstand across from the bunk.

She was tempted to tell him that his need for soap and water was greater than hers, but she held her tongue. No need to cause undue aggravation and have the captain turn his wrath upon her even before they set sail. Instead, after he left, she paced about the tiny room, back and forth, to and fro, already feeling caged by the walls of her seafaring prison. Fatigued and overwhelmed, she heaved a weary sigh, plopped down on the bunk, and listened as the aged timbers of the groaning ship began to move, steadily taking her farther and farther away from those whom she knew and loved.

Chapter 2

Apersistent pounding resonated in the distance. It continued to grow louder until finally Qui Jin awakened and bolted upright from her bunk. Someone was beating on the cabin door. Stumbling, Qui Jin wiped the sleep from her eyes and pulled open the door.

"Thought maybe you was dead. Eat this," the captain bellowed as he thrust a wooden bowl toward her.

Qui Jin stared down at the mixture. "What is it?"

His face was filled with disdain. "It's your supper. What else would it be?"

She cast another glance at the lumpy, congealing concoction and stood motionless. It looked like nothing she had ever eaten before, and although her stomach growled for food, hunger seemed a better option than attempting to eat this strange-looking substance.

"Ain't nothing in there gonna hurt you. In fact, it's a mighty fine stew. Just wait until we've been at sea for a couple of weeks. You'll wish you had something this good. But you suit yourself. If you want to starve, you'll find it's an exceedingly slow death." He gave a mocking laugh as he walked out of the room and pulled the door closed behind him.

She waited—silently listening yet hearing nothing but the creaks and groans of the ship as it cut through the water. She gathered her courage, took a deep, cleansing breath, and tiptoed across the small room. Placing her ear against the door, she stood quietly for a moment. Carefully, she opened the heavy door just wide enough to gain a view and peeked down the dark corridor. Seeing no one, she cautiously made her way to the stairs and stopped, taking note of her surroundings. She could hear the distant voices of the sailors, but it was quiet directly above the steps. Placing a sweaty palm on the wall alongside the stairway, she slowly began her ascent. With her heart pounding wildly, she finally reached the opening and slowly raised her head just high enough to gain a limited view of the deck.

Were her eyes deceiving her? There was a man standing at the railing. A man in a loose, black silk, Chinese jacket with a tightly braided queue of shiny black. Rubbing her eyes, she took another peek. He was still there. She hissed between her teeth as loudly as she dared. Why didn't he look? "Psst! Psst!"

"Over here!" she commanded when he finally glanced in her direction. Lifting her arm above the stairway, she waved him toward her. "I'm over here. I need to talk to you." She watched him scan the deck, then move slowly toward her. Reaching the top of the stairway, he stopped.

"Who are you?" he asked without looking toward her.

She bowed her head. "Suey Qui Jin from Kwantung Province in the Pearl River Delta. Are you going to America?" She sneaked a glance from beneath her lashes.

He smiled. "I certainly hope we're going to America. If not, I'd better jump overboard. Is that your only concern—if I'm traveling to America?"

Qui Jin shook her head and flashed him an embarrassed smile. "Do you think you could help me? I am being transported to America and. . ."

"You were kidnapped?" he interrupted before she could finish.

"Not really. My father sold me. To the captain," she added.

"And the captain has mistreated you?"

"No, unless you consider that foul dinner he served me to be mistreatment. I'm not sure how I expect you to help—or anyone else, for that matter," she replied, now wondering why she had been so brazen. "It appears my future has already been decided. Do you think I would get in trouble if I came up on deck with you? It's so dark and gloomy down below."

"I don't think there will be a problem. I've sailed with this captain before. He's rough-spoken and permits no nonsense on board his ship, but he's always treated me fairly. Besides, I doubt anyone will notice us. They're all too busy at the moment."

Ever watchful, she stepped up onto the deck and surveyed her new surroundings. The crew was hard at work, and if they noticed her, they appeared indifferent. Carefully, she made her way toward the ship's railing and felt her confidence begin to surge as she leaned forward and watched the sleek bow of the ship slice through the rising swells. A toss of spray shot upward, then showered down upon where she stood. She giggled, the coolness of the water surprising her. Perhaps everything was going to be all right.

The man had moved back, capably avoiding the shower of water. She turned toward him and was met by his grin. "The wind will dry you quickly," he said.

Qui Jin returned his smile while smoothing back the wet strands of hair that had escaped from her braid. "You said you've sailed with this captain before. Have you already been to America?"

He joined her at the railing just as the ship began to plow through a giant swell. The vessel listed, and he reached out to grab her hand, but he was a moment too late. She went sprawling across the deck before finally coming to rest a few feet from the stairway.

"You'll become accustomed to the ship's movements after a while. The Americans say that you must get your sea legs." He offered his hand.

Embarrassed, she kept her eyes lowered while allowing him to assist her. "I hope it doesn't take too long to gain those 'sea legs' you speak of."

"You'll be surprised how quickly you will learn to move with the rocking of the ship." He nodded as she gingerly moved back toward the railing and grabbed hold.

"You see? You've already begun to master the technique."

There was no doubt he was merely being kind. She knew she resembled a scrawny duck, wobbling side to side as she maneuvered her way across the deck. "I was asking you about America before I fell down and made a spectacle of myself."

"Yes, I have been to America. In fact, California is my home."

"You live in America?" She was incredulous. "I've heard my parents speak of our countrymen who have gone to live in foreign countries, but I didn't believe it. Why would you want to live in America?"

"I was born in America."

Qui Jin giggled and shook her head. "You are teasing me. You are Chinese. What is your name?"

"Chinese, yes—but born in America. My name is Sam Ying. You will soon learn that living in America is not such a strange thing. Many Chinese live there."

"Sam Ying? That is a funny name."

"It's part American and part Chinese. Names in America are different. In fact, Americans place the family name last rather than first. So, in America, my friends call me Sam."

"How is it that you were born in America?"

"My father left China after his family members got killed in the Punti-Haaka Rebellion. He had heard stories about the gold in California and sold his belongings. He made enough for his passage and the beginning of a new life. He traveled back to China several years later and married my mother. Soon, they returned to California. He's never regretted his decision to live in America."

His explanation sounded reasonable, yet she could not imagine voluntarily leaving one's home. However, before she had time to ponder the idea of such a risky undertaking, her feet began to slip from beneath her. As the ship began pitching downward, Sam's arm came around her waist, holding her fast against the rail in a secure embrace.

She glanced up at him from beneath her lashes. Their eyes met. For a moment she stopped breathing, unable to comprehend the strange stirrings within her. It was oddly wonderful—exciting and exhilarating. She wondered if he felt the same sensation. He smiled down at her, his tempting good looks causing her heart to race at a wildly erratic pace. She could feel a hot flush creeping upward into her cheeks and quickly glanced away, hoping he would not notice her embarrassment.

Almost as quickly as it began, the pitching motion subsided, and the ship resumed its gentle rocking sway across the whitecapped waves. Sam released his grasp from around her waist. For a moment, Qui Jin wished the ship would once again return to its somersaulting antics. His arm about her waist had been breathtaking, and if the truth be told, she longed to have him hold her even more tightly. Ashamed, she quickly forced the thought from her mind.

"If America is your home, why were you in Canton?" She carefully kept her gaze away from his luminous, dark eyes.

"I travel there frequently. When I was young, my parents brought me to visit

China. They wanted me to learn of my heritage and be familiar with the country of their birth. Now my visits have more to do with commerce than learning about my ancestors. My father owns several businesses. One of them is a supply house that furnishes merchandise to many of the businesses in Chinatown. He also owns an apothecary and emporium."

"What is—?"

"Say, what's going on here? I told you to stay down below!" The captain loped toward them, his long legs reaching out in angry, giant strides across the wooden deck.

"It was very warm below deck. I merely came up to get some fresh air," Qui Jin stammered, cowering behind Sam.

"You need to get down there and stay out of the way."

"She meant no harm," Sam said to the captain, easily switching to the English language.

"Maybe not, but she's an investment, just like the rest of the cargo I'm hauling. She's better off below deck where the men won't see her and get ideas."

"Your men know better than to disobey your commands, Captain, and what harm is the fresh sea air? She'll be sick and lifeless if you keep her stowed away below deck the entire voyage," Sam replied.

"She's gonna be sick and lifeless anyway if she don't start eating. She's a puny thing. Look at this." The captain reached out and wrapped his thick hands around Qui Jin's waist. "I can latch my fingers around her midsection with room to spare. Who's going to pay a decent price for such a skinny girl?"

Qui Jin shrank away from the captain. His hands felt rough and callous, a far cry from Sam's gentle touch a short time ago.

"She can take her meals with me. I'll convince her to eat," Sam quickly replied.

The captain's lips began to curl into a devious grin. "You got your eye on this one for yourself?"

"No, I just thought I could be of assistance to you."

"All right then, you've got yourself a bargain. She can join you for meals so long as you make sure she eats. You tell her that if she don't eat, she don't get to come up on deck and see you. For now, she needs to get back to her room," the captain ordered.

Qui Jin watched as the two men nodded at each other and the captain strode off. Sam turned toward her and interpreted the conversation, then asked, "Do you understand?"

Qui Jin nodded. She would force herself to eat anything for the privilege of spending a bit of time in the fresh air, especially if she could be with Sam. He was the kindest man she had ever met, and deep inside, she somehow knew he was going to help her. She wasn't sure how or why, but he would help—of that she felt certain. Obviously, he knew about America, and perhaps he would know of a family with whom she could obtain employment. The captain would surely listen to Sam's suggestions.

"Thank you for your aid," she softly said.

"You are most welcome, but I'm not sure how much I've helped. You must go back to your cabin now. I will see you tomorrow for the morning meal. In time, I am certain that the captain will permit you to spend more time on deck."

His smile reassured her. She nodded and made her way toward the stairway before pausing momentarily to look back at him. He leaned against the railing in his black silk tunic, a perfect silhouette against the pink-and-gold sunset. She rushed down the stairway, wondering what he must be thinking of her, dirty and unkempt in her faded, worn, blue tunic and shabby cloth slippers.

Chapter 3

Sam Ying stood by the railing for several minutes, his gaze resting upon the fading sun as it descended into the distant horizon. He wondered what the future held for such a pretty young girl in San Francisco's Chinatown. Since the captain seemed concerned only that she gain weight and stay out of his way, perhaps he would at least permit Sam an opportunity to make the voyage more bearable for her. He attempted to concentrate on Qui Jin's well-being, yet he realized he was thinking of himself as well as the beautiful young woman. A longing or sadness surrounded her—he wasn't sure which, but he knew he must somehow help her.

Sam had chosen to once again sail on the *Falcon,* a smaller and slower ship than many other clippers. The larger vessels sailing out of Canton dwarfed the *Falcon's* mere 130-foot length and three canvas masts. Unless troubled by storms, the lengthy voyage would provide him with a brief respite from the ever-increasing duties of managing his father's burgeoning business enterprises.

"You thinking about how much you'd like to own that girl?" the captain asked as he approached the railing.

Sam turned and looked upward, meeting the captain's stare. "I wondered how you happened to have her on board. Never knew you to be a man who traded in human flesh."

"Never have before, but her father wouldn't turn loose; kept up his incessant chatter until I finally agreed to buy her."

Sam shook his head slowly. "I've known you for five years, and I've never seen any man who could force you to do something you didn't want to."

The captain nodded in agreement, his hearty laughter filling the air. "Guess you're right about that! Don't rightly have an answer, but no matter. If I hadn't bought her, there were plenty of others who would—and her voyage would have been much less comfortable."

"That's true. But what are your plans once you get her to California?"

The captain looked away and shifted from the rail. "Haven't had time to give it much thought."

"No? Then why are you trying to fatten her up? Appears to me you have something in mind. I thought perhaps you planned to sell her to one of the Tong

264

members for use in their brothels."

"I will admit I figured she'd fetch a good price—got a pretty face for a Chinese. She's just too scrawny. I don't know if I'll even be able to smuggle her in. You know as well as I do that I'm going to have a problem getting her past the inspectors when we dock."

"I agree. Getting her off the ship will be difficult—perhaps impossible. I think you're going to find that those Exclusionary Laws the Congress was so anxious to pass may work against your gaining a profit on the girl. Didn't you consider the problem of the inspectors before you bought her?"

" 'Course I did. I'm not stupid," the captain barked. "I'll come up with a plan before we arrive. I might even get some ideas from you," he said with a wink.

Before Sam had an opportunity to reply, the first mate called the captain to the stern for assistance. "We'll talk about this later," the captain called back over his shoulder.

Sam waved in agreement as he watched the captain rush off. "Perhaps I will have an idea for you, Captain Obley," Sam muttered to himself before turning his attention back to the greenish-black waters that swirled and foamed around the hull of the ship.

🐝

As the days passed, the captain readily acquiesced to Sam's request that Qui Jin be permitted to spend additional time with him. At first, she had been interested only in hearing about the Gold Mountain of which her parents had spoken. But once Sam convinced her that the streets were not paved with gold and California was a land of poverty as well as opportunity, she became convinced learning the language of her new country would be beneficial. Slowly, painstakingly, he began to teach her. She proved herself a capable student, and daily her skills increased. Her ability to learn continued to amaze Sam—perhaps because he tended to compare her with his sisters. Although their father insisted all of his children receive a formal education, Sam's sisters had been uninterested students.

"Soon you will understand the language better than I do," he remarked after she quickly interpreted a passing sailor's remark. "It's probably best that you forget most of the words you hear from these sailors, for many are unacceptable."

She nodded and bowed her head. "I know; you have told me so before." Blushing, she lifted her head and graced him with a delightful smile. "Why don't you tell me more about your family? You already know a great deal about my relatives, but you have not spoken of your family since we first met. I would enjoy hearing more—if you would like to tell me," she added quickly.

He laughed and leaned back. "I'm not sure we have sufficient time for me to tell you about my family before we arrive in California."

"There is that much to tell?"

He nodded his head. "Once I get started, it's difficult to stop. Are you sure you want me to begin?"

"Oh, yes, please."

Her enthusiasm touched his heart. "I'll do my best not to bore you. My father is a fine man, highly respected throughout Chinatown and even among some of the American businessmen in San Francisco. He has a good mind for business and enjoys his work. The family business has expanded, creating almost more work than my father and I can manage. That's one of the reasons I chose to return on the *Falcon*. I needed a little time alone to relax. On the other hand, my father never seems to need time to relax. He's up at sunrise each morning, ready to conquer another day. Most days he works fourteen hours, although he does come home for his meals and takes a short rest each afternoon. That's his daily routine except for Sundays, of course. My mother has attempted to get him to slow down for many years, but thus far she has been unsuccessful. I think she's concluded that he will slow down when he's ready."

"And does your mother help with the business?"

"No, Father forbids it, although she sometimes visits the shops. She always offers suggestions about how Father should rearrange the merchandise and immediately begins moving things about. Unfortunately, her actions make Father so anxious, he immediately hastens her departure. It's become a family joke that whenever Mother arrives at the shop, Father will find a reason to send her off to the back rooms to inspect new inventory. Personally, I believe my mother has learned that when she wants a new piece of fabric for a dress, she need only enter the building where he is hard at work."

The family's secret joke caused him to laugh. Qui Jin returned his smile, yet he wasn't sure she understood the humor.

She leaned forward, and the sparkling intensity of her dark-chocolate-brown eyes captivated him. "You have brothers and sisters?"

"No brothers. Three sisters."

Hesitating for a moment, Qui Jin gave consideration to her next question. It was a brazen thing to ask; yet Sam had given her permission to inquire about his family, so she forged on. "Your father was very sad when he had only one son?"

"I am not certain about that. I suppose he would have been pleased with more sons to help in the business, but my sisters enchant him. I don't think he would have considered trading any of them for a son, if such a thing were possible."

Qui Jin's eyes grew large at the revelation. "He is not ashamed to have so many daughters and only one son?"

Once again, Sam was enthralled by her innocent charm, her desire to understand and learn whatever he could teach. "No, he is very proud of them. All of my sisters are married. The youngest wed only days before I set sail for China."

He waited. She fidgeted with the frayed edge of her tunic and tucked a stray wisp of hair behind her ear, while her gaze remained fixed upon the worn sandals covering her tiny feet. "And you? Have you taken a wife?" she asked, her voice a mere whisper.

"Not yet, although gifts have been exchanged. My mother feared I would not marry unless she became involved in the engagement process. She insisted Li Laan was waiting for me. We have known each other since childhood, and our parents planned for us to marry from the time we were babies."

Why was he rambling on? And why did he feel such a need to defend his engagement to Li Laan?

Once again it was quiet between them. "So marriages are arranged in your country—just like in China?" she ventured, finally breaking the silence.

"Not always. Two of my sisters had arranged marriages, but both of them loved their intended husbands. My youngest sister chose her husband—or I should say, they chose each other."

"How could your sisters love their intended husbands? Were they also childhood friends?"

Sam laughed and shook his head. "No, their husbands attended the same church. They first became acquainted with them at the church services. In America, young men and women are permitted to know each other before marriage. They go to dinner and attend activities together. It is how they become better acquainted and find out if they are suited for a lifetime with each other. Not all Chinese people permit their children this opportunity, but my parents wanted happy marriages for their children, so they have given their permission."

She appeared to be contemplating her next question, so he waited, wondering if she would ask if he loved Li Laan. "How was it possible for your sisters to meet their husbands at the temple?"

Her eyes were filled with confusion. Sam had prayed for an opportunity to tell Qui Jin about his faith. Unlike his mother and sisters, who wanted to miss an opportunity to share the gospel, Sam and his father both waited, hoping to find God's perfect timing for sharing their belief. Perhaps it was merely the fact that his sisters followed their mother's enthusiastic zeal for sharing, while Sam followed his father's thoughtful consideration and careful planning.

He measured his words for several moments before speaking. "I am what is known as a Christian. Have you ever heard that word before?"

She shook her head. "No. What is a Christian?"

Her question gave him the freedom to speak the words he had longed to share with her for days. He issued a silent prayer of thanksgiving before speaking. "A Christian is someone who believes that Jesus Christ is the Son of God. The Bible is God's message to us. It tells us Jesus was conceived of a virgin, lived here on earth, and was crucified to save us from our sins."

"So your Jesus is dead?"

"No. He died, but three days later He arose and once again reigns in heaven with God the Father. When Jesus returned to heaven, he left the Holy Spirit here to comfort and be with us. Do you understand?"

Qui Jin's face was etched with confusion. "You don't pray to Buddha?"

"No, I pray to the one true God, the Creator of the universe. Whom do you pray to, Qui Jin?"

"I don't pray to anyone. My father did not speak of gods or religion. He believed he was cursed since he had so many daughters."

Sam nodded. There was a crushing sadness in her voice, a tender ache that revealed wrenching pain, for she believed she was a disappointment to her earthly father. "Qui Jin, you need to believe that you are exactly the person God intended you to be. He has a plan for your life, and He is delighted with you. Most of all, I want you to know God loves you very much. Can you believe that?"

She shook her head. "No. I don't think any god could love me if my own father considers me a curse."

Sam stretched out his arm and lifted her chin with his finger. "Look at me, Qui Jin. Look into my eyes. You are not a curse; you are a child of God. He loved you so much, He sent His own Son to die on a cross—just for you. I pray that one day this will become clear to you."

"If my new Chinese family believes as you do, perhaps they will teach me," she replied. "Do you think that is possible?"

"It may be very possible," he said, while jumping to his feet. "Go below. I must talk to the captain," he ordered.

"I have offended you?" She backed away from him.

He was such a fool, jumping up and ordering her about. His actions frightened her. She probably thought he was some sort of lunatic. He needed to assure her everything was all right. But when he moved toward her, she ran across the deck and down the stairway. He wouldn't follow her—not now. Instead, he would find the captain.

Chapter 4

S am knocked on the door leading to the captain's quarters. He had searched the deck and questioned the crew, but no one had seen the captain for several hours.

"Who's disturbing my peace and quiet?" Captain Obley roared from the other side of the door.

Sam hesitated for only a moment. "Sam Ying. I need to speak with you when you have a few minutes."

He waited. Finally, he heard a chair scrape across the wooden floor, followed by the thud of footsteps. The door swung open. The captain filled the small doorway, his bloodshot eyes squinting to focus in the bright morning sunlight.

"Get in here," he snarled, pulling Sam inside and slamming the door. "Sit down," he ordered, pointing to a wooden chair as he fell into another. "What's on your mind?"

"The girl, Qui Jin. I wanted to discuss her future."

The captain licked his lips and leaned across the small table by his side. "I thought maybe that was it. You're wantin' her, ain't ya?"

"Not in the way you're thinking," Sam answered, "but I am concerned about your plans for her. You mentioned at the beginning of the voyage that you might need my help getting her off the ship."

"My plans are to sell her and make a tidy profit. What's your plan?"

"There is no way you'll be able to get her past the immigration inspectors. There is no plausible reason for you to have a female Chinese peasant on board this ship. We both know that."

"Some of my mates have told me the inspectors can be bribed," the captain argued.

Sam remained unmoved by the captain's words. "Possibly, but that would certainly cut into any profit on the girl. Besides, I've heard stories of the inspectors taking bribe money, then arranging to seize a ship and its captain for breaking the law."

The captain glared across the table at Sam before running his broad hand against the stubble that splotched his beefy jowls. "You got this all figured out, ain't ya? You think I'll just give her to you so's I don't have to worry about losing my ship. I'm right, ain't I?"

"No, I don't have it all figured out. That's why I'm here. I thought we could

269

reason this out together. I'll be honest with you, Captain Obley. I think the girl deserves better than a life of prostitution. What if she were your daughter?"

"Don't be trying to turn the tables on me, Sam. She ain't my daughter, and it was her own father who was so willing to get rid of her. And remember, it's your own people who are using these women as prostitutes."

"I know that, and it shames me greatly. That is why I am here."

"Then make me an offer I can't refuse. You can afford to buy her, and we both know you can get her past the inspectors. You're a businessman; the law permits you to return to the United States with a Chinese wife." The captain slapped his knee in delight. "It's a perfect way out of this mess—for all of us."

"Except for the fact that I do not believe in buying and selling human beings."

"Oh, I get it. You want me to give her to you. That would be mighty nice, now wouldn't it? I'll take my chances sneaking her by the inspectors before I give her away. I could even keep her on board and let my men have at her. They'd be willing to pay for the use of her. I'd have my money back in no time."

"You know better than that, Captain. You'd have more fights on board this ship than you could handle if you did such a thing."

"Well, pay me for what I've got in her. That's the least you can do. Don't think of it as buying her. Think of it as a creative settlement of a difficult situation."

Sam wasn't sure how to resolve the matter. On the one hand, he knew bartering in human flesh was morally wrong. Yet to turn his back would mean that Qui Jin would surely be doomed to a life of misery. "Give me time to consider your offer," he finally replied.

"If the winds stay with us, I'd say you've got about six days to decide. Just remember: If you don't take her, I'll find some way to get rid of her."

Sam nodded as he left the room. He knew the captain meant to frighten him— and he had. It was obvious that the captain regretted purchasing Qui Jin, but he also knew Captain Obley would want a fair return on his money. Sam leaned his arms along the railing of the ship and thought of his parents and sisters. How would they handle such a situation? Most likely, his sisters and mother would immediately pay the money and consider it well spent. His father, on the other hand, would look for another way. He would insist that correcting one wrong with another was not a proper way to proceed. *Look to the ways of Jesus,* he would advise. "Look to the ways of Jesus," Sam said aloud. Immediately, he rushed to his cabin and opened his Bible. Surely his answer must lie within these pages. "Give me wisdom, Lord. Show me how I may please You," he prayed.

Sam rose early the next morning and made his way to Captain Obley's cabin. Sometime during the night his answer had come. Now he must see if the captain would agree. Sam rapped on the door and waited.

"Made your decision so soon?" the captain inquired as he pulled open the heavy door.

"I have a proposal to place before you. I do not know what you paid for the girl."

"Well, I. . ."

Sam held up his hand to stave off the attempted interruption. "Please do not tell me. I have sought the Christian way to handle this matter, and here is my offer to you: I will pay for the girl's passage from Canton to San Francisco. I can give you the same amount I paid for my own passage. Although you may choose to believe you are selling the girl, please understand I am paying for the cost of her journey—nothing else. Do you agree?"

The captain grinned and spat on the floor. "You got a deal. Hand over the money and she's yours, or she's free—whichever you want to call it."

Sam placed the money in the captain's outstretched hand. "Please let me explain this transaction to Qui Jin."

"I wasn't planning on telling her anything. Haven't said a word to her since the day after we set sail and don't plan to start now. Guess you know I would have sold her for a lot less," the captain said as Sam walked toward the door.

"Perhaps. . .but I didn't purchase her; I paid for her passage on the ship," Sam replied without looking back.

His plan had worked. It didn't matter what the cost or what the captain thought. Qui Jin was free.

Chapter 5

Qui Jin made her way down the hallway and up the steps to the deck, her heart quickening when she saw Sam watching for her. He motioned to her and smiled. Apparently, she had misinterpreted his actions the day before. She had been certain that he was angry when he sent her off to her cabin.

"You are not annoyed with me?" she questioned in a barely audible whisper.

"Of course not. Come closer—I want to talk to you."

She moved by his side and returned his smile. "I heard the sailors talking. They say we will soon be in San Francisco. Is that correct?"

He nodded his head. "Yes, possibly five or six days. That's why we need to talk. You misunderstood the captain's plans for your future in America, and he permitted you to believe whatever you wanted. He had no plan for you to become a servant to a Chinese family. In fact, there are laws that prohibit him from bringing you into the country."

She felt confused. Why would the captain purchase her if she was not allowed into the country? "I don't understand."

"I know. It is difficult. The captain thought he might be able to smuggle you past the inspectors. If he had been successful, he planned to sell you to one of the Tong leaders, who would use you as a prostitute."

His voice grew so quiet, she needed to strain forward in order to hear him. As he completed his explanation, she jumped back. "I am to be a. . ."

"No, listen—I went to the captain and agreed to pay for your passage if he would give you your freedom. He agreed. You are now free."

She stared at him in disbelief. "Free to do what? I will die in this country of strangers." Uncontrollable fear welled up inside her, a giant volcano threatening to erupt at any moment.

"I am going to help you. My family will help you. It's going to be all right—you'll see." He gently wiped away a tear that glistened on her cheek. "Trust me."

"What else can I do?"

He smiled. "I don't know that you have many choices right now, but one day you will. I hope when that time comes, you will have wisdom to make all the right decisions."

"I hope so also. You were reading your Bible?" she asked, pointing toward the book in his hand.

"Yes. I was looking for answers."

"And did you find them?"

"Some of them. A few questions still remain unanswered. I am hopeful that with prayer and God's help, the answers will come when they are truly needed."

Qui Jin nodded. "Perhaps if we continue to search your Bible, we can find the remaining answers. You said we have five or six days until we arrive, didn't you?"

Sam gave her a broad smile. "Why didn't I think of that?"

Unable to hide her enthusiasm, Qui Jin clapped her hands together. "Let's begin!"

Sam handed her the Bible. "You choose what you would like to read."

Thumbing through the book, Qui Jin looked at Sam in dismay. It was difficult to make a choice among so many pages. Finally, she shrugged her shoulders, looked heavenward, opened the Bible, and handed it back to Sam.

He gazed down at the page. "The tenth chapter of Romans." He contemplated the passage, then began reading the plan of salvation aloud to Qui Jin.

✤❧

With deliberate determination, Sam handed the Bible to Qui Jin each time they began their Bible readings. On every occasion, she looked heavenward and opened the Bible. They read the seventeenth chapter of John, the thirteenth chapter of Luke, and the third chapter of John. And so it continued. Sam would read; she would listen. He was sure she understood, and yet she gave him no indication of her own willingness to accept Christ as her Savior.

He prayed for the words to speak—to convince her. None came. And so he remained silent, handing her the Bible, waiting to read the Scripture. On their final day at sea, Qui Jin handed him the open Bible. "Luke, chapter twelve," he read, surprised at the choice, for he knew the Scripture spoke more of hypocrisy than of salvation.

"Wait, wait. . . ," Qui Jin interrupted as he finished reading the seventh verse. "God cares not just for people but for even a tiny bird?" Her eyes were filled with wonder.

Sam nodded his head. "Yes, every creature, even a tiny bird."

"And surely if a tiny bird is of value to God, a girl-child must be of some worth also—wouldn't you think?" she timidly questioned.

"Oh, yes, Qui Jin. You are worth His life. He died for you—that's how much He loved you."

"I think what you have been trying to teach me has now become clear, Sam. I, too, want to belong to your God."

✤❧

That afternoon, the *Falcon* docked in San Francisco. "Go to your cabin and put this on. We will be going ashore in about an hour," Sam instructed while handing her a yellow silk dress.

273

Qui Jin eyed the costly garment and looked back at Sam. "Is this for your betrothed?"

"No, it is for my mother. I never return home without a gift for her. I thought she would like a new dress."

"It is beautiful. I cannot wear such an expensive piece of clothing."

"We haven't time to argue, Qui Jin. You must trust me. If I attempt to take you off this ship and you wear your tattered clothes, we will be questioned and possibly thrown in jail. Please do as I say."

He kept his voice firm and gave her a stern look that made her rush off with the dress under her arm. When she reappeared on the deck, Sam's breath caught in his throat. She had braided her hair and fashioned it into two large coils that rested at the base of her head. The dress fit her perfectly, and the red embroidery along the neckline emphasized the pink tinge in her cheeks. The captain was right—the few extra pounds she had recently gained turned her into a beautiful young woman.

"Am I presentable?"

"You are more than presentable. You are lovely."

The color in her cheeks heightened with his praise, and she immediately looked downward. "Do you think they will notice my shoes?"

"I doubt it, but if they ask questions, let me answer. You must act as though you understand nothing they say. I don't expect any problems, but keep this with you." He pulled the golden cord he used as a bookmark from his Bible and placed it in her hand. "Should we become separated, find some trustworthy person and ask him to bring you to the Tongantang Apothecary. My father owns the shop, and generally some member of my family works there. If for some reason the man is afraid to escort you, ask him to deliver the cord to the shop and say it is for me. Do you understand?"

Sam watched the fear begin to etch itself upon her face as he spoke, yet he needed to protect her. There were too many of his fellow countrymen who would be delighted to take advantage of her, should the opportunity arise.

"I understand, but I will stay close to you," she promised as she took the cord from his hand.

"Good. I am praying God will go before us and give us a clear path."

She nodded. "Tell Him I would like that also."

"I will. Now come along; it is time." Sam turned toward the captain. "Thank you for providing us with a safe journey, Captain."

"Glad to have you aboard anytime, Sam. Good luck to you. Your cargo should be unloaded in a few hours," Captain Obley replied while gesturing toward the dock.

Sam nodded, then led Qui Jin down the gangplank and into a dilapidated building at one end of the dock. A weatherworn sign had come loose from one of its hinges and now balanced precariously over the door as they entered.

"Papers?" one of the officials barked while holding out his hand.

Sam complied and said nothing. "What about her?" the inspector asked, using his club to turn Qui Jin's face toward him.

"She is with me," Sam replied.

"Went over there and brought back a wife, did ya? She ain't half bad for a slant-eye. Go on! Get outta here. Just what we need—another Chink," the inspector muttered before he turned back to continue his game of cards.

"We are safe now?" Qui Jin whispered as they turned away from the ocean and began to make their way down a narrow street.

"I'll get a carriage to take us to my home," Sam replied. He motioned to a Chinese man standing down the street. Moments later, a shiny black carriage pulled by two brown mares came to a halt in front of them. Slowly, they moved down Jackson Street and then Dupont. They passed the corner of California and Montgomery Streets and continued onward, each street lined with its share of red-and-green barber stands, bazaars, and emporiums, along with a Chinese theater, and the large, granite-faced Wells Fargo Bank.

"That is one of my father's apothecary shops," Sam remarked. "Now tell me, what do you think of our little city?"

"It is larger than I thought it would be, and there is much to see. Most of all, I enjoy seeing so many of our people, especially the children." She pointed toward two small children toddling alongside their father. "It makes me feel more at home to see familiar sights; yet at the same time, it makes me long for home. Does that make any sense at all?"

He smiled. She was so lovely in the yellow silk with her velvet-brown eyes staring up at him as though he had all the answers to every problem in the universe.

"Yes, it makes sense. I feel a bit the same way when I visit China."

"But you know you will come back home to what you love, to a family who is waiting for you. That is a huge difference."

"Qui Jin, what would you have me do? If you want to return to Canton, I will purchase a ticket on the next ship. Is that what you want?"

"In here," she said, placing her hand firmly on her chest, "that is what I want. But here," she continued, pointing to her head, "I know I cannot return. Yet what is to become of me? I have no home, no place where I belong. I don't mean to sound ungrateful. You have been very good to me."

"You need not apologize for anything. Just know for now, you belong with me. We'll figure out the rest later."

"I hope your family will feel the same way," Qui Jin replied, though a note of trepidation caused her voice to falter.

Chapter 6

Ying Kum Shu stared at his son in disbelief. "You purchased this girl and brought her home? What were you thinking? What happened to your values and beliefs? I cannot believe my son would stoop so low as to buy another human. Did you think this girl was no different from glassware at the bazaar? You just pay your money and bring her home?"

"No, Father. Please permit me to explain. I did not purchase her. I merely agreed to pay her passage. I don't own her. She is free, and she knows that, but where was she to go? I prayed about her situation and what to do. I believe I was meant to help her. We both know that if she had left the docks alone with no money and no place to go, she would have ended up in one of those cages on Bartlett Alley, working as a prostitute. Tell me, Father, what would you have done?"

Kum Shu shook his head. "I do not know. There is truth to what you say. It would be tragic to have her end up in a brothel, and yet. . ."

"He did the right thing," Sam's mother interrupted.

"Your mother has been away from the homeland too long. Not only does she interrupt her husband, but she now disagrees with him."

Their gentle laughter broke the tension and released the mantle of gloom that had cloaked their conversation over the past hour. Sam leaned toward Kum Shu, his arms resting on his knees. "You know my heart, Father. I would not intentionally do anything to disgrace you, and I try very hard to live by God's Word."

"I know you do, my son, and I am sorry for my hasty remarks. Sometimes I need to spend more time in thought and prayer before I open my mouth. Your intentions and your heart were in the right place. But what do we do with this girl?"

Ying Ah Ching fervently shook her head. "Such foolishness! You make it sound as though there is no need for a beautiful young Chinese woman in all of this city. Most likely, you could have her betrothed by nightfall—but that is not what I recommend."

Kum Shu's lips turned slightly upward as he listened to his wife. "I am sure you have already decided upon the perfect plan for Qui Jin's life."

"Since you asked, I think she should remain with us. She can work here in the house. You know there is more than enough work for two women in this house. It would be a pleasure to have another woman here with me, now that all of our daughters are gone."

"You already have another daughter to help you. Li Laan will be here tomorrow," Kum Shu reminded.

Sam turned toward his mother. "What?"

"While you've been off to China, Li Laan's mother received word that her parents are ill. Naturally, Li Laan's parents wanted to return to the homeland and offer their assistance. They sail at daybreak. Li Laan did not want to leave her teaching position at the school. Of course, she could not remain alone in their house. . . ."

The words hung in the air, begging for completion for several minutes. Sam looked back and forth between his parents. His father finally spoke. "Your mother suggested Li Laan come to live with us until her parents return to San Francisco."

"I see." Sam nodded his head. "Well then, Mother, having Li Laan and Qui Jin in the house will be very similar to the days when my sisters were living at home, won't it?"

"Exactly! You see, this is not a problem. I managed to keep three daughters busy for many years. Besides, Li Laan will be teaching at the school most days."

"As you wish, Wife, but you may find that you can't control Li Laan and Qui Jin in the same way you controlled our daughters."

"You need not worry. I'll take care of the household, just as I always have. I think I'll go upstairs and see if Qui Jin is rested and would like to join us for some tea."

A smile played at the corner of Sam's lips as he watched his mother walk from the room.

"You are pleased that Qui Jin is going to be close at hand, aren't you?" Kum Shu asked.

Sam stiffened at the question. He hesitated a moment while glancing down at the floor. "I am pleased she is going to be safe."

"I see how you look at her, Sam. It is not the look of someone seeking safety for a stranger. I fear your eyes betray your true feelings for the girl. Can you tell me otherwise?"

"I do care for her, Father. We were companions throughout the voyage. Her life has been difficult, and it brought me pleasure to help her. I told her about life in California and began teaching her English. She is bright and wanted to learn. Is that so wrong?"

His father's dark-brown gaze remained fixed upon Sam for several minutes. "If that is all that you truly feel, there is no need for concern."

"Here we are," Sam's mother said as she led Qui Jin into the room. "You two continue your conversation. We're going to make tea, and we'll be back to join you in a few minutes."

Kum Shu smiled at his wife. "That would be very nice. I trust you find your room adequate?" he asked Qui Jin.

"It is lovely—much too nice for me. The sleeping room you have provided is larger than the entire house where my family lives. I am in your debt." She kept her head bowed.

"I am pleased we can help you in this difficult time, but you need not bow to me,

Qui Jin. This is America, and my family no longer adheres to some of the Chinese customs practiced in the homeland. Most of those rituals have been replaced by our religious beliefs. I am sure my son spoke to you of our faith?"

Qui Jin nodded. "We studied much about God. Sam used stories from the Bible to help me learn English. I accepted Jesus as my Lord only a short time before we arrived. I still have many questions, there are matters that still confuse me, and the Bible has many words to learn."

"Yes, it does. I'm sure my wife will be happy to assist you. And Li Laan, Sam's future wife, is a teacher at the Christian school. She can answer many questions for you also."

"Sam told me that Li Laan is a teacher. I look forward to meeting her."

Kum Shu returned Qui Jin's smile, then turned back toward Sam as the two women left the room.

"Your eyes sparkle when she enters the room; you watch her every movement, entranced by her beauty and grace," Kum Shu accused.

"You think she has beauty and grace also?" Sam flinched at his father's stern look of disapproval. Why had he asked? But it was too late to snatch back the words.

"Sam, have you forgotten that you are engaged to marry Li Laan?"

"Not for a moment, Father." It was the truth, but he dared not elaborate upon the answer. His father would not be pleased to hear Sam's particular thoughts about his engagement to Li Laan. Those distressing thoughts had been in the forefront of his mind on both the journey to China as well as his return.

"Your wedding date is set. You will not bring shame upon me, will you?"

"If it is in my power, I will never do such a thing. But tell me, Father, why are you willing to let some rituals die yet insist that others live on? Why are you willing to accept your wife as an equal but continue to choose the marriage partners of your children? If you have trained us properly, surely you must trust our ability to choose a life partner."

"We arranged marriages for only two of your sisters, but they are happy with the husbands we chose for them. And you are so involved in work, I doubt you would have ever chosen a wife. I thought Li Laan an excellent choice for you. You are well suited, both born in this country, educated, Christians; and our families hold each other in high regard—what more could one desire? You never voiced such concerns before meeting Qui Jin. Until now, you seemed satisfied with our decision. Your question serves only to reinforce my concerns."

"It is not my intent to cause you concern, but I can answer your question in one word, Father. Love—that is the one word that you leave out of your equation for a good marriage."

"As a flower blooms in its season, love blossoms with time. I did not know your mother when we married, but I grew to love her over the years. With time and patience, you will learn to love Li Laan. Don't cause me to regret showing kindness to Qui Jin. I fear I've already made a mistake by giving my permission for her to stay—"

"Here we are with the tea," Sam's mother interrupted.

Qui Jin watched from the doorway as Ah Ching carried a teakwood tray containing the gold-embossed tea-pot and fragile, porcelain cups into the room. "I am not feeling very well. May I be excused to go upstairs?"

Sam rose from his chair and began to walk toward Qui Jin, but she motioned him away. He stopped, hoping she realized that he only wanted to help.

"Do not concern yourself, Sam. I think I need to rest awhile longer. I'm not hungry or thirsty, just weary. I believe it would be best if I went to bed. Thank you for your hospitality," she said, once again bowing her head to Kum Shu. Not waiting for a reply, she rushed down the hallway and up the stairs.

Ah Ching waited until she heard the door latch before she turned to her husband. "We could hear you talking as we came down the hallway," she said, her voice a hoarse whisper. "What were the two of you thinking, to have such a conversation within earshot of the hallway?"

"I suppose I wasn't thinking," Kum Shu replied. "It is my fault. I am the one who pursued the discussion. It should have waited until we were out of the house. Perhaps she didn't hear everything. Perhaps she truly is overtired from the journey."

Qui Jin closed the door and leaned her weight against it. Sam's father didn't want her in his home. She had heard his words: He regretted his decision. There was no choice; she must leave. Once it grew dark outside, she would sneak from the house. She would not remain in a place where she was unwelcome.

Carefully, she spread the yellow silk dress on one side of the bed; she then donned her tattered blue shirt and pants. Laying down on the other side of the bed, she folded her hands and quietly awaited nightfall. Darkness finally descended, and the household noises and conversations came to a halt. Carefully, she turned the doorknob and peeked into the darkened hallway. With her heart pounding, she tiptoed down the stairs, out the heavy wooden door, and into the moonless night.

Chapter 7

Blackness shrouded the streets. Qui Jin fell on the cobblestones in her haste to escape. Perhaps it would be best to retrace the path she and Sam had taken, if only she could gain her sense of direction. The shadowy buildings all looked alike in the disquieting darkness, and she silently reprimanded herself for not paying more attention to the route they had traveled. Instead, she'd been busy gaping at the fortune-tellers and peddlers hawking their wares along the streets.

"I must decide," Qui Jin muttered while turning to look back down the street she had just crossed. Continuing to weave back and forth among the streets, she moved onward. The smell of the ocean made it possible to discern that she was growing nearer to the docks. She slowed her pace and looked over her shoulder. Were those footsteps behind her? The moonless sky made it impossible to see for any distance. Once again, she hastened her steps. Palms sweating, heart racing, she strained to listen for distant footsteps as she scurried past one building and then the next.

Too late she heard him. A scream of fear rose in her throat. An arm encircled her waist, and an open hand slammed over her mouth. Her teeth jammed into the tender flesh of her lower lip. She struggled against the arms that now held her in a viselike grip, his jagged voice hissing curses into the night air as she stomped his left foot.

"You vile little—"

She twisted hard to free herself from the powerful hand that covered her mouth. From the very depths of her being, Qui Jin screamed for help. For the second time, she felt the rough palm slap across her face, thrusting her head back into the muscular chest of her assailant.

"You cannot get away from me. If you know what's good for you, you will cooperate," the man snapped while twisting her head.

He would break her neck—of that she was now certain. Reluctantly, she ceased fighting and allowed her body to go limp.

"That's better. I am going to take my hand away from your mouth, but if you scream, I will kill you. Do you understand?"

He loosened his grip ever so slightly, and she nodded her head in agreement. Slowly, his hand dropped away from her mouth. He pulled her arms back and quickly bound her wrists, the leather strap cutting into her soft flesh. She winced but was cautious to remain silent.

"Listen to me carefully. We are going to walk to my home, where you may remain until morning. Who are you running from? Don't you realize these streets are unsafe? You need my protection."

"You have a strange way of protecting people. If my welfare concerns you, why did you hurt me?" she whispered.

"If I had merely called out for you to stop, would you have done so?"

"No."

He shrugged his shoulders. "You see?"

She wanted to believe him. Perhaps he could help her find work and a place to live. Sam had told her of factories where cigars and shirts were made. She wondered if women were permitted to work in such places. Surely this man could tell her. When they arrived at his home, she would ask him.

He pulled her along until they reached a narrow alleyway. The sun had not begun to rise, but the approaching daylight hour had driven away the deep shroud of blackness that loomed overhead only a short time ago. However, nothing seemed familiar. She struggled to see the address printed on a building above her head. A cold shiver ran down her spine, for it was one of the names Sam had spoken: Bartlett's Alley. She was being taken to one of those places where men paid for sexual favors. She had to get away from this evil man. Without thinking, she jerked her arm from his loosened grip and began running. She heard him laugh as he began chasing after her. With her arms tied behind her, she was easy prey.

She landed with a thud, her face hitting the ground as he tackled her. "You stupid girl!" he screamed, yanking her by her tethered arms. A deep, overpowering wail escaped her lips and echoed through the predawn silence. Searing pain surged through her arms and upward into her shoulders as he jerked her to a standing position. "Did you think you could get away from me? Look what you've done to yourself!" His condemnation was followed by an angry glare as he turned the left side of her face toward him. "Your face is scraped and bleeding. Within the hour, you will be swollen and bruised."

Her face ached, and she could feel the warmth of her own blood beginning to trickle downward, stinging as it seeped from the open wounds on her face. A sharp pain in her left knee caused her to yelp as the man once again pulled her forward. "Why are you so angry? You don't care about me!" she sobbed.

"I care about the money you will be making for me. The way you look right now, I would be lucky to find any man willing to bed you. I have principles. The men who use these Chinatown brothels know that the first time I put a woman in one of my cells, she will be worth top dollar. I treat my women better than the rest of these men—feed them well, make them wash themselves at least twice a week, provide medicine. I know how to protect my investment."

"I am not your investment. I am free."

His look of contempt was followed by a scornful laugh. "You are my investment, because you now belong to me. Now get over here." He placed his key into a heavy lock hanging from one of the doors that lined the alleyway.

Metal bars slashed across a square opening in the wooden door the man now unlocked and pulled open. He jerked her inside, shoving her onto a mat on the floor while he lit a candle that sat atop a small, scarred table.

"This," he said, gesturing with his arm, "is your new home. I will return in a short time with some salve and herbs to tend to your wounds." He grabbed her chin and pushed her head back against the cold brick wall until he was looking directly into her eyes. He spoke to her from between clenched yellow teeth. "For now, sit there and be quiet, or you will incur my wrath. Believe me, you do not want that to happen."

She remained on the mat, listening as he carefully locked the door and scurried back down the alley. Once assured that her assailant was gone, Qui Jin limped to the window and pressed her bruised face against the bars.

"Psst. Can anyone hear me?" she asked in a hoarse whisper.

Silence. She waited for a few moments, then tried again. "Anyone—is anyone awake? Can you hear me?"

"Who are you?" a woman called back. It sounded as though it came from the door to her right.

"Suey Qui Jin. I came here from Canton—just yesterday," she added. "Who are you?"

"My name is Tien Fu Lin. Did Kem Chinn smuggle you into the country?"

"No. I am free. I was walking down the street when a man attacked me and brought me to this place."

"Free? You'll never be free again. Believe me, there is no escape from this wickedness. I have been here for three years. Kem Chinn came to China, saying he wanted to take a wife. In fact, he made grand promises to my parents and spoke of his wealth, telling them we would be married in California. Once we arrived in California, he placed me in this alley. This room is where I have remained ever since. When I asked him why he had lied to me, he said that in order to become prosperous, he needed more women for his business. I am fulfilling his need to acquire more wealth. So will you." Her words were spoken in a sad yet matter-of-fact tone.

"I will not do such a thing," Qui Jin replied firmly.

"That is what I said also. But you will soon find there are no choices for us. I saw you attempt to run away. I was silently cheering for you, hoping you would gain your freedom," Fu Lin replied. "Where are you injured?"

"My face is swollen and bleeding, and I injured one leg. I don't think he damaged my arms, although his leather strap cut into my wrists."

"Kem Chinn will be primarily concerned about repairing your face. The men who frequent the brothels are willing to pay extra money for attractive girls. He prides himself on having the most beautiful, well-dressed girls. If you are a virgin, he will obtain triple price for your first night. That will make him very happy."

"I should never have run away from Sam's home," Qui Jin mournfully murmured as she lowered herself onto the mat. Exhausted, she lay down and dropped off into a fitful sleep.

The sun was streaming through the bars when Kem Chinn reappeared inside the cell, this time with an old woman in tow. "Fix her. I will return for you later," he snarled at the old woman. He glared at Qui Jin, turned, and departed.

The woman squatted down and motioned Qui Jin closer. "You made a mistake wandering out in the night, didn't you?" She didn't wait for an answer but turned to her basket and pulled out a white cotton cloth along with a bottle of clear liquid. After dousing the piece of soft fabric, the old woman gingerly dabbed Qui Jin's swollen cheek.

"You are hurting me." Qui Jin winced and shoved at the woman's hand.

She leaned back on her haunches and cackled. "Stings, doesn't it? But it will heal these cuts without leaving scars on your face, which will please Kem Chinn. Where did he find you?"

"He didn't find me—he chased me down and tied me up. I am free."

Once again the woman laughed. "You may have been free before he captured you, but you are now the property of Kem Chinn and will turn a nice profit for him." She observed Qui Jin's face more closely. "At least once you are healed. Until then, he will consider you a liability."

"And do you belong to Kem Chinn also?"

"Yes, but I am too old to work in the alley any longer. Now I work at the house, preparing meals, keeping you girls in good physical condition, and teaching proper behavior to the new arrivals, girls just like you."

"Proper behavior? I am locked inside four walls. How can I behave improperly?"

"You already have. Look at the damage you have caused your beautiful face and well-formed body. It will be at least five days before you are healed, and Kem Chinn will not place you for bid until he can obtain the highest price. You are a virgin?"

Qui Jin stared at the woman, her mouth stretched with disgust.

"If you do not answer, I will be required to examine you. You don't want that, do you?"

"Yes, I am a virgin," Qui Jin quickly responded.

"You see? It is much easier if you cooperate. You will find that is true in all things, especially when you are with the men. You must do whatever they request of you, and you must do it as though it pleases you to make them happy. If Kem Chinn receives complaints from his customers, you will suffer his rage. He is a cruel man. He will injure you, but not in ways that will prohibit you from servicing his customers. Do you understand what I am telling you?"

Bile rose in Qui Jin's throat, and she swallowed hard before nodding. She knew it would do her no good to disagree with this woman.

"Good. Take off those clothes. I will see that they are burned. You must wash yourself," she said, pointing toward the basin and pitcher of water. "Wear this dress. I will leave the necessary items for you to fashion your hair," she ordered as she pulled a green silk dress from her basket.

Humiliation and modesty caused Qui Jin to shrink into a far corner while she disrobed and began washing her body. The old woman seemed to sense her embarrassment and busied herself rearranging the basket of supplies.

When she had completed bathing herself, Qui Jin pulled the dress over her head and moved to the center of the small room.

"Even with the scratches and cuts, you are quite beautiful," the woman stated as she scooped up the worn blue clothing.

"Stop!" Qui Jin shouted.

Startled, the old woman dropped the clothing into a pile on the floor. Qui Jin rummaged through the inner pocket of her pants and pulled out the twisted gold cord and closed it into her palm.

"Give me that," the woman commanded.

"It is nothing of value, merely a keepsake."

"Let me see it," the old woman insisted. She grabbed Qui Jin's hand and attempted to pry open her fingers.

"You see?" Qui Jin asked as she voluntarily opened her fist.

The woman grabbed the cord and dangled it from one finger. "Quite right. This tiny piece of twine is of no value. It is too short to braid into your hair, and certainly too flimsy for use in hanging yourself. You wait and see. In a few days, you'll be willing to trade that piece of thread for a nice strong rope." Cackling, she shoved the cord back into Qui Jin's hand.

"Kem Chinn is coming. Behave yourself in his presence, or we will both be punished," the old woman hissed.

"Are you done, old woman?" Kem Chinn called out.

"Yes, yes. She is doing well."

"How long before she will be ready for bidding?" Kem Chinn asked as he opened the door and moved inside.

Kem Chinn leered in her direction for a moment, then began walking around her like a hungry tiger circling his prey. Qui Jin shivered in disgust as he prowled about, first touching her arms, then running his fingers down her leg. He turned toward the old woman. "She will make me much money. How long until her face is healed?"

"Four days, maybe five."

"No more than four days. You have her ready," he commanded.

Qui Jin fingered the golden cord as she watched Kem Chinn and the old woman scurry away. "Perhaps the old woman is right. I may be hoping for a rope long enough to hang myself within the week," she murmured, no longer able to stave off the fear that loomed within her.

Chapter 8

Horror filled Ah Ching's eyes. "Qui Jin is gone!"

Sam's jaw went slack as he stood silent, staring into his mother's eyes. When the words finally registered, he pushed past her and vaulted up the steps two at a time. He had to see for himself. Surely his mother was mistaken. His fingers dug into the wood molding that surrounded the doorway. This was a cruel joke, for Qui Jin could not be gone. He had been able to protect her throughout their entire voyage to California, managed to answer questions posed by the inspection officials, gained permission for her to stay in their home, and now she was gone. How could he have ultimately failed so miserably?

"You'll not find her up there," his father called. "Go to the school. Ask Li Laan if there have been any new girls admitted to the mission home. Hurry! I'll go to the shop and gather a group of men to help search. Come on, Sam!"

Retracing his steps, Sam returned to where his father stood waiting. "I should have checked on her last evening." It was all he could manage to say.

"Had you told her about the mission home?" his father asked as they reached the street.

"Only that Li Laan worked at the school."

Kum Shu shook his head. "Then it's doubtful she went there, but it is at least a possibility. Ask Li Laan to report Qui Jin's disappearance to the head of the mission council. Perhaps they will be able to assist in some manner."

Sam forced himself to concentrate on his father's instructions. He needed to keep his wits about him and remain calm. Otherwise, he would be of little assistance. "You think the worst has happened?"

"I don't know. We'll need to check the docks. Perhaps she wanted to return home and thinks she can smuggle herself onto a ship. Who knows what she may have been thinking."

Sam fought back the words he wanted to speak. They both knew what Qui Jin had been thinking when she slipped away. Now was not the time for blame. It wouldn't bring her back, and it would only slow their search.

"Come to the shop after you've talked to Li Laan," Kum Shu called out as he rushed down the street, his long black queue slapping back and forth as he ran.

Sam headed off in the opposite direction, wondering if finding Qui Jin was the primary reason his father sent him to the school.

After entering the gate, he ascended the four steps leading to the front door of the Chinese Christian Mission School. Why was he hesitating? Perhaps once he saw Li Laan, these feelings he had for Qui Jin would disappear and life would return to normal. But how could life ever be normal again? Qui Jin was gone, and he felt responsible for her well-being. What if he never found her? How could he live? Guilt washed over him. He was betrothed to another, yet he wondered how he could live without spending his life with Qui Jin.

"Does no one answer the door?"

Startled, Sam turned to see a man accompanied by a young boy standing beside him. "I just arrived. I haven't rung the bell." Sam quickly reached toward the brass bell and pulled the thick, hemp cord.

"Sam! I didn't know you had returned," Clara Ludwig greeted as she opened the door. "You may go to your classroom," she said to the little boy as his father pushed him forward before rushing back down the steps. "It is good to see you, Sam."

"Thank you, Mrs. Ludwig. I need to speak to Li Laan."

"She's not here, Sam. I'm sure you know her parents are sailing on Friday. She said she needed time off to assist her mother at home prior to their voyage."

He bent his head and placed his right hand on his forehead. Something was wrong. Hadn't his mother said that Li Laan's parents were sailing at daybreak today? They should already be gone. His mother must have confused the dates.

"You did know her parents are leaving for China?"

"What? Yes, yes, but my mother said they were sailing at daybreak today. She must have been mistaken. May I come in and talk to you, Mrs. Ludwig?" he asked, attempting to regain his composure.

"Certainly." She led him into her small office, indicating he be seated in a straight-backed wooden chair. "What can I do for you?"

Without going into great detail, Sam hastily explained Qui Jin's current plight and his growing concern for her whereabouts. "Have you had any new girls come to the house?"

"I'm afraid not, Sam, but I'm attending a meeting with the other mission school leaders this morning. I can spread your inquiry among them. If there's any information, I will send word."

"Thank you, Mrs. Ludwig. You do understand our concern?"

"Of course. Unfortunately, if she wandered off during the night and made her way into the wrong part of town, I fear you may have a struggle gaining her back, even if she should be found."

He wouldn't permit himself to think of Qui Jin in such circumstances. They would find her. Surely God would not allow more pain into this young woman's life. Not now—not when she was searching to find Him and accept the truth. Would Qui Jin think to pray? Ashamed, he admitted to himself that he had not. Instead, he had looked only to his earthly father to solve the problem. Perhaps his mother and father had prayerfully sought guidance in finding Qui Jin.

Sam rose from the chair and moved toward the front door. "Would you pray for her safe return, Mrs. Ludwig? And ask the others also?"

"Yes, Sam," Mrs. Ludwig said. "Please keep us advised of any news—and when you see Li Laan, tell her she will be missed this week. The children love her very much."

"I will do that, and thank you."

He knew that his father expected a report from him, but he must return home first. Surely his mother had been mistaken about the departure date of Li Laan's parents. Or perhaps he had not listened carefully.

Hurrying as he neared the house, Sam pushed open the door and called out, "Mother, where are you?" No answer. Where was she? Rushing about the house, he continued calling out as he moved from room to room and then up the stairs. All the women in his life seemed to be disappearing. Sweat beaded on his forehead as he ran back down the stairs.

"Why are you yelling?" his mother called out from the back of the house.

Relief washed over him as he ran toward her and pulled her into his arms. "Where were you? I need to talk to you."

"I was in the garden, praying."

He smiled while a sense of calm began infusing his spirit. "I should have known."

She returned his smile and took his hand. "Come join me."

Walking side by side, they entered the small garden and sat down on a narrow metal bench. "I went to see Mrs. Ludwig at the mission home—"

"I thought you went to see Li Laan."

"Exactly. I did go to see Li Laan, but she wasn't there, so I talked with Mrs. Ludwig. They have not seen Qui Jin, although Mrs. Ludwig is going to inquire of the other mission leaders this morning. Perhaps one of them will have—"

"Have you told your father?" she interrupted.

"No, not yet. I needed to talk with you first. Mrs. Ludwig said Li Laan requested time off from the mission school to help her parents before they sail for China."

His mother sat listening, nodding approval at the remark. "That was a sweet gesture. Li Laan is a good daughter. But why did you need to tell me this now?"

"Mrs. Ludwig said Li Laan asked to be gone until the end of the week—that her parents sail on Friday. I thought you told me they were sailing today."

He could see the confusion begin to etch itself upon his mother's face. "They should have sailed early this morning. I saw Li Soon at church on Sunday, and their plans had not changed. You say that Li Laan is not at the mission?"

"No, she is not expected back until next Monday."

"This is very strange. She was to come here this afternoon when her last class was finished. Perhaps she is ill. I'll go to the house and see if she is there."

"You know Father would not want you traversing the streets unaccompanied. Besides, I doubt she is ill. She arranged to be away from school all week. I'll go and report to Father. One of us will stop at Li Laan's house today."

Ah Ching took Sam's hand in her own. "Why don't you take a few moments to pray with me? I think you will find it time well spent."

Sam lowered his head, and together the two of them prayed for the safety and protection of Qui Jin and Li Laan. When they had finished, Sam rose from the bench and embraced his mother. "Thank you for reminding me where I should place my trust."

"You must remember that they are both in God's care. Now, go and talk to your father. Perhaps he has some good news."

"Let's hope so, Mother."

Hurrying down the street, Sam broke into a run once he had crossed the street. By the time he entered the apothecary shop, he was gasping for breath. "Any news?" he cried out when he finally spotted his father near the back of the store.

Kum Shu beckoned, and Sam propelled himself toward the rear of the store. His father must have found Qui Jin.

Chapter 9

S am glanced about the rear of the store, quickly looking first in one direction and then the other. "Where is she?"

Kum Shu shook his head. "We have had no success, but I am hopeful."

"I stopped at the house before coming here. Mother and I prayed. When you motioned to me, I was certain Qui Jin was here."

"I assume that Li Laan has heard or seen nothing of a new girl?"

Sam hesitated for a moment, embarrassed that he had not immediately told his father of Li Laan's disappearance. "I was unable to speak with Li Laan. She was not at the mission school today."

"Is she ill?"

Sam recounted his conversation with Mrs. Ludwig as well as the discussion later with his mother. "It appears that I have yet another mystery to solve, Father."

"So it does," Kum Shu agreed. "Ten men have been dispatched, searching in teams of two. They agreed to send someone back here each hour to report on their progress. They've reported nothing substantial thus far, but I remain confident. These men will leave no stone unturned."

"It is gratifying to have such friends."

Kum Shu nodded in agreement. "All these men are from the church. Some of them closed their businesses in order to assist us. Knowing that each of them is praying for Qui Jin's safety while they conduct their search is even more gratifying."

Tears glistened in his father's eyes, which surprised Sam. His father was not a man who had ever displayed his emotions to others—particularly his children. "It is difficult to realize that, even in the midst of this adversity, we still have reason for thanks," Sam said.

Kum Shu cleared his throat. "I think you should go to Li Laan's house and see if she is there. If not, talk to the neighbors. Isn't there another Chinese teacher at the school? Perhaps she knows something."

"You're right. Lon Yoke—they are friends. I'll go to the house first, then on to the school."

"If you are unable to gain any information at her house or from the neighbors, go directly to the school. Otherwise, come back and report your findings. If I do not hear from you, when the other men come back here to report, I will request they add

Li Laan to their search."

Sam shouted his agreement as he hurried out the front door and rushed off toward Kearney Street. Arriving in front of the Tin Fook Jewelry Shop, Sam stopped to regain his breath before ascending the steps that led to the upstairs rooms where Li Laan and her parents lived. When he finally reached the second floor, Sam knocked on the door and waited before he knocked again. No answer. He pressed his ear to the door, hoping to hear some sound of life—anything—but he heard nothing. He knocked one more time.

"There's no one down there," a woman called from one floor up.

Sam loped up the stairway. "Wait, I need to talk to you," he called just as the woman's door was closing. "I am Sam Ying. I am betrothed to Li Laan," he added quickly.

The woman observed him through the narrow opening between the door and the doorjamb for a moment. Apparently satisfied he meant her no harm, the woman returned to the hallway.

"I am searching for Li Laan. Her parents were to sail this morning—for China."

The woman shook her head, agreeing as he spoke. "Yes, I know. They told me they were going. They left very early this morning, before daybreak."

"Have you seen Li Laan today?"

"No. Her mother said she was not going with them, that she would continue teaching at the school and was staying with your parents. She is at the school during this time of the day."

"Yes, I know, but I went to the school, and they have not seen her. That is why I'm here." A hint of exasperation was creeping into Sam's voice as he struggled to remain calm.

The woman shrugged her shoulders. "If she's not at the school, I have no idea where she could be. I thought I heard her leave this morning, perhaps a little earlier than usual, but I may have been mistaken."

"If she comes home, will you tell her of my concern? Tell her it is important she go to the home of my parents, please."

"She is probably sitting and drinking tea with your mother as we speak," the woman said, then quickly added, "but I will tell her if she comes back."

Sam thanked the woman and returned down Kearney Street. If he hurried, he could make it to the school in fifteen minutes, but somehow his sense of urgency had subsided, so he slowed his pace. His compulsion was replaced by a gnawing sensation deep in the pit of his stomach as his mind wandered back to the day of his departure for China. A picture returned to his mind of Li Laan's parents insisting the family accompany him to the dock and his inability to deter their desires—except for Li Laan, who posed no objection to remaining at home. Her parents, however, persevered. Now he recalled the look of detachment in Li Laan's eyes while they discussed the projected date for his return. . .the appearance of disinterest as she assured him there was no need to hurry his voyage. Her parents were engrossed in every imaginable detail of his journey while Li Laan sat in the carriage, strangely quiet and aloof. He hadn't noticed, hadn't even thought about it—until now.

He continued onward, nodding at the occasional passerby, his thoughts focusing on his relationship with Li Laan in the weeks that preceded his voyage. There had been the conversation when she informed him her beliefs regarding arranged marriages differed from those of her parents, her declined invitations to dine with his family, and her seeming lack of interest in their wedding preparations. Her behavior had been a bit unsettling.

Mrs. Ludwig opened the front door. "Sam! I'm surprised to see you again so soon. Did you locate Qui Jin or Li Laan?"

"No, Mrs. Ludwig. In fact, that is why I have returned. There is no one at Li Laan's home. Except for you, everyone I have spoken with tells me she should be here teaching. Would it be possible for me to speak with Lon Yoke?"

"Of course. I didn't think to suggest that you speak with her earlier today. Li Laan and Lon Yoke spend so much time together in the classroom they have become closer than sisters. Let us hope she can help. I'll go and fetch her. I shouldn't be long," Mrs. Ludwig replied as she hurried off.

The sound of footsteps in the hallway caused Sam to turn. He stood still as Mrs. Ludwig entered the room, with Lon Yoke following close behind.

"I must leave, or I'll be late for my meeting. However, please stay and use my office. I'll leave the door open," Mrs. Ludwig stated while hastily running a hatpin through her flower-festooned straw hat.

"We shouldn't be long," Sam replied. He turned toward Lon Yoke. "What can you tell me of Li Laan's whereabouts? She is not at home, and she is not here."

Lon Yoke immediately began twisting her embroidered handkerchief. "I have not seen her today," she whispered.

Sam nodded. "But do you know where she is?"

"Now?"

"Yes, now."

Lon Yoke gazed down at the highly polished oak floor. "No, I do not know. May I return to my class now?"

"No!" Sam shouted. His voice was louder than he'd intended. Lon Yoke cowered back in her chair. "I'm sorry. I should not have raised my voice. Please understand that I am under a great deal of strain. Not only am I searching for Li Laan, but there is another Chinese girl we fear has been abducted. Perhaps Mrs. Ludwig mentioned the disappearance of Suey Qui Jin."

Lon Yoke raised her head ever so slightly, her eyes still focused upon the floor. "Do you fear Li Laan has been abducted?"

"I don't know what to think. The only thing I know for certain is that Li Laan is missing, and nobody seems to know her whereabouts. I think you can help me."

He remained silent—waiting.

Finally, Lon Yoke shifted in her chair, moving forward to the very edge as she reached into the pocket of her shirtwaist. Pulling out an envelope, she extended her arm and handed it to Sam. "I was not to give this to you until she was gone for two days. I told her I would not lie, that surely someone would come looking for her before two days had passed. I truly do not know where she is right now, but I do know she has left the city. She hopes you will not follow her, Sam. I am sure Li Laan is safe, but I doubt the same is true of Qui Jin. It appears Qui Jin is the one who needs your immediate attention."

Sam ripped open the envelope, unfolded the letter, and quickly read the message. He could feel Lon Yoke staring at him, obviously awaiting his response. After neatly refolding the letter and returning it to the envelope, Sam looked at Lon Yoke. "Thank you for providing this information," he said quietly. He tucked the letter into his pocket.

"You have nothing else to say?"

The envelope rustled as he patted his jacket pocket. "No, Li Laan has said it all."

Chapter 10

You are healing nicely. I think you will be ready sooner than I imagined. Kem Chinn will be satisfied with my work," the old lady announced proudly.

"Would you consider telling him I need more time to heal?" Qui Jin begged. "This is only my second day."

The old woman looked directly into her eyes, and Qui Jin thought that for a brief moment she saw a flicker of kindness. "We shall see," she replied after a moment. However, the woman's voice lacked commitment, and her words gave Qui Jin little encouragement. Soon Kem Chinn appeared to take the woman away. Qui Jin sighed with relief when he didn't enter the room to examine her.

The hours passed slowly. Occasionally, a man would be escorted to one of the cells during the early evening hours, but most of them came under cover of darkness. The clanging of the locks and noises that filtered into her room from the alley made it impossible to sleep. She covered her ears to muffle the sounds, and then she began praying to Jesus. All through the night she uttered prayers, urgent pleas that Jesus would rescue her from this place.

"Qui Jin!" the girl in the next cell called out.

Qui Jin moved to the barred window. "Yes?"

"I heard Kem Chinn tell my customer he would have a virgin up for bid in two more nights. He spoke of your beauty and asked that my customer share the information with his friends."

The words struck fear in her heart. Lacing the golden cord through her fingers, she stood staring out into the ugliness of the alleyway. Was this to be the end of her life, living in a brothel, making money for Kem Chinn? Did Jesus die on a cross to save her from her sins in order for her to live out her days as a prostitute? *Surely not,* she prayed.

"You should be pleased. He will treat you better, give you more food and prettier clothes to wear," the girl continued.

Qui Jin ignored the comment. Clothes that men would force her to remove at their pleasure—clothes to wear within the confines of a tiny cell. What did she care about pretty clothes? She stood at the barred window of her room and stared across the narrow street. "Across the alley on that far cell—what is hanging from the window?" Qui Jin called to Fu Lin.

"Sometimes Kem Chinn will move us to different rooms. He says he does it to be kind, but I'm sure there is probably some other reason. For a short time after he moves us, a few of the girls hang a piece of silk or a scarf from their cells so that their customers know where to find them."

"They want the men to find them?"

"Of course. Some of the girls are working here until they repay their debt to Kem Chinn for passage to the country. For those like you and me who will never get away, it is not as important. However, if we don't make enough money for him each day, he withholds our food or punishes us in other ways."

"How much more could he punish us? We are already prisoners."

"You do not want to know. Believe me when I tell you that you do not want to anger Kem Chinn. But if you are as beautiful as I have heard him say, you will have many customers."

Once again, a shiver of fear coursed down Qui Jin's spine. She tucked her hands into the pockets of her dress and paced. Back and forth, back and forth she walked, her fingers wrapping in and out of the tasseled cord until finally she stopped pacing and pulled the cord from her pocket. The fringed tassel appeared to glisten in the sunlight as she held it to the barred window. She would use the cord to mark her cell—not so that men would know her whereabouts and come to abuse her, but so she could tell them the golden cord was from a Bible that spoke of God's love. Carefully, she wrapped the twisted length and then drew the tassel through, pushing the loop down the bar until it hung outside the window, with the fringed end blowing in the warm afternoon breeze.

Qui Jin smiled. There was a bit of comfort in knowing that the same cord that had marked God's Word now identified her cell. On the final days of her and Sam's voyage, she had read a story of Rahab, a woman who had marked her home by hanging a rope out her window. Perhaps someone would come down the alley and see the cord. . .perhaps that person would know it was a Bible marker. . .perhaps that person would realize she believed in Jesus. . .and perhaps that person would save her. "Probably not. Why would a Christian come down one of these alleys?" she murmured in a dejected whisper. The spoken words caused her fear to return anew.

❧

Sam rushed toward Dupont Street. His father would already be on his way home for the noonday meal. Explaining the facts surrounding Li Laan's disappearance would be less complicated with both of his parents together, for there would be less chance of confusion and misunderstanding. At least, that was his desire as he loped into the small courtyard where his parents were beginning their midday meal.

Their joy at seeing him was evident, his father rising as Sam drew nearer. "I have news," he panted.

His father nodded. "Take a moment to catch your breath, and then tell us."

After several moments Sam regained his composure. What he was going to say would be unpleasant. There was no way he could paint a lovely picture. Simple and to the point would be the best method, he decided. "Li Laan has run off with another man. She says she loves this man and intends to marry him."

Perhaps his simple and to-the-point words were not the best decision after all. His mother gasped for breath, her arms flailing as she reached out toward Kum Shu. There was a look of horror in her eyes that was quickly replaced by a glare of accusation as she glanced in Sam's direction.

As Sam had expected, his father remained calm. He'd reveal his thoughts through his words, not with an emotional reaction. Sam watched as his father comforted and calmed his mother until her breathing started returning to normal.

His mother now turned and looked directly into Sam's eyes. "What have you done?"

The words stung. Each one was a punctuated stab that caused surprising pain. "I did nothing, Mother. I honored your wishes in regard to Li Laan and our marriage," he responded in a hushed whisper. "It is Li Laan who has chosen to break the commitment." He pulled the letter from his pocket and thrust it into his mother's hand. "Read for yourself."

"You must go after her." Urgency filled his mother's voice as she quickly scanned the page. "There is no time to stand around talking—you must hurry!"

Kum Shu shook his head. "No! He will not go."

"What? We will be disgraced! Every gossip in Chinatown will be speaking of our shame."

"I care little what the gossips will say. As to shame, Sam did nothing to cause us dishonor. Besides, I doubt he could find Li Laan—and if he did, she would probably already be married."

"But what if he finds her and she hasn't married? He could bring her back, and things would return to normal. They would be married. She would learn to love Sam instead of this other man," his mother argued.

Once again, Kum Shu shook his head. "Hear me, Wife. Even if Sam could find Li Laan, they would both be miserable. It serves no good purpose for Sam to chase after her."

"Sam would not be miserable. He loves Li Laan. Over time, he would win her love in return."

Sam looked toward his father, seeking approval to say what Kum Shu already knew. His father smiled and nodded at Sam. "Tell her," he instructed.

"I do not love Li Laan, Mother. I never have. I, too, love another."

"This is impossible. How can any of this be happening? What have I done to deserve such turmoil and horror in my life?"

Kum Shu laughed. "I am sorry, my wife, but you are creating drama worthy of the theater with your weeping and self-pity. If we compared this incident with the injustice that daily occurs on the streets of Chinatown, I think your turmoil and horror would be infinitesimal. Are you not at all curious whom your son loves?"

A spark of interest gleamed in Ah Ching's eyes. "I am sure I already know. It is Sing Lee Lo. She is attracted to you; her father spoke to us regarding her desire to wed with you. You are secretly meeting with her, aren't you?"

Sam smiled at the smugness in his mother's voice. Confidence etched her face. "No, Mother, Lee Lo does not capture my interest. It is Qui Jin I love."

His mother's eyebrows arched, and her tiny lips gathered into a bow. She stared at him momentarily, then nodded her head. "I should have known."

"Did you not notice the way he looked at her?" Kum Shu asked.

"You knew?" Ah Ching directed an accusatory glare at her husband.

Kum Shu smiled, obviously pleased with himself. "Women are not always the first to see a spark of love. Sam and I discussed his feelings for Qui Jin, but he agreed to honor his betrothal to Li Laan. There is no need for further discussion. I now believe Sam is right; God directed their paths, and they are intended to unite."

Ah Ching stared at her husband in disbelief. "You are giving permission for Sam to wed a peasant girl? Perhaps I could more fully understand if you would reveal what caused you to believe Sam's marriage to Qui Jin is a divine arrangement."

"I will be pleased to do so—but at another time. Right now, we must concentrate on locating Qui Jin." Turning back toward Sam, he shook his head. "I am sorry, but there is nothing positive to report from any of the men searching for Qui Jin. We did become excited for a few moments when one of the men reported seeing an unescorted young woman near the docks. After investigating, our man discovered she is the wife of a merchant returning from China. Her husband explained business detained him and caused his late arrival at the wharf. There is nothing else of consequence to report."

Sam paced back and forth in front of the small stone pond in the courtyard. "Has anyone gone to the alleyway brothels to inquire?" The words stuck in his throat. He did not want to think of Qui Jin in such a place. The very idea caused a wave of nausea to wash over him.

"Yes, but the owners of those despicable places reported there were no new girls. Of course, they tried to interest the men in purchasing services from the women. After declining the invitation, Wing Chew attempted to share God's Word with one of the owners. Unfortunately, Wing Chew didn't have any more success converting the brothel owner than he did finding Qui Jin," his father related.

Sam smiled. He admired Wing Chew's tenacity, for not many would go into the brothels and share Christ. "I doubt there is any reason to check with Mrs. Ludwig at the school, either. I'm not sure where I should search, but I can't sit here waiting. Pray that God will direct my feet. I fear that time is our enemy."

❧

Walking down Sacramento Street, Sam attempted to squelch his feelings of apprehension. *Talking about faith is much easier than putting it into practice,* he decided, bowing his head against a salty breeze. The sound of pounding feet caused Sam to turn and look over his shoulder. Wing Chew was rushing down the street waving his arm. "I have news," Wing Chew called out. "A report of a girl. I believe it may be Qui Jin."

🙚🙘

Angry, arguing voices awakened Qui Jin. She turned her back to the door and placed a finger on each ear. If only they would go away and permit her the luxury of escaping back into her dreams of the homeland and her family. Instead, the noise grew louder. Someone banged on her door, and Kem Chinn screamed vile profanities into the night. There was a clanking noise—the sound of a key in the lock at her door. Qui Jin shrank back into the corner. It was too soon for Kem Chinn to bring men to her cell. Why was he coming into her room?

"Get up, Girl!" Kem Chinn screamed as he lit the candle stub. "This man says you are not free—that you belong to him and I have stolen you." He grabbed Qui Jin's arm and pulled her into glow of the candle.

"She belongs to me. Her name is Suey Qui Jin, and I brought her from Canton. I paid for her passage to California. Captain Obley of the *Falcon* will verify I speak the truth. We sailed on his ship. The girl is somewhat insolent and misbehaves—she ran away during the night. I've been searching for two days. When I saw this cord," he said, "I knew she was here. This marker is mine."

She could not see his face, but her heart filled with unabashed joy at the sound of Sam's voice. How she longed to look into his eyes and beg him to forgive her. She ached to be the woman of his desire, to feel his arms wrap around her in love and protection for the rest of her life—but that was impossible! Still, she determined, if he rescued her from this place, she would offer her abiding friendship—both to him and Li Laan.

"Speak up, Girl, and do not lie. You told me you were free, did you not?" Kem Chinn yelled, his words pulling her away from rambling thoughts of love and friendship.

"Yes," she whispered. "But this man speaks the truth. I belong to him."

Kem Chinn's face was wrenched with anger as he paced about the small cell. "What of my investment in this girl? I have spent much money for her medical care, fed and clothed her, and now you want to just walk out with her. It is unjust."

Qui Jin began to feel courageous in Sam's presence. She doubted Kem Chinn would attempt to strike her with Sam close at hand. "You were the cause of my injuries, pushing me down into the street and dragging me by my arms. And I did not ask for food or this dress. You told me that if I did not eat and do as I was told, you would punish me."

Kem Chinn leapt in front of her, leaning down until his face hovered only inches from hers. "You do not speak!" he screamed. "This is between men. What you have to say is of no importance to either of us."

"It is of importance to me," Sam replied in an even tone as he stepped closer to Qui Jin.

Kem Chinn's mouth dropped open at the unexpected comment. He shifted, moving away from Qui Jin. "You must pay me," he insisted.

"I think the opposite is true. You have damaged my property."

Kem Chinn began to sputter. "But if I had not captured her, she would most likely be aboard a ship to China. I have performed a great service for you."

Sam appeared to be contemplating his rebuttal. "On the one hand, you have managed to keep my property in Chinatown." A wry grin spread across Sam's lips as Kem Chinn bobbed his head up and down in agreement. "On the other hand, my property is now damaged. It appears the best solution is that I take the girl and leave this place."

Kem Chinn's head moved back and forth in vigorous disagreement. "You know that if it weren't for me, she would have escaped. You must pay me."

"I don't know if she would have been successful in boarding a ship," Sam replied. "Perhaps she would have become frightened and returned to my home. In that case, she would not have sustained these injuries. I would like to settle this without intervention of the Chinese Six Company. We both know how they feel about your 'business.' "

Qui Jin watched closely as the men bantered back and forth. She had never heard of the Chinese Six Company, but Kem Chinn cowered at the mention of the name.

"Take her. You know I cannot withstand interference by the Chinese Six Company. Get out of here."

Kem Chinn pushed Qui Jin forward. Rage had returned to his face, and his hands were trembling. Yet he stood fast as Sam moved forward and claimed Qui Jin.

Sam took Qui Jin's elbow and guided her from the cell. "Say nothing and do not look back," he whispered.

Suddenly Qui Jin stopped. Sam was urging her forward, but she remained steadfast. "We must go back to the cell. I forgot the cord from your Bible."

"I will get you another one. We must go," Sam replied.

She shook her head. "Another one will not be the same. I must have that one. It saved my life."

"That piece of cord didn't save your life. I did. Come on," Sam urged.

Qui Jin stopped in her tracks. "You are right, Sam. The cord did not save my life, but it makes me remember where I should place my trust. You see, I now realize Jesus truly saved my life. It is in Him I must always place my trust, not in myself or in others."

How could he possibly argue with such truth? Sam nodded his head. "You wait here. Do not move. I will retrieve the cord."

Once again, Qui Jin heard Kem Chinn shouting, but she did as Sam had directed and did not move. Soon he returned and placed the cord in her hand.

"Thank you," she murmured.

"You are truly welcome, but we must hurry. If we don't soon get out of this place, I fear that Kem Chinn will change his mind."

She remained silent, scurrying along as she attempted to keep pace with Sam.

Only when they were a short distance from Bartlett Alley did Sam slow his steps. "This way," he said, while leading her across the cobblestone street.

They had walked only a short distance, both of them quiet, Sam obviously intent on his own thoughts. "You are angry with me?" Qui Jin finally asked, breaking the silence.

She waited. Finally he spoke. "No, Qui Jin, I am not angry. Fear, disappointment, sadness—those words more adequately explain how I felt. Somehow, I should have found a better way to handle matters. I know you heard my father's words and you were hurt by what he said. However, I never imagined you would run away."

"All my life I have been a burden, first to my father and now to you and your family. I doubt you can imagine such a thing. After all, you are a son, and sons are the beloved children—always a privilege, never an obligation."

Sam stopped and turned toward her. "There is something I must explain to you, Qui Jin. No matter what your earthly father may think of you, you are a child of God. When you accepted Jesus as your Savior, God became your Father. God treasures you more than all the riches you could ever imagine. I know it may be difficult for you to believe yourself worthy of such love and adoration, but our God loves all of His children equally. He more than loves you; He adores you." Sam hesitated for a moment and looked into her eyes. "Do you believe me?"

Qui Jin listened intently to Sam's words. She knew he would not lie to her, yet she had to speak the truth. "I believe what you say, Sam, but such a concept is difficult for me to accept."

He nodded and took her hand. "Consider this: You accepted Jesus as your Lord only a week ago. When you asked Him to come into your heart, He saved you from your sins and granted you eternal life. You were born again. At this time, you are still a baby in God's family. A girl baby."

Could this be true? A baby once again? She smiled at the thought.

Sam returned her smile as he continued. "Remember these things. You were on a ship that does not normally carry passengers, yet I was aboard. Captain Obley gave permission for me to spend time with you on the voyage. I was able to gain your freedom by paying for your passage rather than purchasing you. We were able to pass through the inspection without having to tell one lie. You were given protection in a Christian home, and God directed my path to find you when you left the security of the home He provided for you. Can you honestly question God's complete love for you after all He did?"

"It is true that God has done much for me in a short time. I am undeserving of such goodness."

Sam shook his head. "None of us, male or female, deserves God's generosity. We are all sinners, yet God's grace abounds to all of His children. I pray you will learn to accept His unconditional love in your heart as well as in your mind."

"I will pray about this also," Qui Jin agreed as they continued onward.

A short time later, while they walked together in a comfortable silence, she spied Sam's home and began to slow her pace. Kum Shu's words echoed in her mind. How could she return to Kum Shu's home? She had heard him say he regretted having her as a guest.

She stopped and touched Sam's arm. "Is there someplace you could take me other than your home—someplace where I would be safe? You must understand that I do not want to remain where I am not wanted. I don't hold your father's words against him. He should not be required to accommodate unwanted guests. I believe it would be better for all of us."

"I think you will find my father a willing host, Qui Jin—if you will just give him the opportunity. He deeply regrets his behavior. I'm sure he wants to offer his own apology."

The thought of a man apologizing to her was almost as frightening as returning to unfriendly surroundings. "Before we go in, can you tell me what I did to offend him? If I know, perhaps I will not repeat my error."

"You did nothing wrong. My father and I had been having a discussion about you. He feared that I had grown to love you and would dishonor my pledge to marry Li Laan. Although I told him I would never do such a thing, he continued to interrogate me, convinced my love for you would eventually triumph over my honor. You walked down the hallway then and heard him say he regretted inviting you into our home. My father no longer has reason for concern. He will be most pleased to see I have found you."

She thought about Sam's words. Kum Shu was convinced Sam loved her, and the thought made her heart sing with joy. Even if he married another, she would know he returned the love she held for him. Still, she didn't understand how any of this made a difference in the welcome she would receive from Kum Shu, unless—

"You and Li Laan were married during my absence?" she ventured.

Sam laughed, a loud belly laugh. "No, I have been too busy searching for you, and Li Laan has been too busy running off with another man."

"Truly? She has married another and brought disgrace upon your families? Your father and mother will be distraught. I cannot go in there."

He urged her forward. "You can. They will be most relieved to know that I have found you. Trust me. They will be anxious to welcome you home."

Once again she pulled back. "Wait one moment. I have another question."

"Yes?"

"You said your father feared your love for me would overpower your honor."

He nodded in agreement. She swallowed hard. She had to know. "Was your father correct? Do you love me?"

"More than you can imagine," he replied tenderly. "It is my deepest desire to make you my wife."

She could see the adoration in his eyes. No man had ever looked at her in such a manner. Qui Jin struggled to suppress the mix of emotions rising within her.

Sam raised his finger to her face and carefully wiped away the tear that had spilled over onto her cheek. "I have made you unhappy. You do not share my feelings of love."

"I do share your feelings, Sam. These are tears of joy, not sadness. I am overcome with sensations I cannot begin to explain," she murmured. "I would be honored to become your wife, if your parents do not object. But I have no gifts to offer."

"You have everything I need. I have no desire for worldly gifts from my bride, only her pledge to love me as I love her," he whispered. He gathered her into his arms. "Can you give me your love, Qui Jin?"

"Yes," she whispered. "Now and forever."

I TAKE THEE,
A STRANGER

by Kristy Dykes

Dedication

To my hero husband, Milton,
who is my collaborator in
the deepest sense of the word—
he's believed in me, supported me, and
cheered me on in my quest to be
published in CBA fiction.

Chapter 1

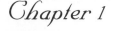

1885—Massachusetts—Large Hill Place

O h, Galen, please don't die," Corinn McCauley said, hovering over the still form of her husband, wiping his brow with a wet cloth. He had lain under their red plaid wedding coverlet for eleven days now, never stirring, her hoping and praying the whole time that he would open his twinkling blue eyes and say, as he'd said many a time, "Corinn, my Scottish lass, all will be well. You'll see. Things will go better for us."

She sat down by the bed and took his limp hand in hers, caressing his wrist, trailing her finger across his palm. "Those calluses, Galen," she choked out, "all for our future. You worked so hard since we came to America. We were going to start a new life...a prosperous one."

She had worked, too, toiling from daybreak to dark, taking in washing and ironing and sewing, baking pies and cakes, recaning chair bottoms—anything that would put dollars in the jar at the back of the drawer. But, between the company boardinghouse and the company mercantile, the level of dollars was always low.

She pleated, then unpleated the edge of the wedding coverlet that lay over her husband, staring at the dingy wall. "Granny Jen, you never dreamed the wedding coverlet you so lovingly made two years ago would one day be a...a death blanket."

Tears streamed down her face, but she ignored them and reached, once again, for the damp cloth on her husband's forehead. She dipped it in a basin of water, squeezed it, and lovingly laid the cloth on his fevered brow. If only she could do something more. Anything to help him. But there was nothing she, or anyone, could do.

When the men from the foundry brought her injured husband home to her, announcing that he would be dead within hours, she refused to believe them. Even when one of the soot-blackened men said, "This happened to Albert Rowe, and he died before daybreak," Corinn made a quiet resolve that the same plight would *not* befall *her* husband.

She took the hem of her apron and wiped away her blinding tears. Then, with fresh resolve to nurse Galen back to health, she fluffed the small pillows that were wedged on either side of his head. Taking a spoonful of water from the cup on the nightstand, she forced a drop of water between his parched lips.

Dr. Robbins would come soon, as he had each day, to change her husband's bandages and offer his grim prognosis. But Corinn refused to give in to despair.

Throughout each long, worry-filled day. . .and night, she had stubbornly held onto her optimism. Until now.

"No," she shrieked, slumping to her knees, pounding the hard wooden chair with her fists, not caring if anyone heard through the thin walls. "I won't let you leave me, Galen McCauley. We've loved each other too long. We have plans, remember? We are going to live in a fine home one day, and our sons and daughters are going to be upstanding American citizens. One of our grandsons shall surely be the president of this mighty nation. Oh, Galen, my heart is breaking in two."

She heard him stir and looked over at him, her soul soaring with joy. "Praise be, you've come back to me." Fresh tears—joy tears—sprang to her eyes. She jumped up, smiling, then laughing.

She leaned over him.

And went cold with fear.

It was the death rattle.

🙰

At dusk, ten days after her husband's burial, Corinn stood on the doctor's doorstep, wondering why he had summoned her. He already had a housekeeper, the position she was seeking.

After Mrs. Mullins showed her to the parlor and excused herself, Corinn settled in a chair and timidly thrust her feet toward the hearth, enjoying the warmth. Nearly every night, she went to bed with cold feet—a phenomenon that had greatly amused Galen.

Tuck them beneath my legs and get them warm, my Scottish lass, he had whispered as he pulled her close each night.

A sob caught in her chest, and a tear threatened to spill over. *Oh, Galen, my bonnie prince. . .*

The door creaked open, and the elderly doctor shuffled toward her. For the first time, she noticed how stiff were his movements, how slow was his gait.

"Good evening, Mrs. McCauley."

"A pleasant evening to you, sir." She made a movement to stand in respect, but he waved her down.

"No need to get up." He shook her hand and sank into the chair opposite hers, pulling an envelope from his coat pocket. "I've an important matter to discuss with you."

He pulled several pages from the envelope and studied them for a moment, then looked up. "I'm concerned about you, Mrs. McCauley. I know what becomes of some women who find themselves in your circumstance. You're an immigrant and a widow. You've no income and no prospects of a job. Soon, you'll be without a roof over your head—"

"How did you know?"

"I made a point of finding out."

She swallowed hard. *Why does this kind man care what happens to me?*

"Women in dire straits sometimes wind up as women of—well, to phrase this as delicately as possible—women of ill repute." He lowered his eyes and stared at the flames. "Or kept women."

Corinn felt her cheeks growing hot as she, too, stared into the fire.

"I don't want you to suffer such a fate." He looked directly into her eyes with fatherly concern. "You are a good woman, one of the kindest and. . .and most industrious I've ever met."

She fidgeted in her chair. She was not accustomed to receiving compliments. Everybody worked hard, didn't they? That was what one was supposed to do.

"I've been impressed with your loyalty to your husband, your diligence. . ."

She fidgeted again.

"Your fortitude, your courage. . ."

She shrugged. "All Scots are brave. It's legendary."

"I've no openings in my household." He hit a sturdy side table with his fist, producing a loud thwacking sound. "If I were a rich man, I'd help you. But, that will never be. I'm tired and old. Soon. . ."

"I'd never ask you for charity." She thrust her shoulders back stiffly. "Even if you were wealthy."

"Yes, I know." His faded gray eyes lit up as he waved the letter he held in his hand, its thin pages rustling. "I have a solution for you—in these pages. The matter is a simple one, really. This letter is from a young man who needs a wife. You are a young woman who needs a husband."

She grasped the arms of the chair, willing herself not to cry out against this travesty, then scolding herself for being outraged. Dr. Robbins was only doing this out of concern.

She stared at the framed landscape above the mantel, not focusing on the details, barely hearing the doctor's words.

He talked on and on, something about how his nephew had gone to Florida, how his mate had recently died from pneumonia, how there were few unattached females in that part of the raw, young state, how he needed a wife. Did his uncle know of a worthy woman who could meet this challenge? In return, he would offer the woman a home—and affection besides. Could the doctor find him such a woman?

"As I said, here is a young man who needs a wife." Dr. Robbins thumped the pages. "And you, my dear, are a young woman who needs a husband. This is the solution to your plight."

"No, Dr. Robbins," she finally said, thoughts of her beloved Galen filling her head and heart.

"Please take time to think about this before you refuse. My nephew is Philadelphia-born and bred and well educated. He's hobnobbed with high society since he was a suckling. Whatever he puts his mind to, he succeeds. Now, it appears he's put his mind to acquiring land in Florida. One day, he'll be an elected official. Mark my words."

She looked down at her worn skirts, at her patched high-top shoes, at her threadbare shawl made of red plaid with a wide band of green. The plaid was her clan's tartan for generations and said by them to be John Knox's tartan—the Great Reformer of Scotland.

What man would want her, especially one with the social standing of which Dr. Robbins spoke? If she looked in a mirror right now, she knew what she would see—not an elegant lady of high society garbed in silks and satins—but a small-statured female with uneven features, thin brown hair, and speckles across her nose.

CORINN, CORINN,
SMALL AND THIN,
SINGS LIKE A ROBIN
BUT LOOKS LIKE A WREN.

The familiar taunt of her schoolmates filled her head, hammering, hammering, hammering. Galen had fallen in love with her when she was a wee sparkly lass, before she had reached womanhood. Even after she had passed the bloom of childhood, Galen had loved her still, despite her plainness.

"Won't you give some serious thought to what I'm offering—what my nephew is offering—Mrs. McCauley? I have no doubt that you could fill the role admirably."

She rubbed her temples in circles, staring at the flames. What had Dr. Robbins called it? A role? Yes, that's what it would be, a role and nothing more, if she were to marry a stranger.

She rose to her feet. "Earlier, I said I could never ask for charity. Something else I could never do is marry a man I don't know, let alone a man I don't love. I may be poor, and I may be uncomely, but I still have my wits. Besides, I'm young and strong and. . .and. . .hopeful."

She faced him squarely. "All will be well. As my husband often said, things *will* go better."

🕮

Two months after Galen's death, Corinn made her way down a busy street. All *was not* well. Things *had not* gone better. She knew what she must do.

She passed a woman wearing bold face paint, dressed in a gown of flimsy fabric that revealed bare arms and a brazen décolletage. A woman of ill repute.

Corinn felt herself blushing, and she rapidly fanned herself with a handkerchief. What was the other type of woman Dr. Robbins had referred to? *A kept woman?* Last evening, when her laird, no, landlord, they called them here. . .when her landlord had evicted her, he had made her an offer. She fanned more furiously, remembering his abominable words.

Another woman of ill repute passed her on the sidewalk. Yes, she knew what she must do.

Woodenly, she plodded down the street, her empty stomach making a thunderous noise. She trudged up the steep steps and grasped the door knocker on Dr. Robbins's front door.

A strange man in Florida didn't seem nearly as frightening as the prospects here in Massachusetts.

Chapter 2

Florida—The Flowery Land

C orinn sat in the minuscule stateroom, thinking of the last few weeks and the grueling trip to Florida. Days and days on a soot-filled train. More days and days on an ocean-tossed boat.

She withdrew Mr. Parker's letter from the sporran that hung from a belt about her waist. Trembling, she held the page in front of her and read the brief note for, it seemed, the hundredth time.

Dear Mrs. McCauley,

Thank you for agreeing to be my wife. I will do my best by you.

We came to Florida about ten years ago, when land was reasonably priced. I now own 2,000 acres. Much of the land is filled with virgin timber, while other portions have been cultivated and are producing sweet potatoes, my main crop.

I have two daughters, ages seven and four. They are genteel little ladies.

When you arrive, I will meet you. Look for a tall man with two children at his side. My uncle, Dr. Robbins, wrote and described you. We will be married immediately. Then we will travel to Sunny Acres by wagon and arrive before nightfall.

With regard,
Trevor Parker

Corinn shivered as she let the letter drop to her lap. What had she done—committing to marry someone she didn't know?

In an effort to comfort herself, she picked up her lap harp and strummed the strings. Within moments, she was no longer in tight quarters on a sailing vessel somewhere near Florida. . .

She was transported to Scotland, singing and playing a lively folk song over the backdrop of droning bagpipes, members of her clan prancing about her in jigs and reels.

Soon, though, she would be in the midst of strangers in a distant land—far away from Scotland and friends and family. As if in a haze, she looked down at her harp and watched her fingers absently plucking discordant, dirge-like notes.

"No," she said aloud, casting her harp aside. "I mustn't think like that." She looked heavenward. " 'Take no thought for your life, what ye shall eat, or what ye shall drink,' " she quoted as she began packing her belongings into the carpetbag beside her. " 'Nor yet for your body, what ye shall put on. . . . But seek ye first the kingdom of God, and his righteousness; and all these things shall be added unto you.' "

She rose and gathered the remainder of her personal articles. The great boat was about to dock. In Florida.

"I shall seek the Lord with all my heart," she whispered. "And all the things I have need of shall be added unto me."

She stopped at midstride and looked down at her left hand. She touched the spot on her ring finger that, for two years, had been encompassed by a band of gold.

What do I have need of, Lord?
The love of a good man.

❧

The boat behind her, the smells of the harbor around her, the honking and geeking of the birds above her, she paused on the gangplank. As she adjusted the beret atop her head and put her plaid about her shoulders, she was trembling again and couldn't seem to stop.

This is no time to be faint of heart, she lectured herself, her throat suddenly feeling like flax. She had made an agreement—to marry Mr. Parker. She had given her word on the matter, and her word was her bond. Wasn't that what her mother had taught her, had drilled into her?

You made your bed—now lie in it, her mother would say if she were here, meaning, *You made a commitment—now keep it.* No turning back.

Telling herself to be steady, she swallowed hard, then took a tenuous step in Mr. Parker's direction. She easily recognized the tall man with two wee girls on either side.

As she walked toward him, she fiddled with the fringe on her plaid. In many foreign countries, women commonly married men they didn't know. An arranged marriage, it was called, in which love eventually came to them. And in the Bible, didn't Rebekah agree to marry Isaac, a stranger? And didn't the Scripture say that Isaac loved her at first sight? And that Rebekah comforted Isaac after the death of his mother?

Perhaps things would turn out between her and Mr. Parker that way. Perhaps Mr. Parker would love her at first sight. And, in comforting him after a dear one's death—just as Rebekah had done for Isaac—Corinn would come to love him too.

"Father God, let it be so." She looked up, squared her shoulders, and smiled. She would face this thing with a cheerful countenance and a hopeful outlook.

She was pleased to see Mr. Parker closing the distance that separated them in long, hurried strides, the wee girls running to keep up.

The smaller girl stumbled, and Corinn gasped, afraid she would land, face-first, in the mud. But he kept up his pace, seemingly oblivious, and the girl righted herself and ran faster on her chubby little legs.

When he reached Corinn, he stopped abruptly, towering over her.

With your physique, Mr. Parker, you could toss the caber, was her first thought. She visualized him participating in the Highland games where only the strongest, most able-bodied men hurled twenty-foot tree trunks into the air and made them land on opposite ends.

Sometime soon, she would share her first impressions of him, perhaps on the wagon ride home. She smiled at the pleasant thought. His strong-looking stature surely bespoke hard work. . .perseverance. . .indefatibility. Her compliments would please him, she was certain. Surely these fine attributes were the reasons behind his success in this untamed land.

"Welcome to Florida," he said in a deep bass voice, extending his hand for a shake.

With a dip of her chin, she said a quiet, "Thank you," then shook his hand.

"Florida means 'flowery land.' " The older girl's voice was a squeak, her posture mouse-like.

"That must mean flowers bloom everywhere," Corinn said, smiling—though her insides were jiggling like droplets of water on a hot skillet.

"Only where they're planted," Mr. Parker remarked, his features without expression.

After formally introducing his daughters, Edith and Adeline, he collected her bags and helped Corinn and the wee ones into his farm wagon. She sat on the front seat beside him, the children on a built-in bench directly behind.

He picked up the reins. "The parson is expecting us," was all he said. All anybody said.

Chapter 3

Sitting in the wagon beside Mr. Parker, Corinn resisted the urge to study him. Proper decorum—well taught by her mother—dictated that she keep her eyes straight ahead. Except for her initial glance and her first impression on the wharf, she had not found an opportune moment to scrutinize his face or even determine his eye color.

From the corner of her eye, she *did* notice that he sported long black sideburns and showed impeccable taste in clothing. From his dark-blue broadcloth coat and his gray serge dress pants to his wine-colored satin tie, he appeared finely tailored.

The children, also, modeled the latest fashions. The older girl wore a flouncy yellow silk frock, and the wee one was attired in pink in a similar pattern. Their matching wide-brimmed, ribbon-garnished hats made them look like the genteel little ladies described by Mr. Parker in his letter.

With a sad pang, she looked down at her own clothing, fingering the folds of her travel-stained brown skirt and jacket, lamenting that she didn't have a new gown to be married in. She tucked a strand of hair under her beret. She hadn't even had time to freshen up for her wedding. Before she and Galen married, she had prepared for months, fashioning a wedding gown and making monogrammed linens.

What would marriage be like to this tall man beside her? She moistened her lips and straightened her shoulders, trying to rally her courage.

At the parson's home, Mr. Parker helped her alight. Within a few moments, all four of them were standing inside an octagon-shaped sitting room, the parson reciting marriage vows.

"Please say these words after me," the parson instructed, standing before them with a black book in his hands. He gestured at Corinn. "You first. Say this, 'I, Corinn, take thee, Trevor.' "

"I, Corinn," she said. *Take thee, a stranger. . .*

"Take thee, Trevor," the parson repeated.

"Take thee, Trevor," she dutifully said.

"To be my lawful wedded husband," he instructed.

"To be my lawful wedded husband." She heard a giggle and looked down to watch the wee girl twist sideways. Then, Mr. Parker snapped his fingers three times. The child grew statue-still.

Corinn repeated the rest of the marriage vows without further prodding from the parson, but her mind was far away.

In Scotland.

At her and Galen's wedding.

Galen, looking lovingly into her eyes.

Family and friends gathered round. Sweet-smelling flowers in her hands. A filmy veil on her head. Music and songs and laughter. . .

"Mrs. Parker?" the parson said.

And then there had been the shivaree after the wedding. . .

"Mrs. Parker, let me be the first person to offer congratulations."

Corinn felt a tugging on her skirts, looked down into bright-blue eyes, saw the wee girl pointing at the parson, then glanced up to see the parson holding out his hand.

"Mrs. Parker, congratulations," the parson said.

She offered her hand and squeaked out a timid, "Thank you, sir," enduring his crushing handshake.

"And congratulations to you, Mr. Parker," the parson offered.

Moments later, she walked across the room, the children on her heels. Mr. Parker raced ahead of her and opened the door wide.

As she stepped onto the porch, she adjusted her beret and touched its red pom-pom.

Then, a staggering thought hit her.

This was the first wedding she had ever been to where the groom had not kissed the bride.

❧

The long ride to Sunny Acres started out as a silent one, and Corinn wondered. Even when they stopped and ate the basket supper that Mr. Parker had purchased from the local hotel, somberness hung in the air.

"For the past three years," Mr. Parker said, after swallowing a bite of biscuit and wiping his lips, "a neighbor woman—Mrs. Henderson—has been cooking and cleaning for us, several days a week." He sighed deeply and added, "But, just enough to keep body and soul together. She has her own nine children to attend to. I've been fortunate with clothing, however. A seamstress in town keeps my daughters well clothed."

"But I thought your wife passed away only months ago," Corinn said. *If that was so, why had he hired someone to do housekeeping three years prior?*

He didn't respond, but she noticed his jaw tightening.

She was puzzled. Had she committed a breach of etiquette? If he asked her about Galen, she would freely give him information. She was only trying to learn something about this reticent man. After all, he was her husband now.

Dead silence reigned as they hurriedly finished their supper. On the road again in the gathering twilight, Corinn sat on the wagon seat, bone weary and heart heavy.

The wee girl began bouncing about, chattering to the dolly she held in her arms, as if she couldn't contain herself any longer.

Corinn turned around, suddenly deciding to do what she'd been wanting to since she'd met little Adeline. She didn't care if Mr. Parker subjected her or the girls to another stern stare.

With sheer joy and abandonment, she scooped up the wee girl and plopped her onto her lap, hugging her, then stroking her springy blond curls. "May I hold your dolly, Adeline?"

The girl giggled, her eyes dancing as she handed over the doll.

"What's your wee bairn's name, lassie?"

"Lathee?" Adeline lisped through her snaggle-toothed grin. "Whath a lathee?"

Corinn laughed. "Oh, that. Lassie is a Scottish term for a wee girl."

"You're from Scotland, aren't you?" Edith, the older girl, asked. "Papa said you were."

"That I am." Corinn touched her plaid shawl, the pride of Scotland welling up in her. "So, Adeline, what's your bairn's name?"

Adeline giggled again. "Whath a bairn?"

"A bairn is a wee babe."

"Mama said I was her baby."

"That's enough, Adeline," Mr. Parker said, a dark shadow passing across his face. "Get back to your seat and settle down."

As Adeline clambered over her in unquestioning obedience, Corinn did what Mary, the mother of Jesus, had done at an uncertain time in her life.

She kept all these things and pondered them in her heart.

❧

When they reached Mr. Parker's house, Corinn went inside at his bidding while he saw to the horses.

As she stepped across the threshold, the wee ones dashed past her, apparently to their bedroom. She stood in the parlor for a long moment, hardly able to keep her mouth from dropping open. Everywhere she looked, she saw elegance. A satinwood upright piano. A rose-colored damask settee and matching chair. A massive mahogany dining table and chairs and buffet. Puffy batiste drapes at the windows. Books galore in glass-fronted cabinets, some with the titles showing, some with the pages facing out.

If clean and organized, the house would have been a showplace. A thick layer of dust covered the piano. Stains spotted the settee. And though the floors appeared to be swept, they begged for a good scrubbing and waxing besides.

Corinn continued in her survey of the room. Apparently the drapes had recently been washed, but their wrinkles cried out for ironing. Ornate gold-framed paintings—landscapes and portraits—hung askew.

She walked over and righted one of the frames. *No picture of the late Mrs. Parker displayed above the mantel? Or on a side table?* Most people who'd lost a mate kept a picture around—at least for a while. She moistened her lips. Perhaps Mr. Parker had put away the late Mrs. Parker's portrait out of respect to her—the new Mrs. Parker.

The kitchen showed the same state of disarray. The cookstove needed scouring. The table needed clearing. The windows needed polishing. The floor needed

315

mopping. Everything screamed out for the touch of a woman. She scanned the room again, resisting the urge to roll up her sleeves and work until everything shone. But she couldn't.

She wasn't the lady of this lair.

Not yet.

"Mrs. Henderson was supposed to come yesterday and tidy things up," Mr. Parker said from behind her as he brought in several boxes from the wagon. "But one of her children fell ill."

Corinn turned and saw that he looked embarrassed. For the first time since she'd met him, she felt kindliness for him welling up inside her.

"I—I apologize," he stammered, still holding one of the boxes as if he didn't realize it was in his arms. "This isn't the way I wanted things to be."

"No need to explain."

"Running the farm," he mumbled. "Seeing to my daughters—" He stopped abruptly and stared through the parted curtains over the window.

"I'll help." Her heart went out to him. "I'm not shy of hard work, Mr. Parker. In my raising, my mother used to say, 'An idle mind is the devil's workshop' and 'The used key is always bright.' By her example, I learned to stay busy always."

"My uncle told me you were of that inclination." Still, he stared out the window. Finally, he turned and faced her. "Welcome to Sunny Acres."

"Why, thank you. Why don't you stow that box in here?" She gestured toward a door behind her. "I assume this is the pantry? That box contains my books. I'll unpack them later." She pulled on the doorknob.

"No." His voice held a loud ring of authority.

"But they'll be out of the way." She jiggled the handle.

In a flash, he set down the box and towered over her, his palm flat on the raised panel of the door, his eyes cold, his mouth drawn into a grim line. "This door always remains locked."

Immediately, she withdrew her hand as if burned by a flame. She could only stare at him. He stood deathly still. Silent. Obviously, she had kindled his ire. Yet, she hadn't the slightest clue why.

She lowered her gaze, ambled to the breakfront, busied herself with untying a box. The realization that she had angered him deeply troubled her. She was the one who always soothed ruffled feathers, not stirred them. What should she do? Should she say she was sorry? But for what? A person couldn't apologize if she didn't know what infraction she had committed.

She heard his long strides crossing the kitchen, and when she turned, he was holding out a brightly wrapped, rectangular-shaped parcel.

"For you," he said, handing her the parcel.

She looked up at him as she accepted it, guarded but wondering. The anger in his eyes was gone, she saw. That pleased her. Nonchalance replaced it. That perplexed her.

"It's fripperies," he said. "All women want fripperies." He turned, not waiting for her response, and made his way outside.

She sauntered back into the parlor and struck a dusty key on the piano, still clutching his package, still wondering, still fretting. Then she roused herself as she looked around the disheveled room.

She had no time for vexation of spirit. She would turn her vitality to more fruitful endeavors. She found herself galvanized by the labors that awaited her, ready to set this house aright, eager to work a cure, willing to double-march.

But she knew she must go slowly, proceed gently. Because of this man and his. . . cankerworm of crossness. And two wee girls who desperately needed affection.

She turned and walked across the hardwood floors, anxious to explore her new home. Her heart stopped when she came to the first doorway on the left.

Could this be Mr. Parker's bedroom?

Their bedroom now?

The only thing she saw was the big bed, bigger than any bed she had ever seen. It was wide and long, and it was centered on the wall between two windows.

His bed.

Their bed now.

Her heart raced.

I take thee. . .a stranger. . . .

Chapter 4

After breakfast the next morning, with the food put away and the dishes done, with Mr. Parker in the fields and the children cutting out paper dolls, Corinn decided to finish unpacking before starting on the housework.

She made her way to the bedroom off the kitchen that Mr. Parker had led her to the night before, a good-sized room that looked as if it hadn't been occupied in a long while. Now, in the light of day, she noticed dusty cobwebs hanging in the corners and saw that the pastel-colored rug needed a good shaking. But the furniture was fine mahogany like the other pieces in the house.

She was thankful for the privacy he had granted her. She wondered how long that would last. After all, they were man and wife.

She drew items of clothing from her portmanteau and shook them out, then hung them in the tall wardrobe. Two skirts, one with a matching jacket. Five shirtwaists—three nearly threadbare. Two nightdresses.

"Oh, I'll take the high road, and you'll take the low road," she sang gustily as she worked. "And I'll get to Scotland a'fore ye."

She pulled out a framed sampler that Granny Jen had embroidered and stared down at it, wondering if she should hang it.

HASTE YE BACK TO SCOTLAND

As much as she loved Scotland, she was ready and willing to cut all ties with her motherland and start a new life. When she lived in Massachusetts, alongside many who had left their homelands and come to America, she had seen what she called "weepy women" who were pining away and useless to their families. She'd resolved that she would be strong and brave in this fine new world. And now, she would be a good wife to Mr. Parker, the best wife possible.

"Ach, dear Scotland," she said aloud. She ran her fingers over the fancy stitch work, then decided that it couldn't hurt to display a sentimental sampler in her bedroom. Within moments, the handicraft was hanging on the wall above her bed, and she stood back to admire it, then returned to her work.

She placed her carpetbag on the bed, then reached for the package Mr. Parker had given her last night.

Fripperies, he had called them. *All women want fripperies,* he'd said.

From the colorful wrapping paper, she pulled a pair of lace-trimmed gloves and a heavily embossed sterling silver glove box. She sighed. She'd never owned such niceties. Then she spotted the three bolts of fabric he'd also given her.

To make yourself some new clothing, he'd said. *In case you need them,* he'd added.

She looked down at her drab brown skirt, the seams shiny from frequent ironings, and her brown print shirtwaist, the flowers blurred from fading. In all probability, Mr. Parker's uncle, Dr. Robbins, had written him about her dire circumstances. Though embarrassed when she accepted the fabric last night, deep down she felt grateful for her new husband's foresight and care.

She recalled the letter he had written Dr. Robbins, when he'd promised he would take good care of the woman who agreed to marry him. Surely Mr. Parker's gifts were an indication of how he would treat her in the days to come. The thought warmed her now.

"Oh, I'll take the high road, and you'll take the low road," she sang as she placed her stockings and underpinnings in the drawers of a mahogany dresser. "Or is it, I'll take the low road," she said, "and you'll take the high road? I always get those two mixed up."

From the corner of her eye, she saw the two wee girls standing in the doorway. She pirouetted around and swung into a low curtsy, holding her skirts out sideways. "Please come in," she bubbled, smiling broadly. "Welcome to my private abode."

"Yippee." Little Adeline skipped into the room and pounced onto the bed, but Edith held back.

"Scots are known for their hospitality. I'm honored that you chose to visit me today."

"What are you doing?" Little Adeline asked.

"Unpacking." She fastened the empty carpetbag and stowed it in the bottom of the armoire, then sat down beside Adeline. "Adeline, sweet Adeline. What a great big name for such a wee little girl."

Adeline giggled, her blue eyes dancing. "Will you play with uth?" she lisped. "My mama did. All the time. We played with the dolls in our dollhouse, and we played dwess-up with her wed parasols and we—"

"Adeline," Edith snapped from the doorway. "You know Papa doesn't want us talking about that."

"Perhaps you can show me your dollhouse another time," Corinn said soothingly, "but this morning, work's awaiting. However, I have time for one song.

"Edith, would you care to join us?" She patted a spot on the bed, then pulled out her lap harp, and little Adeline's face shone with wonder. Edith sauntered into the room and sat down on the bed.

Corinn was pleased at Edith's response. She would win both girls' hearts if the task took every ounce of strength within her.

"What are me and Adeline going to call you?" Edith said in a grown-up voice, far too mature-sounding for her seven years. Her eyes were a brilliant blue; her hair white-blond and full of curls, just like little Adeline's. If they'd been closer in age,

Corinn decided, they would be mistaken for twins.

"What are me and Adeline going to call you?" Edith repeated.

"You mean, *Adeline and I*," Corinn gently corrected, looking across the bed at the two wee girls, her heart going out to them. Here were two lassies who'd recently lost their mother. Though they were sorely in need of a mother's love, she must first gain their trust. Then she could bestow the abundance of affection begging to pour out of her. And she must measure every word she said to them. She glanced beseechingly upward. She needed divine wisdom.

"I called my mother 'Marmsie,'" she said brightly, "but my given name is Corinn. I'd be honored if you chose to call me that."

After she sang them a song, she was amused at Adeline's curiosity and answered the lassie's many questions.

She explained about the sampler.

She explained about the lap harp.

She explained about the sheepskin bagpipes that Galen was holding in the daguerreotype on the bedside table.

She explained about the plaid wedding coverlet on the bed.

"The coverlet symbolizes an old custom my clan adheres to." She caressed the plaid folds beside her. "Every lass is given a wedding coverlet before her marriage. She and her new husband sleep under it their first night as man and wife."

"Papa. Papa." Edith shrieked in delight as she hopped off the bed and ran toward the door where Mr. Parker stood. He dipped under the doorway and stepped into the room, giving Edith a brusque pat as he passed her and came to stand near the bed.

Corinn felt flustered in this tall man's presence, but she pushed her feelings aside. Did he need her assistance? She sprang to her feet, still clutching the lap harp with one hand, smoothing her skirts with the other, then her chignon. "Mr. Parker, are you in need of something?"

"Please keep your seat," he said in clipped tones.

She saw that he was drenched with perspiration. Perhaps the heat was making him irritable. But why had he come inside at midmorning? Something must have happened. "Was there a mishap in the fields?"

He shrugged. "Black Deuce threw a shoe. Had to be seen to. As I passed under the window"—he gestured at the curtains billowing in the breeze "—I heard. . . music."

She held out the lap harp. "It's a jolly thing to make merry. The lassies and I were singing. And having a good time, we were."

His features as still as glass, he didn't say a word.

"She talks funny, Papa," little Adeline piped up.

Corinn laughed, but he remained stoic.

"She says her r's like a whir," Edith said quietly.

"That's known as a Scottish burr." Corinn smiled. "The most identifiable feature of a Scot."

Still he didn't respond. He just stood there, twirling his hat around and around.

Corinn looked down at the floorboard, trying to hide her hurt. Nothing she said seemed to elicit a smile or even a friendly nod from this man. Earlier, she'd made a resolve to win the lassies' hearts if it took every ounce of her strength. She wasn't sure she had the strength to win Mr. Parker's affections.

Why was he so uncommunicative—this man who was now her husband? Yesterday afternoon, on the long ride to Sunny Acres, he'd uttered less than a handful of words. After their arrival last evening, he'd been silent. All through breakfast, his comments had been brief. Now, it was the same. Could she go a lifetime like this? In mournful silence? *I've jumped out of the kettle and into the flames.*

He stared into her eyes momentarily. Then his gaze inched away and came to rest on the sampler hanging above her bed.

She felt the color rush to her face, knew he was reading it, wished she had not hung it. "I—I—"

"No need to explain." He fixed her with another silent stare, then turned and strode toward the door. "I'll be in the fields until nightfall."

Chapter 5

orinn finished her ablutions early one morning, a spark of joy welling up inside her. Today after breakfast, she was going to a quilting bee. A quilting bee was merry, from what she'd heard. There would be new friends to meet and get to know. That was a pleasant thought.

She pulled on her rose-dotted skirt and shirtwaist, then fastened the tiny buttons up the front. Last night, she'd finished making the matching set from one of the bolts of fabric Mr. Parker had given her when she'd arrived three weeks ago. She was grateful for new attire to wear this morning. Soon, she would have the blue calico and green silk dresses completed and hanging in the armoire.

But who knew when she would have another opportunity to sew? The workload seemed to be unending. Daily chores. Weekly chores. Chores that, for some reason, had not been done in. . .a year? Two? Like the awful task of scraping the muck out of the nickel-plated cookstove. Or the backbreaking job of clearing the thick viney undergrowth from the shrub beds surrounding the house so that she could plant flower seeds.

Standing before the mirror, she brushed her hair, pinning it into a chignon, then stared at the rose color of her blouse. Galen had loved this hue, had said it cheered him in the bleakness of their lives. In the tiny room they had occupied in his parents' stone cottage in Scotland, she'd hung ruffled rose-colored curtains—much to her mother-in-law's consternation.

"Abominable," the elderly woman had proclaimed at first sight of them. "Too fancy for poor people. You think you're a Stuart, Corinn? Well, you're not. A McCauley you are, and a McCauley you'll die."

"Enchanting," Galen had said, when they were snuggled in bed that night. "They remind me of dear Scotland's mauve and pink thistle beds that carpet the moors."

Abruptly, Corinn turned away from the dresser, wishing she had time to change her clothing, even if it meant she had to wear her dark-blue walking skirt that bore three patches. Memories were harder to deal with than embarrassment. But she couldn't take any more time for herself. She must prepare breakfast for a hungry family.

Hurriedly, she began to tidy the room. She pulled the red plaid wedding coverlet up over the bed, smoothing the wrinkles lovingly, tucking in the corners at precise angles. Suddenly, as if she had stepped on a thistle, she cried out in pain—yet this pain emanated from deep within her.

"Galen, oh, Galen," she whispered as she stroked the plaid, then sat on the bed, wringing her hands. "How I miss your tender words."

My Scottish lass, he had called her.

A tear plopped on her skirt.

My bonnie prince, she had called him.

Another tear plopped beside the first one.

Since the day she arrived, she had endured impenetrable silence from Mr. Parker.

She clasped, then unclasped her hands, felt her forehead forming into a scowl. A scowl like the one Mr. Parker sometimes wore. He was so drastically different from Galen. Like night and day. Like the Highlands and the Lowlands. Like Scotland and England.

Galen with his lightheartedness...

Galen with his laughter...

Galen with his...love.

She roused herself from her reverie, even reprimanded herself as she stood up and walked toward the door. This was fruitless thinking.

Galen was...gone.

Mr. Parker was...here.

❧

"Thank you for bringing me to the quilting bee this morning," Corinn said as Mr. Parker helped her down from his shiny new Empire buggy. "Adeline and I shall have a grand time today."

"I wish I could go with you," Edith mumbled from the black leather tufted seat.

"You know how much you love school." Corinn smoothed her full skirts with her right hand, then adjusted the brim of her hat as Mr. Parker climbed back up on the seat. In her left arm, she carried a pound cake she had just pulled from the oven, rich with sweet creamery butter and fresh eggs. She looked up at Edith. "You'll have a fine time at school today."

Edith nodded. "Teacher said we're going to cut autumn leaves out of colored paper."

"See? I told you." She patted Edith's leg, and the child did not pull away from her. Her heart did a little somersault of joy as love exuded out of her and into the girl.

Her hand cupped over her eyebrows, Corinn looked up at Mr. Parker through the brightness of the October sun. "You'll be back for us this afternoon? When the quilting bee is over?"

"As soon as I pick up Edith from the schoolhouse."

"Bye-bye, Papa," little Adeline said, standing in the identical position as Corinn, right hand cupped over her eyebrows.

"I'll look for you this afternoon, Mr. Parker." Corinn picked up her skirts and strode across the raked pathway, little Adeline following closely on her heels.

Standing in front of Mrs. Wallace's heavy oak door, Corinn noticed that the gingerbread fretwork on the porch was similar to the trim on Mr. Parker's house. She admired the colorful flowers in the shrub beds. *Soon,* she told herself, *my shrub beds will be profuse with flowers, too.* Snowdrops, wood violets, and hyacinths. She took note of the streak-free windows lining the porch and the white lace curtains that hung inside them. "Adeline, would you like to knock on the door for me?"

Before Adeline's tiny fist hit its target, the door swung open in front of them.

"So you're the new Mrs. Parker," said an ample-bosomed woman with a yellow-toothed grin. "I'm the one that's kept house for the Parkers. I'm Erma Henderson, and I've been dying to meet you."

"Now, now." Another woman bustled past the first one and drew Corinn and Adeline inside. "Welcome to my home. I'm Mrs. Wallace. We're so glad you came."

"Our pleasure," Corinn said, handing her the pound cake. "We've been looking forward to it."

"I can't help wondering if the new Mrs. Parker will fare better than the last one," Mrs. Henderson said, peering closely at Corinn. "Some women can take it; some can't."

Mrs. Wallace tsk-tsked, playfully wagging her finger at the first woman. "Erma Henderson, don't you go scaring off Mrs. Parker with your prattle, good-natured though it is."

"I'm speaking the truth, and you know it." Mrs. Henderson's tone was somber, but her eyes were genial.

Mrs. Wallace tsk-tsked again as she took Corinn by the elbow and ushered her into the parlor to introduce her to a host of women.

Corinn exchanged pleasantries with them. Some she had met at church, and some were new to her.

"Please have a seat beside Mrs. Ross," Mrs. Wallace offered, gesturing at a shiny-faced young girl and the empty chair beside her. "I'll show Adeline where the children are playing," she said over her shoulder as she took the child by the hand.

Corinn tried not to stare at the girl she was supposed to sit by. Had she heard correctly? Had Mrs. Wallace said *Mrs.* Ross? Why, the girl looked young enough to be in short skirts and braids.

Slowly, Corinn scanned the faces in the room again. Of the fifteen or so women present, nearly all of them had streaks of gray in their hair and a wrinkle or two. Three looked to be as old—or older—than Granny Jen. The only one anywhere near her age was the young Mrs. Ross. And she had to be a good eight or so years younger than her own twenty-three. Why, the lass was a mere child.

With a start, Corinn remembered the letter Mr. Parker had written to his uncle, when he was looking for a wife.

There are very few unattached females in this area of Florida, he had said.

With another glance at the young Mrs. Ross, she decided that some men in these parts robbed the cradles.

As she took her seat, the rest of the women sat down, too, around the wide quilting frame. They began stitching the colorful shapes, the wedding ring pattern it was called, intermittently chatting about a myriad of subjects, from husbands to children to school to church to vegetable gardens.

"Was that an orange tree I saw outside, Mrs. Wallace?" Corinn asked timidly, not wanting to be forward among her new acquaintances.

"My, yes. Mr. Wallace planted it when we first moved to Florida." She rolled her eyes. "He insisted that we needed an orange tree, but mostly, the fruit falls to the ground and rots. The children nor I can stand the slimy things. What a mess it makes in my yard."

Corinn tried to keep the look of surprise from her eyes.

"I'm the one who winds up gathering them," Mrs. Wallace said. "I have to haul them across the yard in heaps on a gunnysack and throw them into the woods. I tried giving them to the chickens once, but even *they* turned up their noses. Smart birds, if you ask me."

"May I come and gather your oranges?" Corinn asked.

Mrs. Wallace's eyebrows shot up. "Gather them, you say? Why would you want to do that? Forget the rotted ones. You may have as many as you want, straight from the tree."

"I may?" This time, Corinn smiled—brilliantly—and she didn't care if the women noted her unladylike exuberance. "Long may your chimney smoke, Mrs. Wallace," she added softly.

"What's that?"

"It's an old Scottish saying. It means I wish halcyon days for you."

"Why, thank you, Mrs. Parker. I'll claim prosperity and happiness anytime."

Corinn stared at a red calico quilt square, remembering when she had passed Mrs. Wallace's orange tree that morning, its branches laden to the ground. She looked up and smiled at Mrs. Wallace. "Oranges. . .all I want. . .just for the picking." *Free. I've certainly come into my own halcyon days.*

"Why, a person looking at you would think you had struck gold. What is it about oranges that you love?"

"Marmalade."

"Marmalade?" Mrs. Wallace said, wide-eyed.

"Marmalade?" Mrs. Henderson said, wrinkling her nose.

"Marmalade?" young Mrs. Ross said, pinching her nostrils.

"I cook them up as preserves, using plenty of sugar," Corinn explained. "How I love to make my marmalade."

"And where did you learn to do that?" Mrs. Henderson asked.

"My mother taught me. And her mother taught her. And her mother taught her. And so on. Many years ago, a Scottish woman from the port of Dundee came up with the idea of making marmalade." She moistened her lips, then smiled. "Eating my mother's recipe will make you think you've died and gone to heaven."

"If you can make marmalade like that," Mrs. Wallace said, "I'll pay you a dollar for one jar."

Corinn felt like jumping up and dancing a Scottish jig. Instead, she sat still, hearing her mother's words ringing in her ears. *I'm proud of you, my canny Scot. You're a clever and prudent lass.*

"I'll take the challenge," Corinn exclaimed.

"I'm glad it's you and not me," young Mrs. Ross remarked. "I'm not very good in the kitchen, I'll admit. But give me some knitting needles and yarn, and I can whip out a pair of socks in no time."

"You'll learn," Mrs. Wallace said. "Soon enough. Too soon, in fact. You know what I always say. Love. . .it starts when you sink in his arms. . .and ends with your arms in the sink."

The women cackled. Some even wiped tears from their eyes after their laughter had died down.

"It does my heart good to see these young brides here today," an elderly woman spoke up. "Makes me remember my early days of marriage." Her eyes twinkled.

"You know why we seated you and Mrs. Ross side by side, don't you, Mrs. Parker?" Mrs. Henderson had a mischievous grin on her ruddy face. "Most likely, two new brides have a heap of confidences to share." Guffawing loudly, she elbowed the woman at her side, and several of them followed suit.

Mrs. Henderson rose cumbersomely, her wide girth making it hard to maneuver the tight space around the frame as she bustled out of the room. "It's almost dinnertime. I'll get the food laid out on the trays, Mrs. Wallace. I know where everything is in your kitchen, if it's anything like mine. You all keep sewing. And exchanging confidences"—she let out another loud cackle "—till I call you."

Corinn didn't flinch a muscle, knowing without looking in a mirror that her cheeks were beet-red. Confidences, Mrs. Henderson had said? A heap of confidences, she had talked about?

She cleared her throat, feeling as if she had swallowed a ball of sheepdog hair. The only confidence she had. . .and could never share. . .was an aggrieved heart.

"That Erma," Mrs. Wallace clucked, swinging her head from side to side in exaggerated motions. "She's a sight." She turned to Corinn and touched her arm in a motherly gesture. "She doesn't mean any harm. She'll mind her p's and q's from here on out. I promise."

"There are so few women of marriageable age around here," one of the women spoke up. "New brides are few and far between. We can't let the occasion slip between our fingers without having a little fun with it."

"That's why Erma said what she did," Mrs. Wallace offered. "None of us meant any of this as an affront."

Corinn glanced at Mrs. Wallace, and she was sure she had found a new friend. For life. She looked around the quilting frame at all the women, and she was sure she had found many new friends. For life. Even Mrs. Henderson.

Inwardly, she smiled. Yes, even good-natured Mrs. Henderson. These women sang together in life's chorus—in perfect harmony. She sensed that they understood each other, pulled together, stood beside one another. They were acquainted with—no, akin to—each other's troubles. Surely they poured oil on each other's wounds. They were a sisterhood, a sodality. They were sympathetic, warmhearted, fellow-feeling.

They were just what she needed.

"We didn't mean it as an affront," Mrs. Wallace repeated.

"Affront?" she finally said. "Oh, no. To the contrary. You've endeared yourselves to me this day."

❧

When Mr. Parker arrived to pick up Corrin from the quilting bee, she noticed he had changed from his work attire to Sunday-go-to-meeting clothes. Had he done that for her? When he climbed down from the buggy, Mrs. Wallace insisted that he come in and chat awhile, and Corrin's heart swelled with pride at his impeccable manners and his genteel ways.

Later, on the way home, Corrin sat on the Empire buggy with Edith and Adeline sandwiched between them. When they passed through the pine forest, she didn't even join the wee ones as they counted the tall, skinny trees. Instead, her mind was on the quilting bee.

There are so few women of marriageable age around here, one of the women at the quilting bee had said. *New brides are few and far between,* she'd added.

Corinn drew in a sharp breath of pungent pine as a forceful thought hit her.

I understand Mr. Parker's reason for procuring a wife the way he did. If only I could understand *him.*

She glanced at the tall man across from her, saw the strong set of his handsome jaw, noticed the precise cut of his dress clothing, realized anew how capable he was, how hard he worked, how well-thought-of he was. What was it Dr. Robbins had said about him?

My nephew is Philadelphia-born and bred and well educated. He's hobnobbed with high society since he was a suckling. Whatever he puts his mind to do, he succeeds. Now, it appears he has put his mind to acquiring land in Florida. One day, he'll be an elected official, mark my words.

It didn't matter to Corinn whether Mr. Parker ever became an elected official. He was her husband, bound to her under God's solemn law in the holy estate of matrimony.

If his earthly estate never amounted to anything, she would still be loyal to him as her husband, no matter how unapproachable he seemed to be.

Chapter 6

The next day, Corinn accompanied Mr. Parker to town. They spent the morning running errands, him purchasing farm supplies, her buying household items with little Adeline tagging along at her skirts. She completed her duties and made her purchases, checking "to-dos" off her list, feeling a sense of accomplishment. She and Mr. Parker had agreed to meet at the wagon at noon. On their way home, they would eat the picnic dinner Corinn had prepared earlier that morning.

Now, in the mercantile, amidst bushel baskets of apples and cabbages and bins full of root vegetables, with the smell of coffee beans permeating the air, she gathered up her packages and hurried out the door, nearly colliding with Mr. Parker as he entered the store.

He personified politeness, expressing apologies at his lack of manners, but with a stiff reserve about him.

We may have bumped into each other, Corinn lamented to herself, *but we are as far apart as the North and South Poles.*

Why is this so? she questioned herself. Why were they still a division instead of a convergence? Was the late Mrs. Parker so beautiful that she—the present Mrs. Parker—didn't stand a chance of winning his affection?

"I need to pick up the mail," he said. "And I have a matter to tend to at the livery. Then we'll head for home."

She nodded as she fell into step beside his long strides, their feet making loud plunk-plunks on the boarded walk. "Adeline's been complaining for the longest time that she's hungry. I was on my way to the wagon to get her something out of the basket to tide her over—even though it's a half hour before noon."

"You mustn't spoil her."

Corinn bristled, the familiar chafe surfacing in her chest. Not only had he not greeted Adeline, but he had also been stern with the child, to her way of thinking. When Corinn was growing up, her father had frequently swung her high into the air, smothering her cheeks with kisses, and his bright laughter had rung out, creating memories that would last a lifetime. Did the Parker family never have any merriment? Was it all strictness and austerity?

She tightened her grip on Adeline's tiny hand. It would be easy to fall a sacrifice to resentment.

Mr. Parker pulled open the door of the mail office, then turned toward Corinn. "Why don't you get the mail, and I'll finish up my business?"

She nodded, then swept into the mail office, little Adeline at her skirt tails.

"Good morning," Corinn said. "I'm Mrs. Parker. May I pick up our mail?"

The postmistress stuck out a plump hand over the tall counter. "Name's Mrs. Leah Hancock. Welcome to these parts."

"Thank you, Mrs. Hancock. It's a pleasure to meet you." Corinn returned her shake.

The postmistress turned toward the slots behind her, retrieved the mail, then walked back to the counter, and handed her a small stack of letters.

"Thank you again." Corinn stepped backward, thumbing through the envelopes, studying each one, wondering if she had received any mail from Scotland.

"No mail for Mrs. Parker? Hmmm. That's unusual." The postmistress laughed. "Unusual—that's a good word choice, if I do say so myself." This time she let out a loud peal of laughter then slapped her thigh, like she was laughing at a private joke.

"Unusual? But I've only just moved here."

"The late Mrs. Parker received *lots* of mail." The postmistress put great emphasis on the word "lots," and there seemed to be an air of mystery about her.

"So she was a letter writer, too?" Corinn asked cheerily. Perhaps she had something in common with the late Mrs. Parker. That would be nice. "She enjoyed corresponding with people—as I do?"

"I'll never tell." The postmistress paused. "And I wonder if Mr. Parker ever will."

Corinn looked at her, wondering, then said her good-byes and left, troubled over the woman's comments.

All the way to the wagon, the hammering of her footsteps echoed the hammering of her heart. Not only had she married a stranger, but she had also married one who appeared to be shrouded in secrets.

Chapter 7

As Corinn stirred the bubbling orange concoction in the large pot, she was glad for the warmth coming from the big black stove. For the two months she had lived in Florida, the weather had proved to be sunny and warm. This morning, the first day of November, it was rainy and chilly and had been since dawn, reminding her of the mists of Scotland.

She pulled the pot off the burner, pleased with the way her marmalade was setting up, and decided that this was a good time to take tea—her midmorning respite from her heavy workload.

With precision and care, she laid out a tea tray. First, a lace doily. Then, a china teapot with purple hyacinths and yellow butterflies banded in gilt. A matching footed cup and saucer. Piping-hot scones on a cut-glass platter. Fresh-churned butter in a yellow-lustered compote. Warm-from-the-stove marmalade in a silver jam pot, complete with a miniature silver spoon.

She certainly was glad the late Mrs. Parker had been appreciative of fine things. The lovely appointments were a pleasure to behold.

She carried the tray to her favorite place. She remembered the evening she had arrived at Mr. Parker's house and first set eyes on the big double kitchen windows. She had known that this would be her special spot. Now, two cherrywood rocking chairs and a round table stood in front of the windows, softened by flowered pillows and throw rugs.

Every morning in this sunny alcove, she read her Bible. She loved this place, her sanctum of solace. Besides that, when Adeline ventured outside, Corinn could keep her eye on the child as she played on the oak-tree swing. Today, because of the rain, the wee one was in her room, playing with her dollhouse.

She lit a lamp on the table beside her, and the light dispelled the dreariness of the downpour. As she took a sip of her tea, she heard the back doorknob jiggle. Looking up, she was surprised to see Mr. Parker coming inside, his mackintosh dripping with water.

She jumped to her feet, smiling, at the ready to welcome him and help him. "If I didn't know better, I'd think we were in Scotland—rain, rain, and more rain. When you can see Ben Nevis on the horizon, it's going to rain. When you can't see it, it's raining already."

He didn't respond as he took off his rain gear and hung the heavy coat on a hook, then his hat.

She decided her friendliness would make up for his lack. "Ben Nevis is a mountain," she explained as she handed him a towel to dry his face. "We Scots try to make light of our unstable weather."

"I see," was all he said.

Why was he here? At midmorning? She had never seen him idle. At all times, he labored tirelessly—in the fields, in the barns—wherever his farmwork took him.

He held up a harness. "Mind if I sit in here while I mend this?"

"It's a warm place, this kitchen. Indeed, I'm pleasured at your company. It's time for my morning tea. Would you care to join me?"

"You do this every day, don't you? I've seen you sitting at the window."

She felt like she had been slapped across the cheek. Was he saying that because she had time for tea that she was not working hard? Why, since coming to Florida, she had never worked so hard in all her life, not even when she and Galen had toiled so tediously to make a life for themselves in America.

She resisted the urge to let out a snort of disgust. At Sunny Acres, she had awakened each morning at dawn to prepare a sumptuous breakfast. She cleaned, scrubbed, polished, cooked, gardened, canned, washed, sewed, and ironed. And cleaned, scrubbed, polished, cooked, gardened, canned, washed, sewed, and ironed. Over and over again. Besides that, there had been the children to tend to, though that task had gladdened her heart.

But her labors—they were never-ending. Why, right now, the floors needed sweeping and mopping—a shaft of lamplight revealed a coating of dust—yet she'd just swept and mopped yesterday afternoon. The nerve of him—to criticize her.

"Yes, I'll take some tea." He strode to the washstand and scrubbed his hands, then walked back to the window spot. "My insides could use a touch of something warm."

I couldn't have said it better, Mr. Parker. She gestured at one of the rockers. "Please have a seat." She picked up a cup and saucer from the wall shelf as he sat down, then laid a place for him at the tea table and took her seat opposite him.

Why, oh why, she thought with a sad pang, *couldn't things be different?* This occasion—a husband and wife sitting together for a private moment—should be filled with cordial camaraderie. Instead, she knew from past experience it would be a soliloquy of stony silence. Why was he so unfathomable?

As she poured his tea, she heard the rain pelting the windows. But it was more than raindrops, she was sure. Hail, perhaps? A quick glance told her it was so. Then that meant the temperature had dropped. She glanced covertly at him. Temperature outside—cold. Temperature inside—cold, too.

A moment ago, this line of thinking had saddened her. Now, it rankled her. Immediately, she chastened herself. She must not succumb to the legendary disagreeable temper of a Scot.

Scotland selected the thistle as our national emblem, her mother used to say, *because it reflects a Scot's rough character. Anybody who bumps into it gets pricked.*

Corinn felt like she was in a predicament with no glimmer of hope. Yet, she must display a Christlike attitude. She must. Hadn't she promised God that she would seek Him and His righteousness, and in turn, He would supply all of her needs?

Conjuring up her sweetest smile, she put two scones and generous helpings of marmalade and butter on a plate, then held it out to him.

"Thank you," he said, rather cheerily. "One reason I came inside is because of the weather. Another reason is because I wish to talk with you."

She took a sip of tea, trying hard not to rattle the cup when she returned it to the saucer. *Praise be.* Her patience had paid off. He was finally coming around. Then she remembered she wanted to tell him of *her* good news.

"You're a fine cook," he said, after he'd swallowed a bite of scone and wiped his lips in a mannerly gesture.

This is water to a dying plant, Mr. Parker. Surely the sun had come out. At least in her heart.

"You are to be commended for the fine care you've given my daughters."

Ah.

"They've come to think highly of you."

Her heart was pitter-pattering.

He finished his second scone and asked for a third. "I never liked marmalade until I tasted yours."

Oh, Mr. Parker. Then she remembered what she wanted to tell *him*. "I have customers who love it, too," she gushed, so happy she could burst, happy about the sales, but more than that, thrilled that he was conversing with her in a cheerful manner, elated that he was complimenting her. "I've made sixteen dollars thus far and—"

"That's what I want to talk to you about." His features seemed to darken. "It's come to my attention that you are. . .that you are. . .engaged in selling marmalade."

"Yes. Mrs. Wallace provides the oranges. And I don't even have to use rotting ones. I have my pick of the tree. This isn't costing you a dime."

"That's not the point."

She stared into her tea that was now cold. "I see that you don't approve—"

"A correct assumption."

"I thought you would be proud of me. I thought you would—"

"This is a most embarrassing situation."

"Embarrassing? Any Scot worth his salt is frugal. In fact, thriftiness is lauded in Scotland."

"We're not in Scotland."

"No. . ."

"Neither are we down to cheese parings and candle ends. On the contrary, I am a—"

"Man of means," she said emphatically. She was hurt, wounded to the bone. She thought he'd be proud of her when he found out her marmalade was clamored for and bringing in goodly sums, money that could be put to worthy uses—even though he was a man whom fortune had smiled on.

Unlike her poor Galen.

"I must admit my resources are vast," he said. "I suppose it's time you knew more about my business dealings. . . ."

It's time I knew more about you, Mr. Parker, only you never seem to give me the chance.

"I've worked hard—very hard—to acquire all that I have. And for my efforts, an old saying has proven true for me. 'It never rains but that it pours.' "

She set her cup and saucer on the tea table. Yes, he had spoken a truth. His resources were vast. He was as rich as Croesus. Galen had been as poor as Job's turkey on beam-ends.

She fought to keep her tears in check. She would not lower herself to weep in this man's presence.

He rocked in his chair as he drained his teacup, the runners making *creak-creak* noises, the only sounds in the room save the incessant pelting of the rain against the windows.

She gripped the arms of her rocker, her knuckles turning white. Then, like a bird in flight, she fairly flew across the kitchen.

"Here's something to add to your resources, Mr. Parker." From a high shelf, she pulled down a blue and white soup tureen, removed the lid, and scooped out a handful of money. "I promise not to sell any more marmalade." She walked back across the room and thrust the money toward him, her other hand on the rocker to steady herself.

"I can't accept that." He held his palm up in a stop signal.

"I wash my hands of the whole affair." She was so near weeping, she couldn't even look him in the eye.

He waved her away. "I insist that you keep it. You've worked hard for it, I'm sure." He paused, glancing at the cookstove. "Perhaps I need to give you more household money—"

"No. You've been quite generous." She kept staring through the window, holding the money out to him, hoping he wouldn't see her trembles, impatient for him to retrieve the filthy lucre.

"You take it and use it for something that will benefit you," he said.

Suddenly, a loud clap of thunder sounded, and streaks of lightning flashed, lighting up the room as bright as the noonday sun.

From the hallway, Corinn heard Adeline calling her name. The wee girl came racing into the kitchen crying and burrowed her face in Corinn's skirts.

"There, there," Corinn soothed. In one swift movement, she placed the money on the table, then knelt and gathered the tyke in her arms.

"I'm scared, Co-winn," Adeline lisped.

"There's nothing to be frightened of," Mr. Parker said, his chair abruptly stilled as he leaned forward. "You're a big girl, and big girls don't cry."

"Rain, rain, go away," Corinn sang softly, hoping to allay Adeline's fears, "come again some other day." She hugged her, then smoothed her corkscrew curls. "But truly, lassie, we don't want the rain to go away. Remember my flower garden?"

Adeline nodded, her bottom lip pooched out, tears still in her eyes.

"My anemone and wood violet and snowdrop seeds must have rain to make them grow. Just like you need food to make you grow." She smiled. "Which reminds me. How about a nice hot scone and some of my marmalade—"

She stopped, couldn't help wincing. She didn't want to think about marmalade right now. It had been the source of the disagreement between her and Mr. Parker. Then she continued. "I'll even allow you to have a lady's cup of tea today."

"Tea? I can have tea?" The lassie was all smiles. "Like a real lady drinks?"

"Laced with lots of milk. But yes, you can have your own cup of tea."

"Yippee."

"Mind your manners," Mr. Parker said. "Act like a lady if you want a lady's privileges." He stood.

From the corner of her eye, Corinn noticed that the rain had stopped.

"I'd best get back to work," he said.

A surge of strength hit her, and she turned to face him head-on, her gaze unwavering. "Mr. Parker, I'd like to have a word with you. . . ."

He looked puzzled.

"It's about—" She tipped her head sideways at Adeline. "Mr. Parker, if you'll wait here, I'll get her settled, and then we can talk for a few moments."

"For a few moments, then. That's all the time I have." He sat back down on the flowered cushion and began to rock. "I'll wait here."

Corinn settled little Adeline in the parlor with her lady's cup of tea and scones, giving her permission to rewind the music box each time it wound down. "Enjoy the lively tunes, and I'll join you soon," Corinn promised the bright-eyed tyke.

Then she turned and made her way back to the kitchen, dreading her meeting with Mr. Parker. But the time had come for her to state her opinion on a very important matter.

She sat down in her chair, then looked over at him where he sat rocking steadily. She wouldn't bandy words. She would get right to the point. "I've a matter of grave import to discuss with you."

He crossed his arms, then turned his gaze on her, raising his eyebrows as he did so. "Please proceed."

Was he being smug? No matter. She must intervene. "Mr. Parker, I've no intent to show you disrespect. I've carefully weighed what I have to say for some time, and now is the time to say it." She squelched the case of nerves that threatened to overtake her. "I—I hope you'll take it the right way."

"I would very much like to hear what you've obviously thought long and hard about. You indicated you wish to talk to me about Adeline?"

"And Edith."

"Yes?"

"Sometimes you seem so. . .stern with the children."

334

"I was raised to believe that children should be seen and not heard."

"So was I. . .in certain settings." She took a deep breath and plunged on. "They need more from you as their father."

"I'm a good father," he countered.

"Yes. . ."

"I work hard to provide their food and clothes and baubles."

"They need more than that."

"And just what is it they need, pray tell?"

"They need your love—"

"I love them." He looked smitten, even contrite. "I care for them beyond description."

"Second, they need your attention."

He stopped rocking and glanced at the floor. "There are only so many hours in the day," he said softly. "I want to do well by them, but I'm overwhelmed with the workload. . . ."

How well I know the feeling, Mr. Parker.

"I can only do so much," he said.

She remembered a father who greeted her with a boisterous hug after a long day's absence and made her laugh and told her stories.

He chewed on his bottom lip. "My father. . .was. . . stern."

"Third," she said, "they need their memories of their mother kept alive, perhaps a picture of her displayed. Every time they talk about her, you stop them."

He only glared at her, his brow furrowed, and she visualized Nessie, the mysterious monster in the dark waters of Loch Ness.

"Fourth, Mr. Parker, they need your affection."

Almost lazily, he reached down and picked up her lace-trimmed handkerchief.

She held her hand out. "I didn't realize I'd dropped it."

As if he was ignoring her, he stared down at it, then ran his fingers along the ruffled edging, not responding. When he reached the first corner, he turned the handkerchief and ran his fingers along the edging of the second side. When he reached the second corner, he turned it and ran his fingers along the third side. When he reached the third corner, he turned it and ran his fingers along the fourth side.

She tapped her toes inside her work shoe. She wiggled her foot. She smoothed her skirts. Wasn't he going to say anything? She was anxious to get this interchange over with. Why didn't he answer her? She wanted to say something but didn't know what to utter. No words came.

When he turned the handkerchief for what seemed like the tenth time, she thought she would burst. Instead, she tapped her toes inside her work shoe. She wiggled her foot. She smoothed her skirts.

"I thought we would marry and grow fond of each other," he whispered. "And then. And then. . ." He looked over at her, and she couldn't read the expression in his eyes.

"*Mrs.* Parker," he said, putting great emphasis on the word "Mrs.," his voice low and controlled. "You"—he paused—"are a wife in name only."

She was stunned. This conversation wasn't about them as man and wife. It was about two wee girls.

"And therefore, you're a mother in name only. You have no right to interfere." He drew out his last sentence, six short-clipped words stretched to a piercing allocution.

She squeezed her hands into tight balls. He was odious. Horrid. Execrable. He had forced her to quaff the bitter cup, and she detested him for doing so.

She absently touched her chignon, her fingers shaking, wondering what to do, what to say. She'd been talking about what the wee ones needed. Instead of addressing what had been placed before him, he had skirted the issue and then offended her. Highly.

She stiffened her shoulders. By offending her in this manner, she decided, he had thrown the red rag to the bull.

The Scots are descendants of the fierce, fighting Irish, she wanted to shout at him. *I have Irish blood in me. I'll not sit still and listen to your insults.*

Needs, they'd been talking about? She let out a snort of disgust. "Mr. Parker, all *you* need around here is a workwoman and a nursemaid," she stormed. "You don't need a wife. You don't know the meaning of the word."

"You don't need a husband. Your ghost gives you quite good company—"

"How dare you speak of Galen in that way?"

"Then you admit it? That he's the barrier between us?"

"You're the barrier, Mr. Parker. If you had ever approached me, just once, with tenderness. Or said a kind word. Or displayed a loving gesture toward me—anything. But no, you've stayed behind your stiff facade—"

"And if you'd ever given *me* a moment's notice," he spouted. "All you ever do is cook and clean and care for my daughters—"

"But it was all for you, Mr. Parker—"

"That's not what I need. I need. . .I need. . ." He looked toward the open door of her bedroom.

She followed his gaze and saw her bed, the red plaid wedding coverlet lying atop it.

"I'll tell you what I need. I need you to get rid of that. . .that thing." He pointed at her coverlet. "I overheard you when you told my daughters the meaning behind it."

"Never," she shrieked. Especially not now—after his insults and harshness.

"Never," she repeated, this time more calmly, knowing exactly what he meant, more determined than ever to keep Galen's sweet, tender memory alive. "All I've ever desired is the love of a good man, and the only man offering me such is now dead." She pushed back the tears that burned her eyes.

"For two months, every time I walked by this doorway, I saw that. . .that thing." His tone a snarl; he gestured at the wedding coverlet.

She was so hurt, she couldn't even make the nasty retort she was harboring.

"We'll make a deal, Mrs. Parker." He spat out the words in disgust. "I'll approach you with tenderness"—he paused, like he was formulating his words—"and say a kind word to you"—he paused again—"and what else was it you said *you* needed?"

He touched his temple. "Ah, yes, now I remember. You said if only I'd display a sweet gesture toward you. I'll tell you what, Mrs. Parker. I'll display a sweet gesture toward you"—he stood, then glared down at her and pointed once more toward her bedroom—"when you do away with that. . .that wedding coverlet."

Angrier than she had ever been, she jumped up and whisked from the room.

Chapter 8

"Today, in honor of our twenty-fifth anniversary," the parson announced from the pulpit, his wife at his side, "I'll be speaking on the topic of marriage."

Corinn sat beside Mr. Parker in his pew with Edith and Adeline to her right, wondering at the coincidental timing of their pastor's sermon. She clutched her Bible, running her fingers along the smooth leather surface. Coincidental? No. That was a misnomer. It was providential. For a week, ever since their tempestuous altercation, she had avoided Mr. Parker, and in turn, he had avoided her.

Perhaps it was time for a truce, though what the truce would be and how it would come about, she could not imagine. To her way of thinking, the rift would be healed when Mr. Parker made the first move. After all, he had been the one who had said such hurtful words.

" 'Husbands, love your wives,' " the parson quoted, " 'even as Christ also loved the church, and gave himself for it.' That Scripture is found in Ephesians. Another Scripture I wish to look at is, 'Wives, submit yourselves unto your own husbands, as unto the Lord'—also found in Ephesians. Let us pray."

After prayer, the parson smiled broadly at the congregation. "Lord Byron said, 'Man's love is of man's life a thing apart. 'Tis woman's whole existence.' In marriage, the man's responsibility is to show courtesy to his wife and make her feel cherished. He must initiate love and cause her to feel desired. What a lofty ideal—for a man to love his wife as Christ loved the church."

For close to forty-five minutes, Corinn listened in rapt attention as the parson preached to the congregation, telling them that ultimately, the husband was responsible to God for what the home became.

She sat there, enjoying the parson's command of the English language, feeling smug at how apropos the sermon was to Mr. Parker and his sad lack.

"As for women, dear ladies, you must give up any preconceived notions as to what men in general are like and discover what *your* man is like. Then you must seek to meet his needs, and in so doing, your needs will be met."

Corinn was dumbstruck. Needs? The parson was referring to needs? That's what she and Mr. Parker had talked about. Needs.

"About the role of a wife, Shakespeare wrote, 'Thy husband is thy lord, thy life, thy keeper, thy head, thy sovereign; one that cares for thee, and for thy maintenance!

Commits his body to painful labor, both by sea and land; to watch the night in storms, the day in cold, while thou liest warm at home, secure and safe, and craves no other tribute at thy hands, but love, fair looks, and true obedience, too little payment for so great a debt. Such duty as the subject owes the prince; even such a woman owes her husband.'

"Husbands and wives, I prescribe to you today," the parson continued, "to join your hand and heart to that of your mate's and love each another with sacrificial love, for love is of God, and everyone that loveth is born of God and knoweth God. He that loveth not, knoweth not God, for God is love. Please stand for the closing prayer."

Shakily, Corinn arose, holding tightly to the pew in front of her to steady herself. The parson's words—straight from the Bible—had pierced to her marrow.

❧

On the way home from church, Corinn sat beside Mr. Parker with Edith and Adeline sandwiched between them as they always were when he drove his shiny new buggy. As they *clip-clopped* through the dense green forest on the warm December day, she felt heartened, thinking about the sermon.

Suddenly, a gust of wind blew the wide brim of her hat backward—causing her to laugh out loud—and a fresh burst of hope filled her being. As she righted her hat, she made a new resolve in her heart.

She would make every attempt to show kindness to this man.

She would make every attempt to get to know this man.

She would make every attempt to become acquainted with his needs.

And she would start now.

"When will Edith be out of school for the Christmas holidays, Mr. Parker?"

"December the nineteenth, I believe."

"Hmm. . .that's only two-and-a-half weeks away."

"I had the bestest day of school yesterday," Edith said.

"You mean, best," Corinn gently corrected, smiling, feeling the sunshine flooding her soul. "And it was Friday, not yesterday, that you last went to school."

"I want to go to 'cool," little Adeline piped up.

Corinn ran her finger up one of Adeline's cork-screw curls, then cupped her chin. "You will, lassie. The time will be here before you know it. And then one day, you'll be all grown-up, and handsome young men will come courting at our house."

Adeline's delightful giggles filled the air.

"Teacher said I'm to read out loud more," Edith said. "She told me I need to practice." She held out her Sunday school papers and pointed to a word. "What's that word, Papa?"

"Have her—" he tipped his head sideways at Corinn, his eyes on the road "—tell you."

Corinn looked at the paper. "The word is tenderhearted. It's from a Scripture in Ephesians."

"Read it to me," Edith said.

"Your teacher said you're the one who needs the practice." Corinn smiled down at her. "Read it for us."

" 'Be ye kind one to another, tenderhearted, forgiving one another,' " Edith slowly read, " 'even as God for Christ's sake hath forgiven you.' "

"That's a powerful verse." Mr. Parker looked over at Corinn.

She thought she detected a flicker of. . .something. . .that crossed betwixt them—a knowing between them. That was the only way she could interpret it, and it thrilled her.

"It's a Scripture that should be memorized." He took another long look at Corinn, and there was kindness, even tenderness, in his eyes. Then he looked back at the road.

Her heart raced. Yes, she would make every attempt to get to know this man, her wedded husband.

" 'Be ye kind one to another,' " he quoted—with meaning—glancing at her again. " 'Tenderhearted, forgiving one another. . .' "

Forgive me? his eyes implored, *for hurting you with my caustic words?*

Even as God for Christ's sake hath forgiven you, her gaze conveyed. *And hath forgiven me.*

She drew in a slow, deep breath, her heart flip-flopping in her chest. *Oh, Mr. Parker.*

"Edith," Mr. Parker said, "tonight after supper, why don't you read aloud to us? In the parlor."

"I could pop some corn," Corinn offered, tapping on her chin for a moment. She could make it festive. *Yes, I will do that,* she decided. She would make it a grand occasion—to celebrate the fact that she and Mr. Parker had forgiven each other and made things right between them. She was glowing inside—so vibrantly she almost shouted out an Adeline yippee.

Instead, she patted Edith's shoulder. "Why don't we have a soiree tonight?"

"A soiree?" Edith chirped. "What's a soiree?"

"What's a soiree, Mr. Parker?" Corinn asked.

A long moment passed with him not saying a word, and Corinn was surprised that neither girl broke the silence.

"A soiree is an evening party," he finally said.

"A party?" Edith shrieked.

"A party?" Little Adeline squealed.

Corinn nodded, smiling again, enjoying the twinkles dancing in their eyes. "We'll tell stories, and Edith can read some things aloud to us. And we'll sing some songs and—" She stopped, thinking about what else they would do at their soiree. "And we'll have some party dainties to eat."

Both girls clapped their hands and shouted with glee. Adeline added, "Yippee."

"That sounds like a pleasant proposition," Mr. Parker said, a smile on his face.

Chapter 9

That afternoon, Corinn made preparations for their evening soiree. She decided which stories to tell, selected a few readings of Burns, chose a children's book for Edith to read aloud, and placed her lap harp in the parlor, at the ready to accompany them when they all sang together.

Then she went into the kitchen and put on her daisy-dotted apron. Social gatherings always had delectable food, and for this special occasion, she would make a few dainties. Scottish shortbread would be one of them. As lively folk tunes danced in her head, she laid out the makings.

She passed the double kitchen windows and saw Edith swinging on the oak-tree swing and little Adeline awaiting her turn nearby.

"Swinging on the oak-tree swing," Corinn sang. "Soaring where the bluebirds sing, oh, to be a girl with a headful of curls, swinging on the oak-tree swing."

Under the sprawling branches, she saw Mr. Parker sitting on a bench—a sight she had never seen—him in a state of inaction, his labors in abeyance, enjoying his daughters. Her heart swelled with emotion.

Again, as had happened on the way home from church, sunshine flooded her soul, and hope for their future soared to new heights.

She took the flour canister down from the kitchen shelf, walked to the table, and measured two even cups into a mixing bowl. "Swinging on the oak-tree swing," she sang at the top of her voice, "soaring where the bluebirds sing—"

When she heard Edith scream, her heart stopped, and she jumped up, raced across the kitchen and out the door, frantic with worry.

As her feet flew over the back walkway, she saw Mr. Parker hovering over Edith, who lay on the ground. Nearby lay the swing, one of its ropes severed and frayed.

Edith screamed again, and Corinn saw that Edith's arm was twisted in a grotesque angle. "Dear God. . ." Tears sprang to her eyes, but she forced them back. Edith needed her strength right now.

"Mr. Parker?" she said softly as she bent over him and touched his shoulder.

He looked up, a wide arc of sunlight lighting his worry-filled face. Corinn saw that he, too, had tears that apparently he was trying to keep at bay.

Edith screamed in agony, and Corinn fell to her knees in the dirt and put her mouth in the tyke's ear. "You're going to be all right, lassie," she crooned, seeing the twisted arm, not sure at all if Edith would be all right. Would she lose the use of her arm? The thought made Corinn sick to her stomach.

Adeline whimpered behind Corinn as she kept crooning to Edith.

"It hurts so bad," Edith cried. "So bad."

"I know, my wee one. I know. But soon, we'll have you all righted, and—"

"I want Mama's Bible," Edith wailed.

"I'm going to try to move her into the house," Mr. Parker whispered to Corinn, "and then I'm going for Dr. Adams."

Corinn nodded. Why did a mishap have to happen—just when things were looking so bright? And why did a mishap have to involve one of the wee girls? If a tragedy had to occur, why couldn't she have taken the brunt?

Edith screamed out again, and the pain in Corinn's heart was so great, she wanted to cry out, too. Instead, she stroked Edith's cheek, then dabbed at the tyke's tears with the tail of her apron.

"Please let me have Mama's Bible," Edith begged, great heaving sobs shaking her little body. "If I can just hold Mama's Bible. . ."

"I'll get it," Corinn offered, willing to do anything to help Edith. "Where is it, Mr. Parker?"

A shadow crossed his face. "I'll get you a Bible, Edith. Mine is handy—"

"I want Mama's."

Corinn held Edith's shoulders to keep her from shaking so badly. "If she thrashes about too much," she whispered to Mr. Parker, "it might damage her arm further."

"Papa, please—"

"Let's get her into the house." His face was lined with deep distress.

Corinn nodded.

"You go pull down her bed, while I carry her in." Gently, with the finesse of a musician, taking great care with her twisted limb, he scooped Edith into his arms, then stood up.

"Papa, what about Mama's Bible—"

"After I leave for the doctor"—he looked down at Edith, his voice choked, his words halting—"Corinn will get your mama's Bible for you."

❧

With Edith settled in bed but moaning in pain, Corinn followed Mr. Parker into the kitchen at his bidding.

He stopped and faced her. . .

He peered into her eyes. . .

He grasped her hand. . .

He turned it palm side up.

For a moment, she thought her heart had ceased its beating.

His eyes seemed to search her soul as he placed a key in her hand. "This will open that door," he said softly, gesturing at the pantry. But his gaze never left her face. "Edith's mother's Bible is on the second shelf."

I trust you, his eyes told her.

I know, Mr. Parker, her eyes told him. *And I am glad. So very glad.*

"I'll be back as soon as I can," he said over his shoulder as he dashed out the door.

Chapter 10

As breathless as a burglar on the stealth, feeling like an interloper in this abode, Corinn approached the kitchen pantry with a sense of misgivings and trepidation. Somehow she knew that behind this door, she would find the answer to the many questions she had asked herself throughout the three months she had lived here.

She knew uncannily that, in past years, all had not been sunny at Sunny Acres. What would the pantry reveal? What would she find behind that locked door, besides the late Mrs. Parker's Bible?

She put the key in the lock and turned it, then pulled on the doorknob, but nothing happened. She turned the key again, but still, it would not open. Had Mr. Parker given her the wrong key? She pulled out the key and brushed a few specks of rust tracings from the lock, then thumped on it. Why wouldn't it release its hold?

She put the key in the lock a second time and turned it. Still nothing happened. Her heart lurched within her breast. She couldn't disappoint this tyke, especially in her pain-wracked state. She would rather take a beating than have to tell Edith she could not bring her the treasured Bible.

Edith called out, begging for her mama's Bible, and Corinn heard her—all the way in the kitchen.

"I'm coming, lassie," Corinn called back. "Hold tight."

Turning the key once again, then jiggling it, Corinn felt like shouting in glee when the lock gave way at last. Trembling, she yanked on the knob and swung open the door, its hinges squeaking from disuse.

Before her eyes, on the second shelf of the pantry, she saw stacks and stacks of china plates, cups, saucers, and platters—surely more than one family would ever have need of—all the pieces red-flowered and grotesque.

She stared at the third shelf, lined with exquisite porcelain figurines. Puzzled, she looked more closely at them.

Were there one. . .two. . .three. . .she kept counting. . .half a dozen of the same dancing lady in a tiered red gown? That was odd.

One. . .two. . .three. . .four. . .five of the same soldier in a red uniform blowing a bugle?

One. . .two. . .three. . .four of the same girl holding a red basket on her arm?

And parasols. She quickly counted eight of them, all identical, all bright-red silk. And there were more behind the first bundle.

On the fourth shelf—she was squatting to be at eye level—she saw a towering stack of books—all with the same title—*The Day of the Red Haze.*

She inched back up, feeling dazed. Instinctively, she knew these items had been the late Mrs. Parker's.

On the very top shelf, higher than she was tall, she saw lovely music boxes, all with red bases. When she stood on the tips of her toes, she still couldn't see them all, so crowded were they against the wall.

Words popped into her mind. Eccentric. Unsound. The words kept coming. Delusional. Daft.

Daft? She grabbed hold of the doorknob, trying to summon the breath that had been knocked from her. For that's what she'd experienced—a blow—as surely as she was standing here.

She remembered the day she had arrived and Edith had said, *Florida means 'flowery land,'* and she had replied, *That must mean flowers are everywhere.* Mr. Parker had said, *Only where they're planted,* his features expressionless. By the thick viney undergrowth surrounding Sunny Acres, she had quickly determined that, indeed, no one had planted flowers in years.

She recalled him telling her that Mrs. Henderson had been cooking and cleaning for his family for several years and that a seamstress kept his daughters well clothed. *But I thought your wife passed away only months ago,* she had naively said. He hadn't responded, only given her a stony stare.

She remembered when Adeline had said, *Mama said I was her baby,* and Mr. Parker had commanded her to stop her chatter.

She recalled the sad disarray of the house.

She remembered Mr. Parker's harsh tone when she had tried to open the pantry door. *This door is always locked,* he had said.

She recalled the gift he had given her the night she arrived. *It's fripperies,* he had told her. *All women want fripperies.*

Fripperies? She stared at the music boxes, at the stacks of china, at the dancing ladies and bugle-blowing soldiers and basket-carrying girls, at the red silk parasols, at the books, all with the same title.

The late Mrs. Parker had liked fripperies.

A hard shudder shook her, and she grasped the doorknob more firmly. Then she hugged her upper body, suddenly feeling cold to the bone, despite the heat from the cookstove.

She looked across the kitchen. Had she been standing at the stove only an hour ago? About to begin baking something for some occasion?

Her mind was fuzzy. Hadn't she been planning a special event for tonight? To celebrate something? She glanced back at the shelves in the pantry. Then her mind continued its journey down memory lane.

Edith snapping at Adeline, when she'd said her mother had played with them every day. *You know Papa doesn't want us talking about that.*

Mrs. Henderson's comment. *I can't help wondering if the new Mrs. Parker will fare better than the last one.*

The remarks the postmistress had made. *No mail for Mrs. Parker? Hmmm. That's unusual.*

That woeful word came to her mind again. *Daft.*

Poor Mrs. Parker had taken leave of her senses. Poor Mrs. Parker.

She was stunned. Poor *Mr.* Parker. She rubbed her temples, couldn't think anymore.

"Corinn," Edith wailed. "Are you coming?"

Was Edith calling her?

"Mama's Bible. Did you find Mama's Bible?"

Edith had fallen when the swing snapped.

Edith had broken her arm.

Edith had wanted her mama's Bible.

From the locked pantry.

Suddenly, thankfully, her mind grew clear, and she remembered Mr. Parker saying that the Bible was on the second shelf. She moved the footed teacups. She shifted the stacks of saucers. She pushed aside the china plates. There, shoved against the wall, was a black Bible.

The late Mrs. Parker's Bible.

Poor Mrs. Parker.

Poor *Mr.* Parker. What had all this meant for him?

Without any explanation, she knew.

He would never have to tell her about it. She just knew.

Yes, poor Mr. Parker.

No, *dear* Mr. Parker.

Chapter 11

Corinn carried a tray laden with refreshments into the parlor and set it down on the mahogany table, humming a hymn, thankful that Edith's arm was healing well.

She glanced about the large room, admiring the furnishings, enjoying the scene, absorbing the ambiance. The highly polished mahogany pieces shone in the lamplight, and the fragrance of freshly cut flowers filled the air. Over at the hearth, a fire burned in the grate, its yellow flames saying *welcome*. Next week, when Christmas came, a decorated pine tree would grace the corner.

She peered into the mirror above the mantel, fingering the delicate ruching around the neckline of her green silk dress. The flowing sleeves as well as the cupped-in waistline added a feminine touch, and she was glad she had decided on this pattern. The mirror revealed that her cheeks were glowing with color, and she sighed, knowing it was not from the warmth of the fire.

She strode back to the table and placed the platters of dainties on its polished surface. She had spent all afternoon preparing for an evening soiree, and she was looking forward to it as much as the wee ones. At first, when Edith had asked if they could have it, Mr. Parker said no, that it was only a week after her accident. But when he asked Dr. Evans about it, he had said it would do the child good. After that, Mr. Parker had readily agreed.

I want her to get well soon, Mr. Parker had told Corinn. *I have grand plans to spend more time with her, as well as Adeline.*

She looked at the clock in its handsome fine-grained casing just as the chime bonged out seven bright tones. At seven-thirty, she would usher the lassies into the parlor, as she had promised them, to begin the soiree. She envisioned them in their room this moment, getting dressed by themselves as they had begged to do. *Like ladies,* they had said.

The door to the hallway opened, and Mr. Parker walked in. With her seamstress's eye, she took in his finely cut apparel, from his burgundy waistcoat to his gray serge trousers to his white satin tie. *He looks dashing,* she decided, *as dashing as any man I've ever seen.*

"May I speak with you?" he asked. "I don't want to interrupt your preparations. Do you have a few moments?" Like the gentleman that he was, he stood near the door awaiting her response, as if he were ready to retreat if need be.

"Yes, of course. We've plenty of time." Corinn finished arranging a doily on the table, thinking about the night of Edith's accident, after the doctor had left.

As soon as possible, I'd like to talk with you, Mr. Parker had told her, his eyes troubled.

About the kitchen pantry, her look had said back.

But the entire week, she had run herself ragged tending to Edith as well as her other chores, and so had he. There had simply been no time for them to converse.

Now, as they seated themselves in the parlor, he on a rose damask chair that looked much too small for his tall frame, she on the matching settee, swallowed by the length of it, she couldn't help but feel fidgety, remembering the sight she'd beheld last week when she'd swung open the pantry door. She remembered grabbing hold of the knob, trying to summon the breath that had been knocked from her.

"Edith and Adeline are looking forward to the soiree this evening," he said brightly, smiling at her. "Perhaps there'll be many soirees in the future."

"That would be nice. . . ."

He crossed his right ankle over his left knee. He drummed his fingers on the upholstered chair arm. He stared into the flames.

She glanced at the clock. "You said you wished to speak with me?"

He glanced at the clock, too, then gripped both chair arms, his knuckles white. "Ten years ago, the late Mrs. Parker and I came to Florida. I'd heard about the reasonable land prices and the virgin timber and the rich soil."

He looked down at the hardwood floor. "I had high hopes for our lives in this beauteous new state. My goals were to acquire acreage, establish myself in the area, and do some land prospecting. After that, the sky was the limit, to my way of thinking. And that's exactly the way things turned out. I acquired acreage, established myself in the area, and did some land prospecting.

"And," he continued, "to put the icing on the cake, two beautiful daughters joined our family. They brought us great pleasure. Things couldn't have been sunnier at Sunny Acres."

He crossed his left ankle over his right knee. He drummed his fingers on the upholstered chair arm. He stared into the flames. "It was when Adeline was a year old that I began to notice—"

"You don't have to continue, Mr. Parker. I know."

"You know?" He looked in her direction, his eyebrows shooting up.

She returned his intense gaze with one of her own, a cognizance passing between them.

"Yes, you know," he said quietly. "You know. . .but I need to say a few things."

She nodded, folded her hands in her lap.

"Madeline began to order the. . .the. . ."

"Fripperies?"

"Yes. . .fripperies." He nodded only slightly. "Madeline chose them from catalogues. Red was a fixation with her. They began arriving almost daily. First, the parasols. Then the music boxes. Then the china. On and on it went. It was. . .it was mail-order mayhem."

He looked so pained Corinn wanted to run to his side and draw him into her arms, like she'd done with Edith and Adeline many a time when they were hurt or afraid.

"And there were other things she did. . .and did *not* do. . .many things."

Mail-order mayhem, he had said? She swung her chin up, then down, understanding flooding through her. "The postmistress. . ." *The late Mrs. Parker received lots of mail,* the postmistress had said. Corinn clutched at her throat. "That's why the postmistress said what she did."

It was as if he hadn't heard her. He stared into the flames. "It was so hard, seeing Madeline like that. For as long as I'd known her, she'd been vibrant. . .beautiful. . . capable," he choked out. "I loved her dearly."

His face contorted in agony. "Madeline," he whispered. He sat forward, his elbows propped on his knees, his fingertips rubbing his temples. "I've asked myself a million times if there was anything I could've done. Should've done."

Corinn squirmed in her chair, feeling his misery, wanting to ease his pain, grieving with him over the demise of his beautiful wife. "Mr. Parker, surely you realize it wasn't your fault."

He didn't say anything for a long moment. "Then, I decided to remarry," he finally said, nearly whispering. He pulled his chair closer to her, so close their knees almost touched. "I knew I wanted to give my heart to my new bride—whomever she would be—but I also wanted to honor her tender sensibilities.

"When you arrived," he continued, "I provided a private place for you. I assumed affection would come to us eventually, and I also assumed that our fondness would run its natural course. But I was determined to be very careful. For the marriage ceremony, I even told the parson to skip the part about the kiss."

He looked directly at her, his eyes seeming to mesmerize hers. "I figured. . . ," his voice grew husky, his breathing ragged as his hands found hers and held them tightly, "I figured kisses would come when. . .when. . ."

"Co-winn," shouted little Adeline, running into the parlor, shattering the magical moment.

Neither Corinn nor Mr. Parker made a move, their hands still entwined.

"Co-winn, Co-winn." The tyke tugged on Corinn's skirts.

She stood up, smiled down at Adeline, touched her white-blond curls. "I thought you and Edith wanted to be ushered into the parlor like ladies."

"But Edith says it's—"

"Seven-forty," Edith said from the doorway, leaning against the doorjamb, her right arm cradled around a white sling on her left arm. "At least I think that's what the eight means. Isn't it time to start the soiree?"

"Yes, it's time," Corinn whispered to Edith, but her eyes were on Mr. Parker. "It's time."

All evening, they enjoyed the soiree, telling stories, reading aloud, eating the dainties, and singing songs accompanied by Corinn on her lap harp. She even wound up the music box and tried to teach Edith and Adeline the steps to a Scottish reel, their shoes clacking on the hardwood floor. Over and over, she repeated the instructions until they caught on, stepping forward then backward, right then left, leaping in the air as they held up a knee.

As the music box played for the sixth time, Corinn and Edith, and then Corinn and Adeline, jigged the reel with near perfection. When it ended, the three of them were raucous with laughter.

After their merriment died down, Corinn settled Edith on the settee, her arm propped on a pillow, then Adeline beside her. "One last piece of Scottish shortbread and one last cup of punch for the lassies." She handed the goodies to them.

"These are pretty cookies, Co-winn," little Adeline said, then popped hers in her mouth.

"Yes," Mr. Parker agreed. He picked up a shortbread cookie from the cut-glass platter Corinn held out to him. He studied the fancy edging on it. "It's evident you spent a lot of time making these."

Corinn reached for one too. "And I loved every moment." She ran her finger along the spiked edge. "This is called fluting."

"Fluting?"

She nodded. "It's an old Scottish symbol—the sun's rays. It represents hope for the return of spring."

"Hope?" he asked, his eyes searching hers.

"Hope," she said softly.

"I—I appreciate all that you do for our family," he stammered.

Our family, he'd said? Hope surged through her being. Surely spring was on its way to this household that had been awry for a long winter.

As she sipped a cup of punch, she couldn't help but smile to herself. In nature, spring was a time of growth and development. She thought of the spring beauties she would soon plant, pictured the two-leafed stems bursting forth bearing delicate pink flowers, emerging from the hard-packed dirt though their seeds had long been dormant.

She touched the purple wood violets in the tall vase on the side table. Yes, here in Mr. Parker's household, beauty was emerging, though its seed had long been dormant.

When the clock chimed on the half hour past nine, Mr. Parker announced bedtime.

"Papa, please let Corinn teach you the reel," Edith begged. "Like she taught us."

"Yeth, Papa," little Adeline lisped.

"It's growing late." His voice held concern. "You two need your rest, particularly Edith."

"It's so much fun, Papa," Edith said. "Please? I promise to go to sleep as soon as my head touches the pillow."

Corinn looked over at him, and there were smiles in his eyes. "Sir?" she questioned, her heart racing.

"I'd be honored." With a flourish, he stood up and strode to the middle of the floor.

Corinn wound the music box and set it down, the lively tune filling the air, then walked toward him, feeling awkward and nervous, but tingly, too.

They came together face-to-face, and neither said a word.

"Put your hand on her back, Papa," Edith said, suddenly at his side. She picked up his hand and placed it on Corinn's waistline. "There." Then she moved back to her spot on the settee.

"Yes. . .there." Corinn could feel the color rushing into her face. "We'll go slowly at first, Mr. Parker, so you can learn the steps."

"And hold her fingers with your other hand, Papa," Edith said.

"Like this?" He took Corinn's hand and held it out in midair, his gaze never leaving her face—as if his eyes were memorizing her every nuance.

As if his eyes were. . .feasting on her? She sighed. Was she going to swoon?

"Like this?" he repeated, squeezing her fingers.

She didn't even nod in agreement. She didn't have to. For his thoughts were her thoughts, and her thoughts were his thoughts.

"Start with your left foot," she whispered. "Move one step to the right, then move back in place."

He did as she said, tightening his hold on her waist and squeezing her hand more firmly.

If she had been in a cocoon, she would have burst forth as a brightly colored butterfly. The room was filled with kindness and affection and tenderheartedness, and she warmed to it, embraced it. This. . .was the abode of love.

"Move one step to the right, Mr. Parker," she said softly, "then, move back into place." She paused as they completed the action. "Then raise your left knee while I raise my right one and hop in the air."

As they hopped, not a spot touching save for his light graze on the small of her back and their fingers in midair, their eyes locked for what seemed like all time.

" 'Whoso findeth a wife findeth a good thing,' " he whispered, " 'and obtaineth favour of the Lord.' "

She willed herself not to go weak-kneed. *Oh Mr. Parker. My dear Mr. Parker. My beloved Trevor.*

The music ended abruptly, and Edith and Adeline raced toward them, Adeline burying her face in Corinn's skirts, Mr. Parker scooping Edith up and giving her a hug. "Wasn't that fun, Papa? Wasn't it?" she shrieked, laughing. "See? I told you it would be fun. Corinn's my favored friend."

"Hmm," he said, looking contemplative. "By favor, Edith, do you mean you regard her highly?"

In answer, Edith did as Adeline was doing and buried *her* face in Corinn's skirts, and Corinn thought her soul would burst with happiness.

"Favor also means to win approval." With a thankful heart, Corinn hugged Edith to her. She had finally won the tyke's approval and affection.

She took a deep breath. She had finally won Mr. Parker's approval. . .and affection.

"I'm glad I won yours, Corinn," he said. In his eyes was that familiar knowing again, and she knew exactly what he was referring to.

Chapter 12

Christmas Eve

Corinn left her bedroom and walked into the kitchen, wondering when Mr. Parker would come inside. She lifted the yellow ruffle at the window and peered into the night, dark except for the light shining from the lantern beside the back door.

Earlier, they'd had their Christmas Eve supper. Then, while Mr. Parker had checked on something in the barn—she knew not what—she bedded the lassies. But Edith and Adeline had repeatedly risen, too excited to sleep because of the prospects of Christmas surprises. Now, it appeared they were in dream world, judging by the fact that not a noise had come from their room for a full fifteen minutes.

She sat down in her kitchen rocker, wondering what Mr. Parker would say about her Christmas gift to him. She felt her face grow hot, fanned it with her handkerchief, sighed. Then she settled back against the slats, her heart thumping hard in eager anticipation.

She remembered when Edith had asked her if it was time to start the soiree. *Yes, it's time,* she had whispered to Edith, but her eyes had been on Mr. Parker. *It's time,* she had repeated, knowing full well what she meant.

She fiddled with her chignon, her hands shaking. Was tonight the right time? To—

The doorknob jiggled, and she jumped.

"Are the girls asleep?" he asked as he came inside, then took off his coat and hung it on a hook.

"As far as I can tell." She fingered her buttons as the runners of the rocker *ker-plunked* on the hardwood floor.

He walked over to her. "Mind if I sit?"

"I'd be delighted. Would you like some tea? Coffee?" She made a movement to stand, but he waved her down as he sat beside her.

"No, thank you. Your Christmas Eve meal...I don't believe I've ever tasted better cooking."

"You already told me."

He crossed his left ankle over his right knee. He drummed his fingers on the wooden chair arm. He stared at the far side of the room.

She continued her *ker-plunking*.

He jumped up and dashed across the kitchen, then peered down the hall.

"What is it, Mr. Parker?" she asked.

"I thought I heard the girls, but I guess I didn't." He strode toward her, then stopped midstride in front of her bedroom door.

From where she was sitting, she could clearly see what was happening. She knew why Mr. Parker had stopped in front of her bedroom door. She knew what he had seen. He had discovered one portion of her Christmas gift to him, and her breathing became ragged.

"The wedding coverlet. . .you removed it." He looked at her questioningly.

"Yes," she said shyly.

He rushed to her, drew her up from the rocker, crushed her in his embrace. "My darling. . .Corinn Parker." He kissed her. "Say *my* name."

She looked up at him, wondering.

"Please?" he said.

"Mr. Parker."

"And my given name with it."

"Trevor Parker," she said timidly.

"I'm glad my name's Trevor Parker instead of John Smith," he said with a twinkle in his eye.

"Why?"

"If my name were John Smith, I wouldn't be able to enjoy your Scottish burr."

She smiled.

"I love the way you roll those r's."

"Yes, Mr. Trevor-r-r Par-r-r-ker-r-r, your-r-r name gives my tongue quite a wor-r-r-k-out."

He leaned over and kissed her, squeezing her to him.

When she was able, she murmured, "The rest of your Christmas gift is in *your* bedroom."

He drew back. "My bedroom?"

"Go see."

"Come with me." He took her hand, and they walked to his bedroom.

There, on his bed was a plaid wedding coverlet, only it was blue plaid, not red like the other one.

He smiled from ear to ear, then drew her into a tight embrace as he kept smiling. "You've been sewing it for weeks, haven't you?" He didn't wait for her answer. "I thought you were sewing Christmas things for the girls."

"I did that, too. But I've been working on our wedding coverlet since—"

"Since the sermon?"

She smiled, dipped her chin demurely, nodded. "I bought the fabric in town. . . with the money from the marmalade. . .the money you told me to keep."

He lifted her chin with his finger, forcing her to meet his sensuous gaze.

"The money I told you to use for yourself." Now *he* was smiling, and his eyebrows were going up and down, and he tipped his head in the direction of the wedding coverlet.

She knew her cheeks were flaming as she caught his meaning. She felt her heart racing. Encircled in his arms, she felt *his* heart racing. Love had finally come—to both of them—and she let out a little sigh.

He pointed to the framed sampler she had just completed and hung on the wall above his bed.

FLORIDA, MY HOPE AND HOME

He read it aloud, then repeated it, his voice husky. "Oh, Corinn. . .my darling."

She saw the two of them down through time, husband and wife—*certainly* not in name only—happily rearing a large family in this young, prosperity-filled state. Then a sad thought gnawed at her. If only she were a beautiful woman to grace the side of this tall, handsome gentleman who would one day be a person of public prominence.

"I'm plain." She tucked an errant lock of hair behind her ear, so thin it brushed back into her face.

"You're pretty."

"I'm uncomely."

"You're uncommonly lovely." He kissed the lock of her hair, then her lips, then drew back slightly. "I'll never forget the first moment I laid eyes on you. You were standing on the gangplank with that little beret on your head and your plaid about your shoulders. That's the moment I knew I loved you."

"You knew it then? That's what I was praying for as I stood there, trying to summon my courage to meet you. I prayed that you would love me as Isaac loved Rebekah."

"I do."

She giggled an Adeline giggle, couldn't help herself. "Yippee," she exclaimed, and Mr. Parker grinned.

" 'For sweet is thy voice, and thy countenance is comely,' " he quoted. "That's from Song of Solomon."

She gazed adoringly up at him. "Oh, Mr. Parker. My dear Mr. Parker. My beloved Trevor."

Chapter 13

Edith crept back into bed beside Adeline and adjusted her nightcap with her good arm. Then she snuggled down under the covers, gently elbowing her sister. "Marmsie is sleeping in Papa's bedroom tonight."

"Mawm-sie?"

"Yes. Marmsie. And I heard her say, 'Yippee.' "

Adeline giggled her delightful giggle.

"And there's a picture of Mama in the parlor."

Adeline giggled again.

" 'Night, Adeline."

" 'Night, Edith."

"Sleep tight, and don't let the bedbugs bite."

PROMISES KEPT

by Sally Laity

Chapter 1

1905—New York—Spring

If she lived to be a hundred, the briny smell of the ocean would forever bring joy and pleasure to Kiera MacPherson. The rolling gray-green waves had borne her all the way from northern Ireland to the eastern shores of this glorious new world, all the way to Sean O'Rourke. And if paved city streets, a veritable sea of tall buildings and stately residences, and the incessant cacophony of noises seemed a stark contrast to the verdant peace of their homeland, it was of little consequence. The two interminable years of separation had finally ended. Kiera and the second cousin to whom she had pledged her heart and her love would marry at long last. The very thought all but stole her breath.

She lost herself in fascinating new sights and sounds as a hired driver threaded his carriage through the thoroughfare clogged with pedestrians, horse-drawn trolleys, street peddlers, private conveyances, and chugging motor cars. Just inside her bodice, close to her heart, she had tucked Sean's last letter. She loosened the knitted shawl she wore over her best travel dress, recalling the words forever imprinted on her memory: *We'll have a wonderful life in this new land, I promise. Hurry to me, my love.*

Anticipating those jaunty eyes of his, to say nothing of his all-encompassing smile and manly bearing, Kiera felt her heart contract in exquisite pain. There was so much to tell her beloved. Details of her journey, news of mutual friends back home, the drawn-out humiliations at Ellis Island, and how thankful she was to have actually arrived here in Brooklyn to begin their life together. Within her bags, she had tucked her mother's wedding dress, hoping to wear it as she spoke her vows. Perhaps the gown would ensure her at least a portion of her late parents' happiness, rest their souls.

"We're here, lass," the gangly, black-bedecked driver announced, drawing in on the reins and halting his old mare. He hopped down and offered a hand.

Kiera's pulse raced, causing her fingers to tremble as she accepted his assistance and stepped out. She dug into her reticule for money while he set her bags on the curb. "I thank ye."

"My pleasure." His bony hand closing around the fare, he tipped his head politely and got back into his rig.

Kiera turned and perused the row of two-story brownstone townhomes, verifying the house number before taking a bag in either hand and going up the walkway. Placing her burdens on the stoop, she lifted the wrought-iron doorknocker and rapped lightly, nibbling her lip in anticipation of her betrothed's surprised and delighted expression.

The door opened to reveal a stranger.

"Yes?"

Kiera regarded the rumpled white shirt and dark suit, the thinning hair, the faded blue eyes behind rimless eyeglasses. " 'Tis the wrong address I have, to be sure," she mumbled, her flagging spirit plummeting to her worn button-top shoes. " 'Twas Sean O'Rourke I was expectin' to find."

The aging man offered a smile. "Of course. You must be the cousin. Mrs. O'Rourke mentioned you might be arriving one of these days. Do come in, miss. I'm Dr. Browning." Reaching past her for her bags, he set them inside while she entered.

Her eyes made a swift circuit of the modest but tidy room with its overstuffed furniture draped with Irish linen scarves and fine lace curtains at the windows. Pleasant, familiar sights. Then, the manner in which the gentleman had referred to himself dawned on her. "A doctor, ye say? Is someone ill?"

He nodded, a grim smile deepening the grooves in his already-lined face. "Your cousin has been ailing for some time now. Especially since—" Clearing his throat uneasily, he gestured for her to precede him up the narrow staircase. "Her room's the first one to the right."

Kiera looped her shawl over the banister at the end of the railing and set her straw bonnet atop it, a strange foreboding creeping into her as she climbed the steps.

The bedchamber seemed close and stale as she entered, but Dr. Browning crossed the room and opened the heavy curtains. Immediately, sunlight flooded over the rather ordinary furnishings. The cheery colors of a worn, handmade quilt, turned down to the foot of the bed, seemed somehow out of place.

"Auntie Kathleen," Kiera said softly, using the affectionate title she had adopted since early childhood because of their difference in age. Approaching the still form lying under a sheet and light blanket, her heart ached at the realization of how old and frail her relative appeared in comparison to when they'd bid one another farewell on the quay behind Guildhall two years prior. Hair that once had been bright red and as thick as her son's had thinned and faded to pale blond. Her formerly plump frame had diminished to little more than a collection of angles and hollows.

"Kiera? You've come, lass?" she whispered. Her small, tired eyes swam with tears as she reached weakly toward Kiera.

"Aye, 'tis me." A wave of affection flowed through Kiera as she bent to hug the older woman. "And a fine way to be greetin' your favorite cousin this is," she said lightly, reverting to the easy way they once had of speaking to each other. "And where's that wild son of yours, I ask? I thought 'twould be his merry face greetin' me at the door."

At this, her cousin's breath caught on a sob. Her lips moved, but no sound emerged as she reached out for the doctor before again meeting Kiera's gaze.

The physician stepped nearer and put a hand on Kiera's shoulder. "I'm afraid we have some bad news to convey, miss."

"Oh." She straightened. "So he's still off at his job, is he? The barge canal he wrote about in his letters. Well, after two long years, I'll not mind waitin' another day or so."

But the kindly gentleman remained silent, his expression grave. Grave. . .and something worse.

Dread crept up Kiera's spine as she looked from him to Auntie Kathleen and back again. "Sure and you're not tellin' me he's gone off and married some other girl, now, are ye?"

"There's been an accident," the doctor began.

Alarm weakened Kiera's legs. "Sean's in a hospital, then. Just tell me where he is. I'll go visit—"

A slow shake of the graying head.

Her knees buckled. She sank to the bed. "But you're not sayin'—I mean, he isn't—" Hopelessly she latched onto her cousin's limp hand resting beside hers. "Auntie, please tell me Sean is just sick somewhere. Or hurt, even. I can stand that, if only—"

But the grim faces she searched only confirmed her worst fears. Her head grew light, making the doctor's voice, as he spoke the appalling words, sound fuzzy and far away.

"He was killed, Miss MacPherson. Two weeks ago. I. . .can't tell you how terribly sorry I am."

Two weeks ago. . .while she endured the tedious and meticulous processing at Ellis Island. She had been detained without visitors until a nagging lung inflammation cleared up. Those precious last days they might have been together—now forever wasted.

Kiera saw a huge tear roll from the corner of Kathleen's eye. A lump clogged her own throat, closing her air passage. She couldn't possibly utter a word, even if her very life depended upon it. This was all a horrid nightmare. Surely. Nothing could have happened to Sean, her redheaded giant. He was big and strong, the hardiest of all the young men she had known back home. Why, at any moment he would stride through the door and sweep her off her feet in an exuberant hug.

But as the dire realization slowly permeated her consciousness, she felt the hopes and dreams of a lifetime shrivel and die within her. Along with all of Sean's beautiful promises. And in their place loomed an unspeakable void. Dark. Cold. Far too deep for tears. Numbly, Kiera forced her legs to stand. She had to get out of this room. Go someplace where she could breathe. Think.

A place where she could reconcile herself to the senseless cruelty of fate and decide what in the world she would do now.

The longest fortnight of Kiera's life drew slowly to a close. Sleepless nights of weeping had taken their toll. Utterly spent and emotionally drained, she trudged home after work, her hands still gummy from mounting photographs in the dim confines of the photographer's back room. Each sepia-toned picture she had studied served as a sad reminder. Her mental picture of Sean was already an ever-fading shadow of the once-sharp image. And thoughts of the week's pitiful wages now stashed in her reticule brought a bitter grimace in the fading light of day.

Not one of the glowing reports about life in the New World that she had read in her "America letters" from Sean or heard from the emigrant agents who roamed Londonderry and the surrounding villages had prepared Kiera for reality. Here in New York she had seen so many "No Irish need apply" notices posted alongside employment opportunities that she was teetering on the verge of despair. Finally, she stumbled upon the photographer's establishment. The position consisted of only half days and paid very little. But from what she gathered, women typically earned a mere fraction of what men were paid for similar work anyway.

Not that such things mattered. Nothing mattered anymore. If only Sean had sent her more funds, she would have bought passage on the first ship back to Ireland. But that was out of the question. Auntie Kathleen needed her now. Somehow, Kiera must take care of them both. She had no other recourse.

Reaching their street, she tried to manufacture some semblance of cheerfulness for the moment when she would greet Auntie Kathleen. The older woman had taken her son's death extremely hard, and her health, already poor, had steadily declined ever since. She needed whatever gaiety Kiera could muster.

Oddly enough, she found the front door closed. Normally it stood ajar to permit freshening breezes to waft through the house, as well as to allow their kind neighbor free access to look in on Kathleen. But Kiera attributed the closed state to the growing darkness, and she quietly slipped inside to start supper.

Just then, Dr. Browning came down the stairs.

He did not need to say a word. Kiera could tell from his expression. "Auntie is. . ."

A nod.

In slender currents comes good luck; in rolling torrents comes misfortune. Never had the old proverb seemed so true. First Sean. Now cousin Kathleen. Wordlessly, Kiera sank to the nearest chair and covered her face in her hands.

Almost immediately she felt the doctor's empathetic hand on her shoulder, but it was a long moment until he spoke, his tones gentle. "I'll help you with the arrangements. And afterward, when you are able to consider it, I may have a new position for you, caring for another patient of mine. I've noticed how good you were with Mrs. O'Rourke, and I think this particular opportunity would be to your advantage."

Completely numb inside, Kiera barely listened, hearing the details only on the fringes, as if they were being related to someone else. But slowly they sank in. A place to live. A prominent family. Better wages. She could only nod, and the doctor squeezed her shoulder.

Days later, after Kathleen O'Rourke's ravaged body had been laid to its final rest, Kiera forced herself to deal with the wrenching chore of sorting through the belongings that her cousin and her son had left behind. So many items still bore lingering traces of their owners' scents. She could only hug them and sob until there were no tears left inside.

Coming upon Sean's bank deposit book, she discovered the revelation of a tidy, growing sum. He had obviously been setting aside funds for their marriage. . . until the last large withdrawal for an investment that, according to his mother, had turned out to be a fraudulent scheme. Too late to rue his foolhardiness now.

But other items brought tender memories, thoughts of their former life in Ireland. A treasured pocket watch that had belonged to Sean's now-deceased father, Padraic, still bore the chain Kiera had scrimped and saved months to buy as a parting gift before Sean sailed for America. Not even bothering to dry her cheeks as she wrapped the object in an intricately embroidered linen scarf, she placed the treasure in a trunk containing the other mementos with which she could not part. Others, unfamiliar and meaningless, she would leave to cover the funeral and burial. Then she packed her own possessions and walked out of the rented house without looking back.

❧

"Thank you, Kingsley. This way, miss." Excusing the loyal household servant with a tip of his head, Devon Hamilton led the newly hired Irish girl upstairs to her quarters. Petite, with skin like porcelain and a head full of glorious light-brown curls bent on escaping the prim bun at the nape of her neck, she seemed somewhat aloof, at loose ends. She had barely even smiled. He wondered if such a somber individual would really fit in here with his family, but she came with Doc Browning's highest recommendations. Perhaps all she needed was a chance. "You'll find this room, being next to Mother's, quite handy. If she needs you, you'll easily hear her bell."

With little more than a cursory glance around the comfortably furnished bedroom, she looked up at him. He started at the vacant quality within the blue-green depths of her eyes.

"I thank ye, sir. 'Tis fine enough."

He nodded. "Well, I see Kingsley has already retrieved your luggage, so I'll leave you to unpack. If there is anything else you need, just let him know. We trust you shall enjoy working here. When Mother awakens from her nap, one of us will escort you to her room and introduce you."

Kiera gave another dutiful nod. "When I've put away me things, I'll go down and help with supper, then."

"That won't be necessary, Miss MacPherson. You shall have your own duties to tend. Mother needs someone to keep her company and run for things. With the rest of the staff busy elsewhere, she's certain to find you a blessing."

"Indeed." The word came out on a caustic note. "I'll do me best, sir."

Captivated by her lilting voice, Devon did not miss the sag of her fragile shoulder or the droop of her head as she turned away and started toward the bags left at the foot of her bed. It was almost as if she lacked any spirit at all. Well, whatever the reasons for her melancholy, perhaps she would soon overcome them. If nothing else, he must make it a matter of prayer. Perhaps the reason the Lord had brought her here was as much for her to *find* help as to be a help.

Devon took one last look at the fetching lass then quietly closed the door.

363

Chapter 2

t the faint click of the latch, Kiera released a ragged breath and took a closer look at her new living quarters. The Hamilton mansion, situated on Madison Avenue within strolling distance of beautiful Central Park, had to be the most elegant she had ever seen. Certainly a far cry from either the cramped stone cottage of her childhood or Cousin Kathleen's rented row house in Brooklyn. Were it not for the empty ache inside, she might have thought this all a dream.

Decidedly feminine rose-printed paper adorned the walls, and lush floral-patterned rugs cushioned the polished wood floor. And what hired help would have expected a lace canopy intertwined with a garland of pink roses to crown the cherrywood bed, or a mattress so thick it would likely be soft as heaven's own clouds? Her tattered travel case seemed almost a desecration atop the immaculate satin coverlet—like a dingy blot on the shiny rose and ivory splendor. But aware that she could be summoned at any time to meet the mistress of the house, she sighed and began unpacking her meager belongings.

Her unpacking chore completed, she closed the ornate carved doors of the wardrobe. Moving to the open window, she parted the Belgian lace panels. Her breath caught at the broad expanse of manicured grounds below. Myriad flowers and sculptured shrubbery added to the grandeur of a marble fountain flanked by curved benches. Truly, this place was fit for a king.

If only Sean could have seen it.

But before that thought could render its usual bout of anguish, Kiera took a deep breath and focused her concentration on identifying the blooms whose fragrance perfumed the mild breeze even now stirring the curtains.

A light knock carried through the door, and she went at once to answer.

"Mother has awakened," Devon Hamilton announced with a polite smile. "She'll be having tea shortly. I thought you might take some with her." Wide-set sable eyes the identical shade of his wavy hair and tailored pinstriped suit twinkled as he awaited her response.

"Thank ye, sir." Now that he mentioned it, a cup of tea sounded more than appealing. But following her employer's long strides across the portrait-lined hallway, she felt a nervous chill and shivered, despite the day's warm temperature. What would the lady of the house be like? Hopefully as pleasant as her son, with some of the same handsome, patrician features. Still, Kiera wished she had asked Dr. Browning for his address, just in case this position was unsatisfactory.

Mr. Hamilton paused in the partially open doorway. "I've brought someone to meet you, Mother." He gestured for Kiera to precede him.

Tamping down her apprehension, Kiera schooled her expression into one she hoped appeared calm as she crossed the threshold.

A world of variegated greens enveloped her. Wallpaper, curtains, bedclothes, even the rich Persian carpet—all bore varying shades of the hue, made all the more lovely by an occasional touch of peach and burgundy. Occupying the center of a massive bedstead, a dignified lady in a satin bed jacket reclined against a mountain of pillows. Wisps of silver hair from two thin braids stuck out in disarray around her pasty, lined face, evidence of restless sleep.

"Mother," Mr. Hamilton began, "this is Kiera MacPherson, referred to us by Doc Browning to be your companion."

"Companion!" the well-modulated voice echoed. "With a houseful of loyal servants already, I fail to see the need to take on new help." Her thin lips pursed as she crossed her arms over her bosom.

Feeling like an unwelcome intruder, Kiera flinched.

"Nevertheless," he went on, "Kiera is now part of the household. Let's give her a chance, shall we?"

"As if I have a choice in the matter," the invalid returned. "I still say the very idea is redundant. If you and Alexandria would simply get married, I'd have plenty of. . . genteel company." Then she switched her focus to Kiera. "Well, come closer, girl. Let me have a look at you."

"Mistress," Kiera murmured. And with each dutiful step across the room, she felt keenly aware of the matriarch's critical assessment. Only with the greatest effort could she meet those probing hazel eyes, particularly considering the grim expression on the regal face.

"I trust you possess more presentable clothes." She flicked a glance of distaste toward her son before eyeing Kiera once more. "What is your name again?"

Still smarting from the lady's outright rudeness, it was difficult to answer. "Kiera, madam."

"Irish, no less."

"Aye."

"And as such, it's doubtful you can read."

Rather offended by the queenly attitude, Kiera raised her own chin. "My father was a respected schoolmaster who insisted that I gain an education, mum." At the mention of her dear parent, one of his favorite quotations came to mind, *Character is better than wealth*, but she wisely left the saying unspoken.

The presumptuous mistress gave a grudging nod. "Ah. So you've one point in your favor."

"And likely not to be the only one, Mother," her son declared. "You'll see."

"Humph. I insist you dismiss the girl at once. Companion, indeed."

'Tis fine with me, Kiera nearly blurted. Cutting a glance toward the man of the house, she surmised this to be as good a time as any to bolt.

But the arrival of the tea tray blocked her escape route.

Staying Kiera with a hand on her shoulder, Devon Hamilton didn't seem put off in the least by his mother's ill manners. In fact, he did not even respond to her last remarks. "Thank you, Louella." He took the refreshments from the slim, auburn-haired servant and placed them on the bedside table. "I'm afraid I have other matters to attend just now." He offered Kiera an encouraging smile. "I'll leave you two to get acquainted over your tea, if you don't mind pouring."

She looked at him in confusion. "As ye wish, sir." Having noted a bed tray resting on its side against the wall, Kiera picked it up and positioned it carefully over the invalid's lap. She tried to ignore the disgruntled expression leveled at her in the wake of Mr. Hamilton's departure. Then, willing her fingers to remain steady, she filled a china cup with the steaming liquid and set it before the lady, along with a linen napkin and a spoon. "Will ye be takin' cream or sugar, mistress?"

A grunt. A pause.

Kiera handed the embellishments one at a time to the older woman, paying close attention to the amounts she used. "And there are some lovely biscuits and stewed apricots, as well."

"The kitchen staff is bent upon fattening me up," Mrs. Hamilton said tartly.

"Or perhaps tryin' to restore roses to your cheeks," Kiera ventured. As she served a little of both delicacies, one of her grandmother's proverbs flitted through her thoughts. *Soft words butter no parsnips, but they won't harden the heart of the cabbage either.*

Not even the hint of a smile gentled the woman's features.

Whether a show of good humor might bestow a greater resemblance to her son remained to be seen, Kiera decided. But since her charge had been tended to, she filled the remaining cup and helped herself to a sweet biscuit before claiming the emerald velvet chair nearby. There she sat, prim and stiff, gazing at anything and everything except her mistress. Given the choice, she would have gladly taken her leave from this position, this woman, and even this house, fine as it was. What could the kind doctor have been thinking, to send her here, of all places?

Endless minutes ticked by before Mrs. Hamilton's voice punctured the stillness. "Have you been long in America?"

"No, mum. I've only recently arrived."

"You've no family?"

Kiera swallowed so quickly, she all but scalded her throat. "Not anymore, mum." *And don't be askin' me to explain,* she pleaded inwardly.

A few moments of silence followed, during which the invalid continued to appraise her between sips of tea. "Well, if I'm to be stuck with you, I should like to hear you read."

"Certainly, madam." She returned her now-empty cup to the refreshment tray. Then, noting that Mrs. Hamilton had also consumed her tea, she removed the tray while the woman reclined against the pillows. "Is there somethin' special you'd be havin' me read, then? A book you've started, perhaps?"

"Something from the Psalms. The ninety-first."

"The Psalms, mum?"

A nod. "The Bible is there on the table."

Not exactly acquainted with the Holy Book, Kiera wondered how she might conceal that fact. To her utmost relief, she discovered a list of its contents inside the front cover. She quickly found the correct section and turned to Psalm 91:

" 'He that dwelleth in the secret place of the most High shall abide under the shadow of the Almighty. I will say of the Lord, He is my refuge and my fortress: my God; in him will I trust. ...' "

Even as she continued reading the unfamiliar passage, Kiera wondered at the meaning concealed in the verses. It was not hard to imagine Almighty God living in some secret and lofty place unattainable by mere man. But how could someone call Him a refuge, much less actually place trust in an unknown Being? Those thoughts kept her from concentrating on what else she was reading, until she noticed the end looming near:

" 'Because he hath set his love upon me, therefore will I deliver him: I will set him on high, because he hath known my name. He shall call upon me, and I will answer him: I will be with him in trouble; I will deliver him, and honour him. With long life will I satisfy him, and shew him my salvation.' "

These verses further confused Kiera. Who was speaking? And to whom? But having reached the last verse of the psalm, she hesitated and glanced at Mrs. Hamilton.

"You read quite well." The pronouncement offered mild gratification. "But that is enough for now. You may return to your room."

"Aye, mistress." With a bow of her head, Kiera set the Bible back in its place and picked up the tray of soiled dishes. At least returning them downstairs would occupy some of this strangely long day. . .made all the more uncomfortable as Kiera sensed the woman's stare until she stepped out of her line of vision.

Even while she descended the wide staircase to the main floor, Kiera imagined herself wandering the grand manse in search of the kitchen, but fortunately Kingsley approached her at the landing.

"May I be of service, miss?" The friendly sparkle in the old gentleman's eyes complemented his smile, one incredibly white against his immaculate black suit.

Noting his amiable expression, Kiera liked him immediately. From the top of his snowy-white hair to the soles of his polished shoes, everything about the man exuded an air of pleasant confidence. "The kitchen, if ye please."

He gave a polite tip of his head. "Right this way." He led her down the hall past the drawing room and library to another corridor hung with staid ancestral portraits. At last they reached the kitchen, yet another showplace filled with the very latest in modern advancements.

Kiera tried not to gawk at the wondrous delights gleaming at her from cupboards and walls, where iron hooks held polished copper and tinware pots within easy reach.

And, oh, such a stove.

"Halloo everyone," Kingsley said in a booming voice.

The hustle and bustle in the busy room ceased as two women looked up from their food preparations. Both of them wore crisp uniforms of dove gray with crisp white collars, aprons, and cuffs.

If this is how the servants of the household usually dress, Kiera thought, wincing inwardly, *'tis no wonder the mistress looks with scorn upon someone whose very best attire leaves much to be desired.*

"This is madam's new companion, Miss Kiera MacPherson," Kingsley said. Relieving her of the tray, he took it to the drain board as he gestured with his head toward the stocky, gray-haired cook. "My good wife, Cora, and over at the worktable is Louella. She has her cap set for the butcher man, but we can still claim her for a spell yet."

"Pleased to meet you," slender, freckle-faced Louella said, a flush pinking her cheeks. Her knife remained poised above the fresh carrots she had been chopping.

"Aren't we now," the cook said, beaming. She dried her hands on her apron and crossed the room. "You'll save the lot of us a few steps, I'd say. Welcome to the house, Miss MacPherson."

"Kiera. Please," she urged, smiling and offering a hand.

Immediately her fingers were grasped by ones pudgy and warm. "I trust the mistress was in good humor today," Cora said, and a conspiratorial grin made the rounds at Kiera's silence. "Oh, she does have a good heart inside her. Give her time."

Kiera nodded, hoping they weren't merely being kind.

"Are you hungry, child? We were just about to have some supper. Here, take this seat, and tell us all about yourself while we finish up." Even as Cora spoke, her husband yanked a chair out from the already-set table and nudged Kiera down with gentle pressure on her shoulder while his wife brought another place setting.

❧

By the time she reached the quiet solitude of her own bedchamber after supper, Kiera felt as if she had made some new friends. She truly liked the other staff members and looked forward to the warm relationship that would surely follow. Perhaps one day she would even share her recent sorrows with them.

But Mrs. Hamilton had not rung for her again. Even once. Was the woman so adamant about not needing a companion that Kiera would find herself dismissed on the morrow? And if so, what then?

With Sean gone, was there any point in remaining in America, this land of empty promises? Everything was strange here. Strange and foreign.

Kiera had no living relatives back in Londonderry. Still, the town within those great seventeenth-century walls was achingly familiar. She missed the main thoroughfare of Shipsquay Street and the narrow streets that fingered out from it. She missed the craft village behind O'Doherty Tower...and the splendid views across the sea to the Scottish coast...and Donegal, which she had seen with Sean on the mountain road to Limavady. The Irish way of doing things provided solace. Ireland was home—would always be home.

Renewed purpose flowed through her being. She would work hard here, or at whatever other position she could find, and save every cent. And as soon as she acquired sufficient funds, she would book her return passage for home.

Chapter 3

Rising at dawn's first light, Kiera quickly recited her morning prayers and completed her toilette, then hurried downstairs to the kitchen.

"Well, aren't you the early bird?" Cora Phillips teased, elbowing her husband in the ribs. Already dressed for the day, the couple sat at breakfast.

"I wondered if I'd be expected to take a tray up to the mistress," Kiera admitted. "I shouldn't want to keep her waitin'."

"You can relax on that score, lass," Kingsley assured her, idly fingering a tip of his short handlebar mustache. "Madam never opens her eyes before nine, and we see to her meals. But you come and have a bite with us."

"How about a nice coddled egg?" Cora stood and crossed to the stove.

"Sure and I don't expect ye to be waitin' on me, now. I can do for meself."

"No doubt," the cook answered. "But as it happens, our Louella hasn't made an appearance yet, so this one will soon go to waste."

"Then I shall have it, and I thank ye for it."

The stocky woman removed the cooked egg from the warming oven and brought it in a small bowl to the table, where two more places had been laid out in readiness. She filled the coffee cups and smoothed her apron before reclaiming her seat.

Kiera smiled her appreciation and took a chair, but an awkward moment passed before she touched the food.

"Don't mind us, child," Cora said gently. "If you'd like to say your grace, you just go ahead. We've already prayed."

With a sigh of relief, Kiera murmured the prayer her family had always used:

Bless us, O Lord,
Bless our food and drink,
You who have so dearly redeemed us
And have saved us from evil,
As You have given us this share of food,
May You give us our share of the everlasting glory.

She thought she imagined a curious look pass between the older pair opposite her, but they made no comment as she helped herself to a warm scone from a plate in the middle of the table and dipped the sweet bread into the moist egg.

"Did you sleep well, lass?" Kingsley asked.

"Oh my, 'twas the most restful I've been in ages. On such a grand bed, how could a body do otherwise?" She bit into the buttered biscuit and chewed slowly. "And did ye both have a good night, too?"

Cora nodded. "But we're expecting a busy day today. Master Landon and his bride are returning from their honeymoon and will be here for supper. He's the younger son," she added. "I'm sure Master Devon will be eager to hear about the wedding trip. And Miss Alexandria, what with her upcoming marriage to him, will make it a lively foursome."

"Well," snowy-haired Kingsley cut in, "if you ladies will excuse me, I'd best see to the garden. We'll need flowers for the centerpiece." He lightly tweaked his wife's kitchen cap, then smiled at Kiera. "You take your time, lass." With a last gulp of his remaining coffee, he got up, shoving the chair back with his legs. The sudden force sent it toppling.

Kiera almost choked. A chair falling when a person rose signified an unlucky omen. But the Phillips couple did not appear the least concerned as Kingsley righted the thing and took his leave. She blotted her lips on her napkin and vowed to be extra careful all day. To be on the safe side, she whispered her after-meal prayer when Cora went outside to shake the braided throw rug:

Praise to the King of Plenty,
Praise every time to God,
A hundred praises and thanks to Jesus Christ,
For what we have eaten and shall eat.

With no reason to hurry, Kiera lingered over a second cup of coffee, basking in Cora's quiet chatter before heading back upstairs to await Mrs. Hamilton's bidding. But when she reached her room, a virtual mountain of gray-striped boxes in assorted sizes all but blocked her doorway. Each had a burgundy lid, with the name Hamilton embossed across the top in gold script.

※

Seeing a red-faced Kingsley and a grinning Devon Hamilton approaching, their arms laden with still more, Kiera gasped. "Whatever is all this?"

"We expected to finish before you came up," the old servant blurted.

But nothing caught the man of the house off his guard. "You'll find that the boxes contain just a few things we hope you can use," he said with nonchalance.

"A few things, is it now? And how can I be takin' so much from ye, I ask?"

"It's not that much," he replied. "And surely nothing to trouble yourself over. After all, we do own the store."

Kiera, however, had a different opinion. *Take gifts with a sigh; most men give to be paid*. She could only wonder what particular payment she would be forced to render.

"Why, it's perfectly fine, lass," Kingsley offered in calm assurance. "The madam likes all the staff to look sharp and fashionable."

"Then I'm not to be let go, after all?"

"Far from it," Mr. Hamilton said. "I'm the one who hired you. You stay unless I personally give you the boot, and I'm not about to do so anytime soon." He turned to the older man. "Well, let's tote these boxes into her room, while we're at it. She'll want to put everything away herself, I'm sure."

Kiera stepped aside to allow the two free access. Never had she seen such a quantity of stylish boxes at one time, much less been the recipient. Watching the men as they neatly stacked the packages near the bed, her heartbeat quickened at the mere thought of peeking inside each one. New clothes. American clothes. . .for her. She hadn't expected any immediate personal benefits to her chore of tending a cross-tempered matriarch.

"Well, that's the last of them, Miss MacPherson," her employer announced while Kingsley brushed off the sleeves of his suit and returned to his duties. "If the buyer forgot anything, do let me know, and we'll rectify the situation."

For one terrifying moment, Kiera felt tears gathering behind her eyes. She swallowed the huge lump forming in her throat. "Y–yes, Mr. Hamilton. And. . .thank ye, sir. I've never. . ." Overcome, she lifted a hand in a mute gesture.

He gave an understanding nod. "We want you to feel at home here, Kiera. I trust you will approve the clerk's choices. She's quite knowledgeable about what women are wearing these days."

"But still. . ."

"Remember, as it says in the Bible, our heavenly Father knows when His children have needs."

Against her better judgment, Kiera could not help but speak her mind. "And where might it say that? Seems to me quite a few of those same children have been in need for some time, and still are, in truth."

His dark eyes softened with his smile. "Well, now, I'm not altogether sure of the passage offhand, but I'll look it up so you can read it for yourself, if you'd like."

"Aye. Thank ye. And I truly am most grateful for your kindness."

He grinned and tipped his head, then left, closing the door after himself.

Kiera surveyed her bounty. Where to start. Nibbling her bottom lip as she gazed at the largest parcels, she snatched a smaller one from the top of a pile, to work her way down.

Several pairs of soft kid leather shoes, camisoles, chemises, nightgowns, and bonnets to match a glorious array of summer gowns later, Kiera felt like a princess in a fairy tale. Nothing had been omitted, from lacy shawls to combs for her hair to modest jewelry with matching earbobs. She breathed a wordless prayer of gratitude over her good fortune and began putting her lovely new wardrobe away. All, that is, except for a lavender organdy day gown with embroidered daisies on the bodice. She would wear her favorite color when she greeted her mistress. Slipping off her own worn but serviceable attire, she returned them to the armoire, then donned the new dress, running her hands down the delicate fabric in awe. Even as she brushed her long curls and caught the sides back with ivory combs, she could hardly stop staring at her reflection. She only hoped the mistress would approve.

Soon enough, the bell rang.

Kiera started and jumped to her feet. Then, taking a calming breath, she went at once to the matriarch's bedroom, where she rapped softly and entered. "Top o' the mornin' to ye, mum. Will ye be takin' breakfast now?"

"Yes." The hazel eyes widened, then narrowed again as quickly. "I daresay, you're looking much more presentable today. Not so dowdy as before."

"Thank ye, mistress." Kiera supposed she would get used to the criticisms eventually. She pushed the heavy draperies aside to let light flood the room. "Just look," she exclaimed, admiring the gardens below. " 'Tis a grand mornin'. I'll go see about your tray."

But even as she spoke, Louella Banks appeared at the door with the woman's breakfast. A bit flushed, the servant seemed eager to be relieved of her burden.

Kiera nodded her thanks and had the invalid all set up in short order, somewhat gratified when her charge displayed a bit of appetite. From now on, Kiera determined, a vase with a fresh flower would brighten each meal tray—and perhaps an arrangement of fragrant blooms for the room. No sense in their wilting outside, unseen by the person who had likely planned that wondrous garden. She planned to discuss the matter with Kingsley.

"Is there anything in particular you'd like me to be doin' for ye when you've finished, mum?"

A weary sigh emerged. "Yes. My hair must look a sight. I should like it brushed."

"Certainly. And I can help you freshen up, if you'd direct me to your clean bed jackets. You'll be wantin' to look special for your son and his wife, I'd expect."

Mrs. Hamilton eyed her in contemplation, then gave a nod. "Yes, that is today. I'd forgotten." She paused. "Are you always so. . .cheerful?"

Kiera had to smile. "Morning is my favorite part of the day, mistress. 'Tis so bright with hope and promise, with so many good things likely to happen. To be sure, there's little sense in imagining clouds when the sunshine's so glorious."

"Indeed."

Amazingly, the remainder of the morning passed quite pleasantly, and Mrs. Hamilton, all washed and sporting a pale-green bed gown, actually smiled while Kiera brushed and rebraided her hair. "You have quite a gentle touch, I must say. The others always seem to be in a hurry and invariably yank too hard."

"Well, I've no reason to rush. I'm here to make sure you're rested and comfortable, mum." Returning the costly silver brush to the dressing table, she turned. "Would ye like me to read now?"

But the crowning moment came at lunchtime, with the arrival of the lunch tray.

"A rose!" the older woman cried in surprise. "I'd almost forgotten the lovely garden fragrances, being cooped up in here for weeks and weeks."

Kiera merely smiled. "Perhaps 'tis time we take you out for some sunshine and a stroll around the grounds."

Mrs. Hamilton grimaced. "It's been too much bother for the staff to fuss over an old woman who needs to be carted around."

"Well, 'tis no bother to me. I'll speak to Kingsley."

A noticeable change in atmosphere settled over the sickroom from that point. And not long after eating, the invalid nodded off, providing Kiera with a little time to herself. She dashed downstairs to chat with Cora.

"Oh, just the one I wanted to see," the cook said when Kiera breezed into the kitchen. "Our Louella is a mite under the weather. Could you possibly help serve supper this evening? We do have company coming, if you recall."

"Aye, I remember. I'm as able to be helpin' out as I am to sit in me room with a book, I'd say."

"Thank you, child. I'll get you a clean uniform. You're about the same size as she, though perhaps a bit trimmer about the waist. With a tuck here and there, her things should fit well enough." Going to a small room off the kitchen, she removed a complete outfit and brought it to Kiera.

"When should I be ready?"

"We'll be serving at eight. That's after the mistress has finished her own meal, of course. No doubt she'll excuse you so her sons can visit her awhile."

"Fine. I'll be only too glad to be lendin' a hand. In the meanwhile, is there somethin' I can do to help with the cookin'?"

She shook her head. "No, dearie, not a thing. I've seen to all of that, and there's naught to do but wait for it all to finish."

"And what about the table?"

"King helped with that awhile ago. I won't impose upon you until about seven or so."

"Oh, 'tis no imposition in the least." Kiera regarded the older woman, debating whether to bring up the subject of her morning, yet she saw no reason to avoid the matter. "I. . .suppose you've heard how I happened to come into an incredible variety of new clothing earlier today."

A knowing smile added two more creases in the plump face, and Cora reached across the worktable to give her an empathetic pat on the forearm. "Ah, Master Devon is as generous to us all often enough. Always eager to do for others less fortunate. That's just his way."

Just his way. Kiera pondered that concept as she left the kitchen and carried the uniform to her room. Would the brother Landon be similarly disposed? And what would her employer's fiancée, Alexandria, be like? 'Twould be interesting to see his taste in women. Not that it was any concern of hers. She'd just always been curious by nature.

Chapter 4

At the immense walnut desk in the library, Devon raked splayed fingers through his hair and closed the tiresome accounts folder, pushing it aside. He reached for his Bible instead, opening to the New Testament. He had recently read the passage he quoted to Kiera, and he knew it was in the Gospels.

Sure enough, he came across the passage he sought in the sixth chapter of Matthew. *Consider the lilies. . . .* "Perfect."

Stretching a kink out of his neck, he leaned back in the leather chair and idly scanned the bookshelves lining two walls of the room. His gaze fell upon his grandmother's tattered Bible, the most precious memento of his childhood. Hard to believe a dozen years had passed since Grandma Hamilton had gone to be with the Lord. She had been such a presence in his world. Devon could still envision her spindly frame in her favorite rocking chair on the sunporch, aged head in a ribboned house cap as she pored over the Scriptures. So lovingly she had penned notes in the margins, writing down the insights gained during her times of quiet study and prayer. In the treasure house of his mind, the echo of that quavering voice still proclaimed God's goodness, still encouraged him to be a faithful follower of the Lord. How fervently she had prayed that one of her grandsons would go into the ministry.

Well, at least I came close to fulfilling her desire, Devon reminded himself as he exhaled. He had chosen to enroll in theological college at Princeton, rather than attending Columbia, as his parents preferred. But who would have expected Father to die so suddenly of a heart attack two years ago, leaving the entire Hamilton merchandising enterprise in dire need of a new head? As eldest son and having worked under his father's tutelage for quite a few summers, Devon could do no less than assume the responsibility permanently. Strange, the way life worked out, often so contrary to one's dearest dreams.

But this opportunity to search the Scriptures once more—even though not in the same depth he once did at college—brought back forgotten memories—and forgotten pleasure. Certainly the ministry had to be one of the most satisfying and valuable careers, guiding people in their life decisions, aiding in time of distress, doing something that counted for eternity. High time he made personal Bible study a habit again. Even a lay-person could obey God's instruction to be a workman who needeth not to be ashamed, one ready to give an answer for the hope within.

"Someone in this very house needs some of those answers, Lord," he prayed in the quietness as his thoughts drifted to his mother's new companion. "Use me to help her find them."

He smiled to himself, recalling how Kiera MacPherson had been almost overwhelmed at the paltry items the buyer at Hamilton's selected. A peaches-and-cream complexion like hers couldn't belong to someone more than twenty, yet those ocean-blue eyes contained experience and wisdom beyond her years. And, after listening to Dr. Browning relate the young woman's encounters with hardship in America, Devon felt compelled to make up to her for some of them. . .sort of assist those circumstances in working together for good, as the apostle Paul wrote in Romans.

"And perhaps that old Bible will have new purpose, too," he declared. "Grandma would like that." Rising, he strode to the bookshelf and took it down.

❧

Kiera had never served at a formal supper before, but Cora's advice to stick close and follow her lead went a long way in lessening the possible nervousness. A dutiful step behind the cook as they brought the food into the dining room, Kiera tried not to stare in openmouthed delight. Everything looked exquisite in the light cast by the crystal chandelier—including the elegantly coifed women guests, whose gowns and jewels sparkled with every movement and whose soft laughs could be heard as they sipped lemonade from long-stemmed goblets. The heady perfume of the summer flowers Kingsley had placed in a cut-glass vase on the lace tablecloth almost overpowered that of the Cornish hens in orange sauce on Kiera's tray.

"Mmm. Cora, you have outdone yourself, as always," Devon Hamilton told her upon her approach. "If anyone ever tries to lure you away from us, just tell me, and I'll double their offer."

"Oh, pshaw," she said, obviously accustomed to such good-natured teasing. "As if I'd be happy anywhere but here with you and the madam." Placing one of the golden birds on his plate, she moved on to serve the willowy honey blond to his right.

Noting the perfect oval face, delicate features, and full, rosy lips, Kiera surmised this was his fiancée, Alexandria. The young man occupying the foot of the table had eyes only for the shy, fragile-looking brunette next to him, whose hand rested lightly atop his, their fingers loosely intertwined.

As Kiera drew closer, the blond raised her lashes, revealing the bluest eyes Kiera had ever seen. Though somewhat lacking in warmth, they contained more than a little interest. "And whom have we here, darling?" she asked, favoring Devon with a dazzling smile. "Has little Louella been replaced?"

Seemingly taken aback at the sight of Kiera, Mr. Hamilton tipped his head toward his fiancée. "Actually, this is Mother's new companion, Kiera MacPherson." But confusion colored his tone, and he glanced toward the cook.

"Louella fell ill this evening," she supplied. "I imposed upon the lass to help out."

"Ah."

"Your mother requires a companion?" Alexandria asked him. "When did all this come about?"

He gave a noncommittal shrug. "It was my idea, dear heart. The staff's been so busy lately, she was feeling neglected."

"Oh, what a shame, when something as simple as moving our wedding date forward might have forestalled such a need." Her gaze assessed Kiera more closely. . . as did the others at the table.

"Miss MacPherson has been a real godsend to us," her fiancé quickly added.

The center of attention and discussed as if she wasn't even present, Kiera felt her face heating. She tried not to wilt under everyone's scrutiny while Cora served the remaining hens, and then they both returned to the kitchen. Bringing in the vegetables mere moments later, Kiera was thankful the family's lively conversation had turned to a subject other than herself.

"Paris was ever so romantic," the newly married woman gushed. "What we saw of it, of course, having scarcely left our suite." She blushed daintily.

Her husband, slighter in build and with lighter hair than his older brother's, chuckled. "But then, it's all lovely during the summer, Madeline, my love. I doubt we missed much."

"Yes, I've visited the city several times," Alexandria said wearily. "I'm hoping Devon and I will honeymoon in the Greek Islands."

"Assuming your wedding transpires in our lifetime," the younger son quipped. "Seems my big brother is set on having the longest engagement in history."

Not everyone chuckled.

Kiera remained expressionless as she set the mashed potatoes and gravy in place. But any relief she felt over the fact that this was the last trip she'd be making into the dining room for a while vanished when she happened to catch Alexandria's cool stare on her way out. . .one tinged with ill-concealed distaste and something else. *Could she possibly feel threatened by a newcomer's presence in the house?* Kiera wondered incredulously. Why a woman of quality should look upon an insignificant household servant in such a way was a mystery.

The very thought of trying to compete with such perfection almost made Kiera laugh. After all, she was here only temporarily, at best, determined to flee America at the first opportunity. And besides, she knew her place. Far be it from her to form some foolhardy attachment to her employer, of all people. She was seeking neither close friendships nor love—especially considering the sorry fate that had befallen everyone she had cared about in her life. Obviously she was being punished for something—what other possible explanation could there be for her misfortune?

But thankfully, the evening would not last forever. All Kiera had to do was endure removing the plates and serving dessert. After that, with any luck at all, her path might never again cross that of Mr. Hamilton's betrothed.

❧

Weary and footsore by the time she could turn in, Kiera trudged up the stairs. On the floor just outside her door lay an old Bible. A folded note had been tucked between some of the pages. With a yawn, she stooped to pick up the Book and carried it into her room.

The hour was late, and the house incredibly quiet, for after visiting with the lady of the house, the foursome had gone for a drive in Landon Hamilton's new motor car. Kiera shed the now-wrinkled uniform and donned her nightgown before crawling into bed. But she felt compelled to open the tattered Book despite her tiredness. Pulling the bedside lamp a bit closer, she unfolded the handwritten note.

Kiera,

Please feel free to make use of this Bible during your stay here. It belonged to my grandmother, who was an avid student of the Scriptures. I have marked the passage mentioned earlier and trust that some of her insight may help to clear things up for you. There is a similar account in Luke, chapter twelve, for you to compare. If you have any other questions regarding this or related matters, do not hesitate to let me know.

Cordially,
Devon H.

The fact that her employer had been thoughtful enough to provide a copy of the Bible for her own personal use pleased Kiera. Now, she could search for the answers to the perplexing issues she had raised earlier. And, she could also study the Psalms, which her mistress seemed so fond of, so she wouldn't stumble over the unfamiliar, archaic words.

Stifling another yawn, she noticed that he had marked the ending portion of the sixth chapter of Matthew's gospel, beginning with verse twenty-five. She read the passage through three times, paying particular attention to the phrases and sentences that seemed to stand out. Just as Mr. Hamilton had told her, the Bible did say that God looked after His own. But what did the phrase "seeking after righteousness" mean?

Hoping the rest of the passage might enlighten her along that line, she turned back to the first verse and read the entire sixth chapter. But the extra verses only added more questions to her original one. Who exactly did God consider a hypocrite? And what did He consider vain repetitions? Could this pertain to the short prayers she had recited all her life?

Trying to decipher these new ideas, Kiera's head began to ache. Perhaps in the morning all this would make more sense. Using the note as a bookmark, she closed the Bible and turned off the lamp. Then, with only a slight hesitation, she whispered her customary nighttime prayer as she lay her head on the pillow.

❦

"And you actually believe this girl is an asset to the household?" Alexandria asked.

As the car motored along, Devon watched the play of light and shadow from the street lamps now dancing across his fiancée's fine cheekbones. The night was too pleasant to spoil with an argument. . .something that the two of them seemed to do a lot lately. "Yes, Alex, I do. You heard yourself how Mother sang her praises when we stopped in to chat—and Kiera only arrived two days ago. I've never seen such a drastic change in her disposition."

"All the same, I feel it's *my* place to cheer up your mother. And I will, once we marry. Can't we please set a wedding date?"

Following her line of vision as she turned forward, Devon observed the obvious devotion displayed by the newlyweds in the front seat. He knew Alex only wanted to experience the same heady newness of marriage. And why shouldn't she? After all, they had been engaged for almost three years now. The daughter of his mother's very best friend, Alexandria epitomized Mother's expectations for the bride of her eldest son. She wanted them to marry and produce some grandchildren for her to spoil while she still could. He cupped Alex's cheek with his palm and gently pulled her head nearer to rest on his shoulder. "Soon, sweetheart."

Her soft lips curved into a smile as she raised them to his.

Chapter 5

After breakfast the next day, Kiera ventured outside, the borrowed Bible tucked under her arm. A gathering of clouds appeared to be moving in from the east. But the temperature remained pleasant as she strolled the perimeter of the grounds, admiring the placement of grand shade trees and flower beds, the hem of her periwinkle skirt whispering softly over the grass with each step. The magnificent greens and colorful blossoms made her long for Ulster, with its freshening ocean breezes and mossy places. She hoped that she might soon set sail for her homeland. She hadn't given any thought as to what she would do after she returned to Ireland. . .she only knew she had to go.

As she neared the house, the muted shush of cascading water drew her to the fountain, where glistening arcs spouted from the mouths of the marble dolphins into the fluted pool below. The relaxing sound all but begged to be enjoyed. Sinking onto one of the curved benches, Kiera opened the Bible to the book of Matthew and buried her nose in the passage that still worried her mind. She planned to examine the corresponding account in Luke also, as suggested by her employer. Perhaps that would shed more light on the subject of God's provision for His children.

"Lovely morning, isn't it?"

Kiera sprang to her feet. She had been so absorbed in the Scripture, she hadn't heard Mr. Hamilton's footsteps. "I—I'm sorry. I shouldn't be here, I know."

"Nonsense." He gestured for her to be seated again. "You're not a prisoner here, Kiera. You may do anything you like in your free time."

"Thank ye, sir." The breath returned to her lungs as she regained her composure. "And aye, 'tis as ye said. Lovely."

He gave a polite nod and lowered himself to the opposite end of the bench, gazing off into the distance while he sipped from the coffee mug he held. "Do you come out here often?"

"Until today I've only looked at it from me window."

"My father designed all of this for Mother before the house was even built," Mr. Hamilton said casually. "He was extremely busy. Always at the store. And he wanted her to have grounds she could enjoy in her solitary moments. She occasionally liked to dabble in the garden herself, trying new varieties of roses to see how they'd fare in this climate."

Even as her gaze idly traced his strong, appealing profile, noting how the smart navy suit complemented his coloring, Kiera had no trouble deciding what Alexandria Fitzroy saw in him. She cleared her throat. "If you'll pardon me for speakin' me mind, 'twould do her good to get out again. I was going to ask Kingsley about a wheelchair."

His wide-set eyes turned right to her. "That's an excellent idea. We do have one out in the carriage house. Of course, as you might imagine, after her stroke, Mother adamantly refused to be confined to a contraption designated for the old and infirm. But she might have changed her mind by now. I'll have King dust it off and bring it to the house."

"I thank ye. I'll see that she takes some sunshine every day."

"As you say, it'll do her good." An affable grin spread across his lips.

Kiera lowered her lashes, lest he think her bold.

"I see you brought the Bible with you," he began. "Has it helped you at all?"

"In some ways, aye. In some, nay."

"Mind explaining what you mean?"

Kiera considered her words, hoping to express her feelings correctly. "I understand that the Almighty looks after the creatures He created. He feeds us and clothes us when we are in need. . . ."

"Because He also loves us," her employer cut in. "He knows each of us by name before we're born and numbers the very hairs on our heads. He watches His creation so closely He sees even the sparrow fall."

"It says that, too, in the Bible?"

"It does. I'll look up the references for you."

Kiera gratefully tipped her head, then averted her gaze.

"Then why are you frowning?" he probed. "What else is troubling you?"

She shrugged and drew a deep breath. "I don't know how to put the harder things into words. Such as, if God truly cares for us so very much. . .why does He permit horrid things to happen? Why are there wars? Why do babies die or loved ones get taken from us? Does He care more for birds than He does for His people? And where was He when. . .when my Sean was killed?" Embarrassed that she had touched on her deepest pain, Kiera blinked quickly to stay rising tears.

When Mr. Hamilton failed to respond right away, Kiera feared she had overstepped her bounds. She bit down hard on the inside corner of her lip, wishing she had curbed her tongue. "Forgive me. You're angry that I spoke with such doubt, such disrespect."

Finally he emitted a long breath. "Hardly. You're not the first person who ever wondered about those mysteries, you know. I confess, most of us, at one time or another, wish we could explain them adequately. As to where He was when your friend was killed, I'd say exactly where He was when His own Son was murdered. . . and no doubt with a heart that ached all over again, right along with yours."

Kiera had to look at him as he paused before going on.

"Regarding the other matters, I've asked myself similar questions and come up empty. But tell you what. I'll get out some of my old books and study up. See what I can find out. . .for both of us."

Searching those mahogany eyes, his compassionate expression, Kiera knew he meant what he said, and that, in itself, provided great comfort. She smiled and stood. "Well, in no time a'tall, the mistress will be ringin' the bell. I must hustle up to me room. I thank ye for the—help." Lowering her gaze to the Bible clutched to her breast, she started for the back door.

"Perhaps we'll talk again, another morning," he called after her.

Without turning, Kiera nodded and, with a wave of her hand, went inside.

🐝

The deeper he got into his study, the freer Devon felt in his spirit. How he wished this could have been his vocation. At the store he seemed surrounded by one frustration after another. Trying to keep the staid, older men on the board of directors satisfied with the accounts receivable. The future innovations he and Landon envisioned for Hamilton's. Entire shipments of goods delayed en route, some never arriving at all— or if they did, arriving damaged beyond repair. New stock items, in which they'd invested heavily, scorned by the customers and relegated to discount sales, practically given away. Trusted high-level employees leaving, unexpectedly, for greener pastures. Female employees deciding to stay home with their children or provide new additions to their families. Endless hours confined in that huge, stuffy office.

But here, at home in the quiet, his very soul soaking up the Word of God, he felt a fulfillment that the rest of his life lacked. However noble his intentions, had he made the wrong choice after all? Surely his younger brother expressed more enthusiasm than he, himself, had ever experienced for the family business. But Landon was four years younger than Devon. That fact alone prevented him from finding any opportunity to prove himself worthy of the store's challenge. Perhaps the time had come for him to become more than a mere junior partner.

With a shake of his head, Devon blew out a whoosh of air. Where was he before those conflicting thoughts tangled up his mind? Ah, yes. Romans. Still trying to unearth adequate explanations for Kiera's questions. Would she think it trite if he explained that three wills—God's, Satan's, and man's—were at war on this earth, or that heartaches often came as a result of one's own bad choices? Or that God's thoughts are higher than man's, as the prophet Isaiah had written?

In any event, he doubted he could help her to understand something so complicated by merely passing on a few Scripture references. This kind of thing was better dealt with in face-to-face discussion. And it called for being well prepared. Furthermore, the thought of doing just that exhilarated him beyond measure.

And so did Kiera MacPherson's thirst for spiritual knowledge. That purely lovely face of hers could be scrunched up in puzzlement one moment, and then as understanding set in, every line of concern would dissolve, leaving her expression relaxed in sweet—almost tangible—innocence again. . .the likes of which Devon had never encountered before.

Something about that young woman touched him deeply, stirring chords in his soul that until now had never had a voice.

82

Over the next several weeks, Kiera settled gradually into her new environment, growing accustomed to Mrs. Hamilton's mood swings and the routine of the household. She enjoyed quiet chats with Cora and Kingsley. She admired the unassuming Louella's efficiency as she smoothly ran the household affairs. And she knew enough to stay in her room when the brothers entertained their ladies at family dinners one night a week. With the mistress still confined to the house, Kiera preferred to stay with her on Sundays rather than go with the rest of the household to church. But that hardly seemed a deprivation—considering all that she was learning from one day to the next.

Mr. Hamilton was off managing the store a good deal of the time. Often during the evening he wouldn't come home until the hour was late. No doubt keeping company with his betrothed, Kiera imagined.

But mornings were another story. True to his word, he began meeting her at the fountain after breakfast each day, weather permitting. He listened patiently to her every question then provided explanations that somehow turned the most complex doctrine into simplicity itself. And she heard his counsel, going over various passages with him, then studied them later on her own. Little by little, things were starting to make sense, about God's sovereignty and His holiness, about His infinite wisdom and purpose for mankind. But she couldn't quite grasp the matter of man's need for salvation, how it couldn't be earned, but was a gift freely given by God.

"Ye sound almost like a preacher," she remarked almost in jest after he had finished responding to yet another question she'd asked on the subject.

His gaze clouded over. "Perhaps that's because I almost became one. Lately, I'm beginning to regret not seeing the vocation through." He drew a troubled breath.

In that moment, Kiera caught a glimpse into Devon Hamilton's soul. She recognized that he had shared a confidence with her—one that he hadn't discussed with anyone for a very long time, if ever. Before she realized the words were tumbling from her lips, she was telling him all about Sean. And about the beautiful promises that had fallen by the wayside with his death.

She realized something else, too. No longer did she feel the inferior servant daring to converse with the master. They had come very close to crossing the invisible line into actual friendship. . .a line she knew she had no right to cross.

Kiera deliberately reverted to propriety. "So you're sayin', Mr. Hamilton, that Jesus Christ provided a way for mortal man to reconcile himself to God. And that way is by the Cross, not by our own efforts to find acceptance." The concept, still new to her, bore further pondering within the sanctity of her room.

"Precisely. The third chapter of John explains this truth far more clearly than I ever could. And for pity's sake, Kiera, why don't you call me Devon? Hanging on to that cumbersome formality is more of a hindrance than a necessity, especially when we're trying to sort out the Scriptures."

"Nevertheless," she said, suppressing a blush, " 'tis best I remember me place. And that you do, as well." *Now more than ever,* she almost blurted out.

"Your place." He tucked his chin. "You happen to be part of this household."

"But not part of the family. And as such, I'll be takin' no liberties."

He regarded her steadily for a timeless moment, then acquiesced. "As you wish. Well then, getting back to today's passage. . ."

But Kiera rose even as he spoke. " 'Tis time for me to be seein' to your mother. She'll be wantin' to get dressed for our stroll in the garden."

Mr. Hamilton gave a compliant nod. "I see. Tomorrow, then, we'll take up where we left off." He sobered suddenly. "Oh, wait. I plan to go away for a couple days. We must postpone our next get-together until I return."

"Fine. Top 'o the mornin' to ye, sir. And. . .Godspeed." With a small smile, Kiera traipsed off to her duties. But the day suddenly seemed only half as bright, and the thought of the coming morning brought no enthusiasm.

You're gettin' yourself in too deep with this man, she lectured herself. *Ye can't be gettin' so attached to him that a day without his presence is like a day without the sun itself.*

All the way upstairs, she silently reiterated her intention to return to Ireland. The wages she had put aside would, already, more than cover the cost of passage. The time had come for her to revert to her original plan. The longer she put off her departure, the more difficult her task of bidding farewell to Mr. Hamilton.

For, if the truth were told, she had been calling him Devon in her heart for some time now.

Chapter 6

"Seems a lifetime since I smelled moist earth beneath my fingers," Mrs. Hamilton remarked as Kiera guided the wheelchair over the smoothest route she had found through the grounds, still within sight of the flower beds. "Time was, I'd be out here almost every day, clipping unwanted sucker branches from my rose bushes, choosing just the right gladiolus or dahlias for the evening supper table, tea parties out on the lawn..."

Stopping in the shade of a huge maple, Kiera smiled and plopped onto the grass, her ecru muslin skirts ballooning about her. "No doubt the place has been missin' your touch, mum. 'A garden grows best for the person who loves it most,' me dad always said."

"Strange, to think someone of your tender age is all alone in the world," the older woman said kindly.

"I scarcely think of meself as alone. I've always had people to care for. And I've nothing but good memories of me parents, rest their souls." A soft breeze played around them, tossing a light brown curl in front of Kiera's eyes. She brushed it away and glanced up to the canopy of leaves above, where songbirds flitted through the branches, trilling their choruses.

From the direction of the house, masculine footsteps approached.

"Well, well," Dr. Browning remarked, striding up to them, a twinkle behind his spectacles as he tipped his head toward his patient. "Aren't we looking sprightly these days? Much better than last week when I came by."

"Yes, I'm feeling much improved, thank you. Not quite ready to trust these old legs just yet, but in this thing I make an appearance at the supper table now and then." A droll almost-smile appeared when she tapped an armrest.

"Good. Good. I rather expected you'd flourish under the care of this wee lass." He beamed at Kiera, making her blush.

Her mistress emitted a low laugh...the first Kiera had ever heard from her. "I must admit, this slip of a girl wasn't content to let me wallow in pity, despite the injustices of life. She began whipping me into shape the first minute she set foot in my room."

"Sure and ye jest, mum," Kiera gasped, looking up in denial at her mistress. "I was only tryin' to help ye get well again, so ye could be tendin' the roses. As the old saying goes, 'You'll never plow a field by turning it over in your mind.' "

"Indeed." The aged hand reached down and patted her shoulder. "And well I know, it's thanks to you that I've been regaining my strength. But I am feeling a bit tired just now, if you'd take me inside."

The rail-thin physician stepped forward. "No trouble at all, Daisy. We'll see you back to your bed. It's about time for your nap anyhow." He grinned at Kiera, and she rose from the ground and fell into step beside him.

❧

Devon left home without the foggiest notion of where he was going. He needed to get away—from everyone and everything—long enough to do some serious thinking and praying. Thankfully, Landon's shiny Oldsmobile made that possible. With a tank of gasoline and a suitcase in the back, the miles chugged past in a blur of green hills and valleys liberally dotted with farms and small towns. Occasionally, he passed a picturesque lake shimmering beneath the azure sky, reflecting cloudless glory back to the heavens.

For a brief moment, he wondered how well his brother would handle the business affairs in his absence. But as quickly as the thought had come, the realization overtook him—Hamilton's Department Store had survived the loss of their father, and it would survive Devon's truancy for a day or a week. Even a month, if necessary. *What about a year? Or forever? Would marriage settle his younger brother down enough so that he might take over the store for good?*

Scarcely able to breathe around that possibility, Devon unbuttoned the stiff collar pinching his neck and averted his attention to distant mountains. Row upon row of them in a misty panorama of bluish green. . .the exact shade of a certain pair of Irish eyes he couldn't quite banish from his mind.

And just for a moment he didn't make the attempt.

❧

Having been encouraged by her employer, at their last morning study, to study the third chapter of John's gospel, Kiera spent so much time reading the passage that she could almost recite it from memory. And the story of Nicodemus would not leave her alone. As she lay on her bed in the balmy darkness, she pictured the wealthy ruler, stealing through the night to see Jesus, perhaps on a night like this one, questioning Him about matters beyond the man's understanding. Kiera, too, wondered what it meant to be born again, of water and spirit. Yet, the way Mr. Hamilton had explained man's need for reconciliation to his Maker, and the purpose for the Cross, did make sense.

The thought of God's incredible love for mankind moved her in a way nothing ever had. She tried to fathom the Almighty Father sacrificing His only Son—the Crown Prince of heaven—sending Him to suffer and die an excruciating death for people who neither believed nor cared. These sinful humans deserved nothing less than the eternal wrath of God. Yet, even so, many rejected His gift of love.

But in her heart, she knew it was true. All of it.

And I, too, must make a choice, she admitted. *Whether to remain among the throng who spit upon Him and cried for Him to die. . .or be like the thief on the other cross, who realized in his final moments that he was in the very presence of the Son of God.*

She knew one thing for certain. The short, recited prayers she had uttered dutifully throughout her life had never instilled her with any sense of peace or the presence of God. But since she'd been here, discovering new truths in His Holy Word, witnessing in Devon Hamilton a living, personal relationship between a man and God, the Lord seemed near enough for her to reach out and touch. . .if she would but do so. And suddenly she wanted to do that more than anything in the world. "I choose Jesus Christ," she whispered. And slipping to her knees beside the bed, she confessed her need for the Savior.

❧

After three days of prayer and fasting, Devon purposely returned to the city in time to join the next family supper. He swung by Hamilton's to inform Landon he was back. Then, he drove to see Alexandria and tell her that she would be picked up as usual. Strangely, her ardent embrace failed to stir him the way it once had. But he supposed that was to be expected. He was different now. His priorities had changed. So had his goals. And tonight he must tell the family. He just didn't know how.

He failed to encounter Kiera as he made his way to his bedroom to freshen up and change into his supper clothes. But that was fine. He wasn't quite up to facing her just yet, either. He still had a lot of very personal praying to do.

The afternoon flew by, and all too soon, the supper hour arrived. Family members gathered around the table. . .Mother, Alexandria, Landon, Madeline, and himself.

Even through Devon's befuddled mind, the heady essence of the roses mixed with the tantalizing aroma of Cora's pork roast assailed his senses as he took his seat at the dinner table. Louella served with her usual flair. But in his present state, he could only pick at the food before him, wondering all the while when he should make his announcement. He did notice that his mother's gown matched the asparagus spears, smothered as they were in Hollandaise sauce. In hopes of preserving her good mood, he used this as a springboard to conversation. "You're looking quite well, Mother. I must say, it's been wonderful having you with us at supper of late."

Her cheeks plumped with her smile. "Yes, it's grand to be among the living again. . .even if it is but once or twice a week."

"Soon enough, we'll have you every day," Alexandria gushed, with a subtle flutter of her long lashes in Devon's direction. "Won't we, darling?"

"And when will the happy event take place, big brother?" Landon asked tongue in cheek, while he cut a generous slice from the meat on his plate and forked it to his lips.

Only Madeline remained silent, still retaining her shyness around her new family. Between bites, she sipped delicately from her goblet, seemingly content to let the others converse.

"Well," Devon hedged, "that's what I wanted to discuss with you tonight, while we're all here." Intending to sample another stalk of asparagus, he glanced down at his plate, only to discover it was empty, save for a puddle of sauce. Oddly, he could not remember taking even one bite.

Alexandria swung a puzzled gaze at him. "Don't you think it would be better for the two of us to talk in private, sweetheart?"

He covered her beringed hand with his, hoping she would absorb a measure of the calmness he hoped he portrayed. In truth, however, his insides felt like a dike after a deluge, ready to give way at any second. He drew a long, slow breath.

"I did a lot of thinking while I was gone," he began.

"And where was it you went on this impromptu getaway, dear?" his mother asked. "I'm sure we'd all enjoy hearing exactly where you ended up, wouldn't we?" She circulated a questioning glance and received a trio of nods.

"I headed south," Devon replied. "But that's not important. What is important is that, while I was away, I made some decisions you all should know about."

Alexandria's countenance brightened considerably, and she swallowed a chunk of the roll that she had been nibbling.

Devon knew she undoubtedly surmised he was about to announce their wedding date, and he squelched a twinge of guilt. But he could do little about that now. Nor was there any point in putting off the inevitable. He might as well quit his hedging. "I've decided—I—I—no longer want to run Hamilton's." There. He'd said it. Part of it, anyway. . .

His mother's demeanor froze somewhere between confusion and horror. "I beg your pardon?"

"I'm sure you heard me," he said quietly.

"But—but that's preposterous," she countered. "What would you do, if not head the business your father left you, the business he poured his very life into, in order to provide you and your brother with a prosperous future?"

"I want to go into the ministry."

Two forks clinked onto two china plates. Mother and Alexandria both stared at him aghast, as if he had just informed them he had contracted the bubonic plague.

Landon smirked, one eyebrow hiked, then returned his attentions to his dinner plate.

Madeline's huge gray eyes didn't even blink as she looked from one person to the next.

"I've always admired pastors and their work of eternal value," Devon went on evenly. "The greatest joy comes over me when I study the Bible. I can almost sense God smiling down on me. I did go to Princeton, if you recall. . .and my intention was to prepare for a career in the Lord's service. That's what I've always wanted—more than anything else."

"I have never heard a more ridiculous statement in all my life," Mother finally said, portraying a certain conviction that her eldest son would either come to his senses or she would have his head.

"I agree." Rosy circles came to the fore on Alexandria's high cheekbones. "Why, the last thing I wish to be is the wife of a minister. . . . Just imagine, an entire congregation watching my every step, measuring my every word. Meanwhile, my husband is apt to be called out of our warm bed in the middle of the night to go counsel some drunk or scoundrel who suddenly wants to get religion before drawing his last boozy breath. Pastors put others' needs ahead of those of their own loved ones. No family event is more important than any stranger's request. No, thank you. I don't see myself sharing my husband, my very life, in such a fashion."

"Don't you fret," his mother told her placatingly. "Obviously my son was out in the sun far too long—those automobiles shouldn't be all open like that, you know. All that sun is bad for the mind."

Relief settled over Alexandria's flushed features.

"Wait a minute," Landon piped in. "I happen to find this all quite interesting. I think we should hear what Dev has to say." He switched his attention to Devon again. "Come on. Out with the whole story, man."

Just then, Cora and Louella breezed in from the kitchen. "Is everyone ready for coffee and strawberry shortcake?" They stepped to the table to remove dinner plates, but sensing the somber mood of the family, their movements halted in midair.

"Not just yet, Cora," Mother said, her expression signaling the unlikelihood that anyone would partake of dessert tonight. As the two made as unobtrusive an exit as possible, Mother turned an imperious scowl on Devon.

He felt his neck warming. "I'm sorry, Mother," he told her. "Perhaps the supper table wasn't the wisest place for this discussion; I don't know. Nevertheless, I've spoken openly and honestly. And, in all seriousness, I assure you, I meant what I said."

"Then, I shall be equally serious," she grated, her tone so cold the ensuing words dropped from her mouth like shards of ice. "I will not tolerate such dishonor to your father, who worked so hard to give you every advantage. If you persist in this nonsensical delusion, you will do so with neither the blessing nor the financial support of this family." And with that, she unlocked the wheels of her chair and backed away from the table.

For a full minute after the family's matriarch rolled herself out of the dining room, no one spoke.

Alexandria, her spine rigid as a broomstick, came to her feet. "You made this decision without even discussing it with me. Without a single consideration for my feelings."

"I most certainly did consider your feelings," he told her quietly. "But I can't turn my back on my calling. . .even for you."

"Well, *I* can't live such a thankless life, even for you!" She tore the engagement ring from her finger and dropped it into the watery remnants of lemonade in Devon's goblet, then flounced from the room.

"Well, Dev," Landon said, in a predictable brotherly gibe, "looks like you just managed to throw yourself out into the cold."

Chapter 7

Amidnight thunderstorm drenched the grounds, and Kiera awakened to rainy skies. Filled with the joy of her newfound faith in the Lord, she refused to allow something so insignificant as inclement weather to dampen her enthusiasm. She donned her brightest morning gown, a cheery daffodil yellow, and tied her hair at the nape of her neck with a ribbon of the same hue.

"Top o' the mornin'," she said airily upon entering the kitchen a few moments later.

Cora, at the table with her husband and the housekeeper, peered up at her with a lackluster smile. No one appeared to be eating.

"Why, you've circles under your eyes," Kiera exclaimed in surprise. "All three of ye. Did ye not sleep through the storm?"

"That squall was nothing, compared to the one that blew through the dining room last eve," Kingsley supplied miserably.

"It's Master Devon," Louella said, her fair complexion so white her myriad freckles stood out in prominence. "He's done something that has the mistress all upset."

"Thought you might as well be warned," King added. "This is one storm that will take awhile to blow over."

Helping herself to a fresh muffin and some coffee, Kiera mulled over their words, wondering what on earth could have transpired in a single evening that would have such a profound effect on the household. Thankfully, whatever it was had nothing to do with her. And with all this wonderful new joy bubbling up inside her, surely she had more than enough to share with the lady of the house.

Shortly thereafter, brave hopes notwithstanding, Kiera paused for several moments outside the green bedroom before moistening her lips and rapping lightly.

"Who is it?" Mrs. Hamilton snapped.

"Kiera, mum." Opening the door, she entered without a sound. "I've come to help ye freshen and dress for the day."

"I prefer to stay abed."

"Would ye care for a wash, then? Perhaps a bathin' might make ye feel better."

"Humph. Nothing can make this day any better." She muttered unintelligible phrases, short huffs of breath punctuated with audible exclamation points.

Scarcely able to decipher but a few words here and there, Kiera could only nibble her lip. It had been weeks since she had seen the madam in such a state of mind. Risking her very position here, she ventured on. "Pardon me for askin', mum, but is there something I might do to help?"

"No," she rasped, lying motionless under the light blanket. "No one can help." She went back to mumbling. ". . .stubborn. . .deluded. Ministry, my foot. . .ridiculous notion."

Tidying the room, Kiera held her tongue.

After a short lapse, the volume of Mrs. Hamilton's voice went up a notch in a scornful mimic, as if oblivious to Kiera's presence. "Always loved studying the Bible, did he? Had a dream to go into service for the Lord, did he? Humph. I'll be dead and buried before I see him become some threadbare minister. The ingrate. After his father worked to build that store into something that would ensure a comfortable future for both our sons."

Adding up the various tidbits of information, Kiera felt a chill course through her. Perhaps she had been wrong to assume this trouble in the family had nothing to do with her. In fact, it just might have *everything* to do with her. She'd been the one asking those hard theological questions. Gotten him digging for answers. Quite likely, she'd provided the catalyst for this whole affair. "W–would ye be wantin' your tray, mistress?" she asked, unable to manage more than a whisper.

"No. Nothing. And you may return to your room."

"Aye, mum."

After informing the others not to prepare a breakfast tray, Kiera headed for the library. Her jitters were getting the better of her. She doubted that she'd be able to focus on her daily Bible study. Perhaps amid those endless shelves fairly sagging beneath the wondrous collection of books, she'd find a volume of poetry or a novel, something to take her mind off the tension which seemed to permeate the entire house. And, moreover, assuage her own guilt in the matter. Entering the high-ceilinged room, she began perusing the multitude of titles.

❧

Devon, dozing lightly on the couch facing the library fireplace, stirred from his sleep with an awareness of another's presence. He cautiously inched up a little, just enough to peer over the divan's back. *Ah. A friendly face.* He smiled as he watched Kiera browse the rows of leather bindings, now and then plucking a volume from the rest and leafing through a few pages before returning it to the shelf.

"Looking for something in particular?" He rose to a sitting position.

She nearly jumped out of her shoes. "Forgive me, sir. I didn't know ye were in here." She whirled around in order to make a hasty exit.

"There's no reason for you to leave, Kiera. Make a choice, at least."

Obviously flustered, she inhaled sharply and snatched the nearest title.

Devon chuckled. "*The Care and Feeding of Thoroughbreds?* I had no idea you had an interest in horses."

Despite her flaming cheeks, she calmly replaced the book and slid him a sideways glance rife with chagrin. "Do ye have this entire library memorized?"

"No. But I have a general idea of what's in the various sections. You happen to be standing in front of the animal husbandry books."

Kiera glanced over her shoulder, then turned back, her expression admitting he was right. A small smile tweaked her lips as she visibly relaxed. "Ye had a safe trip, I see."

He nodded. "Right up until I got home, actually." He cocked his head back and forth. "No doubt the entire household is aware by now—the oldest son and heir to the Hamilton empire has gotten himself into hot water."

A tiny shrug indicated her only response. She looked away.

Watching her toying with a fold of her skirt, no doubt wishing she were anywhere but here, Devon couldn't help wondering if she, too, would consider his decision foolhardy. "I. . .told them all I wanted to quit the store," he confessed candidly. "That I wanted to pursue the ministry again."

All the color fled her face. "Ye didn't."

"Yep. Afraid I did."

" 'Tis no wonder your mother seeks that handsome head of yours served up on a platter, then."

"That bad, eh?"

She pursed her lips into a grim smile.

"And what about you? Do you think I've lost my sanity?"

"That's not for me to be sayin' one way or the other."

"Why not?" Hardly caring that she made no reply, he allowed his gaze to linger on her lithe, yet tantalizing frame, on curls that had to be as soft as the finest silk spun in China. . .on those eyes. Eyes that the most able-bodied man could drown in. Suddenly her opinion mattered to him—far more than the opinions of those at supper last night. He moved to one end of the couch and gestured for her to take the other. "Talk to me, Kiera."

"I. . .I don't know what to say," she whispered.

"Then just listen. No one else seems the least interested in anything I have to say."

After a slight hesitation, she took the seat he indicated, folding her hands in her lap.

"Did you learn anything interesting while I was gone?"

"In the Bible? Aye. So much that me poor mind is in a whirl."

He grinned. "Sometimes the truths prove more than one can absorb all at once. Still, nothing ever brings me such pleasure as I find in studying the Word, comparing one passage with another, digging for the clearest meaning. The searching makes me feel. . .alive."

"Aye, I know exactly what ye mean. But what's more important than that, ye have a gift for explainin' things to others," she offered. "I know that for sure."

Devon watched her as she raised her lashes. When she met his gaze, his heart all but stopped beating. Some quality within her eyes lingered unspoken, as if the two of them shared a secret apart from everyone else.

"It's what I was meant to do, Kiera. I see that now as never before. And I've renewed a promise I once made to the Lord. I intend to serve Him all the rest of my days."

🙰

A jumble of emotions assaulted Kiera as Devon Hamilton disclosed his innermost thoughts to her. "But. . .what of the cost?" she had to ask. He could find himself cast out from them all. For good and for always. It just wasn't right, when the whole thing was her fault, not his. Never his. She couldn't bear the thought of his banishment from his own family.

His expression flattened noticeably. "Mother has already informed me of the price she will exact for my brash intentions. Naturally, I wish she felt otherwise. I long for the support of the people I love most—at least emotional support, if not financial." He raised a hand, palm up. "What am I going to do, Kiera? No one understands. None of them." His voice broke on the words, and he bolted to his feet. Crossing the room to the window, he slid his hands into his pockets and stood staring into the rain.

The sight of those manly shoulders sagging in defeat and dejection was more than Kiera could endure. She had no right to care for him. She hadn't planned to care for him. But, gradually, without her realizing it, deep respect and admiration had grown beyond their boundaries and blossomed into something that must never be. She rose and went to his side, knowing that the only comfort she dared offer would be insufficient, at best. Nevertheless, she had to try. Had to say something. "Perhaps. . .in time. . ."

With a low moan, he pivoted and drew her into his arms, burying his face in her hair. For an eternal moment he held her. Wordlessly. His strong, warm arms crushed her against himself so tightly she could hardly breathe. Then, with no warning, he took her face in his palms and covered her lips with his, in a kiss of passion, of desperation.

Kiera's heart skipped in bittersweet joy even as she closed her eyes against the brimming tears. Wishing and dreaming were useless in light of their two different worlds. No matter how special he made her feel when they shared those precious morning discussions, she must put an end to them. Better she accepted that now and seek God's strength in forgetting him. He was merely seeking comfort from the only friend he thought he had, and she would not deny him that. She would savor this one embrace, no matter the cost. . .but it would be all that fate allowed.

When he eased away and brushed a hand down his face, she felt utterly bereft.

He raked his fingers through his hair. "Forgive me," he said incredulously, his tortured eyes searching hers. "I–I'm sorry." And with that, he charged out of the room.

Watching him depart, her own insides a quivering mass of jelly, Kiera envied Alexandria Fitzroy with every fiber of her being.

It's as foolish to let a fool kiss you as it is to let a kiss fool you, the old saying taunted cruelly. Even as the words rang through her mind, Kiera marched straight to her room—to pack.

Chapter 8

W here would you like me to take you, miss?" Dr. Browning asked, his confusion evident as he snapped traces across his mare's back and pulled away from the Hamilton mansion. The rain had stopped within the last hour, but Madison Avenue remained slick and shiny in the late-afternoon light. The gentle breeze carried the promise of autumn.

"Carry me anyplace where I can rent a room until a ship sails for Ireland."

When the old gentleman had happened by, Kiera inwardly declared his arrival providential. While he had called upon Mrs. Hamilton, Kiera stole downstairs with her bags, unseen by anyone. Knowing she could never manage to bid farewell to the dear friends she had made during her stay, she waited outside near the physician's buggy until he reappeared. Then, she prevailed upon his good nature to drive her away.

"I thought you were happy with the Hamiltons," he said, breaking into her thoughts.

"Aye. I was, takin' me in the way they did."

"So why is it you're running away, child?"

The blunt question put Kiera on the defensive. "I'm not runnin' away. Not exactly. I planned from the first to save me money until I had enough to return home to Ireland. And that I have. In fact, I've more than enough. 'Tis time I go back where I belong. Leave them to. . .sort things out on their own."

He chuckled. "Yes. Daisy informed me about Devon's latest escapade. He's sent her into quite a state, to be sure."

Kiera turned to meet his gaze. "Not that 'tis any of me own business, mind ye. . . but do ye think things'll turn out right for them?"

"Wouldn't be a bit surprised, young lady. There's a lot of the adventurous Maxwell Hamilton in that son of his. Just as his dad took a small bit of capital and used it to carve out a name for himself as a merchant, Devon will realize his own dreams. He's a fine lad, one who's likely to succeed in whatever he strives to do. So he plans to step out 'in faith,' as did Abraham of old." The old man chuckled. "Leaving the old life of comfort behind to follow God's call."

The idea of his being cut off from the family he loved so dearly and banished from the home as well cut Kiera like a knife. "Ye think he truly is called to be a minister, then?"

The physician smiled gently. "Now, that's not for me to say, is it? It's between Devon and the Lord. But I'll tell you one thing. . .if God laid something on my heart, I wouldn't want to refuse to do His bidding. Would you?"

She shook her head, and the old straw bonnet she had worn upon her arrival in America felt strangely dowdy, after the more elegant ones she now left behind. Those and all the lovely gowns that had graced her life during the past few months remained in the wardrobe of the guest room. None of those stylish things really belonged to her. Besides, such finery would be out of place in the Old Country.

She switched her attention to the passing traffic, always constant, and counted off the landmarks that had become familiar during her New York summer. Oddly enough, she found herself committing them to memory.

The buggy turned off the street at the next corner, allowing Kiera one final backward glance at the Hamilton mansion in all its red brick splendor. With the dark-haired master of the grand house in mind, her heart breathed an old Irish blessing:

> *May the road rise to meet you,*
> *May the wind be always at your back,*
> *The sun shine warm upon your face,*
> *The rain soft upon your fields,*
> *And until we meet again*
> *May God hold you in the hollow of His hand.*

Only, she couldn't quite picture her path ever crossing Devon Hamilton's again. Not in this life. . .and she hadn't even told him of her newfound faith in Christ. She swallowed her tears and turned forward.

🍀

The hard mattress of the waterfront rooming house provided Kiera precious little sleep the next two nights—especially considering the noisy patrons a mere floor below who were intent on drinking and cavorting the long hours through. Still weary when she rose the next morning, she dressed and went down to settle her bill. Then, bags in hand, she made her way along the wharves, past an endless variety of ships, until she reached the dock where the vessel *Sea Princess* lay at its moorings. She mounted the long gangplank leading up to the passenger deck of the worthy-looking ship scheduled to weigh anchor for Europe within the hour.

The sky lacked the usual cheerful blue she enjoyed, but perhaps was more typical with fall coming. She only hoped for calm seas and that the voyage would be favorable and swift. And she prayed the Irish winter would be mild, so the whin would stay in perpetual flower. She had missed the yellow blossoms that graced the fields and hillsides and longed for their sweet coconut-like smell again. A consolation prize for the heart she would be leaving behind.

Once on board, a young steward in white uniform took her luggage and ushered her to a cabin. "Here you go, miss. Trust you'll be comfortable during the voyage. There's a schedule for meals posted on the wall, along with a map of the decks. If you have any questions, just holler."

"Will I be havin' a cabin mate, do ye know?"

"Don't think so, miss. We seem to have far more passengers sailing *to* New York than *from* it."

"I thank ye." Nodding, she closed the door and sat on one of the two narrow berths lining the walls. The last thing she planned to do was watch the New York skyline and the Statue of Liberty fade into the misty distance as the ship left the harbor. To think of all the hopes she had brought with her to America. . .yet none of them had been fulfilled. All unkept promises. Every one.

As the quietness of her cabin settled around her, she wished she'd brought a book to read. That wonderful old Bible with all its handwritten comments would be one of the two things she would miss most.

The other, she would not allow her thoughts to visit.

🐾

A loud commotion roused her from sleep. Kiera startled to the realization that she had dozed off, and the too-short nap made her head throb. She sat up and blinked to clear her vision.

The cabin door crashed open. "There you are!"

Gaping at the wild-eyed apparition that resembled Devon Hamilton, but with rumpled clothes and hair askew, Kiera had the impression she hadn't awakened after all.

Except he didn't vanish from view, the way mirages were known to do.

And the arms that reached out and drew her to her feet felt amazingly real. As did the muscular frame that nearly swallowed her up in an enthusiastic embrace. And the heart thundering against her own.

"Wh–what are you doing here?" she finally managed, her voice in an unfamiliar, squeaky-high range.

"Looking for you, of course," he replied wryly. "Where are your bags?" He glanced around the small confines of the tiny room, and releasing her, he seized the one most prominently in sight. "Is this all?"

"Devon," she gasped, scarcely realizing she had used his Christian name. "Put that back. I need it."

"No, you don't. Are there any others?"

"Yes. No. Oh, stop! This is crazy. I can't even think." Turning away from the man she was determined to forget, Kiera grasped her temples in her hands.

She heard him express a frustrated breath. But when he spoke, his voice was in a calmer tone. "Look, I didn't mean to startle you, Kiera, but there's no time for a leisurely chat. The ship's about to embark. After a good deal of pleading, I was able to prevail upon the captain to let me aboard so I could take you off."

"But—but I–I'm sailing for Ireland. Going home."

"Home, my dear Kiera, is here. In America. Where I can see you, talk to you, and where we can be together."

"What did you say?"

He grinned then, an amazingly mischievous grin that set her heart to doing unbelievable things. "I'll explain things more clearly in a few minutes. Now, *Kiera, my dear,* must I ask you again to get your things?"

Unable to take her eyes off him and knowing somehow she should do as he wanted, she nibbled her lip, which was so insistent upon smiling. "My other bag is there on the floor by the window."

With a sigh of relief, he grasped both travel cases in one arm, then looped his other around her. And together they ran down the plank to shore, just as the seamen loosened the heavy ropes and raised the wooden walkway.

Devon set her bags into the back of Landon's car. Then he led her around to the passenger door. But before he assisted her inside, he smiled and drew her into a warm embrace. "Thank you. Oh, thank you," he murmured against her ear, "for getting off with me. I don't know what I would have done if you hadn't. I'd have been on the next ship; I do know that much."

"Ye'd have been takin' a lot for granted, I must say," she teased, hardly able to move in her present position and realizing a girl could get used to not breathing. . . .

"No, I was acting strictly by faith," he said seriously, drawing her back to earth. "One of the things the Lord has convinced me of lately is that this life of mine—which has taken a far different turn from what I'd once planned—included a different woman than I'd thought was to be my mate. I have a very strong impression that my future bride is someone with whom I've grown quite close in the recent past. I'm hoping she might feel the same." Suddenly he held her at arm's length. "That is. . .if she'd settle for a poor minister as her husband. Would you?"

He was actually proposing? To her? Was this truly happening? Yet, despite that incredible realization, some of the light seemed to evaporate from the sky with the admission of her worst fears. "So your mother actually did cut you off, then?"

He nodded. "For the time being, at least. Still, you know Mother. She may yet come around. But if she doesn't, I'll take good care of you, somehow. I promise."

I promise. So far, Kiera hadn't had much luck with promises. Yet, gazing into those eyes mere inches above her own, she decided to give this one a chance. Borrow some of Devon's faith. Trust the Lord to work things out. Somehow, this felt more right than anything she'd ever done before.

The driver of a horse-drawn wagon blew a horn as he came up behind their automobile, and Devon waved. "Listen, we have to talk some more. Are you hungry?" But without waiting for her answer, he dashed to the front of the vehicle and gave the crank a few mighty turns before hopping into the driver's seat to start the motor.

A few minutes later, they sat across from each other in a charming tea house overlooking the Hudson River. All the while, Kiera drank in the sight of him, awed at the way this day—her very life—appeared to be turning out. "You never did tell me how you found me," she remarked while they lunched on chicken sandwiches and hot tea.

"Well, it wasn't until quite late in the day that I discovered you were missing," he confessed. "I'd taken a book up to your room, thinking you might find it enlightening. . .only you weren't there. No one had an inkling where you might have gone. And when you didn't show up for hours, I really began to panic. I simply couldn't bear the thought that I might lose you forever. I realized that cabs don't normally frequent our neighborhood but recalled that Doc Browning had paid Mother a visit. So I went to see him.

"Of course," he went on, "as luck would have it, the man was off on a call. I had to hang around his office for heaven knows how long before he finally returned. From there, my search took me to that pathetic excuse of a rooming house. . .and you know the rest."

"Almost like a knight of the realm," she said, half in jest. But remembering the sacrifice he was making, her smile faded. "But what will ye do, Devon? How will ye live?"

"I'm hoping you mean we."

A flush mounted her cheeks.

"Actually, I have some money of my own that should last awhile," he continued. "A trust fund set up by my grandmother. And Landon, of course, says he'll do what he can—as long as Mother doesn't catch wind of our schemes. But I'm not worried. I'm healthy; I can work, if need be. I'm aware it may take awhile before I'm actually established in a church. You'd be taking a lot on faith if. . ."

His gaze warmed as he studied her. "You have yet to answer my question."

"I know."

"Are you ever going to?"

At his incredibly vulnerable expression, her heart contracted. She nodded. "The answer is aye. Be it in the ministry or out of it, with a fortune or in the poorhouse. I love ye, Devon Hamilton. The way ye reached out to a poor Irish girl and showed me how to become a child of God, never makin' me feel beneath ye, always lettin' me speak me mind. . .the way ye look at me sometimes, like now. . . . I'd be proud to be takin' your name."

As the man of her dreams stood and held out his hand, she placed her fingers into it, to be drawn into yet another embrace. The few other patrons in the homey establishment looked on in amusement, but Kiera cared little.

Placing a dollar on the table, Devon led her outside again. But before he helped her into the automobile, he raised her chin with the tip of his index finger and looked deep into her eyes. "There's one more thing I have to tell you, Kiera MacPherson— besides the fact that I love you so much I can hardly see straight. I know you were disillusioned more than once when you first came to America, but I intend to spend my whole life proving something to you. I always keep my promises." Then, lowering his lips to hers, he kissed her breathless.

Aye, her heart fairly sang. . .*I believe ye will.*

Chapter 9

Theirs wasn't the grand society wedding she'd envisioned that Devon would be part of a few short months ago. But to Kiera it seemed somehow. . .better. It was hers. . .and so was he. She would never cease praising God for His goodness.

Dr. Browning, in a gesture so sweet it brought tears to Kiera's eyes, had arranged for the use of a parlor belonging to another of his wealthy patients. The owner had filled the room with flowers and candles to celebrate this wondrous evening.

The one thing that might have made everything perfect would have been Mother Hamilton's presence. But that was not to be. Landon, however, agreed to be best man, though not even Madeline knew of his taking part in the nuptials. But three other dear people knew about the ceremony and came to show their loyalty. Kingsley, Cora, and Louella. . .the threesome provided the cake and punch to be enjoyed after the ceremony.

Wearing her mother's fragile wedding gown, which she had brought with her from Ireland, and a lace veil adorned with white roses with a bouquet of pink and white rosebuds, Kiera felt as elegant as any bride. When the first strains of music drifted up from the parlor, she placed her hand on the physician's arm and all but floated down the stairs to join her husband-to-be.

Her breath caught at the sight of Devon, resplendent in a crisp black suit, wavy hair neatly combed in place, and the light of love radiating from those sable eyes she adored. As she stepped to his side and placed her hand on his, she felt him tremble. But he smiled then, that special smile that made her heart crimp in exquisite pain. . . and she forgot everyone else.

Somewhere in her consciousness she was aware of the candles' glow and the fragrance of the flowers. And the faraway drone of the minister's voice, the repeating of her vows. Then the pronouncement that they were husband and wife, and the permission for them to kiss.

"I love you, Kiera Hamilton," he whispered when they drew apart. . .and she reveled in the sound of her new name.

"We wish you every happiness," Kingsley said, swamping the two of them in a huge hug. Beside him, Cora could only offer a teary smile, but Louella kissed them both on the cheek.

"Just like a fairy tale. Cinderella and her prince," the servant whispered for Kiera's ears only.

But Devon overheard. "More like the princess and her pauper," he said with an optimistic grin. "But at least I know she loves me for myself."

After the refreshments, Devon put Kiera's wrap on her shoulders, and they headed out to his brother's automobile. . .the motor already running in readiness to speed them on their way.

"I'm so glad they all came," she murmured as they waved and took their leave. "I'll always remember this day."

Devon reached over and draped an arm about her with a slightly wicked smile. "And so will I, my love. Today shall be only one of many treasured memories. . .and that I promise."

THE BLESSING BASKET

by Judith Miller

Chapter 1

April 17, 1906

Sing Ho plopped down onto the narrow, quilt-covered bed opposite her best friend, Hung Mooie. As the two oldest girls at the Mission Home, they were now entitled to the coveted small bedroom at the end of the hall—a bedroom they shared only with each other. It seemed fitting. Both of them had become members of the household at 920 Sacramento Street back in the spring of 1894, Sing Ho first and Hung Mooie two days later. Both had been rescued from slave owners who were members of the tongs, the Chinese gangs that victimized and preyed upon their own countrymen. Each of the girls had taken an instant liking to the other, and that had never changed.

"I am so tired! I thought we would *never* finish," Sing Ho stated, her almond-shaped eyes bright with excitement. She pulled her hair forward and began unbraiding the thick black mane.

"We have only a short time to rest before it's time to get cleaned up for the reception. Instead of talking, why don't we take a nap?" Hung Mooie suggested, her eyes already closing as she talked.

Jostling her friend until she finally relented and opened her eyes, Sing Ho gave her a look of disapproval. "Lo Mo is right! You're going to sleep your life away."

"Lo Mo is like all mothers. She never seems to need sleep," Hung Mooie replied. "And you are almost as bad. Why don't you let me sleep? After a week of cleaning and scrubbing every room in this house, I deserve a few minutes of rest."

"You make it sound like you're the only one who was working. Don't forget there are fifty of us living here."

"But not all *fifty* of us did the work," Hung Mooie quickly retorted.

Sing Ho chuckled and shook her head in disbelief. "You expect the three babies and little toddlers to help you scrub floors and dust shelves?"

"No, but the only reason Yuen Kim wants to stay with the babies is so that she doesn't have to do the hard work like the rest of us."

"You don't really believe that, do you? Taking care of the babies and watching all the little ones is *very* hard work. If you felt that way, why didn't you ask Lo Mo if you could trade off with Yuen Kim?" Sing Ho suggested.

"It's not that I *want* to watch the babies. I'm just saying it's easier work," Hung Mooie replied.

"Oh, so you just want to complain, do you?" Sing Ho jokingly countered. "Well, in only a few more days you won't have to worry about anyone else doing less work than you. Once you are married to Mr. Henry Lai, you'll be doing *all* the housework!"

"That's true. But it will only be for two people instead of fifty!"

"Remember, this housecleaning wasn't just for the Mission Board reception and meetings; it was for your wedding also. Perhaps we should have given you the privilege of cleaning by yourself," Sing Ho teased. "Come on! We need to get ready before the guests begin arriving," Sing Ho urged, pulling a white pleated shirtwaist and navy-blue skirt from the cramped, pine-scented closet.

"Now look what you've done! You've cheated me out of my nap!" Hung Mooie replied.

"What is that Bible verse Lo Mo recites? Is it Proverbs 19:15? Something about an 'idle soul shall suffer hunger'? You wouldn't want to sit around and go hungry, would you?" Sing Ho asked and then giggled at her friend's contorted face.

"I prefer to quote the last line of Isaiah 32:18 that says, 'my people shall dwell. . . in quiet resting places.' Not that anyone gets a quiet resting place with you around!"

Sing Ho laughed, a slight blush rising in her saffron-colored complexion. She was going to miss Hung Mooie. At ages twenty-one and twenty-two, the two of them had remained at the Mission Home longer than most. They knew that the younger girls already considered them old maids. At least they had until Hung Mooie announced her wedding plans last winter. Sing Ho was sure they still considered her a lost cause.

It was no matter to her what the other girls thought. She knew that one day God would send the right man into her life—a man with whom she could share her love and respect, someone who shared the same values and beliefs. After all, this wasn't China, where she would be subjected to an arranged marriage and have no say in the matter. Even though Miss Cunningham appeared to thoroughly enjoy matchmaking, she had never forced one of the girls into a loveless marriage. Besides, Miss Cunningham was always telling her she didn't know what she'd do without her, and, for now, she had no urgent desire to leave the only place she had ever considered a real home.

"How are things going between you and Du Wang?" Hung Mooie inquired as she donned a blue-striped shirtwaist with white linen cuffs.

Sing Ho shrugged her shoulders. "He's a nice man, but too old for me. I told Lo Mo he's too old, but she said to be patient—that he's a good Christian man," she answered, wishing that Lo Mo had not given the older man permission to call upon her.

"Did you invite Du Wang to the reception tonight?"

"No, it's only for the members of the board and a few others who have made substantial contributions to the Mission Home. Besides, with his farm so far away, you know he comes to San Francisco only once a month. I'm not sure how Lo Mo thinks we'll ever become acquainted. By the time he completes all his business, there's little time left to visit me."

"It's not fair. A man of forty years is too old for you. I know that Lo Mo wants us to marry good Christian men, but she needs to find someone better suited to you," Hung Mooie agreed. "I don't remember this skirt fitting so snugly. Do you think I've gained weight?" she asked as she tugged at the waistband of the navy serge skirt.

"I warned you that resting all the time isn't good for you. Now maybe you'll believe me," Sing Ho bantered. "We'd better get downstairs. I'm sure Lo Mo would like us to be present before the guests begin arriving."

✌

The two eldest girls stood behind a lace-covered table laden with delicate cookies, pastries, and tea sandwiches, smiling and exchanging pleasantries with the guests as they passed through the serving line. "Who's that man over there who keeps looking at you?" Hung Mooie whispered in Sing Ho's ear, nodding toward the fireplace where a group of guests stood talking.

Sing Ho glanced across the room. "I'm not sure, but I think his name is Charlie Ming. I've seen him at church, and Lo Mo told me once that he owns several businesses in Chinatown."

"Now *he's* a nice-looking man! Is he on the Mission Board?"

"I think so, but—"

"It looks like he's coming over here. I think he wants to meet you," Hung Mooie interrupted as the two of them quickly looked back down at the serving table. "At least I thought he was coming to meet you."

Charlie Ming walked past the girls and stopped at the end of the table where Bertha Cunningham sat pouring tea from a sterling silver tea service. The two girls watched as he stood talking to Miss Cunningham, nodding and occasionally taking a drink of tea. A short time later, Lo Mo looked their way and then rose from her chair and led him to where they stood.

"Sing Ho, this is Mr. Charlie Ming, our newest member of the board. I'm sure you've seen him at church. And this," she continued while nodding toward the other girl, "is Hung Mooie, our bride-to-be."

"Hello," both of the girls replied in unison as Charlie smiled and nodded.

"Sing Ho, why don't you pour yourself a cup of tea and answer some of Charlie's questions about the Mission Home. Hung Mooie can take care of the tea table without your help. Can't you?" she asked the girl, leaving no doubt what answer was expected. Hung Mooie dutifully agreed and gave her friend a look of encouragement.

"Why don't we sit over here?" Charlie asked, giving her an engaging smile.

Sing Ho followed alongside and then seated herself beside him on the silk tapestry of the overstuffed sofa. She tried not to stare, but his jet-black eyes seemed to draw hers like magnets. It wasn't fair to draw comparisons, but she found herself

405

unfavorably contrasting Du Wang, her suitor, with Charlie. Charlie's black hair was neatly braided into a long queue that hung down his back, and his broad shoulders and sturdy build made him appear larger than most Chinese men. Perhaps it was the way he held himself, but he certainly seemed much larger than Du Wang, who would typically appear at the front door of the Mission Home with strands of hair flying out from his queue, his loose trousers and jacket covered in dust, and his shoulders stooped over in an expression of total defeat.

"Do I have something on my face?" Charlie asked, breaking into her thoughts.

"What? No, certainly not," she replied, attempting to regain her composure. Carefully, she balanced the teacup in her hands and turned toward Mr. Ming, attempting to call into play all of the etiquette and elocution lessons she had mastered throughout the past twelve years.

Sing Ho had been one of the brightest students at the Mission School. Her ability to learn, coupled with her willing spirit, had allowed her to develop a close relationship with Miss Cunningham. After attending English classes for only a year, Sing Ho began acting as an interpreter on rescue missions. Miss Cunningham had told her that God would protect them, and Sing Ho never doubted that promise. He had not failed them.

"How are you enjoying our reception?" she inquired.

"It's very nice to have an opportunity to meet with the other board members before the annual meeting begins tomorrow," he replied. "It appears that all of you have been working very hard preparing for our visit," he continued, his eyes surveying the gleaming furniture and floors.

"Lo Mo wanted everything to be in good order for the meeting *and* for Hung Mooie's wedding," she replied, giving him a warm smile.

"I take it that all of you girls call Miss Cunningham, 'Lo Mo'?"

"Yes, eventually we all have—at least all of the girls since I've lived here. The babies just start out calling her Lo Mo because they mimic us. The girls who come when they are older are a little slower to use such an affectionate title. Of course, she was already known as 'Mother' when I came here.

"Miss Minnie, our housekeeper, told me one of the first girls Miss Cunningham rescued began the tradition as a way of showing respect and honor. Since Miss Cunningham is a substitute mother, she decided to call her the Chinese name for 'mother.'"

"And when did *you* come to the mission, if you don't mind my asking?"

"I don't mind at all. I've lived here almost twelve years. Lo Mo rescued me when I was only ten years old. This has become my home and my family, and I have been very happy here," she told him. "It looks as though I'd better get back to the serving table. It appears Hung Mooie is having problems keeping the trays filled."

"I'm sorry. I've been monopolizing your time when you have other duties to attend to. Perhaps we can visit another time?"

"Perhaps. I've enjoyed our conversation," she replied, giving him an engaging smile as he escorted her back to the table and then retreated. Sing Ho smiled when she glanced across the room and noted that his position permitted him a clear view of the serving table where she and Hung Mooie were performing their hostess duties.

By ten o'clock, the few remaining guests were gathering their wraps and visiting near the front door. The older girls, having been relegated to the kitchen for dishwashing duty an hour earlier, were finally released by Miss Minnie.

"I thought we were never going to have a minute alone!" Hung Mooie complained as the two of them raced up the rear stairway. "Did you like him? How old is he? Does he live in Chinatown?"

"Yes, I liked him. But I didn't ask his age or where he lived, you silly girl. I would never ask such rude questions. He would think me impertinent. We talked about the Mission Home. After all, that's why he was at the reception—because of his interest in the home," she replied, revealing nothing further. "We'd better get to sleep. Don't forget, Lo Mo wants us up early in the morning to help prepare for the brunch she's serving the board members before the first meeting."

"I know, but I want to hear more about Charlie Ming," Hung Mooie countered.

"There's nothing more to tell. Besides, you're the one who always complains about not getting enough sleep," Sing Ho replied as she pulled a white cotton nightgown over her head and knelt beside her bed in prayer. A few minutes later, she pulled back the multicolored quilt and slid between the crisp sheets, inhaling a deep whiff of their fresh aroma.

"Good night, Hung Mooie. Pleasant dreams," Sing Ho whispered.

"Good night," her friend replied. Hung Mooie's deep breathing began within a few minutes, and Sing Ho smiled, knowing that her friend was already asleep.

❧

Charlie strode down the sidewalk of the Mission Home and stepped up into his waiting buggy. Come morning, his mother would want all the details of the reception, especially information dealing with any potential brides who might have been in attendance. He smiled to himself. Should he tease her just a little and say there was a minute possibility he had met a young lady that interested him, and then immediately leave for work? He laughed out loud, knowing she would order him back to the breakfast table and question him until she was satisfied he had divulged every tidbit. That was a sobering thought! What would he tell her? A beautiful young girl with sparkling eyes and a captivating smile had stolen his heart? She would think he had lost his senses.

Besides, there was the early morning meeting at the church, and his mother's delay tactics would certainly cause him to be late. He knew his mother well, and her questions would likely lead to an onslaught for which he held no responses. No, he wouldn't tell her—at least not until there was much more to reveal.

❧

A blazing orange sun was beginning to peek out of a pale-tangerine early morning mist as an occasional newspaper cart clattered up the cobblestone street, and a milk wagon rattled along its delivery route. Bags of produce were piled high on the sidewalk, awaiting the vegetable and fruit vendors who would soon begin stocking their carts. An occasional trolley or cable car rumbled by, carrying a few early morning workers while a policeman, swinging a short wooden club, walked his beat. Suddenly a deep, thundering tremor began to sweep across the city of San Francisco—a tremor that swiftly wrenched away the anticipation of a glorious spring day.

"Sing Ho! Sing Ho! What is happening?" a tiny voice cried out.

"Stay there, Ah Chung. I'm coming," Sing Ho called, brushing back strands of hair that had escaped from the long braid hanging down her back. *At least I hope I am,* she thought to herself, trying to remain calm as the bedroom furniture began dancing about the room. Suddenly, shattering glass ricocheted off the walls, threatening bodily injury. *"All of you!* Cover your heads with your pillows!" she screamed, hoping the children could hear her command above the ever-increasing roar.

Bricks were being hurled across the street while telegraph poles rocked and wriggled, shooting off blue sparks into the gray dust-laden sky. The groaning house continued to twist and strain, fighting to hold firm against the quaking earth beneath it. Sing Ho clutched the door jamb, laboring to keep herself upright as she reached the bedroom of the younger children. Terror was written across the small faces of the children that greeted her, their almond-shaped eyes glistening with tears as they peeked from under their white cotton-covered pillows.

"I think it has stopped. Come quickly!" Sing Ho ordered, her petite frame only a bit larger than most of the children. "Bring your pillows, and put on your shoes," she added as they quickly began to desert their beds and run toward her.

"What happened?" Ah Chung whimpered.

"An earthquake, I think. We must gather with the others and move downstairs. Hurry along," she ordered and then watched as the roomful of young Chinese girls filed into the hallway and down the stairs. "Do you need help, Hung Mooie?" she asked her friend, who was leading another group of young girls toward the stairs.

"No, I have all of my group together, and nobody is injured. I think that all of the others have already gone downstairs."

Sing Ho nodded and followed her friend down the winding stairway and into the entrance hall and parlor, where the fifty occupants of 920 Sacramento Street were now gathered.

"Now then, is everyone accounted for?" Miss Cunningham inquired, her dark brown hair hanging loose and unkempt upon her shoulders.

"It looks like everyone is here, Lo Mo," one of the older girls replied, giving Miss Cunningham a halfhearted smile as the older woman began pulling her hair toward the back of her head and into a familiar bun.

"In that case, I want one of you older girls to stay with the little ones. Sing Ho and Hung Mooie, come with me," she commanded. The three walked onto the front porch of the red brick five-story house bearing the inscription "Board of Foreign Missions."

"Look!" Sing Ho stated, her voice a raspy whisper as she pointed toward the columns of smoke rising from the city below.

"The fires are moving this direction. We'll need to feed the children and collect a few belongings. I think we'll be safer if we move to the Presbyterian church."

The two girls nodded. "Whatever you think is best, Lo Mo. Just tell us what we should do," Sing Ho replied.

"With both chimneys down, we can't cook breakfast. Why don't—"

"There's Miss Minnie," Hung Mooie interrupted, pointing toward a middle-aged woman briskly walking toward the house with a wicker basket over her arm.

"I managed to get some bread from Mr. Nettleson's bakery. Mrs. Poon Chew sent apples and is bringing a kettle of tea shortly. God has provided," Minnie called out with a grin spread across her face.

"So He has," Miss Cunningham called back. The three stood waiting as the stout matron hiked up the street and climbed the steep steps to the porch. "I don't recall sending you out for breakfast, Minnie."

"Nor do I," the housekeeper replied, brushing past the three of them and moving toward the front door. "Come along and help me wash these apples, Sing Ho. You watch for Mrs. Poon Chew to bring the tea, Hung Mooie," Minnie continued without further explanation.

"I see that this catastrophe hasn't impeded your ability to take charge," Miss Cunningham retorted, giving the housekeeper a grin.

"Just doing my job—feeding these children is my responsibility," Minnie answered, continuing on toward the kitchen.

"What we gonna do?" Bo Lin asked a few minutes later, holding tightly onto a chunk of bread and a bright-red apple.

"Well, first of all, we're going to say grace and thank God for keeping all of us safe and providing a nourishing meal. Then we're going to dress and gather some of our belongings. After that, we're going to walk up to the First Presbyterian Church and stay there," Miss Cunningham calmly replied.

"Why?" Bo Lin inquired, her five-year-old eyes wide with fear.

"Because I think we'll be safe there. It's farther away from the fire," she explained in a quiet voice.

"I don't want to go," another small child whimpered.

"Neither do I. But we must do what's best, and I'll expect each of you to do as you're told. Sing Ho and Hung Mooie, I need to speak to you," she said, motioning the two older girls toward the parlor. "I want you to take the oldest girls upstairs and have them pack only their necessities. They must be able to carry their own belongings and those of one other child, so they can't take much. The two of you oversee them and gather your own things. I'll stay with the younger children. We must leave *soon*."

"If we try to rush the children, they'll become more frightened. It's only eight blocks to the church," Hung Mooie argued.

"It is eight *long* blocks, and all of them are uphill. We have fifty children to keep in tow during that uphill march. Even worse, the streets are already filling with curious sightseers and people who have been displaced from their homes. And you can be sure that some of the slave owners will be out there lying in wait to kidnap one of you girls. There have been enough small tremors that I don't want to take any chances staying here any longer than necessary. Hurry now!" Miss Cunningham commanded in her sternest tone.

Instructing the children as they ascended the stairway, the older girls watched as the little ones quickly bundled some bedding and a few garments, along with an occasional keepsake.

"What are you doing?" Sing Ho asked, keeping her voice low.

"I can't leave it. If I take nothing else, I'm taking my wedding gown," Hung Mooie answered, as she continued to frantically stuff the white gown into a small valise.

"Lo Mo will be unhappy with your decision," Sing Ho warned, her dark eyes flashing.

"She won't know unless you tell her."

"I won't tell her, but what do *you* plan to say when you need a change of clothing?" Sing Ho inquired. Without waiting for an answer, she motioned the children to hurry. "As soon as you have your belongings, go downstairs to the parlor and wait," she instructed.

An hour had passed by the time the group was assembled, tasks had been assigned, and they were able to get under way. The household formed a tight knot with Bertha, Minnie, and the older girls surrounding the younger children, all of them keeping a wary eye for any stranger that might draw near. Slowly, the procession picked its way up Sacramento Street toward Van Ness Avenue, past the ruined mansions on Nob Hill with their brick-and-stone grandeur now transformed into piles of rubble, and trudged on toward the church.

"You girls collect pew cushions and carry them to the basement. We'll use those for pallets to sleep on," Miss Cunningham instructed as they entered the church.

"Miss Cunningham! I'm relieved to see you and your girls," Pastor Browne called out from the front of the church. "Do you need some assistance getting settled?"

"We can always use extra hands," she replied, watching as the preacher began gathering several men to aid with their baggage.

"Sing Ho! Let me carry that," a man offered and then reached for the bundles that she was carrying toward the stairs.

Startled, she quickly turned toward the familiar voice. "Charlie! What are *you* doing here at the church?"

"Pastor Browne had arranged for the Mission Board members to meet for prayer before the annual meeting. I didn't sleep well last night and finally got up and began walking to the church shortly before five o'clock. You can probably guess the rest," he said.

"Were you already at the church when the earthquake hit?" she asked.

"I had just come inside when the first tremor began. Let me take your baggage," he urged.

"I can carry these. Why don't you help the smaller children?"

Charlie nodded and gave her a broad smile that reached his engaging dark eyes. His black queue was tightly braided and swung back and forth as he bounded down the stairs. Sing Ho watched as he quickly set down his burden and ran back upstairs for another load. Moments later, she spied him with an armload of pew cushions, which he began to carefully arrange into make-shift beds on the floor. She didn't understand her feelings at that moment, but something stirred deep within her as she watched him speak quietly to one of the little girls, give her a reassuring hug, and then continue arranging the cushions as the child followed along behind him.

"There you are, Charlie," Bertha Cunningham called out as she approached her newest board member. "I can't begin to tell you how much we all appreciate your help."

Continuing down the aisle of cushions, Charlie placed a bundle of belongings atop each of the improvised cots. "I wish I could do more," he said, eyeing the group of toddlers, fearful and crying, wandering around the large room.

"I'm sure that opportunity will arise," she replied while surveying their unaccustomed surroundings.

❧

It was some time during the early hours of the morning when Charlie felt himself being roused from a deep slumber. Trying to blink away the sleep from his eyes, it took a few moments before he realized where he was. Bertha Cunningham was leaning over him and shaking his arm.

"Something terrible has occurred, and it must be resolved immediately. Will you help?" she asked, her tremulous voice barely audible.

Chapter 2

April 19, 1906

T
he wind changed as the couple turned onto Sacramento Street, the light breeze now showering them with ashes and stinging their eyes with smoke as they cautiously traced their way through the darkness and descended the steep hill.

"I wish we could have done this during daylight," Charlie stated just as Miss Cunningham lost her footing on a pile of loose rubble.

"So do I, but I didn't remember earlier in the day. I'm sure that God was warning me of the danger, and that's why I awakened. We have to remember that God doesn't always work on our schedules, Charlie," she stated, giving him a reassuring smile.

"Perhaps, but—"

"Hold up there!" a loud voice called out. "Don't take another step, or I'll shoot."

The pair stopped in their tracks as the soldier approached, his rifle pointed toward them as he looked them up and down with a menacing glare.

"Don't you know we're under martial law? Nobody's supposed to be out on these streets," he yelled. "Is this slant-eye trying to rob you?" He spat at Charlie's feet. "Dirty Ch—"

"Stop that!" Bertha commanded, straightening her shoulders and pulling herself into a rigid stance. "This *gentleman* is a member of the Board of Foreign Missions, and he is helping me."

"I don't care *who* he is. You two had better get off these streets, or you're gonna get yourselves shot. Do you understand me?"

"What's going on?" another voice called out of the darkness. "You have a problem, Private Morgan?"

"It's nothing, Captain, just some lady and a—"

"May I please speak with you, Captain?" Bertha called out in a firm voice, ignoring the threatening look of the young private.

"Yes, ma'am," he replied, taking long steady strides toward where they stood. "What can I do for you?"

"We need to get into the house at 920 Sacramento Street; it's the Mission Home," she explained.

"Can't do that, ma'am. We have orders to keep everyone out of the houses and buildings. It's too dangerous to go back in, what with the dynamiting and fires breaking out everywhere. Ain't nothing in your house worth dying over," he stated.

"Oh, yes there is," Bertha argued, "and I'm going to get in there, one way or the other."

"Just what could be so important that you're willing to risk your life, lady?"

"I've spent the last twenty-five years rescuing little Chinese girls from the hands of tong leaders who want to use them in their filthy brothels in Chinatown," she explained. "I've had to go to court and fight these evil men to establish my right to keep the girls. In our haste to leave yesterday, I forgot the papers."

"You want to go back for a bunch of papers?"

"They're not just *papers*. They're proof of my girls' identities and their guardianship documents. If fire consumes our home, I lose all the proof that grants me legal authority to keep the girls."

"Those tong leaders won't ever know your papers burned up," the Captain growled.

"You don't know these men. They're like animals sniffing after a bone. They won't hesitate to take me into court and challenge my rights. These girls are chattels to them, and they don't give up easily. I'm begging you to please show some charity toward these young children."

"So who is this?" the captain asked, poking his rifle toward Charlie.

"This is Charlie Ming, a respected member of our Mission Board and the owner of several prosperous business establishments in the community," she responded. "He, along with Pastor Browne and several others, helped us get settled in the Presbyterian church on Van Ness earlier today."

"Probably not safe to be traveling with a…Chinese man," he stated matter-of-factly.

"I think it's safer than traveling by myself on these deserted streets. Now, are you going to help us or not?" Bertha asked, bringing the conversation back to her intended objective.

"Come on. After all, who am I to interfere with your divine assignment?" he begrudgingly agreed, leading them down the hill until they reached the fortress of red brick with its domed top.

Bertha stood transfixed, staring at the home. It looked much as they'd left it, the subsequent tremors seeming to have had little effect upon the stalwart edifice.

"You just gonna stand there, or you going in?" the captain asked. "We can't be around here for long. You've got five minutes to get your papers and get back out here," he commanded while quickly scanning the area.

Bertha and Charlie scurried up the steps and into the house. The glare of the burning city lit up the rooms. "Why don't you grab some additional food while I get the papers," she hastily suggested as she ran up the steps to her office.

Locating the papers, she quickly stuffed them into a pillowcase, along with the ledgers, some jewelry, and a meager amount of money she'd not yet taken to the bank. Charlie met her at the foot of the stairway with two baskets of food, just as the anxious soldier called out for them to hurry.

"They're dynamiting in the next block. We've got to get out of here!" he shouted as Bertha reached the front porch.

"Thank you, Captain. I know you'll be rewarded for your kindness," Bertha said as he escorted them along the desolate pavement to the top of Sacramento Street.

"If anyone finds out about this, my reward will be a court-martial," he grunted. "By the way, it's not going to be safe in that church for much longer. You'll need to get those girls moved somewhere else tomorrow," he warned as they passed a few scattered troops moving up the hill ahead of the dynamiting.

"Yes, sir. We will leave in the morning," she assured him.

"It's only a couple of hours until dawn. We'd better try to get some sleep. We'll make a decision about where to move in the morning," she said to Charlie as they walked into the church.

❧

Sing Ho spent most of the night going from pallet to pallet, attempting to comfort the younger girls, holding crying toddlers, and feeding the infants. Their strange surroundings and the deep resounding booms of exploding dynamite sent the young children trembling with fear to anyone who would hold them. She breathed a sigh of relief when morning eventually arrived.

"I'm looking for Miss Cunningham," a messenger called out as he entered the church shortly after they had finished a meager breakfast.

"She's over there," Sing Ho said, pointing toward the American woman surrounded by a group of small Chinese girls.

Shoving the paper toward Miss Cunningham, the young messenger rocked from foot to foot, reciting his assigned speech. "Mr. Knoxberry asked me to deliver this message to you. He said to tell you he and several other members of the board were burned out. They've temporarily relocated in Oakland, but he's found a place for you and these children to stay in San Anselmo. You want me to take any message back to him?"

When she declined, the boy took off as if he'd sprouted wings. "Sing Ho," Miss Cunningham called out as she folded the paper and shoved it into her pocket, "would you please go upstairs and ask Mr. Ming and Pastor Browne to come down here?"

Sing Ho nodded and quickly ran upstairs to the sanctuary. "Miss Cunningham would like to see you and Pastor Browne downstairs," she said, giving Charlie a bright smile. "You look tired. Were the benches too hard for sleeping?"

"No, the night was too short. Miss Cunningham requested that I accompany her on an errand early this morning," he confided, returning her smile. "Pastor Browne left a few minutes ago. I don't know when he'll be back, so we might as well go on downstairs."

"Where did you go with Miss Cunningham?" she asked, trying to hide her weariness.

"We made a trip back to the Mission Home."

"Why would she even consider going back?" Sing Ho asked, a look of disbelief crossing her face.

"She forgot the guardianship and identity papers for all of you. Her fear is that if one of the tong members ever takes her back to court, she won't be able to prove she has legal custody," Charlie explained.

Sing Ho shook her head in amazement. "She is such an unselfish person. To think that she would do such a thing isn't surprising. God seems to protect Lo Mo, even when she makes unwise decisions. What would we do without her? Thank you for going along to protect her," Sing Ho said, rewarding him with another radiant smile.

"*She* did the protecting," he said as he gave her a nervous laugh. "We were stopped by the militia."

"What happened?" Sing Ho asked, her eyes growing large as she reached out and took his hand. "Did they harass you?"

"Yes, but Miss Cunningham quickly took my defense," he replied while glancing at her hands, which now embraced his.

She followed his eyes and quickly dropped her hold. *What am I doing?* she thought. *Lo Mo would be dismayed by such bold behavior.* "We should go downstairs," she said, struggling to regain her composure.

"Sing Ho, wait just a moment."

"Yes?"

"Would you...would it be—how do I say this—acceptable if I asked Miss Cunningham for permission to call upon you? When things have settled down a bit, that is," he quickly added.

"I don't know if she would permit it. She has already given someone else permission," Sing Ho replied, trying to hide her excitement at his interest.

"I see. I didn't realize that you are betrothed."

"Oh, no, I'm not betrothed. We are just getting to know each other. He calls upon me once a month," Sing Ho explained.

"Once a month?" he asked with a look of astonishment on his face. "At that rate, it will take the two of you years to decide if you are suited. Miss Cunningham does permit you girls to marry someone you care for, doesn't she? I mean, she doesn't arrange a marriage and—"

"No, she doesn't force us into arranged marriages, but she does encourage us to marry Christians," Sing Ho quickly informed him.

"And what do you think of this young man who is courting you?" he boldly inquired.

Sing Ho gave him a shy smile. "He's not so young, but I can say nothing ill of him. I think we should go downstairs now. Lo Mo will wonder what has happened to us," she replied, quickly changing the subject, knowing she dared not express her true feelings.

What would he think if I told him that Du Wang doesn't meet my marriage requirements? I wonder if he would be shocked to hear that I would dance with delight if given the opportunity to have him as a suitor instead of Du Wang. He would probably think that I was an ill-mannered, impertinent, uncharitable human being, Sing Ho thought, meeting Charlie's understanding eyes.

But she wouldn't say any of those things. She had been taught better. Such behavior was frowned upon, and, as the oldest girl at the Mission Home, Sing Ho was expected to set a good example. Instead, she pulled her gaze away from him, kept her lips tightly sealed, and walked resolutely toward the stairway.

Miss Cunningham, Minnie, and several of the older girls were gathered together in a small group when the pair entered the room. "Pastor Browne has left the church, and we don't know when he's expected to return," Sing Ho stated as the two of them walked toward the clustered women.

"Well, we won't wait. We've been advised that we must leave the church. I've received a message that there is an old barn in San Anselmo where we can make a temporary home. It's a four-mile hike, which will be difficult for the small children, especially since we have all these bundles to carry. We don't want to frighten the little ones, so let's attempt to make this seem as much like an adventure as possible," she suggested.

The group began their hasty preparations and it soon became apparent that much would be left behind. "There's so much we won't be able to take with us," Hung Mooie told her friend as they attempted to make assignments of what bundles each person should carry.

"I have an idea," Sing Ho told the others excitedly. "We can break the handles off the brooms and tie our bundles to them. If we balance the poles on our shoulders, we can carry more."

"She's right," Minnie agreed. "Hurry! Find everything that has a wooden handle that we can use."

Working at a frantic pace, the anxious group soon organized their belongings and began their journey. The little girls' soaring spirits and excitement over their anticipated excursion to the boat docks were quickly subdued by thick smoke, flying cinders, and tired feet. Doggedly, they proceeded onward, a weary, unwashed, uncombed procession tramping through the stifling, crowded streets while the fires continued to rage. Farther on, they passed through the evacuated district that had already burned and lay still smoldering in the aftermath. It seemed an eternity before the group finally reached the foot of Van Ness Avenue.

"There's the pier," Charlie called back over his shoulder, waving them forward.

He smiled as the small children began clapping at the sight. As they drew closer, the winds from the ocean pushed the smoke back, and they watched an empty ferryboat churn through the bluish-green water and maneuver alongside the wooden pier.

"We need passage across the bay," Charlie told the captain.

"Get 'em loaded," he replied. "Haven't seen this boat so empty in two days," the captain remarked as the group began to board the steamer.

"God's watching out for us again," Bertha stated as she stood beside Charlie, who was helping to load the smaller children.

Forcing herself to smile as she approached where the others stood, Sing Ho silently began lifting bundles and passing them into the boat. "You are coming with us, aren't you?" she finally asked Charlie, secretly fearing his answer.

"No, but I've told Miss Cunningham I will come later in the week and bring some supplies. Take care of yourself," he said, giving her a warm smile while assisting her onto the boat.

She thought that he had given her hand a slight squeeze, but perhaps that was just her imagination.

Chapter 3

Positioning herself between two of the younger girls, Sing Ho slipped an arm around each and pulled them close, with her eyes remaining fixed on the pier where Charlie stood waving. She knew that she should stop thinking about him, but it seemed impossible. Unless Lo Mo was willing to terminate the courting arrangement with Du Wang, she felt certain that Charlie would keep his distance. *The only way to solve this is through Lo Mo. As soon as we get settled, I'll talk to her,* Sing Ho decided, glancing toward the household matriarch, who appeared to be deep in conversation with several of the girls. Pulling her thoughts away from Charlie, Sing Ho gave them her attention.

"I still don't understand why God would do this to us. If He is a God of love, why didn't He prevent this earthquake?" Yuen Kim asked in a trembling voice, obviously close to tears.

"That's an excellent question, my dear, but I'm afraid I can't answer the whys and wherefores of God's plan for this universe," Miss Cunningham replied, giving her an encouraging smile. "However, it does seem that we begin to question God's love only when things are going wrong. I suppose it's human nature. But, if you would look at our situation from a different perspective, you would be assured that God loves you very much, Yuen Kim. In fact, He loves every one of us," she continued, stretching her arm outward to include all of them in her declaration. "Do you understand what I mean?"

The boat continued to slice through the calm waters toward the opposite shore. "Not exactly," a bedraggled Yuen Kim answered.

Miss Cunningham scanned the group of girls. "Anyone? Do any of you girls feel absolutely assured that God still loves us?"

"I do," Sing Ho quickly replied. "The Bible tells us that God's love is steadfast and never changing. But we're also told we will suffer and that our salvation is no assurance of an easy life."

"That's true. But can you give me an example of God's love in the midst of all this chaos?" Miss Cunningham urged.

"None of us were injured," Sing Ho replied. "So many people were injured or died during the earthquake, yet none of us suffered even a scratch."

"Exactly!" Miss Cunningham responded while beaming from ear to ear at her protégée's answer.

"And we had a place to stay," one of the other girls called out.

"And food to eat," another cried.

"I think that if we were to list all the blessings God has bestowed upon us since the earthquake, we would all be pleasantly surprised," Miss Cunningham told them. "In fact, why don't we do that?"

"We don't have any writing supplies," Yuen Kim responded sullenly, obviously intent on remaining negative.

Sing Ho reached for the basket that was stowed beneath her feet and lifted it to her lap. "I don't have a paper or pencil, but I do have a small knife," she began.

"What good is *that?*" Yuen Kim asked, her voice now dripping with sarcasm.

"I can make a small notch in the edge of my basket for each blessing," Sing Ho explained as she directed her idea toward the others and avoided Yuen Kim's frown.

"Oh, yes," the smaller girls agreed, clapping their hands.

"I think that's a fine idea, Sing Ho. It will be our blessings basket," Miss Cunningham concurred. "Now, who wants to be first?" she asked, turning her attention to the group.

Sing Ho continued to carve tiny notches around the top of the basket until they arrived at their destination, and even as they disembarked the steamer at Sausalito, several of the girls continued to call out God's blessings. They all agreed, Lo Mo included, that the trip from the dock in Sausalito to the old barn in the countryside of San Anselmo was going to be grueling. But, in spite of their hardships, the girls continued to find blessings. Hung Mooie was first when she joyfully declared that she was claiming their picturesque surroundings as one of God's blessings, and she instructed Sing Ho to immediately carve another notch. Good humor remained intact for the remainder of the excursion, with only an occasional insolent remark from one or two of the girls.

As predicted by the ever-gloomy Yuen Kim, the barn was large, drafty, and uncomfortable. The group was plagued by inadequate bedding, food, and water, all of which Yuen Kim seemed only too pleased to point out. But when Lo Mo asked the other girls for their opinion, she received shouts of jubilation for a roof and dry hay; for the one tin dipper; for the dozen spoons and plates that they could share; for the crystal clear, bubbling stream that ran close by; and for the red beans that Miss Minnie had packed and set to boil over a fire shortly after their arrival.

Hung Mooie made her way to where Sing Ho was fashioning pallets in the hay for some of the younger children. "Would you pray that Henry will find us?" she asked, tears beginning to form in her eyes.

"Of course, I will. Everything is going to work out. I just know it," Sing Ho replied, tenderly wrapping her arms around Hung Mooie. "Come on now—help me with these beds, and then we'll go down to that stream and wash up. That will make both of us feel better."

A feeble smile tugged at Hung Mooie's lips as she leaned down and spread one of the blankets. "I didn't pack any clothes, remember?"

"I know, but I did," Sing Ho answered as she continued to work alongside Hung Mooie.

"Your clothes won't fit me!"

"I know that. When you insisted on filling your valise with your wedding gown, I went back and got two of your shirtwaists and skirts and packed them with my things."

"Really? You are such a fine friend that you make me ashamed of being so selfish," Hung Mooie replied, grabbing her friend's hands and dancing about.

What would it feel like to be so excited about your upcoming marriage that you would pack a wedding gown instead of necessities? What would it feel like to even know you were going to marry? Even more, what would it feel like to be in love and want to spend the rest of your life with another person? Sing Ho wondered as the two young women walked hand in hand toward the stream.

"You need to carve another notch in your basket," Hung Mooie said, interrupting her thoughts.

"Why is that?" Sing Ho asked as they reached the stream. Sitting down by the water's edge, she began to poke through her basket, pulling out several pieces of clothing and a hairbrush.

"For you—for our friendship. What would I have done all these years without you by my side, always a faithful friend?"

"You would have been fine! But I'm going to miss you when you marry Henry and leave for Ohio. I wish you weren't moving so far away."

"You mean *if* I get married. Henry's train was due to arrive on the eighteenth, the day of the earthquake. Even if he did make it to San Francisco, I doubt that he will ever find us," Hung Mooie lamented, running the brush through her long, black hair and then dividing it into three sections. Her supple fingers dove in and out, quickly plaiting the strands into a tight braid as she followed along behind Sing Ho.

Bedding and a few food supplies were being delivered from several of the local churches just as the girls reached the barn. "Another blessing," Hung Mooie giggled as they began to help unload the items.

They completed the task just as a light mist began to fall. Within several hours, it had turned into a raging storm, which soon gave evidence to a multitude of holes in the barn roof. Beds were moved to any dry spot they could locate while the wind whistled through the cracks in the deteriorating wood. And true to form, Yuen Kim gave them yet another facial expression that matched the gloomy weather conditions.

🌿

Two days later, the rains abated and the sun began to peek through a crimson and gold horizon. Sing Ho smiled as she walked outdoors, her arms filled with laundry. The rains had transformed the hills and valleys into an exquisite panorama of reds, pinks, yellows, blues, and purples. The flowering blossoms of the hawthorn trees and a profusion of blooming wildflowers and budding acacia painted the surrounding expanse in a rainbow of color. It was going to be a good day; she could feel it. Maybe, just maybe, Henry would arrive and set Hung Mooie's worrying to rest. And perhaps even Charlie would visit them by tomorrow or the next day—at least she could hope.

Reveling in the beauty, she walked downstream a short distance and began scrubbing and soaking the multitude of small shirts and matching baggy trousers worn by most of the little girls. Carefully, she spread them across the nearby bushes and grass, the warmth of the sun assuring her that they would soon be dry. Sitting back on her heels, Sing Ho brushed a strand of hair behind her ear. It was hard to believe that only a few miles away such devastation existed.

Sing Ho had just finished washing the last shirt when she heard Hung Mooie calling for her. Waving toward her friend, she briskly started walking back to the barn. Was that a man standing beside Hung Mooie? She couldn't quite see. But then, a few moments later, the figure began to take shape. Was it Henry? Could it possibly be? She began to run. It was! Henry had found them. She ran forward and embraced Hung Mooie as she greeted Henry. "I told you he would find us," Sing Ho proclaimed. "This should be worth more than one notch in my basket!" Sing Ho declared as the two girls skipped about, unable to contain their excitement.

"You would think that Henry came to marry *you*," a voice spoke from behind where the happy trio stood.

Sing Ho whirled around. "Charlie! You came! And so soon." She could hardly catch her breath. Her heart fluttered at the sight of him, and her fingers trembled as he took her hand in welcome. "I'm so happy to see you," she blurted out, wishing that she could throw herself into his arms as she had done with Hung Mooie a few moments earlier.

"And I am *very* happy to see you, also," he replied, giving her hand a squeeze. "You're trembling. Are you ill?"

"Yes. No. I mean, no, I'm not ill. I'm just excited. When did you get here? How did you find us, Henry? I can't wait to hear *everything*," she exclaimed just as Miss Cunningham walked out of the barn toward the two couples.

"Why don't you young people walk down by the stream and have a picnic lunch? Charlie went into Sausalito and brought us a supply of food. You girls pack some things and relax for a few hours," she suggested.

"Oh thank you, Lo Mo," Sing Ho replied, giving the matron a hug.

Lo Mo shook her head and laughed. "You're right, Charlie. You'd think *she* was the one getting married."

"Perhaps she will be," he replied, his remark causing Sing Ho to stop in her tracks. She turned toward him, a questioning look on her face, but he merely smiled and continued talking to Miss Cunningham.

Could it be that he cares for me? Or is he thinking that I'll soon marry Du Wang? she thought, running into the barn. Quickly, she grabbed some bread, cheese, and several ripe oranges and tucked them into her wicker basket.

"Where are you going?" Miss Minnie called out. "I'm making chicken and rice for lunch. Charlie brought us all this good food. You won't want to miss it."

"Charlie, Henry, Hung Mooie, and I are going on a picnic down by the stream. We'll have some rice for dinner."

"Ha! You think there will be any left by then? Go along, then—enjoy your picnic while we eat a good, hot meal," she replied, laughing and giving Sing Ho a pat on the shoulder.

Running from the barn with the basket swinging from her arm, Sing Ho joined the others. "I'm ready," she breathlessly announced as soon as Miss Cunningham had finished speaking.

"Then, off with you. Go and have fun, but be back by 3:00," she instructed. "You can bring the laundry back when you come."

"Yes, ma'am," Sing Ho answered as the group meandered down the slight incline toward the stream. "Let's go farther up this way," Sing Ho suggested, pointing upstream toward a small grove of hawthorn trees.

Together they ate and listened carefully as Henry told them of his trip across the country and the final miles into the outskirts of San Francisco. Fortunately, the passengers had been warned of the disaster, but there had been no way to prepare them for the shocking sights that they would see.

"The train stopped several miles outside the city, and the railroad had a few horse-drawn drays to carry us into town. It was gruesome. Cable and trolley tracks sticking up, twisted in midair, injured and dead people lying in the streets, roads split open in great chasms—how do you prepare people for sights such as those?" Henry asked, shaking his head. "But why am I saying this to you? You lived through it," he continued, still shaking his head as if to chase the dreadful scene from his mind. "When I tried to make my way to the Mission Home, the militia stopped me. They said all the homes had been evacuated. When I asked how I would find you, they laughed. But then one man called me back and said most of the refugees had headed toward either San Mateo, across the bay to Sausalito, or toward Oakland. I decided a group of fifty girls would be noticed by at least a few people, so I began questioning anyone who would talk to me. When I arrived at the Embarcadero, there was a man standing on the pier looking out across the bay. It was Charlie."

Wide-eyed, the two girls looked at each other. "This is more than a blessing; this is a miracle," Hung Mooie stated, her voice a strangled whisper.

"It *is* a miracle," Henry replied, placing an arm around his fiancée's shoulder and drawing her close. "I still want our wedding to take place on schedule. I don't want to wait," he continued. "I've told Miss Cunningham, and she promised to check with Pastor Landon. She thought that perhaps we could be married in the chapel at the theological seminary."

Hung Mooie beamed at this suggestion. "I brought my wedding dress," she told him, obviously unable to contain her excitement. "It was the only thing I could fit in my valise, but I refused to leave it behind."

"It's true," Sing Ho acknowledged when both men stared at Hung Mooie in obvious amazement.

"In that case, we had better put it to good use," Henry replied. "I know it won't be the wedding that you planned, but it will still be beautiful."

Charlie and Sing Ho walked toward the fortress-like seminary, which stood several miles in the distance, neither of them saying a word. A screeching hawk flew overhead, and robins twittered about, obviously seeking worms for their newborn babies.

"Tell me about yourself, Charlie," Sing Ho asked. "When did you immigrate to San Francisco, and where is your family?"

He gave her a subdued laugh. "I didn't *immigrate* to San Francisco—I was born here."

"*No!* Really? Your parents lived in California when you were born? That's hard to believe!"

"Why is that so hard to believe? My father was born in this country also. You see, my grandfather came to California during the days of the gold rush, back in 1850. Shortly after he arrived, he sent for my grandmother. My father was born in the gold-mining country up around Placerville in 1852. My grandparents were very fortunate, in more ways than one," he explained.

"How is that?" she asked.

"Well, while panning for gold they met a young missionary couple who led them to the Lord. They soon became Christians and raised their children in a Christian home. In addition to that, my grandfather struck gold and became a very wealthy man."

"I see. So you've had a life of luxury and indulgence."

Charlie laughed a deep, resonating laugh that continued for several minutes. "No, far from it. Even though my grandfather became wealthy, his values and ethics remained the same. And those same values have been passed down to me. My family lives comfortably, but we are far from pampered. Much of my parents' time and money is spent in the Christian work of spreading the gospel," he told her.

"So is that how you came to serve on the board at the Mission Home?" Sing Ho asked.

"Yes. My parents have both been very supportive of the home, and when Miss Cunningham asked that one of them serve on the board, they deferred to me. You see, my father's health is not what it used to be, and my mother would never consider such a prominent position—she prefers to work behind the scenes. Miss Cunningham seemed pleased by the suggestion, so here I am, at your service," he joked, giving her a mock salute.

"What keeps you busy when you're not collecting food for our wayward group?" she asked as they turned and walked back toward the stream, where Hung Mooie and Henry appeared to be deep in conversation.

"Many things, but I will be spending a large portion of my time rebuilding two of the family businesses. We own part interest in a shoe factory on the edge of Chinatown, and my father owns the telephone company in Chinatown. Both suffered tremendous damage," he explained. "Needless to say, there is more work to do than I care to think about right now. When we aren't fighting the devastation of earthquakes, I manage those interests, along with several others, for my family. I am an only son, which means my father relies upon me greatly," he explained.

Giving him a sweet smile, she contemplated her next question. She didn't want to appear bold, but she wanted to know if there was a woman in his life. From some of his comments, she felt that there was no one, but there was no way to find out for sure—no way but to ask. "And what of your evenings and weekends? Do you and your lady friend attend the theater and exciting social events?"

"I attend as few as possible. Those things really don't interest me. By the way, I almost forgot to tell you," he said, but then hesitated momentarily. "Henry isn't the only person who found me," Charlie finally remarked, breaking the silence.

"What do you mean?" Sing Ho asked, her curiosity piqued.

"Your gentleman friend, Du Wang, came looking for me. He asked if I knew where Miss Cunningham had moved you girls."

Sing Ho's breath caught in her throat. "Du Wang? How would he even know to look for you?"

"I'm not sure who, but somebody told him I was a member of the Mission Board. I'm not a difficult person to find—even after a major disaster. He found me at what remains of the telephone company, picking through the rubble."

She wasn't sure she wanted to know the answer, but she asked anyway. "What did you tell him?"

"I told him the truth—that I saw you off on a ferry headed for Sausalito and your final destination was an old barn in San Anselmo, near the theological seminary."

She nodded, keeping her head bowed, not wanting to meet his eyes. "And did he say he was coming here?"

"No, he merely scribbled down what I told him and scurried off without a word. He's a strange little man. He appears too old for you," Charlie added, "although I suppose that is not my business."

Chapter 4

Hearing Bo Lin's soft cries, Sing Ho rose from the rumpled, uncomfortable pallet and carefully threaded her way through the maze of sleeping children on the floor. She stooped down, lovingly gathered the small child into her arms, and began rocking her back and forth. As Bo Lin's whimpering ceased and her breathing deepened, Sing Ho's thoughts wandered back over that day's events.

It had been a good day. The plans for Hung Mooie's wedding were well under way before Henry's departure earlier that evening. The thought of their wedding filled Sing Ho with a strange mixture of excitement and anxiety. Then, too, Charlie had delivered the good news that there was a vacant home available for all of them in San Rafael. One of the board members had offered it as a temporary residence until final decisions could be made concerning rebuilding the Mission Home in San Francisco. But news of restoring the Mission Home had been promising, also. According to Charlie, funds were already pouring in toward repairing the brick edifice on Sacramento Street. In fact, his visit had been cause for several notches in her basket.

After the many struggles of the preceding days, seeing Charlie had provided a much-needed respite. She smiled, remembering how attentive and kind he'd been throughout the day. Yet he *had* masterfully avoided her question about escorting lady friends to social functions. Moreover, he'd told her about Du Wang's visit immediately after she had asked that particular question. Perhaps he was censoring her question, thinking it inappropriate—reminding her that she had no right to ask about his personal life when she had a suitor of her own. However, he had seemed pleased to go walking with her after the picnic and tell her about his family, apparently enjoying her company. It was confusing—that much she knew for certain.

The smart thing to do is put thoughts of Charlie aside, Sing Ho determined. *After all, Du Wang had obviously been concerned about our welfare. Why else would he have made a special trip to inquire about our whereabouts?* Those thoughts, however, did little to curtail her interest in Charlie Ming or the fact that he would be returning with Henry on Saturday. She wandered back to her makeshift bed and slipped into a restless sleep that was fraught with dreams of living on a small vegetable farm with Du Wang, only it was she that was stoop-shouldered with unkempt hair instead of Du Wang.

Miss Minnie's morning rituals were already in progress when Sing Ho awakened. "You're beginning to take up Hung Mooie's habits," Minnie teased as Sing Ho walked outdoors toward the crackling fire where the older woman sat tending breakfast.

"I didn't sleep well," Sing Ho replied, collapsing onto the ground beside Minnie.

"Somebody stolen your heart?" she asked, not looking away from her task. Bright-orange flames licked upward around the bottom of the skillet as a large slice of ham resting inside sizzled and popped in protest.

Sing Ho eyed the woman. *How could she know? Is there some telltale sign?*

"I'll take your silence as a 'yes,'" Minnie chortled, obviously pleased with herself. "Can't say as I blame you. That young man certainly stole my heart, too."

"What? You're in love with Charlie?" Sing Ho asked in a shrill voice. How could somebody Miss Minnie's age possibly be in love with Charlie? It wasn't possible!

Miss Minnie laughed—loud and hard. She laughed until tears ran down her plump cheeks and spilled onto the bodice of her blue print shirtwaist. "I'm sorry, Sing Ho. I shouldn't be laughing at you," she sputtered, obviously trying to contain herself. "It's just that such a thought is so preposterous that I couldn't help myself," she continued, gasping to catch her breath as the giggles began to subside. "Can't you just imagine—oh, never mind," she stopped herself.

"No! You must explain what you meant about Charlie stealing your heart," Sing Ho insisted.

"Any man who would spend his time and money making sure this little band of vagabonds has food and shelter has my love and loyalty. He's a Good Samaritan, if ever I saw one," she explained. "You needn't worry about me trying to steal your beau!"

Silently, Sing Ho watched as Minnie tossed flour into the skillet and stirred until it turned a golden brown. Miss Minnie could make gravy better than anyone. Of course, it had taken several years before Sing Ho had grown accustomed to American food, but now she ate it as often as she ate the food cooked in the Chinese kitchen of their home. At least she had when they had a home.

"Did Lo Mo tell you anything about the house in San Rafael?" Sing Ho asked.

"A little. Why do you ask?"

"Does it have two kitchens like our house on Sacramento Street?"

Minnie tilted her head to one side and gave Sing Ho a kind smile. "She didn't say, but I would guess that it has only one. Most houses don't come equipped with more than one kitchen, but if we can adjust to living in a barn, we can adjust to cooking Chinese and American food in one kitchen. I'm just thankful that we'll soon have a roof over our heads that doesn't spring leaks. At least I hope it doesn't."

Sing Ho nodded and contemplated her next question. Miss Minnie didn't mince words when asked for advice. Not that she was unkind—but if she thought you were headed down the wrong path, a dose of her advice was akin to a spoonful of castor oil, and Sing Ho didn't feel up to that. She needed to word her question carefully, but it soon became obvious that she wasn't quite sure how to ask it.

Minnie finally broke the silence. "Something on your mind, child?"

"Would you talk to Lo Mo about Charlie?" she blurted without further thought.

"Sure. But about what?" the older woman asked. She brushed a wisp of gray hair back from her face and gave Sing Ho an inquisitive look.

"I want her to give Charlie permission to call upon me—as a suitor. Instead of Du Wang," she quickly added.

Miss Minnie said nothing for several minutes. Instead, she sat staring at the bubbling gravy, stirring while quietly murmuring something under her breath. "So he really has stolen your heart. Is *that* what you're telling me?" she asked, breaking the early morning silence. Her tone of voice sent a reverberating signal, and Sing Ho immediately questioned the wisdom of seeking Miss Minnie's assistance. "What's going on between the two of you?"

"Nothing. Nothing is going on. He's a good man, and I find him much more to my liking than Du Wang. I can't help how I feel," she explained, sensing that she needed to defend herself.

"I see. Well, this matter might take care of itself without any interference," she commented as several of the little girls began to gather around, eager to begin their breakfast. "Du Wang probably won't pursue his courtship. He doesn't even know that we've come this direction," she continued.

"That's just it. He *does* know," Sing Ho replied. "He's already talked to Charlie and gotten directions to the barn. Why would he inquire if he didn't intend to continue our courtship?"

"You've got a point, but I think this is something best left in the hands of the Lord," Minnie advised as she pulled a Dutch oven filled with biscuits out of the fire.

"*What's* best left to the Lord?" Miss Cunningham asked as she approached the two of them.

"Charlie Ming," Sing Ho muttered, handing Bo Lin a biscuit.

"Isn't he a fine man? And not yet married, either! I may ask him if he'd like to call on Yuen Kim."

"You're going to give Charlie permission to call upon Yuen Kim? Why would you do such a thing?" Sing Ho squeaked. Fingers of overpowering panic began stretching and tightening their way around her heart. She struggled to regain her composure. "He's too old for Yuen Kim," she offered, stealing a fleeting glance at Miss Minnie.

"Yuen Kim is only a year younger than you," Miss Cunningham replied.

Sing Ho could think of nothing to say. Not one word of rebuttal would come to mind as she sat mutely staring across the fire into Miss Minnie's brilliant blue eyes.

"Your comment surprises me, Bertha," Minnie declared, giving Sing Ho a compassionate look as she spoke to Miss Cunningham.

"What? That Yuen Kim is only a year younger than Sing Ho, or that I would talk to Charlie about courting her?"

"The part about Charlie. He didn't appear interested in Yuen Kim. In fact, if you'll forgive my saying so, he acted like a man besotted with our little Sing Ho."

"You may be right. I don't know what I was thinking to send them off with Hung Mooie and Henry. After all, Sing Ho is already spoken for."

Sing Ho's eyes darted back and forth between the two women until she could no longer restrain herself. "Spoken for? Du Wang has not spoken for *me!* I've seen him exactly eight times since you told him he could call on me a year ago. He has never spoken of marriage, but I now know I could never be married to him!" she exclaimed.

"Just what has occurred in the last few weeks to convince you of such a thing?" Miss Cunningham asked while taking Sing Ho aside and walking toward a small clump of bushes alongside the barn.

"Quite honestly, I never wanted him to be my suitor. I told you before that he's too old for me and I have no feeling for him. But you told me to be patient, so I have tried," she replied.

Miss Cunningham nodded her head, appearing to carefully listen to Sing Ho's remarks. "Yet I feel there's more to this than your earlier proclamation that Du Wang is too old. Is there something else you should be telling me?" she probed.

"It's Charlie. I would like Charlie to be *my* suitor," she honestly replied. "Is that so wrong? He's more my age, and we can talk together. Besides, I think he cares for me also," she quickly added.

"I see. Well, I know Charlie Ming is an honorable man, and he would never interfere with another man's courtship. Besides, if he had plans for courtship, I'm sure he would discuss them with *me* before talking to one of my girls."

"He has said nothing about courtship and he knows that Du Wang is my suitor, but whether Charlie declares intentions to court me or not, I would like you to consider breaking my courtship with Du Wang. Would you at least consider it?" she pleaded.

"I think Miss Minnie was right. This needs some prayer," Miss Cunningham told the girl. Lo Mo placed an arm about Sing Ho's shoulder and led her back to where the rest of their family was hungrily eating breakfast.

✖∂

If one couldn't be married in the Chinese room at 920 Sacramento Street, Sing Ho decided that the ivy-covered chapel outside San Anselmo was near perfect. It was a part of the theological seminary but stood far enough away from the other buildings to give the appearance of sitting alone among the flowering hawthorn and acacia. Sing Ho, Yuen Kim, and several of the other girls had spent the morning decorating the church sanctuary, which now stood in readiness for the afternoon nuptials.

"It looks beautiful, don't you think?" Yuen Kim asked as the group headed back toward the barn.

Sing Ho voiced her agreement and then busied herself talking to Bo Lin, her five-year-old shadow. She knew that it wasn't Yuen Kim's fault that Miss Cunningham considered her a possible bride for Charlie. But Lo Mo's proclamation caused Sing Ho now to view the girl as an adversary, and even prayer had not assuaged those emotions.

"Oh, look—Henry and Charlie have arrived," Yuen Kim declared, a smile lighting up her face.

"Why are *you* getting so excited?" Sing Ho curtly inquired.

Yuen Kim glared at Sing Ho and grabbed her arm. "I want to know why you're treating me so rudely. What have I done to you?"

"Nothing! You've done nothing! Now let go of my arm. We need to get back to the barn," she ordered, attempting to pull her arm from Yuen Kim's tightening grip.

"If I have done nothing, then why won't you talk to me? You act as though I don't even exist anymore. You never used to treat me this way, and I don't see you acting impolitely with anyone else," she persisted. "Is it because I told Miss Cunningham I had no interest in being courted by Charlie Ming? I know he's become your friend and you think he's a wonderful man—not that I don't think he's nice, too," she quickly added, "but I don't want to get involved with *any* man. I told Lo Mo I've decided I want to go to college."

"You do? Oh, Yuen Kim, I think that's a wonderful idea—your going to school, I mean," Sing Ho replied, embracing her in a giant bear hug and giggling.

"You've been acting strangely for the past several days. It must be Hung Mooie's wedding. I know you're going to miss her!"

"I *am* going to miss Hung Mooie," Sing Ho agreed.

Yuen Kim's pronouncement that she held no interest in Charlie was more than Sing Ho could have hoped for. She wanted to take off in a headlong run toward where Charlie stood, but she knew that she dared not make a spectacle of herself. At least part of her prayer had been answered.

It was a beautiful spring day, Hung Mooie would be married in a few hours, and, best of all, she could enjoy the festivities in Charlie's company.

Sing Ho headed directly for where Charlie stood talking with Miss Cunningham, but her thoughts were interrupted by Miss Minnie's declaration that Hung Mooie wanted her assistance in the barn. "She needs you to help her get dressed, so hurry along," she continued, turning Sing Ho toward the barn door and away from where Charlie stood staring at her. Their eyes locked momentarily before Miss Minnie took her by the arm and escorted her inside.

Hung Mooie sat waiting in one corner of the barn, her wedding dress hanging neatly from a nail in one of the wooden braces. "Hurry! You know I want you to fix my hair. What took you so long?" she asked in a voice filled with agitation.

"You need to calm yourself. We have plenty of time. Besides, you wanted the church to look nice, didn't you? Well, that's what I was doing—decorating the church. I see that you found someone to press your wedding gown. It looks lovely," Sing Ho rambled on as she began brushing Hung Mooie's long black hair. Carefully she divided the hair in half and plaited it into two plump braids, which were then coiled on either side of Hung Mooie's head and embellished with wildflowers and ribbon. "There!" Sing Ho proclaimed when she had finally finished the task. "You look especially lovely, and, once we get you into that dress, there won't be words to describe your beauty."

"As long as Henry finds me a worthy bride, I will be happy," Hung Mooie replied. "You'd better hurry and get dressed."

"I wish I had packed the dress I was to wear for your wedding," Sing Ho complained, remembering the royal-blue silk print. "But since I didn't, I suppose you must be satisfied with an attendant dressed in a simple skirt and blouse."

"Just so long as you are there with me, I don't care what you're wearing. Did Miss Minnie tell you that Mr. Haslett from the church in San Anselmo sent over a horse and buggy for my ride to the chapel?"

"No. That's wonderful! Isn't his wife the lady who pressed your gown?"

"Yes. They've been very nice. Mrs. Haslett found out about the wedding, and within two days she had organized the ladies who made the food for the reception! Everyone is being so helpful and kind, that it's hard to believe we're a displaced group of nomads."

"I gathered some lovely flowers for your bouquet—they match what I've put in your hair. We can leave the stems long, and Lo Mo gave me some ribbons I can use to tie around them into a bow. They're over in my basket if you want to see them," Sing Ho remarked while braiding her own thick hair and coiling it into a bun at the back of her head. "Once we remove the flowers, it sounds as though I need to carve a few more notches in the basket."

The flowers looked beautiful lying in the basket—a profusion of colors and sizes mixed with a variety of ferns and green, leafy stems. Hung Mooie stared at them momentarily and quickly walked back to where Sing Ho had just finished styling her hair.

"Instead of making a bouquet, why don't I carry the flowers in the blessings basket, as a remembrance of all the good things God has provided since the earthquake? When I walk down the aisle carrying the basket, it will cause all of us to reflect upon God's mercy," Hung Mooie suggested, holding the basketful of flowers in front of her. "How does it look?"

"It looks splendid! I'll just tie the ribbons to the handle, and I think it will be much more lovely than anything we could possibly create."

They heard Mr. Haslett arrive with the horse and buggy just as Sing Ho finished tying the ribbons. Miss Minnie scurried into the barn, announcing the men had already gone to the chapel and rushing the two girls toward the waiting carriage. They rode in silence, Sing Ho contemplating her life without Hung Mooie's ever-present friendship while Hung Mooie's trembling fingers clung to the flower basket. From the number of buggies tied outside the chapel, it appeared that most of the residents of San Anselmo had decided to attend the wedding.

"I'm starting to get nervous," Hung Mooie confided as they stepped out of the buggy.

"Then you're doing fine. I would have been nervous way before now. Just think how much better you're doing than I would," Sing Ho soothingly replied. They both giggled—a shrill, nervous, cackling noise that sounded strange in Sing Ho's ears. Miss Cunningham met them in the church vestibule, gave final instructions, and then ordered Sing Ho to begin her walk down the aisle. With halting steps, she walked down the long, narrow passageway between the pews.

Henry stood waiting for his bride at the front of the church with Charlie standing beside him, obviously acting as best man. His eyes met hers, and Sing Ho wondered why Hung Mooie hadn't mentioned that Charlie would be Henry's best man. Of course, who else would be? She really hadn't given the matter any thought, but somehow she hadn't expected to see him standing there waiting beside Henry. Something deep inside made her wish that Charlie were waiting for her to meet him at the end of the aisle and become his bride. But this wasn't her day—it was Hung Mooie's, and wishing wouldn't change anything.

Turning, Sing Ho stood with Pastor Landon, Henry, and Charlie and then watched as Miss Cunningham escorted Hung Mooie down the aisle. Poised and stately in a green and gray cheviot dress, Lo Mo tucked Hung Mooie's arm through her own, and together they slowly walked toward the front of the church. No one could deny the fact that Hung Mooie, in her off-white silk gown and gossamer veil trimmed in blond lace, was the focal point of the afternoon.

Several times throughout the ceremony, Sing Ho glanced toward Charlie. Each time she found him staring at her. It pleased her, yet she hoped that Lo Mo and Miss Minnie weren't watching them. Miss Minnie already seemed intent on keeping the pair separated, and she wanted to spend at least a little time with him during the reception. Chords of joyous organ music brought Sing Ho back to the present. She watched as Henry kissed his bride and the newlyweds began walking back down the aisle. Charlie walked toward her and offered his arm. Her heart fluttered, and a slight shiver ran down her back as she took his arm.

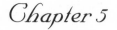

T hree of the girls from the Mission Home stood at white linen-covered tables and proudly served fruit punch and thin slices of buttery pound cake topped with a translucent raspberry glaze. At another table, sterling silver trays were laden with delicate tea sandwiches, fresh fruit, and cheese. The guests mingled and visited, most of them devout members of the San Anselmo church, who had become enchanted by the wedding plans from the moment their assistance was requested. Who could refuse a young couple determined to overcome one of nature's most devastating obstacles in order to proceed with their nuptials?

Miss Minnie fluttered from table to table while dispensing orders and filling trays, her cheeks flushed with excitement. Outside the church, the little girls played in the small fruit orchard. Their shouts of pleasure blended with the polite conversation of the adults who had gathered inside the church parlor to watch the bride and groom open their wedding gifts.

Charlie stood beside Sing Ho as Hung Mooie began to unwrap one of the beribboned packages. "It was so kind of these people to purchase wedding gifts for Henry and Hung Mooie. They don't even know them, yet they've done so much," Sing Ho stated.

"That's one of the many benefits that come with having a Christian family. The family extends and embraces all members of the faith, helping each other wherever and however they can. At least that has been my experience, and I believe it's what Christ planned for His church," Charlie replied, offering her a cup of punch. "Any word from Du Wang since I last saw you?" he asked, surprising her by the abrupt change of topics.

"No, although I'm not surprised. I still can't imagine why he went to the trouble of finding you and requesting information about my whereabouts. He never seemed like a man who would do such a thing."

"Perhaps he cares very deeply, but has difficulty showing his emotions—a lot of men are like that," he commented. "It looks as though the bride and groom are about ready to leave. You'd better get over there, or you'll miss your chance to bid Hung Mooie farewell."

Hung Mooie's arms reached out to hug her approaching friend. "I was beginning to wonder if you would tear yourself away from Charlie to tell me good-bye," she

432

teased as they tenderly embraced.

"You know better than that!" Sing Ho replied, pulling her tighter. "I will miss you so very much, but I know that you and Henry are going to have a wonderful life with lots of lovely children. You must make him promise to bring you back to visit us, and I'll expect letters—lots of them! You can tell me all about Cleveland and those other big eastern cities."

"You know that I'll write to you. I'm going to be lost without all the noise and activity—at least for a short time!" she replied, with a mixture of laughter and tears.

"You'd better go. Henry is waiting, and we're just going to cry if we keep talking. I love you, Hung Mooie, and I know I'll never have a better friend. You'd *better* be happy," Sing Ho said, shaking her finger.

Hung Mooie flashed her friend a bright smile and then took Henry's arm and walked out the double wooden doors of the ivy-covered chapel, into her new life as Mrs. Henry Lai.

🦋

"Sing Ho! Come here, please," Miss Cunningham called out, motioning the girl toward where she stood.

"Yes? Do you need help?" Sing Ho inquired obligingly.

"Would you please go outdoors and check on the little girls? I'm sure that they're fine, but I don't want them wandering too far away from the church."

"Certainly. I'll be glad to," Sing Ho replied, unaware that Charlie followed close on her heels.

"Where are you rushing off to?" he asked, running the last few paces to catch up with her.

"Lo Mo wanted me to check on the children. I suppose it comes from all those years of worrying that one of them will be kidnapped. Quite frankly, it's easier to do her bidding than argue. Besides, I never win an argument with Lo Mo," Sing Ho told him and laughed.

The girls were in a large circle, playing drop the handkerchief, and Sing Ho quickly counted heads. And then she counted again, her eyes carefully scanning the little faces.

"Where are Bo Lin and Yoke Lon?" she asked while attempting to keep her voice calm. Her fists were clenched, and she could feel her fingernails digging into the flesh of her palms.

"They went to play over by those trees," one of the girls said, pointing toward a small grove not far off. Hiking up her skirt, Sing Ho took off, her feet flying through the grass and her voice piercing the air as she called the two girls' names. Panting and out of breath, she was unwilling to believe her eyes. She continued to run between the trees, certain that Bo Lin's head would pop out from behind a bush at any moment. "They're hiding from me. It's just a game," she frantically cried to Charlie, who was searching nearby.

"Keep looking! I'm going back to the church and get some of the other men to help us search," he instructed before rushing back in the direction of the church.

"Bo Lin, *please*. Come out here right now. This isn't funny anymore! Bo Lin, *please, please!*" Sing Ho wailed.

The men flooded out of the chapel doors and came running toward Sing Ho. By the time they reached her, she had fallen to the ground weeping, no longer able to convince herself that the girls were merely hiding. Miss Minnie and Miss Cunningham followed closely behind, fear etched on their faces as they obviously attempted to retain their composure. Meanwhile the children's game had ceased, and, their curiosity piqued, they now began to wander toward the adults who were spreading across the grassy acreage.

"You must gain control of yourself, Sing Ho. We also need to think about the other children. I don't want to frighten them. After all, this may be a false alarm. Now tell me—who is missing?" Miss Minnie pleaded.

"Bo Lin and Yoke Lon," she managed to croak through the lump that had formed in her constricting throat. "My little Bo Lin," she wept, falling into Miss Minnie's arms.

"They may have gone to play over at the stream," one of the men yelled. "Three of you men come with me, and we'll check along the water's edge."

"That's it!" Sing Ho announced, brightening. "They have gone to play in the water. You know how Bo Lin loves the water, Miss Minnie."

"Yes, dearie, I know she does. And perhaps they're having themselves a gay old time splashing in the stream. Now, you need to settle yourself. We need to question the other children and find out if they know anything. Can you help?"

"Yes," she staunchly replied, sniffing one last time before wiping her eyes.

And so they began questioning the children, one by one. *How long had Bo Lin and Yoke Lon been gone? Why did they leave the group? Had they seen the pair after they went toward the trees? Had anyone strange been lurking about? Had anyone heard either of the girls scream or cry?*

The replies were surprisingly similar. The two girls hadn't wanted to play games and decided that they wanted to sit under the trees where it was cool. They had been in view for a while, but then had disappeared. Nobody had heard them make any noise, nor had they seen any strangers in the vicinity.

"It sounds as though they may have wandered off—at least that's what I want to believe. Since none of the girls saw anyone or heard any noises, it's just possible," Miss Cunningham confided in Sing Ho and Miss Minnie. "I don't want to believe that members of the tongs have tracked us down. You would certainly think they would have more pressing matters to take care of following an earthquake—wouldn't you?"

Minnie nodded her head in agreement. All three of them knew that there were a multitude of ways the tong members could busy themselves. But none of those would prove as profitable as securing several girls who could soon work in their brothels.

"I didn't risk my life to save those little girls to see their Christian lives cut short by those evil men," Miss Cunningham angrily proclaimed. "And I don't believe it is God's plan for those children to grow up and be forced to lead lives of depravity and disgrace. If they've been kidnapped, I'll find them and get them back if it's the last thing I do!"

Sing Ho had no doubt that Lo Mo would be true to her word. While accompanying Lo Mo on many of her rescue attempts, Sing Ho had learned long ago why Miss Cunningham was called *Fan Quai*, the "white devil," by the tong members. They found the American woman's uncanny ability to locate their slave girls and spirit them away to the Mission Home abhorrent—and her lack of fear was without dispute. It was because of that success they called her the white devil, certain that if she were merely human, they could stop her.

Sing Ho and the other girls had taken courage as Miss Cunningham had consistently refused to succumb to the terroristic threats and plotting by the tong. Whenever the men came to their residence at 920 Sacramento Street, screaming curses and attempting to instill fear, Lo Mo met the challenge with the Word of God; when they sought to intimidate with the evil messages they attached to rocks and hurled into the windows, Lo Mo placed iron grilles across the glass; when they lurked about attempting to kidnap one of the children, Lo Mo obtained police protection; and each time they took her to court attempting to prove that she had stolen a child, Lo Mo succeeded in producing the necessary adoption papers. In her heart, Sing Ho knew that Miss Cunningham would do everything possible to protect Bo Lin and Yoke Lon—but would it be enough?

Watching as Charlie crossed the grassy field and walked toward them, Sing Ho was sure of his message. With faltering steps, slumped shoulders, and a solemn face, he took Miss Cunningham's hands in his own. "We've found nothing, except this," he told them, holding up a pink satin ribbon that Sing Ho had woven into Bo Lin's hair earlier in the day.

Horror seized Sing Ho as she pulled the ribbon from between Charlie's extended fingers. She screamed inwardly, a prolonged, excruciating wail that never reached her lips. As hard as she tried, she could say nothing. Her voice wouldn't come. She merely nodded when Charlie asked if the ribbon belonged to Bo Lin. She stood mute, listening to Miss Cunningham ask where the ribbon had been found, and Charlie's answer that it was discovered near the road that ran by the barn.

"We think that the girls were kidnapped and that the men headed back toward the dock," Charlie explained. "It's certain they'll want to get the pair back to San Francisco as quickly as possible. Some of our men have already gone in that direction. Mr. Weaver took his horseless carriage. I'll join them shortly, but I wanted to report our findings to you," he told them.

"The girls would scream and holler if they tried to take them on the ferry. Surely the other passengers would be alerted," Miss Minnie suggested.

"You're right, it would be impossible to keep the girls quiet. They wouldn't risk traveling with other people. My guess is that they traveled in a small boat that they rented or perhaps borrowed," Charlie agreed. "Our only hope is that they don't reach the bay before we catch up with them. If I don't return before nightfall, don't worry. I promise you that I will return and report to you—no matter what the news," he assured them.

Without warning, Sing Ho's voice returned, loud and clear. "I want to go with him," she told Miss Cunningham. "I must," she said, so sadly and so simply that Miss Cunningham merely nodded her agreement.

"You're not going to let Sing Ho go off unescorted with the *men*, are you?" Minnie asked, her voice filled with shock.

"Minnie, there's a time to worry about propriety and a time to do what your heart knows is honorable. It is crucial to Sing Ho's welfare that she help find the girls," she replied as the young couple walked away. "I think that I'll head back to the chapel and pray. Care to join me?"

🍂

Charlie and Sing Ho climbed into Pastor Landon's buggy, and the threesome soon caught up to Mr. Weaver and the other men near Sausalito. The pastor said a quick prayer with the young couple and the searchers for the safe recovery of the girls before he returned to the church.

"We've talked with several people who have seen Chinese men with a cart of hay headed toward the bay," Mr. Weaver explained, "but none of them have seen any Chinese *children*."

"We've no time to waste," Charlie said.

"Let's go." Mr. Weaver nodded and helped Sing Ho into his horseless carriage.

Within minutes, the search group spotted some Chinese men with a hay cart stopped by the side of the road just ahead.

"There! There's the hay cart!" exclaimed Sing Ho.

"We'll drive on past them and wait just ahead where we can watch them," Mr. Weaver stated. He slowed down and added, "You two had better get invisible while we pass them, or they are likely to get nervous. We don't want them doing anything stupid if they have the children."

Sing Ho and Charlie ducked down as they passed the hay cart. "Can't we just stop and search the wagon?" Sing Ho asked.

"We can't take the chance that they would hurt Bo Lin and Yoke Lon," Charlie answered. "First, we must see what they are doing, and then we will know what to do."

The closeness of Charlie's warm breath and encouraging smile made Sing Ho want to hold onto him to drive off the chill of fear.

The searchers stopped in a small group along the road, feigning trouble with one of the buggies while they observed the hay cart. Apparently confident that the group ahead was not watching them, the Chinese men moved some hay aside and appeared agitated as they talked.

"Bo Lin and Yoke Lon are in there, Charlie. I just know it," said Sing Ho.

"If you are right, we will need assistance from the police," Charlie answered. "Mr. Baker has the fastest horse, perhaps he could go into Sausalito and alert the police?"

"I'm on my way," Mr. Baker said as he spun on his heel and headed for his buggy.

"And I'll see if these men would like to sell me some hay while Mr. Baker is gone," Mr. Weaver said. "You all stay here unless I tip my hat back. That's the signal the girls are in the cart." He turned and casually strolled down the road.

As Mr. Weaver approached the hay cart, the Chinese men hastily pushed the hay back into place. Mr. Weaver walked past them to the back of the cart, and they followed him. He reached in, grabbed a handful of hay, and inspected it. The men gestured for him to stop, but he reached in again, dredging deeper. Sing Ho gasped as Mr. Weaver leaned back and pushed his hat far back on his head. Charlie and the other men rushed toward the cart with Sing Ho on their heels.

Mr. Weaver reached deep into the hay, and the kidnappers tried to feign shock when he pulled Bo Lin and then Yoke Lon from under the hay and the rescuers collected around them. Sing Ho heard them claim the girls must be runaways trying to escape a cruel master.

"Then perhaps you can explain the ropes around their ankles and wrists and the gags over their mouths," Charlie countered.

The kidnappers tried to run away but were detained by the rescuers and led away from the hay cart. Sing Ho was both relieved and outraged as she helped the girls loose from their bindings. Frightened but unharmed, both girls were talking and crying, apologizing and thanking Sing Ho for finding them.

The police finally arrived, and Sing Ho and the girls watched until the kidnappers were taken away to Sausalito. Charlie returned to the hay cart, where the three girls sat hugging, awash in tears of relief.

&⬧

Shortly before sunset, Miss Cunningham saw plumes of dust billowing in the distance. Squinting into the late-afternoon sun, she finally made out Mr. Weaver's horseless carriage lumbering down the dirt road toward her. An arm was waving out the window, and she could hear excited shouts from the passengers as the car drew closer.

"Please, Lord," she whispered, "let my girls be in that car." Eventually, the automobile was within sight, and she thought she could see Bo Lin. Or was that her imagination? No, it *was* Bo Lin. In fact, she was perched on Charlie's lap, clapping her hands and laughing. But where was Yoke Lon? Surely they hadn't come back with only one child. Surely they had remained and searched further. Rushing toward the car, she grabbed Bo Lin from Charlie before the car came to a complete stop. Tears streamed down her cheeks.

"Thank You, Lord. Thank You," she repeated over and over, clinging to the child while her eyes continued to scan the vehicle that was now stopped a short distance from where she stood. She held her breath as the passengers piled out, one by one.

Sing Ho appeared haggard and near exhaustion as she moved toward Miss Cunningham, a half-smile upon her face. "As you can see, we've returned safe and sound," she quietly reported.

"At least part of you," Lo Mo replied, her voice cracking with emotion. "And what of Yoke Lon? Do you hold any hope that we'll be able to recover her?"

"Oh, Lo Mo, I am so sorry. Yoke Lon fell asleep in the car. I was weary, and she was sleeping so soundly that I let her remain there. You thought—"

"Yes. I thought you had recovered only one of the girls. Praise, God! Our family is reunited!" she shouted.

Before long, all of the girls were outdoors, talking and laughing, shouting questions and showing fervent interest in every detail of the kidnapping.

"Girls, girls! Quit your shouting! I know you all want to know what happened, and so do I. Why don't we all gather together in the barn? That way they can tell the story, and, after they've finished, we can ask any questions we may have."

Quickly, the girls began to scamper back toward the barn. Miss Minnie lifted Yoke Lon from the car and carried her inside as the other adults followed and seated themselves in a circle. Once the group was settled, Miss Cunningham looked toward Sing Ho.

"I'd rather that Charlie tell you what happened," she said in answer to the older woman's look.

"Charlie? Would you care to enlighten us?" Miss Cunningham asked after giving Sing Ho a nod of understanding.

"It's much as we had thought. The girls were playing in the stand of trees away from the church. After a short time, they decided to get some water from the stream. They had gone only a short distance when they spotted the men. Thinking that the men were members of the local community, the girls weren't frightened. Even when the men approached them, they remained calm. It wasn't until they were seized and were being pushed under a pile of hay in the back of a small, horse-drawn cart that they realized they'd made a gigantic error in judgment."

"Apparently, I've failed to make the girls understand the seriousness of their plight," Miss Cunningham lamented as Charlie shifted and crossed his legs.

"This isn't your fault," he consoled her. "The girls need to have *some* freedom in their lives."

"I suppose. I'm sorry for interrupting. Please continue," she urged him.

Charlie spared no details explaining how the girls were discovered in the hay cart.

"The hay kept tickling my nose, and we could hardly breathe," Bo Lin chimed in.

"Who were these men? Were any of them from the brothels in Chinatown?" Miss Cunningham inquired.

"They were opportunists attempting to earn a bounty from the slave owners. It seems that even something as disastrous as an earthquake will not stop these men from their evil ways. In fact, they've already set up their ugly businesses in Oakland and other communities where large groups of Chinese men have begun to relocate. And, as you know, whenever they think they can find girls who will someday be useful to them, they are on the prowl," Charlie replied.

"It seems strange they would come to San Anselmo. So few Chinese migrated in this direction that I'm surprised they chose to search this area. Doesn't it seem odd to you?" Miss Minnie inquired.

Sing Ho and Charlie exchanged a look. "Is there something that you're not telling us?" Miss Cunningham asked.

"I'll tell them," Sing Ho quietly replied as Charlie gave her an encouraging smile. "When the police arrived, one of the kidnappers claimed to have been forced to participate in the kidnapping, in repayment of a debt, and soon divulged everything. It seems that Du Wang conducted business with several of these men, selling them produce whenever he came to San Francisco. And during one of those visits, Du Wang told them he was courting a girl who lived at the Mission Home."

"That was certainly foolish. What could he have been thinking? I can't imagine why he would even conduct business with such people, let alone tell them his personal business," Miss Cunningham interjected.

Sing Ho gave her a weak smile. "It seems that Du Wang met one of the men when he came to San Francisco after the earthquake. The man offered him a large sum of money if he would tell where the girls from the Mission Home had gone after the earthquake. That's why Du Wang went looking for Charlie and wanted to know our whereabouts," she stated.

"Are you telling me. . .do you mean to say. . .surely Du Wang would not consider doing such a thing," Miss Cunningham stammered.

"Not only did he consider doing it—but he did it!" Charlie stated, his voice filled with outrage. "How he could have done such a thing is beyond me, but apparently his love of money was greater than—"

"Than his love for *me*," Sing Ho stated softly.

"Sing Ho, this is certainly no reflection upon *you*," Miss Cunningham quickly interjected. "If anything, it's a reflection upon my judgment of character. I'm the one who gave Du Wang permission to court you. The last thing I want is for you to feel any responsibility for what has occurred," she continued, giving Sing Ho a warm smile.

"Does this mean that Sing Ho's courtship with Du Wang is over?" Chow Kum, one of the older girls, asked as she walked from the side of the room and sat down beside Yuen Kim. All eyes turned toward Chow Kum.

"Well, of course," Miss Cunningham replied. "Why would you even need to ask such a question?"

Ignoring Miss Cunningham's question, Chow Kum looked at Sing Ho. "Now you can carve another notch in your basket, can't you?" the girl asked, a furtive gleam crossing her face.

"What *are* you talking about?" Miss Cunningham inquired.

"Because now she's free of Du Wang. *That's* a blessing, isn't it, Sing Ho?" Chow Kum persisted stubbornly.

"If your remarks are made in an effort to inform Lo Mo that I never cared for Du Wang and that I wanted the courtship to end, she already knows that. I told her of my feelings long before this incident," Sing Ho asserted, her eyes darting back and forth between Yuen Kim and Chow Kum.

"And have you already told her of your feelings for Charlie and that *he's* the one you want to court you?" Chow Kum inquired, her eyes dancing in delight at the surprised gasps from several of the older girls.

Sing Ho jumped up and ran outdoors, unable to withstand the embarrassment of sitting there any longer. Why had Chow Kum said those things in front of everyone? Especially Charlie. How would she ever face him again? And how did Chow Kum know of her feelings toward Charlie? That is, unless Yuen Kim had surmised the truth and discussed it with Chow Kum.

Sing Ho didn't hear the approaching footsteps and was startled when Charlie lightly touched her arm. "Please don't let Chow Kum's foolish actions embarrass you. She has humiliated herself by this reckless behavior. In fact, Miss Cunningham is speaking with her now." Taking hold of her shoulders, Charlie turned her to face him and gently lifted her chin until their eyes met. "However, I hope that what Chow Kum said just now is true, because I would be honored to know that you care for me. And I want you to know that the *only* reason I hadn't requested permission to court you was because of your prior relationship with Du Wang. Surely you've come to realize that I care for you—haven't you?"

"I have hoped for that," she replied, a blush rising in her cheeks.

"Then if I request Miss Cunningham's permission to court you, I need not fear rejection?" he asked while giving her a warm smile.

"No, you need not fear rejection. In fact, Chow Kum is right. I would probably sit up all night carving notches in the blessings basket!"

"One day, you're going to have to explain just what that blessings basket is all about. But for right now, I think I'd prefer to settle for this," he told her, gently gathering her into his arms and placing a tender kiss upon her lips.

Her arms seemed to automatically slip around his neck as she returned his kiss, and her heart beat with excitement.

Chapter 6

April, 1907

The golden poppies, pink rockroses, and woolly blue curls were all in bloom, and the beautiful, ivy-covered chapel at San Anselmo looked much as it had a year ago. "Here we are," Miss Cunningham announced to the group of fifty girls. "You older girls, get busy and begin picking flowers—you little ones, stay close at hand," she ordered. "And be careful," she called after them. "Don't get out of my sight!"

She smiled as they scattered into the field, quickly gathering an array of blossoming wildflowers to be used as decorations in the small chapel. She had tried for several months to convince Sing Ho that the larger church in San Rafael would be more suitable for her wedding, but to no avail. The girl was convinced that the vows should be exchanged at San Anselmo. And, of course, whatever Sing Ho desired was fine with Charlie. Throughout the past year, their dedication and love had developed, becoming a constant source of delight to everyone who knew them, and he seemed unable to refuse any of her wishes regarding the wedding plans.

The Ming family was well-known in the San Francisco area, and their guest list had been extensive. That fact, combined with the number of members of the Mission Board, their families, and Sing Ho's fifty-member family, had initially convinced Miss Cunningham that the chapel was out of the question. The Ming family had agreed. That is, until Sing Ho spent an afternoon at their home explaining all the events that had occurred the previous year and the significance of the barn and chapel located in San Anselmo. The Mings had never heard the entire story of the attempted kidnapping and how it had eventually brought Charlie and Sing Ho together. And in the end, they had agreed with Sing Ho that the wedding should be held at the chapel, even if the guests were a bit uncomfortable.

Minnie assured her that this arrangement would work if Miss Cunningham would leave things in her hands. And so she had—everything except decorating the church and arranging the flowers. Sing Ho had specifically requested that Lo Mo have the children decorate the sanctuary and fill her basket with wildflowers. She had sent along ribbons to tie a small bouquet for Hung Mooie, who had arrived from Cleveland only yesterday to act as matron of honor.

The sound of approaching horses' hooves and rumbling buggy wheels pulled Miss Cunningham back to the present, and she watched in delight as Sing Ho stepped out of the carriage in her ivory satin gown, followed by Hung Mooie and little Bo Lin in pale pink silk.

"Come see what you think of the decorations," she said, greeting the girls as they walked toward her. Three large silver candelabra stood at the front of the church, entwined with lavender and pink rockroses. Two large baskets of wildflowers bursting in a profusion of colors rested on marble pedestals between the candelabra. Large white ribbons were tied to the end of each pew, with different colored wildflowers nestled in the center of each bow.

Taking in the full effect of the decorations, Sing Ho placed an arm around Miss Cunningham. "It looks beautiful!" As soon as she'd made the pronouncement, she began to giggle.

"What? Have I missed something?" Lo Mo asked, quickly surveying the room.

"No," Sing Ho replied, attempting to squelch her laughter. "I was thinking back to a conversation I had with Charlie's mother about Chinese weddings," she sputtered, still unable to contain herself.

Miss Cunningham was clearly concerned that something was wrong with the decorations, and Sing Ho couldn't seem to stop giggling.

"I think she has wedding jitters," Hung Mooie interjected. "The church looks lovely," she added. "It reminds me so much of my wedding to Henry. Don't you think, Sing Ho?"

Sing Ho nodded her head and wiped away the tears that had pooled in her eyes. "I'm sorry, Lo Mo. The church looks absolutely stunning."

"Well, now that you seem to have composed yourself a bit, what was it that Charlie's mother told you about Chinese weddings that you found so humorous?"

"She asked me if I had ever witnessed a Chinese wedding ceremony or knew any of the Chinese wedding rituals. I told her I hadn't attended a wedding, but I knew that the bride wore a red gown and that gifts of money were wrapped in red paper because red is the Chinese color of joy."

Miss Cunningham nodded. "I still fail to see anything funny about that."

"That's not the funny part," Sing Ho replied. "Charlie's mother explained to me that when the bride is dressed in her red gown, a female member of the groom's household staff comes to the bride's house to escort her to the groom's home."

"And?" Miss Cunningham impatiently urged when it appeared Sing Ho was going to once again burst into laughter.

"This woman that the groom sends as an escort is required to carry the bride *piggyback* out of the house to the awaiting sedan chair. Then when they arrive at the home of the groom, the woman must once again carry the bride into the groom's house, because the bride's feet are not allowed to touch the ground until she reaches the home of the groom. Can't you just see me in a billowing red gown with Hung Mooie carrying me on her back into the church?" All three of them broke into gales of laughter, Sing Ho holding her sides as tears streamed down her face.

"What else did she tell you?" Hung Mooie sputtered, attempting to catch her breath.

"Nothing else that was quite so funny as that. The rest was about the hair-combing ritual to find good fortune and the fact that the emphasis of the ceremony is on worshiping ancestors and the heavens and earth instead of God. She told me that all of it now seemed strange to her, too."

"I think we had better quit our chattering before our guests arrive. Here are your bouquets," Lo Mo said, motioning for one of the girls to bring the flowers. The blessings basket was filled with every variety of wildflower that could be found, and lavish white ribbons matching those at the ends of the pews had been tied to each side of the handle. A large coordinating bouquet and ribbon had been made for Hung Mooie, and Bo Lin received a small basket filled with rose petals, which she would scatter down the aisle. "We've even matched the ribbons and flowers on the serving tables for the reception," Miss Cunningham confided, pleased with Sing Ho's delighted reaction.

"It's *beautiful*, Lo Mo! How can I ever thank you?" Sing Ho asked, pulling her surrogate mother into a loving embrace.

"Just be happy, and always remain close to the Lord. That's thanks enough. And by the way, you were right," she replied, returning the hug. "This chapel *is* the proper choice for your wedding. I don't know why I ever thought that you should consider any other."

🐝

Sing Ho stood in the vestibule of the church, peeking around the corner to gain a view of Bo Lin as she preceded her down the aisle. She looked so grown-up in the pink silk dress, with her head held high as she took slow, halting steps, and inched her way toward the front of the church. Carefully, she dispersed the rose petals, a few at a time, until she reached her designated spot beside Hung Mooie.

"It's time," Lo Mo stated. "Are you ready?" she asked, tucking Sing Ho's arm into the crook of her own.

"I think so," she replied, the basket of flowers visibly shaking in her hand as they walked into the back of the church. She took a deep breath and exhaled slowly. There were so many people, and all of them were staring at *her*. Immediately, she began scanning the front of the church, searching for Charlie. Suddenly their eyes met, and he was looking at her with such love and adoration that her heart skipped a beat. She returned his gaze, keeping her eyes fixed upon him as Lo Mo slowly escorted her to where her groom stood waiting.

"Who gives this woman in marriage?" Pastor Landon asked, looking toward Lo Mo, who was positioned to the left of Sing Ho.

"As a blessing from God, *I* give this woman," Lo Mo replied, her voice unfaltering as she kissed Sing Ho's cheek and then released her to Charlie.

The remaining vows were exchanged in loving tenderness, followed by a gentle kiss, which drew applause from the crowd. Turning the young couple toward the assembled group, the minister proclaimed, "Honored guests, I present to you Mr. and Mrs. Charlie Ming."

🕭

"Who would have ever believed that out of the devastation of an earthquake one year ago, our lives would have been so filled with blessings?" Sing Ho asked the small group that remained at the end of the afternoon.

"Certainly not Yuen Kim," Miss Minnie replied, causing them all to burst into laughter.

Yuen Kim nodded her head in agreement. "You're right! I've learned much about God's faithfulness this past year. I just hope that He doesn't need to take such drastic measures to get my attention in the future," she joked.

"I don't think that the earthquake was arranged solely for your benefit, Yuen Kim. I think there are a lot of us that needed that same lesson!" Miss Minnie replied as they moved about the room, packing up dishes and cleaning the tables and floor.

"It's time for us to leave," Charlie stated, giving his bride a smile. "We'll miss the last ferry across the bay if we wait any longer."

"Just a moment," she said, walking to a nearby table and picking up the basketful of flowers. "Come here, Bo Lin," she called to the child, who was carefully watching her every move. "I have a very special task for you," she explained. "Now that I'll be leaving to make my home with Charlie, I'd like for you to be in charge of the blessings basket. Do you think you can do that?" she asked in a solemn voice.

"I might cut myself. Maybe you should stay and live with us," she said, giving Charlie a doleful expression.

"I can't do that, Bo Lin, but Charlie has told me that you can come and visit us as soon as we return from our trip to China. It would make me very happy if I knew that you were taking care of the basket. And perhaps Miss Minnie will help you make the notches. How would that be?" she cajoled.

"If you're sure you can't stay with us, then I promise we'll take care of it," Bo Lin replied while glancing toward Miss Minnie, who was nodding her approval.

"Thank you, Bo Lin. I know that you are the very best choice to take care of the basket," Sing Ho replied, gathering the child into a tight embrace.

"I'm ready," she said, moving toward Charlie. His arm encircled her waist as they walked to the buggy waiting outside the church.

"I've made a decision," he told her as the horse trotted down the dirt road away from the church.

"And what is that?" she asked, giving him a bright smile.

"To purchase a big basket for our home. I think a blessings basket is *exactly* what we'll need!"

ABOUT THE AUTHORS

IRENE BRAND

Irene is a lifelong resident of West Virginia, where she lives with her husband, Rod. Her first inspirational romance was published in 1984, and presently she has more than twenty-five novels published or under contract. She is the author of four nonfiction books, various devotional materials, and her writings have appeared in numerous historical, religious, and general magazines.

Irene became a Christian at the age of eleven, and continues to be actively involved in her local church. Before retiring in 1989 to devote full time to freelance writing, Irene taught for 23 years in secondary public schools. Many of her books have been inspired while traveling to 49 of the United States and 35 foreign countries.

KRISTY DYKES

Kristy—wife to Rev. Milton Dykes, mother to two beautiful young women, grandmother, and native Floridian—was author of hundreds of articles, a weekly cooking column, short stories, and novels. She was also a public speaker whose favorite topic was on "How to Love Your Husband." Her goal in writing was to "make them laugh, make them cry, and make them wait" (a Charles Dicken's quote). She passed away from this life in 2008.

NANCY J. FARRIER

Nancy is an award-winning author of numerous books, articles, short stories, and devotions living in Southern California. She is married and the mother of five children and one grandson. Nancy feels called to share her faith with other through her writing.

PAMELA GRIFFIN

Pamela lives in Texas with her family. She fully gave her life to Christ in 1988 after a rebellious young adulthood and owes the fact that she's still alive today to an all-loving and forgiving God and to a mother who steadfastly prayed and had faith that God could bring her wayward daughter "home." Pamela's main goal in writing Christian romance is to help and encourage those who do know the Lord and to plant a seed of hope in those who don't.

JOANN A. GROTE

JoAnn lives in Minnesota, where she grew up. She uses the state for most of her story settings, and like her characters, JoAnn seeks to serve Christ in her work. She believes that readers of novels can receive a message of salvation and encouragement from well-crafted fiction. With over 35 books to her credit, including novels, "The American Adventure" series for children, and the "Heartsong Presents Inspirational Romance" series. She captivates and addresses the deeper meaning between life and faith.

SALLY LAITY

Sally considers it a joy to know that the Lord can touch other hearts through her stories. She has written both historical and contemporary novels, including a co-authored series for Tyndale House and another for Barbour Publishing, nine Heartsong Romances, and twelve Barbour novellas. Her favorite pastimes include quilting for her church's Prayer Quilt Ministry and scrapbooking. She makes her home in the beautiful Tehachapi Mountains of southern California with her husband of fifty years and enjoys being a grandma and great-grandma.

JUDITH MILLER

is an award-winning author whose avid research and love for history are reflected in her novels, many of which have appeared on the CBA bestseller lists. Judy makes her home in Topeka, Kansas.

JANET SPAETH

In first grade, Janet Spaeth was asked to write a summary of a story about a family making maple syrup. She wrote all during class, through morning recess, lunch, and afternoon recess, and asked to stay after school. When the teacher pointed out that a summary was supposed to be shorter than the original story, Janet explained that she didn't feel the readers knew the characters well enough, so she was expanding on what was in the first-grade reader. Thus a writer was born. She lives in the Midwest and loves to travel, but to her, the happiest word in the English language is *home*.

If you enjoyed
The Immigrant Brides Collection
look for

The Prairie Romance Collection

The Bartered Bride Collection

The Stitched with Love Collection

The Texas Brides Collection

The Farmer's Bride Collection

The Lighthouse Brides Collection

The Brides of Chance Collection

The Alaska Brides Collection

Available wherever books are sold.